Juliana Choo '97

CLOUD MOUNTAIN

Also by Aimee Liu

Face

(Nonfiction) *Solitaire*

AIMEE E. LIU

CLOUD MOUNTAIN

WARNER BOOKS

A Time Warner Company

Warner Books, Inc., 1271 Avenue of the Americas, New York, NY 10020

 A Time Warner Company

Printed in the United States of America

ISBN 0-446-51987-1

In memory of
Liu Ch'eng-yü (Don Luis),
Jennie Ella Trescott Luis,
and
Blossom Luis Robertson

AUTHOR'S NOTE

This book is a work of fiction. While it follows the general chronology of the marriage between my grandparents Liu Ch'eng-yü and Jennie Trescott Luis, and incorporates versions of stories told to me by various family members, it is in no sense a family history. I never knew my grandparents and have specifically *not* tried to make Hope and Paul Leon "true" to their characters, as this would do a disservice both to their memory and to this novel. I have, however, tried to be true to the history of the times that my grandparents and their children lived through. To this end, many of the events recounted in this book are drawn from a collection of my grandfather's "Reminiscences" published in 1946 and from other firsthand accounts of the early 1900s in the Bay Area and succeeding decades in China. The poems that appear in this book are adapted from my grandfather's verses.

Just as I have reconfigured personal stories, I have shifted certain dates and events to fit the needs of fiction. Most of these incidents are historically insignificant. However, it should be noted that my fictional portrait of Shanghai's May Fourth riot, while more violent than the actual 1919 event, does reflect the brutality of later clashes between Chinese protesters and foreign police.

For the sake of historical consistency, the Wade-Giles system of romanization, rather than the modern *pinyin*, is used for all Chinese words, names, and places mentioned in this book. I have also kept the spellings of common terms and place-names that were in use during the period in which this story takes place.

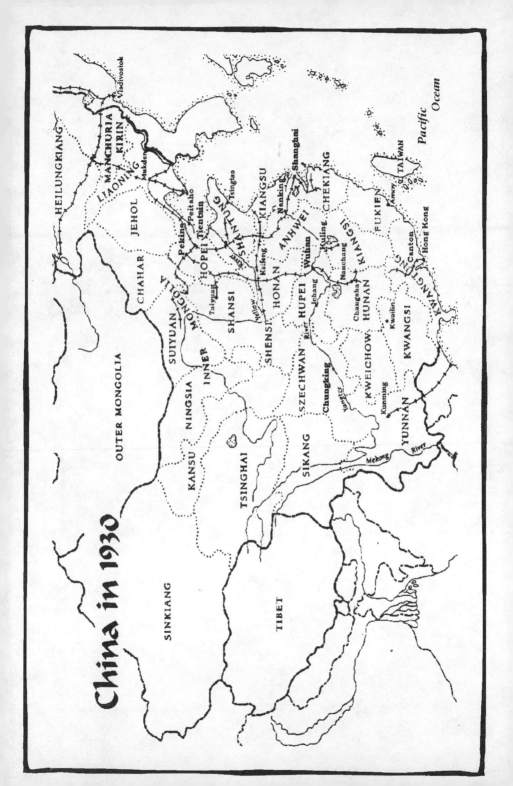

China in 1930

PROLOGUE

Over the three cliffs of fog
Descends the chill of August.
Animals in the forest cry in alarm.
Yellow leaves are marked by worms.
Autumn surprises this old man,
And crossing the stream becomes arduous.
Winds and clouds are of one kind.
My dreams span the four mountains.

REQUEST

LOS ANGELES

(OCTOBER 1941)

I have a letter from my husband. A small, tailored man wearing a Panama hat brought it to the gate a few minutes ago. He had weak shoulders, this man, a complexion like butterscotch, and he started at the sight of me. My marbled hair and faded blue eyes were not what he was expecting, and then, when I spoke my Chinese name, *Liang Hsin-hsin*, the tones went flat from lack of practice. He hesitated, clearly torn between duty and doubt, before handing me the envelope. He said he'd received it from his cousin. I did not recognize the cousin's name any more than I did the young man's own. I understood this much, however: with the war in China, such human chains are the only sure way to get a message through.

Though I knew it was futile to hope for additional information, I asked my caller to come in, have some tea before starting back down to the city. But he cast a wary eye over the tiered patio and black-bottomed pool, the whitewashed walls and terra-cotta roofs of this sprawling Spanish-style compound where my daughter and her husband have decided I must live with them. I couldn't blame him. He must have thought he'd stumbled into some gangster's or movie star's hideaway. To me, too, this hilltop villa feels as remote as a cloud from the rest of the living world.

As the children were not home to persuade him, I let my visitor go. Still, I waited to open the letter. It's been years since the last one. To hurry now seemed pointless, and the sun was going down.

From the guest cottage where I am staying I can see a thin band of Pacific Ocean floating above the crisscrossed sprawl of Los Angeles. Throughout the day this band turns from green to blue to silver to gold and then, precipitously, to black. Of course, I know better than most the connection between this shimmering line and the other side of the world, yet I still rely on the sun, after slipping over the edge each evening, to send back its report. When the sky ignites above the dark horizon, I feel reassured that Paul is seeing the opposite glow as dawn.

Now I draw the curtains and inspect the letter. Under the glare of my desk lamp the envelope appears tattered and grimy with the oils of a hundred hands, but the paper inside bears only my husband's markings. It is addressed from a numbered apartment in Chungking and dated April 2, my birthday six months—no, two *years* and six months ago. I stare at the number, 1939, with a curious mix of sadness and reproach, as if the long delay en route were somehow our own fault. I know it is only the war and time, geography and history that are to blame, yet my inability to accept these particular opponents was always our deepest problem. Now I don't know how to proceed. What relevance can words written two and a half years ago have to me today?

But the immediacy of the brush-worked letters overwhelms the numbers at the top of the page. Paul's hand is so evident in these jerking strokes, I can just see him leaning over his table, eyes pinched with effort behind their round glasses, a ruff of gray hair skimming the tops of his ears, the wide sleeves of his scholar's gown fanning down from his shoulders. He writes English like the stranger he has become, awkward with his calligraphy brush, using as his tablet not the elegant rice paper he once demanded but crude sheets torn from government issue pads. Before I read the first word, I feel all that he has spared me by sending me away. By allowing me to leave. After nearly a decade apart I still don't know which is the truer version.

He writes that we have lost everything we built together. Everything he owned. He has escaped the bombings and firestorms and fled across China with nothing but one bag of summer clothing and the Shetland blanket I gave him our first Christmas in Shanghai. He has survived the Japanese and the Communists and Chiang's scorched earth policy just as he survived the blacklists and firing squads that regularly took aim at him during our years together. I was the one who could not survive.

But now his brushstroke wavers. He writes in the language of mourning.

Dearest Hope, here all is gone for me, everything change. I do not know how to do in future. I think, if I come to you, now will be better. Only so much time passed. Do you keep place for me in your heart, your home? I cannot be certain unless you answer.

I await your answer,

Your husband, Paul

The light flickers. Two and a half years. I stare at the letter, dry-eyed, no longer reading. Laughter at the gate signals the children's return. I don't know if or when or what I will tell them. Even if I should tell them. So I turn out the lamp. Let them believe I'm sleeping, Mama needs her rest. My daughter is parading these days as a "Eurasian" starlet and her doleful young husband supports us all off his father's investments in the railroads. They think I'm old at sixty. That my hardest choices are over. They don't know me any better than I know the man who wrote this letter.

Yet Paul knows what my answer must be. He remembers when our story began . . . and so do I.

BOOK ONE

Three hundred white strands are suspended.
Together they fall like the roots of clouds,
Splitting the cliff and leaping from the sky,
Hanging streams among the rocks.
Yin and Yang form twin towers,
Mist and fog mysterious gates.
The drunken sky weaves its summer brocade.
Mountain spirits dare not touch it.

I

MEETING

BERKELEY, CALIFORNIA

(1906)

᠍᠍᠍᠍᠍

1

I remember that the young woman I was then had no intention of celebrating her twenty-fifth birthday. Hope Newfield preferred to keep her age to herself, and the day, in any case, was too warm for festivities. Unreasonably warm, she thought. Berkeley in April should be either crisp and breezy or drenched in mist. Instead, from the verandah of the house where she boarded, Hope could see particles of dust shimmering like fool's gold. The lawn had a withered look, and all the moisture it seemed to beg for was pouring down the crease between Hope's imprisoned breasts, pasting that old whalebone corset to her back, and steaming her feet in their proper but insufferable laced black boots.

"Many younger girls," said Eleanor Layton, peering over Hope's shoulder at the letter in her lap, "would give their souls to marry Professor Chesterton."

While waiting for her next student, Hope had been reading her father's birthday apologies, a confession that the Oregon gold mine he'd bought in '04 probably had been seeded. *My girl, I promise, I'll have a little something to send your way by Christmas. Hard times, but thanks to your Professor Chesterton, least you're safe and sound . . .*

Eleanor stepped back waving her garden shears. "Delay much longer, you'll be worse off 'n me, Hope. Maybe my dear husband's gone, but I do have my memories."

And a reliable income and property, thought Hope, and, through that, the conviction that all of Berkeley society embraces you. Eleanor was an officious, middle-aged widow, hardly taller than Hope but several times as wide, who favored crinoline bows, velvetta hats, and was perpetually struggling to reduce. Hope worked hard to view her with sympathy or humor, rather than annoyance—her five-dollar rent was a bargain she could ill afford to jeopardize—but the landlady's busybody ways did get tiresome.

Eleanor picked the yellow leaves off her potted gardenia. "You know," she said, as if the thought had just occurred to her, "you'll never do better."

Hope rolled her eyes. "Whether I will or will not *do* better is irrelevant."

"Ah, *irrelevant* is it!" Eleanor cried. "Well, if it's love you're after, you'd best hurry. Love's a game for the young and lovely, and the mirror, my dear, never lies." She snapped her clippers for emphasis and let the screen door slam as she went inside.

"Happy birthday to you, too," Hope said under her breath, turning defiantly to her reflection in the parlor window.

In any ordinary looking glass, the bright blue of Hope's eyes and the paleness of her skin left no doubt as to her "loveliness." Unfortunately, the play of light in this dark glass stripped away her color while highlighting the ambiguities of her face. But, she reassured herself, her aquiline nose could as well be the legacy of English or Roman forebears as her one Seneca grandmother—who had died long before Hope was even born. And her hair, though dark, was fine and wavy as no Indian's she'd ever seen. If Hope's bloodline had not been public knowledge among the boys in Fort Dodge they surely would never have guessed it. And here in California, not even Eleanor Layton suspected she was part native. No, the mirror never lies, Hope thought, and precisely for that reason, she had nothing to worry about.

"Hulloo-oo!"

She looked up, startled by the casual tone of the greeting. But shading her eyes she saw that it was not the new student, but Collis Chesterton swinging around the weeping willow at the foot of the yard. In spite of the heat, he wore his signature tweeds and bowler, and moved with lumbering precision, as if his upper body were precariously balanced. His recent trip to Los Angeles, Hope saw, had poached his nose and forehead.

She stood as he reached the top of the steps. "I didn't expect you back so soon."

He took her hand and gave it a kiss that was more mustache than mouth. "I hurried back."

She reclaimed her hand. ". . . how was your interview?"

"Superlative!" He grinned, stuck his thumbs in his vest pockets. "G. R. Granville—that Pasadena construction tycoon I told you about—he's put up five thousand dollars for a department he's calling—" he cleared his throat "—Modern Austro-Germanic Studies. Granville's decided Austria is *the* cradle of twentieth-century civilization."

"And your role . . . ?"

"What would you say to department chair?"

"I guess I'd say congratulations."

"Thank you, my dear." A courtly bow.

"I'd ask you in, Collis, but I'm expecting that new student. Mr. Liang?"

"Yes." He drew a yellow handkerchief from his breast pocket and blew his nose. "That's one of the reasons I came, to warn you. I'm told he's something of a troublemaker."

As faculty advisor and Hope's referral to the Asian students she tutored in English, Collis had a credible interest in such matters, but his timing today made her suspicious. "In what way?" she asked.

"Oh, nothing serious. Celestials and their mystical cults and intrigues. But best be on your guard. You know."

Hope knew little of the kind. Of her ten Chinese and Japanese students, not one had ever directly met her eyes or shaken her hand, and questions regarding their personal lives or beliefs were invariably answered in monosyllables.

"Mr. Liang is a mystic then?"

"Hardly! One of the moderns, calls himself a republican. Wants to overthrow the imperials back home. Other fellows call him a traitor."

"I see." Hope had read in *Harper's* about these revolutionists, their campaign under Dr. Sun Yat-sen to bring democracy to China. She thought Mr. Liang sounded interesting.

Collis took a step toward her. "It's been three weeks, Hope."

At that, a floorboard creaked inside, and Eleanor's shadow drew away from the screen. Hope took her suitor's elbow and steered him back down the steps.

"I have been considering," she said.

"Well, I should hope so!"

And she did like the way he towered over her. He was fair, strong, accomplished, respected. It should be a simple matter to say yes. But at close range, Collis Chesterton smelled of breakfast meat, and he was just so *positive* about everything . . . especially his future with her.

"I'm sorry, Collis," she said. "But he really will be here any minute."

He tugged on his ear, eyes on the scrubby grass, then snapped his fingers. "I left out the best! Granville wants me to make a study expedition to Europe this summer, and when I mentioned *our* plans, he suggested you come along as my—well, researcher. Charge to the department, see. Cagey old bastard, said to consider it his wedding present."

"Collis—"

"No, now not a word. I'll call in a few days."

As he leaned forward and planted a kiss on her cheek, Hope reached—fought—for some shred of sensation she could associate with passion. All she felt were his whiskers.

When he had gone, she returned to the verandah and flipped through the new *Leslie's Weekly*, but as often happened after Collis's visits, her thoughts were back with Frank Pearson.

Hope would have said yes to Frank without question—and she knew it the first moment she saw him, four years ago now, helping a little boy fallen from a wagon down on Adeline Street. Frank was brawny and warm, a compassionate physician with a voracious appetite for books and exploration. Together they rode up into the Oakland hills and walked the shoreline all the way to Albany. One day they borrowed a boat and sailed around the point to Cliff House and on, clear down the peninsula, so far they had to return after dark, navigating by moonlight. But all the time they were together, Hope never felt the slightest twinge of anxiety or fear. Frank's protection was like a glove that held her close, kept her warm and dry, yet left her free to move. He thought women should have the Vote. He considered education a lifelong pursuit. He believed the world was waiting to be seen and there was nothing so suffocating as the smug complacency of American high society.

This comment prompted Hope to put their relationship to the ultimate test. After swearing Frank to secrecy, she revealed that her mother's mother was Indian. Frank responded by sweeping her into his arms and, laughing, said he knew there was *something* wonderful about her. The son of a Baltimore steel baron, Frank Pearson offered Hope the tantalizing prospect of snubbing the same elements of society that scorned her while, at the same time, marrying among them.

The next evening Frank was summoned to the Barbary Coast to patch up some casualties of a dockside brawl. A stevedore found him the following morning with a harpoon through his throat.

Hope's first public appearance after Frank died was a suffrage rally, and though everyone was cheering and stomping, the crowd's exuberance reduced her to tears. She'd plowed blindly into Collis Chesterton, and he insisted she make it up to him by letting him buy her a cup of coffee. When he learned she'd just graduated from Mills College and was supporting herself by tutoring spoiled rich children by day and immigrants by night, he presumed her distress was financial. He explained that, as de facto advisor to the university's Asian students (he taught European, not Asian, history and was filling in only because no one else would volunteer), he was always looking for able English tutors. Though Hope spoke not a word of Chinese or Japanese, Collis assured her that such knowledge would only lead to her coddling the boys. He also promised a reliable income of ten dollars or more per week—nearly double what she had been earning.

She never did tell Collis about Frank Pearson, never enticed his courtship, but it was enough that she accepted the work. In the second year of this arrangement, he invited her to the theater, lectures, concerts in the park. In the third, he began to hint of "intentions." When she casually remarked that she'd "give anything" to tour Europe, Collis promised to take her to Vienna—if she would give him her hand.

The *Leslie's* slipped from her lap, falling open to the advertisements at the back: combination washers and Acme cook stoves, silver-plated tea services, croquet sets. Embroidered bed linens and antimacassars. Security. Comfort. Children. A home. All of which Collis would happily provide.

She shut her eyes and listened past her own breathing. A magpie was singing. A squirrel chattered. Cartwheels rolled up the hill accompanied by the heavy clip-clop of hooves. But now she sensed a change. A split second, something so small it would go unnoticed a thousand times out of a thousand and one, except that she was listening. A current of cooler air shifting the breeze? A lark ascending from the Procters' field? Or something even more subtle, like time's rearrangement of light. Whatever the prompting, she looked up and discovered she was being watched.

Ordinarily such a discovery would alarm her—would alarm anyone, surely, the way her watcher had silently approached. Yet she felt no such disturbance. Neither fear nor surprise, nor even the casual whirl of embarrassment. He stood at the foot of the steps—tall and slight with lank black hair scissored close to the head, ears as precise as shells, skin the color of sand. His face, dominated by high, smooth cheekbones, was broad and square at the forehead but tapered to a gentle chin. Nose a bit too delicate for the breadth of the face. Curving lips—a question hovered—and tender eyes beneath smudgy brows. He wore not a suit but a navy cutaway mismatched with gray trousers and a celadon tie. His white shirt collar lifted in wings, and he held his derby between fingers that stretched so long and smooth she thought of feathers.

"Miss Newfeel." The voice did not break the quiet between them but moved on it, low and luxuriant, his alteration of her name giving it a drape that was both innocent and seductive.

"Yes?" She came to the top of the steps.

"I am Liang Po-yu."

But the watcher bore no resemblance to the student she'd been expecting. "I'm sorry, Mr. Liang, I didn't realize . . . Please, do come up. Yes. I am Hope Newfield."

It was the cropped hair, combed and parted to one side, that had misled her. She was accustomed to shaved-back foreheads and long submissive pigtails. Her students had told her their Manchu rulers would execute them if they returned to China without their queues. Of course, they were not revolutionists.

She started to bow . . . hesitated. He extended his hand. She accepted, but he seemed to be new to the art of the handshake, for their fingers were soon entwined, snagged between American and European-style contact. She laughed, tilted her head to look up at him.

At that moment Eleanor's voice hummed off-key from the other side of the house. Eleanor, who insisted that even the most educated Chinese were, deep down, shiftless gamblers and layabouts. Hope let go of Mr. Liang and brought him inside, down a musty corridor lined with portraits of the widow's relatives, and into the office Hope had made her own.

Here a soft breeze ballooned white lace curtains. A small leather-topped desk, high-backed chairs with embroidered seats, and a pale blue divan filled one side of the room, while a round walnut table large enough to accommodate books, writing paper, and full tea service dominated the other. Perhaps because it was less intimidating to deal with a woman only from the elbows up, most of Hope's students seemed more at ease working across the table from her than sitting in parlor positions, but Mr. Liang seated himself on the divan. She took the chair opposite.

"Please." He held out an envelope and she saw that his fingers were misleading. Though smooth and slender in their length, the tips were blunt, nails bitten to the quick.

Mr. Liang's letter of introduction was written in meticulous block lettering on translucent rice paper, in English except for the scarlet seal at the bottom of the page. She read the first line four times before the words began to register.

18 June, 1903
Honorable Sir,
This letter will introduce Mr. Liang Po-yu, son of Liang Yu-sheng, venerable Viceroy of Canton. The Liang family ancestors reside in Wuchang, Hupei Province, China.

Mr. Liang Po-yu, styled Yu-fen, was born to a most learned family. He trained in the classical studies from an early age. After reaching his adolescence he was admitted into two colleges in Hunan and Hupei provinces where he excelled particularly in history of ethnic groups such as Liao, King, and Yüan, and in geography of northwest China. Mr. Liang studied English and Russian languages and composed three volumes poetry before traveling to Hong Kong and Japan to continue his studies. After composing sixteen volumes history of the wars of Taiping Heavenly Kingdom, Mr. Liang returned to China to distinguish himself in the study of Latin at Chen-tan College.

By then he was no older than twenty-six. At this writing Mr.
Liang is to embark on a voyage to the United States to study at
the University of California. He surely will bring honor to his
family and his nation during his studies in America.

Please to welcome this esteemed scholar to your great country.

Signed most humbly,

Ma Hsiang-po, Instructor of Latin, Chen-tan College

When Hope looked up, he was watching her again. She dropped her
eyes. *By then he was no older than twenty-six.* Was this even possible? That
beardless skin, the slender length of him . . . Yet he must be at least thirty
to have accomplished all the letter told. If even half of this were true, he
would be the intellectual superior of every man in Berkeley!

"This isn't right." She thrust back the paper. "I don't know enough to
teach you, Mr. Liang."

"Ah, no! I am nothing." He leaned forward, and she was afraid he might
reach out and touch her again. Instead he slapped the letter against his
palm. "These words not true!"

"Of course they're true."

"I am no good, no show——" He stopped, started again too quickly.
"Too much I know——should not Mr. Ma write——*pu chih i t'i!*"

She would have thought it an act except that his face reddened and he
was breathing hard. He pulled a pair of rimless spectacles from his
pocket, fumbled the stems around his ears, and spread the letter with
trembling hands, as if to prove the lie.

"Please. It's all right. I'll fetch our tea."

She escaped to the kitchen, where the kettle proceeded to burn her
thumb, the sugar spoon clattered across the linoleum, and wafting in from
the garden came Eleanor's spirited rendition of "Castles in the Air."

ॐॐॐ

Liang Po-yu had lived in America for over a year, but never had his
poor command of the English language shamed him more than in these
few minutes. When Chesterton told him that his tutor was to be a
woman, Po-yu had envisioned an elderly missionary with pasted hair and

brittle eyes and enormous camel feet. He could have borne the shame of error before such a *yang kueitsu*, he thought, but Hope Newfield was young and delicate, small as a child yet so graceful . . . He was not only ashamed of himself, but furious.

In fact, from the moment he first caught sight of her as he entered the garden gate he had strained against a pressure in his chest, like the lid of a box from which something dangerous is trying to escape. It had nearly succeeded when his words ran away with him. Now, while she was preparing their tea, he reminded himself of the story his shipmates had told of a visiting scholar from Kwangsi who developed feelings for the daughter of a San Francisco fireman. The father became suspicious and enlisted his squad to kidnap the scholar, tie him by the wrists and queue to the back of their fire wagon. They drove that wagon up and down the city's hills in the hours before dawn, did not stop until the scholar's hair had pulled from his head and the steel cords with which they'd tied his wrists had severed the hands from his arms. Then they left him in the middle of Chinatown to bleed to death.

But there were different stories, as well, which Po-yu had heard from men he respected far more than those cowards on the boat. In Hong Kong several years earlier he had become the disciple of an elderly man named Jung Ch'un-fu who had graduated from Yale University, the first Chinese to earn an American degree. Jung had married the daughter of a Connecticut senator, who bore him two American sons before her early death. Yet Jung still considered himself a patriot, and traveled often to China to negotiate with the foreign powers for his homeland's modernization. Jung was a man of the world, thought Po-yu, and although it could not have been simple for him to love and marry a white woman of such high class, he had survived and perhaps even benefited from this marriage. Two decades after her death the eighty-year-old Jung had confided that he still mourned his wife every day.

Po-yu shook his head, berating himself. He had displayed such ineptitude that Miss Newfield had all but run from the room to escape him, and here he was fantasizing about marriage!

"I speak like child," he apologized after she returned. They sat across that round, dark table from each other, and the tea she had brought tasted like decayed grass. This helped to ease his shame.

"Mr. Liang, it is customary in this country to look at the person with whom one is conversing."

He lifted his eyes as far as the white ruffle at her throat.

"Did you bring any of your books with you to America?"

He did not understand.

"The poetry and histories that Mr. Ma mentioned."

"Ah. Yes. A few."

"I would like to see them."

He glanced up just long enough to discover her blue eyes, smiling.

"Collis says you are a republican," she continued.

"Collis."

"Mr. Chesterton."

"Ah."

"He says you believe the imperial system is wrong. But isn't it true that system is all China has ever known?"

He nodded slowly. Collis, she called him.

"Do you think, then, there will be a revolution over there? In your country?"

Your country. My country. He could just see the two of them, laughing, hooping hands through the air. This American beauty and that red-whiskered barbarian, Chesterton.

She raced on, "I know embarrassingly little about China, but it seems to me our countries are so different. And this would be such a radical change. Do you really think democracy could work in China? Collis—"

"Yes! I think!"

She looked straight into his eyes. "I didn't mean to insult you."

"Mr. Chesterton mean this," he mumbled.

Her left thumb rubbed the table. After a pause she answered, "You're right. It isn't really malicious, though . . . Collis is incapable of violence. It's more his—limitation . . ."

But he could see she was making excuses. She was embarrassed. "*Che shih wo te pu tui,*" he said, leaning forward. "I speak too bold. My friend say I borrow trouble."

"Mr. Liang, however troublesome the truth may be, that does not make it less true."

The pot shook as she poured out more tea, which they did not drink.

She offered him a wafer from a silver plate, which he accepted but did not taste. Finally she broke the tension with a hard laugh. "Oh, I don't *care* what Collis thinks! Tell me about China."

So he took a deep breath and told her, or tried, in his haphazard English. The imperial system must be toppled, he explained, because each time the Westerners pointed their guns, the Empress Dowager would give whatever they asked—even if it meant starving entire provinces. Foreigners controlled China's railroads, mining rights, customs and treaty ports, and every time the ruling Ch'ing dynasty ran out of money, the Western powers would write new loans at higher interest rates, increasing their hold over the Ch'ing government. Chinese people had no rights.

When she asked why, if he felt this way, he would come to the land of the enemy to study, he praised the question. Chinese asked this often of foreign-bound students, but he had never heard it from a Westerner. He explained that although he loved his country, he felt it could not defend itself against the outside world until its leaders mastered modern technology, politics, and warfare. And China's Han majority, who had been ruled by Manchu emperors for more than two centuries, could reclaim their government only if they applied the same principles of self-rule and self-determination that had made America a free nation.

She challenged him. "America's revolution was terribly bloody. And it was followed by the Civil War, which cost even more lives."

"Ah." He sighed. "You wish peace revolution."

"I wish *for* peace*ful* revolution," she corrected. "Here—" She nodded toward a large and ugly brown moth that had settled on the plate of wafers. "Let's say he's the enemy and I want to get rid of him." She cupped her hand over the insect, took the plate to the window. When she turned back, the moth was gone. "Revolution accomplished!"

He grinned. "Lucky bug have no gun."

"Aye, there's the rub." She laughed, and for a strange, rounded moment they sat, mischievous as children. Then, like a child, he grew careless.

He reached into his jacket.

"What's this?"

"My newspaper. *Ta T'ung Jih Pao. Chinese Free Press.* You can read Chinese, please to give opinion."

"Your newspaper?"

He nodded, urging it into her hands. "I am editor."

But the longer she stared at the paper, the more he grew disheartened.

Gently, he reversed the pages. "Chinese read this way. Back front. Right left."

"Oh! I'm so sorry." She brought the back of her wrist to her mouth, and when she looked up he saw that her cheeks were flaming. She had only inquired about his books out of politeness, to ease his humiliation. She could not begin to read them.

"*Mei yu kuan hsi,* how you can know?" He retrieved the paper and folded it into his pocket.

"Mr. Liang," she said, "I really don't think I am qualified to teach you . . . but I would be honored if you will allow me to try."

He bowed his head. "Thank you, Miss Newfield." He bit hard to produce the proper *d*, then added, "I do not enjoy to speak like child."

The corners of her mouth twitched. "I can tell."

And so they arranged to meet Monday and Thursday mornings. He asked if she would do the honor of giving him an American name. She answered that it was a great responsibility, but she would do her best.

༄༄༄

2

"Pass the green," said Mary Jane Lockyear.

Hope pushed the tin of spools across the banner. EQUAL PAY FOR EQUAL WORK the satin letters would read when they finished. But it was after nine already. The last trolley from Oakland left at ten, and they were not half done.

"You'll stay the night," said Mary Jane, reading Hope's mind. "You have an early lesson tomorrow?"

Hope nodded and shook her head in reply.

"You're not getting much done. And if you've spoken more than ten words all evening, I haven't heard them."

"Sorry. It was sweet of you to bake that cake."

"You hardly touched it."

Hope sighed. "Birthdays are for children."

"And you're an old maid." Mary Jane gave the table an impatient tap with her thimble. "I'll be forty next month. Remind me not to invite you to *my* party!"

Hope forced a smile. Mary Jane was her closest friend, and she didn't mean to cut her off. "Collis is back."

The violet eyes narrowed. "And you've given him your answer."

"Briefly."

"I hardly think three years is brief!"

"He's a good man." Hope stared at the flashing steel point of her needle.

"You're too soft, Hope. There are some men who won't take no for an answer unless you're downright brutal."

"I suppose you're so experienced!" The words leapt from her mouth before she could stop them. "Oh, Mary Jane. I'm sorry, I didn't mean it like that."

Mary Jane stood and turned up the lamp. In her checked gingham wrapper, fading hair in wisps, she seemed more matronly than usual this evening, but she was no spinster. If Hope could bring herself to speak the truth, she knew her friend would repay her in kind.

But Mary Jane spoke first. "So you're actually considering accepting."

"I don't know. Sometimes I think I'd be better off."

"Married to Collis Chesterton?"

"I still think about Frank."

"I don't blame you." Mary Jane had run into them together once on their way into Demetrak's to buy a picnic for the beach. She told Hope that Frank Pearson was the handsomest man she'd ever laid eyes on. "But all the more reason to end this nonsense with Collis."

"I'm not so sure. If I leave myself free, I may just make another terrible mistake."

"Nothing terrible about Frank Pearson. I've never seen a girl so in love—*you* had nothing to do with his death!"

"It's not that. But his kind of man . . . the effect he had on me. What if I had married him? If we'd had children? Would that have stopped him

getting himself killed? Even worse, sometimes I wonder if the only reason I still love Frank is that he *did* die—before he had the chance to disappoint me."

"Hope Newfield. If you bind your life in what-ifs you'll never live at
all."

"That's exactly what I'm afraid of."

Mary Jane's needle stopped in midair. "Have you met someone else?"

Hope tried to laugh, but the sound was more of a gasp. "I do have a
new Chinese student."

Mary Jane resumed her sewing. "Just as well. If you took up with another man now it would only make matters worse."

Hope looked away. "You know I'd tell you if there were anyone else."
But for the first time in their friendship she didn't trust Mary Jane any
more than she trusted herself.

ৰৰৰ

When she returned home the following day she took her tattered Chinese dictionary and looked up *Po-yu*. Always difficult to tell, given the variations in Chinese tones and translations by the Britishers who put those
early, pre–Wade-Giles dictionaries together, but his name seemed to mean
Joyful Spirit. A wonderful name. Unfortunately, she could think of no English equivalent. Nor did her other Chinese students provide much inspiration. Ho Han-chang, Yang Kuo-kan, Jin Feng-pao, and Willy Chang were
earnest young men, products of missionary zeal or royal privilege. They did
their work and paid attention, but she often felt when addressing them that
it was all a game of masks. Han-chang was the splay-toothed smiler, Yang
the sullen prince, Feng-pao the glowerer, and Willy the gray and sickly one.
It made no difference that one was called Willy, nor would it matter if the
others were John, Sam, or Charley—blatant Chinaman names. These young
men would neither be insulted nor cajoled into revealing their true selves.
But Liang Po-yu was an exception.

On Thursday morning she was hanging out the wash, with just an
hour until his lesson and still no name. *Adam*, she thought. *Walter.
Nathaniel. Ralph.* The weather had cooled. The sun dove in and out of
great frothy clouds. She stared at the flapping sheet as if it were a canvas
and she the painter working from memory. She could see his features eas-

ily enough, the restless measure of his eyes, the fullness of his mouth, that look of cautious pride . . . but she knew she could never capture him.

"Po-yu," she whispered.

"Paul," snapped the wind.

Paul! She put her hands on her hips, lifted her face to the winking sun. Raised rather lackadasically as a Presbyterian, she had never consciously demanded much of God and so, rarely attributed the turns in her life to His will. This time she saluted Him.

ॐॐॐ

Po-yu, in his turn, had spent three restless days and nights trying to decide whether his teacher would prefer jasmine or chrysanthemum tea. There was much to be said for the chrysanthemum, apart from its being his favorite. The sweetness and weight of the tea gave it an invigorating power. Chrysanthemum symbolized long life and duration. And then there was Tu Mu's great lyric poem:

Put chrysanthemums in your hair!
You must be decked in blossoms when you accompany me home.

The truth was, he could not free himself from the yearning for her touch. As he sat through the drone of his university lectures, he imagined her fingers still threaded through his. In his Chinatown newspaper office he recorded a woman's pulse in every thud of the printing press. And when he clapped his colleagues on the back, the texture he felt was not the cheap nub of Western-style jackets or the floss of scholars' robes but the silk of Hope Newfield's palm.

This was an unprecedented obsession—and not a welcome one. True, in Japan there had been much discussion of the West's free love and he had been as enticed by this notion as the next man. He agreed that the abolition of arranged marriage should be a revolutionary mandate. Yet, at the same time, experience taught him that sexual desire was best restricted either to the marital bed or flower house. It did not chase him into the company of men, did not shadow his work or thoughts. And it must not be allowed to influence his dealings with American women.

On Thursday morning, he considered the two scarlet boxes on his night stand and selected the jasmine, quite simply, because the flower was the more beautiful. Miss Newfield said the tea was heavenly and promised that, from this day forward, she would serve only Chinese teas at their lessons. He said that her pleasure pleased him.

"What do you think of the name Paul?" she asked.

He nodded at the smooth roundness of the sound. But it cracked the first time he tried, coming forth in three chunks—Pa-ou-ah. Then two—Pau-eh. Finally he conquered the roll of the l, and she applauded his achievement.

He practiced a few more times, assessing. "I like this Paul. Very much. Thank you."

"What's my name, then?"

"Chinese name?"

She nodded. "I know in Mandarin, the word for hope is *chin-chin*. Would you advise simply using that translation?"

He bit back a smile at her butchered pronunciation. "You know Mandarin."

"Hardly! I've learned a few words, for my students' sake, but I'm very much an amateur. Perhaps you could help me."

Paul nodded, then cautiously demonstrated how to place the tongue close against the front teeth, a cross between an s and sh sound. "Hsin-hsin," he said. "This your Chinese name."

"Hsin-hsin." She laughed. "Yes, that sounds much better. Thank you—Mr. Liang?"

"You give me this name, Paul. No need say Mr. Liang anymore."

"Well, that creates a dilemma for me. Will you call me Hope or Hsin-hsin, then?"

No hesitation. "Hope."

Unlike her other students, who preferred the security of primers and textbooks, Paul wanted to read the classics he'd spotted on Hope's shelves. Poe, Melville, Tocqueville, Rousseau. He read out the names as though they were state secrets. Perhaps in China they were. Hope promised they would get to these, but suggested they spend the first few lessons tackling conversation. She made it sound as if she did this with all her students.

"Begin with what you know best," she proposed. "Your life."

And so he began, "I am only son of Liang Yu-sheng. My mother, Nai-li, third concubine . . ."

He spoke haltingly at first, approaching unfamiliar words like treacherous currents, but each time he was about to go under, she would reach and pull him back up. The faltering Mandarin she'd absorbed from her other students counterbalanced his fledgling English to give the illusion of equal footing, and soon his delivery became more relaxed. Hope found herself translating his story into a world that tantalized even as it appalled her.

Though born in Canton, where his father served as viceroy, Paul had spent most of his childhood in the Liang ancestral home in Wuchang. From the age of five, at his father's insistence, he was tutored by Fong Yao-li, an enlightened scholar of the old school who wrote with a red brush in red ink, and received his payment in a special red envelope. Fong began the young Po-yu's education with a single line from Confucius: "To study is great pleasure."

"And did you agree?" Hope asked.

Paul grinned down at his folded hands. "My great pleasure is gold fish." His hands came up around an imaginary carp, lifted it to his lips for a kiss, then opened, palms up. "I do not study, Master Fong will beat me, no can catch fish."

Hope laughed, imagining the dark child-eyes innocently imploring this cruel tutor. "So you agreed at least that study made pleasure *possible.*"

Paul tipped his head to one side, almost, but not quite meeting her gaze, then repeated, carefully. "Yes. Study make pleasure *possible.*"

To her horror, Hope felt her face flush. She busied herself refilling their teacups, and urged him on with his story.

Paul's childhood, as he described it, was a swirl of ceremonial ritual, sharpened criticism, recitation, and repetitive brushstrokes. He slept, ate, studied, and dreamed within the high walls of his compound, rarely even venturing to the courts of his father's other wives, let alone to the city outside. When he was six, Paul remembered, his mother caught him playing chase with the first wife's daughter and a friend, around and around the spirit wall with the green-backed dragon and curling clouds that was supposed to deter evil spirits. His mother dragged him to her room and forced him to kneel with his palms up, waiting for a thrashing that never came. On and on he waited, until his knees turned white and then purple, his hips and ankles throbbed. When his arms began to shake, she pulled out a long tapered box, which housed a crescent sword.

"This belong to my father when he is Imperial examiner." Paul showed how his mother tipped the sword, that her son might appreciate its cutting edge. "She say he use this hay chopper one time cut Fukien student. This student lie, cheat, but he not die right away, first write with tongue in dust, 'tragedy.' "

"How hideous!" Hope cried. "Your father . . . and your *mother* showed you this, threatened you, her own child!"

But from the way he pursed his lips, she saw she had misunderstood. "My father is official," he explained, "very busy, much away. I must respect my father, obey my mother."

Hope swallowed hard, at once chastened and repelled. Yet when Paul called her attention to the chiming clock, she could not bear for him to leave on this note. "Please," she said. "I shouldn't have spoken. My own mother died when I was a baby, and my father, like yours, was away much of the time."

He studied her with sudden concern. "Who will take care of you?"

She smiled, overlooking his mistaken tense. "I was raised by another family, Paul. Friends of my father. It's all right, I was treated well . . . But I shouldn't presume to judge your parents."

"I am sad for you, Hope," he said. "Every baby need mother." His dark eyes rested on her, for once not pulling away, but when she did not answer, he started to rise.

"Wait." She stretched a hand. "My next lesson isn't until this afternoon. Would you stay? I'd like to hear more."

He lifted his chin, and she could see he was flattered, but he protested that he was not worthy of her time. Only when she insisted, did he settle back down and resume his story.

He was years older when a cousin informed him that the tragic Fukienese was not an errant student at all, but a corrupt official who took a bribe to pass a less-than-able scholar. By then, however, the hay chopper had already accomplished its purpose. Paul worked hard at his studies and strove to be a dutiful son.

"I do not chase my sister friend," he said with a comic sigh. "My friend all boy."

Hope burst out laughing, relieved at this opening even as she felt compelled to correct him. "My friends *were* all boys. Tell me about them."

Because he had no brothers of his own, Paul said, he adopted his cousins and classmates, and even some of the village merchants' and farmers' sons as "spirit brothers." There was Chen who laughed like a bird, Deng who talked in rhyming couplets, and Shi who kept lizards for pets. Together they climbed trees, explored the abandoned temples and ancient ruins outside the city walls, or made excursions across the river to Hankow or Hanyang. They entertained each other with stories of brigands and Taoist mysteries, wild tales of Western barbarians, the evil power of foreign gunboats, and the magic that caused glass to burn like lightning, metal to move by itself.

Paul smiled at Hope apologetically. "We do not yet study the Western Learning. We do not have electricity. We never see white person."

But in Master Fong's classroom the boys would recite the poems of the Song and Ming Dynasties, the history of the Warring States, the Five Dynasties, the Ten Kingdoms, all proof (justifiable proof, Hope thought, imagining herself in Paul's place) that China was indeed the center of the universe, and had been for more than three thousand years. Translucent copy books, carved sticks of ink, the imprint of a bamboo brush left in finger flesh. These testified to the passage of hours and weeks and years as Paul moved through his classical training, memorizing the teachings of Confucius and Mencius, preparing for his Imperial exams.

His father, an elderly man whose long gray beard Paul described as "a fading stream," made it a point to advise his son whenever he returned to Wuchang—two, maybe three times each year. They would sit for hours in the Hall of Ancestors reviewing the illustrious history of the Liang clan, many generations of scholars and governors. Liang Yu-sheng expected his only son, too, to bring honor on the family. He recognized that China was changing and Paul must prepare himself for a very different future than any his ancestors had known. But he must still pass his examinations.

Again the clock began to chime, and again Paul protested that he should leave. For the first time, it occurred to Hope that she might be keeping him from other obligations—his classes, his newspaper . . .

"I'm so sorry," she started, but a rap on the door interrupted.

Eleanor poked her head in. "You all right, Hope? I just noticed you've been in here since nine." She looked pointedly at Paul. "Your lessons don't run but an hour, do they?"

"Thank you, Mrs. Layton." Hope stood up. "We are perfectly all right."

"Well—"

"Thank you," Hope repeated. Eleanor withdrew in a huff.

"Now I truly am sorry," Hope said. "I didn't mean to consume your whole day. I'm sure you've better things to do."

"No," said Paul. "This my pleasure. Please."

She held his gaze. "So you tell me. To study is your pleasure."

When he had gone, she fell back against the door, half laughing, half aghast. What on earth was the matter with her?

"He's a Chinaman!" But even though she said this out loud, she found it impossible to accept.

ॐॐॐ

He arrived ten minutes early for his next lesson, but she was already on the verandah waiting. She ushered him quickly to her office lest Eleanor see him, and when she poured out his tea, which she had steeped in advance, its perfume filled the room.

"Examinations," she prompted.

He smiled as if she were the teacher's pet, not he, and obediently followed her cue.

Every Liang male for more than three centuries, he said, had passed through the grueling succession of examinations leading to admission into the Imperial college. Every Liang male for generations had worn the furred hat topped with golden canary that signified scholarly success, had ultimately borne the official *t'ing tai* cap plumed with pheasant feathers, and the robes bearing the golden pheasant insignia of a magistrate or minister.

"Only most pure oil rise to top," Paul recalled his father warning him. Hope understood that Paul's purity was never, for one instant, in doubt. And as his father told him it must, the Liang name invariably appeared among the ranks of qualified students. Yet Paul's fear of failure was so great that for weeks before and after each exam he would wake screaming at the vision of the candidates' poster with only the outline of a crescent blade where his name should be. Not the three-cannon salute, or the band that accompanied the admission poster as it was paraded through the streets, or even the abundance of congratulatory gifts sent by his bride's family—

"Your bride?" Hope interrupted. She searched Paul's ringless hands, his smooth cheeks, and dropped gaze for evidence, but again it seemed that his appearance belied his true age and experience.

He hesitated, then lowered his voice. "My parents choose their daughter, arrange wedding after examination. I go then, study Western Learning in Hong Kong, Tokyo. Soon my father, my wife also die."

Hope looked away. "Paul, I didn't mean to . . ."

He waved his hands back and forth. "No problem." And continued talking.

On the day in late spring, 1901, when he received the news that his father and wife had both died in a cholera epidemic, the staff of the *Hupei Students' Journal*, of which Paul was editor, insisted on taking him to the beach to toast the departed spirits with wine and eat in their honor a ham brought all the way from Chekiang. The talk, as usual, circled to their shared hatred of the Manchus, and in an act of spontaneous freedom and foolhardiness, they borrowed fish knives from the local villagers and hacked off their queues. Then they piled the shorn pigtails onto scavenged planks, adorned then with flaming paper candles, and wet their trousers to the knees delivering the little ships into the tide. From that day on, Paul would dream no more of failed examinations or crescent blades, but instead of the future, the free and modern West, scenes from books such as Jules Verne's *Around the World in Eighty Days*, which one of his friends had recently translated into Chinese.

The rules by which they'd been raised were dead, Paul informed his fellow revolutionists. The past was a trap from which China must be freed, and it was their job, their duty to become its liberators.

He lifted his eyes to Hope. "This day, everything change. Everything new. Everything can be."

"Everything is possible," she corrected, more moved than she dared let him see.

Now, when their hour ended, she did not detain him, and after he had left, she sat for a long time staring at the thick green scrim of leaves outside her window. Eleanor had gone out. The house was silent, but she could still hear the uneven rhythm of his voice, still smelled his scent, like fragrant wood, mingling with the jasmine tea. And she could still feel the revulsion that had gripped her as the truth of his life finally registered. This idealist! This brilliant innocent who had married and left his bride to die. Of course, the marriage was arranged. Could she reasonably blame him for not resisting? Did any man in China resist? After all, once he married the bride chosen by his parents, he could collect as many other wives—concubines!—as he pleased. As his own father had. Was Paul, then—Po-yu—even capable of love?

Love or no love, he had experienced his bride, surely. Had worked his strong, lean frame against her thighs. Entered and planted himself inside her. She who had no face or name. Had she pleased him? Had she known the secret rules, the tricks and treacheries of the flesh? How? Had she learned such things from a mother, a sister—or from her husband's own moans and whispers? This woman who died for him.

She brought her diary from its secret drawer. She had written her way through dark times before; if she could just get this insanity out on paper, perhaps she would be rid of it.

What is this terrible storm chasing through me? Is it madness, as my mind insists, or the criminal workings of an errant heart? Paul is a man to me. A dear, tender, dangerous man. An overwhelming stranger. But a man in every sense, and when I speak to him I feel fully a woman.

Would that I could will him to leave. When I close my eyes even now his sweet face is here. I am drawn to him. I abhor him. I listen to his story of hardship and duty, and I think I would have clawed the eyes out of his father and mother, while he instead mutilates himself (those torn and bitten nails). I will never understand his world, but against my will I know what it is to be misunderstood. We are nothing alike. We are the same. He terrifies me . . .

⋙⋙⋙
3

What happened, she asked the next time, after the burning rafts? She spoke in a low, measured voice, addressing the pages of the notebook that lay before her on the table. She made notes, she explained, because it was difficult to remember all the names and places that were so familiar to him.

Paul wished she would speak more about herself, but what American woman would confide in a Chinaman? He could only hope she might feed him an occasional morsel in return for his offering a feast, so he resumed his story as if delivering the next of many courses.

He told of the New Year's gathering of the Chinese Students' Union in Tokyo, 1903, when he rose before an audience of one hundred fellow students and the Chinese Imperial Minister to Japan and called for the overthrow of the Ch'ing Dynasty. "Dr. Sun Yat-sen give me courage. I know many students believe with me, but when I shout, no one will answer. No one drink. No one eat. All eyes turn to Minister Ts'ai. He will not look, too, only point. Then police come."

"This most bad," he tried to make her understand. "No one do such thing ever."

"This was very bad," she spoke to her bobbing pencil. "No one had ever done such a thing." She stopped writing and looked up. "What exactly was it that you said?"

"I say, Han people no more can give destiny of China to invaders! We rely only ourselves. We must drive Manchu from power!"

"I *said*, Paul. We *can* rely only *upon* ourselves. What happened then?"

"I *was* arrested. Minister have me deported. Shanghai is only place in

China where I am safe. I stay there one year until Dr. Sun Yat-sen arrange me come to San Francisco, run his newspaper."

She frowned and did not correct the mistakes he was certain he had made. "I thought you came here as a student."

"Yes." He paused, considering her fair hand as it skimmed across the page. If he were not a student he would have been denied an entry visa, but of course she would not think of this. "Yes," he repeated.

"What would have happened if you had gone outside Shanghai?"

He said simply, "I will be executed."

"For giving a speech!"

"And my queue. Treason."

She shook her head. "The Manchus must be terrible cowards."

He smiled grimly, coiled his hands and placed them one atop the other. "In China, power squeeze from top. Foreigner squeeze Manchu. Manchu squeeze Chinese. Wealthy man squeeze poor man." One hand surrounded the other. "Is like box pushing small, small. Must explode."

"In revolution," she said quietly. When he did not reply, she asked, "Were you imprisoned . . . in Japan?"

He shrugged, at once pleased by her breathless tone and uncertain how much he dared to tell her. "One night only. Japanese police good friend with Dr. Sun Yat-sen."

She toyed with her pencil. "And so, by coming here and running his paper, you were repaying Dr. Sun for rescuing you?"

"I am honored to work with Dr. Sun," he said firmly.

"Oh, of course. I'm not . . . It's just that your story, Paul—your courage is remarkable."

"And you story, Hope. Also remarkable. Young woman, educated, so independent."

But she did not smile, as he'd expected. Instead, she acted as though she had not heard. She stood and pulled a volume from her bookshelf, walked to the window, thumbing pages. She wore a dress the color of apricots that lifted just above the toe of her boot, and for the first time, he noticed her feet. They were smaller than his hands.

"What you were describing," she said when she had found her place, "the *way* you described it . . . Listen to this."

He felt a surge of relief. She was simply preoccupied by what he had said before, by her desire to answer him. But as she began reading, her tone darkened, and he was flung unexpectedly back six years. She spoke of a dungeon with creeping walls. Rats. Dripping water. An invisible well and a blade that swung ever nearer as the walls closed in until the prisoner "struggled no more, but the agony of my soul found vent in one loud, long, and final scream of despair." He could almost smell again the stink of fear in his own drawn blood. Was it possible that Hope Newfield knew of his imprisonment by Chang Chih-tung?

"Who write these things?" he demanded.

She glanced up. "Edgar Allan Poe." She laid the book aside and returned to the table, watching him curiously. "One of this country's greatest writers. But the feeling . . . it's just like what *you* were describing."

No, he thought. She knew nothing, this American girl—imagined torture a literary device! But her blue-eyed innocence was too powerful for him to fault her. He grasped at the only word of her speech he could now recall. "Despair?"

"It means suffering so much that you lose all thought of escape. Hopelessness."

"Ah. Chinese say *chüeh-wang*. Only no Chinese will write such story."

"Why not?"

He considered, then said, "I am angry, compose verse about black mountain, snow lion, hunter. Maybe this man and lion die in fight. Still that mountain is beautiful. You know?"

She hesitated. "I think so."

"You Mr. Poe will say no. Black cloud swallow that mountain. All is dark. Or all light. That is his way."

"Not *my* Mr. Poe." An awkward smile. She tilted her head. "*You* are a true believer!"

"Believer?"

"You believe life is essentially good, that black is white."

He let his hands fall outward to the table. "Not all white, all black. White *and* black. Day, night. Good, bad. Chinese say *yin* and *yang*." He paused. "Like man and woman. Always two opposite together make one."

These last words dropped like pebbles. Suddenly she was rubbing the table again, circling her thumb until the wood paled with her warmth, and he realized this was a nervous habit. That he had made her nervous. The thought released a deep shudder of confusion. He wanted nothing more than to cover her circling hand with his own, to calm her and possess the fears he had unleashed, but what other terrors would follow then?

The clock struck. He stood, hesitating. "Two officials from Manchu government give speech at university tomorrow. Perhaps you will be interested to see?"

She looked up. "Your Minister Ts'ai?"

"Different ministers. Manchu think maybe constitution give power. But ministers do not know constitution, so must travel to West, learn what we students study many years!"

"And you? Are you planning to stand up and give another of your speeches?" She pursed her mouth as if unsure whether to smile or frown.

He jingled the change in his pocket. "I have not decided."

"But you'll be there?"

He nodded.

"Well. Perhaps I'll see you then."

ॐॐॐ

April 13, 1906

I didn't mean to go. I still don't know what prompted me, unless it was Collis's telephone call this morning—and my need to manufacture an excuse to avoid meeting him. Throwing myself in front of the Key trolley might have been a better strategy.

I thought I was safe when I entered the hall and saw those two Manchu ministers. Straight out of Hans Christian Andersen they were, in their brilliant brocade robes and tasseled button hats. Another world. Another century. Nothing to do with me. Then Paul spotted me at the back of the auditorium, came to stand beside me, and though he was polite, perfectly reserved, my heart started pounding so I was sure he must hear it. And when he mentioned that the visiting minister Tuan had presided over his examinations in Hupei and therefore considered him his student, the strangest chill—like an ache—ran through me. I looked from Paul, in his smart, manly suit, to those two old men in their fairy-tale robes, and the true enormity of his violation struck me—the distance he has traveled, not only from his homeland but from all the traditions and expectations that once ruled his every move! It was as though his ancestry had sprung to life in these two fawning ministers, and I had no choice but to believe it.

Yet I admired his rebellion all the more as the "lecture" dissolved into buffoonery. The ministers turned out to be the Chinese twins of Tweedledum and Tweedledee. First they argued over who should have the honor of speaking. The one who was senior deferred to Tuan because he was more familiar with Westerners. But after every sentence, Tuan would turn and ask, "Is that right?" "Yes, yes," the other would say, and so it went, back and forth, as they boasted of the Ch'ing government's grand plans for modernizing China. Every single line punctuated by, "Is that right?" and "Yes, yes." Paul stood through it all with his arms folded, grinning like the Cheshire cat.

Afterward, a young reporter for the student newspaper came over and asked why it takes two Chinese to give the speech of one. Paul gave an elaborate answer about China's ancient code of respect, implying that the ministers had performed in this manner as a way of showing reverence to the host university! The young man dutifully scribbled this down, and I fully expect Paul's "wisdom" to become Chinese gospel in tomorrow's *Berkeley Banner*.

"Is that true?" I asked when the reporter had gone.

"Oh, no." Paul smiled. "Ministers are Manchu. Always go in circle, no one dare to lead."

But now the audience was dispersing. I was one of only a handful of women, and people had noticed me standing with Paul. I was about to say goodbye, when who should come hurrying toward us but Minister Tuan! He took Paul aside and began waving his big sleeves, talking fast and hard, his frustration clearly mounting as Paul remained deadpan as a vaudevillian. I was transfixed. Then suddenly Tuan left in a huff. Paul returned with an amused expression, and I requested a translation. He seemed only too pleased to oblige . . .

Tuan: Before I came to San Francisco, I read your articles in the *Ta T'ung Daily*. Let me say to you, after today do not say those things anymore.

Paul: I do not know what things you mean.

Tuan: Those things you say.

Paul: I did not say anything.

Tuan: I mean the things you say every day.

Paul: I do not say anything every day.

Tuan: You do not know yourself? Those things that come out of your mouth. You know. I know. After today do not say them. We Chinese must deal with the foreigners as one. When we return from this trip you will benefit from our friendship. Give me some face. Brother, do not say those things anymore.

When he finished, Paul looked at me with such a devilish twinkle in his eye that we both burst into laughter. I said he should quit spouting revolution and become America's first Chinese comedian. Then it occurred to me that Minister Tuan was serious. I asked if it was wise to tease him so. Paul sobered immediately, and I felt that chill again. But his reply took me aback.

"You are right, Hope," he said. "These things you and I think funny may bring hardship to Minister Tuan."

I will never forget the combination of regret in Paul's voice with the kindness in his eyes, his genuine concern for Tuan . . . and his confiding in me. In that brief glow of laughter I'd allowed myself to imagine I might sidestep my obsessive longings by befriending Paul as a sister. Now I am, again, submerged.

ॐॐॐ

4

That weekend Hope was to help Mary Jane Lockyear host a garden party to raise funds for Donaldina Cameron's Chinese Presbyterian Mission

Home. Donaldina, a longtime friend of Mary Jane's, was known throughout the Bay Area as the savior of Chinese slave girls. For over a decade she had waged a largely single-handed war against the merchants and highbinders who controlled the filthy back-alley "cribs" and hidden chambers in which Chinatown's prostitution trade was conducted. She identified newly arrived slave girls, arranged police raids to rescue them, then housed and educated these girls in her Home on Sacramento Street. Many in San Francisco hailed Donaldina as a saint, but there were also those, both within and outside Chinatown, who benefited from the prostitution trade and would have been pleased to see the Scottish do-gooder dead. All of this Hope knew from Mary Jane and the papers. She herself had not met the woman, until now had never felt more than passing curiosity about her. Even though she tutored Chinese men, Hope had always preferred to think them immune and apart from the evils of Chinatown. But Paul forced her to recognize that her Chinese students were as capable of taking the ferry across the Bay as any foul-minded white man. Every day, in fact, he made this trip, to go to his newspaper office on Grant Street, and he must be at least as familiar as Donaldina with Chinatown's inner workings. But what, Hope wondered, was the *nature* of his familiarity? And could she bear to find out?

Sunday morning she arrived at Mary Jane's with armloads of flowers, cookies, and cakes for the reception. The two women hauled chairs and tables, assembled trays of dainties, and decanted sherry and port. As they worked, Mary Jane peppered her with questions about Collis, but Hope would say only that he had requested a visit and she had agreed to receive him the following Tuesday.

"My, how formal," Mary Jane remarked. "An audience with the queen. Promises a warm and cozy bridal chamber."

"Mary Jane!"

"Just an observation, my sweet."

"Collis is trying to respect my wishes."

"Some of the same men who call themselves gents for holding a door for a lady think nothing of barring and locking that door once the lady's inside. If you're not careful people will think your deviled eggs are filled with blood."

"Oh, shoo!" Hope slammed down the jar of paprika and took a spoon to the red dust mountain rising from the bowl of yolks. "Now look what you've made me do!"

Mary Jane's strong fingers closed on her shoulder. "No one can make you do anything, Hope, that you don't choose for yourself."

"No one can make you do anything," Hope snapped, "if your father makes a bloody fortune and leaves it in your lap!"

Mary Jane's father and grandfather had possessed every bit as much practical acumen as Hope's own father lacked. They had built a small manufacturing empire in Missouri, first supplying Conestoga wagons for the Oregon Trail and, later, steam engines for Mississippi River boats. Mary Jane was the only heir when her father and mother drowned in a holiday boating accident the year Mary Jane completed college. Hope had never before allowed her envy of Mary Jane's fortune to overshadow her sympathy for her friend's tragic losses, but it was hard to accept criticism from someone who really could do whatever she pleased!

Mary Jane's voice was terse and brutally blunt. "This has nothing to do with money."

Maybe not, thought Hope, but I've been made to do plenty that I never chose. In school she was made to wear feathers in her hair. When her class studied fractions, she was brought up in front of the class to prove that one fourth could be a quarter-blood Indian. Then there was the day Lester and Duncan Beasley, sons of the local judge, toppled and rolled her in the mud, smeared their hands across her chest and belly and told her *that* was how filthy she was inside.

"If you marry that man," Mary Jane pressed, "you are saying to him, and to the entire world, that you have chosen to lie with him, to strip yourself naked before him, to let him enter you, body and soul. To bear his children, to give up your life—to belong to him, Hope! I know you well enough to know that you will never surrender your will to any man you don't love. And I know you don't love Collis Chesterton."

"Well, you're wrong!" Hope cried, whirling so Mary Jane couldn't read her eyes.

"About which part?"

"About everything!"

They continued working for the next hour without uttering one word. By three o'clock a looping breeze had risen, offering slight relief from the oppressive heat. Donaldina Cameron arrived towing two scrubbed Chinese girls, one as small as a porcelain doll and the other tall and sturdy. Sample products, thought Hope bitterly, to prove the nobility of woman, the savagery of the native.

But Donaldina was a compact burst of efficiency with prematurely silver hair and an oversized nose and a voice so gently positive that Hope could not dislike her. She clasped Hope's hands and thanked her for all her generous work, making Hope feel woefully inadequate. The girls curtsied, enchanting in their broadly sashed frills, eyes on the table of sweets. Hope made sure they each had a petit four before the other guests arrived, but their delight did little to salve her conscience. Not only had she failed to commit her life to saving other people's lost souls, but she was likely casting her own to the winds at this very moment. Fortunately, this line of self-flagellation was cut short by the arrival of Donaldina's "donors."

In no time the terrace was crowded with white organza, flowered hats, monocles, and morning coats. Here were the cream of East Bay philanthropy, keepers of the flame of social conscience. As they bent to Donaldina's "Chinese daughters," their remarks made Hope cringe.

"How *well* you speak English!"

"Why, you're a little doll!"

"Such an excellent job you've done, Miss Cameron. They're perfect Celestial princesses."

"What a lucky, lucky girl you are to be saved by the likes of Miss Cameron."

While in a lower tone, cupped behind men's palms and rippling beneath women's parasols: *She knows the bowels of Chinatown like the back of her hand, stomps right into their brothels she does. If there's a trapdoor she'll find it, drag them little girls out of stalls that smell like pig chutes. Some never seen daylight since they come off the boat. Whip 'em and burn 'em, use 'em ten, twenty times a night. Down in the cribs it's twenty-five cents a pop, and special rate, fifteen cents for boys. Y'ever seen 'em? Like caged animals behind those barred windows, down the end those gummy black alleys. Gotta lure their own customers to buy 'emselves free, they'll call y'over and tell you they just had your father. Chinese think it's some kinda honor, like father like son. Aye, this Donaldina's a saint to take on those miserable monkeys. Stark, staring depravity, that's what they are.*

Donaldina stood beneath the big leafy alder, flanked by her honorary daughters, and gave a rousing speech about dignity, faith, and the resilience of the human soul. Then, as illustration, she cupped a hand around the older girl's shoulder and asked her to tell her story.

The child's name was Li-li. Her English excellent. Her story harrowing.

"I come from Mukden," she began, "to the north of China in Manchuria. When the Russians and Japanese invade my homeland, my village is burned and many uncles and neighbors taken away. My family walked many weeks through snow to the port city, Tientsin. But my father have no money. My mother tried to stop him, but he said he have no choice."

Then Donaldina took over, alluding to the more distasteful details in such a way that the ladies in the audience covered their mouths. Li-li's father had sold her and three sisters to a broker who packed the girls into steerage on a freighter bound for San Francisco. The sisters died of dysentery within the first week at sea, but Li-li, the "oldest and fattest" by her own reckoning, survived by clinging to the single vent through which fresh air pierced the sealed compartment. Donaldina, who had been alerted to the child's arrival by another passenger on the ship, claimed Li-li in a split-second seizure while her Chinatown "father" was distracted paying off his personal customs official. Reprisals were anticipated, but Li-li had lived at the Presbyterian mission for the past three years without incident. She planned to graduate high school and had expressed an interest in becoming a teacher. (A murmur ran through the gathering at these final details, as if they were the most astounding of all.)

Compassion and courage, Donaldina concluded, spanned all races. "And the evils of slavery and perversion must not—*will* not be tolerated on our shores." The combination of saintliness and revulsion produced the desired effect, and hands fluttered like wings over open checkbooks, though, as the guests were leaving, Hope heard more than one mutter, "Cost a whole lot less just to send 'em all back where they come from."

Later, as they were cleaning up, Hope asked Donaldina what did happen to her girls after they left the Mission Home.

"Some get jobs," she answered. "Others marry or are adopted into families."

"White families?"

"And Chinese."

"Then you're not entirely at war with the Chinese community."

"Heavens, no!"

"But how can you make your peace, when what's done to these girls—" Hope glanced to the children, giggling on the other side of the garden. "I've heard the ones you don't save die of disease before they're twenty."

Donaldina sighed. "It's true more often than I can bear to admit. But you know, every race has its evils. Our own enslaved the Negroes; shall we then condemn the white abolitionists along with the cotton growers simply because of their skin color? Many Chinatown residents work harder than I to end these evils. I consider it a sorry side effect of my work that my staunchest white supporters include some of the most rabid anti-Chinese."

"And yet you accept their donations."

"I do. And I try to educate them."

"Are you successful?"

Donaldina whisked a palmful of crumbs from the table toward an expectant robin. "One man took one of my girls for his wife. I believe he treats her well, but he's completely cut her off from her race. I'm afraid that's sometimes the best I can expect."

"But you do allow the girls to choose whom they marry?"

"Of course!" She looked shocked that Hope could think otherwise.

"Even Chinese men?"

"Yes, surely."

"Then there are Chinese men you would consider honorable," Hope asked, at last gaining the courage to voice her own personal concern.

"Oh, many. Especially among the educated—I should say, those who prize education over money. Sadly, money can be an even more powerful engine among the Chinese than among our own, and that makes many of them callous." She picked up a stack of plates and turned toward the kitchen. "There are no easy answers in such matters, my dear. One thing I have learned from my Chinese friends is to appreciate—and accept— the complexities of life. We Americans have a bad habit of always wanting things in black and white."

So Paul had said. Perhaps this was Hope's downfall, as well. But it seemed there were some matters that brooked no compromise, and the more muddled they were allowed to become, the more harmful the consequences.

When the others had left, Hope said to Mary Jane, "Donaldina told me that sometimes her girls end up marrying white men, or being adopted into white families. I wonder if the reverse ever happens."

"White families being adopted into Chinese girls?"

"Oh, you!" Hope shook her head. "A white *woman* marrying a Chinese man."

"Can't," said Mary Jane flatly. "It's against the law. 'Course, I've heard there's a few do live in sin. Lower-class women. Laundresses and divorcees. Gives me the shivers to think about."

"Why do you say that?"

"Ugh. Something about a man without body hair. Like making love to a child, I imagine. It just seems . . . unnatural. And their food and all those strange evil smells."

"But what if the man were American in his ways?"

"An American Chinese! Really, Hope. Donaldina's girls are a rare breed, and they owe who they are entirely to her. There's a reason the Chinese are called Celestials. They belong to a different universe."

Like making love to a child, Hope repeated to herself as she walked the darkened block to the trolley, and over and over again through the long ride home.

In the morning she telephoned Paul's boarding house and left a message that she was ill, canceling their lesson.

II
RESCUE
BERKELEY
(APRIL 1906)

☙☙☙

1

The morning of Tuesday, April 17, brought more heat and humidity under a sky the color of sea glass. As Hope braced for Collis's visit, Eleanor Layton readied herself for a trip to San Francisco and a cousin's society wedding. The carriage had been summoned for eleven o'clock to take her to the noon ferry. Unfortunately, it overturned on the way. Another cart was sent, but when Eleanor smelled whiskey on the driver's breath, she ordered him away and began babbling about this being a sign she should not go at all.

Hope offered her landlady sherry for her nerves and called for a mule-drawn hack. By the time it arrived she had succeeded in persuading Eleanor that her cousin's wedding was sure to be San Francisco's event of the season, and Eleanor would never forgive herself if she didn't attend. The landlady, two drinks for the better, even allowed herself to be persuaded that the unfortunate green tint her hair had acquired when she colored it for the occasion was actually quite becoming. She clamped Hope in a weepy embrace as if she were going off to the South Seas instead of across the Bay for four days.

"Do be careful, dear girl. I feel horrible leaving you like this——" The

driver snapped his whip. Eleanor fell back. "Goodbye!" she sang out with
a feeble wave.

Hope stared at the garden. Not a blade of grass, not a leaf moved. It
was like the stillness before a storm. Maybe that had contributed to
Eleanor's jitters, and Hope had been too harsh in shooing her away. But
she couldn't let her stay.

She knelt by the border and dragged her fingers through the warm
spongy earth. After Eleanor's weeding frenzies Hope sometimes
covertly sowed wildflower seeds here. Indian pink, fairy lantern,
columbine, and gentian, the little shoots would come streaming out of
the churned soil, and the landlady would throw up her hands. "How
did *they* get in! What are they, anyway?" The unintended nature of wildflowers bedeviled her, and the beauty of those that survived her rake to
bloom infuriated her. "They're no better than weeds and just as much
trouble."

Hope smiled grimly, shook the earth from her hands, and was rins-
ing them at the pump when she spotted Collis across the street. He was
whistling, arms full of stall-bought gladiolus. Funeral flowers, to
Hope's mind. But expensive and well meant. She slipped into the
kitchen.

As she entered the parlor with a tray of lemonade, he pressed his nose
to the screen. "You look beautiful."

"Come in, Collis. It's cooler inside." She put down the tray. "Thank
you. So are the flowers."

She escaped to plunge the stalks into water, leaving him to pour out
their glasses, but in the kitchen, the scarlet packaging of Paul's jasmine tea
caught her eye. She stood wavering for several seconds, then tossed the
box into the trash.

"Eleanor here?" he asked when she returned.

"She's gone to a—" Hope checked herself. "No."

"Well, all right. I'll have you alone, then. Sit here beside me?"

They sat on balding velveteen upholstery and inhaled the parlor's overlapping scents—lavender sachets, the oil that lubricated Eleanor's
Graphophone, the vapors of her chicken soup. The hallway clock punctuated every second.

Hope took a glass from the tray and rolled it against her cheek. She moved her eyes around the pieces of Collis's face. The metallic curl of his mustache and sideburns. The mole above his right eye. His soft pink mouth and the beads of perspiration beneath his lower lip.

He thrust a hand into his jacket pocket. "Close your eyes."

She hardly needed to look to know the ring was exquisite. Gold set with rubies encircling a teardrop diamond. When she said nothing, he slid it awkwardly onto her right ring finger.

"It fits!" A boyish grin.

"It's lovely."

"Why, Hope, you're crying! Here." He wiped her face with his own pale yellow monogrammed handkerchief, edging closer and closer until his features blurred. She shut her eyes and held her breath against the smell of him, then pushed away on the pretext of looking at the stones by the window's light. He followed, dropped a hand to her shoulder. "Yes, then?"

She turned the gleaming gems. They were hard and smooth and unmoving as rock, yet leapt with the illusion of life.

There followed an intimate celebration lunch, one-sided discussion of dates, guest lists, reception sites, services (Collis, though Episcopalian, was solicitous of Hope's Presbyterian upbringing), and, of course, dangling like a poisoned carrot at the end of the stick, their European honeymoon. Somehow she made it through the afternoon. But once he had finally gone, her teeth began to chatter. In spite of the day's lingering heat, in spite of sweaters, scarves, woolen socks, and, later, her heaviest flannel gown, she could not seem to get warm.

Alone in the empty house, she turned every lock and checked each one twice before retiring upstairs. She sought refuge in Elizabeth Cady Stanton's *Solitude of Self*, but her brain refused to absorb the proud and confident words. Her engagement notwithstanding, Paul's dark eyes appeared between the lines. And the sight tormented her.

She considered the stones sparking against her skin, saw in them Collis's numbing gray gaze, his thick white fingers with their tufts of hair. She slipped off the ring, hid it as Mother Wayland had taught her to do with all jewels, in a stocking in her underwear drawer. What would her real mother have advised, she wondered. But diphtheria had killed her mother when Hope was just two months old.

Now, abruptly, she was hot. She peeled away all the layers she'd piled on until her gown rode against naked skin. She decided a cup of cold milk would help and started down through the empty house with a smile at the updraft, like cooling hands between her legs. In the kitchen she hauled open the ice chest, found the milk bottle, and started to reach for a cup. But the polished, sweating surface, the bottle's sliding weight against her palm caused her to reconsider and, instead, skate the glass up the inside of her free wrist, then to the elbow, and on, pushing her sleeve all the way up over her shoulder. She closed her eyes. The sensation, as if her skin were itself becoming liquid, unleashed a different sort of thirst. Not an unfamiliar one—she had quelled its kind more than once before. But this time she put up no resistance. She lifted her nightdress and rode the bottle over the flat of her belly, now into the hollows between her ribs. She brought it down smooth against her hip and lowered herself to the chair, then, suddenly impatient, she flung her gown above her waist. She raised the moist surface to her sternum and across each breast, grazing the bluish tips lightly, again with more pressure, and again, cold and hard so her nipples tightened into knots. The curtains were open. Any backyard trespasser could see her, watch her exploring herself, but the spell was such that she did not notice, indeed, could not have stopped if she wanted. She slid the instrument of this strange luxury downward, slowing along the inside of her thighs. From knee to knee, she pulled against the contraction of muscle and nerve, slowly—still more slowly— until the pressure reached her very center. And the cold hard whiteness melted into her and gave silence to what she only at this instant understood was her despair.

She let her gown fall back into place, then fastidiously wiped the bottle clean and returned it, with an ironic smile, to Eleanor's hardwood ice chest.

She dreamed, that night, of a high, gateless wall snaking for miles under stars that flowed like an ocean.

᭞᭞᭞

2

When Hope next opened her eyes she was flying. For the briefest of seconds she actually believed she had magical powers. Then she slammed into a wall. But the pain was barely noticeable for the violence she now felt and heard around her. Shattering. Shaking. The darkened room heaved, floor rippling beneath a cascade of glass and crockery and books. A nightmare. Must be. Trapped in a ship inside a gray bottle that some giant was rattling—hard—while the surrounding seas erupted with pounding and clanging, animal screams and yelps.

She had to get up, pull herself together, and go help whoever—whatever—was making those ghastly noises. But when she lifted her head the floor tipped again and the massive oak bed that had sent her flying hurtled into the closet, missing her shoulder by inches. Sobered and profoundly awake, she tucked herself into a ball and made a helmet of her hands. She would wait this out. But the seconds stretched on these monstrous waves. The house would not stop swaying. She heard the rain of chimney bricks, and within the frame of her busted window a crescent moon jittered across a smoky green sky.

It seemed to go on and on, and even after the shaking finally subsided she did not trust the stillness. The room had filled with unrecognizable shadows and the sinister glint of night glass. She extended her arm and felt the wall, lifted the ghostly shape of her hand as if it were a foreign object. It was a relief when the swirling dust made her sneeze, the first familiar sensation since she'd awakened. Now she recognized the clang of church bells and the patter of hoofbeats outside. The animal screaming had ceased.

She had no experience of earthquakes, but she had heard the temblors could continue, with varying intensity, for days. This house didn't feel as if it would stand through another upheaval. She needed to get out and away. But everything she owned was here, and Eleanor had gone off entrusting her with all her worldly possessions as well—Eleanor.

Was it conceivable the quake had struck only this side of the Bay? The thought of all San Francisco being twisted and thrown as she had been, of her landlady perhaps dying or maimed—and she had insisted Eleanor leave, all but roped her into that hack. Eleanor, Mary Jane, Collis—Paul. Hope crushed her palms to her eyes. She must keep control of herself. Get out and see what needed to be done. What she could do to help.

She climbed to her feet and pulled open the door. The hall was pitch black and quiet except for the creak of fractured wood. She moved cautiously, sliding barefoot through rubble, but had covered only a yard or two when the giant hand seized the house again, then twisted and tore at it, ravaging. Plaster showered from the ceiling, knocking her to her knees. She heard the staircase shimmy. The floor buckled, walls tilted. Then a sudden deafening reverberation, like the explosion of solid stone.

When the aftershock subsided she was crouching farther down the hallway, a little more bruised but otherwise intact. The air had turned ghostly with dust so thick she could feel its grain in her throat, against the surface of her eyes. She pulled up the neck of her gown to mask her nose and mouth and berated herself for the childish pique that had left her exposed underneath. No time to find clothes and change, she'd have to face the world like this. At least, she reminded herself, she was alive. But she had to get downstairs.

From the corner where the hallway turned she was able to make out a few familiar shapes. The dark plane of the opposite wall. The striped shadow of the balustrade. The paler expanse of the open stairwell. But what was that draft? She took a step. Another. The floorboards groaned beneath her weight. She flattened herself against the wall and stared.

The falling chimney had obliterated the staircase, leaving a three-story drop.

The recognition that she was trapped stopped the rocking in her legs, banished all concern for her friends, modesty, the screams outside, and reeled her back toward her room. She was the one who needed help. She had to get to a window. Someone would come. Surely someone would come. But now, though she shoved with all her force, the door refused to open. The bed or dresser must have wedged against it during the last seizure.

Again she hurled herself at the panel. And again it repelled her. On the third futile assault she thought, I am going to die here.

భోభోభో

In Chinese superstition, the earth rests on the back of a sleeping dragon. When this Earth Dragon is irritated he responds by squirming and scratching. Sometimes he awakens, stretches high and wide, rolls over. Chinese call this *ti lung chen*. Earth Dragon shake.

That morning, when he was tossed from sleep in the greening dark before dawn, Paul's first thought was that the Earth Dragon must be very angry. His second was that he must rid himself of such feudal superstitions. His third thought, as the Dragon gave another stretch and the residents of his boarding house began yelling, was for Hope Newfield.

He did not pause to question this impulse or even to dress himself. He regretted the lack of shoes when he finally noticed the street was laced with shattered glass. But, as in a dream, he was immune to injury, ran like a child's toy on a string, without feeling the ground. He ran the stricken avenues of Berkeley from Addison to Telegraph to Stuart Street seeing the houses as cutouts—broken squares of gray and terra-cotta roofs, the blood-red and brown of dropped chimneys, falling waves of purple vines. Paul was familiar with the colors and designs of nature's fury. He had been in Japan ten years ago when the great earthquake and tsunami had killed twenty-eight thousand. Berkeley, it appeared, had been lucky. If only this luck would extend to Hsin-hsin.

He passed dozens of distraught people out in robes and wrappers staring up at their broken roofs or talking among themselves, but on Stuart Street the houses were farther apart, and no one was outside. His teacher's house, like the others, had lost its chimney and the surrounding patch of roof, but otherwise was standing. The front door had sunk inward off its jamb, giving access to the parlor. Walls broken and smoking dust, furnishings split and cast aside, the room might have been ransacked by bandits. At the back, where the staircase should have been, a pile of tumbled bricks and timbers rose higher than his head. The well above was empty.

He listened but heard no sound of life. If she'd been on those stairs when they collapsed, she might now be lying beneath them. He inhaled sharply, cupped hands around his mouth, and, tipping his head back, howled her name.

"I'm here!" She scrambled to her feet. "I'm up here, Paul. Help me!"

An instant, and their voices were flying. She must find her way to a window. Her bedroom was blocked. Another room, then. The spare room! In the madness of fear, the most obvious solutions go unseen. And yes, there was a ladder in the shed out back. He must bring that around. She would make a rope to lower herself. He would climb to meet her. "I receive you," he called.

"You *will* receive me," she teased, giddy with her reprieve, though he was already gone.

The door to the spare room opened just enough for her to twist through. The bureau here was on its side, surrounded by shards of broken window and mirror that reflected the brightening dawn. Spilled cedar chips and dried lavender carpeted the floor, along with skirts and stockings and corsets and waists out of the fallen armoire: Eleanor's off-season wardrobe. Hope registered another clutch of guilt and took a step without looking, was sliding in blood.

"One thing at a time," she told herself, extracting the sliver from her right heel. A Bible and a Sears Roebuck consumer's guide lay within reach. She shook their pages free of debris and skated on the splayed bindings over to the window.

The world outside lay rearranged, but subtly. The front of a nearby barn tipped forward as cleanly as the lid off a crate, while the three houses within view all appeared undamaged except for their fallen chimneys. Down by Telegraph Avenue a motorcar sprawled, wheels to the sky, with a goat stepping circles on its upturned belly. Now two riderless horses tore uphill, but overall the scene was as quiet as if everyone had gone back to sleep. There had not been an aftershock in what seemed like hours, and the soft pewter light of daybreak promised the worst was over.

It occurred to Hope that she could simply pull back inside and wait. Paul would not be able to reach her without her throwing down a line. He would have to get help. Then they would not be alone.

But here he came now, hauling the ladder around the corner. He wore loose black pants and a blue tunic that sailed behind him as he moved. Long bare feet. Square shoulders. His dark hair still tumbled from sleep. She strained against herself, hoisting the sash, leaned out the window and waved.

"Hurry," he replied, already positioning the ladder below.

Among the garments at her feet lay winter wrappers, nainsook skirts, muslin corset covers, and woolen stockings. She tied the sturdiest fabrics into a chain and secured one end around the leg of the bureau, dropped the other over the ledge. Below, he pulled to check its strength, then called that he was ready. She was reaching one last time into the pile of clothing when another aftershock rippled the house, driving clean out of her mind whatever she had been reaching for. She threw one leg over the windowsill, grabbed the rope with both hands, took a deep breath and brought the other leg over, and started down.

Hand over hand, soles clenched, she had descended only a foot or two when she felt her gown billowing out, the cold air painting her legs. Drawers. She'd been reaching for a pair of black and white striped drawers when the last shock emptied her mind.

The sudden dawning of her exposed and irretrievable condition caused her to clap her knees shut, skinning them on the shingle siding as she swung against the house. She clung to the rope with one hand and cinched the gown with the other, but it was impossible. She curled inward like a snail and dangled. "Go away," she called over her shoulder. "Please."

"*Pu yao chin te*," he pleaded unintelligibly, still holding the rope beneath her.

He did not go, and she did not move. How long she would have hung there is difficult to say. She was stubborn and strong for her size. But the knots were slipping, the fabric stretching. The absurdity of her position came to her at last, along with the recognition that they were both equally compromised. Both compelled to see and feel nothing. She told herself this as she traded hands, dropping and clutching, dropping and clutching. She told herself he would not dare.

Then, as promised, he received her. His fingers encircled her ankle. The span of his palm covered her entire sole, but the intimacy of his touch and his relative size neither terrified nor humiliated, and for this reason posed a greater threat than if he had opened her flapping skirt and thrust a hand between her legs.

He guided her to the ladder's top rung, then quickly let her go.

As soon as he had seen her safely on the ground, Paul started back up the ladder.

"This you room?" he called, pointing.

"Yes, but how will you get over there?"

He shook his head against her worry and pulled himself up the rope, then crept along the outer ledge and entered her bedroom through the broken window. It was not a selfless act. Although he had averted his eyes, he had seen enough during her descent to understand that she must be dressed before they were discovered together. Beyond this practical assessment he forbade his thoughts to travel.

Her tumbled belongings lay in a haze of fragrance—foreign flowers pulsing so strong he let out a violent sneeze and nearly cut his foot on her shattered mirror. Her dressing table stood in the center of the room surrounded by its former contents, which he combed through while berating himself for not being more observant. American women did not use sticks to hold up their hair. What, then? Hooks? Or pins? He swept the hardwood floor with his hand. Whatever she used, he must find it. He had not imagined such hair, the longing its dark, emancipated weight would arouse in him.

Among spilled powder and towels, the remnants of a pitcher and basin, he located ten brown hooks and a silver-backed brush. He pulled a tuft of her hair from the bristles and rubbed it between his thumbs as he considered what else he should bring her. On the floor beside the bed he found the white shirtwaist with the ruffled throat and black skirt she had worn the day they met; the high-collared dress, apricot with jade stripes, from his last lesson; small, brown buttoned boots; kid gloves; a jacket to match the skirt and another blouse. He made a bundle of this clothing and knelt to inspect her scattered books and papers.

There was the volume of Poe from which she had read to him, a photograph of an older man who might be her father, and here, a leather-bound notebook that swam with the markings of her pen. Page after page of fragile waves. He was not familiar with Western script, was about to fold the book closed when his name rushed out at him. LIANG PO-YU. PAUL LIANG. This alone she had inserted in legible black letters. He squinted, stared, but the surrounding lines tangled, obscuring whatever emotion or accusation they contained.

"Paul!" she called from outside. "Are you all right?" He tucked the diary inside the rolled clothing. Better he did not know her feelings. He had no right to know.

He was about to announce his descent when he noticed a heap of soft, pale garments. Lustrous pink and ivory fabric, with ruffles and tucks and long bony ridges. He held one of the corsets in his arm and traced its elaborate shape, lifted it to his nose and breathed a scent that was lighter, softer, more intoxicating than any supplied in a bottle. He had not touched the hidden clothing of a woman since leaving his wife for the last time, six years earlier. That was in summer, and the fabric had been silk of the finest quality, the fragrance within them like a thrilling mountain fog. The woman herself was something quite different.

He added the garments and several pairs of stockings to the bundle already assembled. Hope Newfield, he told himself firmly, was nothing—nothing—like his wife.

While Paul was up in her room, Hope had safely retrieved from her shambled office her money purse, which held twenty-seven dollars, her bankbook, which registered another sixty-one in savings, and her black serge cloak and felt fedora. But the wreckage of the stairwell, now fully visible in the morning light, warned against spending any more time in the building than was absolutely essential, so when Paul descended with her clothing, she went to change in the cramped but intact garden shed out back.

Opening the bundle in the dusty light she expected at most a dress, a pair of boots, perhaps a jacket and hose. She was stunned to find as well her most intimate possessions. Her petticoats he had touched, her corsets, her drawers. He had found her journal, with his name printed boldly inside, and surely his decision to salvage it showed he had read her mindless ramblings. Embarrassment scalded her. Even the inclusion of her father's portrait seemed a presumptuous insult, the presence of the volume of Poe a humiliating reminder of her own carnal weakness and stupidity. But her rescuer's gravest transgression was the burial, at the very center of this package, of those inlaid tortoiseshell hairpins. Those pins had been Frank Pearson's final gift to her.

Hope felt that she had been rendered transparent, as if this man she barely knew could see through walls, her skin, her mind. She dressed in a rush, stumbling among the filthy tools, and a wave of nausea swept her. Then she was angry.

She had to get away. He would be waiting outside, but she could switch to the left around the side of the house and on out into the street. There must be people about by now. Perhaps even Collis. The thought of her suitor—fiancé—only stoked her fury. Of course, though he lived on the other side of Albany, Collis surely was on his way. Had she but waited he would have been her rescuer. She pinned her hair with tight, skewered twists and pushed it inside her hat, then rolled her remaining possessions into her cloak. She would leave, she decided, and if the Chinaman followed, she would scream.

But when she stepped from the shed, the small kitchen yard lay empty.

Good, she thought. She must walk toward town. If the streetcars, by some miracle, were running, she would board one for Oakland. If not, she would hire a cart to take her to Mary Jane's. From there, she would figure out what to do about Collis. She would not think about Paul.

What prompted her before leaving, then, to glance back toward the kitchen garden? A prodding breeze, perhaps. The call of a bird. Or a sudden shift of light.

He was barely visible, a line of darkness in the darker shade beyond the old moss-covered privy. He had found a discarded bench overhung by ivy, and there sat erect, motionless. One bare foot rested on the opposite knee while his hands lay upturned in his lap in an attitude of serenity and complete detachment. His long neck rose like a stem from his mandarin collar. His eyes were closed.

She inched forward, stepping softly between rows of lavender and thyme as her anger turned to dust. She should thank him, she thought, and say goodbye. But he would not look up. She moistened her lips and cleared her throat. No reaction. A cold, certain knowledge rode through her now: he did not want her at all.

When at last his eyes fluttered open, they faced each other in unexpected but absolute stillness.

∂∂∂

What were they thinking? Had they a plan as they set off that morning, her belongings under his arm, striding into public scrutiny? Certainly there were no stated intentions. They had to get away from that house, from the solitude it afforded and the resulting temptation, but they did not have to stay together. At the first raised eyebrow they would have parted. However, Berkeley was in a state of shock and utterly self-absorbed.

Before they'd even left the yard, one of the Burgess boys called to them from across the road. His parents lay pinned in their bed beneath a fallen bureau. By the time Hope and Paul had freed the trapped couple, helped to set their broken legs, and seen to the needs of their three young children, two hours had passed. The family found them food and water and put Paul in a pair of Mr. Burgess's socks and bluchers. They offered a jacket and pants as well, but Hope's neighbor weighed well over two hundred pounds. It was a miracle the shoes fit.

As they left, Hope glanced at Paul and was surprised to find him grinning broadly. She asked what was so funny. He pointed out that during all that time, Mrs. Burgess had never changed out of her nightdress or pinned up her hair.

"She does not even cover herself before a Chinaman."

Hope asked if he thought Mrs. Burgess a loose woman because of this.

Whether he honestly didn't understand, she would never know, but he answered with a quizzical, "She is not loose. She is broken."

Hope laughed. Oh, how she laughed! Relief, gratitude, wonder flooded through her. It was going to be all right.

Of course, there were no streetcars, no electricity, no telephones or wire service, but there were plenty of carts and rigs for hire, and Hope still might have gone to Mary Jane's. But she couldn't imagine bringing Paul there. And she couldn't leave him now. Every window on Shattuck was broken, and the street was awash with milk from tipped wagons and whiskey from capsized saloons. Turnips and onions that had rolled from the shops filled gutters and trolley tracks. Merchants stood scratching their heads and exchanging doomsday estimates of their losses, while the few shops that managed to open that day had customers lined up around the block. The talk was all of damage, of the fires flaring across the Bay, refugees coming. Someone shouted that they needed help over at the temporary hospital being set up at Hearst Hall. Paul never asked why Hope welcomed this announcement. But he came along.

In the makeshift hospital they were treated as partners for walking through the door together. Once the supervising nurse had established that neither of them needed treatment themselves and that they could communicate with each other, they were put to work rolling bandages, inventorying ointments and gauzes, setting up cots, and generally making ready for casualties from the city. According to the latest reports, San Francisco's entire business district was on fire, with new flare-ups by the minute. The nurse said Hope and Paul should work as a team, because they'd be more efficient that way. Perhaps she meant it. Perhaps she didn't trust Paul to work alone, but circumstances soon distracted her. Refugees from San Francisco were already streaming in. Burn victims, people with broken bones, lacerations, and shock. Paul and Hope worked as far from the injuries as possible.

They did not talk much—the din of arriving patients and shouting would have made even casual conversation difficult, if casual conversation had even been desired. Sometime during the afternoon they were given sandwiches and milk, which they might have taken outside to the grass, but instead they gravitated to a couple of chairs in the central hallway. The unspoken reason was to avoid any semblance of intimacy, but Hope wasn't prepared for the implicit intimacy of eating and drinking together, just the two of them in that sea of strangers. She noticed how he blotted his lips on the back of his hands after swallowing, that he handled the sandwich suspiciously, wouldn't touch the milk at all. For most of the meal, however, her eyes were fixed on a rosette knot in the floorboard beside her right foot.

They had not really come as Samaritans, of course. That large, bustling hall was a safe zone. Hope could stand in public close enough to touch him, and occasionally their hands would meet, and no one else thought anything of it. While they were there, aid was their mission—and noble enough justification for Hope's abandoning the wreckage of her home.

(She did inquire about her landlady, and was assured that no E. Layton had been posted on any casualty lists.) But Hope's and Paul's medical skills were minimal, and once all civilian preparations were in order, their "team" was dismissed.

It was five o'clock and the western sky was solid with smoke. Hope could taste the creosote, see the ash descending in a lazy snow. Animals shaken to flight that morning formed roving packs that grew bolder as their numbers swelled. Rats streamed like shadows out of alleyways and basements. There were also packs of stray men. Signs had been posted warning that looters would be shot, and most merchants had already boarded up their shops in anticipation of trouble.

ॐॐॐ

Hope and Paul found Miss Bertha's boarding house vacant but unbroken. In Paul's second-floor room fallen papers littered the floor, the desk stood askew, and the lacquered hide boxes containing his Chinese robes, scrolls, and what remained of the dried and pickled vegetables and medicinal roots he had brought from Hupei lay strewn about like dominoes. The heavier camphor chests containing his furs and winter garments remained securely wedged inside the small corner closet, while the limbs of his Western suits poked out from beneath the walnut dresser.

Paul pushed his narrow bed to the wall, tugged the covers taut, and sat down. Hope had not asked, simply followed him upstairs, and now she knelt among his belongings, pushing books and ink sticks and papers into aimless piles. The light from the lantern washed her skin gold. She had removed her hat, let her hair slip loose about her face. One stray curl clung to her cheek, below a smudge of soot. She yawned broadly and rocked her upper body, never lifting her eyes. He could see she was exhausted. Yet she was alone with him in his room.

Outside men yelled and clattered dimly. He could not feel his own fatigue.

She picked up one of his writing brushes and drew it across her wrist. "What do we do?"

"You must rest."

"Here?"

"You are safe here."

"Am I?" Her voice arched, then she laughed and jabbed the brush be-hind her ear. A tear ran down her left cheek.

"I will sleep some other place," he said.

She did not answer.

He came to her, bending, placed his fingertips lightly on her upturned wrist. "First I bring some food and water."

"Paul?"

He pulled away.

"Thank you."

A short while later, after he had left Hope to sleep, the two other boarders, Ma Lung-sing and Ho Yao-fan, burst into the kitchen. Their talk was all about the white devils they had watched struggling with their disaster. Ho was just asking where Paul had disappeared to that morning, when they were joined by Miss Bertha Miles. The landlady was so tall she had to bow to pass through the doorway, and she had a habit of rocking from one square hip to the other as she talked. Paul had lived in this house since his arrival in America more than a year ear-lier, but he never tired of looking at Miss Bertha. The first person with black skin he had ever met, she was so dark that in the beginning he could hardly believe her face and hands were not painted. They had be-come friends when she said she used to think exactly the same thing about Chinese eyes.

The landlady told them she'd just returned from the wharf where the Salvation Army was setting up a tent city. The refugees already numbered in the thousands. She made no comment when Paul informed her that an-other guest would be staying overnight.

"These is strange times," she said, turning away. "Worrisome times. Can't nothing be the same after a day like today."

A few minutes later they heard Miss Bertha's voice rise up out of her bedroom like a long streak of coal dust singing sharp and deep with the love of her Christian lord. Ma and Ho demanded information about Po-yu's guest. Assuming they would see her eventually, he told the truth.

They both sucked air between their teeth. "*Chipa jen!*" You are a crazy man.

"Doomed!"

"She can't stay here—they will chop our cocks off."

"If you cannot contain your appetites, Liang, you know there are slave girls in Chinatown!"

"I hear Chinatown is burning now."

"No!"

"I hear everybody has run away."

At the medical shelter Paul had heard no mention of Chinatown, but Ma claimed the destruction was total: not one block had survived. That meant the offices of the Chinese newspapers, including the *Free Press*, must also have been destroyed. The loss of the newspapers would cripple the republicans' political activities. Dr. Sun's followers would need to work double time to reclaim whatever equipment was salvageable, find a new location, reconstruct a press. As editor, Paul thought, this should be my first concern. And yet . . .

No water can be pulled from a dry spring. Chinatown's rebuilding of homes and businesses would drain money and attention away from the revolution in China for weeks, perhaps months to come. People helped only themselves in such times.

కుకుకు

3

Paul woke at dawn after a night filled with enough wheezing and moaning to sound a Peking opera. From the small dormer window he could see the continuing climb of smoke, pale gray and black, above San Francisco, blotting the early light. The street in front of the house had come alive with makeshift fires and encampments. Families in odd combinations of dress clutched whatever they had managed to salvage: tattered pillows, jewelry boxes, one-eyed toys, mewling cats, and caged canaries. They wore nightmare masks, which Paul had seen so often on refugees in China, though he had not thought he would see them here.

Taking care not to rouse the other men, he dressed in the vested herringbone suit he had gathered up after delivering Hope's supper last night. But when he checked his room now it was empty, and when he got downstairs he found Hope already at the front door, pulling on her gloves. "I'm going back," she said without looking up. "If Eleanor survived, she'd come home. I should be there."

A pink crease notched her cheek where it had rested all night against his pillow. Her packed belongings lay at her feet. He took them wordlessly and followed her out.

They could see the transformation all the way from the corner of Telegraph Avenue. Mrs. Layton's lawn had sprouted mushroom tents. Cooking smoke spiraled up from the side yard, and the verandah was walled with paper bags, boxes, valises, and crates. Babies shrieked from one side of the house. Men wielding tools attacked the other. Women in tarnished evening gowns chattered, while children dressed for a beggars' banquet ran races back and forth. In an upholstered armchair just inside the front gate sat a woman with matted green hair underneath what appeared to be a dead bird in a nest of shriveled straw. She wore a curious, mawkish smile and wave the singed remains of a Chinese fan back and forth below her chin.

The thought came to Paul of reproductions he had once seen of paintings by the Flemish artist Hieronymus Bosch. Strange images in which humans appeared as small and numerous as insects in a landscape of yawning wounds. The paintings had seemed unlike anything in life, until today.

Only when Hope cried out her name and hurried through the gate did Paul recognize the green-haired woman. He immediately pulled back. Eleanor Layton had no use for him, nor he for her.

"I'm so relieved you're safe, Eleanor," said Hope, "but who are all these people?"

"We're the wedding!" A small, sharp-voiced girl glared at Hope.

"The Mackays," Mrs. Layton nodded toward the gathering by the house, "and the Breckinridges."

"They made everybody leave the hotel when the fires came," the girl started up again, whirling as she talked. "We had to walk and walk to get away and then we had to wait forever before Papa could find a boat to take us. It stank of dirty fish and it was after *midnight* when we came here. I had to sleep on the grass with my cousin Delbert snoring in my ear. Uh oh. Dizzy!" She fell dramatically, arms overhead.

"My great-niece Jennifer." Mrs. Layton shook her head at the prostrate child. "So now that you know our story, Hope, tell me where have *you* been, leaving my house in such a shambles?"

"Oh." Hope shrugged, speaking into the wind. "With a friend."

But looking back now, she saw no sign of him. There was a team of shirt-sleeved men at the gate, hauling lumber. Nearby, two little boys tore up tufts of grass and threw them at each other. Hammering poured from the house, women's voices from the side yard. Hope scanned up and down the street, to the edges of the garden, among more clusters of children playing marbles and jumping rope. There must be twenty people here, or more. But Paul had disappeared.

She told herself it was for the best. She had not intended for him to come in the first place. It was quite disturbing enough to have slept in his scent all night, and there was no reason for him to be here. But this way he had of appearing and vanishing made her fitful. And he had her clothes—that journal, which she should have burned as soon as she wrote his name. How could he have left!

"Yes, I saw your Rapunzel rope and ladder." Eleanor grinned. "You're a wicked one, you are, but I'm glad you've come to your senses."

Hope only half heard her. She was remembering Paul's face leaning over her last night, the dazzle of heat that shot through her when he stroked her upturned wrist. She shuddered, forced her attention back to the situation at hand. Yesterday she had heard reports of flames tall as Russian Hill, buildings exploding from the heat, streets melting into rivers of liquid macadam. Trampled children. Police shooting to kill anyone who crossed them. She looked at her landlady's tattered clothing—that mangled hat!

"I shouldn't have pushed you to go into the city, Eleanor. It must have been an agony over there."

"Agh! We were lucky. An adventure I'll never forget. Excitement's grand when you've come out of it alive. Besides, my house will soon be good as new, and I'll have a family to fill it at last."

"What do you mean?"

Eleanor waved her fan toward the group by the verandah. "You see that broad-shouldered man up there and the tall, pretty woman beside him. That's Reggie and Stella Mackay, and eight of these children are theirs. They barely got out of their house on Dupont, poor things, and Reggie's saying he'll never go back, so I told him, why not live here with me?" She smiled at Hope. "You know I always wanted children."

"But where will we put them all?"

The landlady winked. "Good you're moving out, dear."

Hope struggled to reconstruct the day before the quake. Eleanor had left a good half-hour before Collis arrived, so she couldn't possibly be referring to Hope's engagement . . .

At the other end of the house the bride wailed and broke free from a man who had been trying to embrace her. She tripped on her long train and sank to the ground shuddering like a crippled moth. Eleanor said, "That's Prudence and Robert. Poor thing insists it's bad luck to change out of that gown—however soiled—until they've seen this wedding through. As if she could have any *more* bad luck."

Hope looked away. She had read in *National Geographic* that Chinese brides always dressed in red, with one notable exception. If the groom died before his wedding, the bride was still expected to become his widow and his parents' obedient daughter-in-law, so a spirit wedding was held. Only on this occasion, when a girl was marrying a dead man, would the wedding garments be white.

"Hope!"

It was Collis, coming across the street.

"There's your shining knight. Could be a double wedding, Hope," Eleanor suggested. "Preacher's on his way."

"Double wedding!" That annoying little girl clapped and spun toward the house.

Hope opened her mouth, but the wind silenced her. The same wind that was driving the fires, leveling the city.

The widow rolled her eyes. "Already one night into it. Tongues'll wag if you don't tie the knot now."

Finally it dawned on her. No wonder Eleanor had received her with such relish.

Collis rushed through the gate. His trousers were spattered with mud, his shirt collar half out of his jacket, and he'd misbuttoned himself so one lapel flopped over his hastily knotted tie, but he had that tie on and, as he neared them, he straightened his gray Dunlap derby as if making a formal call.

Hope cast one last glance down the street, though she could not have said whether she was dreading or praying Paul would be there. It didn't matter. He was gone.

"Where in hell have you been, Hope? I spent all night searching, out of my mind with worry."

She moved away from Eleanor to meet him. "Collis, I'm sorry—"

"Took hours to get here, and no sign of you." He put his hand on her shoulder, and she flinched. His tone altered. "It'll be all right, Hope. You're safe now—"

The width and height of him closed around her like the walls of a tomb. Safe. She was anything but safe. She pressed her cheek into the gray of his shoulder as he talked on in that possessive tone and held her, and she said nothing. But around them the wind continued to blow, whipping at the treetops, lashing the long green branches of the willow outside the gate. And suddenly, from beneath those branches, Paul appeared. He had been watching her all along.

She tried to shake her head, to signal him that what he saw had nothing to do with her, that it was another girl in Chesterton's embrace, but Paul made no further movement or gesture. Do what you will, he seemed to say. What you have to.

No one can make you do anything you don't choose for yourself.

She brought her hands up flat against Collis's chest and roughly pushed him away. His eyes gave off a brief, injured spark, then retreated to their persistent dullness as he mistook her rejection for spunkiness. "There's my girl," he coaxed.

She quickly scanned the yard and saw that no one else had noticed Paul, though she and Collis had drawn everyone's attention. A line of women near the pump were shading their eyes for a better view, the children were loudly smacking their lips, and Eleanor was clucking like a matron of honor. Only the man they did not see understood the true meaning of Hope's withdrawal. He revealed this understanding through the slow shift of her belongings in the crook of his arm, the quiet parting of his lips. He never took his eyes off her.

She drew her purse from her cloak pocket. "I've made a mistake," she said.

Collis gave her a benevolent smile. "Mistake?"

"I can't marry you."

Collis watched her as if he hadn't heard. "What are you doing?"

"Here." Hope reached for his hand and pushed into it the ring she had found in her stocking that morning.

"She's mad," shrilled Eleanor, starting forward. "Don't believe a word she says, Professor."

"Mrs. Layton, please!" Collis bellowed and lifted the back of his hand, stopping himself within inches of her face. Eleanor shook all over like a dog and grabbed her great-niece as if to shield herself against further insult.

"What is it, Aunt," said the oblivious child as she was being steered away. "Double wedding?"

"Not on my property, it's not," muttered Eleanor. "Come away, all you children. Let them clean up their own mess."

"What's happened to you, Hope?" said Collis when the landlady was out of earshot. "Where were you last night?"

"Don't use that condescending tone. I didn't suffer a blow to the head, and I have not taken leave of my senses."

"You were perfectly happy to marry me the day before yesterday."

"Was I?" She didn't dare look at Paul for fear that Collis would follow her eyes, but she could feel him tensed and waiting, measuring every move.

"So you led me to believe."

"You've been too good, Collis." She swallowed. "It's no fault of yours."

"Well that makes all the difference, doesn't it?"

She glared at him. "You force me to say I don't love you!"

He laughed. Fat tears glistened in the corners of his eyes. He brushed them away with the back of his wrist and looked down at the ring he was still holding, as if mystified by its presence. "I never said love was a condition."

For the first time it occurred to Hope that Collis would have been as miserable with her as she would have been with him.

From the corner of the yard a lilting, little boy's voice started up the old nursery chant—"Chinky chinky Chinaman! Yellow-face, pigtail rat-eater!"—but Collis, already turning away, paid no attention. He batted his arms back in Hope's direction. When she failed to reach out to stop him, he kept walking. Only when he turned outside the gate did he notice Paul standing before him. Collis looked him up and down as if assessing a cut of pork.

"You might have known there'd be no lesson today, Liang." Collis went on a few paces, then paused and looked at his hand, glanced back, and tossed the ring into the dirt at Paul's feet.

4

They walked quickly, urgently uphill, kicking dust and sending gravel skittering from beneath their heels, and were soon breathing hard with exertion at the steep incline. Had she been with a different man, in other circumstances, Hope might have reached for his elbow or hand, leaned against him to ease the climb. But even when they had passed well beyond the last house into the higher pastures where their sole witnesses were grazing cattle, she kept her hands to herself and maintained a distance of several feet. Occasionally they would glance at each other, sparking mutual confusion. Hope would blush violently and yank the brim of her fedora back down. Paul would tip his face to the clouds. Neither spoke.

After twenty minutes without crossing another human being, they arrived at the skirt of forest below Grizzly Peak. Here the canopy of cypress and eucalyptus formed a shady den where Hope had often come to write in her journal or simply admire the view, which stretched all the way across the Bay. Today it was a view of disasters. The sunken rooftops of their own broken city. The harbor clotted with boats. The remains of San Francisco crouching beneath a mountain of smoke so enormous and black that by rights it should swallow the entire sky. But it didn't. Here, where they stood, the morning sun shone hard and polished as silver, and shade fell clean as rain.

Hope scooted herself up onto the flat of a boulder and drew her knees to her chin. Paul laid the bundle he had been carrying beside her. For a moment he stood near enough that she imagined she could feel the heat from his body, but then he stepped back.

He held up the ring that Collis had thrown at his feet. "What do you call this?"

She tugged off her gloves with fierce attention. "Collis called it an engagement ring. You may call it whatever you like. It's yours now."

"Why do you decide this way?"

"Not to marry him, you mean?"

He nodded.

"I don't love him." She yanked a handful of the tall grass growing beside the boulder. "I tried to, but I couldn't."

Paul slid the ring back into his pocket. "But first you agree?"

"Yes."

"Your family will be displeased?"

"My family!"

"In China, when a man wish to marry, he will ask go-between to make arrangement with family. Your family . . . ?"

"There's only my father." She chewed on her lower lip, considering. "He's never met Collis, but he's a romantic at heart. He'll understand."

"Romantic."

She ripped apart the grass she'd been braiding. "He wouldn't really want me to marry someone like Collis."

"Why do you choose this day to say no?"

"I—" She winced. "You know why."

"I see my name in your notebook."

"You did read it, then."

"I see my name. The rest—your markings are like knots."

A wave of relief swept through her. She laughed. "Yes, you're right, they are."

"If a man does not ask father, then how it is done?"

"What do you mean, Paul?"

"I wish to marry you."

The combination of this proposal's bluntness and its impossibility caused her to pull away, but he reached up and caught her wrists, drew her down toward him. His arms went around her back, and she was surrounded again by the warmth of his body, inhaled the same sweet spice that had disturbed her sleep all night.

"No!" she cried. "Paul, we mustn't."

"Why no?" he said softly.

But his closeness crippled her powers of reason, and for a second, two, she was so lost in the sensation of his breath on her ear that she could not imagine an answer. Then he started to pull her nearer, and she blurted out, "It's against the law!"

"*Pu*," he whispered. "Not in Wyoming."

She arched her back, abruptly rational, and stared at his long boyish lashes, that confident gaze. "What are you saying?"

He stroked her eyelids. Her nose. Her lips. She waited.

He slipped off her hat, touched her hair. "In Wyoming is allowed. We go there, marry."

"But *marriage* . . . children—"

"We will have beautiful children," he murmured.

And suddenly she was crying. He took her face between his hands. "Do not be afraid, Hsin-hsin."

The intensity of his gaze, his voice was like a promise. She realized she trusted him absolutely. Then he squeezed his eyes as if testing whether this could really be happening. It was this that lifted the last of her defenses and drove her to kiss him.

Swift and breathless, she had to go up on her toes to reach his mouth, stayed barely long enough to register the surprised softness of his lips and their dark, salty flavor, but as she dropped back he bent forward, catching her up again. Suddenly she was breathing him, tasting and touching, her hands amazed at the smoothness of his cheeks and throat and hair, and she felt his desire so keenly that it became indistinguishable from her own.

III
WEDDING
FROM BERKELEY TO
EVANSTON, WYOMING
(1906)

ॐॐॐ

1

May 2, 1906
c/o Mary Jane Lockyear
57 Hawthorne
Oakland
Dearest Dad,

I trust you received my telegram all right and are not sitting up there in Oregon—or racing down here!—full of worry about your daughter. The Quake *was* very dramatic, like some great bucking bronco had gotten underneath the earth's skin. But Berkeley came through without a single fire and few injuries. I was shaken, but not harmed. As you can see by the return address, I've been staying with Mary Jane Lockyear since the disaster. Eleanor Layton needed the room for her homeless relatives from across the Bay. Yes, she does have some nerve but I prefer it here, truth be told, as the company is considerably more enlightened than Eleanor could be. Mary Jane has taken in several of us unmoored friends, and we're all for the Vote and more humane treatment of the colored races, so conversation is not the chore it was with Eleanor.

But here's the big surprise. Are you sitting down?

I'm getting married, and it's not to Collis Chesterton. (I should never had led you on about him—I never loved him at all and would have been miserable married to him.) My future husband's name is Paul. Paul Leon. He's an educated man—a graduate student at Berkeley—and his family is enormously wealthy. They live abroad and will surely be as surprised as you when they learn of our plans. I know it's sudden, but perhaps you'll understand when I tell you Paul saved my life. That's a bit dramatic, but if he hadn't come along and gotten a ladder up, I might still be trapped on the third floor of Eleanor's house! The staircase collapsed during the Quake, you see, and I had no way to get down on my own.

Now, Dad, thanks to Paul, I am safe and healthy and happy and soon to be a married lady, and we fully intend to entertain you like royalty the next time you venture out of the mountains, but I would feel beastly to make you come all that way just to watch us tie the knot, and as none of his family will be on hand either, we have decided to join a group of chums for a quick and simple ceremony later this month. With the whole Bay Area still digging out, no one is in a mood for grand celebrations, so you mustn't feel you're missing much. By the time you read this, the deed will be done. By the time I next see you I hope to be ensconced in a lovely home of our own with room for you to visit.

I do so miss you, Dad, but I know you will approve of Paul. Please wish us well.

Your loving daughter,
Hope

She lied. Not just about Paul, but about Mary Jane. Those interim weeks were anything but rosy as Hope's dearest friend did all in her power to discourage this marriage, enlisting everyone else in the house to campaign against it as well. For one part of Hope's letter to her father was accurate: she did have lively and unusual company in her temporary home. Dorothea Marr, the French literature scholar, had founded the Mills College suffrage group. Antonia Laws wore an eye patch and smoked a pipe, and Antonia's younger sister Anne spent her youth as a rodeo rider. These were no more the primrose princesses of Berkeley society than was Mary Jane, but each in turn took Hope aside and appealed to her "horse sense," her "superior feminine wisdom," her "uncommon intellect," her "independent nature," her "able character," and—Hope's favorite, coming from the black-patched Antonia—her "impressive moral breeding." They warned of irreversible consequences. Hope would be persecuted. Ridiculed. She would live in poverty. She would lose her country and her birthright. Paul will try to convert you, Mary Jane predicted. He'll have you cooking eel and bear paw. He'll put you in silk robes and expect you to follow five paces behind, or worse, keep you locked up for fear other men might see you.

"I can see how much you love him, Hope," she said when all other arguments failed. "That's none of my business, and I heartily apologize if I ever said anything mean in that regard. But it'll take more than love if you marry this man. The world's not going to change just because you've decided it should. And it could be brutal in its refusal."

Hope stayed with Mary Jane for want of anywhere else to go. Paul's boarding house was now filled with Miss Miles's San Francisco friends and relatives, and Paul no longer had his own room. Besides, she dreaded being seen with him. Chaos had buffered them the day of the Quake, but order had been restored now, and the tedium of relocation and rebuilding only made people greedy for gossip. Talk in the markets was full of scandals about adulterers caught with their mistresses in the Quake, or prominent citizens seen fleeing bordellos, or the haste of certain marriages among refugees in the tent cities. But the talk had a darker edge, as well. People were worried about all those thousands of Chinatown Chinese who would relocate in Oakland if no one stopped them.

More than that, said a puffy-faced woman in the grocer's one day, since the immigration files had burned in the fires, all the Chinamen were now claiming they'd been born here, that they were American *citizens*. Who could tell which ones were lying? There'd be no way to get rid of the yellows now.

Sure enough, answered her companion, her husband had the way to get rid of 'em, and it stood loaded with the trigger cocked next to his bed.

The Yellow Peril was glowering again, as it had twenty years earlier at the height of the anti-Chinese fever. Hope knew that if she and Paul ventured out together now, their feelings for each other would be visible to everyone they passed. Even when in public on her own she felt as if she were wearing a scarlet letter. M for miscegenist.

She told herself none of this would matter once she and Paul were wed, that the legal and religious institution of marriage would be their shield. In the meantime, they visited privately, with restraint, in the small enclosed sun room behind Mary Jane's parlor. The oak settee would creak, the golden dust motes fly, and the world's disapproval settle between them like a cold snap. Paul kept his hat in his lap and his boot heels clamped together, the rimless glasses on the tip of his nose aging him by decades. Hope occupied her hands packing charity baskets for the refugees, and they would talk, not of love—never love—or intention or the craving for each other's skin that underscored everything, but of their future as the logistical enterprise it had become. Eight hundred miles was no mere possibility but the actual distance between this room and the line that would set them free. The multifaceted problem of crossing that line only made it seem more tangible, the ultimate goal of marrying more real. And every new difficulty that presented itself served to drive Hope more stubbornly to Paul's side.

They had between them barely one hundred dollars, not including the value of Collis's ring, which Hope insisted Paul keep in his possession. If and when the San Francisco bank where Paul did his business rebuilt itself and honored past accounts, he would have access to another fifty or so, and in mid-June he would receive his quarterly stipend of two hundred dollars from home. He could wire his family for emergency support, but there were complications there. Although he was reluctant to state the problem directly, Hope understood that the Chinese could be every bit as racist, particularly when it came to white women marrying their sons, as Americans were toward Chinese. Paul was convinced his mother would do everything in her power to block their marriage, and since his father had died and she held the family purse strings, her first recourse would be to cut him off financially.

Having supported herself since she was eighteen, Hope encouraged Paul to write the truth and let his mother do her worst. They were so many thousands of miles away, and there were plenty of students for Hope to tutor, even without Collis Chesterton's referral, and once the *Free Press* resumed publication, Paul would have his salary.

"We'll manage," she assured him.

"You do not understand," he said.

That first of so many times he spoke those words he was standing in a flood of late afternoon sun with his hands clasped behind him as if manacled. He had his back to her. There was no anger in his voice, never anger, but such sadness, a resignation that rose like a thick pane of glass between them. She wanted to hurl herself at it, smash it with promises of freedom and love. She wanted to bury her face in his shoulder.

"No," she said, keeping her distance. "I don't suppose I do."

He sent no news to China; their one hundred dollars was more than enough to pay for their journey to Wyoming. But there were further considerations besides money. The permissiveness of Wyoming law toward mixed marriage was at odds with the state's history toward Chinese. Some twenty years earlier the white miners in a town called Rock Springs had, in broad daylight, attacked their Celestial counterparts, burning down their tents, shooting dozens in the back, and running hundreds out of town. It seemed to Hope that, rather than simply set off blind, she and Paul had better first locate a minister of the peace who recognized the current latitude of the law and agreed in advance to uphold it. Through his network of Chinese Freemasons, fellow revolutionists, students, and journalists, Paul learned of two other mixed couples in the area, and a plan quickly unfolded for this "group of chums" to make the expedition as a single wedding party. A Berkeley law graduate named Donald Lim, engaged to a young Irish dressmaker, had already contacted a Presbyterian minister who would marry them in Evanston, the first stop on the Union Pacific over the Wyoming border. Reverend Leander C. Hills had written that he held no grudges against the Orientals or against couples in love, and since Wyoming required none of the standard waiting periods other states required, Donald and his friends could be married and back on the train in a matter of hours. It was decided that the wedding should take place on the last Tuesday in May.

ও ও ও

2

Hope and Paul arrived at the Oakland terminal at six on the morning of their departure, though the dense fog made it feel more like evening. The surrounding ships, ferries, and trains were visible only as looming shadows, and the figures of porters and dockworkers appeared and faded like ghosts. Hope half wished the fog would swallow her and Paul as well, at least until they were boarded and underway. As it was, they skirted the passenger waiting rooms and went directly to the platform nearest the train, where they found the rest of their "wedding party" also just arriving.

Paul and the other two men exchanged broad smiles and greeted each other with energetic nods. They all wore similar dark Western suits and carefully brushed and banded black derbies over cropped haircuts. At a glance, they might have been brothers. The women, however, eyed each other with reserve and waited to be introduced.

"Please, ladies," Paul said, "I am—" He hesitated, glancing to Hope, then straightened his shoulders. "I am Paul Liang. And my—This Hope Newfield."

Hope smiled inwardly at Paul's struggle over the appropriate graces, language, and role description, but she maintained her surface composure. Here, then, was the law student Donald Lim, a skinny, tense boy-man, and his Irish dressmaker, Sarah. She was beautiful, in an edgy way, with hard green eyes and bright auburn hair, and a smile that Hope didn't trust. She laughed as Donald introduced her and insisted on shaking everyone's hand. This befuddled the third couple, a barrel-chested dry goods merchant named Ong Ben Joe and his Kathe, a round and ruddy Scandinavian who spoke English even more haltingly than Ong. These two, Hope recalled Paul telling her, had met while trudging toward the Presidio to escape the Great Fire. Ong had won Kathe's confidence by standing guard outside her tent and by carrying wherever they went the big oil painting of swans that was her prized possession.

Now, as the men drifted off, Hope recounted the story and asked Kathe who had painted the picture. She was only asking for the sake of conversation, but Kathe frowned in all seriousness and answered, "I do not know."

Sarah wondered aloud, "Why go to such lengths to save it, then?"

Hope said, "Maybe she likes swans."

"Risk her neck and marry a Chinaman all because she fancies the pretty white *birds!*" Sarah whooped at the thought.

Hope looked to Paul for moral support and found him leaning against a lamp post. They had agreed to maintain a certain distance, there was to be no touching, no display, no public evidence of their intentions. But he was watching her. Go on, he seemed to say, bite back.

"And how did you and Donald meet?" Hope asked Sarah as Paul turned back to the men.

Sarah replied curtly, "Donald and I met five years ago on the sailboat of a mutual friend. We disliked each other on sight, but our paths kept crossing until we had no choice but to marry."

The train whistle blew. Across the platform a cluster of squatting, queued coolie miners wolfed down the last of their breakfast. Surely no white woman would marry a Chinese if she felt she had a choice, thought Hope, but Sarah spoke as though someone were *forcing* her. Between this Irishwoman's coarseness and Kathe's limited English, there seemed little chance of friendship, which was a pity considering all they had—or would have—in common. As Hope gathered up her valises and handed the hamper of food and water to Paul, she felt a stab of loneliness. The conductors' swinging arms were directing them toward the second-class Pullmans at the middle of the train. For reasons of economy and propriety, Paul would leave her there and go on with the other men to the coach section. She was to travel alone with these two strangers. On her wedding journey.

Before they could reach the Pullmans, however, crowds of passengers swarmed out of the depot and, for the first time, Hope experienced the attention she had been dreading all this past month. Eyes screwed open and closed like jar lids, chins swerved and dove back toward them. Women wagged their heads in disbelief, and Hope steeled herself against the same unabashed stares she had seen on Kansas cowboys, the same filthy sneers the Beasley brothers flashed when they rolled her into the dirt.

She whirled, pretending to shield her eyes from a flying cinder. Paul had fallen behind, or she would have scorned them all by grabbing his arm. Instead she plowed into Kathe, sent the heavy blond sprawling headlong into the squatting coolies.

What happened next Hope saw as a series of images stacked like segments of a dream. There were the stricken, invaded expressions on the journeymen's faces, Donald and Ben Joe reaching among them, Kathe like a tumbled ninepin. Then a conductor materialized out of the mist. He had feral eyes and grimaced as he shoved the scholar and merchant away. The men bent together, all those hairless, unshaven cheeks conferring, the crude sling of their language. And Paul . . . Where was Paul? Behind her somewhere, she couldn't see him, only Kathe now leaning against Ben Joe and the dawning revulsion on the conductor's mouth, the peasants with their rope-belted pants hastily packing bowls and chopsticks into baskets, as appalled as the conductor by the sight of a white woman on a Chinaman's arm.

Hope wavered. She started to back away, but Sarah caught her, turned her, green eyes blazing. "Get used to it," she said. "Or quit now."

Hope let Sarah's unexpected heat whip her. Not another word was uttered. By the time Paul caught up with them, her pulse was no longer pounding in her ears.

"I—" She fumbled for some explanation to ease the concern in his eyes. "I thought I heard the whistle blow, and—" Sarah rolled her eyes and marched back to Donald. Hope began again, "I'm nervous, Paul. I panicked. I'm sorry."

He studied her. "I am sorry. You should have true wedding. Friends. Family—"

"I wish I could kiss you. Or just hold your hand."

"I know."

"But it's forbidden."

"Three days, Hope." He smiled.

"Three long days."

He looked down at the ticket in his hand. "This your car."

Their fingers brushed in the transfer of her bags, and then she was standing between Sarah and Kathe, watching from their compartment window as Paul and Ben Joe and Donald waved and walked away. She thought of how Paul had persuaded her that he and his friends had chosen to ride third class. The women should be comfortable, he had said, but the men had no difficulty sleeping in their seats. When she had tried to discuss it, he provoked a quarrel about the color of her wedding gown that ended with his making her a gift of the ruby peach silk she had fashioned into matching waist and skirt now packed in their own special carpetbag. She hadn't given the rail accommodations another thought until this moment.

This moment when she realized, leaning from her window and squinting against the fog, that that snarling conductor was automatically shunting all Chinese together, from her future husband and his friends right down to the last of those pantalooned laborers, to the same third-class car at the end of the line.

ॐॐॐ

The women settled into the narrow wood-paneled confines of their compartment with few words among them. Kathe pressed her nose into a Swedish dime novel with a golden-haired couple kissing on the cover. Sarah flipped through the pages of *Vogue*. The compartment brightened dramatically as the train left the coastal fog and rolled into farm country, but the two of them barely glanced up. You would think, Hope thought as she rocked from side to side, that they made this trip all the time.

She took out the new Moroccan-bound journal that she had bought especially to record her wedding journey, but after several false starts, she laid down her pencil and felt inside her hidden belt pouch for the gold band her father had given her on her sixteenth birthday. "If you take this as your wedding ring when the times comes," he told her, "I guarantee your marriage will be blessed." There had been tears in his eyes. The ring was inscribed *To my beloved Jennie. Always.* And yet, Hope thought darkly, in spite of this ring, in spite of a husband's eternal love, her mother had died at the age of twenty-one, her marriage not two years old. There were no guarantees.

She tried again to concentrate on the passing countryside, jotting down impressions now of sunshine and growth, endless orchards and white clapboard farmhouses. Kathe brought out a pack of cards and engaged Sarah in a game of all fours, and Hope once again wondered at their dispassionate manner, as if they were—well, as if they were on a business trip. Hope's romantic instincts rebelled at this notion, and yet, the more she thought about it, the more she saw that it could offer a kind of protection. She imagined herself lifting her head high, looking at Paul and announcing, "This man and I have business together." Had she been thus armored this morning she might have been able to deflect those stares at the station, to nod at that insolent conductor and walk on. Pretend they were partners in a Colorado general store returning from a purchasing trip. Or administrative assistants to Donaldina Cameron checking on the whereabouts of a slave girl last seen in Sacramento. Or diplomats traveling to Washington to petition President Roosevelt to support the Chinese bid for independence.

Hope smiled as she noted these fantasies in her journal. Was it so preposterous, really, that she might have a hand in Paul's revolutionary business? She had been his teacher, after all, and once they were married she would doubtless help him with his correspondence. She might even learn Chinese and translate some of his writings into English. Her mind leapt with the possibilities.

❧❧❧

They started climbing into the Sierras by late afternoon, crossed the snow line at Cape Horn, and shortly after nightfall the snow sheds began. These protective tunnels, made of sheet metal and steel staves, arced over the tracks for miles.

"I feel as if we're in one of Jules Verne's science fictions." Hope stared over the remains of their dining car supper at her reflection in the otherwise blank window. "We might as well be traveling to the center of the earth."

"Yes, and won't we pop out in China," Sarah said. "And our dear mothers-in-law will be waiting with red veils and the wedding sedans."

Hope stirred her tea, trying to conceal her surprise that her companion knew the first thing about Chinese weddings and mothers-in-law. On the few occasions all day when Sarah had mentioned Donald, it was only to boast about his prospects with a law firm on the East Coast or to describe the maroon Fredonia runabout he had promised to buy her for their first anniversary.

"And what would you do, then?" asked Hope.

"I believe I would catch the next train back." Sarah took the apple from her plate and polished it on the white damask tablecloth. As with the rest of her meal, she seemed to prefer toying with the fruit to eating it.

"What if Donald wanted to stay there?"

"China?" Kathe was struggling to make sense of the vowels and syllables speeding past her. "China is not good. No pigtails." She drew a confident finger across her plump neck and shook her blond curls emphatically.

"That's right," said Sarah. "Our boys would be dead men, sure. Anyway, Donald's no thought of going back."

"Ever?" said Sarah.

"Don't tell me you see yourself as a Chinese wife!"

"Well—" Hope stared as the electric lights dimmed, then flashed off, plunging them into utter blackness before sputtering back to life. "After the revolution," she continued, "everything will be different in China. Modern."

"You're a dreamer," said Sarah. "And a fool if you believe your dreams."

"You will eat?" Kathe eyed the apple.

Sarah handed it to her. "I'm not hungry."

That night, after the awkward tussle of unpacking, changing, and restowing luggage, Hope stretched back to stiff back with Sarah behind the heavy drawn curtains of the upper bunk while Kathe, to whom they'd given the lower bed on grounds of her girth, murmured an evening prayer. But their earlier conversation kept replaying in Hope's mind. How could anyone marrying an alien be certain that he would not return to his homeland—that he would even be *allowed* to stay on in this country! Chinese students and merchants had so far been spared from the Exclusion Acts that banned new immigration of Chinese laborers, but who could tell how long their exemption would continue? Perhaps Donald and Ben Joe would be among those thousands who planned to take advantage of the Great Fire and claim they were born in America, but Hope doubted they'd get away with it, and she knew Paul would never stoop to such lies. A man who believed as fervently as Paul in the democratic future of his homeland would surely be among the first to return when the Imperial system was toppled. Much as this prospect daunted her, it also excited—and even reassured—her, in a way. China could hardly present more obstacles than America had thrown up against them, and what could be more fascinating than to witness the transformation of an ancient empire into a modern republic?

Sarah jerked violently and rolled over, asleep. Hope pulled the muslin sheet to her chin. Whatever happened in the future, what mattered now was that she and Paul find some sanctuary where they could be alone—really alone. Last week they had met in the secret glen where he had proposed and, feeling she could bear it no longer, she had taken his hand beneath her skirts and begun to unbutton his collar, and it had been Paul who stopped her, gathering her into him, crushing her against his chest. "Soon," he had said. "So soon." She had loved him all the more for that, for making her trust that he loved her, though he never said so. Could not say the word for love, she thought, yet demonstrated with every fiber of his body that this was what he felt.

She pressed her nose against the frosty window. The snow sheds had lapsed and Donner Lake appeared, mirroring the moon and clouds and black, leaning silhouettes of trees.

℘℘℘

The next day carried them across the scorching wastes of Nevada and the third morning across the Great Salt Flats to Ogden, Utah, at the base of the Wasatch Mountains. Here, amid clusters of parch-faced, calico-clad Mormons, the wedding party changed trains from the Central to Union Pacific, boarding the end coach to ride, together at last, the final brief leg to Evanston. But Hope's excitement at rejoining Paul dimmed before they reached their seats. The atmosphere could not have been more different from their genteel Pullman. Here in coach, families spread their breakfast into the aisle. Miners, trappers, and frontier homesteaders hawked morning phlegm into clay spittoons. Babies squealed, and boys shot spitballs. There were no fans, and though all the windows were open, the air was a swill of smoke and dust, the hot breath of burning metal, the stink of unwashed bodies. Hope, Kathe, and Sarah squeezed into one cushionless wooden bench, while their men occupied another. Paul looked exhausted. He refused to meet Hope's gaze, and did not even glance back when the conductor—a whistling, grandfatherly conductor, this time—came to check their tickets. Yet ten minutes later, after they were underway, Paul stood and crooked his finger for her to follow him outside, and Hope rose quite as casually as if they had planned this all along.

She found him alone on the platform between the coach and the first of the train's many freight cars. The wheels made a frightful racket and the motion was so jarring that they had to hang on to the railing to keep upright. Before them loomed the gray-green and purple span of the Wasatches. Behind, the white-hot desert. Hope felt less casual now that they were actually alone. There was something in Paul's expression—like a shadow—that warned against either talk or touch.

When he finally spoke, his voice was so low she had to read his lips. "These days," he said, "I have chance to think. There is much you do not know. I did not think to tell you. My father arrange my first marriage when I am seven years old. After I marry, I go to study in Hong Kong. My wife is dead five years." He paused. "Cholera." He passed a hand over his hatless forehead and gave a start, as if the sensation of his own hairline surprised him. Hope realized with some alarm that she had seen those coolies rub their foreheads in just that way when Kathe fell among them. A nervous reaction, a habit. Paul had expected the same smooth sensation and was surprised to find it changed.

They were climbing and the temperature was dropping. Hope shivered. "You told me all that," she said.

But before he could answer, they entered a tunnel, and in that sudden, unexpected blackness he pulled her into his arms and held her so hard that she could feel the reverberation of stone and iron and steam in his bones as well as her own. The smell of his skin and hair seemed inseparable from the damp mineral smells of the mountain. She closed her eyes, and the darkness deepened, the magnified clattering of the wheels seemed to merge with Paul's heartbeat. It was a terrifying and wondrous sensation that left her aghast when, just before the darkness lifted, he released her.

"You must know." He watched her closely. "I have one son, one daughter."

Nothing he had ever said or done, least of all in the preceding moments, prepared her for this announcement. She had known—assumed—

he must have made love to his wife, but he had left her so soon and so young. Hope had told herself that he was hers now, that they could discover each other through the light of marriage as if they had been reborn. But here, in one simple statement, Paul had not only wiped away her naive fantasy but cast into doubt her judgment of him and possibly their entire future together.

She clutched the railing as the train swerved. "Did you plan all along to tell me like this? Here? Now?"

Before he could answer they plunged into another tunnel, but this time the blackness and noise fell like an impenetrable wall between them. Her quip about dropping through the core of the earth echoed in her ears—and Sarah's bitter reply. She was right, Hope thought, I am a dreamer. What could he possibly say that would soothe me? That his life in China doesn't matter? That he has no intention of ever returning to the family he left behind? That he was terrified if he told me, he'd lose me?

When they emerged, Paul stood as before, one shoulder braced against the door into the coach, both hands thrust deep in his jacket pockets.

"I might never forgive you, you know."

"In China—" he began, but his pedagogic tone inflamed her all over again.

"I don't care how it is in China!" she shouted. "Don't you understand, Paul? Your children will be my stepchildren. They will be brother and sister to our children. How *could* you not tell me this!"

"I tell you I married. I think you do not wish to know more."

Hope shuddered. "How old are they?" she said, looking away. "Where are they?" But her voice sprang up again as she suddenly understood the true source of her distress. "How could you leave them and never even mention their existence!"

Paul rubbed his lips together. He waited until the thunder of the wheels had drowned out the last echo of Hope's cry. Then he answered her. "My daughter, Mulan, is eldest, eleven years. My son, Jin, now nine years." He leveled his eyes to Hope's. "They live in Hankow, Hsin-hsin. They live with my mother."

                    *   *   *

Over the next three hours, as she resumed her place beside Sarah and Kathe, Hope's anger over Paul's revelation subsided, but it left in its place a weight that filled her whole body and dulled her senses. She had no access to the excitement that should surround her wedding day. Instead she mourned the fact that she would not wear white, that her father would not give her away—was, by her own choice, not even here. She was about to become daughter-in-law to a Chinese concubine, stepmother to two children who would surely be poisoned against her before she ever laid eyes on them. The worst was that she could not tell whether this last detail was a source of sorrow or relief.

Kathe interrupted her thoughts with a hushed but urgent question. "Why so much kiss-kiss?"

Hope followed her gaze across the aisle to a young couple locked in passionate embrace. She shrugged.

"No," insisted Kathe with a wave of her arm. "Everyone!"

"Didn't you know?" said Sarah too loudly. "Evanston's a conjugal boomtown. A regular Niagara Falls."

For the first time Hope lifted up and saw that, in addition to the hardbitten miners, homesteading families, and Chinese journeymen, a disproportionate number of seats were taken by intensely preoccupied couples. Some were dressed in farmer's denims, some in dandy suits and frills. Some were old, some young, some giddy, some numb. Some had their arms intertwined while others sat biting their lips. With a shock Hope realized that all these couples were suffering from variations of the same premarital jitters that she herself was feeling. Well, not quite the same. None of these husbands-to-be, she imagined, already had children in China.

"I know why *we* had to come here," said Hope, "but why so many of *them?*"

"God is business," answered Donald, standing behind her and stretching his arms to the rack above his head.

"Excuse me?"

"Other states demand long wait." Paul spoke quietly, leaning forward with his elbows on the back of Hope's seat. "But not Wyoming. Evanston first train stop over border. This why so many lovers."

"Lovers." The word spun her around to face him. "Like us?"

It was a direct challenge. And a plea. To heal. To promise. To put a name to this business they had together.

His face tightened.

"Why can't you say it?" she demanded.

The train stopped, pitching them and all the other passengers backward and forward in a wave. Around them, their companions busied themselves with their bags as if none had heard Hope. Paul stooped to pick up his black satchel, then reached for the carpetbag containing her wedding clothes. There was a spacious dignity to his movements, a smoothness as hard and obdurate as granite.

"Please." It was no request. He was directing her to step into the aisle, place one foot in front of the other, and join him in the procession of men and women who were leaving this train to be married.

Hope swallowed hard and followed him. Just as Mary Jane warned she would.

Why, she berated herself. Why did love and stubbornness have to make a person so blind! But then there was Paul at the foot of the steps, his weary face upturned, hands reaching to help her down, to lift her toward him.

"Yes," he whispered when only she could hear. "Yes. Lovers."

ॐॐॐ

3

Spread along the southern bank of the Bear River, Evanston was a bustling town with wide mud streets and wooden sidewalks, electric lights, abundant saloons, an opera house—and, to Hope's surprise, throngs of Chinese conducting all manner of business. Celestials laced their way through the crowds around the depot, rode horses, and reined in mule teams. They appeared in upstairs windows and on hotel verandahs, in shop doorways and beside corner fruit and vegetable stands. With their crisp white serving jackets or loose blue coats, swinging queues, and penchant for hats—everything from Stetsons and derbies to ribboned straw boaters—they did not so much stand out from the crowd as quietly dominate it. All the laborers driven out of Rock Springs, Hope thought, must have found refuge here in Evanston. Strip away the tourists and it looked as though the Chinese might comprise the majority. Yet these were not their businesses, their hotels, their homes facing Front Street. The Chinamen lived in a collection of shanties submerged in cook smoke, barely visible from the white town and downwind of the tracks.

Hope looked to Paul, who was walking apart from her with the other men. How different they appeared, these handsome young moderns. The best of both worlds, she told herself. How could anyone confuse Paul with a common laborer? Certainly, these sojourners would not make that mistake. Just see how they looked at him, with awe, dumbstruck. The way they unconsciously reached up to assure themselves that their own pigtails were still securely fastened to their heads. How many of them had ever written poetry? Could they read Latin? Had they memorized the entire Constitution of the United States in Chinese? She looked beyond the journeymen to the grimy blacksmith down the street, or that cat-eyed grocery boy atop his cart. She thought of the conductor's withering glance in Oakland. None of them, of either race, were fit to black Paul's boots.

Hope's mental pep talk aside, Donald did not lead the group to the grand and comfortable Union Pacific Hotel across from the depot, or to the Hotel Marx, a rather more severe but ample structure one block over. Instead, he led them with their arms full of baggage, hats tilting in the warm breeze, across oozing mud and around behind the Front Street lodgings to a small disheveled house that advertised rooms for fifty cents. There Mrs. Cassandra López greeted them with the face of a milkmaid and the voice of a goat, but she was courteous and directed them to rooms arranged in advance, where they could prepare themselves. Reverend Hills was expecting them at the Presbyterian Church at four o'clock, just one hour away.

Hope bit back her frustration and shame, joined Sarah and Kathe to change in one room while the men piled into the other. The place was clean and cheap and available, Sarah announced as they shook out their petticoats and wedding blouses, "And we were lucky to get it. There's a convention of sheepherders in town, if you can believe such a thing. Besides, one night hardly matters, does it?"

Hope looked to see if Sarah was just putting on a brave face, and was stunned to catch her tippling from a tin flask. Kathe smiled and wrung her hands, signaling that Sarah must be nervous, but Hope doubted that, at least in the sense that she herself was nervous.

" 'Tis for me throat." Sarah lowered the bottle. Her excuse was defiant, her brogue exaggerated. "Got to make sure I've me voice for me vows."

Hope could see that neither Sarah nor Kathe cared about the shabbiness of their honeymoon accommodations. Or minded the fact that, with three couples in two rooms, only one would have privacy tonight.

ᢒᢒᢒ

Paul had never set foot in a church, but he remembered how Europeans in China would hover in clouds outside the great cathedrals after services. Beggars would descend to prey on the Christians' Sunday conscience. Itinerant candy makers and puppetteers would appeal to the swarming children, and rickshaw drivers would compete to whisk families away before either the enterprising or the maimed could touch them. The atmosphere surrounding China's churches was a cross between festival and battleground, but as the wedding party approached the plaza outside the Presbyterian Church of Evanston, it became evident that, here, the festival reigned supreme.

A fierce mountain sunshine seemed to squirt the whole scene with gilt, and as couples awaited their turns at the altar they could bargain with jewelers, florists, and musicians, vendors of salted meats, sandwiches, even portable wedding cakes. Elderly townspeople offered signatures as witnesses for five bits apiece. "Just think what a savings, we'll witness each other for free!" Hope whispered to Paul.

Sarah, overhearing, said, "Well, I don't know about you, but I aim to charge. It's no less than a dollar if ye want my John Hancock." She thrust her arm under Donald's and his face paled at the public contact. He straightened his elbow and she fell away, laughing broadly as her drawstring purse thumped against her hip.

"What is in this pouch of Sarah?" Paul asked.

"She said it was tonic. For her throat."

"Tonic." Paul turned in time to see Donald pull the flask from Sarah's purse and empty it against the church wall. Sarah stood with her arms crossed, feathered hat askew. A brittle smile was pasted across her lips.

"Paul." No longer watching Sarah's antics, Hope was drawing a circle with her toe in the dirt. "I've been thinking. It might be best—for the marriage certificate, you know—if we use an Anglicized name."

"You give me American name. Paul."

"I mean our last name. We could just drop the g, spell L-E-O-N. It's nearly the same . . ."

"Leon." Paul stroked his chin. "Leon is Spanish name."

"People *might* take you for Spanish. It's possible."

Paul drew a mental image of the Spaniards he had encountered. Broad, bulky men who walked with their shoulders flung back, carrying their chests like trays. Winding black mustaches. Pirate skin and devil's eyes.

"Never."

"It's not what *I* think, Paul. But it could make things easier for us. We have to be practical. In California, it's better to be Spanish than Chinese."

"Better Spanish than Chinese." He stared at her.

"Oh, sweet. You know what I mean!"

He knew that in China names change easily. Babies are given "milk names" at birth to position them within a particular generation of their family—all the Liang cousins of his generation were named Po- something. Later, children acquire nicknames such as Stumpy or Bald or Muscles, reflecting personal idiosyncrasies or skills. Girls, when they marry, become their husband's *taitai*—if Hope were Chinese she would be addressed as Liang Taitai. And students who pass their examinations are rewarded with "style names" to be used in scholarly pursuits. His own style name was Yu-fen. But not even women change their family name. Lineage is sacred, and the family name is the key to one's lineage. Though many of Paul's friends and associates had had their names butchered by immigration officers in coming to this country, none had voluntarily forsaken their ancestors' names. Let alone masquerade as a Spaniard.

"No," he said.

"Paul." Hope lowered her voice, speaking sternly and deliberately, as if about a business arrangement. In spite of his annoyance, he was impressed by her persistence. "Your Chinese name will never change. Your friends

will know you as Liang Po-yu, just as they do now. This will have no effect on the characters with which you sign your articles—" She hesitated.
"Or your letters home. Only the bill collectors and the tax man will see
this other name, and then they won't try to cheat us because they won't
know we're Chinese. If we want to buy property, perhaps under this name
we'll be able to."

"Why they won't cheat us?" He could not keep the smile from his voice
as he repeated her phrase.

She straightened herself and looked him square in the eye. "Because
they won't know *we* are Chinese."

He sighed and shook his head. She was speaking of business. American business. It was his first glimpse that the woman he loved was a master of disguise.

"All right," he said. "American name for America only."

"Understood." She removed her left glove, inserted her fingers into the
belt of her skirt and extracted the gold ring she'd instructed him to place
on her finger after they exchanged vows. He wondered whether she still
would have passed him this ring if he had refused to change his name and,
if not, what they would have done then. But before this question could
fester, the church doors swung open and a man the shape and color of a
carrot leapt over the rough wooden step whooping and waving a swan-
white cowboy hat. He turned back and lifted by the waist a young lady
wearing what Paul first thought was a Chinese wedding robe, but it was
only the scarlet color that confused him. She kicked her heels as the man
held her like a wiggling child, locked her arms around his neck and
smeared his mouth crimson with her own painted lips. Then she yanked
his hat from his hand and flung it into the street. The man crowed like a
drunken rooster as the woman leaned back and brayed, "Ne-ext!"

The wedding party entered a bare, dimly lit room to stand before a
man who might have been Collis Chesterton's father. The same stretched-
thin head, bony limbs, colorless eyes gave Paul an involuntary chill. But
the minister's voice was as quiet and amiable as his name.

"I am Reverend Leander C. Hills." He nodded and gave each of them
an earnest smile, jotted down the names as they were to appear on the
marriage certificates, then clasped his Bible and began, "We are gathered
in the sight of God . . ."

As Paul stole a look at Hope beside him, she turned from the minister's sleepy voice and lifted her face to his.

". . . if any among you," said Reverend Hills, "has any preexisting matrimonial bond still in effect?"

Paul broke from Hope's gaze and found Donald with his eyes trained firmly on the plain wooden cross above the altar. Sarah's face was pinched and down-turned. Ong appeared on the verge of dozing off, and Kathe's expression was blank with incomprehension.

"Law requires a response," said Reverend Hills. "On account of this is Mormon country."

"I'm sorry," said Hope. "I—I wasn't paying attention."

"I need you to state if you're already married."

"Why, no!" she answered. "Of course not."

"No," said Sarah firmly.

"No," Kathe repeated after the others.

"And you fellas?" said the preacher.

"No," answered Paul.

Ong Ben Joe blinked. Paul suspected he still did not understand the question, which was just as well. "No."

"Where?" asked Donald, the lawyer.

"I beg pardon, young man?"

"Where should I have these matrimonial bonds?"

The Reverend shifted his weight from one hip to the other. "You tell me, son."

Sarah made a sucking sound, and Paul saw the dawning awareness draw Hope's mouth into a perfect circle.

"I—" Donald's voice pitched high and inward as Sarah ground her heel into his toe. So she did know, thought Paul. Donald had told her of his first wife still in Wuhan, and she would marry him anyway. No wonder she had been drinking.

"You got somethin' to tell me?" The minister's words pressed among them. Paul could not decide if the Reverend wanted to hear the truth or a made-up story, whether he cared at all or was merely obeying the law, but he could feel Hope beside him holding her breath.

"No." Donald bent his head.

Sarah coughed spasmodically.

Reverend Hills said, "Well, let's get on with it, shall we?"

Kathe's and Ong's paltry English spared them any inkling of the drama that had just played out, but Hope stood rigid next to Paul, and he could only imagine the thoughts that must be running through her mind. He straightened his arm by his side and took the fabric of her skirt between his fingers, surreptitiously drew her toward him. She resisted at first, but as the minister droned on, Paul kept up, and she gradually relented. He imagined the tension breaking within her as she moved against him, and through the powers of his mind, he tried to reassure her.

Reverend Hills turned to them. He glanced at his notes.

"Do you—" He paused to check again. "Paul Po-yu Leon, take this woman to be your lawfully wedded wife?"

Paul took a deep breath as Hope stepped away from him. "I do."

"Do you promise to love, honor, and protect her as long as you both shall live?"

"I do."

The minister repeated the vows for Hope. She answered as Paul had, keeping her eyes locked on Reverend Hills.

"Do you have the ring?"

Paul fumbled in his pocket and brought out Hope's mother's gold band. She lifted her hand, which seemed impossibly pale and small. But he was surprised at the coolness of her skin when he touched her, the absence of the slightest tremor or hesitation. He placed the ring on her finger and moved it into the position that would mark her for the rest of their days as his wife.

ᏸᏸᏸ

The preprinted certificates were each engraved with a drawing of palm fronds and trailing ribbons and the Holy Bible. Reverend Hills spread three such forms on his battered desk behind the altar, and they stood in a circle filling blank lines with names and the date. The Reverend affixed his signature last and blotted the ink with a hide-bound rolling pin, then collected five dollars apiece. Hope did not realize her mistake until the ink was dry.

This is to certify
That on the 29th day of May in the year of our Lord 1906
Paul Poyu Leon
and Miss Hope Jennie Newfield
were united by me in
Holy Matrimony
At Evanston
according to the ordinance of God and the laws of the State of
Wyoming
Leander C. Hills of the Presbyterian Church
Witnesses:
Sarah O'Malley Lim
Ong Ben Joe
Kathe Nilssen Ong

Paul Poyu Leon. The name leapt at her. This made-up name. If anyone challenged the validity of this marriage, what proof would they have that Paul—her true Paul—had even been present today? This was no idle worry, she knew, for immigration officials were sure to question their marriage if she and Paul ever tried to leave this country. They would never issue her a visa to accompany him to China unless she could prove he was her husband.

She felt him reading over her shoulder. "How do you do?" he said. "My name is Paul Poyu Leon."

"I'm too clever for my own good by half," she said.

But Paul had an idea. Outside, across the churchyard stood a large black cart with ornate gold lettering that read: LANDSCAPES, PORTRAITS, KEEP-SAKES. At Paul's approach the cameraman, a smooth-shaven young man who knew a good picture when he saw one, offered to make a portrait of the wedding party for free.

"It's n-n-not every day I see a g-g-group like you f-f-folks."

"Why free?" asked Donald suspiciously.

"Oh, hey." The photographer threw up his arms in mock surrender. "I know what y-y-you're thin-thinking, and you g-g-got nothin' to worry about here. I respect the p-privacy of my subjects, but Ko-kodak's got this contest. P-Prize is a trip to Shang-Shanghai." He removed his hat, exposing a long, unruly mass of orange curls. He offered Donald his hand. "Name's J-J-Jed Israel."

The stammering young man—hardly more than a boy, really—was so good-natured and guileless that Donald soon backed down. They positioned themselves against the church's clapboard wall and froze as he vanished beneath his black drapes. Then a gust of wind caught Hope's hat, sent it tumbling into the weeds, and Sarah was inspired. "No, no, no!" she cried, darting after the fedora. "We all look like bloody corpses standing here! Let's have some fun."

Ignoring the cries of protest and her husband's embarrassed grimace, she switched the men's hats with their wives'. Hope took one look at Ong weighted down beneath Kathe's fake tropical fruit and burst into laughter. "It's brilliant," she said, pushing the rim of Paul's derby up out of her eyes. "Donald, you must agree, it's a funny picture."

Donald examined Sarah's dyed green and red plumes as if they might be alive. "*Ni yeh lai ma?*" he asked Paul. *You will do this?*

Paul lifted his hands. Hope thought her fedora might have looked quite smart on him had it not been four sizes too small. "*Hao pa,*" he said, grinning.

"She's right," called the photographer, coming out from under his drapes, his stammer curiously vanished. "It's a prize-winner for sure."

"Then it's settled," said Sarah, taking Donald's arm. "Now, deadpan, everyone. It's only funny if we all look utterly sober."

Hope thought this an odd comment, considering Sarah's prenuptial cocktail, but she held her peace. Everything about Sarah and Donald was odd or worse, and she decided she was better off not knowing what had really brought them together. In fact, she would be perfectly content to escape with Paul now and never see the other two couples again. The wedding was over. Weren't they finally entitled to some time alone?

But the men had other ideas. Donald, claiming his privilege as organizer, had already made it clear that he and Sarah were to have one room to themselves, though for loving or fighting was at the moment less clear. And even before they reached that stage, there was the wedding banquet.

❊   ❊   ❊

Hope understood that this grandiose title could in no way match the event that awaited them, but the phrase seemed to spring automatically to Paul's lips when he took her aside to explain. "In China we do not take bride to church, only kneel before ancestors. Give feast for friends and family. This way show respect." He tipped his head toward the others, who were admiring the young photographer's camera. "So Ong and Donald and I decide, yes, we make wedding banquet, American style. Surprise you."

He seemed so pleased with himself that she didn't have the heart to protest, but she found it impossible to force much enthusiasm. "Where?"

"Union Pacific Hotel."

"How'd you arrange that!"

He winked. "*Kuan hsi.* Connections."

These "connections" consisted of a liberal bribe to the Union Pacific's Chinese night manager, one Mr. Fu. This elderly, bullet-faced man met them at the hotel's rear entrance and hurried them into a small rear dining room draped in maroon velvet and lit by brass wall lanterns. The chairs were ornately carved and upholstered, the linens crisply starched, the silver lay heavy as money on the pure white cloth, but all this was bitter consolation. Hope longed to grab Paul's hand and storm out into the lobby, commandeer a table in the main dining room, dine defiantly, uncompromisingly, but with enormous public grace, and then step up to the register and demand a private room for the night.

Paul's leg moved against hers under the table. He was watching her with a bemused smile.

"Must we go through this?" she whispered.

"You are not hungry?"

"Far more tired than hungry." She glanced around the table, at Donald and Sarah in their corner arguing, Kathe tucking into her butter and roll as if she had not eaten for months, Ong imperturbably filling his nostrils with snuff. Two Chinese waiters padded about on rope soles, assiduously avoiding all eye contact, especially with the ladies. She could not imagine how she had come to this place, and the only thing that kept her from tears was the unwavering touch of Paul's knee.

"I thought—" he started.

"Never mind." She lay her hand over his, lightly but confidently reassuring that she would not shame him, and pulled away before the gesture could be noticed by anyone else. Paul's hand remained where she left it, cupped around the base of his glass, but beneath the table, she felt him press harder in apology and promise. He maintained that pressure for the duration of the meal, and this single, continuous sensation became the thread on which all memory of the evening would be strung. It was as though she and Paul occupied a separate zone of intense focus while the rest became a blur of reflected light and noise. The food, the drink, the hotel's smells of must and aged wood, the moving faces and hands of their companions all became background music. As for Sarah's unfolding performance, Hope felt she was watching a sideshow that fought shamelessly for her attention but was simply no match for the main event.

"If this were China," Sarah announced, "we brides wouldn't be allowed to attend this banquet. Isn't that so, Donald?"

Donald repositioned the bowl of tomato soup that had just been placed in front of him. He did not answer his wife.

"No, in China," she continued, looking now to the rest of them, "the wedding is not about the marriage at all, is it? No. Acquisition, that's the real reason for celebration, isn't it? That's why the brides are not invited. Because we are the acquisitions. Like precious vases or antique scrolls. One more for the trove, isn't it? Parade us through the streets with all the clang and bang. Announce to the world that you've won another prize, then lock her away with your other valuables for your own private consumption." She swallowed a mouthful of wine. "What I don't understand is what a man's other wives do on his wedding night. Do they go into the wedding chamber and prepare the new girl? Do they spill the secrets of his fancies? Do they hide under the bed and listen? Or do they just breathe a huge sigh of relief and enjoy their night off?"

Ong belched loudly and barked a string of syllables at Donald, waving his spoon and laughing. Donald's face relaxed as he took his instruction, and lifted his glass to Ong. The two men toasted each other back and forth, rapidly emptying and refilling their glasses. Sarah waved for her untouched soup to be removed as Kathe signaled that she'd like some more.

"Tell me, Ong Ben Joe," said Sarah. "Do you know of any good wet nurses in Chinatown?"

Ong set down his glass and stared at her with his watery eyes.

"Well, we're all going to need them soon enough." She raised her glass to Hope. "Chinese ladies never nurse their own babies, you know. It spoils their figures for their husbands."

Hope studied the next arriving course. Turkey with relish, boiled potatoes, beets. Familiar as Mother Wayland's kitchen. She couldn't begin to name the foods on which Paul had been raised.

"Just how do you know so much about Chinese culture, Sarah?" she asked.

"Donald," answered Sarah. When Hope's face betrayed her surprise at this, she insisted, "My darlin' husband has taught me everything I know about his beloved homeland, you can be sure of that."

Maybe so, but Hope doubted that Donald had provided these lessons so his wife could skewer him with them on their wedding night. Nevertheless, neither Donald nor anyone else seemed willing to stop Sarah as she deliberately drank down one glass of wine after another while pronouncing the specially ordered food inedible and demanding why her husband had not had the chef make chow mein. Kathe ate on, undeterred, and the men took refuge in a drinking game of finger throws. Paul managed not only to play but to consistently win at this game while still holding Hope in their secret embrace. Ignored, Sarah's diatribe dimmed to a mutter.

At last came the wedding cake, a small white circular confection dusted with candied violets, and to go with it a bottle of *pai kan chiu*—a special gift personally delivered by their host. Mr. Fu addressed his presentation to Donald.

"*Che chih shih yi tienerh hsin yi. Chu nimen yung yüan hsing fu.*" Mr. Fu wheezed slightly and fluttered his hand, nodding vigorously as he pushed the bottle at Donald's chest. Donald responded by pressing it back on their host, who bowed, shaking his head and insisting. Paul and Ong nodded their approval from the sidelines. The women exchanged mystified glances. None of the men apparently saw any need to translate.

Mr. Fu stretched his neck and issued another string of syllables. Donald protested one last time, and the manager thrust the bottle at one of the waiters, with a circular motion commanding that drink be poured all around. However, at no time did the night manager indicate that the women were present or visible to him. When he turned to speak across the table to Paul,

Hope was fascinated by his ability to time his blinks to the exact moments when his gaze crossed hers.

The instant the glasses had all been filled their host's face split in a jack-o'-lantern smile. He bowed to Donald and raised a toast. "*Pan nimen taso sheng kuei tsi.*"

Sarah started to lift her glass. Donald glared at her, stood and beamed at Mr. Fu. He emptied his glass, then returned the toast. Only when this double-sided ritual had been repeated by Paul and Ong, and the host had bowed his way out of the room, did the women move. Sarah didn't say a word but drank three glasses of the liquor in a row, gagging a little on each one but refilling the glass herself. When she looked up her eyes seemed to be filled with the same pale liquid, and Hope expected these tears to release a new wave of hostility in Donald. She didn't know what form it would take—quiet, crippling words, perhaps, or another look like the one that had crossed his face just before he lied to the minister—but she was unprepared for the sight of him now leaning toward his wife in an attitude not of anger but concern. He reminded Hope of a father, the way he was speaking now softly, cautiously pushing the table setting out of the way as if they needed more room. And finally, she understood. "She's carrying his child," she whispered to Paul. "Isn't she?"

He shrugged. "Donald say nothing. I believe you are right."

"What was the toast Mr. Fu made to him?"

Paul grinned. " 'Hope you blessed with precious children very soon.' "

"I see." She felt herself blushing as she struggled with competing reactions of amusement and mortification. To Paul's right, Kathe was mechanically devouring Sarah's rejected portion of cake, Kathe's third slice, and pouring as much sugar into her cup as tea.

There was nothing Hope could do to help these women, to change the course of the lives they, for whatever reasons, had set in motion. Nor had they asked her to try. But the loneliness she had felt at being *different* was nothing compared to her sadness now at the realization that she and Paul alone of the couples had chosen each other out of love.

ⓑⓑⓑ

Darkness and a fine rain had fallen by the time they left the hotel, and the air was dense with the smells of burning piñon and freshly churned mud. In the near distance savage, drunken shouts and hard shapes of light sprang from the doors of saloons, while farther off a single melancholy gong sounded from the direction of Chinatown. Mrs. López's rooming house was lit as brightly as any saloon, but here the clamoring voices, piano playing, and the stomp of dancing feet from the parlor served as a shield past which the newlyweds slipped unnoticed. The gabled room where the men had dressed earlier was now divided into two by a blue muslin curtain strung from the ceiling. This was to be the wedding chamber Paul and Hope would share with the Ongs, their serenade the din downstairs.

Unfortunately, neither this reverberating noise nor the thin curtain could block out the sounds that soon erupted on the other side of the room. For a moment after the couples said good night, Ong's silhouette loomed, a gigantic projection against the wavering wall. Then the light flicked off. The room swelled with the rustle of fabric leaving skin, the unceremonious slap of muscle against softer flesh, a strange curdled grunt, then breathing, harsh and rapid as batwings, escalating within seconds to the graveled moan of sexual release. And, almost as quickly, snoring.

Through all of this Hope stood motionless by the open window, and Paul sat fingering the moth-eaten blanket on the single, dipping cot where they would sleep. As his eyes adjusted to the darkness, he studied the muted shapes of debris where the floorboards met the sloping roof. He felt the soft collision between the wood's hoarded warmth and the night's cool, invading air, and as shadows rippled across the blue curtain and the noise from the other side waned, his thoughts turned relentlessly to another wedding night. Red silk then, cascading from ceiling to floor around a square bed and the figure of a woman draped in more red, head to foot. Draw one curtain, tear away the other. Lift the veil. Lift the veil. Voices pry and whisper in the room outside. Fingers poke through oil-paper windows. Beneath the silk and dangling jewels, beneath rigid face paint waits a girl with skin like ice and eyes that burn. In the morning his mother will inspect the sheets for crimson stains.

Paul looked up abruptly. Hope was kneeling in the corner. Slowly, consciously, she unfolded herself, and he saw that she had changed from her wedding clothes into a loose silken shift that floated with the breeze. Paled and grayed by the absence of light, she seemed to be watching him, but he couldn't be sure.

Then she turned. Moonlight, freed from a passing cloud, splashed in through the window and ignited the garment's brilliant color. Paul gasped. She knew. For him, this color. For him alone.

"When babies born," he whispered, "old man in moon take his magic thread, tie girl child to one boy. Later those babies must marry."

He reached across the short distance separating them and drew her to the narrow mattress, then guided her hands to remove his jacket, his tie, unbutton his shirt. She pulled her knees up under the flaming cloth, curling against him as she explored his skin. "That explains arranged marriage," she said softly. "But what about us?"

His fingers traveled slowly up the smoothness of her arm, and he felt the answering tremor run through her entire body. "Destiny is arranged."

"Destiny." She tilted her head back. Paul kissed her throat.

He smoothed the wisps of hair from her forehead, then lifted the scarlet veil.

ভভভ

4

Later they could not remember whose idea it had been, for it seemed they both woke with the same thought. Honeyed light streamed through the window. The blue drape shivered against their bed. Stomps of early risers issued from other rooms, though there was no sound from Kathe and Ben Joe. Paul cupped his mouth against Hope's ear and breathed the obvious question. "How?"

She turned in his arms, her mouth twitching. "Ever been camping?"

"Camping."

"We sleep outside. Away from town. Under the stars."

"Like cowboys?"

"Yes." She laughed, and kissed his disbelieving mouth. "And Indians."

They kept their plan secret through a breakfast in Mrs. López's kitchen of bacon, biscuits, refried beans, and chicory coffee. This was no difficult task since they shared the table with three bloodshot sheepherders who stared at the newlyweds as if they were part of some dark and unforgiving hangover. The brides all had buttoned and belted and laced themselves as strenuously as nuns, but the rings on their fingers, the tinged paleness of their cheeks (bordering on a bleached green, in Sarah's case), the shy wonder in their eyes as they watched their husband's hands touching, lips tasting the food before them—all of these betrayed the knowledge freshly steeped within their flesh. Carnal truth hung over this table like a fierce and inescapable perfume.

The first business of marriage is procreation, thought Hope, and everyone in this room knows that as well as they know that white women do not marry Chinese men. As well as they know that we three women have violated one order that we may fulfill the other. But this recognition came to her in a dreamy, slipshod fashion, stripped of fear or anger. The long awaited sin of her union with Paul had bestowed on her a feeling of transparency, as if in this one forbidden embrace she had entered a spiritual truth so powerful that it would protect her from all the meanness and ignorance the world could dole out. To all but Paul she would, in effect, become invisible. To her beloved alone she would reveal her true self. And because others saw only the shell of the woman she had become, nothing they could do or say or think would any longer affect her.

Picking at her own food, she allowed herself only the briefest sidewise glances to Paul and each time was rewarded with an answering gaze so full of amazed delight that she immediately looked away for fear she would either throw herself against him or burst out weeping or laughing. She was grateful for the concealing clang of Mrs. López's pans on the stove, the herders' slurps and belches, the tidy clatter of utensils at table, the wreathing smells of food and wood smoke and the white men's sweat and rawhide hats. But when the herders had finished, they shoved back their heavy wooden chairs, tipped their hats to Mrs. López, and walked out disgustedly shaking their heads. As if ashamed to be left with the couples, the landlady abruptly wiped her hands and followed them out, mumbling something about seeing to her other "guests."

"They've seen it all now," Hope whispered to Paul.

"And nothing," he answered, holding her gaze.

Ong stood, waving his pocket watch, and announced that their train was due in thirty minutes. He was interrupted by a scratching at the kitchen door, which stood open to help clear the cook smoke.

"Folks?" A wiry figure wearing a dilapidated hat pressed his shadowed face to the mesh. "I g-g-got your pictures."

Paul opened the screen. The photographer removed his hat and took a cautious look around the kitchen, then slowly uncrooked his arm, extending a small black paper portfolio.

They closed in around him. "It's all r-r-right." Jed Israel pressed a cardboard-mounted copy of the photograph into each couple's hands. Hope smiled as she peered over Paul's shoulder, then laughed aloud. "We look positively stunned!"

It was most definitely not your typical wedding portrait. They had their hands on each other's shoulders and waists so that it was impossible to distinguish one couple from another. Their clothes were trim and appropriately formal, jackets and ties and lace-encrusted dresses. Most of them looked as though they would expire from boredom. But then, inexplicably, there were those silly hats, the men all feathered and fruited and ribboned, the women stern beneath manly brims. The flash of magnesium reflected off Paul's spectacles, so that he seemed to be peering through two puddles of milk. The church behind them was obscured. The portrait might have been taken in the dark of night on an empty sand lot.

"No," said Sarah smirking. "We look . . . shipwrecked."

Jed Israel, taken aback, started to mumble an apology, but Hope touched his elbow. "Don't mind us. It really is a lovely picture, only it's different than looking in a mirror, you know. We don't see ourselves this way."

The young photographer twisted his lips together, rocked back on his heels, his body stiff with disappointment. Hope was afraid she'd only made him feel worse and patted his elbow ineffectually. Suddenly Paul let out a belly laugh and turned to Donald, waving the print. "You can see Minister Tuan present this at court. 'See how these young rebels disgrace us!' Very good. I think this very good!" He grinned at the startled photographer. "Thank you, Mr. Israel. Thank you very much."

They left the awkward boy standing in the kitchen still clutching the fifty-cent piece that Paul insisted on paying him, and ten minutes later they joined the throng at the station watching for the westbound train. While Paul explained his and Hope's change of plans to the others, Hope approached the bench where Sarah was sitting alone, hollow-cheeked now and lost in thought.

"We're not coming with you," she said. "But I promise to call after we get back to Frisco."

"Will you." Sarah's tone was biting, but Hope refused to let it invade her. She pitied Sarah. Sarah intrigued her. But she was nothing like her.

"I will." She hesitated. "That is, if you'd like."

Sarah squared her eyes on her. "You think you know why I married Donald, don't you? Because I'm with child. Yes, but whose child?" She paused to let her implication sink in. "You understand now? Donald's my savior, isn't he? And I must forgive him his faults as he forgives mine. It's not about love. It's an arrangement. A negotiation."

"Business," murmured Hope, horrified.

"So," said Sarah, her voice flattening, "you and Paul are staying. Here." Hope didn't answer. "I've never held much faith in love," Sarah went on. "Surely would never believe a white woman could marry a Chinaman for love. That's why I called you a fool, you know. But I suppose I should tell you, I was wrong. I saw, this morning. You and Paul, you're different. You're one of the lucky ones, Hope. Or perhaps you're even more doomed than I, I don't know. But I envy you."

Sarah's ugly revelation, followed by this confession, the unexpected tumble into softness and raw truth made Hope feel as though she'd been turned inside out. The train was pulling in. Paul beckoned.

"I'm sorry," she said, wrapping her arms around Sarah. "I'm so sorry."

"Don't be," said Sarah. "Just take care of yourself."

ဢ ဢ ဢ

After the train had gone, Hope and Paul followed the railroad tracks along the river to the beginning of the shanties that made up Chinatown. They stopped outside a ramshackle building with shredded tarpaper for roofing, a sagging half porch, broken windows patched with newsprint, and a sign of flaking green and white paint that bore a series of Chinese characters and, in crude lettering, JOE GON GENERAL STORE. Paul said,

"Mr. Fu tell me this store owner from Hupei. His cousin friend of Sun Yat-sen. He will help us."

A quick glance around the dingy interior told Hope that Joe Gon could outfit them with whatever they needed—and more. The plank tables and shelves were laden with food and dry goods, many of which bore Chinese labels. A rack of sausages and jerky hung behind the counter—along with the shrunken, eyeless head of a boar, painted red as a Paiute—and the far corner was piled with miners' gear: kerosene lamps, tin pans and utensils, oilcloth tarpaulins, mosquito webbing, axe flints, shovels, drill bits, canvas tenting, flints, stick matches, black tar soap.

But the merchant was understandably cautious. A Chinese man leaving town alone with a white woman was bound to be noticed, and on the outside it was even more difficult to predict the actions of men than in town. Some of the local homesteaders were friends of the Chinese, but then again Joe Gon, a stocky, wizened man in his fifties, had lived through Rock Springs. His nightmares still rang with the white miners' rallying cry, "The Chinese must go!"

"Sometimes," he told Paul, "this American wilderness is not as wide or empty as one would wish." He shook his head ponderously from side to side.

Hope stepped closer. They were speaking in dialect, but the merchant's attitude was plain enough. "We will pay."

"This is not—" Paul started, but Hope cut him off.

"You take pawn? Paul, show him Collis's ring."

"Hope, money is not the problem."

But she could see by the knit of Joe Gon's heavy eyebrows that this was not strictly true. "Some Indian pawn," he said, too casually.

Paul reluctantly handed her the jeweled band. She started to set it on the counter, but Paul immediately snatched it back and drew her out of the man's earshot. "No good. He will gamble this."

"If that thing brings old Joe Gon bad luck, I'd rather it be him than me. He knows this area. He must know a place we can go where no one will bother us. And he obviously has all the provisions we'll need. Let him keep the ring as security."

Still Paul hesitated. "You have no feelings for these jewels?"

"No more than I have for the man who threw them at your feet."

When the merchant understood that he was truly to be granted the use of the ring, he flashed four wooden teeth and ducked down behind the counter. Sounds of shuffling and folding, then he came back up with an armload of dusty black clothing and two floppy felt hats. He thrust one bundle at Hope, the other at Paul.

"More safe." Joe Gon pointed to Hope's dark hair, shaped the smallness of her figure with his hands. "Like Chinese boy." He motioned her through a curtained doorway into a sliver of space outfitted with a cot and Coleman and a crude plank washstand, where she was to change.

She wrinkled her nose as she shook out the garments. They smelled of grass and sand and onions and smoke—and human sweat. But her inspection revealed no evidence of vermin, no stench of disease. The smell, she instructed herself, was not bad, only strange. Still, she pulled a vial of rose water from her bag and splashed it across the cloth, then under her arms, her throat, behind her knees. She was still wearing her corset, camisole, drawers, and stockings when she climbed into the rough coverings. The pants could be tightened about the waist with a rope, and the length would serve to conceal her boots. The jacket fastened to her chin and coughed dust when she raised her arms. Heavy dust, it seemed, powdery white like the limestone they mined in these hills. It occurred to her to wonder how the merchant came by these clothes, but she firmly put the thought out of her mind and yanked the pins from her hair. She combed out the tangles with her fingers and braided it the way she used to as a girl, into a long, dangling pigtail. Then she pulled the hat brim down to her eyes and marched back into the store.

Paul whistled softly at the length of her braid, and when he lifted the brim of her hat she grinned to find him identically dressed—except that any passersby would have to believe his queue was coiled up under his hat. Joe Gon grunted as her body gravitated toward Paul's. She quickly stepped away and bowed. After they had selected their provisions, the merchant loaded them into two wicker baskets, which he strung to a bamboo pole. Paul balanced this contraption over his shoulder with the aplomb of a born journeyman.

Hope had to laugh as they set off. All the prideful energy she had poured into mentally segregating her husband from the peasants—what perfect irony that they should both now, by choice, outfit themselves as Chinaboys!

But the irony shriveled when they passed a couple of deerstalkers at the edge of town. From deep beneath her down-turned hat Hope watched the hunters elbow each other at a distance of about twenty yards. The men changed direction to avoid coming close, but at the same time lifted their rifles so Hope could see the black nostrils of the gun barrels pointing straight at her and Paul.

"Keep walking," Paul breathed when she stumbled over a rut. The men had dropped behind them.

Then she heard them groan with laughter. "Goddamn Chinks. Even deer got 'nough guts to look y'in the eye fore ya shoot 'em."

ᗏᗏᗏ

They kept on in a stricken, fearful silence, but after the hunters they encountered only a white-haired sojourner crouched by the river with his basket of washing. The Bear River led them to a stream that branched left, then they struck off through a meadow solid with yellow mustard plants and brilliant blue lupine. The meadow was triangular in shape, an arrow dipping down to a shaded pond where a family of elk had stopped for a drink. Following Joe Gon's instructions, they continued along the stream, entering a high, narrow canyon. It was hushed here, the race of water fusing with the rustle of wings and paws in the undergrowth. Live oak and sycamore and enormous lodgepole pines grew sideways in the canyon walls. There was no trail or other evidence of humans, which was reassuring but also inconvenient, as it meant they had to cut their own path. Paul suggested stopping at several points, but Hope insisted if they kept going, the canyon would eventually widen out.

"We need a flat area to pitch the tent," she explained, and when he asked how she knew such things, she told him of the trips she used to make with her father, childhood summers and holidays when he was a traveling naturopath. She told about their red and gold wagon, with DOC MIRACLE'S CURES emblazoned on the sides, how proud she was to ride beside her father, how he called her his "assistant," even though she was just five years old. She was never as happy in Fort Dodge with the Waylands as she was out traveling, and their adventures only got more rugged when

Doc took up ranching. They'd pitched tents during lightning storms and on Indian ruins. One night they'd been awakened by a herd of stampeding longhorns. And there was the time they'd fed two strangers supper only to learn in town the next morning that their guests had robbed a bank just three days earlier.

"You are afraid?" asked Paul, extending a hand to help her over a wide, knuckled root.

"Were," she corrected. "I had no reason to be. The bandits did me no harm. In fact, they told me stories. Jack and the Beanstalk, Robin Hood, of course. But most important was my father's reaction. He laughed. Nothing scares Dad."

"He teach you to be brave," said Paul.

"Or foolish, if you believe Sarah."

Paul grimaced. "Sarah is no good."

"I feel sorry for her."

"Do not waste time for her."

As if in proof of Sarah's destructive powers, an uncomfortable silence descended between them now as they plunged deeper into the narrowing canyon. For the better part of a mile, this shadow danced between them, then suddenly the ravine widened.

"Look!" Hope clapped her hands. "Isn't it perfect!"

Ahead, in a clearing lined with berry thickets, blooming apple and massive old oak trees, stood an abandoned miner's hut. The structure had long ago lost its roof, but the fieldstone walls stood firm. Mourning doves had nested atop one corner, and a family of chipmunks used another as a storage den. Fallen leaves and pine needles padded the dirt floor, and sky was visible through the stovepipe still in position above the fireplace, though no fire had been built here in decades. The only other sign of human occupancy was a tin washtub overturned by the stove, now home to an active universe of spiders.

"You see!" Hope hung their hats on a rusty nail beside the door. "It's *sanctuary*. That's what it is."

Paul smiled, indulgent as a father, and wondered if they could eat the raspberries just coming ripe outside the hut. After a lunch of this fruit, some crackers and sausage from their provisions, and stream water, which Paul insisted on boiling into tea, they set to work. He constructed a broom from birch-wood branches and swept the floor, scrubbed the hut for cobwebs, scoured out the tub, and hung an oilcloth roof across one corner in case of rain. Hope washed their utensils in the creek, unpacked the rest of their provisions, and ordered a kitchen from a ledge beside the fireplace, then explored around the house until she located a ring of spruce trees that would serve as screen for a privy. Using a large flat rock, she dug a pit in soft dirt as her father had taught her, and spread a carpet of clean pine needles around what Dad had always dubbed "the wilderness throne."

When she returned, Paul stood barefoot to meet her. He took her hand and drew her to the mattress he had fashioned by spreading their bedrolls over a cushion of lavender and sweet grass and feathery sage. "I wish look at you," he said simply.

∞∞∞

Afterward, she wondered how she could have failed to see, when his clothes fell away, when her hands ran, trembling, down his back, or when she clasped him to her during their lovemaking. Was it her own innate desire to avoid his suffering, or had he orchestrated his body, even in the throes of passion, to shield her? Whatever the reason, it was only after they had lain together, after the tenderest murmurs of inquiry and exploration had subsided, after Paul rolled away from her and stepped across to the brimming tub that her eyes discovered what her hands had missed: a net of white-blue and purple wheals that stretched from the small of his back all the way to the crease of his buttocks.

It looked as though an etcher's burin had dug across Paul's flesh, and again, and again, and again. Some of the gouges ran straight, some quavered. Reading the scars Hope could see that the lacerations had cut to bone. How many years earlier she could not tell, but no mere accident could have produced such trauma.

She was paralyzed by two competing impulses: to caress the damaged flesh in a futile, womanish attempt to comfort, and to withdraw in revulsion.

As he turned, bringing the tub closer, she held her breath and clutched her arms across her breasts. He said nothing, but reached his fingertips into the water, ran them across her cheeks. He unfolded her arms and touched the hollow at the base of her throat, and the cold moisture forced her to breathe, though what came forth was something between a gasp and a cry. He wet her lips then to silence her, kissed her firmly and bade her stand in the tub. He bathed each breast as if it were some rare fruit. He gently unfolded the place where he had entered her, washing away his own seed and sweat now as something unnatural. Undesirable.

"No!" She grabbed his wrist, afraid suddenly to lose his scent from her skin, as if the man would go with it.

He stopped and lifted her like a child out of the tub, stepped in himself. "Now you," he said, as much with his eyes as his voice. And he turned, that she might begin by cleansing his scars.

"Tell me," she said.

"Long story," he warned.

She stroked the marbled flesh. "When did it happen?"

"Western calendar, nineteen hundred. First, you need know about one man Chang Chih-tung. Chang is my teacher many years in Hupei. He is very powerful, viceroy of Hupei and Hunan Province both. Chang start Two Lakes Academy. I am student in first class. Chang change whole education system, stop classical examinations, open to modern learning. He do many good things, also can be evil. Very interesting, but—"

Paul knit his fingers together to illustrate the word he could not locate.

"Complex?"

"Complex, yes. Chang admire Jesus, Socrates, so he follow their example. Some time every day he bring his students and followers around him this kind discussion. This way he hear many ideas. He take many ideas, decide which followers he can trust."

"And you were one of those he could trust?"

He took her hand and led her back to the bed, where they lay down, facing each other. "Chang enjoy me. I study him. I memorialize him. I teach him about foreigners and the West. He will use this. He say Japan is good place for Chinese to study—modern country, very good military training, but still Asia, so better than West. Many Chinese now think this, but Chang was first."

"It was Chang, then, who sent you to study in Japan?"

"At first. Yes. I attend Seijo Gakko military academy."

"You trained to be a soldier!" Hope was stunned. In spite of Paul's rev-

olutionary fervor, there was nothing remotely militaristic about his attitude or bearing.

"I learn military arts. Troop movement. Strategy." Paul smiled.
"Chess."

"What about weapons?"

He shrugged, wrapped her damp hair like a bandage around his hand.
"I learn artillery, ballistics, ammunition. Price of these things."

"You learned to organize a revolution."

"In Japan I meet Dr. Sun, who teach me revolution is only way China
can be free of Manchus and foreigners."

"But all of this is before you got up at that New Year's party and called
for the Manchus' overthrow."

"That is 1903, yes, this only 1900. Through Dr. Sun I join plot to take
Hankow. I arrange funds, make connection with Chinatown donors in
Honolulu, Singapore. I return to Hupei to plan with revolutionary leaders. But there is fire in Honolulu, and the money is slow. We must postpone. Other donors pull back. Some men turn, confess to Chang
Chih-tung in trade for their lives. So arrests begin. It is not like Japan or
Shanghai, where police are cautious with Chinese prisoners. In Hupei,
questioning is never words alone. Chang takes heads of ten my friends,
some same students he sent with me to study in Japan."

"And he had you marked for life."

"Chang does not know how to do with me. My father has been viceroy
of Canton, you know. My mother is sending gifts every day, pleading for
my life. One day she comes in person, offering Chang statue of goddess
Kuanyin, Goddess of Mercy, apple jade more than five hundred years old.
Base of this statue is hollow. Inside, three gold bars. Next morning, door to
my prison cell is open, no guards. I escape. You see, this Chinese justice."

Hope shivered. "Your mother saved you."

"My mother gives to me two times life. This is true."

"Then I owe her my thanks also." But the words stuck in Hope's throat.
Paul noticed.

"My mother have one child, Hope, and he is son. This center everything in China."

"In *your* China, or in hers?"

"Hope." He shook his head.

"I can't help it, I'm afraid of her, Paul. Of the power she wields over you. Everything you tell me about her seems to add to that power, and yet I can't picture her. I have nothing to compare her to except the queens of fairy tales. In fairy tales, the queen can become invisible, can turn lovers against each other without their even knowing she's there."

"You worry too much."

She placed her hand over the tracery of his lower back. "Do I?"

"I should not told these stories. I think you can understand, I want you know me, care for me. You ask questions, I give answer. But you listen to words you hear, not words I speak."

"Have told," corrected Hope, retiring to the shelter of literacy in order, they both recognized, to sidestep the words he had spoken. "*I should not have told you these stories. I want you to know me.* But, Paul?" She pushed herself up onto her elbow so she was looking down at him. "I'm glad you did, and I don't want you to stop. Some things are so different—I can't help but feel threatened. Yet if you don't teach me where you come from, what forces made you the way you are, then I'll never truly know you. And when the world starts to close against us, as we both know it will, we won't have a chance of surviving—together or apart."

"And you?" answered Paul. "You wish to know me, but you say little about yourself."

A sudden movement caught her eye and she looked up to see a squirrel spread flat as a kite sailing between the branches above them. "My stories are not as interesting as yours."

"I like these about your father. Camping with bandits."

She shook her head, still facing upward. "That world is behind me. Yours is ahead." And then, unexpectedly, "Did you understand your first wife so well?"

"Hsin-hsin." He started to reach for her, then pulled back. "I know more about my wife maybe I can ever know you. I can name her parents, cousins, ancestors, village, birth sign, history of her clan. I learn these things like lesson to pass examination. That examination is marriage. But I never understand her. I do not try. This way is easy to leave her."

He held his hand to her breast, not quite touching but close enough that she felt her skin lifting toward him.

"Help me to understand you, Hope."

ﾎﾟﾎﾟﾎﾟ

The next morning, they ventured deeper into the canyon. The air was hot and dry, and mosquitoes nipped at their throats. Hope rejected her boots, rolled up her pant cuffs, and walked in the stream, stepping stone to stone. Paul kept to the bank, hands clasped behind his back, head tilted upward, silent. He might be composing a poem, Hope thought. Or pondering the mysteries of the universe. If there was a difference. For the first time, she had a clear vision of him as a scholar, could see him trussed in a mandarin's gown, leaning stiffly over a scroll with pen—no, brush—in hand. She pictured herself tiptoeing around him so as not to disturb.

But while Hope's attention narrowed to her husband, Paul's concentration opened outward. Far from being lost in thought, he was absorbed by the world around them. He wanted to record in his mind the slats of light between the trees, the spongy texture of this forest earth, the music of the stream, and the tantalizing grace of his wife as she moved beside him. Paul's were the eyes of a poet and a military strategist and, in this country, a fascinated tourist. They attributed meaning to details that others would never even notice. "Look." He pointed.

Ahead on their right, growing up from the stream bank, rose a massive tree whose upper half looked as if it had once been split by lightning. Paul pushed up his glasses. "They are like us."

"They?" Hope splashed closer.

"It is two trees. Look, two colors."

Though identical in size and planted so closely that their seeds could have grown from the same pod, one of the trees had the deep gray bark and clustered leaves of a live oak while the other had the pale skin and larger fisted leaves of a sycamore. They were clearly two different species, yet they had literally grown into and around each other, the two skins pressed so tightly that the transition from one body to the next was perfectly seamless and they appeared to share the same trunk. In fact, it defied belief that they had not managed to organically enter each other's systems.

Hope and Paul clasped hands as they circled this strange botanic monument. Every detail suggested the intensity of embrace, from the interweaving of limbs and leaves, to the roots, which held stones and moss and petrified nuts in their combined grasp. Unlike the trunks, the roots grew equally dark in color, so it was impossible to tell which belonged to which parent. One span of roots laced together into a bench that stretched out over the water. "A love seat," Hope pronounced, pulling Paul down.

He, too, removed his boots now, let the icy water pummel his feet. "I think these lovers forced to part in past life. Now for eternity, they will be together."

"Eternity." Hope leaned back and stared up through the fretwork of leaves. "My father used to tell stories like that. About lovers. He said they came from old Indian tales."

Paul thought for a minute, then asked, "Will I meet your father?"

"Oh, I hope so!" She looked at him sharply. "I wouldn't be surprised if he's waiting for us when we return to Berkeley."

Paul unhooked his glasses, folded them, then waved them at the tree. "I think these lovers part because bride father disapprove."

"You needn't worry about Dad. I told you, he's a romantic."

He glanced at her. "You do not speak of your mother."

"I don't know much about her. Only . . ." She chewed her lower lip. "These stories of Dad's. He was talking about himself and my mother. I could feel it in his voice."

"Why Indian stories?"

She leaned forward and dipped her hand, felt the current push against her. *You wish to know me, but you say little about yourself.*

She came back up and forced herself to look at his face. His coloring. The arching cheekbones and flat sweep of his lids above those dark eyes. "My mother," she answered slowly, "was half Indian. Her mother was from the Seneca tribe, but she died in childbirth. My grandfather was post commander at Fort Dodge. He was from England. My father was always respectful, said my mother's Indian blood made her very beautiful and headstrong, but I was raised by a white family in a white town. My father was from Boston, and if I had any living Indian relatives, we never knew them. Do you understand?"

Paul lifted her chin with his fingertips. She felt him reconsider the shape of her nose and eyes, the tint and texture of her hair, and there was an irritating eagerness in his gaze, like that of a scientist examining a rare specimen, but that same gaze was so utterly devoid of prejudice that she found it impossible to begrudge him his curiosity.

"When I study history," he said, "I think Europeans do to native people in America same way foreigners and Manchus do to Chinese. It is good you tell about your mother. And father. Yes." He nodded slowly. "Yes, Hsin-hsin. I understand."

He touched her cheek and smiled, first at Hope, then up at the intertwining branches above them. "This tree is our children's history," he said. "We must remember this place, always."

IV
HOME
BERKELEY
(1906–1911)

1

BERKELEY DAILY GAZETTE, June 21, 1906

OBJECTS TO THE CHINESE
CITIZEN FEARS THE ORIENTALS MAY SECURE VALUABLE HOME PROPERTY IN HEART OF TOWN

When the frightful calamity to San Francisco brought thousands of homeless ones to this side of the bay a few buccaneering individuals have not only been guilty of renting a home on Grant Street to a half dozen or more Chinamen but have also a scheme to sell the adjoining property to another batch of Orientals. These houses are located in the heart of town, within two blocks of the high school and a region where many comfortable and tasty homes have been erected. Now these arc threatened by an influx from Chinatown and a certain deterioration of the value of property.

If this horde of yellow Chinese, with all the filth and disease there [sic] presence means, are to remain within the town limits let it be in some locality apart from decent residences where they can herd together under proper surveillance. . . .

"Baboon!" Mary Jane hoisted the paper like an enemy flag. "What's the Chinese word for abominations like this man?"

Paul peered at her over his glasses. He and Hope had debated whether to show the article to Mary Jane, but Hope had insisted—to prove to him that her friend would stand by them. "*Sha jiba,*" he answered.

"I hope that's worse than what I said."

"I do not speak its meaning in company of ladies," he answered with a gallant nod.

"Unfortunately, there are plenty of others exactly like him," said Hope. "And far too few of these 'buccaneering individuals' for us to find a home. What are we going to do?"

"Just stay put," said Mary Jane, returning Paul's nod. "Since the Three Musketeers decamped, I'm crawling with room, and your company has spoiled me for solitude."

It was when Mary Jane started calling Dorothea, Anne, and Antonia the Three Musketeers that the trio decided they'd overstayed their welcome and found an apartment together in Albany. Hope and Paul would have heeded the cue as well, if they'd had a choice, but while housing for Chinese was limited—and disputed—housing for Chinese who had taken white wives seemed to be nonexistent. Kathe and Ben Joe had given up the hunt and moved to a Chinese community near Fresno, and Sarah and Donald had stolen away even before Hope and Paul returned from Wyoming, supposedly following an offer of employment in Maine. Mary Jane was the only friend Hope had who could, and would, take them in. But they had been here nearly a month.

Paul cleared his throat, nodding in time to the Mozart concerto playing on the Gramophone. With his legs outstretched, their host's enormous mustard cat in his lap, and his feet propped on the chintz ottoman, he looked a picture of comfort. Hope wondered at this with some resentment. Tensions that buffeted her seemed to pass right over him, and he sometimes acted as if he didn't care whether they ever found a place of their own!

Gingerly, so as not to disturb the cat, Paul eased a slip of paper from his jacket pocket. "Tomorrow morning, ten o'clock, you meet me at this place. If you like, we live there."

Hope stared, dumbfounded. "But how in heaven—"

"Forget heaven," said Mary Jane, crowding in for a look, "how on *earth* did you manage to find a place smack in the middle of Berkeley!"

The address was 1919 Francisco Street, just around the corner from the university and a block from the Key trolley to the ferry. It was indeed a good location, Hope thought with a glance to the newsprint still crumpled in Mary Jane's fist. There were far more "comfortable and tasty homes" on this block of Francisco than on the Chinamen's block of Grant.

"You've actually spoken with the owner?" she asked.

"Yes, yes." Paul stroked the purring cat.

"Don't look a gift horse in the mouth, child." Mary Jane tossed the newspaper into the fire. "If you like it, I hope it works out. If not, don't worry. I'm going to bed. Remember to put old Methusaleh there outside to do his business before you close up for the night."

But Hope could not let it go. She had a nose for a story, and Paul's benign masks didn't fool her one bit. "Tell me," she begged when Mary Jane had left them. "What's it like?"

"I have not seen it."

"Not seen it!"

"Not this house for us."

"Well, what have you seen, then?"

"This gentleman's house."

"What gentleman?"

"Landlord."

"Honestly, Paul. Start at the beginning."

He kept on with that cat, as if in a trance. Hope stamped her foot and pulled the needle from the recording. The room swelled with Methusaleh's purring. Paul's lids, like the cat's, remained half closed.

"Which came first, the man or the house?"

"Man," he murmured.

"And how did you meet this man?"

"He was crossing the street. Truck was coming. I pull him away."

Her hands went to her hips. "You mean you saved his life."

Paul shrugged. The cat twitched and cast him a warning glance.

"So just like that, he offered you a place to live?"

"This happen before his house. Big house, many rooms. I ask maybe he will rent to me and my wife." Paul frowned and slid his hands under the beast, gently removed it to the floor, and they both stood, side by side, stretching. Paul yawned. "He shaked my hand. Say he will give me cottage behind, I come see tomorrow, ten-thirty. Then he walked away and another wagon almost hit him."

Hope pushed the cat aside with her shoe and came into her husband's arms. "You lead a charmed life."

"I think so," he agreed, and kissed the tip of her nose.

ᔥᔥᔥ

Mr. Thomas Wall lived in a handsome, ivy-covered mansard, with a tall verandah, gables, and huge bay windows. "Like Shanghai," Paul remarked as they stood looking up at it from the front gate.

"What's like Shanghai?" Hope searched in vain for a pagoda, a golden deity, any exotic flourish.

"This style. All foreigners build like this."

"Ah. *Foreigners.*" She felt a pang of dismay. The contradictions of her husband's world never seemed to cease.

They knocked four times and had almost given up when the door fell open, and there stood before them a figure of gloom for which Paul's story had in no way prepared Hope. The man he had rescued was tall, rangy, with a beard like a bear's and bulging bloodshot eyes. His skin was lined and unnaturally pale, and his black wool suit, far too warm for this weather, looked as if he had slept in it. He used only his shoulders to signal them in, did not invite them to sit down, did not offer refreshment, and asked no questions. Indeed, he seemed utterly indifferent to their identities or backgrounds, leading them more like a butler than master through a dingy, untended kitchen and down some steps to the yard, which sloped to a large carriage barn on one side of the property and a white clapboard cottage on the other. The latter was small and dear, with a front porch and trellis bursting with yellow roses.

"I built this," Mr. Wall said in a deadened voice, "for my wife's parents. Before the Quake."

Hope tugged on the corners of her jacket, checking Paul for signs that he'd heard this before, but he seemed as mystified as she. Mr. Wall stood,

silent again, arms lifeless as the stopped hands of a clock. It was not difficult to imagine him stepping, oblivious, into traffic.

"My wife," he concluded, "and her parents are gone. The cottage is no
use to me now. I am happy you are here." Before they could answer he
leaned into a turn and lumbered back to the house. Hope thought she'd
never seen a man who suited the word "happy" less than Thomas Wall.

"What do you think?" asked Paul.

"I think he's very sad. Do you suppose they were killed in the Quake?"

"Perhaps." He eyed the cottage. "Do you wish to look?"

"I don't see that we have any choice."

The previous occupants must have been short, to judge by the doorways—Paul had to duck as he moved from room to room—and the
kitchen and bathroom fixtures were set unusually low. But the latter fea-
ture was a boon for Hope, who had to stand on tiptoe to see into the mirrors on most people's walls. And though the furnishings were a bit stuffy
for her taste, with crocheted dustcovers and needle-pointed love songs
from the nineties, she didn't imagine Mr. Wall meant them to keep these
things. The rooms were generous, full of light but cool, thanks to the
steeped roof. There was a large plastered fireplace in the parlor and a
wood stove in the kitchen. Paul's Chinese scrolls and lacquered trunks
would look handsome here, and with two bedrooms and an indoor flush
toilet, the little house surpassed Hope's wildest expectations.

"Look here," Paul called from the larger bedroom.

She found him in front of a corner étagère displaying a collection of
framed photographs, including one of Thomas Wall gazing deeply into
the eyes of a fair-haired young woman. Behind them stood an older couple arm in arm.

Paul said, "Some believe it unwise to begin marriage in such a place."

"Unwise?"

"If spirits are not settled, they will maybe return."

"I thought superstition went out with the revolution." She patted his
hand. "Anyway, if these American ghosts wanted to keep their home,
don't you think they'd have helped us find another?"

"I do not know." He scanned the room, considering, then gave her a
slow sidelong look. He clasped his hands in front of him and bowed
solemnly three times to the picture, murmuring some sort of incantation

under his breath. At the end of the final bow he closed his eyes as if gathering his nerve to make some special, arduous request. Hope held still, a little embarrassed by this ceremony and at the same time awed that he would allow her to witness it. Paul had told her he was raised a Buddhist, had shown her the fragrant wood worry beads that he sometimes wore around his wrist, had described the ornate temples to which his mother took him as a child. Still, she had never seen him perform devotions, and her sense was that the Chinese religions were so closely tied to superstition that her revolutionary husband had disavowed them all.

At last Paul's eyes fluttered open. He dropped his hands, stood for a moment as if in a daze. Then he spun and lifted Hope by the waist. It was such an exuberant, impious notion that she burst out laughing. "You madman! Put me down!"

He beamed at her flailing above him. "Say you are happy."

"I'm happy."

"Loud."

"I am happy!"

He grinned and set her down. "Chinese lie to fool evil spirits. Maybe American ghosts respect truth."

June 28, 1906

Whatever race or religion our gods may be, they are certainly smiling on Paul and me. We have a home beyond my dreams for which we pay just $5 (and that to satisfy my pride only, Mr. Wall offered and Paul was ready to take it for free!). My one regret is that our good fortune is due to our landlord's tragic loss. After nearly a week here, we have finally pieced together his sad tale.

It seems that Thomas is an architect. A few days before the Quake, he had gone down to Santa Cruz, where he was finishing a house. While he was away, his wife and her parents were visiting with friends across the Bay. The friends' home burned to the ground the morning of the Quake, and Thomas's family was last seen loaded down with satchels near the civic center. Moments later that whole area was incinerated in a firestorm.

I cannot imagine a greater horror than to know your loved ones perished in such a ghastly way, or a greater guilt than having been the lone member of the family to survive. Every sound that falls from Thomas's mouth is weighted with sorrow. His entire body shows his pain. I think if Paul met such an end, I would better go after him into the flames than suffer a minute of the hell poor Thomas is enduring.

However, Paul is so full of energy and life that such a fate is inconceivable. Every morning, he is up and off at dawn to his other world across the Bay. In these two months his people have already raised a new building to replace the offices that were burned, and in another week he expects to bring his paper back to press. Afternoons he spends in class, since the university has reopened for summer, and his evenings are devoted to writing—poetry, translations, articles, volumes of correspondence in his eternal fund-raising quest for Sun Yat-sen. I, meanwhile, strain to keep myself busy making curtains and learning to steam a proper pot of Chinese rice! Money is tighter than ever, and I feel like a sloth by comparison with Paul. I will not crawl back to Collis, but I must find work. The Mason sisters, who run the Berkeley Chinese Educational Mission, have advertised for an English tutor, and I plan to call on them this week.

ৡৡৡ

2

BERKELEY DAILY GAZETTE, July 13, 1906

CHINESE WEDS LOCAL WOMAN JUSTIFICATION FOR RACE PREJUDICE IN BAY AREA

Friends have learned of the recent marriage of Miss Hope Newfield, lately of Berkeley, to a Chinese student, Po-yu Liang. This pair's elopement, with two other interracial couples from San Francisco, brings acutely to the front one of the indisputable hazards arising out of the matriculation of Oriental students at the University of California. The Orientals exercise a fascination over certain American females, and as long as they are allowed to attend U.S. colleges, studying alongside coeds and, as in this case, enjoying personal contact with female teachers, we must brace ourselves for increasing waves of mongrelization.

Although the Berkeley interracials traveled to Wyoming to escape local anti-miscegenation laws, it was inevitable that friends and colleagues would discover their act when they returned as husband and wife. This has brought social ostracism for the bride, who formerly tutored foreign university students in English. And when news of this marriage is spread beyond our city walls, more than one father and mother may worry that their daughter might acquire an Oriental husband along with an education or paycheck if she comes to the University of California to study or work. University officials take heed!

"University officials indeed!" cried Hope. "Collis planted this sewage, I'm sure of it."

"Be still," said Paul, trying to read over her shoulder. His insistence on finishing the article before reacting infuriated her so that she thrust the newsprint into his hands and stormed across the room.

"We should sue them for slander! He's a vicious little toad, is what he is. Doesn't even have the nerve to fight this out face-to-face, but goes broadcasting it to the entire city. How I despise that man!"

Paul finished the article and folded it in half, half again, then sat slapping the resulting packet against his knee and watching her over his glasses.

"Don't give me that paternal stare! And don't tell me this doesn't make your blood boil, too!"

"It is odd thing," he answered, unflappable. "Americans treat Chinese worse than dogs, but fear us like dragons." He prodded his glasses back into place and, smiling, scanned the article again. "They object because I *exercise fascination* over you. I am interested that Americans see themselves so weak, Chinese so powerful."

"It's no joke, Paul! You don't know what these people can do. Collis is a coward and a weakling. That's why he's put this out to the public—so others will punish us for him."

He laid the paper aside and came to her. She allowed him to calm her. But three mornings later they were wakened by a fusillade outside their window.

The concussions were prolonged, overlapping, and sharp as knife thrusts. Hope dove for the floor, and Paul curled his body to cover her as the room filled with black powder and smoke. After several deafening minutes the explosion withered to a few muffled pops. Then silence.

Paul slowly pulled back, turning Hope in his arms. "All right?"

She nodded, but trembled as he pulled her up and they moved cautiously down the hall together, checking the other rooms. The inside of the house appeared unscathed, but outside a heavy metallic cloud draped the porch and yard. No birds sang. No squirrels chattered.

Paul left Hope at the front door and felt his way to the end of the porch. A moment later he was back, his face ashen.

"What is it?"

"No matter." He shut the door.

"Is someone out there?"

"No." He was blocking her deliberately.

"Let me see," she said with more bravado than she felt, and pushed past him.

The smell made her gag. It was more than the dark, leaden Fourth of July stench of explosives. This had a thick, organic quality, piercing to the nostrils and stomach-wrenching, the smell of burnt hair and flesh. She crept forward but, halfway down the porch, stopped abruptly. The roses had changed. Their yellow and green were suddenly flecked with darkness. Bits of flesh and fur, brown and white and a deep, sickly red. She sagged back against Paul as her eyes finally, ruthlessly dropped to the source of these exploded fragments.

At the bottom of the porch steps lay the disemboweled carcasses of some twenty rats, bits of black and vermilion scattered over them, remnants of the firecrackers that had been planted among the bodies.

"Damn them! Damn them all!"

He tried to draw her back onto the cottage. "They have not hurt us, Hope. They will not hurt us." But she would neither be consoled nor moved.

"I hate them," she kept saying, even as she stared with dreadful fascination at the tiny, shattered skulls.

"Hope, please," he begged. "What they think does not matter. They are nothing."

Her teeth began to chatter and she hugged herself. She wanted to take Paul's hand and go in, slam the door and never come out. He was right, they were nothing. But what they thought controlled the world.

He brought a blanket and wound it around her shoulders.

"I knew something like this would happen," she said.

"I tell you." He stroked her hair. "They are afraid."

"Yes, and so am I. But what now, Paul! What do we do now?"

He looked past her. "Thomas."

"Oh, no." Whatever they had brought upon themselves, Thomas Wall was innocent and too fragile to be subjected to it. He came toward them like a wakened scarecrow in that rumpled black suit, in his hands a small silver derringer.

"No problem," Paul called. With a quick, steadying glance to Hope, he hurried from the porch, skirting the carnage. "No damage. No harm done."

Hope clutched the blanket and followed her husband. "It was only a prank," she said hoarsely. "Chinese firecrackers."

They thought they could stop Thomas, turn him around, steer him back to bed, and along the way relieve him of the gun, but he would not be maneuvered. In fact, he became more alert and commanding with each step. At the pile of exploded flesh he stopped, sniffed, glanced back at his tenants' bare feet. "You didn't touch any of this?"

Hope and Paul stared at him, perplexed. "No."

"Good. Let me clean up then. If these are plague rats, they could be as lethal dead as alive. Better soak your feet in disinfectant, just in case."

"Plague rats?" Paul looked to Hope for translation.

"Bubonic plague's been in the city for years." Thomas waved them back toward his house. "They try to hush it up, 'cause it's carried over from Asia. Old Mayor Ruef takes so many cuts out of the Chinatown trade, he couldn't afford having those ships turned back." He glanced at Paul apologetically. "I did a stint on the Board of Supervisors. Long as it was only Chinese dying, they figured no one'd notice. But since the Quake's stirred things up, the rats are all over."

"And you think—" Hope ducked Paul's worried eyes.

"I saw what they wrote against you," Thomas said.

Paul winced. "We have endangered you."

Thomas ran a hand through his rangy brown hair and sighed. "You two are the least of my burdens. Anyway, you're not to blame. Now come on. Jeyes' Liquid for both of you and some gloves and a mask for me. I'll have to dust the yard—it's the fleas that actually carry the disease. Anyway, by tomorrow, you'll forget this happened."

But they did not forget, and neither Hope nor Paul was now willing to let the attack go unanswered. Thomas Wall gave them just the ammunition they needed. Galvanized out of the stupor of his grieving, he took the remains of the rats for analysis that very morning and discovered that fully one third of them did indeed carry the plague virus. Whether the rats had been purposely brought from the city for this devious purpose, or had migrated before being captured, no one could tell, but, after conferring with Mary Jane, Hope and Paul decided to proclaim the worst.

Two days after the explosion, the *Berkeley Gazette* published the following:

Vicious Prank Endangers Lives of All Berkeley Residents
Racial Prejudice Is a Threat to All

To the Editor:

Last Friday this paper published an unauthorized announcement of our marriage which all but instructed the local populace to take up arms against us. Less than one week after this publication we were subjected to a vicious and cowardly attack that put the lives of every resident in Berkeley at risk. We are writing today to protest this paper's policy of encouraging racist sentiment, and to alert the public to the grave and immediate menace that prejudice poses not only to those who belong to or choose to associate with the non-white races but to every member of this society. The person who penned those public words against us is as much a vandal, violating our private lives, as the person or persons who endangered all of Berkeley by physically assaulting us yesterday morning.

What was this vicious act? We will not dignify it with detailed description, but say only that it involved the distribution of rats, which had been infected by bubonic plague, around the premises of our residence. Fortunately, we recognized the risk that these animals posed not only to us but to the surrounding neighborhood. All threat of disease from this incident has been eradicated, as verified by the health authorities.

Surely we need not elaborate on the degree to which this hostility dismays and disheartens us. Is not America the Land of Liberty and Justice? Is it not the Home of the Free? Should we not all be entitled to love on right principle, to become true husband and wife by the laws of both holy gospel and the land? We fervently believe in the principles of justice and fairness on which this nation was founded. We believe that China, the world's oldest civilization, has much to learn from America, the world's greatest republic. However, we also believe that our two peoples will mutually benefit only if we can forge a secure foundation of friendship, tolerance, and trust between our races. We intend to do all in our power to this end.

Sincerely,

Mr. and Mrs. Paul Leon

Over the following weeks a flurry of answering editorials protested that the majority of Berkeley's citizens fully endorsed the civil rights of Oriental students, and if an American woman should, of her free will, choose to marry a Chinaman, then it was no one's business but her own family's. Eleanor Layton, of all people, joined the chorus with a public announcement that Hope Newfield had been a model tenant, and, while stopping short of condoning or even acknowledging Hope's marriage, averred that the Oriental students in Eleanor's experience had always shown exemplary behavior. (Oh, what a conveniently flexible commodity is hindsight, Hope thought.) From Collis Chesterton, of course, there came not a peep, but exactly two weeks after the explosion, the *Gazette*'s Campus Column announced "the appointment of East-Asian language scholar John Marion as the new supervisor of Oriental students, replacing Professor Collis Chesterton, who has accepted a position at the University of Southern California as chair of a new history department."

Hope showed the announcement to Paul, who studied it with his usual thoroughness, then pressed it back into her hands. "He has brought us together. I take you from him. Now we have driven him away. It is enough, I think."

"You forgive too easily."

"You believe Chesterton made this attack on us?"

"I *know* he wrote that article—and was not man enough even to sign it."

"And the rest?" Paul pressed his fingertips together. She noticed with a shock of pride that he was no longer biting or tearing at his nails. Even with all that had happened.

"The rest," she said. "No. No, I don't think Collis, even in the lowest depths of his soul, could conceive of such savagery."

"Then it is enough."

Unfortunately, while Hope and Paul were ready to put the attack behind them, the town's curiosity would not subside. Invitations were extended from prominent matriarchs for the young couple to attend formal dinners and teas. They received calls from church deacons urging them to join this or that congregation. A lawyer sent his card with an offer of six hours of free consultation if they wished to press charges against the newspaper. Such invitations were transparent lures to bring her and Paul out for public viewing, and so Hope declined them all, but enough people in Berkeley had passing acquaintance that their identity was soon common knowledge. Overnight, Francisco Street became a favorite destination for strolling couples and families, nannies with prams, or giggling schoolchildren who clustered outside the front gate, hoping to catch the scandalous interracial pair in a kiss.

In self-defense, Hope and Paul took to coming and going at different times, so as not to be seen together. But even apart, they were recognized, sometimes followed, and not always by well-wishers. When Hope set off for the Berkeley Chinese Educational Mission (where the charitably Methodist Mason sisters had hired her on the spot as the new tutor) men would tip their hats and leer. At the same time, merchants who used to place change directly into her palm and wish her a good day now served her closemouthed and left her cash on the counter. Women frequently blushed and giggled when they spotted Paul on the trolley, but he was also attacked twice on the ferry landing by gangs of stone-throwing boys. On campus Paul was treated with deference by Asians and whites alike. However, upon entering the lecture hall one day he found his seat coated with semen, and the whole room filled with chortling as he bent to wipe the chair clean. Hope and Paul did not speak of these insults, but they could each see how the other stiffened before leaving the haven of their cottage. At night they lay back to back, staring sleepless at the moon-shadowed walls, alert to the slightest skitter of leaves, the thud of the smallest seed pod hitting the roof. Separately and silently, they imagined eyes at the window, footsteps on the porch, the creak of the screen door being pried open. A two-by-four lay under the bed, within Paul's reach, and he would use it, too, if it came to that, but they both recognized that the consequences of defending themselves could be far graver than any injury at the hands of assailants. Even the most carefully wrought public opinion would backlash if a drop of white blood were shed by the Chinaman, whatever his provocation.

The mystery of their attacker's identity continued to weigh on them until late one night in early August when a single shot rang out, sending them racing for Thomas's. They found him rocking on his front porch, the derringer in his lap.

"Stupid kids," Thomas said. "Too young to be prosecuted, too ignorant to be blamed."

The lawn lay still and ominously dark. "You didn't shoot them!" Hope whispered.

"Over them. Scared the bejeezus out of them, though. They ran like the devil was at their tail." He shifted the pistol and yawned.

"You sit here watching every night?" Paul asked.

"Can't sleep much anyway. Makes me feel useful."

Paul stuck out his hand. Thomas looked up in surprise, smiled as he met it with his own.

ৡৡৡ

3

A man's silhouette filled the screen door, solid black and unfamiliar, its borders blurred by the sunlight shimmering through the trellis behind him. Hope, coming into the hallway, saw him first and caught her breath as he pounded the frame. The screen was fastened but flimsy, no match for the pounding, and the inner door stood wide open against the August heat.

Paul came out of the bedroom behind her. They'd been let alone these past few weeks (public attention blessedly diverted by a spectacular society murder), but uninvited guests, like sudden noises, still put them on alert. "Dolly!" shouted the visitor. "You in there?"

Hope turned, whispering frantically to Paul. "It's my father."

That she didn't rush to fling the door open surprised neither of them. Except for a brief note, responding with predictable relief and astonishment— and terse congratulations—to her letter following the Quake, she had heard nothing from Doc Newfield since their marriage, and the only other communication Hope had sent him was a breezy update, before the troubles, giving their new address.

The shadow yanked at the door, cursed, and called again.

"Dolly?" said Paul.

"His pet name for me."

Paul smiled. "Because you are small as a toy." He pushed her gently. "Go to him."

Hope's father crushed his hat in one hand, reached the other like a giant paw as she unlatched the door. He was a tall man and sturdy, flesh boiled by long frontier days to a lavender pink. His eyes roared, luminous blue, and his graying whiskers drooped in a hood above large tender lips. He lifted her off the ground like a child and gave her a syrupy smack on the cheek.

"Dad. This is Paul."

He set her down, grinning hard. "Leon, is it? Hell, son, you sure don't look like a Spaniard."

By the time Hope worked up the nerve to look, her father had an arm clapped around Paul's shoulders. "I am honored to make your acquaintance, Dr. Newfield," Paul was saying stiffly.

"Come in, Dad," she cried. "Look at you! All dressed up in city clothes. You must be thirsty. Tea, or lemonade?" An inventory of the pantry compressed her mind, forcing more severe thoughts off to one side as she led them back to the kitchen. She could offer shortbread and tea biscuits. Or some of Paul's dried pork sticks. Not far off from the jerky that had sustained her father over long weeks riding over cattle lands, or on the road with his wagonload of tonics . . .

Paul placed himself directly across from his father-in-law and waited while the huge man's gaze scaled and descended and scaled him again. Doc took breaths that doubled his chest, let them out with gusts of Sen-Sen. Paul held his eyes below his father-in-law's chin and did not speak.

"Chinese," the older man muttered at last, glancing starkly to Hope. "Damn."

She placed a plate of food on the table between them. Paul shook his head. Chinese sausage and English biscuits.

"I'll be damned," Doc repeated as he, too, inspected the plate. He took a piece of dried meat between his fingers and dropped it into his mouth. "Jerky?" He chewed.

"In a manner of speaking." Hope smiled, turned from her father to Paul. The strain in her expression was as subtle as a shift of tenses, but Paul noticed and understood at once. He had seen the same expression on the street last week when he and Hope dared to go out for a short walk together, and they had talked about the power of people's stares to construct a wall between them.

"*La jou*," he said.

The meat descended, a wad in father-in-law's long throat. "Pardon?"

"Chinese jerky," Hope translated.

Doc set a biscuit on his tongue and appeared to swallow the pale circle whole, washing it down with tea. He wiped his perspiring forehead, then fanned his knobby hands flat on the table. "You children love each other?"

Paul looked to his wife. She sat straight, watching the plate of food.

"I am proud to have your daughter for my bride," he answered.

"Not what I asked."

"It's too personal a question, Dad," Hope said.

Her father filled his mouth with sausage. He showed his food as he chewed, Paul noted, broad and wide as a peasant.

"Seems to me you've gone out of your way to make your personal business public." Doc pulled from his pocket a wadded newspaper, spread it open to another defamatory report of their marriage, and stabbed it with his finger. *The Portland Herald.*

Hope grabbed the paper as if to crumple it, but Paul shook it from her grasp, handed it back to his father-in-law without a word. Hope's palm fell to the table, thumb angrily rubbing the green paint.

Doc Newfield held Paul's gaze, then drew Hope's in as well until the three of them were linked. "You know, I understand love. I understand pain. And I know how one can lead to the other." His bright eyes dimmed and lowered, rose again. "Take more than a name change to hide behind."

Suddenly Paul felt as if his skin were on fire. He bent his head, mumbled an inarticulate excuse, and thrust his chair back, escaping to the bedroom, where he plunged his face into a basin of cold, numbing water.

As she entered the room Hope saw herself reflected in Paul's spectacles, unrecognizable. "I never said—"

"Paul Leon."

"I told him your name. Yes."

"This name you choose. This Spanish name."

"Paul, we've been over that—"

"You are ashamed of me to your own father!"

"At least I told him that I'd married. That you even exist!"

It was not what she'd meant to say. They needed his regular stipend from home, and Paul seemed so sure of the consequences if his mother learned of his American marriage, they'd agreed it was best that his family not know. But the words slipped out.

Paul removed his glasses, placed them on the dresser and stood for a long moment, watching her in the mirror. "I will write to my mother."

"I'm sorry, Paul. I shouldn't have spoken."

"But you are right," he said softly. "So is your father. We cannot hide what we have done. Or who we are."

He took the white, dripping cloth from the basin and touched it to her chin, her nose, her cheeks and forehead. The cool water, the slow gesture had the feel of ritual. She made no move against it, but let the moisture coat her eyes and skin.

"In China," Paul said, "every new bride must leave her parents, journey alone to family of her husband. Here in America, you and I journey together, make new family."

Through the closed door Hope could hear her father coughing, rattling his newspaper in the sitting room. The last thing he'd said to her was that he would only stay the weekend. As far back as she could remember, his initial greetings always included a deadline for their time together, a point beyond which he'd resume his separate life and send her back to hers.

Hope pushed Paul's hand and the cloth aside, and buried her face in his shoulder.

঩঩঩

4

A few days later, Paul posted the following:

> Revered Mother,
> I hope this letter finds you and my children in excellent health and abundance. It is long since I have sent word to you and much has changed in this strange country. The broken city of San Francisco is rising like a phoenix from its ashes and soon will be as new, with towering buildings and splendid palaces. But the greatest change has transpired within your own son's humble heart.
> I beg your forgiveness, my Mother. I have taken a bride without first consulting you. But she is a wife of my true heart. Her father is an American landowner. The family name is Newfield. My bride is exceptionally beautiful, well educated, slender as a Han, with natural lotus feet. Her hair is black as ebony, her skin as pale as the plum blossom. She is strong and healthy. I call her Hsin-hsin.
> I entreat you to welcome your new daughter-in-law to our

family, Mother. She pleases me greatly and assists me in my work and studies. She is eager to meet you and my children and to make her home with us in China. She is a devoted wife and will deliver many sons. Together we ask for your blessing.

I wish my family peace, health, and harmony.

Your respectful son,

Liang Po-yu

Mails to inland China took months. Hope and Paul had discussed sending a cable instead, but agreed finally that there was no point to that now. It would only give his mother the idea that she could still intervene. The form of a letter was more graceful, less threatening, and more conducive to diplomacy. Besides, after the attacks they had suffered already, they were in no hurry for Nai-li's reply.

By September life had fallen into a semblance of routine. Though they still did not go out publicly together, they had their evenings at home with Thomas or Mary Jane or both. Paul had his work and school, and Hope's job at the Mission, while less lucrative than her work under Collis's patronage, was gratifying nevertheless. Her new charges were younger, from poorer backgrounds, and, though most still wore pigtails coiled under their hats, they were more Western in dress and manner than most of her past students. And they were Christians. As a result, she felt freer to question them about their families, themselves, their villages—in short, about the land and culture into which she had married. Yang, her pigtailed student from the north, described the walled cities of Peking with their rooftops covered in gold. Mao, from Kunming, remembered a melting orange sun like a paper lantern over purple lakes. Little Pan from Soochow told of a city gridded with canals, like Italy's Venice. He also explained to Hope that girl babies were frequently left to die in fields or at the base of neglected temples or were given away to Buddhist nunneries, but that boys were cursed in another way, because they could be commandeered at will by the roving armies and bandits that dominated rural China under the Manchus. Soldiers were feared and hated in China, Pan said, because they took their pay in plunder. "In China everyone is in debt, everyone hungry. But you must know. All these things your husband write."

Hope started. "You know my husband?"

"I read his newspaper. I read his book on Taipings. I even read some journal he edit in Japan—*Hupei Student Circle*, yes?"

"You're quite the celebrity among my students," she told Paul as they got ready for bed that night. "Seems young Pan's read everything you've ever written. I think he knows you better than I do."

Paul draped his jacket over the wooden valet and turned with an indulgent smile. "I promise, he does not."

Hope plucked at the folds of her nightgown, smoothing and fanning it for Paul's benefit, then snuggled provocatively under the covers. She was vexed, after all this, to look up and find his attention had left her.

He stood removing his collar and cuffs, his pale yellow silk vest. He unbuttoned his shirt and slipped out of his trousers, perched on the bed as he peeled off his socks, and never once did he so much as glance at her. It was infuriating. And yet, at the same time, Hope appreciated the casual way he stood naked before her. The pink-shaded lamp deepened his color, softened the long, straight lines of his body, and when he turned, those silent scars across his back stirred such feelings of tenderness in her that she knew she must love him forever.

He put on his nightshirt and got in beside her holding a volume of Conrad. That morning he had pointed out that their lessons had lapsed and wondered, if she wasn't willing to teach him, should he find another tutor? She'd cuffed his ears, and told him to bring his reading glasses to bed. Now she asked, "What would you think if I learned to read Chinese?"

He looked at her over the top of his spectacles.

"I mean it, Paul. If I'm teaching you my language, shouldn't you teach me yours?"

"You never ask this!"

"Well, I am now."

"Hope. You are busy with so many things." He gave *Heart of Darkness* an impatient tap.

"You don't think I can!"

"I do not say this."

"Why, you!" She seized a pillow and pummeled him with it, knocking off his glasses, but in one easy movement he rolled her over. The book slid away, and he imprisoned her wrists, then arranged himself on top of her.

"Teach me," she said.

He moved his hips, coaxing. "Why?"

"For one thing, because I want to be able to read what you write!"

"You are my wife," he said, still coaxing. "Not my business partner."

The smoothness of his voice, the smug certainty she detected within that smoothness irked her so that she gave a quick jerk and flipped him to one side. The confusion that now sparked in his eyes was surprisingly gratifying. "That's just it," she said. "I don't want to be your wife!"

Now he was really confused.

"Oh, I don't mean that," she said quickly. "I mean I don't want to be *just* your wife. Never, I never wanted that. Even on the train going out to Wyoming, I was thinking that's exactly what we must not be. No, we *must* have business together, don't you see? A shared mission. Work. Some larger enterprise that we're in together, equally."

He gave a long, low sigh and flopped back, shaking his head.

"I even thought how," she said. "If I could read your work, I could translate it. I could write articles, drum up support for China among American readers the same way you do with your paper."

Outside, it began to rain. "Too dangerous," he said.

"Oh, pooh! Dangerous. There are lots of magazines—*The Independent* or *Harper's* or *Leslie's*—they run China articles all the time written by missionaries and diplomats. Why wouldn't they jump for stories about the *inside* of Chinese life? Your stories about growing up. About the makings of the revolution in Japan. The hardship of peasant life under the Manchus. How the republic will change everything. We'll write them together."

He locked his eyes on the ceiling. "Americans want to believe their own stories about China. And about Chinese."

"The magazines would pay us, Paul."

"They will not pay a Chinese man. They will not publish article under Chinese man's name. So what name do you use?"

"They will!"

"And if you give them your name, how do you explain your knowledge of such things? Do you write to them, I have married a Chinaman?"

"Paul!"

"Or do you use this Spanish name you make up for the marriage paper? And then why does this Spaniard know so much about China?"

"You're wrong."

"Am I?"

The rain quickened, causing the little bedside lamp to waver. Paul slid a hand over her hip, slowly up the folds of her gown to her breast. He lay his head on her shoulder, and she stroked his hair, simultaneously marveling and despairing at her willingness to accept tenderness and touch as substitutes for genuine understanding. "Would you love me more if I were Chinese?" she asked.

He lifted up and gave her a stern, almost rigid kiss on the mouth, then hovered over her as he spoke. "If you are Chinese, then you are not Hope. But Hope is my wife."

"Why can't you ever answer directly?"

"Your question is not direct. It is hypocritical."

The giggle erupted before she could stifle it. "I think," she said, "you mean hypothetical."

Paul sighed, regarding her fondly. He waited for her laughter to subside. "Are you happy with me?"

"Oh, my darling, yes. More than I have any right to be. But you are a little intimidating."

"Intimidating?"

"I mean, sometimes I feel . . . in awe of you. When we're together—" she took his hand and placed it back on her breast, held it there to show what she meant "—everything else melts away, and all that matters is that we *are* together, but when we're apart, sometimes even if you're just sitting at your desk across the room, I feel I'm on the other side of an ocean."

The shower let up. Paul said, "When you come to China you can understand. You can learn, feel, breathe these things."

"Yet you don't want me to read your work," she said stubbornly.

He sighed. "Hope. I have begun studying from the age of seven to learn classical Chinese. Sometimes I write in this language, sometimes vernacular. These two separate languages. To print the *Free Press* we use twelve thousand ideograms, only for most simple, direct ideas." He shook his head. "Of course, I am happy for you to learn, but you must not think I expect this."

She chewed her lip, considering. It was daunting. "I'll strike a bargain with you."

"Bargain?"

She retrieved the volume that had fallen by the bed. "We'll read the books in English that you want, but every other night you tell me one of your stories." She gave him a hard look. "To prepare me for the day we go back."

☙☙☙

Over the next few months, Hope pulled Paul's past from him the way a fisherman culls from the sea. She threw out questions and hauled in names, dropped lines and brought up memories. He told her about his boyhood tutor who fell asleep in the middle of lessons and recited Mencius in his dreams. He told of the sit-in demonstration he and his fellow students in Tokyo staged to protest school admission policies favoring Manchurian candidates. He remembered tricks that he'd played on friends in his youth, tragic tales of love and reversals of fortune among his old classmates, and the endless rumors of scandal and intrigue that surrounded China's ruling elite. She learned of the so-called Mutual Love Association of Chinese girl students in Japan (actually a revolutionary group) and one member who masqueraded as a sailor's mistress to bring coded instructions onto freighters bearing Sun Yat-sen's armaments.

The seriousness with which Hope approached their nightly sessions amused Paul. She would stretch out in bed with her delicate feet crossed at the ankles, her journal propped on her stomach, and take notes like a stenographer while he, for his part, lazed with hands clasped behind his head in a chair across the room. They were not far apart, but neither were they linked in any way, and occasionally, when he had been talking for some time about Chang Chih-tung or Yüan Shih-k'ai or Li Yüan-hung, he would ask if she was following, and she would purse her lips, busily continuing her note-taking, and shake her head as if annoyed. But when he tried to steal a look at her journal she would pull it close like an unfinished drawing.

"No article," he warned.

"No," she said. "Just notes for me, so I won't forget."

October 19, 1906

I think the real reason Paul opposes my idea of articles for the American press may be that he doesn't trust me to deliver accurate information, but I've come up with a way around this. I can call Paul simply The Revolutionist, put down his stories directly as he relays them (plus or minus a small bit of my own editing) and sign a pen name. No one need know our relationship or even our actual identity. I know in my bones that this will work. For all the "as told to's" about natives in New Guinea and the Amazon and excursions to the heart of Africa, I've never seen anything like the tales in Paul's repertoire. Like the one he told me last night, which gives a new glimpse into his egalitarian views on women—and at least the beginning of some sympathy for his mother. I want this to work because *we* need it to work. Hearing him talk, replaying his words, making them part of myself is the closest I can come to slipping inside his soul, to smelling and seeing and *entering* this world to which otherwise I have no access.

Here, then, is how this most recent story would appear, if I should work up the courage to go through with this plan.

Red Beards and Big Feet
The Taiping Rebellion Retold

"I would like to set the record straight," The Chinese Revolutionist began, "as to the true story of the Taiping Rebellion. I would relate not the slander spread by the embattled Manchus and foreigners who stood to lose their vast holdings if the Taipings had been victorious, but the stories my mother told of the days when the Taipings came to our city."

"I know little about the Taipings," I urged him, "except that they were Christians, and that China's new revolutionists have taken them as heroes. I am eager to know their true story."

This, then, is what he told . . .

The Taipings captured my province in 1867, eight years before I was born. The official story is that Taipings were barbarians, devils with red beards who pillaged and slaughtered. That is what the people were told, so that they would fear and resist the Taipings. But my mother told how it really was when the Redbeards came through Hankow.

At the time, my father was in the capital taking his examinations, and the family was living in our home village of Pai-sha-chou. Of course, the whole province was in chaos. Taipings already occupied Hong Mountain and the river was filled with warships all lit up like dragons. The family managed to get across the river to Hankow just before the Taipings landed at Yellow Goose Jetty and began their attack. People said the Ts'aohu city gate had been breached and scores of women were drowning themselves to avoid being raped by the Redbeards. My elder brother and sister were still in swaddling then, and my mother dared not flee. She locked the doors and waited.

Before first light, Taiping soldiers filled the street blowing an ox horn and shouting, "The Eastern King has ordered that all people be settled this morning. All with a home should return home. The homeless should go to our shelters. Men to men's and women to women's. Any man attempting to enter the women's shelter will be beheaded. Any woman going to the men's shelter will be strangled. Any Taiping brothers who rape, rob, kill, or burn will be beheaded. This is the order of the Eastern King and must be immediately obeyed."

Before noon a woman with big, unbound feet, bright red pants, and a tightly belted white shirt led a group of Taiping soldiers wearing red turbans and wielding swords down our street. They searched the home where my family was staying and confiscated all red material. They asked if my mother was hiding evil spirits. My mother did not know what they meant, but she answered, "Our home has never had evil spirits." Only later did she realize that the Taipings called Ch'ing soldiers evil spirits.

The next day a relative who had joined the Taiping Army

came to tell my mother that he was leaving to fight the wind. The troops were fanning out from the city in all directions.

My mother visited the women's shelter several times. The women in charge were all big-foot barbarian women from Kiangsi. The Taiping women cooked and brought fuel for the shelter and kept order, one bigfoot for every ten homeless women. There was no charge for room or food.

When the soldiers came back from fighting the wind they called together several tens of thousands of the brothers. They gave every person one piece of red cloth for a turban, and they arrayed several thousand red ships on the river. At the time the water was very low, and from Hanyang gate the ships were lined abreast so that they appeared as a floating bridge all the way to the Dragon King Temple. At the sight about fifty Ch'ing soldiers still hiding in Hankow lost their courage and came forward. At the shout of a single Taiping soldier, the Ch'ings all threw down their swords and knelt, allowed their hands to be tied so that they could be taken prisoner.

Ten days later the Eastern King boarded a large ship and led the flotilla downstream. Ch'ing troops moved back in behind him. But the people of our province had learned that the stories spread about the evil Taipings were not true. They had seen how quickly the Ch'ing troops would run and surrender, how little they would do to protect the people. Half a century later, the Ch'ings have not changed. And the spirit of the Taipings lives on in the hearts of revolutionary leaders like Dr. Sun Yatsen and the thousands of Chinese—men and women alike— who have vowed to bring democracy to China.

Even as I set these words down I am filled with something akin to dread. Would I have possessed the courage Paul's mother showed? Stranded, with two young children, amid chaos and terror, yet she stood up to the invaders and was courageous enough to see them as humans instead of the monsters she had been taught to expect. Like mother, like son, I suppose, and perhaps this explains how Paul could journey to the land of the barbarians and see me clearly enough to take me for his own.

He says that age and loss have hardened his mother. Those two young children died before Paul was born. His father was away for months at a time, leaving his mother at the mercy of his first two wives, and though finally he sent for her to join him during his appointment as viceroy in Canton—Paul's birthplace—she contracted malaria there, and was left barren.

Oh, so much about the life of this woman makes me quail. Starting with the ghastly practice of footbinding and carrying through that hideous tradition of concubinage, in which the only measure of a woman's worth is her ability to bear sons! Paul does not subscribe to the views of his countrymen toward the female sex, and yet he cannot help but be a product of his culture even as he fights it.

I find myself wondering about his wife, the way he left her to go off on his revolutionary escapades (making friends with that "Mutual Love" group!). I sympathize with her in spite of myself. And I worry for Paul's children. When will they see their father again? Will I ever meet them? Is there any way I can find acceptance in the hearts of people whose ways are so completely alien to mine? That we all share this man is a source of continual fascination and amazement to me. It is a tribute to his breadth of knowledge and sensitivity that this is possible, but there is another side of the equation that gives me pause. He seems so content to keep me in my world, so reluctant for me to probe into his. Why does he discourage me from learning his language? Why not tell me about his children? Why not introduce me to his friends? If I were to draw a diagram, I would show our situation as a straight line, with Paul in the center holding me by one hand and his Chinese family by the other. In my fantasy, I would change that drawing to a circle by linking my free hand to that of his family. I've no idea what concessions we would all have to make, but after speaking with Donaldina I am sure of at last one imperative. I must bear Paul a son.

All my visions of business together—of serving as a help-mate in Paul's revolution, of making him a safe home and schooling myself in his political ambitions—are well and good, Donaldina told me, as long as I am thinking like an emancipated American. But it counts for nothing in the Chinese mind. And deep down I must reconcile myself with the fact that Paul's mind *is* Chinese. My task as wife is to bear him children. That he does not mention my failure to conceive in our half-year of marriage bespeaks his respect and love for me, but it does not mean he is not waiting.

Donaldina's plain language has forced me to look my predicament squarely in the eye. I, too, want children. And what heavenly children we will have! But they cannot be the hallowed offspring of a typical Chinese marriage. They will be called mongrels. They will be despised as half-breeds. And unless I do everything in my power to protect them, they will endure worse prejudice than any I myself ever knew. But I will protect them. I will love them with all my heart, and we will prove that those who despise us are wrong. They are nothing.

5

The long-awaited answer arrived by telegram in late October.

Marriage forbidden. Bride Ling-yi awaits your return.

"Who is Bride Ling-yi?" Hope asked, judiciously disregarding the first comment as moot.

"Youngest daughter of my father's friend." Paul chewed on a thumb-nail. "She used to play at our house with my sisters. She had teeth like a beaver's and on her cheek a purple birthmark in the shape of an axe."

"Mm," Hope said. "Pretty, then?"

He grunted and folded his arms. "This is the first I hear of her in twenty years."

"And what exactly is this you're hearing?"

He looked at her gravely. "I will cable," he said. "I will tell her it cannot be."

His telegram read: *Marriage cannot be undone. Hsin-hsin is wife of my heart. I take no other.*

Within days came an extravagantly long reply instructing that Paul's duty was first to his family, and this marriage caused his whole clan to lose face. Having one wife did not prevent him from taking another, and Nai-li had betrothed him to Ling-yi.

Unlike Hope's father, her mother-in-law made no mention of love.

For the next month the arguments slid back and forth across the ocean. Neither Paul nor his mother would relent, and by Thanksgiving the cables ceased. When it became clear that she could not persuade Paul to give up his alien bride, his mother simply pulled away. As he'd predicted, she cut off all financial support. Paul's son and daughter became Nai-li's hostages.

This turn of events redoubled Hope's determination to bring in some extra income. She sent off the article about the Taipings to *The Independent*. She increased her tutorial hours, milking her students even more for background details to fortify her understanding of China, and during the early evening hours before Paul's return home, she applied herself to learning five new Chinese ideograms per day. Though she could not account for the feeling with any rational explanation, she felt she was fighting for her life. None of this did she reveal to her husband.

For his part, Paul was philosophical. "Nothing to be done," he said simply. The moment he said this, as they were standing in the kitchen looking out on a scene of flying, withered leaves, a chill ran through her. There was a flatness to his voice that made her turn and stare at him. His face was as passive and accommodating as a blank slate, and the words, still bright on his lips, seemed to rise of their own accord. How could she know then that in future years she would come to view their Mandarin translation, *mei fatse*, as China's fatal mantra? She could not possibly, and yet the ease and naturalness with which those words coasted from Paul's mouth utterly paralyzed her. Only after he'd come back to himself and gruffly left the room did she realize why this simple phrase had such an effect on her: it was utterly at odds with the man she thought she had married.

But Paul's fatalism was like a charm, and once he'd surrendered the notion that he and Hope could exert any further force on their destiny, events shifted as by some heavenly hand. "Remember Minister Tuan?" he called out one December evening, seconds after walking in the door.

"Minister Tuan?" In the kitchen Hope wiped her floury hands on her apron and glanced to make sure the soup was not boiling over.

"You remember. He and Minister Tai gave lecture here last spring."

"Mm." She came out to meet him. "Supper's not ready yet. You're early. Tuan. The comedian?"

"Tuan is a good man." He held up an envelope with an official-looking seal.

Hope recalled Paul's protective stance toward this Minister Tuan, how she had loved him for it. Now, it seemed, his solicitousness was to be rewarded. While traveling in Europe, Tuan had heard of the earthquake— and of Paul's marriage. He was sending five hundred dollars from his own purse because, as his note explained, Paul's membership in the rebel party had cost him the support of officials of Hupei who would ordinarily have been obliged to support a scholar from their district in such an emergency.

"I don't believe this," she said. "Why should he want to help us?"

Paul flopped down on the divan and said grimly, "He has put himself at risk to warn me."

"Warn you?"

"He hopes I will take this money and stop my writing."

"Surely that's not a condition for accepting it?"

Paul's expression softened. "Don't worry. I am a rebel but not a fool. I know we need this money." He gave a terse laugh. "Everyone knows."

Hope sat beside him, thinking out loud. "You could write and thank him, assure him somehow that you won't— I know! Treat it as a wedding gift. Nothing more or less. That would implicitly let Tuan know that we'll respect his wishes to the extent of keeping the money confidential, but your work will go on as before."

She could all but hear the gears of his brain turning in the silence that followed, each passing second strengthening her conviction that the suggestion she had made was good. Finally he turned, placed a hand on her knee, and asked with the barest glimmer of a smile, "How can my American wife have such a Chinese mind?"

જીજીજી

6

Midway through January came one of those glimmering, blustery, yet unseasonably mild winter mornings when the mere act of pushing back the drapes is an electric experience. Sweet and bright, the sun played hide and seek among rolled satin clouds. The air, when Hope lifted the window, was so fresh that each breath made her lungs sizzle.

As usual, Paul had been up and out before daybreak. For the past month the wires had sizzled with reports of famine and rice riots in China's coastal provinces, and of the Ch'ing's brutal suppression of these riots—without providing the people relief from their starvation. Paul pounced on these reports, for starvation and riots made excellent fuel for revolution. Several secret societies had already mounted revolts, and though they had been suppressed, public support for the rebels had never been stronger. As Hope understood it, Paul's task, through his editorials, was to excite interest and financial support from Chinese societies in America for more revolts. However, this was not as simple as it sounded. Paul had explained to her that Chinatown was a cauldron of factions with varying positions for or against Imperial rule. Paul's group, the Hung-men Society, were the most democratic and Western in their thinking, while their arch-adversary, the Royal Preservation Party, supported the continuation of Imperial rule through constitutional monarchy. The two groups had long competed for donations and political support and watched each other covertly, and though no blood had been shed between them, sabotage had been common—vandalism of news offices, spies in the triad meetings, heckling and threatening of audiences at some of Sun Yat-sen's early appearances in 1904. Before the Quake, Paul's editorial staff spent more energy fending off the Royalists than they did criticizing the Manchus. But the devastation and rebuilding of Chinatown had forced a truce between the factions, and the news from China now seemed to be dealing the Royalists a natural death. All of this cheered Paul no end, and he went forth each dawn with an eager set to his jaw, hands impatiently fumbling with his tie and buttons as the door fell closed behind him.

Ordinarily Hope kissed her husband goodbye, dressed leisurely, tidied the house, and walked over to Shattuck to do the day's marketing before her afternoon lessons. If there was time, she would write in her journal or draw up a leaflet or poster for Mary Jane's latest trade union or suffrage project. Or she would work on her "Revolutionist" articles, which she was proceeding to write in secret. Today, however, the two students she was scheduled to tutor were both in quarantine with measles—mild cases, thank goodness—and this left a tantalizing stretch of free time.

What could be more natural, she thought defiantly, than to visit her husband's office and meet his colleagues? Nevertheless, the idea was intimidating. Mother Wayland warned her even before she left Kansas that white slavers would pounce on any girl foolish enough to walk alone in Chinatown. Hope had gone once anyway, with a group of classmates early on, and although that pre-Quake Chinatown was a compressed, otherworldly place, at turns gaudy as a carnival or bleak as the worst Dickensian slum, no ill had befallen her. Then last May she had returned again with Mary Jane and Antonia Laws. San Francisco was a seething mass of rubble and dust, with only the husks of buildings and vacant lots where reconstruction had not yet begun. The women visited the old site of Donaldina Cameron's Mission Home and found nothing but charred bricks and mortar. Then, stiffening their backs without a word of discussion, they proceeded downhill to the blocks that had been Chinatown. Mary Jane had said as they marched, "However different you believe your husband to be, you cannot afford to ignore this place, these people, for they belong to him more than you do." To which Hope threw back, "I know that, and I will embrace them, just see if I don't!" But her resolve had faltered before the swarms of black, bent figures carrying lumber, mixing mortar, hoisting shovels and picks. No wagons, no mules, no

muscle-bound giants assisted these slight, straining men. Neither sanctioned nor aided by the town fathers, they were, in fact, racing against
Mayor Ruef's campaign to relocate the Chinese outside city limits. Paul
predicted his people would triumph, and Hope that day was convinced he
must be right. But she also was repelled by her own embarrassment at having invaded this tableau as a tourist. "I feel like a man who has stumbled
into a birthing room," she said as they watched an elderly man a fraction
of her size breaking rocks with his bare hands. So the intervening months
passed, and she had not returned, even though Paul made the crossing
every day.

Then, in an Oakland stationer's a few days before Christmas, she
chanced on a selection of pictures by the photographer Arnold Genthe,
a white man whom some had accused of being "obsessed with the Yellows." Genthe was an acquaintance of Mary Jane's, a sweet, sentimental
man who acknowledged that his affection for the Chinese was surpassed
only by his mystification at their ways. His pre-Quake photographs captured both, but the decided emphasis was on his subjects' humanity. Hope
had selected two portraits for Paul's Christmas gift, which now hung here
above his desk—one of a merchant father in black skullcap holding a
swaddled infant, the other of a silk-skirted father and small son holding
hands. Hope had presented these images to Paul that they might prompt
some discussion about his own children, his feelings for them, his expectations of her role in their lives, but instead he'd kissed her forehead and
said simply, "When?" Horrified at her misstep, she'd had to tell him, no,
that wasn't what the gift meant at all, there was no child coming. Then she
had started crying and he'd had to comfort her, and nothing more was
said.

Now for the past week she'd suspected he was right, after all, and this
morning she decided she was certain. That was the news she would bring
him. She threw off her wrapper, dressed quickly in her black worsted suit,
did her hair in a low bun, Chinese style, and pulled down her brown felt
fedora. Dark gloves, walking boots. Incognito. But this time she was no
tourist. She had a destination and a right to it.

Hope was wound so tightly into these thoughts that she walked smack
into the postman at the gate. A bulky, florid man, he was completely flum-
moxed, thrust the mail into her hands, and huffed on down the street be-

fore she could apologize. She was about to call after him when she glanced down and saw, on the top of the stack, the envelope for which she had been waiting. She tore it open and read in a state of high anxiety, then shoved the rest of the mail into the box, and set off for the Key trolley at a near trot.

She knew that Paul's office was located at 717 Grant Street in the Freemasons' headquarters. What she had not foreseen was that few of the buildings in this new Chinatown bore any numbers, and on fewer still were the numbers painted in Arabic numerals. She located a restaurant at 684 Grant, and a bazaar at 739, but the addresses in between were impossible to calculate, and most of the ground floors were occupied by fishmongers, grocers, restaurants, laundries, or banks, sometimes two or three to a storefront. Paul must work up one of these dark, unmarked stairwells, she decided, but she could not remember the ideographs for *Ta T'ung Jih Pao* or Chih Kung T'ang, the Freemasons' Chinese name. Finally she stopped and bought some almonds from one of the street vendors. Though he would not make eye contact, he would accept her money, and she was heartened when he named the price in halting English.

"*Ta T'ung Jih Pao tsai nar?*" she asked.

The young man, whose brushlike hair gave him a rather electrified appearance to begin with, turned a violent shade of purple, and Hope feared her mangled pronunciation had asked him something unspeakable. She retreated hurriedly, forgetting the almonds, which forced the poor boy to run after her, head twisted almost backward as he dropped the parcel by her feet. A moment later a nearby door swung open and a man wearing a brown serge suit and matching Homburg emerged, the picture of cosmopolitan elegance. Hope felt sure he spoke English.

"Excuse me," she called, "but could you direct me to the offices of *Ta T'ung Jih Pao*—the *Chinese Free Press?*"

His broad lips parted. "I've just come from there. Top floor."

She clapped her hands with relief. "Thank you so much. I don't know what possessed me to think I could find it alone."

The man, rather stumpy in build but with bold, wide-set eyes, was so clearly Westernized that Hope nearly gave him her hand, yet such a gesture in this place could be cause for scandal. Already they were drawing scores of curious, if covert, stares.

"You are Mrs. Liang, I think." He tipped his hat and bent from the waist, taking her startled silence as assent. "I am William Tan. Your husband and I were schoolmates in Hupei. Now I am his counterpart in New York. I am honored to meet you at last."

Hope had never imagined Paul mentioning her to his friends. It both pleased and unnerved her to think what he might say to a dandy like William Tan. "How do you do?" she said.

"I do very well." He lifted his left eyebrow. "I am only disappointed that I must leave this afternoon—I am on my way back east, and my train leaves at five. If not, it would be my pleasure to entertain you. Perhaps another time."

She nodded stiffly. "Perhaps." He continued to stare at her. "If you'll excuse me, then . . ."

"Yes, of course, Madame Liang. Goodbye."

"Goodbye, Mr. Tan." Hope stepped past him and escaped into the doorway. William Tan reminded her of Collis Chesterton, but she was at the third-floor landing before she realized why. It was that both men made her feel obligated to simultaneously thank and escape them.

The stairwell was steep, thick with the smells of new lumber and cement, and there was no railing, little light. By the time she reached the fifth and last floor she was panting. Fortunately there was only one door. At her tap it flew open, and a young boy wearing a peaked cap and suspendered knickers staggered out under a shoulderload of papers. He gaped at Hope, incredulous, stepped without looking and teetered on the top step. With visions of him plunging headlong down the steep drop, she instinctively reached out and grabbed him by the shoulders. You'd have thought the wicked witch had snatched him, the way he shot down the stairs.

Hope steeled herself and stepped inside. She was in a printing office— she could hear the press and feel its vibration in the raw pine floor—but all she could see were two slanted banks that stretched from the door some forty feet to the opposite wall. Halfway down this aisle, a man in a blue coolie jacket and navy beret stood beneath a dangling lightbulb, plucking at the left embankment. He wore yellow Turkish slippers with upturned toes and had not noticed Hope.

She let the door fall closed behind her. The man's hands worked the laddered wall like chickens pecking for grain, and Hope felt a despairing pang as she realized that these embankments were, in fact, type cases to hold the thousands of characters needed to print Paul's newspaper. How had any brain the capacity to store, much less process, such a code?

"*Ni hao.*" The man in the beret was coming toward her with eyebrows up.

"Hello," she said. "I'm looking for Liang Po-yu."

"Ah, *shih, shih.*" He nodded and hurried off down the aisle, leaving her to follow or not. She followed, but slowly, still struggling to absorb the reality of this place. Through a break between the cases she could see tables laid with print racks half filled with type and, beyond, a machine spitting large white tongues of paper. Three young men stood feeding and emptying the machine, two dressed in western denims, the third in journeyman's garb, with a queue. Hope had stopped to watch them when Paul's voice breathed in her ear.

She jumped, then started laughing. His face, however, was stern. "What is wrong?"

"Nothing! You startled me."

He glanced to the typesetter, who nodded and went back to work.

"I wanted to surprise you." Hope began, but soon the words were tumbling over each other. "I didn't expect you to be so hard to find. Fortunately, I ran into William Tan downstairs. How well he speaks English! Hardly a trace of any accent. Oh! Now I remember, you've told me about him, haven't you? He runs Sun's paper in New York? I *wish* I'd remembered that when we were talking, he made me nervous, somehow—"

"Hope," he interrupted. "Why are you here?"

"I thought—" But the light struck his glasses so she could not see his eyes. He was in shirtsleeves, his fingers pinched around a reed brush with wet black bristles. One cheek wore a slash of ink like a scar.

"I wanted to see where you work," she said.

He pulled off his glasses, and his eyes narrowed. Suddenly it dawned on her. What but disaster would bring his American wife to this place?

"I was curious," she said. "That's all."

He chewed his lip, frowning, then beckoned her to follow him.

"Paul, if it's too much trouble—" But the look he tossed over his shoulder told her she should have thought of that before coming.

They walked past three more young men hunched over writing tables, and Paul ushered her into a small office the size of their bedroom. Light from the brilliant day outside drizzled though clerestory windows. A slab of oak held up by sawhorses formed Paul's desk. His chair—the only one in the room—was massive, more oak, but so battered it must have been scavenged. Piles of old newspapers and books filled the corners. Across his desk were strewn pages of his hieroglyphic scrawl, the palm-sized slate in which he mixed his ink, like a pool of liquid tar, and his onyx seal with the carved lion head.

Paul shut the door.

Her shoulders went back at the disapproval in his face. "Paul, I'm sorry I barged in like this. I wanted to see—"

"What you think you will find here!"

"You! I wanted to see you."

He placed his glasses and brush on the desk, went around and sat down so that Hope was standing before him like a petitioner. "Why?"

"I wanted to see where you work, this part of your life." Why was it so hard to explain herself?

"You do not trust me."

She nearly threw herself into his lap. "No, no! Oh, Paul, that's not it at *all*." She began to laugh, squeezed his hand. "Such a thought never entered my mind, I swear it."

He seemed to relax finally, smiling a little abashedly, then gave her his chair. He perched on the corner of the desk.

"I told you. I woke up this morning feeling—well, left out. Not in the way you were thinking. You would never take another woman, I know that, and I'm really not the jealous sort. But this—" thumping his desk, his papers "—your work is a mistress, too, in a way. It takes you away from me."

He started to interrupt, but she shushed him. "No, hear me out. I would never interfere with your work, Paul, but I thought if I came here, I wouldn't feel so disconnected. At least I would know where you go when you leave me."

He squinted at her. "Your place is in my heart. My home. Is this not enough?"

"Not when so much of your time is spent away from me."

"You want me to stay home more."

"No! Nor do I mean to invade your office. But to be able to envision you here when you are gone from me—this helps."

His face softened. She could almost feel the thought coalescing. *This is another of Hope's ways of expressing her love. I must be tolerant.*

But she didn't want to be tolerated. She swiveled in his chair, touched the grain of his desk. His gold pocket watch lay under the goose-neck lamp, beside marching columns of brushstrokes. She leaned closer to see if she could interpret any of them. A few numbers, the simplest of characters, looked back reassuringly. The rest might have been cipher.

He picked up his watch, snapped it shut. "Hope, they are waiting for my copy to print the final pages. I am late with it now."

"You were right," she said. "We are going to have a child."

"A—" His voice stalled as she caught and held his gaze.

"A baby."

He took a deep breath, pulling his shoulders to his ears, then dropped them and, laughing, cupped Hope's face between his hands. "You cannot wait until I come home?"

She smiled sheepishly. "Do you blame me?"

"No, but—" The door opened and one of the junior editors barked out a question, ignoring Hope's presence. Paul answered, and the young man went out.

Paul said, "You bring good news, Hope, but I must work. Tonight I bring a special tea, make our baby strong."

"Our baby." She rose reluctantly, then remembered. "There's more good news." She drew the envelope out of her skirt and waved it in front of his nose. "*The Independent* will pay us ten dollars for your story about the Taipings!"

In his methodical way, Paul took the letter, shook it out, and read through word by word before his face revealed any reaction. Hope's excitement drained as she waited.

"This letter is addressed to Hope Newfield," he said, replacing the paper in its envelope and handing it back.

"Yes. I thought a pen name best. In case of . . . well, repercussions."

"We talked about this."

"You said nobody would be interested. But they are, Paul. See, all I must do is sign this and they'll send the check and, did you read, they want more stories. They'll publish them as a series."

But his face had darkened. "I do not even know what you have written."

"I wrote only what you told me!"

Another boy appeared at the door, but Paul snapped him away. "How can I believe you when we say one thing, you do another?"

"We need the money, Paul. Five hundred dollars won't last long with a child coming, and I won't be able to continue tutoring after the fifth or sixth month. But I *can* continue writing—" Her voice broke. "I don't understand why you're not pleased about this."

"You want too much."

"Is it too much to want to share your passion?"

"When one acts in secret, this is not sharing."

Hope's face started to burn. She could see from the set of Paul's mouth that it was useless to argue, and she knew from the stony weight on her heart that she had already gone too far. Yet she had only the faintest notion how or why, what rules had been violated, what borders transgressed.

"No more secrets, then," she said suddenly. "You read everything before I send it."

He sighed and shook his head.

᭜᭜᭜

May 12, 1907
Mr. Harrison Wofford
Literary Editor
The Independent
Dear Mr. Wofford:
I realize that months have passed since your kind invitation for me to submit a series of articles based on my conversations with a Chinese revolutionist. I apologize for the delay in composing these, but I have worked hard to pull the material together and bring it to what I feel is its rightful form. I enclose two works herewith and have several others in progress, which

I shall send, if you wish, after you have had a chance to respond to these.

With my most sincere thanks for offering me this opportunity.

Hope Newfield

A Literary Prank

"Americans often say," The Revolutionist recently said to me, "that Chinese have no humor. But the keys to humor lie in language and heart, and it is only because few Americans can understand Chinese language or see into our hearts that they think we have no humor."

"Can you give me an example of something you find funny," I goaded him.

"I can tell you a true story," he replied. "A prank involving the language and hearts of young men, who are often the most amusing when they try to be the most serious."

"Please," I said.

And this is the story he told . . .

In China under the Manchu reign, the publication of revolutionary materials is punishable by death. For this reason, Chinese students have taken full advantage of the press freedoms in Japan to experiment with a wide variety of journals, including literary, scientific, and political articles. However, the zeal of young editors to publish these journals sometimes outpaces the ability of writers to fill their pages. Competition for talent can be fierce and occasionally devious.

Early in my own student days, I learned of a brilliant scholar named Ma Chun-wu. He had several times contributed revolutionary writings to the *New Citizen Journal*, published by some Chinese friends of mine in Yokohama. Ma's writing was much admired, but he was a reluctant contributor, for fear his articles would lead to his arrest. There came a time, however, when the *New Citizen Journal* lacked quality submissions, and the editors devised a scheme to lure Ma into their net. I was their unwitting pawn.

Editor Lo Hsiao-kao published one of my poems under a woman's pseudonym, then wrote to Ma exclaiming over this woman's great talent and beauty.

"Is it possible to meet her," Ma wrote back.

"I will be the go-between," Lo promised, "if you come to Japan to study. But first, you must write to her."

Ma delivered eight verse poems, which he entrusted Lo to send to the woman. The opening couplet read:

Melancholy flower stem and willow branch

For whom do you knit your far mountain brow?

All the poems were published in the journal, and before long Ma received a poem from the woman. Lo told Ma he would have to write more articles. Otherwise Lo would not introduce them. So Ma continued to write day and night until finally he could wait no longer. Arrangements were made, and he arrived in Japan, where Lo showed him a photograph of the woman and a letter in which she wrote that she was soon to travel by boat from the West. Fully aroused now, Ma gave to Lo a photograph of himself, along with many boxes of fine Japanese delicacies, to be sent to the woman to hasten her arrival.

Lo tweaked his chain again. "You have not been writing much. I will not introduce you unless you get back to work." Whereupon Ma went back to his room and threw himself into another spate of poems.

Several days later I arrived in Yokohama with a group of students from Hong Kong, and Lo met us with armloads of delicacies. To Ma he reported, "She is here."

Ma came to Lo in the middle of the night, demanding to meet the woman and threatening blows if Lo put him off any longer. As I was in the next room, I heard them and came to see why they were arguing.

"There is your woman!" Lo pointed at me.

Realizing that he had been duped, Ma threw him back and turned on me, waving the woman's photograph in front of my nose. "I have written to the point of spitting blood! I have spent a fortune! Where is she!"

"She is only a Cantonese singsong girl." Lo dared smile. "Nothing to smooth a melancholy brow."

Ma ransacked Lo's room, destroying his manuscripts, and left Japan the following day. I am happy to say that he continued to oppose the Manchus, but he never did write for *New Citizen* again, and some months later the journal ceased publication.

Girl at the Teahouse

"I understand that you admire democracy," I said to The Revolutionist one day. "But China has been under Imperial rule for hundreds of centuries. Why do you believe that now is the time to change?"

"Because the throne and all who answer to it have fallen into decay. The rulers see the Chinese people only as slaves, to be used and discarded at their pleasure."

"Can you give me an example?" I asked.

And so he did.

After passing my examinations and before traveling to Japan, I spent several years in the service of then viceroy of Hupei, a man named Chang Chih-tung. Chang was a most powerful man, a politician in the true Chinese sense, with such personal cunning and practical sense that it was impossible to tell whether his instincts were noble or base. In matters of the heart, however, he was as weak as any man.

During the course of his duties, Chang, like all provincial officials, rode in a covered sedan chair. But Chang liked to look out on his subjects, as he thought of them, without their seeing him, so he arranged for his sedan to be outfitted with a window covered in dark mesh that appeared solid from the outside. One day after making a routine inspection of the textile mill near Hankow's east gate, Chang happened to look through his window toward a nearby teahouse. There stood a young girl of exceptional beauty.

When they arrived back at the governor's yamen Chang

summoned a former Manchu cavalier who owed his current position as Middle Army official to Chang. "The girl who serves
behind the counter of the teahouse at Wen Chang gate is a real
beauty," Chang said. The official made his own interpretation
and approached the girl's father next day.

"If you allow your daughter to serve the governor's third
concubine," the envoy said, "your family will be promoted and
get very rich."

That night the girl was brought to the yamen. Chang kept
her constant company for two months, not even pausing when
she was inconvenient. It wasn't long before she became ill with
infection and died. Chang ordered her body removed out the
back door, but everyone who served in the yamen, including
myself, knew the truth. Moreover, we had predicted from the
start that it would end exactly thus.

ॐॐॐ

7

June 1, 1907

So quickly I have my reply. Serves me right for resisting
Paul's intuition, but I was seduced, plain and simple. An offer
made, a promise tendered, and I accepted in good faith and was
only a bit tardy in fulfilling my end, to be kicked in the teeth
and humiliated in return . . .

"While your article about the Taipings offered a unique view
into the history of the Orient, these new pieces concentrate on
obscure, incidental, and wholly unbelievable details about insignificant characters with unpronounceable names who, to our
readers, are indistinguishable one from another. I do not know
if this revolutionary of yours is based on a real acquaintance or

an imaginary figure, but in any case he fails to inspire my belief. It is with great regret that I must return these works to you. I had hoped for an intriguing series. My advice in light of this recent work, however, is that you follow the old adage and write what you know instead of reaching for the exotic."

WHY? Is this, as Paul insists, proof that Americans must view Chinese as either chessboard figurines or yellow heathens? Or is Harrison Wofford right in skewering my ability? I am hardly a seasoned writer, and certainly no China scholar. I have trusted that Paul's stories, by themselves, would infect others as they have me, but it seems I have failed to this end.

Oh, what hubris to think I could achieve in a few pages the bridge between cultures that has eluded generations of the East's most brilliant scholars and noblemen! Well, it's over now. I will write no more except, as before, for my own education. Paul, I think, is relieved, and perhaps he is right. We could have used the money, but maybe, after all, raising our family should be my first and highest order of business.

བ྇བ྇བ྇

July arrived in a storm worthy of March. Gale winds kicked up the Bay, slanted walkers, flogged treetops, and sent currents of cold, damp air through Paul's office, finally chasing him home for fear the ferry would shut down. The rain was gusting sideways by the time he burst through the front door, peeling off his sopping jacket and calling for Hope. Their baby was due in a month, and she had now entered her confinement, but the sitting room was dark.

As he started down the hall he saw Mary Jane Lockyear's broad figure turning in the bedroom doorway. Beyond, a yellowed light curled around a crooked, unreadable shadow. He heard a metallic splash, distinct from the rain on the roof. Mary Jane laid a weightless hand on his shoulder. Behind her, in the bedroom, a short, buxom woman with iron gray hair wrung a bloodied cloth in the basin.

"It's all right, Paul," Mary Jane said. "She's all right."

But Hope lay on the bed in a coil of blue and gray blankets. As he approached, her face remained colorless, her expression emptied of all emotion as it fixed on the oblong parcel in her arms. "A boy." She stroked the still-damp shock of black hair, the forehead blue and small as a bruise. Suddenly her eyes brimmed with tears. "Paul, I'm so sorry."

They wrapped the infant with their own hands. Hope wept silently, motionless. She did not hide her face or shut her eyes to the unbearable smallness of the casket. But as they were leaving the graveyard where they had placed their boy alongside the memorial to Thomas's wife, Hope clung to Paul's hand as to a lifeline.

"Do you think it was a curse, Paul? My mother's death, and hers before her? Maybe I'm not *meant* to have children."

"No, Hsin-hsin," Paul murmured. "He came the wrong way."

"I was afraid to die, afraid of our child. It was my fear that killed him."

He stopped walking and held her firmly. "That midwife explained to us. The baby is sideways. The cord is around his neck. Nothing you can do."

"But there is now, Paul." Flushed and panting, she turned her face up to his with sudden urgency. "We must have another child, and I mustn't be afraid. We must have a child and give it all the love our little boy was denied. Don't you see, it's the only way!"

"When you are well," said Paul. "We will see."

"No, we mustn't wait," she cried. "We mustn't be afraid, Paul, please. Please."

He led her to the victoria waiting outside the cemetery and held her quietly against his shoulder as she continued to whimper, "Please!"

᭙᭙᭙

August 5, 1907

Nothing. That is what has happened. That is what I see, what I feel. I fear our child has left his death in me. Certainly he has marked my dreams. At night I am visited by my mother and grandmother shouting and pointing as if to show me a turn I have missed in the road. When I go back I meet my baby, grown to a man but still blue-skinned with those deathly accusing eyes. And I scream and Paul reaches to soothe me, but his hand passes through my flesh.

October 19, 1907

This lost boy will not leave us. Everyone tries to make him go. My father came last weekend, full of jokes and cures. Mary Jane drags me out to union halls, to rallies and work meetings and strategy sessions. The Mason sisters load me down with cookies and pies to sweeten my mood while my students fill our "lessons" with rote recitations from McGuffey's reader and pretend not to notice my distraction. Paul feeds me, bathes me, puts me to bed, as if I were the baby I've killed. His patience and attentiveness crucify me.

"A son," I want to scream at him. "Your precious son."

I want to accuse and blame and come to blows, and instead he kisses my eyelids, his lips like fluttering butterfly wings. I want to hate him until one night I reach out and discover that his pillow, too, is soaked with tears.

January 25, 1908

Our season of sorrow is finally ended. A new life has entered me, and I can feel its strength and comfort like a magical potion coursing through my veins. Only Paul knows. We are taking no chances, but everyone has noticed the change in me. My boy still comes to me in my dreams, but now he stands between my mother and grandmother and they are all three holding hands and smiling. He has made his crossing at last.

ややや

Jennifer Pearl Leon, destined to be called by her middle name, sailed into her own at midnight one year to the day after her brother's stillbirth. Hope labored for nine hours but with little pain until the end, and that was over quickly. The Swedish midwife gave the baby a lusty smack and beamed at her squalling reply, then washed away her milky coating, swaddled and placed her in Hope's arms, and set to cleaning up the birth.

When mother and child were sufficiently presentable, Mary Jane summoned Paul, and they all gathered to admire the thick, black mane of hair, pink cherub's cheeks, and eyes so dark and alert they seemed to possess the wisdom of the ages.

"She's your girl," said Hope, lifting their daughter for Paul's inspection.

He touched the newborn skin hesitantly, held his thumb for the tiny fingers to grasp. The child, all wrinkles and pink purple blotches, yawned broadly.

"Take her," Hope urged.

He shied back as if she'd asked him to put his hand to a flame.

"She can't bite you, Paul. She has no teeth."

Mary Jane gave Hope an understanding nod and led the midwife out, but in the women's absence the shadows across the dimly lit room seemed to lengthen, and Hope was suddenly aware of the wind outside. The baby studied her calmly, as if waiting for her to act.

"Come." She shifted the child to release an arm, patted the bed beside her. Though Paul sat, his discomfort was palpable.

"She does not seem human," he said.

"She's your daughter, Paul. She's miraculous, I know, but she has as much right to have you hold her as she does me." Hope gave him a curious look. "Did you never hold your other son or daughter?"

"I was away." He looked into the infant's wide eyes.

"And you're still away from them," said Hope. "But you're here for Pearl. She's different. *We* are different, and so you must be. Take her, Paul. Hold her and love her. She's a part of us—our greatest triumph. You must realize that."

She sat up with effort and showed her husband how to open his arms, to support the wobbling head and cradle the narrow back. She had never seen him so terrified, and he jumped with panic when the baby opened her mouth and let out a stream of pleased, gurgling sounds, but gradually he relaxed and began to rock shyly side to side. A sweetness came over him as the small eyes closed to sleep.

"She is both of us," he said.

"Why, what did you expect?" Hope would have laughed if it hadn't hurt so.

He looked genuinely bemused. "American. I think, we will have an American child."

"And so we have."

"But in China—"

Hope cut him off. "I know, and in America, too, she will be mistaken. That's why she needs us both, Paul, to protect her and teach her who she really is."

He delivered the sleeping child back to Hope's arms and kissed her doubtfully.

🐛🐛🐛

8

November 17, 1908

Dearest Dad,

Bizarre, wonderful, scary news from China this week. The cables have been flooding in from Paul's friends in Hankow and Peking (several of whom serve the revolution by spying inside the Forbidden City!). The wording of these cables is too priceless for me to paraphrase, so here's how Paul read them to me.

FIRST: Emperor suffering from constipation. Empress diarrhea due to cream and crab apples with Dalai Lama. Imperial seesaw in balance.

THEN: Kuang Hsü has drunk Yang's special "wine" and wins the race. Empress finish hours later. Baby P'u Yi playing Emperor. China poised and ready.

FINALLY: Eunuchs and regents in command, promise constitution, parliament. Provincial assemblies organize.

Need a translation? So did I, and even Paul isn't entirely sure of the truth, since the odd language is a form of cipher, but he believes that the Empress Dowager Tz'u-hsi and the Emperor Kuang-hsü, whom she has kept a palace prisoner for years, finally succeeded in poisoning each other (by playing favorites with the court eunuchs, you see!). The Empress Dowager managed to outlive the Emperor by just enough hours to appoint her three-year-old grand-nephew as the new Emperor. Theoretically the boy's father rules in his place, as Regent, until the child comes of age, but in reality no one has enough authority or vision to buck the mounting demand for change. Now the court is trying to pacify the revolutionaries by promising some of the most basic reforms, but Paul doubts they'll follow through. A true constitution and parliament would strip the Manchus of too much power, and many of the people now running the court care even less for the country than the Empress Dowager did.

What does this mean for us, I hear you asking. I ask the same of Paul and he just bunches up his nose, looking eager and worried. He says it means the revolution will succeed, but whether in months or years is still impossible to predict. I am relieved that he is not talking about hurrying back yet. It is still too dangerous for him at home, I gather, and Dr. Sun still depends too heavily on the funds and goodwill that Paul rallies in this country.

I confess to having very mixed feelings about this development. Our life has settled at last into such a peaceful pattern. Thanks to Thomas and Mary Jane, we have a dear home here, and Paul and I both have our work and studies. Pearl is a delight, an easy baby made that much easier by the addition to our household of a young "amah" named Li-li. She's one of Donaldina Cameron's girls whom I first met two years ago when her childish sweetness and harrowing tale of rescue from the slavers made her a powerful fund-raising accomplice for Donaldina's Mission. Now she's sixteen, too bright and beautiful to be kept in the environs of Chinatown (now more enticing than ever to the traders) and too independent yet to be married. You might say we're offering her a "halfway house." She cares for Pearl in exchange for room and board (in the nursery), and this enables me to return to tutoring for the Mason sisters—essential since

Pearl's birth has done nothing to loosen Paul's mother's purse strings. It is not always easy, but we have achieved, I think, a good balance of the elements required for a sane, happy married life. Though it would be a great adventure to bundle ourselves up and off to China, there would be so many unknowns, and even in the best of circumstances, there would be dangers. Yes, Dad, you who have ridden bareback across the wilderness and traded recipes for headache medicines with hostile tribes and worked yourself numb on the frozen mountaintops must be having a good laugh at your spoiled, selfish daughter. Where has my pioneer spirit gone? I suppose it's fallen sound asleep in the warmth of this sweet nest. I finally feel as though I know what's good for me. It's everything we have here.

I must close. Paul is due home soon and Li-li is calling me to taste her sweet-and-spicy soup. Pearl and Paul join me in sending our love.

Hope.

჻჻჻

Over the next two years, Hope juggled the demands of her growing daughter, her students, and Mary Jane's perennial reeducation campaign for suffrage. Paul, meanwhile, was increasingly preoccupied by events six thousand miles away. Reforms promised by Prince Ts'ai Feng, the father of P'u-i and now Regent of China, were repeatedly postponed, while taxes escalated convulsively as the Manchus scrambled to repay foreign loans taken out by the late Empress Dowager to fill the Ch'ing's jewel chests. Peasant and merchant classes alike were rioting, and although the Manchus still had the power to quell Sun Yat-sen's New Army revolts, for the first time the majority of revolutionary troops were Imperial turncoats.

In the fall of 1909 Paul traveled to New York to meet Sun Yat-sen and escort him across the country. Over the next four months they traveled with a company of musicians and actors, staging revolutionary operas in t'ang halls and mining camps. They made stump speeches in Chinatowns, took collections from laundrymen, fruit pickers, explosives experts, greengrocers, and houseboys. They distributed pamphlets written in English to American politicians, businessmen, and churchmen propagandizing democratic revolution as "The True Solution of the Chinese Question." Ultimately, they landed back on the West Coast with a platter of lies tailor-made for American mercenaries. They met in Los Angeles with "General" Homer Lea, the eighty-eight-pound, Stanford-graduated hunchback who, for the past decade, had been the Royalists' military advisor. Now Lea and a retired New York banker named Charles Boothe had decided they might better make their fortune by investing in the soon-to-be Republic of China. Paul sat mute and amused as Dr. Sun tendered to the two men and their proposed Syndicate full or leased control of China's railroads, central bank, coinage, and mineral deposits. Dr. Sun, whose woolly eyebrows and wiry mustache concealed any trace of dissemblance, was fully aware of the racist prejudices both Americans harbored, and he was prepared to do unto them as they would do unto him. If they could come up with four million dollars for New China, then Sun had no compunctions about numbering his forces at thirty thousand intellectuals and ten million secret society "volunteers."

"It will be commercial suicide for the American capitalists," Sun said on the March evening he spent with Paul and Hope before sailing for Honolulu. "But better to make a net than to pine for fish at the edge of the pond."

Paul and their other guests, newspaperman and Presbyterian minister Ng Poon Chew and his wife Chun Fa, with whom Dr. Sun was staying, nodded sedately behind identical pairs of wire-rimmed glasses.

"But nets are full of holes," Hope said, "and some fish always manage to wriggle through." She saw Paul wince, and added pointedly, "Forgive my impertinence, Dr. Sun. I only wish to understand your strategy."

Reverend Chew smiled broadly. A sturdy, compact man in his forties with a square head and straight mouth hooded by a neatly clipped boxcar mustache, Chew edited the *Chinese Western Daily* in Oakland but had also served as pastor of Donaldina's Mission. He had cut off his queue nearly thirty years earlier. So when he said, "Your American wife is not afraid to display her intelligence," Hope wondered whether he was poking fun at her or at Paul.

Mrs. Chew showed no confusion. A tiny but spirited woman in her thirties, she lifted her chin to her husband. "Nor are our own daughters."

He laughed. "Because they, too, are Americans!"

"You have no plans to return to China after the revolution, P'an Chao?" Dr. Sun asked, giving the newspaperman's name its proper un-American pronunciation. (Confused by the Chinese order of last and first names, immigration officials had noted Chew as the family name on Ng Poon Chew's 1881 entry documents, and so it had remained ever since.) Reverend Chew used his newspaper and frequent turns at the lecture podium to denounce the Chinese Exclusion laws, but although he had once rescued Sun from deportation and was also a member of the Chinese sect of Masons that supported the *Free Press*, he was not an active participant in the revolutionary cause.

"This is my home and my children's home," Reverend Chew said. "Besides, if I can improve understanding between whites and Chinese in this country, then some of those whites may be more inclined to support your revolution."

Dr. Sun pursed his lips, nodded once, and turned back to Hope. "I, too, am sometimes accused of impertinence, but I consider this a compliment. As for your observation, Madame Liang, I would say that the fish I wish to net will be too large to slip through the holes. However, they may prove too wily to enter the net, which will lead to the same result. So I lure them with promises I know I cannot keep, and hope that they cannot detect this."

"They understand nothing but their own greed," said Paul. "You read them perfectly."

"The ends justify the means, in other words," said Hope.

Ng Poon Chew and his wife exchanged glances and blew on their tea.

"We are trying to overthrow a government, Hope." Paul uncrossed his legs and spread his hands over his knees. "Profit motive is a useful tool."

"I see it as prospecting," said Sun Yat-sen. "How different from a wealthy man paying for an expedition to open a mine in search of gold. Maybe it pays off. Maybe not."

"Yes." Paul nodded emphatically. "Yes."

But Hope wondered at her husband's willing participation in this deceit. Sun Yat-sen struck her as a good man, earnest and intense, but there was also a palpable ineffectuality about him that undercut his daring words. With those brushlike eyebrows and sleepy eyes, the slicked-back hair like a little boy's and those querulous lips, he could easily be mistaken for a poet or an absentminded banker. She could understand why, on his early trips through America, this slight, almost effeminate man had been more of an irritant than an inspiration to the *hua ch'iao*—overseas Chinese—who had blown tunnels through mountains and built the railroads with their bare hands. What was astounding about him was that he kept coming back, had circled the globe multiple times, and, though there was a price on his head and he had several times barely escaped arrest, he continued, like Paul, to pursue his vision of a free China.

Hope relieved Li-li of the chattering cup and saucer she was attempting to hand her. The girl had been tongue-tied all day at the prospect of Dr. Sun's visit, had burned the first batch of biscuits and put too much salt in the stew and forgotten to put Pearl down for her nap until the poor baby was screaming with exhaustion. Hope finally offered to serve supper herself so that Li-li could remain in the nursery. With that, the young amah had pulled herself together and served the meal—a simple American repast, by Dr. Sun's request. But her awe was starting to show through again.

Hope directed the girl to check on the sleeping Pearl. By the time she turned back to her guests the men had lapsed into Cantonese. Chun Fa, seated to Hope's left, wagged her black-slippered foot in the air like a baton. As Westernized as her husband, Mrs. Chew wore a trim visiting gown of aquamarine taffeta with satin trim and a matching feathered hat over her pompadour.

"Your children," said Hope. "Do you think you'll take them back to China someday?" She nodded toward the men. "Assuming they get their way?"

Mrs. Chew dropped her foot to the floor. "You say this word 'back' as some say all Chinese should go 'back where they came from.' But I am born in America. All my four children are born in America, and my husband has not seen China in almost thirty years, since he was fifteen years old. I would like my family someday to visit China, yes, but we will not be going back."

The words were delivered in a gentle voice, but the undercurrent of resentment was unmistakable. Hope felt she had been chastised and was now expected to apologize, but as after any scolding, apology came hard. Instead, she gave a tough, small laugh. "Between Paul and my students and my amah, I sometimes imagine that I, too, am from China, and when I think of our going someday, I always think in terms of going back."

"Then you are fooling yourself. Your husband will be going back, as mine would be. But you will be going away. The two are not at all the same." With that, the older woman leaned across and patted Hope's hand. Seeing the pale skin against her own, the narrow, delicately knuckled fingers, Hope was startled to realize that she and Chun Fa were almost exactly the same size and height and, except for their eyes, had the same coloring. Moreover, the broad neatly lined face staring back at her was filled not with resentment at all, but with something dangerously resembling pity.

She blanched and pulled away, turning toward the men. Paul was tossing a handful of sugared pumpkin seeds into his mouth. Dr. Sun was examining his pocket watch and yawning. Ng Poon Chew was straightening the pleat in his pin-striped trousers.

"Do you have children, Dr. Sun?" Hope asked.

"Why, yes." He snapped the gold watch cover shut and looked up with a benign smile. "One son and two daughters."

"It must be very difficult for them, with you traveling so much."

Paul threw Hope a warning glance. "Forgive my wife, Dr. Sun. I try to explain to her that Chinese families are different from American families, but she cannot understand."

Sun Yat-sen drew a finger along the left wing of his mustache.

"I ask," said Hope, "because these past months, when my husband was traveling with you, our daughter asked for him every night. I was able to reassure her that her papa would be home in just a few days, but I thought how sad we would both be if, instead of days, it was to be years before we were reunited."

"One of the differences between Chinese and American families," said Dr. Sun, "is the marriages that produce them."

Reverend Chew pressed his hands together, forefingers touching his lower lip. "Jung Ch'un-fu once said that American-style marriage is a precious gem that one carefully selects, polishes, and treasures, while Chinese-style marriage is a stone that one is obligated to carry. You know Jung, don't you, Po-yu?"

Paul nodded, his gaze falling to Hope. "He was my teacher in Hong Kong. Dr. Sun and I stopped in to pay our respects last autumn when we were east."

"He was devoted to his American wife," said Sun Yat-sen.

"Then you must understand my concern, Dr. Sun." Hope clasped the seat of her chair, leaning forward. "Because ours is, as you say, an American-style marriage, I am not eager to see my husband leave, whether for weeks or months or years. And as your ambitions point to his destiny, I feel I must ask how you see China's future unfolding."

"And what role I see there for your husband?" Dr. Sun made a show of lifting his cup and studying the swirl of tea leaves. Hope flared at his mocking her, but held her tongue. "I am afraid I never learned the art of tea leaves, and I have too much respect for you to make the kinds of promises I hold out to certain other American friends. However, I do believe our revolution will succeed and your husband will hold a prominent position in our new republic within the next ten years. Is this satisfactory?"

She curled her arms around her waist, suddenly chilled.

"My wife is of two minds about our success," said Paul.

"I can see that," said Sun Yat-sen. "But so, too, are many of our own countrymen, even those who can only benefit by it."

"It's the blood that's spilled on the way that scares them," said Hope.

"No," said Dr. Sun. "There I must disagree. In China, few are frightened to die, and many look forward to the end. But change—that is a source of terror. And that terror is our greatest enemy."

"To Americans," said Paul, "change is like opium. It fascinates them and beckons them. They read in it the illusion of happiness, and so pursue it at the cost of their spirits and even their lives. I think this is why white men are such a restless breed, never truly content or at peace, why they must forever go forth and conquer new lands and people."

Hope opened her mouth to disagree, but Reverend Chew diplomatically raised a hand. "It is late," he said. "We thank you for a most enjoyable evening, but Dr. Sun's ship sails at an early hour."

Hope and Paul escorted their guests past Li-li's energetic bowing and out to the street. It was cold and damp with a full moon gleaming behind shredded clouds. Up on Shattuck the ten o'clock trolley clanged, but Ng Poon Chew was chauffeuring his esteemed guest in a forest green Packard coupé, borrowed for the evening from Oakland's wealthiest curio dealer. The three figures looked almost furtive as they ducked into the glittering car, Chun Fa slipping alone into the cavernous rear compartment. Again, Hope felt a pang of recognition, empathy for this other American married to a Chinese man. Yet Chun Fa pitied her.

The large globe headlamps burst to life, and the Packard growled up the street, leaving Hope and Paul waving in the gaslight. They stood so close that when she shivered he noticed and wrapped an arm around her—American-style.

"I think you have shocked Dr. Sun," he said as they started back.

"I think you were more perturbed than he."

"He is my teacher and my hero. In history, he will be known as the father of the Chinese revolution. Think how you would feel if George Washington or Abraham Lincoln came to dinner."

"I would be no less direct with them," retorted Hope. "Even heroes are human. What is his wife like?"

"She is the bride his parents arranged for him. He is duty-bound to her, but he does not love her."

Hope reached up and found Paul's hand at her shoulder. They walked in step, his longer legs shortening stride to match hers. "Three children," Hope said, "and no love?"

"You heard, Chinese marriage is founded on obligation, not love."

"His poor wife."

The moon slid behind a cloud and the yard seemed to recede beyond the lights of the cottage. "I am sorry that Thomas could not join us tonight." Paul motioned toward the darkened main house. For the past month their landlord had been working late almost every night on the new Northbrae subdivision. "Dr. Sun would enjoy asking him about city development."

"You're changing the subject. Is that the real reason Sun spends all his time charging around the world? To avoid the home front?"

"I think Sun Yat-sen's true love is revolution."

"Then he should divorce his wife and let her find someone who will be true to her."

"That would dishonor her. This way she is cared for and treated with respect."

Paul started to turn toward the cottage, but Hope tugged him in the other direction. There was a wooden bench across the yard, near the swing that Thomas had hung from the big elm for Li-li and Pearl. "Let's sit and talk awhile."

"You are cold."

"No, it's all right. Just keep close. You're warm enough for two."

"What if Li-li sees us?"

"What if she does?" Hope stretched up and kissed him on the ear. "Do you think she doesn't notice that we share the same bed?"

"She is a child."

"A child well acquainted with the facts of life. I think we do her a favor by showing what love looks like."

He let her pull him down beside her, let her curl against his chest. The clouds parted and the moon sallied forth, majestic and brilliant through the leafless branches.

"Tell me about your first wife," said Hope.

"I have told you."

"You told me only that she existed. What was she like? How did she act? Was she pretty? Young?"

Paul did not change his position, did not move away from her, and yet she felt something in him tighten. "She has no importance," he said.

"She was the mother of your children. She is important to them."

He took a deep breath and dropped his hand to her waist. "I have told you she died in the cholera epidemic. This is true, but she did not die of cholera." He hesitated.

"Tell me," Hope urged.

"Always she was a nervous girl. Temper——?"

"Temperamental?"

"Yes. Always looking in the mirror."

"She was beautiful."

"Yes, at first, but she was her father's favorite and so considered herself like the Empress. Very demanding."

"Your mother must have loved that."

"She and my mother fought from the start. More she complained, more punishment my mother thought for her. They hate each other, and they are just alike."

"And with the children?"

"She had no interest in our children. She would spend all day coloring her nails or making her face. When I come home, she begs to stay with me. When I leave, she begs to come away."

Hope drew back a little, searching for his eyes through the darkness. "You don't think it's just possible that she loved you?"

He shook his head. "When I refuse to take her away, she screams and threatens me, says she will hurt our children. I think it is only her—temperamental—nature. I do not have time for her tricks anymore. I have to worry about Chang Chih-tung. It is the time I am plotting the Hankow revolt."

"When you were arrested." She slipped a hand around to his back. "When your mother saved your life."

"Yes, but this only angers my wife more."

Hope nodded. "Because the two of them were locked in battle, and this gave your mother more power over you."

He studied Hope with an expression that hovered between admiration and suspicion. "How do you know so well how my wife thinks?"

She sighed, shaking her head. "So what happened then?"

"After I escape to Shanghai my mother discovered my wife has taken a lover."

"Paul! How did she find out?"

"In China a woman has no secrets from her mother-in-law. For three months my wife had no bloody rags to wash, and I had been away six months. When I had been away eight months I learned that my daughter had taken ill with cholera but had been cured, while my father and wife had died. Much later, I learned that my wife had not died of the fever but had eaten gold."

Hope shut her eyes. She could see them all in their lavish gowns, paste white faces and ruby lips, sidestepping the children and hating each other. Characters in a nightmare. Except Paul. When she tried to set her husband into this mental tableau he would have no part of it. Yet even in absentia, he remained its very center.

She shivered. He took her hands between his and, shaking his head, breathed on them to warm them. "Why do you force me to tell these things?"

"You have managed not to for four years. It makes me wonder what else you're hiding."

"We cannot know everything about each other."

"You're right," she said. "And if we did know everything, we'd probably lose interest. But it's the *striving* to know that holds us, don't you see that, Paul?"

He kissed each of her fingertips in turn, then guided her arms around his waist and kissed her softly on the mouth and eyelids and nose. The low, sonorous hoot of a barge whistle floated up from the Bay, and the mist spread its fine veil over their skin. Hope was chilled through now, yet when Li-li opened the door and peeked out, she pushed Paul back into the shadows. The door closed, and the dark peach of Li-li's dress moved from one window frame to the next. The door to the nursery opened, and they watched through the sheer curtains as the amah bent over the crib, then lifted her arms to undo her braids. Across the property, the spray of gravel and guttering of a motor announced Thomas's return.

"Come," said Paul.

"No, wait," whispered Hope. She couldn't describe what held her. Inertia, fascination, fatigue. The sense that she and Paul were at once hiding and watching. Not quite spying, but it had that same clandestine quality. She wasn't ready to give it up.

The door of the Model T shut with a bang. They couldn't see him for the tree, but they could hear Thomas's footsteps sinking into the grass, moving down the hill toward the Y where the drive split toward their cottage. Hope lifted her head off Paul's chest—his heartbeat was so loud that she could not tell if what she thought she detected was so, but yes. She could see Thomas now. Slowing. Turning. He stood at the crossroads for several long seconds, his domed hat falling forward as he craned his neck toward the cottage lights.

Hope heard Paul's breath and clapped her hand over his open mouth. She grinned up at him, pleading, put a finger to her lips and signaled for him to watch.

Over the two years since Li-li had come to them, Thomas had been restored. Not only had he plunged back into his work, but he had put on weight. His cheeks were flushed, his step buoyant. He dressed with a flare that Hope would never have imagined he possessed, and he proved his skill as a builder at home, with Pearl as his excuse. The swing was his first gift, constructed like a bowl with holes for the baby's chubby legs, so she could not fall out as Li-li pushed her. Then he erected a folding rail, so they could play out on the porch in summer without Pearl tumbling down the steps. Then a little wagon, painted red and yellow, in which Li-li could trundle Pearl up and down the drive. Often Thomas would walk along with them or come out to push the baby on the swing. Hope had welcomed these attentions, thinking he was experiencing through Pearl the fatherhood that had been denied him when his wife died. Now, as she watched the way Thomas stood outside the nursery window, she realized she'd had it all backward.

He was watching not the baby but Li-li, as she stood in that peach dress in her lamp-lit room, slowly brushing her waist-length hair.

෨෨෨

January 5, 1911

My father came for three days over Christmas and Thomas fed us a standing rib roast, which he and Li-li cooked entirely by themselves. There was a magnificent blue spruce in the parlor and a crackling fire. We drank whiskeyed eggnog and pretended not to notice the mistletoe dangling like an errant cupid in every doorway. My father made one of his typically pungent remarks about the powers of Chinese aphrodisiacs, sending Mary Jane into gales of laughter while poor Thomas and Li-li turned red as tomatoes. Paul saved the day (sort of) by asking Dad if he'd ever tried any of those magical herbs and, when Dad said regrettably that he had not, offered to procure some for him. This was Dad's cue to color. He only saved himself (sort of) by announcing that he's finally given up his mining fantasy at La Porte and is moving down to Los Angeles to go back into the naturopathy business. Said maybe he and Paul could trade a few herbs, see whose worked the best. We drank to that.

Throughout the evening Thomas and Li-li couldn't take their eyes off each other. There was a sparkle in Li-li's laughter that I've never heard before, and Thomas poured so much wine that I started to wonder if *that* were the aphrodisiac. Finally, as the flames danced around the plum pudding, Thomas made the announcement we've all expected—and I've been dreading—for months.

The good news is that they are planning to wait until the spring, and they insist that the only significant change will be Li-li's move across the yard. Paul and I are to "stay put," in Thomas's words, and Li-li made me promise not to hire another amah for Pearl. So everyone is happy. We all told them how glad we were. We all held our tongues with regard to the prejudices they well know they are going to encounter. Then Pearl, little queen that she is, demanded Thomas and Li-li each give her a kiss, and everyone agreed that the union had now been officially blessed.

What mystifies me are the strange currents of jealousy that have been dogging me ever since the announcement. I find myself watching as they sit together up on Thomas's porch after supper. I note the attentive cock of his head whenever she is speaking, the flush that comes into her cheeks at the least sight of him. I am forced to admit that Paul and I have already slipped out of this magnetic newness of love. We are married folk. We have a life together. A different magic holds us now, a sense of comfort and trust, but also a kind of melancholy dawning.

Sometimes in the middle of the night I'll glance over at Paul's lovely sleek head curled asleep like a child's in his pillow, and this melancholy will settle its gloved hand at my throat, pressing softly but steadily until I cry out against it. Then Paul will curl an arm and hold me, murmur something I can't understand, and I will at once feel soothed and lonelier than ever. Last night when this happened I lay there for a long time awake in his sleeping embrace, and I thought about Thomas and Lili, and finally I saw the true source of my jealousy.

I realized that when we fell in love, we also fell into an illusion. We believed—I believed—that by joining together as close as a man and woman can possibly be, we would come to *know* each other. Here was this other person, a finite body with finite experiences—like a treasure chest. By loving enough, by giving ourselves to each other completely, we would be able to take that treasure in hand and possess it physically, spiritually, emotionally. Totally. What we didn't realize, and what perhaps new lovers can't bear to believe even if someone is stupid enough to try to tell them, is that this treasure, which we desire so deeply and hold so dear, is not finite at all but ever expanding. Now the instant I touch Paul, he seems to multiply before my eyes. He is not one man but five, has not one life but twenty, not ten ambitions but hundreds, and not a hundred friends but thousands. The extensions and folds in his experience are limitless, as are mine, I suppose. But the more I know him the less I know of him. That is the hard truth that comes only with marriage. And there is nothing—absolutely nothing for it.

ৡৡৡ

9

The next months for Hope had a bittersweet quality, like the end of a long holiday. She reveled in her hours with Li-li and Pearl, in the celebration of Thomas and Li-li's wedding, in her afternoons with students at the Mission, and evening chats with Mary Jane. But these days were shadowed by the steady procession of events in China.

After a stall of nearly two years the Manchu government had finally allowed provinces to elect representatives for a National Assembly, however they had refused the representatives' demand for an opening of parliament. Some of Paul's former classmates attempted to assassinate the Prince Regent, but were arrested, tortured, and executed. Others of his confreres in Wuhan established a secret revolutionary organization under the decoy name, Hupei Literary Society, funded largely by *hua ch'iao* contributions collected by Paul and funneled through the *Ta T'ung Daily*. All of this meant that Paul spent more and more of his days either at the paper or in smoke-filled halls lecturing to merchants and sojourners. He attended classes rarely, delegated his schoolwork to underlings at the paper, and shrugged off Hope's occasional reminders that his visa status depended on his at least pretending to be a student. He was too mired in strategy and scheming on a grander canvas.

For the first time Paul's political dedication began to encroach, as well, on their private life. He barked at Pearl when she toddled up and searched his jacket pockets for the sweets he used to bring home every evening. Hope often had to ask a question three or four times before he heard her, and in bed he would lie for hours with his open eyes fixed on the ceiling. Their lovemaking alternated between a perfunctory, almost impersonal release of physical tension, and a desperately hungry act that made Hope feel as if he were searching inside her for some secret balm, a solution to some puzzle within himself. When she tried to soothe him, her hands slipped on the sweat running down his back, tangled in the scars that seemed to grow deeper and more violent at night. She could not hold him, and she felt helpless to heal him.

"You wish you were back there launching the final revolt," she said one evening as he sat at his desk studying the day's telegrams, which numbered more than the cables he had received in the whole first year of their marriage.

"I am living in exile." He pulled off his glasses and rubbed his temples, switching into Mandarin. "I am following orders and saving my neck while men who once admired me are risking their lives to save China."

Hope tugged off his jacket and unbuttoned his collar to massage his shoulders. "You know, Paul, without you here those men would not have a prayer. Now more than ever."

He reached up and stopped her hands. "You will come with me," he said, "when it is time?"

She swallowed and shut her eyes against the ocher glare of his lamp. Down the hall, Pearl was crying out in her sleep.

"I don't know," she said, tears that she had not foreseen spilling as she turned away. "Please don't ask until it's real. Pearl needs me. Paul, please let me go."

He released her and she fled, like a boat jerked from its mooring. She was nearly two months pregnant.

అలఅలఅల

The cable she had been dreading arrived the afternoon of October 13, 1911. Four nights earlier, Paul's friends in the office of the Progressive Society in Hankow's Russian Concession accidentally exploded a bomb intended for an uprising later in the month. Scores were arrested and executed, but the following day the surviving rebels, supported by mutinying government troops, seized the armory in the neighboring city of Wuchang, Paul's hometown. In another twenty-four hours the revolutionaries controlled all three of the sister cities—Wuchang, Hankow, and Hanyang—that together formed Hupei's provincial capital, Wuhan. Now armed revolts ignited across China like firecrackers on a winding fuse. One by one, then in twos and threes, cities and provinces were proclaiming their independence, and the last of the Manchu armies were crossing over to the revolution.

That evening, as Hope stood watching from the doorway, Paul hugged his three-year-old daughter so tightly that she squealed, "Papa, too strong!"

He smoothed the bedclothes and rubbed a thumb over her thick dark eyebrows. "And you, my precious Pearl? Are you strong?" The child drew her lips in, scowling and dimpling in the very image of power. "You must be strong, my daughter."

"Why?"

A glance to Hope. A smile. "I must go far away, and you take care of your mama. Soon, I send for you and Mama to come to me."

"Where?"

"To China. Your other country."

"What a country, Papa?"

"A country——" But he could not think how to explain the idea of statehood to the child. She was like a little Dowager Empress, his Pearl, so sheltered from the larger world.

"Let me tell you a story," he said instead. "When I am a little boy I live in China. Every day I eat candies—horses and tigers and pigs of spun sugar. In winter, snow falls white and cold and taller than you. In spring, jugglers and puppet man and acrobats come. We make a festival with flowers and painted banners. I have a pet pigeon and yellow canary, and many kites, shape of snakes and dragons, and on windy days . . ." But his daughter's small fingers had curled into sleep and she no longer heard him. He pulled the blanket to her chin and kissed her dark lashes.

"*Tso ko Chung-kuo men, mei-mei,*" he whispered. "You will be there soon."

"You mean to enchant her," said Hope.

He switched off the light and followed her out. His trunks and lac-quered crates littered the hallway. "I mean she will not be afraid."

"Do you really believe that enchantment will still be there after your revolution?"

"Hope." He started to shake his head, but she laid a hand on his cheek to stop him.

"Pearl isn't afraid, Paul, but I am. What story are you going to use to make me feel better?"

He sighed. The house looked as though a typhoon had struck it. His clothing, papers, open valises, and books were everywhere. He would be up until midnight packing. But first he gathered her against him, resting his chin on the crown of her head. "One month," he said, "no more than two, I will send for you and Pearl."

She held still. "The baby—"

"That is why, no longer than two months."

"And if I want this child to be born in America?"

He stiffened.

"I've chosen to give up my citizenship for you, Paul, but at least if this child is born here, he and Pearl will both be able to make their own choice." She stepped back, lifting her face defiantly. "You don't know what things will be like there for us—for the children. You *can't* know."

Now he gripped her hands tightly, shaking them as if to awaken her. "This baby will not come until April. Do you want to be apart so long?"

"No," she said. "No, of course not, but—oh, *why* must you go!" Her eyes blazed, then brimmed with tears. He bore her anguish at first with-out moving, then softly, gently brought her arms around his waist. He stroked her hair, pressed his lips to her forehead, and for several minutes they stood together. There was nothing more to say.

∽∽∽

October 14, 1911
Dearest,
It is barely ten hours since you left. Too soon to write, I hear

you say, too soon even for the full impact of your leaving to register. You have been away from me before and often enough that I thought I had shed my sorrow at your absence, but tonight it is as if a great spoon had opened a cavity in my soul. I see the curve of your brow in our daughter's sleeping face. I imagine your pulse in our new child. Yet this house is ours no more. This bed is now mine alone. Our children's lives are beginning, and I can hear you say that our life together, too, will soon begin anew, but tonight I am haunted by the specter of finality, the memory of your eyes, the line of sight that stretched between us those few hours ago, pulling, pulling as the ship bore you away and, that fast, you were gone.

I cannot pretend that you misled me. It was I who chose not to see or prepare myself for this parting. I who misled myself into believing that this life we have been living was the same for which we were intended. Will I ever share *your* vision of our life together in China?

If I should have the brazenness to actually send this letter, you will have arrived safe in Shanghai by the time you read it, so at least some of my fears will be moot. Then it will rest with the strength of your Dr. Sun to assuage my other terrors and see us reunited.

There is nothing I long for more . . .

1919 Francisco St.
November 11, 1911
Dearest,

What times we live in! In a way, you could not have chosen a better time to leave, as the Vote has given me little opportunity to wallow in my sorrow. Mary Jane came and roused me at six in the morning on Election Day. "It's history, girl," she kept saying. "You have the rest of your life to weep, but only this day to win us the Vote." I carried our sleeping daughter over to stay with Li-li and Thomas, then we hauled armloads of voter instruction pamphlets over to Shattuck and set up camp at the voting booths.

The ward heelers and barkeeps were out in force, matching

every two of our shouts with four of their own. If we did not cast an eagle eye, the announcer would call off "no" instead of the voter's "yes" to our referendum. The clerks would mark down a nay vote when a yea had been cast. I was near exhaustion when I finally stumbled home, after 11:30 p.m. Next morning the papers were cheering with news of our defeat and it seemed we would have to wait still more years for this most basic right. But, Paul, the most miraculous thing occurred. The early reports reflected the urban vote only, and much of that had been tampered with. As the rural returns came in it appeared that we *won California!* That still leaves thirty-nine states to persuade, and yet my faith in democracy has been renewed. If you can make this system work in your China, dearest, it will truly be cause for celebration.

Fresh on the heels of victory, with love and kisses to you always,

your Hope

P.S. Nearly forgot one hugely important bit of news. Li-li is expecting a baby, too! This means either you must fetch us soon, or, you will *have* to come back to us here, as our two babies will undoubtedly be inseparable!

Aboard the SK *Korea*
December 2, 1911
Dearest Dad,
This is surely the most difficult letter I have ever written. I dread hurting you. I refuse to say goodbye. But what has happened must come as no surprise. We all knew that my future and that of my children lay with my husband—whether he remained in America or returned to China. Well, he has returned to China, as you know. It appears the violent revolution we all feared has not come to pass, the Manchus are in the process of capitulating with barely a whimper, and your son-in-law is preparing to take his place as senator from Hupei in the newly forming government of the Republic of China. Last week he wired the arrangements for Pearl and me to join him in Shanghai.

It all has happened so quickly, Dad. I knew you would oppose us. I would in your position. But I am a grown woman and a wife, and my allegiance now is to my husband. And I know you will not argue the truth or appropriateness of that.

Dad, you have been a pioneer all your life. You have bequeathed to me that same spirit of discovery, and you have supported me—against your instincts, I know—in marrying the man I love. Now I count on you supporting me in this greatest of all pioneering acts of my life, in traveling halfway around the world to discover a whole new continent.

I exaggerate only to win your smile. Paul is the true pioneer, for it is he who will bring democracy to this ancient empire. He has assured me that we will suffer neither hardship nor discomfort. Certainly nothing to compare with the hard knocks you and Mother must have endured. Some small part of me actually regrets Paul's promising ease and luxury, for I love you all the more for what you've lived through. I wonder, if we are truly to be pampered in this strange new world, whether I will be able to live with myself!

If this ship is any indication, the answer is a resounding no. By Paul's arrangement our cabin was equipped with champagne and chocolates and a bouquet of long-stem roses when we boarded! We have everything we could possibly need, including our own private washroom, and we dine, when the seas are not too rocky, on white linen set with china and silver so sharply polished that Pearl uses the spoon for a mirror—taking great delight, as you can imagine, in her upside-down reflection! So you see, my husband is already delivering on his promise, and my only complaint is that he takes too good care.

I will post this letter from Hawaii so it reaches you at about the same time we are landing in Shanghai. Think of us on our great adventure, and do not worry too awfully. We will be well taken care of, and when we are settled you will come visit. Oh Dad, please, please understand. This is not, will never be goodbye.

Your loving daughter,
Hope

BOOK TWO

Delicate trees paint the peaks green.

Through the window I see an abandoned castle.

A womb of clouds carries the coming rain,

In the mountain ranges the bubbling of springs,

Rays of sunshine peal off the golden tower.

The scent of spring coats the growing grass.

Every morning I watch without tiring.

It holds the love of a woman.

Shanghai

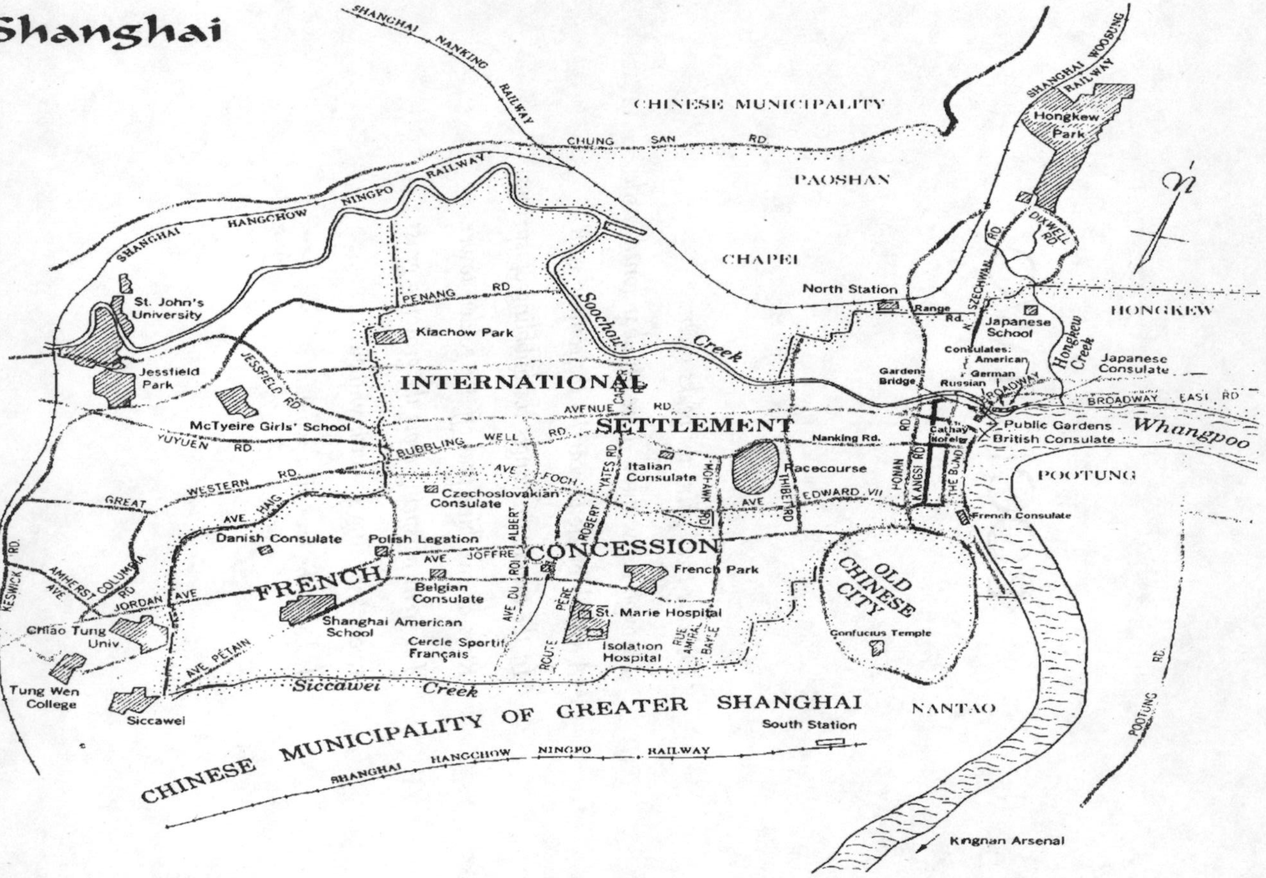
CHINESE MUNICIPALITY
SHANGHAI NANKING RAILWAY
CHUNG SAN RD
PAOSHAN
CHAPEI
SHANGHAI HANGCHOW NINGPO RAILWAY
SHANGHAI WOOSUNG RAILWAY
Hongkew Park
DIXWELL RD
SZECHWAN RD
North Station
Range Rd.
Japanese School
HONGKEW
Hongkew Creek
Japanese Consulate
Consulates: American German Russian
Garden Bridge
BROADWAY
EAST RD
Public Gardens
British Consulate
Whangpoo
Cathay Hotel
Nanking Rd.
THE BUND
KANGSI RD
HONAN RD
POOTUNG
French Consulate
St. John's University
Jessfield Park
Soochow Creek
PENANG RD
Kiachow Park
JESSFIELD RD
INTERNATIONAL SETTLEMENT
AVENUE RD
CARTER RD
McTyeire Girls' School
YUYUEN RD
BUBBLING WELL RD
AVE FOCH
YATES RD
Italian Consulate
MOHAWK RD
Racecourse
THIBET RD
EDWARD VII AVE
GREAT WESTERN RD
AVE HAIG
Czechoslovakian Consulate
Danish Consulate
Polish Legation
ALBERT
ROBERT
CONCESSION
French Park
OLD CHINESE CITY
Confucius Temple
KESWICK RD
AMHERST AVE
COLUMBIA RD
JORDAN AVE
FRENCH
AVE JOFFRE
Belgian Consulate
AVE DU ROI
PERE
St. Marie Hospital
Chiao Tung Univ.
Shanghai American School
Cercle Sportif Français
ROUTE
Isolation Hospital
RUE AMIRAL BAYLE
AVE PETAIN
Tung Wen College
Siccawei
Siccawei Creek
CHINESE MUNICIPALITY OF GREATER SHANGHAI
NANTAO
South Station
POOTUNG RD
Kingnan Arsenal

V
CROSSING
SHANGHAI
(1911–1912)

᭑᭑᭑

1

Beyond the horizon crouched a great horned lizard, fuming, claws dug deep beneath the sea. The image arrived in a dream and would not let go, so that each time Hope looked up from her blanketed deck chair while reading to Pearl or watching the shuffleboard champions spinning their discs, she braced for the sight of the lizard lifting its craggy head over the rail, blinking cruel, hooded eyes, and bellowing a fearsome warning. But after two erratic weeks, when their steamship at last approached the coast of Chekiang, the beast of China was only a dull green shadow, slumbering in the fog.

As Hope and Pearl stood watch from the bow, beads of ocean cold frosted their hair, the nap of their coats, their cheeks. Pearl laughed and stuck out her tongue. She took a child's delight in weather, ignoring all discomfort and measuring temperature, it seemed, by some internal thermostat entirely disconnected from the surface of her skin. Pearl imagined no monstrous reptiles. Even during the week of high seas, when they had to lock themselves in their cabin and strap themselves into their berth, her daughter's sleep seemed so peaceful that Hope would marvel at her trust. She could feel this same trust even now in the warmth of the small bare hand pulsing through her glove, and in the new baby's firefly movements.

Yet the utter dependence of one child by her side and another in her womb, the resounding soul of a third left far and forever behind, evoked a terrible unease within Hope. She had already failed one of her children. Whatever awaited her when this great slumbering lizard awoke, she must not fail another.

"Look, Mama!" Pearl was jumping, poking sausage fingers through the mesh guard. "Castle!"

"Woosung Fort," corrected an elderly Britisher standing beside them. "Have to go to England for a proper castle." As they drew closer to shore, the decks had crowded with passengers venturing from their warm compartments for a glimpse of their destination, but here on the cabin-class deck, where the majority were American, English, or Japanese, expressions of grim resignation rather than excitement reigned, and this Englishman was no exception. As he tugged his gray flop-hat down over his ears and fixed his horn-rimmed spectacles, he looked as if he'd rather be anywhere but here.

He turned and scrutinized Pearl more closely. Her black curls, her caramel cheeks and dark, elongated eyes. Then he squinted at Hope.

"I don't believe we've met," she said briskly. "Our name is Leon. We're from Berkeley." She extended her right hand.

The man lifted his chin and strode away.

What difference, Hope wondered watching him flee, between this pompous bigot and her childhood tormentors in Fort Dodge? Only age and accent. And degrees of cowardice.

She shook the tension from her hands and knelt beside her daughter, whose rapture at the advancing scenery had spared her the Englishman's contempt. "This is the mouth of the Yangtze," Hope said. "We'll be with Papa any minute."

Native craft appeared in ghostly formations, barbed with the voices of occupants made invisible by the mist. Hope pointed out the rounded hoods of sampans, slender hulls of slipper boats, the huge square riggings of junks. Houseboats, trawlers, slipshod rafts. "Bird!" Pearl clapped at each new shape, as if expecting it to fly.

"No, sweet, not birds," her mother said. "See, they're boats." But she could understand Pearl's confusion as the vessels came closer. Many of the wide, spread sails did resemble wings, and vivid round painted eyes protected the hulls from evil spirits.

Then, shoving between the small craft, came the obdurate lines of an unmistakably man-made hulk. The gunboat pulled alongside the steamer and a British voice pumped through a megaphone. The SK *Korea* slowed to follow its escort into the delta, where the passengers would board tenders for the last stretch up the Whangpoo to Shanghai.

The water thickened now with coastal steamers, barges, and launches flying flags of Japan, France, Russia, Germany—and some stars and stripes. This new activity seemed to clear the air and abruptly heightened the noise level. There were foghorns, sirens, the splash of paddles, and the continuous scrape and suck of dredgers working the banks. Hope lifted her mesmerized daughter, held her so their cheeks pressed together. Whatever adventures lay ahead, she thought, they would share at least this first impression—

Frank Pearson.

She nearly dropped Pearl. There on the bridge of the gunboat! Of course, it couldn't be. This was a mirage—a mistake. Frank was dead, she told herself roughly. But the resemblance . . . that sandy shag of hair, the height and build, as if constructed of broom sticks, and the angular profile—like Chief Joseph, he used to joke, though he confessed he had no Indian blood, the only man she'd ever met who regretted such a lack. Unlike the sailors around him, this man wore no uniform but a sharp brown suit. Sharp. The image surrounded her like a drop of pond water caught in the twist of a microscope. A split second later, it was gone.

Pearl, in her excitement, had put her hands to Hope's cheeks and tugged her face to one side. "Bird!" She was pointing at a boatload of cormorants with irons around their necks.

Hope twisted back searching among the figures on the bridge, but the uniform whites formed a solid bloom. There were no sandy-haired men in brown suits.

She clung to the child as the frantic whip of her heart subsided. She couldn't afford such fantasies. Paul was her husband, father of her children. He, not regret, was the reason she had traveled so far.

"Papa told me about those birds," she said as the gunboat finally slipped behind them. "They dive for fish, catch them in their beaks, and come up into the air to eat them. But the iron rings stop the cormorants from swallowing their catch. They'll dive over and over, and the bigger the prize they bring back up, the less chance they have of keeping it."

🐦🐦🐦

2

The crowd on the customs jetty had been waiting more than an hour for the *Korea*'s arriving passengers. The white men were passing the time with flasked whiskey while the women complained of the stench, holding perfumed handkerchiefs to their noses, drawing veils, lifting elbows, raising parasols against any accidental contact with the native haulers and compradors who scurried between the docks and customs office.

Up on the Bund a coolie foreman chanted: "See that fat foreign camel-foot there."

And his gang answered, "Look at her. Look at the camel-foot cunt!"

"Just try mounting her jade gate!"

"What a fate. What a fate! Just try mounting her white jade gate!"

Paul bit the inside of his cheek. Even if Hope eventually mastered Shanghainese, it was unlikely she would ever be able to decipher coolie vernacular, but the chant galled him nonetheless. It embodied everything that ailed China: the pathetic and irredeemable stupidity of China's poorest; the arrogance of the Westerners whose contempt for the Chinese invited the same in return; the swift, mindless ease with which one wrong idea was embraced and amplified by the masses. Revolution! Back in his homeland barely two months, already he was bitter and cynical.

A convoy of tenders was approaching the wharf, but the brims and feathers of foreign hats made it impossible to make out the faces. The waiting crowd surged forward. The first boat emptied, cast off again. He heard a child cry, "Papa!"

He elbowed his way among the shoulders and parasols, bellowing in that peremptory way of the Westerners. They stepped back automatically, not realizing until they yielded that the speaker was Chinese, and in seconds he was through to the front. The next boat slammed and tilted, passengers scrambling to keep their footing. Through the weaving bodies he spotted them huddled in the farthest seat.

He could have cried out, eased the anxiety in Hope's eyes and given Pearl's roving gaze a focus. He could, and perhaps should have done this, but instead he held still, savoring the sight of them. Pearl's red tam-o'-shanter was like a flame, her little mouth gulping the wind. Next to her Hope sat quietly, almost pensive beneath the familiar gray fedora, a single black and white feather tucked into its band. Though her cheeks, like Pearl's, were bright from the wind and cold, there was a hollowness to her eyes that seemed more haunted than weary. For a moment he was afraid, but then she lifted up, and he was reassured by the fullness these ten weeks had added to her figure. He remembered his own feelings upon arriving in America, knowing no one, unable to speak the language—that sensation of exile. This must be what his wife was feeling as she searched for the one connection that would make sense of her presence here. The thought aroused an almost unbearable tenderness within him.

He waved, and suddenly her eyes came alive. Pearl was up and wobbling, Hope bending to catch the child's arm as the tender bumped the dock. They fell forward. Paul reached and scooped his daughter onto his shoulder, cupped his free hand beneath Hope's elbow. She stepped up.

"Paul, I—Oh!" She stumbled against him. "Sea legs." She laughed, her lashes dark and lacy against those flushed cheeks.

He longed to sweep her into his arms, but instead gently pressed her away. He kissed only his daughter, but he kissed her greedily and so loudly that her shrieks of laughter drowned out his grateful murmur to them both. "You are safe."

Hope gave him a hurt and curious look. "Paul?"

He winked one eye as he had seen American boys do, a signal of secret intimacy, and returned Pearl to her mother while he hailed a porter for their hand baggage. The trunks would come the next day. The house he had rented was not far. Hope and Pearl should rest, meet the servants; tomorrow he would show them the city. He talked, resisting Hope's disappointment even as he hurried them up the crowded ramp and the city assaulted them. Beggar children pressed dirt-black fingers against the hems of their clothing. Trams hurtled past. The smells of European colognes and pig leather competed with the dead-fish stink and fumes from the Pootung mills across the river. Two bar girls in plum-colored satin fought over a grinning Portuguese sailor, and all the while, the coolies continued chanting their abuse.

At last they were seated in their carriage and off, though Paul wished now he had hired a closed cab. Hope had shrunk back from the onslaught of the wharf and sat staring at the foreign buildings along the Bund, above them the iron sky.

Pearl, though bewildered, was easily distracted with a gift from his pocket. While she busied herself with unwrapping, Paul brought Hope's hand into his lap and peeled down the top of her glove. Then he bent, as if to reach something by his feet, instead pressing his cheek to this un-covered skin. He shut his eyes at the familiar scent, like lilies.

"So it's against the law to touch here, too," she said when he came back up.

He pushed their joined hands down between their coats. "In public only."

"Always in public."

"Even if you are Chinese."

"But not if you were American, I'll bet."

"Ah, but if we both were British, yes."

And suddenly she was smiling, relaxing into him. Pearl gave a shout. Her gift was a bear with clapping cymbals, and they were three, nearly four, a family again finally, on their way home.

༄༄༄

The house stood at the intersection of two broad tree-lined boulevards, Avenue Foch and Avenue Pétain, in the French Concession. French in name, French in architecture, French in government and attitude, and thus more hospitable to Chinese revolutionaries than the British-dominated International Settlement, the Concession had been Paul's haven when he escaped Chang Chih-tung in the summer of 1900 and again after his ex-pulsion from Japan in 1903. Now he had borrowed a house here from a fellow revolutionary who was currently studying in Paris.

A tall plaster wall ran around the compound, broken only by a round red-lacquered gate which swung open at the carriage's approach. They did not drive in but alighted outside, while the driver, or *mafoo*, attended to their baggage and a small man with bristling black hair and a wrinkled grin appeared through the gate, bowing deeply. *"Huanying. Huanying."*

"This is our gatekeeper, Lin," Paul said.

But before Hope could respond, Mr. Lin raced off, shouting to the rest of the household, *"Laoyeh! Laoyeh!"* Master!

Hope helped Pearl over the wooden threshold, and they entered a sheltered entryway facing a massive stone tablet, which Hope identified from Paul's stories as a spirit wall. A carved dragon writhed from bottom to top, spitting flames against evil spirits. Evil, she recalled, traveled only in straight lines and could not lift its legs, hence the knee-high doorsill and spirit screen blocking the full width of the gate. Humans, wily creatures that they were, could step over and around and thus be safe from evil when inside their homes. If only it were so.

"Ready?" Paul asked.

"I suppose," Hope answered. He seemed oddly apprehensive, nodding for her and Pearl to follow him into the courtyard. It was only when she saw the waiting line of servants that she understood his hesitancy. There was doubtless a protocol to follow.

Paul strode to the head of the line and began introductions with a man whose most remarkable of several unnerving features was his height. He was inches taller than Paul, which meant he towered over Hope. His face was wedge-shaped—very broad and flat at the cheekbones, then tapering to a dimpled chin. He was thin, but had powerful shoulders, and his dark eyes glittered beneath wide bandy lids. Above his plain cotton jacket he wore a perfectly domed black bowler.

"Yen Ching-san is our majordomo," said Paul. "He will take care of you."

As Pearl hid her face in her mother's skirt, Hope nodded with what she hoped was appropriate respect, and delivered the words she had practiced with Li-li in preparation for this moment. *"Ni hao ma?"*

A vast and instantaneous grin took hold of Yen Ching-san's face. The large block head ducked, and ducked again. The wide lips drew back, showing a mouthful of yellow teeth, like old piano keys. The three other faces beamed on cue. Paul, too, was smiling expectantly.

"Tui pu ch'i," she apologized, and spread her hands to preclude saying more.

Paul cleared his throat as the servants smirked. "Yen is our Number One. He has been with me a long time. But Pearl, this is your new amah, Joy."

Pearl peered around Hope's leg. The nut-faced girl blinking back at her looked no older than fifteen. She wore a starched blue jacket and white Peter Pan collar, loose pants, and shocking pink satin slippers. Her mouth formed a tight rosette. Pearl stayed where she was, but smiled.

"Dahsoo," Paul continued, "is our cook, and Lu-mei his wife." The two faces split into grins. The woman's graying hair was held in a low, tight knot. The man's was shorn as if someone that morning had cut it with a knife. They wore identical black jackets and trousers.

"Taitai," they greeted her in unison. "Liang Taitai." Mistress Liang.

"We are pleased to meet all of you," Hope said finally in halting Mandarin. She didn't know what a Number One majordomo did. She had never had a cook or gatekeeper. What work was she expected to assign the cook's wife? And how on earth could they afford all this?

The answers would come, she told herself as Paul, in a series of quick, pointed commands, dismissed all the servants but Joy. If she labored over the questions raining down on her now she would be buried within seconds.

She looked up, feeling through her still rocking legs the slickness of the stones beneath her. The square courtyard was bounded on two sides by low Chinese houses with white plaster walls and curling black-tiled roofs. An aged ginkgo tree dominated one end of the court, a spreading maple the other. All this was perfectly quaint, as appropriately picturesque as a scene from a gazetteer. The main house, however, was confounding.

A pink Italianate villa. Two stories of meringue offset with white shutters on arching windows, a pitched terra-cotta roof and columned portico. Plaster cherubim under the cornices. Swan-shaped corbels. Polished brass trim.

"What do you think?" Paul's soft voice unaccountably alarmed her.

"I'm too amazed to think. This can't be real."

"It is not real. It is Shanghai. I tried to warn— Here, you are cold. Come inside."

Hope nodded, shivering. "Pearl?"

But while Hope was distracted, Joy had lured Pearl with a fistful of pretty stones. Already they were laughing together in what appeared to be a secret language, neither English nor Chinese, but nonsense noises as they gazed down into a low porcelain vat.

Feeling her mother's eyes on her, Pearl looked up. "Fiss, Mama!" She pointed delightedly to the sluggish oranges and blacks in the water. "Look, fiss!"

"We're going inside now, Pearl."

The small face crumpled.

"You like to stay with Joy, watch the fish?" Paul asked.

The little girl pursed her mouth. Then she looked at her mother and slipped her hand into her new amah's. "Fiss," she answered decisively.

Hope hesitated. It was chilly and damp, and Pearl had not left her side for two weeks. "The water is only for looking, Pearl. Don't get wet."

"*Come.*" Paul held the door open. "You were not so protective in Berkeley."

Hope chose not to answer. She was on Paul's territory now, and she could feel the rules subtly changing. She had to keep faith, that was all— "Oh, Paul!"

Just inside the foyer, which was a tall, white, rounded space defined by a curving staircase, he had erected a monkey pine. The anemic, drooping branches were strung with garlands of dried jasmine blossoms and dotted with gold and red paper stars. A tinsel crown perched precariously at the top.

"You see," said Paul. "Christmas comes even in China. But only by special permission." She followed his voice up the wall to a rotund gold Buddha sitting in an alcove with one hand raised, a beneficent smile.

"You know," she turned back to her husband's pleased eyes, "I'm dying to kiss you."

"Yes?" He pretended confusion. "I bring my wife ten thousand *li* to have her die for a kiss?"

Then he took her hand and led her upstairs, down a narrow hallway and through an open door, which he closed softly behind them.

彭彭彭

Supper, like the house, was a conscious collision of East and West. Steamed pork ribs, Chinese broccoli, baked potatoes, and butter from a tin—chopsticks and silverware.

Hope toyed with the stalk of broccoli between her chopsticks. "Have you been in touch with your mother?"

"I have been to Wuchang."

"You told them we were coming."

"My mother will come to Shanghai maybe after our baby is born."

"If it's a son."

A smile crept into his eyes. She blushed. As they had lain together that afternoon, he had examined her swollen belly with lavish, uninhibited care.

"I think he will be," he said.

But Hope was not so easily mollified. "Has she changed her mind, then?"

He held her gaze briefly. The smile faded, and he picked up his rice bowl. For several minutes the sounds of his eating filled the room. Dahsoo came in with a bowl of spicy soup, but Hope was no longer hungry.

She said, more out of obligation than interest, "The captain on the *Korea* said Dr. Sun is on his way here."

"Two days, he will arrive."

"On *Christmas?*"

"He is overdue."

A new, grimmer strain in his voice caught her attention. "What do you mean?"

He put down his half-gnawed sparerib. He picked up his chopsticks, then put them down, too, and wiped his hands. "If he had come last month maybe everything will be different. Instead, he thinks only about money, investors from America, Europeans. Meantime, China has no leader." His hands struck the table with accidental violence. "Senator from Hupei—wah!"

"Paul." Hope leaned forward, thoroughly contrite now, and alarmed. "I'm new here. I need you to explain."

So, in a voice fluctuating between despair and fury, he told what his life had been these two months. He told of shuttling between Shanghai, Wuhan, and Nanking, trying to mediate between warlords and bureaucrats, monarchists and revolutionaries. He told about the uncertainty and confusion that dominated the leaderless "provisional parliament," the endless wrangling over trivialities, the evasion of critical decisions. The senators could not even agree on a capital for the new government!

Too many years in the West had deluded Paul into believing that knowledge and determination could catapult his country from revolution to instant democracy. He returned home to find instead that the Manchus had been toppled by bandits with the revolution footing the bill. Most of the gentry and scholarly literati who were Paul's peers had no interest in democracy at all but clung to the fantasy that China could be united under a new Han Chinese Emperor who would honor their traditional claims to power and wealth. Meanwhile, the local warlords whose peasant soldiers had actually carried out the rebellion were intent on dividing the nation among themselves into personal fiefdoms. Paul's country was no more receptive to true revolution than his mother was to her foreign daughter-in-law.

They stared at each other for several minutes without speaking. In the harsh yellow light of the electric candelabra, Paul appeared to Hope exhausted—drawn and pale and frightened, disillusioned and out of place. She might have been looking into a mirror.

჻჻჻

3

The next day, he dutifully toured them around Shanghai, and Hope began the long, ambivalent process of adopting a new hometown. Setting aside for the moment Paul's grim prognosis for the new Republic—and forbidding herself to give another thought to his pigheaded mother—she decided that Shanghai at least lived up to its reputation as a city of paradox. There were streetcars with bells that a blind man would swear sounded just like San Francisco's, gleaming Packards with canopy tops, victorias drawn by ponies that looked almost like horses, if smaller, shaggier, heavier-hoofed. There were the facades of great imposing banks, office buildings, department stores with flashing electric billboards, shop windows festooned with Christmas evergreen and tinsel, signs worded boldly in guidebook English . . . SINGER MANUFACTURING COMPANY: *Needles, Patterns, Oil, and Parts.* RUSSO-CHINESE BANK. INTERNATIONAL BICYCLE COMPANY: *Bicycles, Typewriters, Sporting Guns.* WALTER DUNN: *Wine Merchant, Bookseller, Generalist.* MAITLAND & CO., PUBLIC AUCTIONS. DENNISTON & SULLIVAN: *Kodak Film, Development, Cameras.*

But the streets were also filled with hooded rickshaws, wheelbarrows heaped high with cargo and passengers, sedan chairs swathed in silk—all pulled by ragged, starve-faced men. Every block had its beggars and sidewalk vendors, peasants trotting with impossible loads strung from shoulder poles. And while most signs along the wide avenues were painted in roman letters, the vertical banners that festooned the side streets bore exclusively Chinese characters.

As contradictory as Shanghai's sights were its smells, which seemed to Hope to mingle the highest and lowest elements of humanity. Urine from the open latrines, incense from the open temples, rotting garbage from the open sewers, fumes of ammonia and Jeyes' Liquid from the open windows of European-style villas and apartment blocks. All of this swathed in the briny mist that welled up off the open Whangpoo. "If the spirit is willing," Hope found herself muttering as their carriage skidded on the icy cobbles. It was a favored phrase of Mother Wayland's in times of distress—as when young Frank sliced the last joint off his finger while chopping wood or Margaret was knocked unconscious by a falling tree and didn't wake up for a week. Thinking about her foster family right now hurt, but at least she had the consolation of having said goodbye to them. Her father—well, he'd always told her, as a child, *he* would never say goodbye, because he would never really leave her . . .

"This is the Chinese City," Paul said.

She looked up, startled.

"You must understand, Hope. Shanghai is not China. It is taken from China as a spoil of the Opium War. Only seventy years ago Britain brings her gunboats, the coward Manchus bow and quiver, and now here is this Western city, ruled by foreign powers according to foreign law. Great center of foreign commerce and opium trade, where Chinese people are the conquered natives. In Shanghai, Chinese have their Chinatown just as in San Francisco."

He stopped the carriage and pointed toward a high crenellated wall pierced by an open gate and surrounded by a moat filled with reeking, trash-strewn mud. The street life visible through the gate made Hope think of a squeezed accordion. Dark, slicing corners teemed with buyers, sellers, deal-makers shouting and raising fists. Men wore felt hats pulled down to their eyes—hats filled, Paul told her, with queues that they refused to cut for fear the Manchus would rise again. Above the medieval alleys jutted poles dangling trousers, vests, long streaming white bandages.

Made stupid by the collision of images and smells, and Paul's cynical tone, she asked, "Why so many bandages?"

"Binding cloths. Women's feet."

She shuddered. "I thought that was going to be outlawed under the new Republic."

He pointed grimly at an ornate sedan chair being trumpeted through the pinched streets. Accompanying musicians banged gongs and cymbals, while the bearers leapt side to side. Hope thought the chair's occupant must be green with seasick, especially as the heavy red enclosure permitted no view out.

"Chinese wedding," Paul said. "This, too, was to be outlawed."

ᏸᏸᏸ

On Christmas morning beneath the crippled monkey pine, he showered them with gifts. For Pearl, a set of polished black wooden peaches, the largest as fat as a cantaloupe clicking open to reveal another and another and another inside, the smallest the size of a pea. And a baby doll with porcelain head and lace cap and gown and eyes that rolled open and shut—a deep oceanic blue. "Like Mama's," Paul said, meeting Hope's gaze. There was a jade horse, a small satin jacket embroidered in the design of a phoenix. And finally, wheeled in with a flourish by Joy, a red-enameled tricycle tied with a chrysanthemum bow.

Pearl squealed and flung her arms around her father's neck. He lifted her high and dropped her down onto the tricycle's seat. Her round legs did not quite reach the pedals, and she didn't understand the principles of propulsion, so had to be pushed at first, but she inched forward and found her footing and soon was off down the parlor with a whoop of freedom that made Hope want to cover her eyes. Instead she and Joy flew through the room gathering all the vases, sculptures, and breakable *objets*—which was to say virtually everything in the room—and placing them out of harm's way.

"Pearl, the tricycle is for outside, please!"

But Paul said, "Let her enjoy her first Christmas in China. I want her to remember this day." He turned. "And you, Hope." He laid in her palm a cerise silk pouch that felt like a heavy cloud.

She hesitated. Paul had always given her Christmas presents. In their five years together he had given her a blue fountain pen, a tortoiseshell comb, a book of poems by Emily Dickinson, and a genuine Dunlap fedora. She, in turn, had given him sweaters and mufflers she'd knitted, a porcelain jar for his writing brushes, a pair of genuine Australian kangaroo bluchers, and the Genthe photographs. This year she had brought him a blanket, butterscotch color, in soft but durable Scottish shetland wool. By mutual understanding, their gifts had always been sensible, secular, economical. She could tell at a glance that this one broke form.

Clucking his impatience, he took the pouch back and emptied it unceremoniously into her hand. The blue stones shimmered like drops of water.

"Paul! What have you done!"

"You do not like?"

"Of course, it's exquisite, but it's too much! What will I do—"

Pearl came barreling over, colliding with Hope's slippered feet and jumping for a peek at the necklace. She held it up. "Ooh, flowers, Mama. Bootiful flowers and pearl, like me! Ooh la la!"

They both stared at their daughter. "Ooh la la?" Paul repeated.

"Joy taught me. Ooh la la!"

The amah's face turned as red as the pouch. "I hear the French girls say."

They looked at each other then, a moment of utter, delicious disbelief, before laughter swept them away. It burst the tension that had been pulling against them for the past two days, and they swooped their daughter up between them, sounding a singularly undignified and impromptu chorus. "Ooh la la!" The other servants came running. Yen appeared, his shaved head hatless, with his usual consternation. Hope took one look at him. "Ooh la la!" Renewed gales overtook them. Pearl pumped her arm and escalated the cry, the chrysanthemum ribbon a crown in her hair. "Ooh la la! Ooh la la!"

Paul waved his hand ineffectually at the servants, who stared as if he were mad. He was chortling, crying, clutching his foreign wife and child. Yen didn't recognize him. Paul didn't recognize himself. The servants fled. Pearl went back to play, and gradually the spell subsided, but now he felt a new wave of emotion.

Hope was holding up the necklace, smiling and shaking her head. "How can we afford this? And where on earth would I wear it?" He led her to the foyer looking glass before fastening the strand around her throat. The aquamarines and tiny seed pearls were even more beautiful against her skin than he had expected.

"I tell you. Everything is different here, Hsin-hsin. You are my American princess. You will wear tomorrow night."

She eyed him suspiciously in the mirror. "What is tomorrow night?"

"Governor's ball. To welcome Dr. Sun."

"A *ball?* Paul, you must be joking."

But he had dropped down and was searching behind the spindly tree for one last gift.

"Really, I—"

He stood up holding a large oblong box covered in blue sateen. *A La Parisienne* was stamped in gold filigree on top. She groaned. "What are you thinking? I've never been to a ball in my life, and I'm five months pregnant! I thought you Chinese kept your women out of sight."

He grinned at her teasing. "No, no. I want all Shanghai to know my wife."

He pressed the box on her until finally she relented, lifting from the tissue the first ball gown Paul had ever purchased, the first she had owned. As the Spanish shopgirl had described it, the dress was midnight blue silk velvet with cap sleeves, a dipping neckline that would expose enough skin to show off the necklace but not as much as Europeans considered vogue, and an Empire waistline that would help to disguise his wife's *"embarazo."* The fabric had felt as supple as flesh when he touched it in the store. Now his eyes did not leave Hope's. "Good?"

"Tomorrow." She pursed her lips doubtfully, holding the dress up to the glass. "You don't give a girl much time, do you?"

ᏸᏸᏸ

4

By six o'clock the following evening Hope was bathed and dressed and nervous as a fish on a line. Sun Yat-sen's homecoming, with the requisite meetings, receptions, and banquets, had kept Paul out all the previous evening and today since early morning. Now, as the hours passed and her husband still failed to return, she began to fantasize that the ball had been called off and she would not have to go through this public exposure after all. But just as Hope was settling down to read Pearl her bedtime story, Paul stormed past the nursery. "It's all a sham," he said when she caught up with him in their bedroom. "Sun has caved in. Yüan Shih-k'ai has played the mirror game."

"You mean Sun won't take the presidency?"

"Oh, he takes it—and then he will give it away."

She trailed him into the bathroom, watched the knobs whirl, drops fly. Stripped to the waist he attacked his exposed flesh with a steaming white cloth that left patches of hard red burn. He grimaced at the scent of her lavender soap. He delivered a muffled yell into the cloth when he held it over his face, then balled the cloth and hurled it into the tub so hard the copper reverberated like a bell. Hope stood out of the way as he strode back into the bedroom and attacked his evening suit. She expected him to calm down at some point, but he was trembling so he could not deal with his tie. She took it into her own hands and began folding the bow. "Is this going to be the tenor of the whole evening?"

"This evening is a farce."

"Then why are we putting on these silly costumes? Why pretend to honor Sun Yat-sen if you don't believe in what he's doing—"

He had reared his head back, squeezing his eyes so tightly his whole face seemed to fold over. At first she thought she was choking him, and released the bow. Then, astonished, she realized he was crying. "Paul!"

But he shook his head so violently she was forced to back away.

"Go," he said. "Wait downstairs."

"But we don't have to—" He silenced her not with thunder or rage but by hiding his face in his hands.

An hour later their hired carriage drew up before a massive gothic establishment, whether consulate or private estate was unspecified, but it had all the trappings of arrogant European wealth—carriage gates leading from Bubbling Well Road to a long macadamed drive, vast lawns and formal gardens, a ponderous porte cochere attached to four stories of stone intercut with small leaded windows. All this wavering in gaslight.

"I feel like Cinderella," whispered Hope as they stepped down.

Paul, who had sat rigid and speechless during the twenty-minute ride, attempted a smile. "Do not dance with the prince."

She met his eyes gratefully. "I can't dance any more than you can."

"Good."

Whatever he was suffering, she thought as he helped her from the carriage, he had never looked stronger or more handsome than he did tonight. His top hat was set at a rakish angle, and though the borrowed evening jacket pulled a little too tightly through the shoulders, this forced him to stand straight and tall. She was tempted to remove those spectacles—he didn't really need them except for reading, and he looked so much more elegant without them—but eyeglasses were perceived among the Chinese as a mark of education and distinction, and Paul insisted on wearing his for all public appearances. Besides, the lenses helped to screen the anger and frustration still burning behind them. By the time she thought to ask, "What prince?" his expression had already hardened again.

"You will see soon enough," he said.

Before she could press him further a white-jacketed servant had ushered them into the massive oak vestibule and another stepped forward to take Hope's cloak, yet another to direct them toward the ballroom, and suddenly her concern for Paul's grim mood was overtaken by the pageantry of their surroundings. It *was* like a scene from a fairy tale. Red carpet flowing down a long marble staircase. Chandelier dripping cut glass tears, which in turn scattered rainbow diamonds across the cream-colored walls. Polished brass rails and potted palms and more mute, white-gloved attendants lined the upstairs foyer, which otherwise was empty, as most guests were already in the ballroom. Hope walked by Paul's side without touching him or speaking. He did not offer his arm.

As they approached the ballroom, a tide of light and music poured toward them, but before they could enter they were accosted by a dwarf with a pale mustachioed face pinched between top hat and frock coat. "Liang!" he shrilled. "So they let you back in."

"Homer Lea, I present my wife, Hope."

"Enchanted, madame." The hunchback, for she now realized he was not actually a dwarf, grabbed her hand and very nearly rubbed it against his sickly lips. She pulled back, reflexively, but was then ashamed of her repulsion. She relaxed her arm, even nudged forward, but he shrugged as if to say, it happens all the time.

"Could I borrow you for a few, Liang?"

"I—" Paul's dark eyes lowered apologetically to Hope's.

Lea stroked his sateen lapel with imperious patience. "Sun wants to make sure we're all on the same battle plan."

"I'll wait over there." She nodded past the sea of heads to a windowed alcove in the corner.

"I return soon," Paul promised.

But as he vanished behind the wall of strangers, she realized this was the first time she had been out alone since leaving San Francisco. On the trip, she'd had Pearl. Then Paul had met them, and in the last few days, if no one else, there had been the servants. She smiled, scolding herself. What were Joy and Yen and the others if not total strangers become familiar? She must find someone here to talk to, that was all. Only, where to begin? The diversity of this gathering was as daunting as it was impressive. There were bright kimonos, dark scholar's robes, both Victorian and décolleté ball gowns, full tuxedos, military men dressed in the uniforms of the Kaiser, the Tsar, American and British Marines. The fluid tones of French and Mandarin and the rapid fire of Japanese syllables collided with the heavy clip of Queen's English and the guttural pounding of Russian and German. Meanwhile, the orchestra's merry waltz promised to weave them all peaceably together. The music tweaked Hope with the memory of Frank Pearson trying to teach her to dance. They'd been standing on the verandah kissing good night when Eleanor started up the Graphophone inside. Frank had insisted and she protested, and finally he'd instructed her to stand on his toes and she'd clung to his neck and tried to follow, instead managing to trip him. "That's the trouble with you damn suffragists," he'd said in exasperation, "you always want to lead."

A passing waiter offered her champagne, and she gratefully took a glass. How often since marrying Paul had she told herself what a disaster life with Frank would have been?

"Don't you love it! Here we are, their worst nightmare being trotted out like mascots."

A kid-gloved hand descended on Hope's wrist and she realized with a start that the voice was addressing her. She looked up into a pair of laughing green eyes set into a face of handsome angles. They competed for attention with opulent breasts and an emerald necklace that made Hope's aquamarines and pearls look like trinkets.

"No need to look so shocked." The woman released Hope and adjusted her auburn curls with one hand while the other fingered the plunging neckline of her sea green shantung gown. "It's all in the architecture. French woman over on Nanking Road works wonders. I'm a good bit smaller than you, as I recall."

Hope was squeezing her glass so hard that it cracked. "Sarah Lim," she breathed. "I don't believe it."

"Chou, now." Sarah handed Hope a napkin to blot the wine from her gloves and deposited the oozing champagne flute in a nearby spittoon.

"What are you doing here! And where— What did you say?"

Sarah laughed. "Chou. Yes, dear, I've moved on. Tsing-lee, otherwise known as Eugene. He's a banker, up to his sweet ears in the change from Manchu taels to Republican dollars. Paul knows him, I think, has courted him for Sun Yat-sen over the years, but Gene's thrown his hat in now with the prince."

Hope was lost. "What prince?"

"Yüan Shih-k'ai. There, that fat man. And the broad-shouldered fellow with the big chin is Eugene." She nodded toward a cluster of bowing Orientals on the other side of the ballroom. The man she'd described as Eugene was turned sideways to Hope, but even from this distance, she could see the power and confidence in his bearing. He talked with his hands, and snapped his head back for emphasis. His animation contrasted with Yüan

Shih-k'ai, who posed beside him in full military regalia, one hand planted on his gold sword and the other in Napoleonic fashion across his ample chest.

"Why does everyone call him that?"

"Because he tried to usurp the prince's position in the old Manchu court, and now some say he aims to crown himself Emperor of the Republic."

Paul hardly need worry about her dancing with *him*, thought Hope, but she could understand her husband's concern at this cold-eyed martinet presiding over China.

"All right." She pointed Sarah to a pair of chairs by the wall. "Tell me what has happened to bring you here."

"What has happened to *me?*" Sarah lifted one eyebrow as if Hope had told a naughty joke. "No more than's happened to you by the look of it. When's your baby due?"

"April."

"Is it your first?"

Hope flinched "Second." She paused. "We have a daughter, Pearl. She's three."

"Well, you'll need some help with her, then, at the—"

Hope cut her off. "How long have you been here, Sarah?"

"Ah, you sense a good juicy story, don't you?" Sarah stretched her arms in their long white gloves. Something in the motion reminded Hope of swan's necks, and for the first time in years she thought of Kathe and Ong. The whole wedding journey, in fact, flooded back over her, but Sarah would not feed her nostalgia. "It is and it isn't," she continued. "Donald brought me back nearly two years ago."

"You said you'd never come."

"I said a lot of things."

"The baby?"

"Oh, that was true enough. He's a big boy now. Gerald. Poor thing, he's been through the wringer, but he's a toughie. Five years going on sixteen, and dark as a Chinaman in spite of my coloring—I suppose I never told you his father was a sailor, a South American with some sort of native blood. Enough to pass around here for Eurasian anyway. Eugene's decent to the boy."

"But Donald . . ."

"Well, yes, Donald. He died."

"Sarah, I'm sorry."

"I'm not. Not in the way you mean. He was a good egg to me and Gerry. That's what I'm doing here, after all. For everything they say about 'em, Chinese men have done all right by me—better'n any white man I ever crossed paths with. But they've more than their share of weaknesses, too, and don't let 'em tell you they don't. Funny, remember all that ruckus back in Wyoming about the Chinese wives?"

"What do you mean?"

"Well, Ong had one, too, you know. It wasn't only Donald. But such are the tricks fate plays on the foolish. Though another woman in my place might call it luck."

"I don't understand."

"Little I knew, Don wasn't the *marrying* kind at all."

"He wasn't . . ." The band struck up a martial waltz, and a slow spin of dancers took the floor.

"At first I thought it was because I was preggers. Then because of the birth. Then, when I insisted on nursing Gerry myself, I pretended this, too, put him off. I went nearly two years blaming Chinese superstition before I finally noticed how Don favored certain of his male friends. Can't begin to tell you how stupid I felt then!"

A sudden revulsion took hold of Hope as she recalled Donald's insistence on taking one of the rooms in Evanston for him and Sarah alone, the strangeness of Sarah's behavior throughout that whole trip. She wasn't sure she could stand to hear the rest of the story.

"How did you end up *here*—and with him?" She pointed across to the banker.

"Ah, I remember now. Squeamish over the details. I knew that about you the very first day. Remember how you fell to pieces when poor Kathe fell in among those coolies? I warned you then, and I'll warn you now. You're going to have to buck up even more if you expect to get by in this country. My business is nothing compared to what you'll hear—what you'll see going on before your very eyes in China."

"But what *is* this business?"

Sarah smiled. "When I confronted Donald about his—ahh—preferences, he was really quite gracious. I'd given him a son, which was all his family cared about. Number One Wife had failed to produce, for obvious reasons, and even a 'Eurasian' grandson was better than none at all. Donald offered to keep Gerry, let me go off as a so-called free woman, but I pointed out that—even if I'd consider leaving my boy—being the castoff of a Chinaman was no step up from being an unwed mum. So we came to an understanding. He'd support us, and we'd live together, but separately, you see. Only Donald's plan to become an American lawyer wasn't working. Then Standard Oil offered him a position as a clerk here in their Shanghai office. It was one of those arrangements people make to get by."

Hope shook her head. "Seems to me, you make more than your share, Sarah."

"I won't disagree with that, but you must admit it keeps life interesting."

"Does it?" To Hope's mind, however interesting Sarah's life might be, certain essential ingredients were missing.

"To shorten a much longer story," said Sarah, "I would have stayed with Donald and gone on with the pretense of being mother to his child—it wasn't all bad for Gerald, really. But shortly after we arrived here, Donald got sick. Tuberculosis. And then his family descended, and I couldn't bear it, Hope, the way they swarmed over us and all but plucked my little boy right out of my hands. I could see what would happen after Donald died. He could, too. Eugene was a friend. I liked him well enough. And he was rich and powerful in that Chinese way that entitles him to collect certain types of women as trophies. I was his first white trophy, you might say."

"Oh, Sarah!" Hope covered her mouth in disgust.

"The position comes with a good number of privileges, my dear. Not the least of which was permission for me to keep Gerry. Eugene's given us our own house in Frenchtown."

"I can't—" Hope stood, suddenly dizzy. The story. Sarah's cool, disengaged smile. The implied warning underneath it all. "I have to find Paul."

Sarah shrugged her freckled shoulders. "You and I, my dear, have the distinction of being the only two Americans married to Chinamen in all the Settlements. I'm not as bad as you think, and you may not be as good as you think after this place is through with you. Don't be too quick to pass judgment."

But Hope was already among the waltzing couples, pushing her way as if through tall grass. Paul had been right about Sarah all those years ago: she did somehow bring the worst on herself. But had he also known, as Sarah suggested he must, that she had preceded Hope in coming to Shanghai? If so, he should have known she would be here tonight. There he was, finally, emerging from a door at the opposite end of the room.

Paul frowned at her breathlessness.

"Sarah's here! Sarah Lim—Chou." Hope motioned with her eyes to the slim, redheaded figure still standing alone where she had left her. "Why didn't you prepare me?"

"Prepare you." He followed her glance. "Yes . . ." But his voice trailed off. The throb of bodies and music was louder now, and he turned abruptly, leading her through a pair of French doors to an empty balcony above the darkened garden.

Though the night air was biting and damp, Hope breathed it with relief after the crush of perfumed skin and clothing—Sarah's hideous tale. She hugged herself. Paul was leaning away, turning his top hat between his hands and looking out into the shadows. From below rose the urgent whispers, in French but unmistakable, of a man and woman plotting an assignation.

"I must go to Nanking tomorrow," Paul said, loud enough to disperse the whisperers.

"Nanking!"

"With Homer Lea and Dr. Sun. It is decided. Inauguration will take place there next week."

"Nanking." Hope tried to grasp what Paul was telling her, but the geography of China was still as foreign to her as its politics. She had only a vague sense of this inland city as a spot on the map connected to Shanghai by an indeterminate mileage of rail and river. The guidebooks identified Nanking as the capital of the last Han Chinese dynasties and of the Taiping rebels. Paul had told her the provisional parliament had been meeting there, but she had given this little weight, as he'd also told her the site for the Republic's new capital was undecided. And if he'd settled them in Shanghai, surely he believed the government must seat itself here. Why, this ball was an indication—

"I will return soon as possible," he said.

She removed her wine-damp gloves and stood wringing them for something to do with her hands. When she spoke, her voice was too bright. "Couldn't we go with you?"

He turned toward her. "You do not know what you are asking."

"But—"

"There is no foreign concession in Nanking."

"That doesn't matter! We came here to be together."

"Hope. There are no Western doctors. No hospital. No cow's milk. No foreign court of law." His narrow chest lifted and fell. Behind those round glass spectacles, he was again refusing to look at her.

She felt her trained inclination to appease, submerge, and accept now buckling under the more instinctual yearning for reassurance, yet the words that flew out of her were barbed with sarcasm. "What right do I have to complain, after all. I'm only your wife!"

He gave her an equally sharp, quick glance, then rolled his shoulders back, straightening his spine. After a moment he set his hat square on top of his head. "Dr. Sun always speaks of you with much respect. You must greet him. Then we go home."

"That's all you have to say?"

"Hope." Paul's voice strained against itself. He removed his glasses and stood briefly staring down at them in his hands, then sought her with his naked eyes. He said gently, "That is all I can say."

֍֍֍

5

January 8, 1912
Dear Mary Jane,
Still no answer from Dad to my bombshell. The slowness of

the mails across are a horror to one so far from home, and there's a part of me that warns, wait and find out how large a wound I have gouged before rubbing salt in it. This is but one reason I am writing you my first report from China instead of directing it to him. Coward that I am.

There is, predictably, good news and bad. The good is that this is a fascinating place, and Paul has planted us in the lap of luxury. You thought perhaps we would be living in a pagoda à la Chinatown? Or one of Lafcadio Hearn's courtyard palaces? Not with Paul in charge. For the next year we will be residing in what must surely be Shanghai's only pink Italian villa! It belongs to a friend of Paul's who was smitten by Italy. This young Mr. Huei had an architect make some renderings and bought up half the antiquities in Florence, then came home and built this place as a showcase for his treasures. Like many wealthy Chinese, Mr. Huei's father had invested in property here in the French Concession because the taxes, while higher than those paid by whites, are stable and low when compared to fees levied by the Manchus outside the Concessions. Also, no matter how much the Chinese rail about "foreign imperialism" and "gunboat diplomacy," those with large enough purses have invested heavily in the international settlements as a hedge against times of unrest, when the curse of foreign domain, or "extrality" (extraterritoriality), magically transforms into sanctuary.

This is what I mean about good and bad! Everything is all mixed up here, more than ever in the States. Servants are another example. Yes, we have five full time, plus a second amah, no doubt, when the baby arrives and a rickshaw puller and *mafoo*—carriage driver—whom we share with the neighbors. They all speak colonial pidgin, a jumble of British and Portuguese that is even more offensive to the ear than the talkee-talkee hurled at Chinese journeymen back home. They call me Missy and Paul Master, and promise to do everything "chop chop." Paul says pidgin is the worst sort of compromise between the races—the result when neither side is willing to do the work to really understand the other. What he means, of course, is that the foreigners have not made the effort to learn Chinese. Since most servants are illiterate in their own language, pidgin represents a heroic effort on their part. No, Paul's absolutely right, and I've made it my first order of business to get at least a functional handle on Shanghainese (a totally different lingo from Mandarin!) so that we can avoid this charade.

Pearl, meanwhile, is in hog heaven. So happy here that I think she must possess some core biological component that responds to this continent as her proper home. I have taken her out for an excursion every day since we arrived, and while I am at times overcome by the sense of confluence that pervades this city, she is enthralled by it.

You want particulars, I know. It's so overwhelming though, Mary Jane. Perhaps best to describe as if I were a camera some of what we saw on our outing yesterday. In the same frame, I was looking out from our carriage and saw an emaciated man, muscles standing out from his bare neck and chest and legs in cords as he dragged a towering load of scavenged paper by means of a cloth strap around his forehead *and* another man dressed in blue silk brocade with a coral-buttoned scholar's cap and a gold cigarette holder casually dangling from his lips as he rode *piggy-backed* on the shoulders of a young, perspiring serving girl. There is the Bund, the riverfront avenue with its facades of imposing European colonnades and parades of carriages and lorries and couples dressed in fine English tweeds, while there in the lower right-hand corner of the frame—can you picture?—squats a young mother in rags clutching the body of her limp boy-child, a baby daughter lying silent as a stone beside her, and the woman rocks, howling like an animal, and not a single head on the promenade turns in her direction.

Pearl says, "Why's that lady crying, Mama?" When I tell my daughter that the lady and her children are very poor and sick (I do not tell her that I suspect the boy is already dead), she says, "We can bring them to our house." And I am confronted by the fact that I host the same monster within myself that grins with evil pleasure from the fronts of these British banks and mercantile houses, that glints in the corners of all those blue and green eyes so carefully turned away from the doomed woman and her children. That monster is content to wait and watch, to taste the pleasures of this exotic realm, to convert the foreign into the familiar, to tame that which is primitive or rude, but it will send up shields, post guards at the gates if China's deeper terrors veer too close.

"Because we're not doctors," I said to my daughter, "and because what they have may be catching."

"But what will happen to them?" she insisted.

"Someone will come," I told her. "Someone will help."

"Like Miss Cameron back home?"

"Yes."

"Miss Cameron will know." She nodded with certainty, then, "Look!" And she was up out of her seat pointing at a street corner juggler twirling five plates on the tips of chopsticks while hopping on six-foot stilts—the woman with the dying child no more than a lingering question.

I am not proud of my reply to Pearl's question, but I find this place forces all notions of self-protection to a new level. You see, we are alone, Pearl and I with our houseful of servants. This is the rest of the bad news. Paul's government is to be seated in Nanking, former capital of the Ming Dynasty (the last rulers who were not "barbarian invaders"). And because Nanking is one of the few major cities that has no international concession, Paul feels it would be unsafe for us to move there with him. He has promised to return whenever he has a break in his duties. It is just a day's journey. But it is not what I had expected, and I am so hopelessly unprepared for all of this, Mary Jane!

Please do not say I told you so. The fact is, I do not want to return, and I would not have chosen differently. Seeing Paul for a few days a month is better than not knowing if we would ever meet again. And once I recover the liberty of my own body, my outlook surely will change. But my confinement looms like a door that is about to spring shut . . . How I miss you!

Please write to us, dear heart.

The letter she had been dreading arrived in the following week's mail.

Dr. Herbert Newfield
Naturopathic Physician, Nervous and Chronic Diseases
Vibration, Electricity, and Herbs, Mineral Baths
1311 South Hill Street
Los Angeles, Cal.
Broadway 3777; Home 24053   December 16, 1911
Dear Dolly,

I received your letter this morning and I think a spanking would do you good. Last I heard you were sick in bed in Frisco and I wrote there and received no reply. I did not know whether you were dead or what—you can write fast enough when you want assistance but not otherwise. I hightailed it up, found your house empty, Thomas and Li-li off who-knew-where, was about to get on to the police and likely would have lit out after you myself if I'd known what you were up to. Might even now if Mary Jane hadn't got her thumbs into me. That woman could make a lion purr if she had a mind to. You've still got the goddamnedest way of saying goodbye I ever did hear of, though, daughter.

Mary Jane said you were ashamed, and I won't deny there's reason, making a decision like this without a word to those who love you. But to cross the Pacific Ocean not even bothering to tell me! You're right, girl, you're on a great adventure, bigger'n any of mine, but you're my only child, and you might have given me something as Pearl's granddad. I don't blame Paul. I don't even blame you for the going . . . Well, you're gone now, nothing for it. Just see you keep yourself and that family of yours safe and come back to us someday soon—sooner if Paul's grand plans don't come together for the good. Anyhow, you can use this fiver on a late Christmas present for Pearl.

You know you have my love if not my endorsement of your tactics. Better write and tell me how it is.

Always,
your Dad

How it is. Hope dragged the coarse white stationery across the back of her hand. How it is to come halfway around the world to be with a husband who is not here. How it is to live in someone else's home which, at that, belongs on yet another continent. How it is to live with servants and a bodyguard who look at you like some strange Arctic specimen, who never ever meet your eyes, who steal your daughter's heart and talk about you behind your back but in a language and at such speed that you cannot guess whether they speak with malice or mere ridicule.

How it is to be summoned to tea, as she and Pearl were last week, by the only "society" for which they might conceivably qualify. Renata Hwang, wife of an immensely wealthy Chinese usurer, had spied Hope with Sarah at the Republican ball and had desired to satisfy her curiosity about this new arrival. Hope believed that, since Renata, too, had a Chinese husband, they would find much in common, so she anticipated the visit with some excitement. As it turned out, Renata was a young, radiantly lovely, and thoroughly spoiled Parisienne whose daughter, only a month or two older than Pearl, appeared in a swirl of pink organdy. Pearl was dazzled and unaware of the comparative plainness of her own smocked pinafore. The two girls played in the Hwang nursery while Renata, who did virtually all the talking, informed Hope about the social hierarchies that dominated Shanghai society—the ladies clubs and Cercle Sportif, the racecourse, symphony, and rituals of tea at the Cathay and dancing at the Palace. "If you have enough *richesse*," she said, "perhaps you may be admitted. And if you have some *courage ici*," she tapped the emerald brooch fixed to her bosom, "then you may enjoy. But for all that, you and I, *cherie*, we shall never be accepted."

There was one British wife, she said, flicking her thin white hands like handkerchiefs, who was so tormented within the International Settlement for having "married Chinese" that she left her husband and *two children*, taking nothing, and went in secret to the British consulate where she begged the ambassador for repatriation. Which he granted without argument. Found a home-bound English couple to escort her and booked passage within a week. Renata concluded this story by kissing the large diamond on her left hand with a reverence that both appalled and unnerved the silent Hope. The visit was abruptly terminated when Pearl came running into the room in tears because Renata's daughter had told her she looked like a

Chapei half-breed. Pearl didn't fully understand what that meant, but Hope did. Chapei was the neighborhood for poor and working-class whites—mostly Portuguese or Russians—who married Chinese.

How it is—now thinking of the previous day's outing—to sit pinching one's skirts for three hours in the outer room of a medical office where the secretary keeps telling you, "The Doctor has not yet returned from luncheon," in spite of the fact that you have a confirmed appointment and other patients are admitted with the regularity of a metronome. And then, when you finally are shown in, the doctor is not the doctor at all but his half-baked son with gin on his breath and jagged ice in his eyes who asks, "So the father's a Chink, eh?" and kicks at your skirt with the steel-tipped toe of a boot still muddy from his morning at the racetrack.

Should she tell her father how it is to take your little girl to play in the park and hear women who would not be hired as scullery maids back in Yorkshire instruct their fat, pop-eyed preciouses not to play with your daughter because she's a mongrel. Or how the men lean back on the polished brass railings outside their clubs and leer at you as you pass, saying to each other but loudly enough for you to hear, "They take it in their mouth, you know," or "The concubines give 'em lessons, else they can't stay in the game, and sometimes there's three or four in the bed." Or, simply, "Slut."

ᛒᛒᛒ

Nanking
February 15, 1912
My Hope,

It is done. Three days ago the child Emperor abdicated his throne. Next day Sun submit his resignation. Today, like sheep, we bow and elect Yüan Shih-k'ai provisional President. This breaks my heart, to see Dr. Sun walk away from this moment. He walks erect but I can see that, inside, he trembles with anger and disappointment. He will say that Yüan favors him with this new post, Director of National Railroads, but he fools no one. Even Homer Lea has given up and returned to America. Yesterday I say to Dr. Sun, "I, too, will step down from my office to show support for you." But Dr. Sun says no, I must contain my feelings, work within this government for sake of Republic.

Do you remember that first day I come to you, our first lesson, when you take that moth out the window, and say, there is peaceful revolution? I think of this time every day now. I remember your eyes, so full of certainty, as if you have power to cast the future. It is I who disbelieved your idea of peaceful revolution. Then last October comes, and China rise up, Manchu armies fall. The boy Emperor now sits, like your moth, alive and well but stripped of his rule. And your powers are proven. Only Western nations do not share your respect for justice and honor. They have prospered by trading with Manchu tyrants and fear true democracy in China. So they circle their gunboats and whisper their bribes, knowing Yüan will do their bidding.

In this historic time, I feel not excitement and pride, but deep and terrible sadness. So many years I have dreamed of China's Republic, and now I feel that we are but children playing at government, imitating process we do not understand. For this disappointment I leave you and Pearl so many weeks, but there is no other way.

We must now revise the constitution and decide some other matters. Yüan wants to move capital to Peking, where he can remain living in his palaces like a Manchu. Dr. Sun is opposed, but I suspect that Yüan will prevail. If yes, this can be better for us than Nanking, as Peking is treaty city with foreign legation, perhaps we can live together there. For now I do not know how long until I can return to Shanghai, but I have send to Yen's care $200. These should pay your needs for this time.

My Hope, I cannot say what is in my heart as I know you would wish. When we are together, there is no need. Only this distance gives words importance. I try to remember this day when you come to me across the ocean. I have enclosed my poor effort and hope that you will understand.

My love and most tender kisses for you and our daughter,
Your husband Paul

Enclosed with the letter was a poem, written in brush-worked English on a slip of pearlescent rice paper.

Across Ten Thousand Li

The door to my humble home swings open,
Winter's frost melts to summer rain.
The morning boat brings you back to me
On a river that shines like silver mirror
Reunited at last.

Hope read this letter and poem in their entirety three times. Then she folded them into her pocket and, dry-eyed, called Pearl for her lessons. She spent the next hour teaching her daughter to add and subtract using the hard polished pits of lychee fruit as counters. She read aloud Kipling's tale of "How the Rhinoceros Got Its Skin." They had Oolong tea and some of the corn cakes she had taught Dahsoo to make the day before. Then she kissed her daughter on the forehead and sent her off with Joy for a nap. For the next hour Hope sat alone in the courtyard watching Paul's beloved fish swim circles in their porcelain prison.

ৡৡৡ

6

The first face she saw when she came out of the ether was Sarah Chou's, with an angel looming behind her. "Are we dead?" she whispered.

"Worse." Sarah wagged a long, bony finger. "You've a little boy. Ah, you'll be in for it now."

The angel lifted her wings, coasted back. Those ridiculous hats. Hope laughed at herself—with effort. "There's a girl," crooned Sarah, helping her to sit. "Sore? I don't doubt it, such a little thing you are."

"Where is he?"

But nurse angel had a way of reading mothers' minds and was already swooping back down on them. "He looks just like Paul," Hope breathed, opening her arms to the swaddled newborn.

"He doesn't!" said Sarah, leaning closer. "Look, his hair's wavy, and his eyes are nearly blue, like yours—"

"All babies have blue eyes," retorted Hope. "Look at the gorgeous long lashes."

"Well! You should be glad enough for the distinction."

Hope lifted the baby to her breast. There was the forgotten awkwardness of latching on. The tiny blind mouth rooting. The small desperate gasps and grunts, impossible fingers like anemone wands pulling toward her flesh, the nipple huge—too huge for that mouth, and the spasm of panic that nature would fail at this critical juncture. Then magic. Like some organic puzzle, the pieces all fit and her milk let down, a warm tide of pleasure and sadness rushing through her as her child took hold and began to suckle. She remembered when this baby was conceived. Sprays of night-blooming jasmine by the bed. Rain purring on the roof. She and Paul had kicked off their covers and lain naked and shivering, clinging as if to take refuge inside each other's skin. Another world. An eternity ago. Yet here was the living proof.

"No wet nurse for you, either," Sarah said archly, and when Hope did not respond, she continued, "As I always say, you can marry a Chinese man, but that won't make you a Chinese wife."

"Paul has never made the slightest effort to direct my instincts as a mother."

"I see." Sarah plucked at her skirt. "Well. And what will you call this baby, then?"

"We haven't decided."

"We?" Sarah turned her head to the right, to the left. "I don't see any we, dear. Only you."

Hope held her tongue. She had asked Sarah to come, had leaned on her far more than she should have these past weeks. With Yüan Shih-k'ai's transfer of the government to Peking at the beginning of April, it became clear that Paul would not be present for the birth, and in any case, he knew nothing about Shanghai's foreign doctors and hospitals. It was Sarah who referred Hope to Ste. Marie's, a large austere missionary hospital in the French Concession with hard mattresses, an overwhelming odor of ether, and religious icons above each bed, but also a reputation for professional and impartial medical treatment for both Chinese and foreigners. It was Sarah who kept her company during the final days of her confinement, Sarah who brought her son, Gerry, to play with Pearl, Sarah who, for all her broad and unabashed ways, was Hope's only friend in Shanghai. Yet Paul was one topic Hope refused to discuss with her.

"He is coming back in two weeks," she said evenly. "Right after the Senate's inauguration."

"Ladies?" The voice, low and polite, came from outside the curtain that ringed the bed. Sarah put a finger to her lips and shook her head for Hope to play mum. The speaker's shadow turned to a trim profile, raised the shape of a clipboard, and merged with the fanned silhouette of a passing nurse. Sarah squeezed Hope's fingers, suppressing laughter, but the baby, pulled loose from his nipple, gave them away with a gas-filled squall.

The curtain opened. "I'm Dr. Mann."

Hope shifted awkwardly to cover herself and pat the baby quiet. The doctor, a lean, youthful sandy-haired American, gave a cursory nod and reached for the chart at the end of the bed. "Mrs.—mm—" He glanced not at the mother but the child. That mop of glistening black hair and eyes—two dark dashes over high moon cheeks. He checked the chart again. "Mrs. Leon?"

"Yes." Hope's voice pinched. She had thought there was something familiar about the doctor's appearance but now decided it was just that patina of efficiency that so often camouflages prejudice.

"You've a fine boy there. May I?" He took the squirming bundle with a peremptory nod.

As he checked the baby's pulse and heartbeat, Sarah eyed him curiously. "Are you new to Shanghai, Doctor?"

"Few weeks," he mumbled.

"Where're you from?"

He inspected an ear. "Seattle."

Sarah tossed a conspiratorial grin. "My last stop in the States was New York, but I've been here three years now. Practically an old hand. How are you liking it?"

"There's plenty of work." Dr. Mann tidied the swaddling, returned the newborn to Hope. "Any other children?"

Hope kissed her baby, ignoring the question. She distrusted this man's offhand manner and was embarrassed by Sarah's forwardness. She wished they both would leave.

"She has a daughter," Sarah answered for her. "Three years old and already a heartbreaker."

"I imagine you're eager to get back to her."

"I wouldn't be if they'd let her stay with me," Hope flung back.

He shook his head. "I know. We have patients going home days, even weeks too early because they're worried about their families. But the chief here is manic about young children and germs." He lowered his voice conspiratorially. "It's a bit late for this now, but if you have need again, you might consider Shanghai Native Hospital. There you may have your children and even your amah stay with you. It's much more humane."

"I'll remember that," Hope said coldly. She laid the baby, now fast asleep, in the wicker bassinet by her side. "You won't mind approving my release for this afternoon, then."

He had strange eyes, she noticed, meeting them for the first time. Hazel shot through with strands of pale blue and green. They clouded over. "As I say, in my opinion, you and this child would be safer here."

"But," Hope said firmly.

He hesitated. "But I understand."

"You know, Doctor," said Sarah, "there's more goes on in Shanghai than work."

His ringless hands rested on the collar of his stethoscope. "Good day, ladies."

"Cretin," muttered Hope as the curtain dropped.

"Adonis!"

"Hand me that chart."

"You can't tell me that's not one handsome man." Sarah gave her the clipboard from the end of the bed.

"There." Hope stabbed the sheet with her index finger. "Mother's race: white. Father's race: Chinese. That's all they care about! Shanghai Native Hospital, indeed!"

"None of it's untrue," said Sarah.

"None of it *matters*." She crumpled the pale blue paper.

Sarah dropped onto the end of the bed. "Now there you're wrong, dear. In this town, it matters more than anywhere."

She was dressed in jade-colored taffeta, her flaming hair piled beneath a round hat draped in matching ribbon, yet for all her jauntiness, there was a darkness about Sarah. While Hope would never permit herself to fully trust this woman, she was beyond—far beyond—ignoring her.

Hope laid a hand on the baby's forehead, felt the tiny muscles already knotted with dreams. "How do you stand it, Sarah?"

She didn't get an answer right away, but when she did, the glibness was gone. "My father kicked me out when I was twelve," said Sarah. "He was drunk and I was a handful. I still am, and I think that's what's saved me. I'm sure no romantic. Had the wind knocked out of me too many times to be ruffled by insults or misunderstandings. But I'm not entirely cynical, either. I don't think that doctor meant to slight you, Hope."

Hope sighed, shaking her head and reluctantly smiling. "I don't know whether to give you a hug or turn the other cheek."

Sarah laughed. "I'll settle for a chance to hold that baby."

உ௭௭௭

Two weeks later Hope was coming up out of a nap when she heard Paul bellowing in the courtyard. "Where is my son! Where is my wife!" The usual commotion of servants, then a burst of giggles. "And my big, big daughter, Precious Pearl." Minutes later the door flew open, and he entered the room like a gathering wind.

Grinning and rumpled, hat askew, tan wool coat thrown carelessly over his shoulders, he looked as though he could swallow her whole, but first donned his spectacles and reached for his son.

"Are your hands clean?" Hope demanded, as if it were hours instead of weeks since she'd last seen him.

"My hands."

"You've been traveling. They're probably cold, too."

Paul let out an exasperated grunt. "Millions of babies born in fields and mud huts, no one washes hands."

"And millions of them die. Now do as I say."

He inhaled sharply, but did as she said, returning scrubbed and combed, relieved of his coat and chafing his hands, the look of a chastened schoolboy in his eye—but a schoolboy fond of his teacher withal.

"That's better." She lifted an eyebrow and passed him the baby, who in his turn regarded his father with a solemn gaze.

Paul studied the child's face only a moment before flipping him across his lap. He peeled away the layers of swaddling, undid the diaper, and bent squinting over the infant's backside.

"What is it?" Hope asked, alarmed. "What are you looking for?"

The baby gurgled and kicked, enjoying his freedom as Paul's finger described a circle at the base of the spine. A chill went through Hope as she leaned to see the small flat brown mark. But Pearl had one there, too, when she was born. Hope had thought nothing of it, Paul never mentioned it, and in time it had disappeared.

"He is Chinese!" Paul declared, triumphant. He kissed the mark. Then he leaned across and kissed his startled wife. "You give me a Chinese son, Hsin-hsin. This Mongol spot is our proof. First son of Liang born into the new Republic!"

Hope's throat tightened. She reclaimed the child and began methodically to rewrap him. Paul stretched his arms and took a turn around the room, drumming his fingers on the bureau as he passed. He paused to look out the window, called encouragement to Pearl, whose tricycle answered with a metallic clatter. At length he turned.

"You are well," he said quietly.

Hope looked up. Her mouth twitched, but before she could frame a reply there was a rap at the door, and a young, polished brown face peered in. Yen had hired Ah-nie while Hope was still in the hospital. She was from Shantung, strikingly handsome and with excellent references but also smileless and taciturn. She frightened Pearl and intimidated Joy and was, in Hope's opinion, efficient to a fault. Yet when Hope demanded why Yen had failed even to consult her on this selection, he showed the wire from Paul, dated three days before the baby's birth and accompanied by a money order made out to Yen's care, giving explicit instructions to have a new amah in place before mother and child returned home from the hospital.

"You might at least have trusted me to hire the amah myself," Hope said when Ah-nie had taken the baby out.

"Are you displeased?"

"Displeased." Hope chewed at the edges of his word as he approached the bed. "No, really, Paul, I'm pleased as punch. I've moved halfway around the world to be with a husband I love and who gives me in return as much as one or two whole days a month. I'm living among total strangers, have just given birth at a Catholic hospital because it's the only one in town where the doctors won't assault me. I have a servant who acts as if he's my keeper, because my husband trusts him with his money and his business and even the most basic knowledge of his whereabouts more than he does me. Why ever should I be displeased?"

He sighed, lowering himself to the bed. "You welcome me by driving me away."

"I can't help it." She leaned away from the dip his weight carved in the mattress.

"You are my wife. Should I leave you on the other side of the world?"

He took her hand then, working it delicately between his fingers as his eyes played across her face. It was the old ploy, substituting touch for reason, but it was as effective as it was transparent. She hated to quarrel, and now that he was finally here, the last thing she wanted was to spoil it. Yet she heard herself persisting. "You could have stayed, you know. We had a home. If it weren't for a fluke of history you wouldn't have been able to come back at all."

"You wish this."

"If it meant we could be together." She gripped his stiffened fingers. "That's all I want, Paul. You know that. Can you really blame me?"

The compressed lips, the hard blinking down and shake of his head— she struggled to read her own will into these gestures. No, he did not blame her, he was wrong to abandon her, wrong to undermine her authority, even—perhaps especially—wrong to believe in Sun Yat-sen's idyllic vision of a democratic China. But the more she sought to exonerate herself, the more she recognized in his dejected pose the falseness and arrogance of her demands. Here they sat, in a chamber thick with the sweet-sour smells of breast milk and talcum and newborn flesh, the soft fragrance of lilies and freshly starched sheets. Lace curtains stirred on a sun-drenched breeze, and their daughter's high reedy voice came floating in a counting song through the open window. Here in this room, at this instant, she had everything she was asking for, and yet if this were all she had, whether here or in Berkeley or anywhere, it could never be enough. What she wanted was not for Paul to sacrifice his dreams but to incorporate her into them.

"Well, I blame myself."

He lifted his eyes warily. She touched his cheek. "It's just that I've missed you so," she whispered. "You can't imagine."

Paul cocked his head. He brought a finger to the tip of her nose, then traced it down over her lips and chin, down to the hollow at the base of her throat just above the eyelet of her nursing gown. He stared for several seconds at the point where he'd come to rest, then inched forward and kissed her lightly there, and again on her lips. He pulled back with a quizzical expression, then kissed her yet again, thoughtfully. When he came up this time his smile was softer, more relaxed. He threaded his fingers through hers.

"I think we must name our son Morris," he said.

Hope fell back against the pillow. "Have you heard a word I've said!"

He brought their hands together. "Listen. You remember I tell you about my teacher Jung Ch'un-fu?" She shrugged. "If not for Jung Ch'un-fu, I would not have dared to ask you to marry me, Hope."

"I feel another of your tricks coming on."

"No trick. I met Jung's son last month in Peking. He is a parliamentary clerk there now, but he tells me his father has died this year. In Connecticut."

"He was an old man."

"Eighty-four years. Many of those devoted to modernizing China. And to forming a bridge between China and America." He studied her. "This son is named Morris."

Hope sighed, and shook her head. "Do you know you have a very sentimental nature?"

"No sentiment." He smoothed the counterpane over her legs. "Jung Ch'un-fu is a godfather to our marriage in same way Sun Yat-sen is godfather to Chinese Republic. By honoring his family, we safeguard our own, just as those who honor Dr. Sun safeguard the future of China."

"All right. Not sentimental. Superstitious." She grinned and tweaked his ear. "I can hardly wait to hear what you have in mind for our boy's Chinese name."

"With your approval." Paul cleared his throat, a grin tugging at his lips. "I think Ch'eng-yü is a good choice."

"Which means . . ."

He was beaming now, unable to contain his glee. "Clear Language."

"Clear Language." She mentally twisted and scrutinized the phrase. She considered Paul, her own past lives, how they'd met, the divisions between them. And always the one sustaining force that held them. She met his grin. "I take it all back. You're neither sentimental nor superstitious. You're devious, Paul. Devious and dear and perfectly brilliant. What would I do without you?"

ॐॐॐ

He remained in Shanghai for two weeks, shuttling between the numerous political parties now vying to represent China's gentry—the educated scholars, landowners, and merchant classes who were the financial base and the electorate for the new government. "The greatest threat to China is disintegration!" he warned them. "Yüan's command of the military will hold the country together long enough for us to establish the Republic and get the government on its feet. He is the only hope we have."

The very words sickened him. Yüan was a tyrant and a buffoon. When the Senate had opposed his demand to return the government to the north, Yüan had prompted "renegade" troops to loot and burn property throughout Peking, including the homes of foreigners. Within four days this "mutiny" had spread to the treaty port of Tientsin, and the foreign powers had called in more than two thousand British, American, French, German, and Japanese troops to help Yüan "restore order." Clearly, the situation around Peking was too precarious (and foreign holdings there too precious) for Yüan and his "loyal" troops to leave. Western pressure was exerted on the Senate, and Peking was named the Republic's new capital. Now Yüan was using equally devious tactics against anyone who publicly opposed him. But Paul's democratic idealism had been so thoroughly punctured since his return to China that he saw pragmatism as the only alternative. Everything he said in these meetings was true.

On May 5 the rival parties merged to form the pro–Yüan Shih-k'ai

Republican Party. The next morning Paul would leave for the north to report that he had secured the support Yüan needed to install his cabinet. As he packed his bags, Hope sat on the bed listening to him mutter under his breath. "You know you're making a pact with the devil," she said finally.

"In China we have many devils." He snapped his valise shut.

"And many gods. Why not do your business with them instead?"

"Gods are scarce now, Hope. It's the devils who are in charge."

"That's cold comfort as you walk out the door, back into their company."

The amber lamplight flickered across his face. *"Mei fatse."*

"You don't believe that."

"No? What is to be done, then?"

"I don't know, but you mustn't give in. Everything has happened so fast, Paul, and all of it can change just as quickly."

"Change." He sat beside her. "Most of us in the new government have devoted our lives to bring change to China. Yet nothing has really changed."

"All right, then, nothing has changed. You're proving my point, you know."

"What we need is more idealistic students," he continued thoughtfully, "to give the revolution new life. It is the Western Learning that inspires them, of course. When I was young we had to go overseas to receive the Western Learning. But now that we have returned . . ." He sneaked a look at her.

"What *are* you going on about, Paul?"

"You know," still he spoke as if the idea were just now coming to him, "my friend Wan in the Ministry of Education tells me that some universities right here in Shanghai have called for returned students to lecture."

"Lecture." She tugged him by the shoulders so he faced her. Only his eyes gave him away. "You're talking about teaching! Getting out of politics?"

"You would like this?"

"Like it! You goose! I'd give anything to see you happy again, Paul. It's perfect."

"Lecturing is not full-time job," he warned. "And I am not ready to retire from government just yet."

"But you've already spoken to the schools, haven't you? I can tell, you have. And they want you."

"Few days each two months. Literature and political science. Hope, it is not much money."

"Never mind that. You'll be here. That's all I care about." She flung her arms around his neck.

He let his hand drift down the curve of her breast and on to her uncorseted waist. At his touch her body pulled against him, her fingers roamed his collar and throat. "We're a week short of a month," she whispered. "But I won't tell the doctor if you don't."

After all the separation, the discord and abstinence during the last months of pregnancy—they had not made love since the day of her arrival—their coupling this night was like the meeting of two friends who have changed in unexpected ways and are surprised to find these changes pleasing. This did not prevent Paul's rising before dawn and kissing her goodbye, but Hope, half ashamed that she had allowed herself to fantasize it might, made no further move to hold him.

♌♌♌

A few mornings later found her with Pearl in the parlor, all windows open to a clear May breeze overflowing with birdsong. Ah-nie had just taken the baby for his nap, and Hope was reading to Pearl from a tattered and much beloved *Peter Rabbit* when Yen appeared in the doorway bearing a large brown paper package. Bright stamps—American, Philippine, Indochinese—straggled like the shreddings of a tropical flower above Mary Jane's bold script.

"A present!" cried Pearl.

"Probably something for the baby." Hope wrenched the flap and plucked the letter from atop the excelsior before turning the box over to Pearl. "Go ahead and open it, but let Yen help you, so nothing gets broken." It was one thing she could not fault in this tall, sober northerner. However inflexible his dealings with Hope, Yen was all grins the instant permission was granted for him to serve Pearl. His long thin frame would accordion down, flat hands flapping with an animation kept under strict lock and key at all other times, and Pearl would address him with absolute authority and trust. Now this meticulous child was stymied by the problem of unwrapping the gift without tearing the paper or cutting the bow. All must be preserved. This notion appealed to Yen's native respect for paper, and so they proceeded slowly, with matched caution and care, while Hope opened Mary Jane's letter.

It was dated nearly three months earlier, which explained the plethora of stamps acquired during the package's roundabout passage. Such misroutings were common enough in trans-Pacific post, yet in the split second after this information registered, Hope felt a disappointment as keen as grief. She was separated from her friends and home not only by distance but, even more acutely, by time.

> February 20, 1912
> Dearest Hope,
> I enclose my suggestion to ease your soul. I was thinking about this as a going-away gift, but in the whirlwind of the election I plum forgot. Perhaps it's just as well, since the tone of your letter suggests you are now good and ready to make use of this offering. Already, you describe in picture terms, and so I expect you to accompany future letters with the pictures themselves! Your new home, your Paul, little Pearl, your servants—the baby, when your time comes.
> What originally started me thinking of giving you a camera was those pictures of Chinatown by Arnold Genthe. I remember the way you would study them when you didn't know anyone was watching. There was a look in your eye, more than admiration or any memory the images provoked. As if you wished *you'd* taken them. I detected that same spark in your letter, and I remembered how, even here in Berkeley, whenever Paul would get involved in his revolutionary business or go off on his cross-country trips, you'd be out of sorts, at cross purposes until you threw yourself into your own mission. We in the Movement were the happy beneficiaries of your frustration, but now you're in another world, dear, and you must make your

own mission. The more, with all those servants to take care of your children! Perhaps this little Kodak holds a key.

Well, I could go on with pages of questions and suppositions, but am chomping at the bit to tell you the news from this side of the sea. Since it's not fully mine to tell, however, I'll turn the pen over to one better qualified—on condition he let me add my final dime's worth . . .

Hope, it's Dad. Yes, here with Mary Jane. Sharing her letterhead and her pen and desk. And her future. Guess impulse runs thick through this brood, but if you can up and off to China without so much as a say-so, then your best friend and old dad can tie the knot just as quick. I love her. Seeing as you do, too, I can't see you'd have much to say against us. That is, if you can figure how she could love a codger like me, but she claims she does, and I'm so far under her spell that I believe any damn thing she tells me. Besides, since I have neither youth nor money, why else would she marry me? Honey, you should see us. Never met a woman who enjoys a good spat as much as your Mary Jane, or who's as quick to make up afterward. She's taken thirty years off me and hasn't begrudged a second of the ten I've still got on her. I know in real time there's a couple decades between us, but you, of all people, must understand that love can lead folks to foolish choices. The only other woman who ever lit up my life the way Mary Jane does was your mother, Hope. Please give us your blessing.

I'm up here with her now, helping her pack. Those friends of hers the Laws sisters are buying the place so she can move down with me to Hill Street. Says it's high time the lady Angelenos joined the suffrage bandwagon. If anyone can make 'em, Mary Jane can, and I'll be right behind her pushing.

I thank you for bringing us together, honey. If only you and Pearl were here my life would be as perfect as could be. But know that I love you all, and if we have a good year, maybe we'll take a late honeymoon to Shanghai so you can show us the sights. I'm sure Paul will settle back down once the government finds its course. He's a brave soul and a patriot, and it's possible that combination is even harder in a husband than if he were a ne'er-do-well like yours truly. But I know he loves you and that little girl of yours. He'll do anything for you, and he'll always come home. If you trust that, it'll help.

I send you all my love and joy. Now here, as promised, my bride again . . .

[It's Mary Jane] Surprised? It was your leaving that did it, you know. He came banging on my door after midnight demanding what had happened to you, and I stumbled downstairs in my nightgown and when I saw the expression on the poor man's face we both started bawling for you, and we had no choice from that moment but to spend the rest of our lives together. How he can make me laugh—but also feel like such a lady—imagine *me* liking that sort of thing! What he failed to mention was that we truly did get married, legal and proper, last Thursday at four o'clock at Justice Donnel's house down on Adeline, with Dorothea Marr and the Laws sisters as witnesses, and we missed having you there almost as much as we enjoyed the cake and champers at the Shattuck Hotel afterward.

Well, my darling. That's a bundle to travel such a long distance. The camera is really from both your dad and me. Consider it a large hint, and let your wedding gift to us be photographs of your new life to keep us company in ours.

With love to spare,
Mary Jane and Dad

"Look, Mama!" Triumphant, Pearl held the Kodak aloft. Its chrome fittings glittered. The black morocco gave off a pungent smell of new leather. The bellows crackled as Hope haltingly pulled on the lens, but by the time she lifted the viewfinder to her eye, her vision had dissolved in the first tears she'd allowed herself since arriving in China.

VI
FAMILY AND FRIENDS

SHANGHAI

(1912–1913)

ও৶ও৶ও৶

1

Political events that first summer played out as Paul predicted. Sporadic mutinies against the central government erupted, but Yüan Shih-kai's loyal warlords quickly put them down. In Peking, several leaders of the original government, including the Premier and four cabinet ministers—all old friends of Paul's—resigned, and Yüan replaced them with his yes-men. Meanwhile, the British pressured the new government to reverse the few fundamental policies on which the sparring Chinese factions agreed—notably the new ban on the opium trade. Britain had originally introduced opium into China, had fought the Opium Wars to protect its right to sell the drug to the Chinese, and had no intention of giving up this lucrative business now. The implied threat of British warships pa-trolling the coast and Yangtze gorges didn't need to be spelled out.

"But that's immoral!" Hope cried when Paul, back for a surprise visit in July, reached this point in his account. "Opium's as bad as slavery."

"You begin to understand our feelings toward Westerners."

"The British, yes."

"All the Western powers have benefited. Even the Americans with their Open Door Policy. Let the vultures have equal rights to descend on China's bleeding remains." The bitterness of his words belied his deep ambivalence toward the Western powers—his abiding admiration for the inner workings and principles of their governments coupled with his almost visceral loathing for the men in these same governments who had imposed their predatory policies on China. The underlying historical attitude of the West—and Britain, in particular—was that what works for the white man is beyond the ken of the yellow, the black, or the brown. For centuries the corresponding attitude in China had been that what the white man—and particularly the Englishman—thought good and noble was, in fact, contemptible. Paul's was the first generation of educated Chinese to try to reach across the breach, to borrow from the West as equals rather than surrendering as slaves or compradors. But just as there was a certain duplicity in living under the protection of the foreign concessions while at the same time protesting the rule of Western, rather than Chinese justice in these territories, so he could not champion Western ideals of democracy without admitting that he and his fellow governors and literati would be the first to benefit from them—perhaps at the expense of his poorer, illiterate countrymen. As if to prove the point, there was Hope standing by the drawing room window in a sheer white dress with Belgian lace, while outside Ah-nie hovered protectively above Morris's white wicker perambulator and Pearl and Joy played badminton, as immune to the sweltering heat and political chaos as two sparrows.

"I thought one reason for getting rid of the Manchus was to finally put the foreign powers in their place," Hope said.

"You thought. I thought. But in order to achieve our revolution of the heart we have joined hands with some whose motives differ."

Her fingernails made a rasping noise as she trailed them down the window screen. "Do I hear another change of allegiance?"

"China cannot be governed without a strong united army. That is Yüan's strength. By whatever means—bribery, blackmail, he is above nothing—he has gained the support of provincial warlords throughout the north. But if he cannot be persuaded to reform, then we must beat him at his own game—by attracting the warlords of the south to a different leader."

"Sun Yat-sen again." Her voice tightened. "And you're the messenger."

"Only one of many."

"So you'll continue running from one end of the country to the other, but now dealing with butchers and thugs."

"With power. Those who wield power are rarely noble, Hope, except in fairy stories."

"And how do I know you won't end up in one of their prisons with another knife in your back!"

He pushed himself up off the sofa and approached her warily. She stood with her hands on her hips, as slender and headstrong and delicately formed as the day he first saw her. Yet these years with him had left their mark in the tension that tugged at her mouth, the uncertain shadows around her blue eyes. Though he now returned to Shanghai every other month, his visits were crowded with banquets and government business, preparation for his lectures and discussions with students and, increasingly, secret meetings with members of the opposition. His teaching was failing to bring the relief Hope had expected, and his prompting for today's unplanned return was even less likely to please her than the news of his changing politics.

"You must not worry about these things," he said.

"How can I help it?"

He met her eyes. "My family is here. In Shanghai." He paused. "My mother has requested that we visit her tomorrow, Hope."

Her lips parted briefly, then closed. Her only other response was to lift her left hand, curled, and tap her ring against her chin. She did not speak, and he could not read her expression.

At last she said, "Your children will be there."

"Yes." He swallowed. Her voice was calm. Best put it all out. "In fact, Mulan was here all spring."

He felt the blue of her eyes like a slap.

"I think it was better you do not know," he continued. "Mulan attends Aurora University. She is busy with her studies. In any case, my mother has forbidden her to visit us."

Hope folded her arms and walked away from him, saying nothing. When she reached the opposite side of the room she stopped, still holding herself. Finally she turned, stretching and shaking out her hands, her breathing jagged. "Sometimes I wonder if you would prefer me to know nothing at all."

"Hope—"

"No, Paul. No, it is not better, don't you see? It's just easier for you. It's more comfortable, simpler, requires less of your attention." She flung her arms violently down by her sides. "Can't you see that it makes *me* feel you're ashamed of us?"

"You know that is not true."

"Do I? Even now, looking into your face, I can see I'm embarrassing you. You think I'm acting like a hysterical foreigner. You wish I would simply nod and smile and tell you everything is fine. You can't bear it when I tell you what I'm really feeling, except when——" She broke off, covering her face with her hands. He was afraid she was crying, that she really would become hysterical, but he could not move either to relieve her distress or to chastise her. She was right, such behavior did embarrass, even sicken him.

But she was not crying, and after a moment she regained control of herself, dropping her hands. She licked her lips and took a breath. "Are you quite sure I'm included in this invitation?"

"I am certain."

"Then I don't suppose I have any choice." To his surprise, her eyes were clear and serious. "But even if I did, I wouldn't say no."

"What you would say?" he asked, cautiously smiling.

"I would say, *why* couldn't you give me time to prepare?"

"Six years is not enough?"

"Six centuries would not be enough." She sighed. "But maybe lightning will strike. Once your mother sees the children, sees us all together . . ."

"Hope." His smile stiffened. "My mother is a stubborn woman. Set in her ways. You must not expect to change her."

"Why not? I changed you, and you're her son."

"Yes," he said. "But you are her daughter-in-law."

"So . . . ?"

"I have arranged for us to go to the mountains at the end of this month. It will be cooler." He went over and took her hands. "Maybe we find another tree, like Wyoming."

"That's wonderful, but you're changing the subject."

"Yes," he said. "I am."

The following afternoon gatekeeper Lin readied the two ceremonial rickshaws that were stabled next to the kitchen. The tarpaulins were thrown off, the black lacquer woodwork and brass side-lamps polished until they shone. The cushions were encased in snowy starched covers, and the canvas hoods folded down. Special pullers were hired—tall, strong northerners whose neat jackets and cloth slippers complemented the dazzling vehicles, and at two o'clock Paul and Pearl settled themselves in one rickshaw, Hope and the baby in the other. Morris was drenched in a long white gown that Mary Jane had sent from Los Angeles. Pearl wore a pale yellow frock with pleated skirt, black patent strap shoes with white silk anklets, and a taffeta bow in her hair. Hope, after considerable agonizing, had settled on a summer waist and skirt of peach muslin, demurely cut about the throat and sleeves, while Paul suffered the torrid heat in a beige linen suit and straw skimmer. The silver and jade bracelets weighing down the children's wrists were Hope's one sartorial concession for Nainai, or Grandmother, as Paul instructed them to call her.

They followed a long, leisurely route that led along boulevards lined with poplars and plane trees through the French Concession and into Nantao, the district surrounding the walled Chinese City. At first Hope had faulted Paul for not telling her that his family owned a home here— a home where Hope was not permitted to live. Like his failure to tell her of Mulan's presence in Shanghai, it forced her to wonder what other secrets he might be keeping. And like his insistence that Yen's marketplace savvy made him better qualified than Hope to run the household accounts, both these omissions suggested a paternalism on Paul's part that rankled her. Yet she had to admit she had been more comfortable believing Paul's family away in Wuchang, and now, as they crossed over Siccawei Creek and left the groomed boulevards of Frenchtown behind, she understood why she and the children could never live in his family's house, with or without his mother. Like those inside the European Settlements, the high brick compound walls here were spiked with broken glass and barbed wire; however, these were footed not in scrubbed paving stones and flower beds but caked mud and squatting throngs of beggars, peddlers, and mangy dogs. People were shrieking, wailing, bargaining, and pleading, and for all the heaving humanity that suddenly clogged these narrowing streets, there was not a white face in sight. The last gendarme was a mile behind them, in the kiosk at the Concession boundary. This section of Shanghai was governed not by the Municipal Council but by Chinese law.

The rickshaws stopped before a pair of heavy, double-leaved doors and the front puller sang out, "Open! The lord and his foreign family have arrived." The gatekeeper bowed, murmuring greetings to "Laoyeh" alone.

The compound was built in Chinese style of cedar wood and plaster with black tile roofs. The first courtyard (Hope could glimpse others through two circular gateways) was dominated by a recessed pool filled with dappled carp, two thickly blooming white magnolias, and an artificial hill capped by a small pavilion and red-leafed maple. The surrounding walls were intercut with latticework windows, and an oiled parchment panel stood open to a reception hall. Here the family was met by a wizened serving woman who greeted Paul with a toothless wail. He returned the greeting soberly and explained that Winter Plum had been with the Liang family for four decades and was his mother's favorite maid.

Hope smiled and bowed her head over Morris, asleep in her arms, but the servant's eyes never lifted. She said something to Paul in a dialect that Hope did not recognize. "My mother wishes to see me alone first," Paul said to Hope. "Maybe Pearl would like to watch the fish."

"Don't be long," Hope answered, too gaily. Paul gave her a warning look and pointed her back toward the courtyard.

While Pearl dangled a bamboo frond to tease the carp, Hope settled with the baby under the pavilion. When Pearl tired of the fish, she set about walking the grid of moss that grew between the paving stones. She plunged her nose into the trumpet of a coral hibiscus, conversed with a cicada, and chased a small green lizard up the wall. The child's almost simpleminded ease never failed to amaze her mother. It was a function of youth, of course. Pearl was still too innocent to notice the slights from strangers, the barbed comments and sidelong glances the followed them on the street—or even, it sometimes seemed, the absence of her father. She cared only for her mother, baby brother, Joy, and, with steadily increasing affection, Ah-nie and Yen. Hope wished she could bottle her daughter's cheerful purity and hoard it as an antidote to all the pain that awaited her.

One patent leather Mary Jane in front of another, Pearl was pretending to walk a tightrope when suddenly she pointed and called to her mother. A scarlet butterfly was flitting about one of the magnolia trees. "Isn't she lovely," whispered Hope.

"Can I catch her, Mama?"

"Oh, no. I don't think—" She left off without even realizing it.

The butterfly had drawn Hope's eyes to one of those open latticed windows in the wall to her left. Through it she had a clear view of Paul. He was kneeling, hands splayed flat in front of his knees, knocking his forehead on the floor. Over and over, with mechanical precision, he would rock back and rise, eyes lifting as before an altar, then down again collapse, crawl forward. He was prostrating himself like a slave.

Hope squirmed, horrified and embarrassed but unable to look away. Had Paul not confessed, and in their earliest hours, to the cruelty he had suffered in the name of filial duty? He had told her. She had listened, even written it down as a mesmerizing story. And she had tried to understand, believed in some small way she'd succeeded. But this man throwing himself on his knees was no one she had ever known. He was no child to be pitied. No slave to be freed. No prisoner forced to this humiliation. He was a grown man. A revolutionary, of all things! With no more pride than a dog on a leash.

Sadness, disgust, rage, shame—oh, all of these coursed through her, but none compared with the utter desolation she felt at the failure of her own imagination. Surely she misunderstood. Maybe this room was not, as she supposed, his mother's apartment, but rather some sort of shrine. Perhaps his contortions were, in fact, religious rather than filial. She wasn't sure why, but she could stomach that, could respect and even condone it. But then a woman's voice squawked imperiously from the depths of the chamber, and Paul kneeled again, head bowed, facing straight, his very silence visible in the crosshatch of light pouring over him. Hope wanted to scream at him to rise. Come to his senses. Stand like the man she knew him to be and leave this place at once. Instead, the baby screamed, and she realized she had been squeezing the breath out of him in her agitation.

The maddened infant was blood-red in the face, hungry, hot, wet, and clearly incensed at her rough treatment. Pearl was at her elbow babbling consolations, and all Hope could think about was getting the three of them safely away. She jiggled the baby against her shoulder and was halfway to the gate when a young woman stepped from the reception hall. She was several inches taller than Hope, slender with broad, straight shoulders accentuated by her green mandarin dress. Her hair was pulled

into two braided coils, studded with pomegranate blossoms. Her eyebrows were plucked to slivers. She stood staring coldly until Hope had
stopped and turned fully around to face her, then said in exacting English,
"Nainai wishes you to come."

She didn't bother to introduce herself. She didn't need to.

"The baby is unwell," said Hope. "I must take him home."

"Home?" The taunt percolated across the courtyard. Pearl drew back
behind Hope's long skirts while Morris grabbed her top button, tried to
shove it into his mouth.

Mulan's vermilion lips formed the shape of an inverted butterfly
against the powdered whiteness of her skin. She planted one hand on her
hip, shook the other so that her fat jade bangles clattered like laughter,
then turned on her heel and sailed back inside.

"Where's Papa?" Pearl whimpered. "Is Papa all right?"

Hope freed one hand from the baby and slid it down to meet Pearl's.
"Are you ready to meet your *nainai?*" she said, breathing lightly.

"I don't want to," said Pearl.

"I know." Hope smoothed the dark hair back from the child's damp
forehead. "I know, but it's only for a little while. We must do this for
Papa." She struggled. "It's not a choice, you understand?"

Pearl nodded, slipping her fingers back trustingly into her mother's
hand.

They proceeded to the chamber where Paul and his other family were
waiting, but for all her desire to get through this with grace, Hope's long
skirt snagged on the wooden threshold, causing her to stumble and pitch
forward. Morris let out a yelp at the spasmodic jerking of her arms,
Pearl's ruddy face turned up, and Hope felt momentarily skewered by the
volume of eyes trained on her. The blue-black orbs of painted dragons
and cranes staring from their overhead beams, the not-so-benevolent leers
of Confucius and the Buddha from their dangling scrolls, even the brass
wall studs seemed to mimic Paul's and her stepchildren's silent rebuke.
Only as Hope proceeded and her vision adjusted to the smoky light, did
she realize that the three of them had their eyes fastened firmly on the
slate floor. The boy, Jin, was bareheaded, jug-eared, and carried his long
dark robe with such reticence that he seemed poised to disappear. Mulan,
by contrast, stood taut and threatening as a bird of prey. But it was Paul's

downcast gaze that bore the heaviest weight, not because of its implicit disapproval or even its exposed weakness, but because there was no way around it.

A peremptory cough. The clack of metal and stone. Pearl tugged at Hope's elbow, furtively pointing, and with relief Hope realized the stage was being reclaimed by its rightful owner. For the first time she allowed herself to meet the only eyes that had actually watched them enter. They were hard and bright as two lumps of anthracite beneath unblinking hoods, though one drooped lower than the other, giving the impression of a perpetual wink. The surrounding face stretched wide and round, the skin unreasonably smooth and the roundness enhanced by the plucking of the eyebrows into spindly crescent moons, of the hairline into a perfect circle lifting behind the crown. The charcoal hair was oiled flat against the skull, showing off to effect two small ears adorned with modest gold hoops, the thin crimsoned lips tugged in a toothless grimace beneath a wide equilateral beak. Imperious. Mischievous. Brittle. Alarming. Nai-li's small back never touched the broad rosewood throne or the scarlet cushions on which she was perched. Her bound feet in cornflower blue silk lotus shoes rested stiffly on a low stool And though the skin of her hands showed they'd never been subjected to either work or sun, the constant click of her rings and gold bracelets told that they never rested.

Now the matriarch reached to the tray Winter Plum held out, put a long-stemmed pipe to her lips, and inhaled slowly, elaborately. When she laid the pipe aside, her cough reverberated across the bare floor.

"Kuo lai!" she screeched.

The glittering eyes had dropped with a sudden predatory glee to the squirming morsel in Hope's arms. Instinctively, those arms tightened. The acid smell of wet diaper hung about the baby and the back of his white voile gown stuck to Hope's sleeve. A bubble of drool had formed on his lips, his tiny fingers groped her breast, and he was making hungry grunts. Hope started to turn, her mind peeling away from the larger event and escaping into the needs of her child, but she was stopped by a pair of reaching hands, tattered fingernails scraping her wrist, the infant's eyes widening as he looked up and recognized his father.

Not a word was exchanged. Only the briefest of glances, but it was enough.

Hope let go. In that instant, she felt herself vanish. Not from Pearl, who remained half buried in her skirts, and surely not from her tormented Paul or Morris. But as far as everyone else here was concerned, she might have stepped to the other side of the looking glass. All her fantasies of reconciliation were, in this instant, dashed. Yet with these fantasies went all the shame, the yearning and regret that had driven them. It had been folly, she thought with a shock of relief. She might as well have dreamed of being embraced by the painted dragons above her head.

As if from a safe distance now, she watched Paul lower the baby to his *nainai*'s lap. She saw Mulan casually drape herself into one of those rigid blackwood chairs and inspect a dish of candies, Jin stay planted where he was, only wiggling his ears at Pearl.

"Pao-pei," cooed the matriarch, turning little Morris this way and that. She held him up for Winter Plum, who wrinkled her nose at his smell and plucked with disapproval at his soiled white gown and bootees. Nainai agreed the child was poorly cared for, but look at his fine black hair, fat cheeks, and grasping hands heavy with Liang silver. When the novelty of this inspection wore off and Morris began to cry, the old woman dipped her finger into a cup beside her seat, then popped it into his mouth.

Forgetting her newfound disconnection, Hope cried out and started forward in protest, but Paul caught her arm and yanked her to silence. The baby took the syruped finger and smacked his lips. Nainai cackled, with a triumphant glance not to Hope but to Paul, then dipped again. With supreme effort, Hope kept still. Morris sucked contentedly. Now Winter Plum beckoned to Pearl. She held out a plate of candied melon strips and lotus seeds. Paul took the child's hands and pushed her forward. Delivering his lambs to slaughter, thought Hope. But how proud she was of Pearl. Once committed, her little girl neither shrank nor shirked this obligation, but approached it on her own terms. Marching straight ahead, she smiled at the withered old servant, curtsied to her grandmother, plunged her hand deeply into the sweets, and before either of the women had a chance to criticize, she cried *"Hsieh hsieh,* Nainai!" at the top of her lungs and raced back to her mother's side.

Paul moved almost as quickly to reprimand his daughter as Hope did to shield her. Nainai shrieked for silence. The girl-child was nothing, she was saying, not worth the foreign clothes she was dressed in. Hope covered Pearl's ears, but the child's command of Mandarin was far better than her own, and none of this escaped her.

"I hate that lady," Pearl whispered, scowling even as she fisted her small hand over her trove of candy.

"Take her out," ordered Paul.

But Hope stood her ground. Slowly, pointedly, she surveyed the room, her eyes digging into one face after the other. She caught Jin's wan lips stretching to conceal a giggle, Mulan studying her fingernails with precarious indifference, Winter Plum busying her shoulders and arms like some decrepit locust preparing to sing. And Nainai, finger still plugging the baby's mouth as her own lips worked in righteous outrage. Lastly Hope leveled her gaze on her husband.

"It is time for us to leave, Paul. Together. As a family."

Perhaps it was her pioneer upbringing, memories of Mother Wayland laying down the law, or Mary Jane's earnest exhortations to stand up for her rights. Whatever prompted this defiance, Hope had fully intended to sound tough and resolute. Fire with fire, if Paul would not stand up to his mother then she must defend the children herself. Surely he couldn't expect her to leave that room without her son! But she was unprepared. When Paul's eyes came up they wore an ardent, pleading expression that was like nothing she had ever seen. With the simultaneous force of a blow and the frailty of a feather, it threw her completely off guard. She let out a gasp. Pearl grabbed her hand, and together they took several tripping steps backward. They did not leave the room, but it was enough—just barely, she now recognized, to restore to Paul a modicum of the face that she had cost him. He drew a breath and spread his hands, closing them loosely as he turned and advanced toward his mother. They exchanged a flurry of words in which Hope recognized the phrases "camel-foot woman" and "big-nose ghost," "dishonor" and "never again." Then Paul bowed from the waist, retrieved his son, and, finally, was dismissed.

Though the children and Paul would make regular pilgrimages to Nainai's house each year when she came to Shanghai, by mutual unspoken consent Hope would not face her mother-in-law again for nearly a decade. Nor would she ever reveal to Paul—or anyone—what she'd seen that day through the latticed window.

᠍᠍ ᠍ ᠍

2

Luling, Lu Shan, Kiangsi Province
August 1, 1912
Dearest Mary Jane and Dad,

I am writing from Kuling, a mountain resort where Paul has blessedly installed us during these hottest weeks of the summer. I know this must sound incredibly decadent, but to understand why it's not only lovely but *lifesaving*, you must try to imagine what an infernal, smoldering cauldron Shanghai becomes this time of year. Everything stinks of a high, nauseating putrescence, as if the very soil beneath our feet were an open cyst, and by mid-July, poor little Morris was covered with prickly heat, there was a cholera outbreak in the Chinese City, and I was quite frankly afraid for our lives. Paul's announcement that a friend would lend us his summer house was like manna.

Getting up here was another matter. First off, we took an English steamer for seven days up the Yangtze. This would have been all right except that Paul was not permitted to travel first-class, and he said it was too hot for us down below, with the baby in his condition. So for nearly a week we slept, ate, and journeyed apart, even though on the same boat. Yes, we were able to go down to the second-class deck to see Paul, but the gawking and stir we caused there was intolerable. In the end, Paul spent most of the trip working on his papers, and I spent what free moments I had during the children's naps putting your little Kodak to full advantage, as you can see. What these poor fledgling photographs cannot show, alas, is the exuberant color along the Yangtze. The green fairly blazes off the fields, and the sky's vivid blue is mirrored in the busy water. The Yangtze has been called the lifeline of China, flowing as it does all the way from Tibet past the inland's Chungking and the three-city area known as Wuhan, where Paul's mother lives. I certainly saw every conceivable cargo being hauled in every manner of vessel. The true river people, however, live on those round-hooded sampans you see in the foreground. They are said to give birth on these boats, make their living on the water trade, marry their children to each other, and die, in some cases, without ever having set foot on solid ground. For all of this, they seem amazingly cheerful, waving to us with big toothless smiles and offering for sale fat fish or baskets they've woven from river reeds. Meanwhile, in the background you can see the other denizens of the Yangtze, the considerably less picturesque European gunboats that patrol this vital trade route.

We left the steamer at last in the treaty port of Kiukiang. The harbor area swarmed with vendors and drivers and sedan chair bearers, all shouting to outbid each other. Paul quickly hired a carriage, which got us back together and across the plains to the foothills of our mountain Lu Shan. That was where the real fun began. The journey up to Kuling, which hundreds if not thousands make every summer, can be accomplished only by foot, meaning one's own feet or the feet of bearers. There is no road, no horse trail, and the stone steps up are centuries old. Everything, from visitors to provisions, construction materials and kitchen appliances, must be hand-carried up rocky paths full of hairpin zigzags and forty-degree inclines, all too often less than three feet wide with hundred-foot drops over the side. I made this ascent holding little Morris, with Pearl and Paul and our man Yen and our baggage each in their own separate chairs. I tried very hard to appreciate the spectacular view of that emerald valley and the gold-tinged clouds, but I confess my heart was in my mouth. I always feel such humiliation in a rickshaw or sedan chair, and the fact that no other mode of transportation was possible did not assuage my misgivings. What did was the ease and good humor of the bearers as they climbed, switching off at intervals without losing a step, so that one of the three assigned to each chair was always resting. They called to each other, laughed often, and though I could not decipher their dialect, I'm sure they were plenty interested in Paul's and my relationship.

After such a journey I was set to despise this place that was achieved at such a price, but I confess, the first sight of it won me. You can see from the picture what I mean. The valley stretches back in terraces overhung with pine-clad slopes and wispy clouds and, like a benevolent grandfather above it all, the snowy peak of Lu Shan. The main valley floor has served the Europeans for many years as a summer resort. They say it's just like Switzerland, though I doubt many tourists in Switzerland arrive on the backs of men. Anyway, the road through Kuling's main valley runs along a rushing stream and is flanked by blue-trimmed fieldstone cottages. We kept on about ten minutes to the next higher valley, a narrower, less developed place where a handful of wealthy Chinese keep summer homes. Here Paul brought us to a lovely little compound, all whitewashed with black tile roof and sliding screens, where we are now happily ensconced. The only blot is that we are rather isolated, so the local mountain people feel free to spy. They will come right up to the house, by placing a wet finger against the paper make a perfect hole in the window, and you'll look up from dinner or putting the children to bed and discover this huddle of little black eyeballs watching your every move. At first I was appalled, but it's really quite amusing, and they don't mean us any harm.

Every day since we arrived we have made an outing to explore the surrounding sights. Yen engaged a local couple to cook and care for the baby, so I've been free to take Pearl on almost daily outings. She and Paul have become champion swimmers in the glacial pools, and today we walked across a bridge rumored to be more than a thousand years old! I think this place is very nearly paradise on earth, and as you can see from the final group snapshot in this packet, we are together and happy as a family in a way we have never been before. God and the Republic willing, our life in China has finally taken root and will continue to grow and thrive.

With love from all of us,

Hope

P.S. You must be wondering how I could have gotten these photos developed in such an outpost. Our man Yen took the film all the way down to Kiukiang, where there is a photo shop, that you might have these prints with your letter. I was unsure of Yen at first—he's that giant glaring out from under his black bowler—but he is utterly devoted to all of us, even *yang taitai* (Foreign Wife!).

Sunset occurred suddenly in Kuling. One second the sun rode high overhead, bathing the valley in silvered heat. In the next, it dropped below the ridge, exploding the sky into color and pitching the earth into dusk. The display was so magnificent that each evening Hope and Paul would come out into the courtyard to watch it.

"Promise me we'll come back here every summer," Hope said as twilight descended on evening number eight.

"I do not like to make promises that I cannot control."

"But you love it here, too. I can see it in you, Paul. A load's been lifted these past days. You've laughed and played with the children as you never do in Shanghai. And you can't tell me you didn't enjoy our swim yesterday . . ." Up in the next valley they had found a small lake fed by hot springs at one end and a waterfall at the other. They had taken both children in with them, and later returned by themselves.

"I do enjoy," he said. "But most I enjoy that you are contented here."

"How could I not be? You know what Pearl has christened this place? She calls it Cloud Mountain."

Paul studied her in the dwindling light, neither responding nor retreating from the hand she had laid on his arm. "When the poets write these words, 'cloud mountain,'" he said, "they mean separation, longing. It is an image filled with beauty, yes, but also regret."

The sky had turned violet now, the air chilled. Yen crossed the nearest window, taper in hand. He was lighting the lanterns, but even when every one was lit, the center of the sloping yard, where Hope and Paul sat, remained in darkness.

Hope drew the shawl from the back of her chair and pulled it around her shoulders. "I wish I'd never mentioned it." When he did not answer she said, "When do you leave?"

"Tomorrow."

She wondered how—when—he would have elected to tell her had she not thrown him this convenient metaphor. Tonight in bed, after making love? In the morning over breakfast? When the coolies trotted up, waggling the sedan chair, or, better yet, while she and Pearl stood idiotically in bathing costumes waiting for him to come swim? "Will you tell me, at least, *where* you are going?"

His tone was measured. "I must first visit Wuhan, then return to Peking for elections."

The elections. Of course. Though she had forgotten all about them in the pleasure of these days, and though Paul's general cynicism about Yüan's Peking made the prospect of a ballot seem almost farcical, they had not magically faded away. She tugged at her shawl and finally contained her disappointment. "I'm sorry. I know you must go. There's no chance you'll lose your seat, though, is there?"

"The vote is not in doubt. Question is whether Yüan will honor the results. He prefers to hand-pick his parliament."

"Surely the numbers are against him."

"Perhaps, but there is no unity. This is the reason I must stay in Peking until the end of the month. Dr. Sun and Senate leader Sung Chiao-jen have persuaded the United League to call for a Party Congress on the twenty-fifth. Our plan is to form a Kuomintang—Nationalist Party—to campaign in general elections opposite Yüan's Republicans. Kuomintang candidates will stand for democracy and constitution and a strong independent China. The people will understand this when they cast their votes. And when Yüan sees *our* numbers, he will think before he acts."

Hope shivered and pulled her knees up, tucking her skirts around her. If Paul were American, she thought treacherously, he would move now to hold me. Instead, he merely said, "I will return as soon as this Congress ends. I will accompany you back to Shanghai."

"You said you would go first to Wuhan. Is your mother back there, then?"

"Yes." He leaned forward—the sharpness of the movement visible to her even in the waning light—and dug his elbows into his knees. "Mulan is to be married."

"Married!"

"She is already eighteen." His voice rose defensively.

"But you've never spoken of this. Who is the man?"

"He is from Yünnan. His family manufactures firecrackers."

"Is that all you know about him?"

"He is a Muhammedan. Forty years old."

Hope started at a muffled squall from inside the house, but it was only the amah giving Morris his bath. "Surely," she persisted, "Mulan would not choose such a husband for herself?"

Paul did not answer.

"It's Nai-li's doing, isn't it!" The thought sickened her, but she knew it was true. What was worse, Paul would not oppose her. "Last spring when Sun Yat-sen banned footbinding and opium and the buying and selling of human beings, you stood up and cheered, yet now you've let your mother sell your own daughter—"

He stirred. "You and Mulan have no affection between you."

"What has that to do with anything? You allowed this. How can I trust you won't let the same thing happen someday to Pearl!"

Paul stood abruptly and walked to the courtyard gate. He faced away from her for a full, punishing minute. When he turned back his arms were crossed, the whiteness of his Western-style shirt and trousers ghostly. "Mulan has chosen this man herself. They met in Shanghai this spring. I do not approve, Hope. For many years this man Dalin has sold more than fireworks to the Manchu regiments, now he supplies any warlord who will meet his price. I do not trust him. I do not wish him to enter my family, but my mother has agreed and too much face will be lost if I intervene."

"Face! You're saying this man could damage you politically! He's more than twice Mulan's age, and you, her father, were never even consulted! You're the one who's been dishonored!"

"Maybe." There was a long pause, then, to her astonishment, a smile crept into his voice. "You never did consult your father, Hope."

"That was different!"

" 'He will understand,' you said." He started toward her.

"I'm trying to argue with you."

"Yes." He came behind her, stroked the fine wisps of hair at her neck.
She twisted to look at him. "You're not even concerned!"

"I am very concerned. As was your father, I think."

"But she couldn't *possibly* love him?"

"Your friends said the same about you." He moved his hands to her
shoulders, gently signaling for her to come with him inside. But when she
still did not respond, he said, "I cannot see into my daughter's heart any
more than I could see into her mother's. You understand, Hope. This
thing is not within my control."

❦❦❦
3

Balance is key," said Sarah. "You must never forget—or let the servants
forget—that you are in charge. And *don't* make that fatal mistake of going
Chinese. You'll inevitably fail to live up to their standards, and you'll look
and feel a fool for the trying."

Hope looked doubtfully out the tram window. Sarah had insisted that
rather than meeting for another stuffy tea or tiffin (lunch, in Shanghai
parlance), they make an outing to the racecourse. It was opening day of
the Autumn Race Meet, she said, and all Shanghai society would be on
display.

"But Paul is Chinese," Hope reminded her.

"So he is, and that must never be forgotten, either. Balance, as I said.
Take food, for example. My personal advice is never to serve both Western and Eastern food at one meal. Choose one menu or the other, keeping Paul's preferences and whereabouts in mind. Eugene can't abide
Western-style breakfasts but is quite enthusiastic about a full roast beef
and Yorkshire pud dinner, so if and when we breakfast together I order
up salted fish and congee and satisfy myself with a stuffed bun. Then dinner can be the reverse."

"I'm not sure I see the purpose."

"The purpose, dear Hope, is to maintain at least the illusion of respect and purity. Don't mix things up too much. Don't confuse. And don't dilute."

"But we are mixed up. We're married! There's no point pretending otherwise."

"I repeat, Hope, you are not Chinese, whoever marries you. And Paul will never be American."

"He wears foreign clothing. And I've always served him the foods he likes in whatever combination strikes me. He's never complained." They had passed out of the crowded downtown area with its square-cut department stores and leering billboards and were nearing the towers and angled rooftops of the Race Club. The street was packed with rickshaws and touring cars, Western women trailing furs and feathers, men in top hats and beaver coats, and upper-class Chinese gowned in padded silk and brocades, many of them offsetting their robes with tweed jackets, heavy leather brogues, and sharply creased Homburgs. Hope drew Sarah's attention to this mixing of cultures, but to little avail.

"They're posing. Playing costumes. When they go home they won't wear those things. C'mon, we're here. Now stay close, Hope. I've a pal who'll get us into the grandstand."

Hope clutched the Kodak under her arm and swung down into the throng. The air was cold and mossy damp, the horsy smell from the stables wafting in equal measures with the spectators' colognes and brilliantine. On the far side of the yard huddled scores of less affluent Chinese in worn blue cotton—most, like their better heeled countrymen, sporting Western-style haberdashery.

Sarah's pal, an usher, was short and squat with quick darting eyes and a nose like a rat's. He greeted Sarah with an unctuous grin and led them up a rear stairway to prize seats in the second tier. "How'd you know *him?*" Hope whispered when he was gone.

"Friend of Donald's," Sarah answered with an offhandedness that reminded Hope of the secret behind her friend's first marriage—and shocked her all over again.

"I never thought I led a particularly sheltered life," she said. "But I'm beginning to wonder."

"I think there are no more sheltered people in the world than Americans," said Sarah. "The British, too, are easily shocked, but at least they understand *why* they're shocked. Americans haven't a clue."

"That's a rather harsh pronouncement, isn't it?"

The two women turned of a single accord toward the quiet male voice behind them. Its owner cupped his pipe in one hand and lit it with the other. He glanced at them over the starting smoke with amused eyes. Hope had the feeling she'd seen him before—a lean, handsome man with sandy hair combed straight back—but she could not place him.

Sarah had no such difficulty. She boldly extended her hand. "I'm sorry if you disagree, Doctor, but I'm very pleased to see you again anyway."

The man flicked his match expertly, tucked the pipe into his left hand and greeted Sarah with his right. "Pleasure's mine. And how's that baby of yours, Mrs. Leon?" He paused. "Stephen Mann. We met at Ste. Marie's."

Only at that instant did her mental pathways unjam and Hope recognize those strange swirling eyes. "I'm sorry, Doctor! I guess I didn't recognize you without your white jacket. They're quite well. Thank you for asking. For remembering, my goodness!" She gave him her hand, blushing, and glanced away . . . only to lock eyes with Renata Hwang. The Frenchwoman was studying her from the far end of the stand, where she sat beside a stuffed, monocled Chinese man who must be her husband. She wagged her fan, gave Hope a slow, measured nod, and raised her binoculars toward the track.

"I have a good memory," Dr. Mann was saying, "but I would have remembered the two of you, even if I hadn't."

"You're a gallant one, you are," Sarah said.

At that, a horn blew. The ponies and their *mafoos* had lined up at the starting gate. Now they were off, pounding up dust and sending a tremor like an earthquake through the stands. With relief at the diversion, Hope lifted the Kodak to her eyes, focused as best she could on the biscuit-colored oval of the course with its flashing spots of color and mane, and snapped the shutter.

"That must be very fast film," said the doctor.

Hope kept the camera to her eye. "Fast enough."

A bell rang as the first ponies crossed the finish line, and at the other side of the course, a line of boys held up the winning numbers.

"You know about photography, Doctor?" Sarah asked.

"A bit. I've found it a helpful tool—to document unusual cases. And, of course, China invites the camera. I'm afraid I don't have a very artistic eye, though."

"Why don't you practice on us," said Sarah. "Hope and I haven't had our picture taken together in years."

"In—" Hope threw Sarah a puzzled look.

"You're old friends, then?" Dr. Mann drew on his pipe. "Even before Shanghai?"

"Oh, long before. Look, there's a balcony on the other side where you can pose us."

"Mrs. Leon?" said the doctor. "I'm more than willing, but it is your camera."

"Please," she said, surprised all over again at his recollection not only of her circumstances but her name. "To tell the truth, I'm just muddling through. Maybe you can show me the proper settings."

The trio made their way out just as the starting bell sounded for the second race. They drew some curious glances for leaving at such a critical moment, which prompted Mann to say in a loud voice, "I've never been the betting kind, but I do find the scenery entertaining."

"Oh!" whispered Sarah. "You'll have them throwing spears at your back. The races are sacred in Shanghai, Dr. Mann. Fortunes are made and broken here—both financial and social."

"Which did we come for?" asked Hope.

"We just came to give them all a tweak, which apparently, dear doctor, you did, too."

"I'm a sheltered American, remember? I have no idea why they should be shocked at anything I say or do."

They stepped out onto a tiled balcony with a view of the exercise fields adjoining the course. It was a gray day, the city spires obscured by drifting fog, but every now and then the sun would break through, gilding the nearby roofs and treetops. Against this uncertain backdrop, the doctor positioned his two subjects, then told them to bear with him while he fiddled with the camera's knobs and cranks. Hope was impressed by his confidence and even more by his ability to explain the mechanics of camera and film. She had accepted the assurances of the printed directions that arrived with the camera, and simply pointed the lens at subjects that interested her and clicked the shutter. She had attributed the disappointing results to the inexperience of Chinese developers, but Dr. Mann explained that the fault was most likely her own.

"Each variation of light, movement, or exposure requires its own adjustment."

"You're telling me that picture of the race will be nothing but a blur," said Hope.

"Probably, but you never know." His free eye squinted. "Sometimes serendipity takes over when you ignore the rules. Cheers!"

They smiled. "Perfect," said the doctor. "In this case, I *know* you have a keeper." He handed the camera back to Hope. "Now I'm afraid you must excuse me. I have afternoon rounds to get back to."

Sarah said, "I hope we'll meet again, Doctor."

His return glance went to Hope, not quite disapproving and not quite amused. He bowed gravely, and was off.

"What do you think you're doing?" demanded Hope.

"I don't know what you mean."

She tapped Sarah's bejeweled wrist, lifted the fluting of lace at her throat, the egret plume on her velvet hat. "Your husband is a wealthy man."

"The races are a sporting event," said Sarah. "It's all just good sport, Hope."

"Well, I've had enough sport for one day. And Pearl's waiting for me for our afternoon lesson."

"You go ahead, then. I'm feeling lucky." She smiled at Hope's stricken look. "There aren't many ways for an honorable woman to feather her own nest. But at least in Shanghai, this is one of them."

Hope collected herself. "I'll leave you to it, then."

But as she started off down the gallery Sarah called after her. "You'd best find your way, too, Hope. Fortune and love are as fickle as fate."

ॐॐॐ

"You will never believe who is here in Shanghai," Hope said, when Paul returned the following week.

"And why not?" He was looking over the piles of chits and letters that had accumulated on his desk in his absence. Why hadn't Yen sorted these?

"Because it's too amazing. Here, I can't tell you who without telling how I discovered him!"

"Him." Now she had his attention. The bursting animation of her eyes and mouth, the way she was twisting and turning, excited as a child. "Sit down, Hope."

Laughing at the still untold story, she pulled up a chair opposite his desk. "You see, I went to the racecourse with Sarah last week, and we ran into the doctor who examined Morris right after he was born. I had my camera with me, and he seemed to know quite a lot about photography, so Sarah suggested he take our picture, which he did. When I came home I finished the roll of film with some shots of the children, and next day took it down to Denniston's for developing. Nothing unusual about that, but when I returned to pick up the prints, the clerk refused to give them to me. He said I had to wait for the new house photographer to return. I couldn't imagine what was going on, and the clerk is such a dour boy that I was about to quit the whole business when the door swung open, and who should walk in?" She looked at Paul expectantly.

He let out an impatient sigh. "If I know, you would not tell this story."

"Jed Israel!"

At the blankness of his answering look she tucked in the corners of her mouth, went to the low blackwood table in the corner, and picked up the framed photograph Paul kept there. The wedding picture with the traded hats.

"Our photographer! You remember. He had that painful stutter. Said he was going to enter our picture in some contest? Well, he did, and it won him a trip to Shanghai! Now he's living here. Can you believe it?"

He took the picture and set it on his desk. The point of her story did not interest him, but its beginning did. "I heard about your outing to the racecourse."

His tone brought her up short. "From whom?"

"Hwang Yun-shu came to visit me in Peking. He said he and his wife saw you that day."

"Yes, I saw Renata, but—"

"Hwang has much influence in many places. Eugene Chou also is well known. All Shanghai is aware that he has taken an American concubine. All Shanghai knows her name." His hand had curled into a fist as they talked. They both now became aware of this, but he chose not to unfold it.

"You are not my concubine, Hope. No one must be allowed to think—even suspect such a thing."

A liquid movement that he could not decipher rolled across Hope's face. She sat down. After a long pause, she said evenly, "You know Renata Hwang invited me and Pearl to her home after she'd seen me talking with Sarah at the ball last winter. After that visit, I sent three invitations for her to come here. She declined them all without even offering an excuse. I don't think we can blame that on Sarah."

"You do not understand."

She leaned forward. "Then make me understand."

His gaze fell on the two sparring, fire-breathing dragons carved into the ebony highboy beside his desk. "You remember this letter my mother writes to me after we marry."

"I hardly think I could forget."

"In this letter, she writes of a bride."

"Ling-yi."

"So. I did not discover until I return to Wuchang from America that my mother has already paid the bride price, wedding gifts are exchanged between the families, and Ling-yi is performing her duties as my mother's daughter-in-law."

"What—" Hope's voice caught in her throat. "But how could she . . . without you even knowing!"

"The news of the earthquake was very bad. When my mother hears, she thinks I cannot survive, or if I live, then I cannot be whole. When she does not hear from me for many weeks, she thinks she must act for herself. So she arranges a spirit wedding."

"I don't believe it." Hope paced to the middle of the room. "To wish you dead!"

"Her wish is for a daughter-in-law. Perhaps with a bride waiting, the gods will preserve her son. This is her thinking."

"But we wrote her that you were well and married and refused her wishes!"

"It was already done," said Paul quietly.

She leaned against his desk, circling her thumb on the wooden surface. He touched her hand. "You are my only wife, Hsin-hsin. My chosen wife."

"All these months," she said. "Jin. And Mulan, that day at her house. *How* could you never tell me!"

An ugly twitching had taken hold of her left eye, and her lip curled. He let go of her. "I do not tell you because I know you cannot accept. But now you see that you must not go out with Sarah Chou. Surely you understand that."

"I understand more than that." Their eyes met but jerked away as if from an electric shock. Hope had her hand on the doorknob before she spoke again. "I will comfort myself with the belief that this woman stays in Wuchang." She did not turn to face him. "But I would like to know for a fact if you—if you've lain with her."

"Hope. She is nothing to me."

"Have you slept with her, Paul?"

"No."

ॐॐॐ

December 1, 1912

I have lived in this city of the damned for almost a year, but I am only now beginning to feel the true horror of the place. Oh, gay, yes, it is very gay, as Rome before the fall. The streets ring with laughter, hotel lobbies bounce with song, ballrooms throb with the music of twelve-piece orchestras and sigh with the world's most accomplished dance hostesses. Meanwhile, in the darkened alleys, children are bought and sold and left to die, beggars lift up oozing stumps, and opium addicts lie in a stupor, prize patrons of the commerce that keeps the ballroom ladies in silk. And my own place in this world of false mirrors—ah, yes, my position as wife to the despised and mother of the despised, and then you flip the mirror over and it's neither my husband nor children but I myself who am the vilest of them all.

I begin to understand Sarah and the hardness of her shell. And also her advice that I should feather my own nest. Through all of this I persist in loving Paul, and yet my respect—and trust—for him falters with each new evidence of his weakness, the passive restraint with which he endures his mother's machinations, even the wilting way he bows along with his hero Sun before the ogre Yüan. If only he would withdraw, tell his mother and this other wife that he will not see them again, tell Sun that his stomach for politics is gone. If only we could start over.

᠅᠅᠅

4

Early in 1913 the family moved to a terraced row house on Pushi Road—brick, with three narrow stories and a small paved yard. Rented rather than borrowed, its modest dimensions reflected the limitations of Paul's income.

"Hush," Hope said when he started to apologize. "There are other families near, which is good for the children, and as renters we can feel free to make this a real home."

Making a home had taken on new importance for Hope in light of Paul's revelation. No matter that he had always assured her he did not want a Chinese wife; now he had one, and Hope could not help but view her as a threat. If Paul felt a foreigner in his own home, wouldn't Ling-yi, with her familiar ways, inevitably tempt him? Hope knew he *had* felt out of place in that Mediterranean villa—so had she! But the new house gave her a chance not just to balance (as Sarah advised) but to integrate East and West, with comfort as the moderator. To this end, she bought a Western-style easy chair for Paul, but upholstered it in the same celadon Jacquard she had noted on his mother's reception hall chairs. She ordered a sofa made for the parlor with the classic Chinese blackwood frame—but very un-Chinese springs and soft pillows. She laid rush matting over the bare and otherwise drafty tile floors, Oriental carpets in the bedrooms, and from Antique Street hauled a rosewood headboard carved with two magpies ("symbolize married bliss," the dealer had informed her) for the new four-poster. She had Yen hang a swing for Pearl from the Chinese elm that shaded the backyard, bordered the front walk with pots of vibrant red geraniums, and, at either side of the gate, planted night-blooming jasmine.

As the house took shape Hope noticed the children becoming more boisterous, the servants more relaxed. Paul smiled more, joked, and seemed less inclined to work late into the night. Nothing more was said of his mother's other daughter-in-law, as Hope now thought of her, nor did he issue further prohibitions against her fraternizing with Sarah Chou, though he knew she did continue to see her friend discreetly, inviting Sarah to bring young Gerald to play with Pearl or arranging to meet at French Park (as opposed to the British playgrounds, where their "half-breed" children were not allowed). Hope had no other women friends, and Paul was well aware how difficult it would be to make any. For the moment, however, she was happy.

One afternoon toward the end of March, after weeks of fog and rain, spring arrived in a blast of sunshine. Hope had just finished shooting a series of photographs of the house for her father and Mary Jane. Joy had taken Pearl up the block to play with some Danish neighbor children, and Paul was not due back from Peking until later that afternoon. Plenty of time, Hope decided, to put Morris in his pram and walk downtown to the photo shop.

The sky, as they set off, was a joyous blue. Plum and cherry blossoms drifted like snow. The girls from the mills, packed nine to a wheelbarrow, sang as they went by, and on Nanking Road, electric billboards shimmered, horns tooted, and Gramophone marches blared from loudspeakers outside Robinson's Piano Company. When they arrived at Denniston's, Jed Israel greeted Hope warmly, coming out from behind the counter to help her bring in the pram.

Jed's appearance had changed little in the seven years since Evanston. He still looked a gentle cross between boy and man with a stiff handle of cayenne-colored hair falling into his eyes. He had not surrendered to the typical young man's compulsion to facial hair but was smooth-shaven and freckled, with sea-green eyes staring voraciously over wide, sharp cheekbones. He reminded Hope of her young foster brother Jimmy Wayland, always eager, fearless, and incurably merry. At seventeen Jimmy had followed Doc to Oregon in search of gold and was crushed in a mine cave-in.

"He's p-p-p-pretty," said Jed, studying the sleeping Morris.

Hope smiled.

"I g-g-g-g-guess you're not ssss-posed to say a boy's p-pretty," he apologized, twisting his mouth as if to unscrew his speech impediment.

"It's all right." Hope lowered herself into a corner chair and rubbed her tired ankles. There was no one else in the store. "I think he's pretty, too. Not many men even look at babies."

"I l-l-l-look at everything."

"I suppose you do. Is that a natural instinct for a photographer, do you think? Or is it a skill you cultivate?" She gave a laugh and straightened up. "Or is it just an excuse to snoop?"

Jed continued to watch the baby. "I'd c-c-call it a p-privilege."

Hope peeled off her gloves, at once chastened and envious of the young man's passion. "Well." She drew the rolls of film from a pouch inside the pram. "I'm almost afraid to let you see what's on these."

"M-m-m-m-missus Leon, don't s-say that. You're just l-l-learning. Kodak lies—that 'You press the button, w-we do the rest'—not if you want to make a real sta-statement."

"Make a statement," Hope repeated. Jed's crippled talk made her head hurt, yet she genuinely liked the boy, admired the ambition that had brought him halfway around the world. And, as she followed his gaze now through the shop window to a red-turbaned Sikh performing a ballet of traffic direction atop his crossroads pedestal, she suspected Jed had a good eye.

"You know S-s-s-stieglitz?" He beckoned her to a shelf of books on the opposite wall and opened a volume of *Camera Work* to a photograph called *The Steerage*. It showed an immigrant ship from the upper deck, with nattily dressed men in boaters and suits looking down on the kerchiefed women and children, the hanging laundry and squall of the steerage class. The image started a knot in Hope's stomach as she remembered the steamer trips to and from Kiukiang, with Paul forced down below, and that despicable Brit on the ship coming over . . .

She heard the door swing open behind her, Jed move to help another customer. A moment later Hope glanced up to find Stephen Mann peering over her shoulder. "Looks like young Mr. Israel is turning you into an aficionado. Good to see you again, Mrs. Leon."

"Dr. Mann." To her annoyance she felt herself coloring.

The doctor blithely turned to the pram, running a practiced eye over Morris. "He looks well."

"I've been taking him to the Native Hospital," she lied, "for his examinations. You were right, they are most humane." She was gratified by his answering wince.

The doctor pulled out the film he had brought for Jed to develop. "It's a personal project," he explained, as if she had inquired. "The hospital doesn't know and wouldn't approve if they did."

"Oh?" Hope pretended only polite interest.

"The street children. Almost all of them are diseased or crippled or maimed, but no one knows how much of the damage is inflicted intentionally, either by themselves or their parents."

"Intentionally!"

"A god-awful sore can increase a street urchin's income dramatically."

Hope cringed at the thought of the little girl who often stood waving her fly-covered stump outside the house, how readily she would dole a tael to the mother to make them go away.

"And then there are the girls who are left to starve, or whose deaths are helped along before they're abandoned." Dr. Mann spoke around the stem of his pipe, his brow furrowed and his eyes stern. He had an air of quiet solidity that made him impossible to dislike but also difficult to penetrate.

She broke from his gaze. "So you're documenting the damage. What good can that do?"

"The Chinese authorities refuse to see what's under their noses, and as long as they're allowed not to see, they won't begin to do anything about it. Understand, it suits them to let the beggars do themselves in. They pretend the numbers aren't there, the problem is a trifling—"

Hope checked her watch. Paul should be home soon. Not that she objected to Mann's noble goal, but it seemed to her classic missionary posturing—the benevolent white man stepping in to show his yellow brothers the way. What were Paul and Sun and the rest all doing if not to turn this society around, in Sun's words, to "give people livelihood." She smiled at Jed, who had been listening with interest, and said in a tone that addressed both men, "I'm sorry, but my husband's train is due in shortly. I didn't realize it was so late."

"Could I walk with you?" Dr. Mann replied.

For some reason that she couldn't identify, this offer irritated Hope. Instead of answering, she began maneuvering the pram toward the exit. The men were moving to help her when the door flew open and a young Chinese hospital attendant summoned the doctor.

"Shooting at North Station! I think is important senator."

Hope froze, her breath caught in her throat, the man's words reverberating through her with such force that she probably would have fainted had Dr. Mann not laid a steadying grip on her arm and Morris chosen that moment to whimper in his sleep. "Which senator?" she managed to ask.

"We do not know—"

Before he could finish, Hope had wrenched herself away from the doctor, was scooping the baby into her arms. "I'm coming," she said, in a voice that permitted no argument.

The attendant had two rickshaws waiting, and Dr. Mann quickly hailed two more, for Jed insisted on coming, too, closing the shop behind him. But the day that only minutes ago had struck Hope as cause for celebration now pained her. The light seemed blinding, the air caustic, the throngs of shoppers and beggars and vendors suffocating. Hope shrank back into the rickshaw and curled herself over the baby.

After what seemed an eternity they crossed over Soochow Creek, and were proceeding with speed along Honan Road when the traffic pulled to a halt. Sikh policemen waved batons. Outraged foreigners shouted from rickshaws, threatening to see what's what.

Dr. Mann came back on foot to Hope's cart. It seemed all roads had been blockaded around North Station. Immediately, she was down and hurrying alongside him, shushing the baby, who had awakened and was now writhing against her grip. Jed and Mann seemed to know instinctively not to challenge Hope's persistence, and by flanking her they pushed a wedge through the crowd. But the guards who had been posted at the barricades might have been carved of granite. They held steel bayonets across their chests. Their helmet straps dug into their chins, and their eyes were cold and automatic. Dr. Mann showed his identification, and the hospital attendant barked his orders, at which the soldier he was addressing flicked his eyes for them to pass. But when Jed and Hope tried to go, too, the same guard brandished his weapon and roughly pushed them back.

"It's all right," said Mann. "You two stay where you are, and as soon as I know anything I'll send Tsu-chu here back with the news." He indicated his attendant, then hesitated. "Or I'll come myself."

They disappeared among the green and blue uniforms.

"It'll t-t-t-turn out all r-r-r-r-right," Jed said, and Hope looked at him for the first time since they'd left the shop. Somehow, quickly as everything had happened, he had still managed to equip himself with two cameras.

"Go ahead," she said softly. "We'll be fine." He leaned toward her and brushed a hand over the baby's head, then edged off along the barricade, snapping photographs of the soldiers, the gawking crowd, the British captains of industry miffed at missing their train.

Momentarily composed, if the sensation of having molten lead poured through one's veins qualifies as composure, Hope gripped the wiggling Morris and combed the crowd for evidence that her fears were unfounded. Through the patchwork of dialects she was able to make out snatches of the rapidly fomenting rumors, but every detail seemed to point to the worst.

"—on the afternoon train."

"Yüan's men—"

"—victim a Nationalist."

"Try get to Sun—"

"*Ch'ing,*" she said, approaching the guard once again. "*Shei ssu le?*" When not a muscle moved in response, she lifted the baby for him to see. "*Wo hsiang yeh hsü shi wo hsien sheng.*" I think the dead man may be my husband.

The soldier's chinstrap quivered as he shot her a disgusted look, ignoring the child. "*Pu k'o neng,*" he muttered. "*Ssu te shih ko Chung-kuo jen.*" The dead man is Chinese.

"*K'o neng,*" she threw back as Morris let out a wail. "*Wo hsien sheng shih Chung-kuo jen.*" My husband is Chinese.

The man's eyes widened and his grip on the bayonet tightened, not so much out of malice, Hope told herself, as disbelief. After a long hesitation his lips moved, and the air streamed between them in a barely audible confession. "*Wo pu chih tao.*" I don't know.

She drew a shaky breath and begged Morris to stop crying, stay still. He was nearly a year old, and ordinarily she wearied after holding him more than a minute or two, but although she had been standing here nearly half an hour, her arms felt nothing, her legs and feet nothing. Only her heart seemed to be ripping in two, and her head clattered with the constant dodging of the shadow looming ever closer. *What would she do?*

"Hope!" Jed's head wagged between a pair of shoulders and he flung an arm to direct her attention back toward the station. Stephen Mann was throwing a thumbs-up from the platform.

For a moment the mixed signal of this victory gesture and Mann's grim gaze confounded her, but then another voice, closer, cried out her name, and her attention swerved downward, through the drab colors to her husband pushing toward her. At the sight, the tears she had managed all this time to fend off, rose in a cold tide, obscuring her vision and flooding her cheeks. It was no use trying to blink them back, she was weeping, sobbing now uncontrollably as Paul—it really was Paul—rushed past the disbelieving soldier and swept her and Morris into his arms.

"Silly wife," he murmured. "I am not important enough to be in danger."

ও ও ও

But Sung Chiao-jen, the Kuomintang's thirty-one-year-old leader and constitutional hard-liner, was important enough, most notably because he had publicly spoken out against Yüan Shih-k'ai's autocratic leadership. Sung's assassin was identified as a soldier who had been hired by a Shanghai gangster, but it was understood that the gangster was serving Yüan's agents.

That evening, as Paul and Hope lingered alone and silent over the remains of their supper, Paul foresaw the worst. The past year of round-table meetings, posing for pictures, listening to speeches in chambers designed to imitate those of the great Western congresses, strategizing endlessly in smoke-filled banquet halls—it all added up to a wishful charade. Sung's assassination proved that Yüan Shih-k'ai had no interest in democracy, even with himself as President. He wanted to be Emperor.

"Paul," Hope interrupted his thoughts. "I can't bear this."

He swallowed. "I know."

"Then you'll stop. You'll give up your seat and come home. Teach full-time. Get out of politics for good." The anguish in her voice forced his eyes up to hers. That blue.

He shook his head. "Perhaps."

"No perhaps!" She reached across the table and touched his arm. "I'm asking as your wife, for my sake and the children's. Please, Paul."

He studied her small, slender fingers, the pale oval nails with their pearly moons. She did not rip at her hands as he did when agitated, did not tear her own flesh to obscure her fears. No, his wife contained herself inside her skin with the discipline of a general. Only the timbre of her voice, the changing blue of her eyes, her touch betrayed the true intensity of her emotions. "If I resign right away," he said slowly, "this will call too much attention. But by summer, I think so."

Hope slipped her fingers into his palm. "Then we can return to Kuling . . . and you won't leave us?"

"I will not leave you, Hsin-hsin."

☙☙☙

5

Three months later, Hope sat with the children on the back terrace reading poetry about cold, wet gloom. She meant to wring some psychological relief from this steaming June afternoon by evoking hurricanes and blizzards, but the children would have none of it. They squirmed and whined, were tired and sticky and wanted a drink. She was midway

through Longfellow's "Rainy Day" when Yen appeared with their reprieve. "Missy and Master have guests."

"We're not expecting anyone."

"Master say Taitai must come," Yen elaborated. Hope scowled. If these
were Paul's guests they should have no desire for her presence. "Babies
come," he added significantly.

Oh dear, she thought. We're being *presented*. She glanced at her wrinkled
blue dimity, at Pearl in her stained pinafore and Morrie's frayed romper.
"Hurry," she said to Pearl, "go comb your hair and change your dress."
She picked up Morris, who'd gone scrambling on all fours after a lizard,
and called for Ah-nie to put him in a clean suit.

Paul met her in the hallway. He had arrived from Peking only that
morning. "Why didn't you tell me company was coming?" she demanded.

He put his finger to his lips and whispered. "I want to surprise you."

"Surprises again! I look a fright."

He turned her around appraisingly, and with his fingertips gently
pushed the damp strands up from her nape. "You look well, I think. My
old friend William Tan has brought his wife Dai-tzi to live in Shanghai."

"But—"

"No but," he said firmly, pulling her hands from their smoothing and
straightening and crossing them demurely in front of her. "You remember William?"

Hope grimaced. "Yes," she said. "I remember."

William had changed little since Hope's encounter with him in San
Francisco. The same broad squareness of shoulder and head, half spectacles balanced on a nose that seemed far too delicate for the sturdy face.
His young wife, Dai-tzi, also seemed too delicate for William Tan. Slender and fine-boned as a sparrow, she swayed beside him on bound feet,
whatever pain that entailed well concealed behind a bursting smile.

With the ebullience he seemed to reserve for Chinese social occasions,
Paul greeted William like long lost kin. The men bowed and laughed and
nodded, stretching their necks against their starched collars and complaining of the heat in a mixture of English and Mandarin. Dai-tzi giggled, lifting her hand to cover her mouth. Not knowing what else to say,
Hope suggested they sit on the terrace, where there was at least a slight
breeze.

When they were settled William said to Hope, "My wife has been eager to make your acquaintance. She is from the interior and has not met American ladies before." Dai-tzi leaned over to pat Hope's knee. Then she pointed to herself and sat up expectantly. "She would be honored if you will choose for her an American name."

Hope glanced at Paul. He could not have been more pleased with himself. Surprise, indeed.

"Dai-tzi," she said thoughtfully, considering the girl's sunny face, the crisp green of her dress, the white flower in her hair. "Why not Daisy?"

"Day-see?" The young woman cleared her throat, elaborately serious. "Daisy." She lifted her hand and again giggled behind it. William nodded his approval. Daisy, she was.

The amahs appeared holding the children's hands, and Daisy clucked over them unabashedly, touching their hair, fondling their clothing, and pinching them under the chin in the way Hope knew Pearl loathed. It never failed to amaze her how a people so rigid about physical contact between consenting adults could be so uninhibited—even offensively intrusive—when it came to touching children. She rewarded Pearl and Morris for their forbearance by allowing them to load their plates with cakes and sandwiches before escaping to the nursery.

William turned to Paul with a question about the latest outbreak of fighting against Yüan Shih-k'ai in the southern provinces—which some were optimistically calling a Second Revolution.

"They don't stand a chance," answered Paul. "There is no central leadership, little popular support. Yüan has the money and the strength."

"Then maybe it will end soon, and we can go up to Kuling," Hope said, only half joking. She'd had her heart set on Kuling this summer, and if the rebels couldn't possibly win, what was the point of their blockading the river?

William gave her a benign glance and stroked his chin. "I met with Dr. Sun on my way through Japan. He seems to have made his peace with Yüan."

"If he admits the truth, all his work is in vain. So he takes the gold Yüan throws at him and makes speeches in Japan. Sometimes dreamers can bring about miracles, but sometimes those miracles fade like a dream."

"You sound bitter, old friend. Have you given up *your* dream so soon?"

Paul stared absently at the plate of cakes. "Sometimes I think it was a mistake to stay away so long."

William snorted. "Our mistake was not distance but age. Youth believes all things possible."

"And you?" Paul asked. "Where do you stand?"

"I believe Sun will return to his senses and lead the Kuomintang to victory."

Hope was straining to interpret all this (the men had reverted to Mandarin), when Daisy abruptly reached over and touched one of the damp ringlets on her cheek. Hope started so violently that she splashed tea all over her feet. Not the least perturbed, Daisy bent down and yanked up the hem of Hope's dress, not to help wipe the mess as Hope supposed, but to admire her white button-strap shoes.

"*Chen mei*," cooed Daisy. She cupped her hands together with a questioning expression and lowered them beside Hope's feet.

"No." Hope laughed, looking to Paul for assistance, but he and William were deep in talk now, paying no attention. Unable to think how else to respond, she put her sopping napkin aside and reached down to unbutton her shoe. "You see, I just have small feet. No binding."

Daisy stared, mesmerized. Then she put out one of her own tiny feet. No more than three inches long, it was about half the size of Hope's, but shaped more like a hoof than a foot. Hope winced, but complimented her guest on the intricate floral embroidery that covered her homemade shoes. It was the ultimate insult, in Hope's opinion, that after crippling themselves to satisfy this barbaric custom, Chinese women were then required to make by hand the delicate slippers that would conceal the true horror of their maiming.

"*Wo hsiang mai i shuang yu ken de hsieh!*" Daisy clapped her hands and bounced in her seat.

"I'm sorry to interrupt, Paul," said Hope. "I know she's saying she wants something, but I can't make out what."

Paul, who had been paying more attention than he let on, arched an eyebrow. "She says she would like a pair of Western-style shoes with heels like yours."

"But that's not possible, is it?"

William tugged at his lapels. "Even though Daisy is from a very old landowning clan, she has grown up in Hankow. She is literate, and she is very interested in revolution. She understands China must modernize, and ladies, too, must change the old ways. Only yesterday she asks my permission to remove her binding cloths. I have discussed this with your husband. He says maybe you can help my wife. Take her shopping for Western shoes, teach her to walk like a modern lady."

Hope was at a loss. "I'm afraid this will be very painful for Daisy, but of course I'll do what I can—if this is what she genuinely wishes."

William nodded. "As I recall, you have also worked as an English language teacher. I wonder if you will consider teaching Daisy . . . We will pay, of course."

"I wouldn't think of taking your money!" Hope glanced at Paul for approval and found him beaming. "I'm delighted to teach Daisy English. And she can help me polish my Mandarin."

William turned, spoke rapidly to his wife, who blushed and nodded. "She says she, too, will be delighted."

Hope clasped her hands and bowed to Daisy. "I look forward—"

She was interrupted by the unmistakable stutter of gunfire in the distance. By the old Chinese City, from the sound of it.

"So they're going to try," said William calmly.

"Try what!" Hope was unable to conceal her alarm.

"The Chiangnan arsenal near the West Gate. And maybe the *yamen*."

Paul waved a hand. "No need to worry, Hope. They won't dare to touch the Concessions."

"Well, I don't see how you can be so sure! What if Yüan decides to make a purge of the Kuomintang members hiding here?"

"French law protects us. Anyway, it sounds as if Yüan's troops have plenty to keep them busy by the river."

Hope followed Daisy's panicked gaze to the dark bluff of smoke now filling the southern sky. As her fear for the immediate family receded, she thought of Paul's mother's house in Nantao, a mile, maybe less, from the arsenal. Her stepson, Jin, was staying there while attending summer courses at St. John's. Theoretically, he was "looking after Nainai's courts," and this was why he had not been free to visit his father's house. Hope understood the real reason: Nainai had prohibited him from setting foot in the home of the *yang p'otse.* However, if his life were endangered by staying in Nantao . . .

"Paul," she said over another sputter of gunfire, "don't you think Jin had better come stay with us?"

He glanced at her mildly. "The house is not in danger—"

"Regardless, he's only sixteen. He's bound to be frightened staying there with no one but servants for protection."

Paul demurred. He was not willing to violate his mother's orders. He did not speak these words, but they were clear in his eyes—and in his abrupt haste now to bid their guests goodbye. However close a friend William might be, Paul would not air their family business in front of him and Daisy. Hope waited, determined not to cost him face, but with each passing second her will became more inflexible. By the time the door shut and Paul turned back she was absolutely convinced of imminent peril if Jin remained in Nantao.

"You will never forgive yourself if anything happens to him," she said. "And neither will your mother."

Paul would not look at her. He withdrew to his study. By nightfall, Jin had been quartered in Hope's sewing room.

இ)இ)இ)

The bombardment continued through the next month, with attacks focused on the arsenal and *yamen*—the Chinese governor's compound—and on the Woosung forts at the mouth of the delta. Within certain blocks of the fighting, the flag of victory might be traded back and forth after every five rounds, but as Paul had predicted, neither Yüan nor the rebels dared violate the international zone. Within days the *North China Daily* was advising foreigners to resume their routines with only a casually cocked eye for stray shrapnel or shells. Not even the missionary schools and hospitals immediately around the arsenal were evacuated.

Despite all these reassurances and Paul's own unhappy assessment of the rebellion's futility, Hope insisted that Jin remain with them. In truth, she was delighted by the excuse to get acquainted with Paul's son. Removed from Mulan and his *nainai*'s influence, he proved himself a sweet, gentle-spirited boy who, if anything, was as glad for the contact with his stepmother as she was. Though his scholarly upbringing had given him a basic command of written English, he was eager to practice speaking and so became an enthusiastic third once Hope and Daisy's lessons got underway. (These tended to center conversationally around Hope's experiences as a suffragist, her youth among the American pioneers, and her reminiscences of San Francisco during the Gay Nineties—subjects that aroused, in Jin and Daisy, romantic fascination, and, in Hope, a surprisingly cathartic nostalgia.) At the same time, Jin was more than willing to be distracted whenever his half-brother wormed into his lap. Hope would hear laughing and find the two of them tumbling across the floor, or Pearl clambering onto Jin's back yelling "Giddyap, Jin! Giddyap!" Often he would return from his day's classes at St. John's bearing English nougats and butterscotch. He staged a puppet show for Pearl's fifth birthday, and most afternoons he played ball with the children or organized games of tag with the neighbors. At bedtime, he would cast paper-cut shadows of dragons and ponies across the nursery wall.

After his initial reluctance had passed, even Paul seemed to relish Jin's presence. The two often sat late into the night talking about Jin's schoolmates, many of whose fathers were old friends of Paul's, and about the divisions that were forming between the scholars who believed in traditional gentry class rule and those who were convinced the country needed modern leadership. Occasionally they argued.

"I am no soldier," Jin would say, clasping his bony fingers around one knee, "but I believe China's fate lies with its generals." And Paul would light a cigarette and begin to smoke, a habit he had discarded in America but resumed while in Peking. Hope, watching silently over her sewing across the room, thought she detected an aggrieved brightness in his eyes.

"Generals are bandits," he said. "They care only for riches, and they will buy or sell their own families if this bring them personal gain. It has always been and always will be. If our country's fate lies with these warlords, then China has no future."

"But Father, Sun's revolution was won by soldiers—"

"And handed to a warlord, and look at us now!"

Jin's liquid gaze met Hope's in bemusement. Poor boy, she thought, he must have been raised on stories of his father's heroic idealism. And here Paul's become a pessimist.

∽∽∽

August arrived as usual, muggy and hot. The leaves of the plane trees hung motionless. Even the most lightweight clothing stuck to one's skin, and even the children grew listless. But the rebel fighting along the river droned on, and Paul was engaged in endless secret meetings with Sun Yat-sen, who had returned to Shanghai after Sung Chiao-jen's assassination but still refused to end his "retirement" and take a public stand against Yüan. In this atmosphere, the slightest breeze, even a whisper of relief from the stalemate of weather and politics inspired celebration. And so, one Saturday after a morning thunderstorm, Hope invited Jin to come out for a stroll in the cool, freshened air. Yen had taken the children to a moving picture show, and this was a rare chance for them to talk alone.

She tucked her camera into her purse, lifted her oiled paper parasol against the lingering drizzle, and turned arbitrarily toward downtown. Jin walked with his hands thrust into his pockets, a flat-brimmed derby worn so low that it folded the tops of his big ears. He kicked a ginkgo nut as he walked, head down, and though they were attracting the usual disapproving stares from foreigners and predatory harangues from vendors and beggars and rickshaw pullers, Jin did not seem to notice. He had Paul's ability to withdraw into himself, to pull the shutters down against everything around him. Hope supposed they both had developed this skill as a defense against Nai-li's raucous invasions, but, if so, this only made her more resentful at having it used against her.

"You said the other night you were no soldier," she said. "What will you do, then, when you complete your studies?"

He gave her a sidelong look. She had thought the question innocuous, but it seemed to disconcert him, and when at length he mumbled, "I am undecided," she suspected this was not the case at all.

She was trying to think of something reassuring to say when a loud boom issued from the riverfront. Across the avenue a man in a straw boater with red, white, and blue ribbons tooted the horn of his roadster at a young brunette carrying a lace parasol. He swung the door open and she jumped in, laughing, the parasol jerking as the car started forward. Hope got the Kodak up in time to capture the pair just as the bloom of gunsmoke rose above the trees in the background.

When she lowered the camera, Jin was watching her with an expression of such undisguised envy that she asked if he wanted to try a picture himself. He hesitated only a moment, but once the Kodak was in his hands, he seemed overawed, examining the pebbled leather casing, the hardware and lens, as if the contraption were some priceless wonder.

"It's only a Kodak," she said. "It won't break easily, and even if it did, it's not costly to repair."

He sighed. "Do you know this man Diga?"

Hope thought hard, but finally shook her head.

"He paints pictures," Jin said softly. "First he uses the camera. Dancing girls. Singsong girls. Some old men. Then he makes paintings." He made a circular motion with the camera. "I see photographs of these paintings he makes from photographs."

"And you like them?" Hope smiled.

"Very much."

Perhaps it was the wistful tone of his voice or his tremor as he lifted the camera to his eye, or the way he absently wet his lips as he trained the lens now on a flame tree blooming over a garden wall, now on an elderly gentleman taking his canary for a walk, now on a young Chinese girl in bright embroidered silks and her Western-dressed beau—but suddenly Hope said, "Are you thinking of Edgar Degas?"

Jin returned the camera with a respectful bow. "*Shih*," he said. "Diga."

They resumed their walk. The sun, forcing its way through the mist, made the air quiver with the threat of resumed heat, and the traffic now seemed to speed up, as if to pack in as much activity as possible before the next onslaught of lethargy. It was risky to push Jin, Hope realized, but having gained this unexpected opening, she could not resist. She said, "Do you have any of your drawings here in Shanghai?"

He pretended not to understand.

"I've tried drawing," she persisted. "I'm not very good, but I admire artists."

He answered without breaking stride or looking at her. "This kind of art is despised in China."

"Surely not! Painting is honored here. Like poetry."

"Classical painting," he said in a voice raw with contempt. "Classical verse."

So that was it. Jin had fastened his ambitions on Western art. She could just imagine what his grandmother would say about that!

Another cannonade rumbled across the city as they came to Nanking Road. The busy shoppers hardly looked up, but the servants and vendors, whose families lived in and around the Chinese City, studied the skies with concern. Jin turned abruptly. "Please do not tell my family about this conversation."

The guilt in her stepson's eyes seemed vastly out of proportion to his transgression, yet Hope chided herself for presuming that she understood anything of the pressures on Jin to conform, obey, uphold his family's expectations. Pressures perhaps even more overbearing for his father's revolutionary ambitions. And for Paul's violation of Nai-li's will by taking an American wife. "No," she said. "No, of course not."

Suddenly it occurred to her that Jin might enjoy meeting Jed Israel. They weren't far from the photo shop now, and the boy seemed in no hurry to go back, so she turned up Chapoo Road.

Sarah and her little Gerald were poised to leave Denniston's when Hope and Jin entered. Sarah was little interested in photography unless she was the model, but, like Hope, she had gravitated to the guilelessly American Jed Israel as a pal, and now he was infecting Sarah's six-year-old with his passion for the camera. Hope often ran into the two of them here, and since Paul still tacitly disapproved of Sarah, she was glad for these neutral and unplanned meetings. She was not, however, glad for the opportunity of introducing Sarah to Jin.

"What a lovely young man, Hope," Sarah gloated. "Is he *yours?*"

Hope felt herself turning a dark purple under Jed's amused watch. "Sarah Chou," she said coldly. "This is Paul's son Jin."

"Ah!" Sarah pressed her lips together and dipped her head. "Honored to meet you Mr.——eh——Liang, I suppose it is."

"Yes," said Hope. "It is."

Jin bowed noncommittally and smiled at Gerald as Hope nudged him on to Jed. She explained her stepson's interest in painters who worked from photographs, and soon the two of them were nose deep in Jed's library.

"He's a beauty," Sarah whispered. "Can you keep him?"

"Must you?" said Hope.

Sarah feigned a pout and smoothed her son's dark curls. "I'm soft on men. Can't be helped." They stood awkwardly for a moment as Gerald demonstrated the pinhole camera Jed had given him.

"You're making inroads with his family, then?" Sarah asked, the mockery gone.

"Only with Jin."

"Well, be careful. Chinese families are like two-headed snakes. Just when you've got one head tamed, the other whips around and bites you."

"I've known *that* for years," said Hope.

"Still bears keeping in mind."

Having completed his demonstration, Gerald was tugging at his mother's skirt, impatient to get outside where he could experiment with his toy in the light.

"It's good to see you, Hope." Sarah made a fist and brought it against her mouth, frowning. "Oh! I know what I wanted to tell you. That doctor we like so well. Mann? I heard the other day he's moving on."

Hope felt a confused twinge, remembering the doctor's kindness that day at North Station—but also the strange hard tension in his eyes as he signaled Paul's safe passage. "What do you mean, moving on?"

Sarah sighed. "Tragic loss, isn't it? I don't really know. Up the coast or upriver, going to run his own hospital or something. Seems he got himself in a bit of a ruckus with some of the municipal fathers."

"His work with the street children," Hope suggested.

Sarah straightened her hat. "I wouldn't know, but at least he's still in the country, there's hope. Oops!" She giggled. "No pun intended."

Hope groaned, and embraced her. "Sarah, you are incorrigible."

"Do my best." Sarah waved to the preoccupied men and hurried after her son.

A few minutes later the Chinese clerk returned from an errand and Jed announced he was due for a break. Why didn't they take their cameras to the Bund and see if they could get some pictures of the fighting? Hope's better judgment was no match for Jed's enthusiasm. Ten minutes later they were hanging over the stone embankment by the river, aiming across the glittering tin godown roofs and snapping pictures of a crew of Chinese rebels like small black spiders overtaking a German gunboat.

Hope and Jin shared her camera. Jed showed them various ways to frame and focus. The cannons thundered. The flags along the Bund snapped in the breeze. The fighting seemed disconnected, harmless.

"It's obscene to be having such fun in a war zone," Hope shouted over a spurt of gunfire.

"We are not in a war zone," Jin reminded her. "Only watching."

"I g-go closer s-sometimes," said Jed. "Better shots when y-you can see the soldier's face—"

He was interrupted by a sudden escalation of shelling. Downriver, upriver, toward the opposite shore—the commandeered gunboat's artillery men were firing anywhere but toward the arsenal where the rebels had doubtless ordered them to fire. The shrapnel started rattling the trees along the Bund, and the photographers beat a prudent retreat.

"Not in a war zone, eh?" said Hope.

But all three of them were laughing and breathless, still more exhilarated than afraid. And Hope agreed as readily as Jin when Jed Israel asked if they would come out "scouting" with him again sometime.

On the tram back to the house, Hope and Jin made a pact. Hope would not reveal Jin's secret ambitions if Jin would not tell his father what they had done today.

♫♫♫

By September, the "Second Revolution" had gone down in defeat. Troops loyal to Yüan Shih-k'ai celebrated their victory by looting, raping, maiming, and generally sacking the city of Nanking for three straight days. Hundreds of Kuomintang members were executed throughout the country, and in Peking the few governors left with Kuomintang ties were replaced by Yüan Shih-k'ai loyalists—the so-called Republicans. Sun Yat-sen once again took refuge in Japan.

In October the ministers of the Western nations formally recognized Yüan Shih-k'ai's government, and President Woodrow Wilson sent personal congratulations on Yüan's election as President. One month later Yüan ordered the dissolution of the Nationalist Party, canceled its parliamentary membership, and dismissed all Kuomintang members of the assembly. Paul at last withdrew from politics and accepted lecture positions at Shanghai, Fudan, Nanyang, and St. John's University, where Jin had entered the freshman class. He taught political science, Chinese poetry, and New Meiji and American literature. Before the first firecrackers marked the Chinese New Year, the Leons were expecting their next child.

ভ্ভ্ভ্

6

Shanghai Native Hospital
August 13, 1914
Dearest Mary Jane and Dad,

Short and sweet, we have a darling baby girl! *Weeks* overdue, she was painfully big, but with a thick head of hair and round pink cheeks. This time I had lots of company and support, what with my friends Sarah Chou and Daisy Tan and everyone at this hospital so jolly. Yes, Paul was here and a prince with Morris and Pearl. And Paul's son Jin was on hand—the nurses all went into a swoon over him! The embarrassing thing is, we can't decide what to call our new princess. I think maybe Jade (goes so well with Pearl), or perhaps she'll be a flower—Rose or Lily or Jasmine. Anyway, Paul says not to worry. The Chinese custom is not to name a newborn until the one-month mark—like giving a boy baby a girl's name or heaping false insults upon a little one, it's one of a thousand tricks the Chinese play so the evil spirits won't try to take their children.

Well, here comes little no-name now for her supper. I just wanted to dash this off to let you know how very happy and well we are. Will write again after we're settled back home.

With all my love,
Hope

1311 S. Hill St., Los Angeles
August 25, 1914
Dearest Hope and Paul,

We are writing with sad news. We made a visit up to Berkeley last week and found the Wall house boarded and empty. A quarantine notice was flapping around the yard, and the neighbors told us Li-li and the little boy had died of the influenza. Thomas apparently went on a rampage, putting his fist through windows, building a sort of pyre with all Li-li's and the child's belongings and setting it afire in the backyard. He howled for days, they said it sounded like an animal being strangled. Finally he did quiet down—if he hadn't, the neighbors said, he would have been put into an asylum. But then when the news started about the war in Europe, Thomas said there was nothing left for him to live for, but maybe there was something yet worth dying for. And the next anyone knew he was gone.

Oh, this is a hard, hard burden. That man was golden. Seemed everything he touched was beautiful and good. Especially Li-li and that baby—imagine if this were your own Morris! We think of this over and over, and pray that such a tragedy never strikes your babies, Hope. But it tests one's faith to see two such souls as Thomas and Li-li so doomed.

Even as we write this, a check of the calendar tells us that you must have your new one by now. A baby girl or boy? We pray for health for both of you, and are glad for your last piece of news that Paul would be there with you this time.

Here, times are hard. Mary Jane's investments have been dashed to pieces by the market, and it's slow to grow a practice with money so scarce. But we take comfort from each other. In spite of everything there is still much to cherish and be thankful for.

You have all our love and dearest wishes,
Your Mary Jane and Dad

39 Pushi Road, Shanghai
September 30, 1914
Dearest Mary Jane and Doc,

I have just received your letter of August telling this sad news about Thomas and Li-li. You will forgive me, I do not to show this to Hope just now. You see, our own new baby is no more and I do not think Hope will bear to know more sadness.

We had little warning. Hope and the child were home. All was well. In the night the baby amah came to us, very worried. The baby has a fever so high she does not cry, all her bedclothes wet. The foreign doctor came. The Chinese doctor came, but no remedies could help. In one day the little heart stops beating and last week we laid her in her grave.

The foreign doctor has given Hope medicine to make her sleep. You remember her quiet grief after our first child died. She is this way again, but more. She does not weep or speak, barely eats. She stands at the window and watches Pearl and Morris at their play and forbids them to leave our home. She will not see her friends, does not even touch the camera you sent, of which she has become most fond. I can give her no comfort except to sit and quietly hold her hand. She tells me this helps, though I see no change.

I trust you will not think me hard, my wife's parents, but I do not know what to do. I think no man can comprehend a mother's bond to her child—a bond that grows like a vine even before the birth, and multiplies its growth in every day that follows. This child lived long enough for Hope to think of her as a daughter, and so for her this is not the loss of possibility, as it seems for me, but the loss of a true person. She blames me, then, for not understanding and for caring more about her than about our lost child. But I cannot change this. I will do anything to restore my wife, yet I do not know what to do.

Please forgive me. I will deliver your letter to Hope as soon as she will come back to herself. Thank you for your kind thoughts and wishes.

Yours,
Paul

VII
RENEWAL
PEKING
(1914–1916)

જ⁀જ⁀જ

1

Whike Hope grieved for the child that, by Chinese custom, had never existed, the world was rapidly changing. In June, Serbian nationalists in the Balkans had assassinated an Austro-Hungarian Archduke. Now all of Europe was spiraling into war, and the Continental powers that had been so intent on dominating China were forced to turn their attentions back home. Britain, France, Belgium, and Russia summoned back their warships from the Shanghai delta, their key diplomats from the treaty ports, their fittest young soldiers from prime Asian garrisons to battle the troops of Germany's Kaiser on distant fronts with names like Marne and Ypres, Tannenberg and Verdun. In Shanghai's International Settlement, on the streets, in cafés, on the trams, and in Paul's university classes, all talk turned toward Europe, with betting decisively in the Allies' favor.

That August, when Japan seized Germany's underdefended treaty port in Shantung, Paul and his friends were outraged but hardly surprised. Japan's position in China had long been that of a kindred adversary. The two countries were both Asian, shared many similar customs and attitudes, in particular a suspicion of Westerners. Yet when Paul had studied in Tokyo, he was impressed by Japan's modernization and by her ability—unlike China—to turn Western ideas and technology to her own expansionist goals. Unfortunately, most of this expansion was at China's expense. Twenty years ago the Japanese had taken Korea and Formosa from Chinese control. Later, Manchuria. Now Paul saw clearly that the real reason Japan had declared war against Germany was to gain Shantung—a prize toehold on China's central coast. At the same time, Japanese attachés were descending on Peking to offer their "support" to Yüan Shih-k'ai. It looked to Paul like a ploy to turn Yüan into Japan's puppet and, through him, to control the Chinese government.

In October Sun Yat-sen decided Paul should return to Peking. Paul's command of the Japanese language and contacts among Japanese diplomats, Sun reasoned, could make him indispensable to Yüan as he was being wooed by Tokyo. Paul could thus funnel vital information to Sun from inside the Presidential Palace, while Sun worked to reorganize Nationalist forces in the south against Yüan. As long as Paul was cautious and discreet, his personal safety would be assured by his longtime association with Li Yüan-hung, the powerful general from Hupei whom Yüan had appointed as his Vice President. It was Li who, at Sun's discreet suggestion, named Paul to the critical but inconspicuous post of director of the Government Printing Office, overseeing official propaganda.

As Paul sat packing the contents of his study for this return to the north, he thought how fortunate it was that he had not told Hope of the assassination he'd witnessed in Peking during his last visit. Two generals, revolutionary heroes from Hupei, had been invited to the capital to meet with Yüan. At a banquet at the Legion Hotel, Paul listened to the two proclaim their support for Yüan's government. Afterward, he'd emerged from the hotel to see Yüan's secret police surround the generals' car. The men were arrested along with scores of their supporters and summarily shot within hours. Since one of the generals had been Li Yüan-hung's rival in Hankow, it was widely believed that the execution was ordered to solidify Li's support for the President. A favor, one might say.

If he had a choice, even now, Paul thought, he would leave Hope here in Shanghai, where he could be assured she and the children were safely removed from Yüan's madness. But there were other dangers in that course. The loss of their baby had left a sadness in Hope that alarmed him. Her eyes were hollow, her body gaunt. Her hands moved listlessly, and her voice seemed to echo with a darkness that not even Pearl or Morris could ease.

"I want to go home," she had said one day, in a voice so low and tone-less that it seemed inhuman. Her eyes were hard, their blue like ice, and savage. He had recoiled at her ugliness, and then she had folded in on her-self and said nothing more. The words lay between them still. Home was a place she would go without him, from which she would not return.

And so he had promised when he told her of his new position. "This time will not be like before. First thing, I make arrangements. My family comes with me."

Three weeks later, Hope and the children boarded the British coastal steamer SS *Kashing*, bound for Tientsin. They were accompanied only by Yen and Ah-nie, as the other servants were unwilling to move so far from their native soil. Paul had written, in any case, that a new home with staff was already awaiting their arrival.

ॐॐॐ

Pearl had been just three and Morris not yet born the last time they nav-igated this harbor. Now, as the flags and domes and marble spires of Shanghai slipped behind them, Hope recalled her excitement at the first sight of these waters, the red junks with their enormous square sails and painted eyes, the slipper ships and sampans, chained cormorants diving for fish. Then that strange apparition, Frank Pearson stepping onto the bridge of that warship, in a blink disappearing. A curse, she thought now. Had she taken heed, caught the first ship back to the States, how much anguish would have been spared. A life, in any case. One less grave to leave behind.

They turned up the coast into a cold, gusting wind. Paddyfields and low villages replaced the city skyline. Tsungming Island lifted its small but treacherous hump amid warning buoys and the algaed hulks of vessels that had ignored the warning. The river churned now, changing color from the yellow silt liquid of the Whangpoo to the viscous green of the Yangtze delta. Beyond, lay the open blue of the Pacific and, all those thousands of miles across, home

She shaded her eyes as the steamer pulled north, like a toy drawn by a distant magnet. Someone else held the controls. Who was to say whether that someone was Paul, or Sun, or Yüan, the Japanese, or simply fate? The one certainty was that she and her family had become hostage to this bru-tal country. Whatever fantasies she'd entertained after her baby's death, she had no more real power to leave China than had this shabby little hulk of a steamer to break the pull of the shore and head for open seas.

The sun beat down for three long days as they skirted the Yellow Sea. When they rounded the jutting cape of Shantung, Yen swore at the Japanese under his breath, but Hope felt only a stony neutrality. The warship flags with their imperial suns hung wilted, barely recognizable, and from her vantage point, the small, rigid figures that guarded the shoreline looked no more threatening than scarecrows. Though she knew the Japanese invaders were responsible for her forced move north, whether she should curse them or thank them remained to be seen.

Late on the fourth afternoon, they docked at the port of Tientsin. Yen took charge, hailing coolies to carry their bags and herding them all to the nearby train that would carry them on to Peking. The taste of coal and metal, the fuming of the rails, the snap of steel sent Hope's thoughts tumbling back eight years.

The compartment in which Yen settled them, of course, was far grander than the second-class Pullman she had shared with Sarah and Kathe, but it bore the same scents of wicker and plush and mahogany, iron and steam. Here were the same white lace antimacassars. Lamps of frosted glass. Here she and Paul would not have been forced to ride in separate classes. But Paul was still not with her. And her companions now were even more the victims of circumstance than her wedding companions had been.

"Mama, Mama!" Pearl cried. "Look what Yen brought!"

The whistle was screeching and Yen stood outside, hoisting a basket lined with their own starched linens. "What on earth? Here——" Hope swung open the door.

"*Mienpao.*" He thrust the basket into her hands. "I buy, all clean. See, Taitai? No *ping chün.*"

Hope followed his eyes across the crowded platform to the vendor's portable charcoal oven. "Please, Mama," Pearl begged. Hope shook her head. With cholera, yellow fever, tuberculosis rampant, the risks were simply too great.

But Morris was smacking his lips at the sweet spice fragrance. "I take from oven with Taitai's own fork!" Yen said, brandishing the silver utensil.

Hope grudgingly peeled back the napkin and found ten stuffed buns, small and glossy as egg yolks.

"This is how the Empress Dowager killed off the Emperor," she warned, but the children already had dug in and Pearl would not be happy until her mother, too, tasted the steaming bread.

"I suppose," said Hope, "there might be worse ways to die."

"Oh, Mama," Pearl squealed. "You're too silly!"

"Am I?" Hope turned her gaze out the window to the treaty port's dull gray Western architecture. "I think my problem is I'm just not silly enough."

But her mood lifted when they passed out into the countryside. Here the hills swelled and rolled like an ocean. The fields burst with late crops of winter wheat and *kaoliang*, soybeans, rhubarb, and corn. The villages were clusters of small mud-brick dwellings capped by the graceful black-winged rooflines, which Hope often thought constituted the single most unifying image in China. After nightfall the oil lamps burning inside the houses wavered like fireflies over shadowy men riding babies on their knees, families bent over evening meals, mothers putting children to bed. These glimpses of strangers encased in the countryside's immense blackness tore at Hope's heart in a way the grasping, fetid limbs of beggars never had succeeded. These were the people who paid, she thought. When drought withered their crops. When floods washed away their homes. When plagues killed their children and animals. When their sons were taken at gunpoint for soldiers, or the current tyrant residing in Peking doubled and tripled their taxes. And this was the China Paul loved. A China that could be loved because it was still innocent and vulnerable.

With scheduled stops and unscheduled delays and "routine" inspections by government soldiers searching for "rebels and criminals," the hundred-mile journey took hours longer than expected. It was after midnight when the train finally pulled into Ch'ien Men Station, at the edge of the old Tartar City—a torch-lit scene straight out of the Middle Ages. There were clusters of laughing, silk-gowned men still dazed by their evening's debauchery; a train of camels laden with baskets of dried meat and leather, copper and coal from the western provinces; ragged night vendors warming their hands over braziers and offering tea and rice in dispirited tones. Hope scanned up and down the platform, knowing it

was futile to expect Paul after all the delays, feeling disappointed nevertheless by his absence.

Yen hurried them into one large two-seat carriage while ordering their
baggage into another. Morris lay sound asleep in Ah-nie's arms, but Pearl
seemed invigorated by the cold. "Is this the Great Wall?" she asked as they
passed through the tunneled Ch'ien Men Gate.

"No, it's a city wall like the one around the Chinese City in Shanghai."
Hope forced a smile as they emerged on the broad Hatamen Maloo. "But
the Great Wall is not far. Maybe Papa will take us there."

"Oh, please, yes!" The electric lamps along the inner avenue reflected
in Pearl's dark eyes, and Hope envied her craving, her willingness to embrace every myth and fancy this strange country held out. Six years old,
Pearl plunged headlong and with equal enthusiasm into wonder and disaster. She had inherited this trait from her father, Hope thought. And it
was this in both of them that could make them so irresistible, and worrisome.

"Look, Mama. A palace!"

Hope glanced up and gasped. They were poised at the crown of a long,
outstretched hill with the moon hung like a lantern and, below, the roofs
of the Forbidden City sweeping back, successive leaves of ignited gold.
Hope recognized the Imperial Palace at once from Paul's descriptions.
Jewel-like in its beauty and intricate form, this enclosed maze seemed as
remote and uninhabitable as the perfectly preserved ruins of some extinct
civilization. As if to prove the thought, the *mafoo* snapped his whip, the
carriage turned into an unlit *hut'ung*, or alleyway, and the palace vanished.

Hope leaned forward as the carriage slowed to a stop. Yen hopped from
the second carriage, pounded on one of the unmarked doors that lined
the street. While Peking did have its international Legation Quarter, Paul
had warned her they would be living outside it, in the city proper. Unlike
Shanghai, this city was proudly Chinese.

The sound of iron rasped on wood, and the doors groaned opened.
The gateman stepped over the high wooden threshold, bowing and stifling a yawn. Hope helped Pearl down, and Ah-nie followed with Morris
still asleep, as two more drowsy servants shuffled forward. Yen introduced
the slight, bandy-legged man as Kuan, the new cook, and the maid, who
had chewed lips and slightly crossed eyes, as Ju-hua—Chrysanthemum.

Hope gave a perfunctory nod. "Where is my husband? Laoyeh?"

Yen turned to supervise the unloading of baggage. The cook and maid remained with their heads bowed as the gatekeeper lifted his hands.

Paul had promised to be here to meet them. "Without fail," his letter had said.

ᔫᔫᔫ

Hope woke the next morning in a canopied bed weighed down by a brocade counterpane. She rose, dressed quickly, and, pausing at the connecting room only long enough to see that the children were gone, stepped through to the gallery to look for them. In that instant, she was dazzled.

Between the cloudless cobalt sky and the sheer desert air, there was a clarity to the light here that made every surface it touched seem perfect. Pearl and Morris, crouching with Ah-nie beside a sunken goldfish pool, looked like figures from a picture book, and around them, the courtyard could have passed for a stage set. There were miniature fruit trees in porcelain pots, carved stone benches, a massive jujube shading one corner, and terraces of gold- and rust-colored chrysanthemums. Along the raised walkway on which Hope was standing rose scarlet pillars so fat and smooth they might have been enormous candles holding up the dragon- and cloud-painted ceiling. After all her valiant work to "integrate" their last home, Hope almost laughed at this wonderland scene. It looked as though Peking would make them "go Chinese," as Sarah put it, whether they liked it—whether it was *wise*—or not.

Pearl noticed her mother and stood up. "Take us on an explore, Mama? Yen wouldn't let us without you."

"Esspore!" echoed Morris, clapping hands.

Hope sighed. She had been too tired and angry to do more than glance at their new home last night. She was not really any less furious now, but with rest and this sun-drenched splendor, the children's high spirits became contagious.

Their living quarters consisted of the first two courts in a compound owned by a Manchu family who had lost their royal entitlement after the downfall of the Ch'ing, and now lived in the walled-off rear courts while renting out the front. The first yard, through which Hope and the children had entered last night, contained the study and reception hall where Paul would conduct his business. Both these rooms were simple and spare, furnished with low, straight-backed chairs and occasional tables, a black-wood desk, and brass-studded chests. Paul's writing set was arranged on the desk. Hope recognized the carved casing of his ink slate and the mottled bamboo handle of his favorite brush. She supposed the papers stacked in the corner were also his, and, inhaling, she thought she detected the raw, earthy smell of his cigarettes, but before these thoughts could go any further, she slid the door shut and shooed the children back the way they'd come.

Though the courtyards and galleries gave the illusion of spaciousness, in reality there was little to explore. The first court was clearly intended to be Paul's domain, and though the third stood vacant and accessible through the side walkway, Hope did not want to encourage the children to trespass. No, their territory was limited to the second court. The yard, the pool, the bedrooms where Hope and the children had slept last night, and an adjacent dining and sitting room. As Hope had already discovered, there was no plumbing. Washbasins and covered chamber pots were stationed in the bedrooms behind flower-painted screens, and last night Chrysanthemum had brought a lidded wooden cask full of scalding water for Hope's bath. But, she reminded herself firmly, she had grown up in far more primitive conditions, and the children were hardy enough. Now they had discovered Kuan drawing water from the hand pump next to the kitchen (a separate building with sleeping quarters for the servants tucked behind the main hall) and were pestering him to show them how.

"Come away," she called. "Let Kuan get our breakfast, and after we've eaten I'll have Yen hire a cart to take us around the city."

The children cheered, and Hope knew exactly how they felt. She'd been lonely, insecure, and necessarily defensive herself as a child—as she prayed Pearl and Morris never would be—and yet in the rawest physical sense, she'd been free. In China, such freedom was not only dangerous but condemned. The walls around this compound were the height of three men. And above them now, as if on cue, appeared a flock of pigeons with tiny bells fixed to their legs. There was a feeling here, she thought, of being imprisoned in Eden.

But the Peking that waited outside their walls was more like a circus than Paradise. Even the donkey cart that collected them, one of thousands that rattled through the streets, was as irreverently cheerful, with its sky blue canopy, as it was uncomfortable to ride. That same union of cheer and discomfort applied to the veils of dust swirling off the Gobi. They were arid and at times blinding, yes, but they also shimmered like so much gold powder tossed from a passing cloud. It was difficult to stay miserable in such an atmosphere, in such light and (recoiling from the zap of an unseen current as she touched Morris's cheek) such *electricity*. But most of all, Hope decided, it was the color that seduced her. Even those drab gray compound walls sprang to life when the sun caught their vermilion gates, and the hues only intensified in the markets where, beneath intricately carved teak and cedar archways, peddlers sold crimson, blue, green, and gold hats, painted paper lanterns strung like beans, mounds of orange saffron, red sumac, black tea, ceramic pottery, and glassware. Crimson squares of cotton formed tents above makeshift food stalls that reeked of peanut oil and garlic, but more delicate scents surrounded the gilded pagoda restaurants serving merchant and gentry classes. And then there were the other smells of the street, of dust and dung and animal dander, the rough odor of unwashed hair and the pungent fragrance of punk burning at roadside altars that were every bit as numerous, colorful, and well attended as the noodle shops and teahouses.

Yen, who had grown up in nearby Tientsin, reveled in his role of tour guide. He pointed out bird men with golden canaries and finches, brown-faced peasants selling grain out of sacks, barbers scraping foreheads in the old fashion and shearing off pigtails in the new, and especially the audiences of transfixed children watching itinerant puppeteers. ("Next time we'll stop and you can watch," Hope promised her own pleading children. "Today we must see as much as we can so we'll know where to ask Papa to bring us back.") Yen showed them streets festooned with kites in the shapes of dragons and roosters and grinning snakes, others where only fans were sold, or firecrackers or flutes or incense or fur. In Peking, Yen called back from his seat beside the driver, one could buy smoking pipes tall as a man, jewelry dating back to the Shang, and porcelain thin as paper.

Hope, who felt as if she'd been brought up out of some deep cave and was witnessing life for the first time in months, gave her head man a grateful smile. "If only I had my camera," she said. "I'd love to take your picture against all this, Yen."

"Oh, Missy," he answered. "No problem."

The black derby dipped forward, and he came back up cradling the Kodak, which Hope had neither seen nor thought about since the week her baby died.

❦❦❦

2

It was three days before the cry went up. Yen flew across the courtyard drawing his black satin *ma kua* over his gown. Hope gathered the children and instructed them to wait with her on the gallery outside their rooms. There was no telling if Paul would be alone, what business he was returning from. But he was calling for them as he stepped through the moongate, and Pearl would not be confined. She scrambled down and skipped across the flagstones, raising her arms as if she expected her father to shower her with rubies. He answered with a delighted whoop, spinning her above his head.

"My precious Pearl!" He set her down and brought from his pocket a silver-wrapped parcel. Her small fingers shredded the paper.

"A fan! Look, Mama. Papa brought me a fan with roses just like the ones on our house in America!" Pearl spread the ribs wide and fanned her face in broad guileless sweeps.

"Did you really?" said Hope, doing her best to remain stern against the glee of Paul's entrance.

"Actually," he said, coming to stand below her, "I believe they are camellias."

"Papa?" Morris held tight to Hope's skirt, but having watched Pearl receive her gift, his sense of sibling justice was clearly piqued.

"My son." Paul extended his arms and waggled his hands. The two-year-old advanced solemnly, casting Hope a dramatic glance, and let go of her fingers the way a clinging drop lets go a melting icicle. But in an instant all this tragedy dissolved in gales of effulgent laughter as Paul's arms clamped shut and drew the child into a gobbling bear hug. When Paul threw him into the air, Morrie let out such raucous, uncontrollable squeals that Hope was sure the Manchus in the rear court must be plugging their ears, but just as she was about to lodge her own protest, Paul flipped the boy into his arms like an infant and crooned him a song.

Morrie gasped for breath and begged, "Present?"

"Ah, Ch'eng-yü." Paul grinned down at him. "And I thought I could make you forget." Morrie's gift was wrapped in lucky red. He was even swifter than his sister in unwrapping, and it was a miracle he didn't destroy the fragile toy inside: a wire monkey strung between two long sticks, which spun when the sticks were pulled apart just so. The little boy was immediately enthralled, with his sister bowing over him to instruct as only a more experienced elder can do.

Hope stood alone on the gallery watching Paul watch their children. "And where have you been?" she said finally, putting her hands on her hips for effect.

He turned, his smile suspended as if he had no control over it. "The day before you arrive Yüan sent me to Tientsin to meet with the Japanese ambassador. I could not say no."

"Tientsin!" She wavered. "But we came right through there, Paul. You must have known . . ."

He summoned Ah-nie to look to the children, who had stopped playing with their gifts to listen. Then with a single high step he was up on the gallery nodding Hope into the bedroom. He slid the door closed and drew her down onto the bed, his voice abruptly grave. "Last week in Hangchow, Yüan's forces raided the Chinese Revolutionary Party. Twenty people were arrested and shot on suspicion plotting against government. Right now Yüan will take any sign of disloyalty very badly. He needs my help, but also he knows my old friends. I make this trip to Tientsin in secret, Hope. For this reason I cannot meet you."

"But I thought his Vice President was your old friend."

"Yes, yes. But Li's position also is tenuous. The Japanese are putting tremendous pressure on Yüan. He is like the cornered rat, too weak to strike at the large, waiting cat, so he pounces on every midge that will cross his path."

"Was it wise to bring your family into the rat's corner?"

Paul sighed and let her hands go, but he did not rise or move away from her. His lips formed a taut line, and she braced herself for anger as she sought his eyes, but the expression waiting there was something else. Tenderness. Concern. Fatigue and confusion. She realized with a start that Paul's youth was fading. There were creases gently laddering his forehead, shallow pouches beneath his eyes, and that new pinched set of his mouth, more disappointed than disapproving, but barely. He still had sufficient grace and vigor that a smile or rage could restore his physical presence to full and irresistible vitality, but in contemplation the change was pronounced.

She stretched a hand to his cheek. "Your life would be so much simpler if the children and I just disappeared."

"If simplicity were important to me," he said, drawing each word for clarity, "I would never have married you, Hope. I would never have traveled to America. I would marry this girl my mother choose. I would be moneylender, come home every night at six o'clock like Hwang Yun-shu."

There was such contempt in his voice when he mentioned Hwang that Hope stifled the retort that immediately sprang to mind: *And you would have a life with your family.*

"But must it always be like this?" she said instead.

"We are here now. All together." He studied her. "Yes. It must be like this."

ॐॐॐ

The next weeks remained warm and clear, and Paul eased back from his official duties to play host and husband and father. He took the children boating on Pei Hai Lake, treated them to lunch at a floating restaurant in Nan Hai and to a moving picture at the New Peking Cinema. He escorted Hope to a tea for foreign wives at the Dutch Legation, where, though she remained the sole American, she enjoyed a far more cordial reception than she had ever known in Shanghai. One weekend they took a picnic to the Western Hills and visited the giant "Sleeping Buddha," the Temple of the Azure Clouds, and, much to the children's fascinated horror, the upright, staring, and smooth-skinned mummy in the Monastery of Exalted Heaven. A few days later, as they peered through the tunnel of Tien An Men into the Imperial Palace grounds, Paul told of the three days he had once spent inside, sealed in a five-foot cell with nothing but a stool, a table, and writing materials while he completed his Imperial Examination. Pearl and Morris clamored to go see, but as this was not permitted, Paul suggested instead an outing to the Summer Palace, which had just been opened to the public a few weeks earlier. There they viewed the bricked-in hall where the Empress Dowager Tz'u-hsi had imprisoned her nephew the Emperor when he threatened her claim to power. They walked the zigzag galleries through her pleasure gardens, and stepped aboard the marble boat on which she had squandered the funds that might have saved her Imperial Navy during the war with the Japanese. Finally, as if to complete his family's tour of Imperial China's ignominious past, Paul suggested that the time had come for their excursion to the Great Wall.

They traveled by train to Nankow, then rode the remaining seven miles by cart under a frozen white sun. There were few villages, no landmarks, and the earth was dry and barren, unremarkable until they lurched over the final ridge, and the wall unfurled before them. Hope remembered the dream she had had before the San Francisco Quake, that high and gateless, snaking wall. She had seen pictures of the Great Wall, of course, and it was doubtless that they had fueled her dream, yet she was jolted now by the vehemence with which she recognized the scene before her.

The cart pulled nearer and finally disgorged them amid the carnival of vendors and performers who camped along the base of the wall and hawked their goods to tourists. For once the children were immune to the cries of the food sellers. They took the narrow steps to the rampart like two intrepid goats, with Yen chasing after them and Paul and Hope following at their own pace. Many of the stones were out of place or missing, and when they reached the top they could see that sections of the parapet had fallen away. Some of the distant inclines were so littered with loose stones and debris that they were impassable, yet still the wall seemed timeless, indestructible in a way that went beyond its physical dimensions.

Hope pulled the Kodak from her carpetbag and fixed the lens on Morris, who was riding Yen's shoulders as Pearl skipped alongside. To the left a Chinese father and his children stood dispassionately watching, while behind, the wall seemed to snap its tail. When she lowered the camera she found Paul leaning against the battlement, watching her.

"It is good to see," he said, indicating the camera.

"Yes." She stepped out of the way of a Western couple who nodded and thanked her in French. "Yes, you were right to get us out of Shanghai."

"I try, Hope."

There was a plaintive note in his voice that jarred her. She put the camera away and came beside him. "I know you do."

He turned so that they were both looking out toward the west. It was only a little after noon, but the sky was purled with metallic clouds, and below it the landscape of violet hills had a cold oceanic quality. Hope shivered and pulled her jacket collar up around her neck, then tentatively drew against Paul's shoulder.

"Always this fear of the foreigner." He rapped his knuckles against the stone. "This gathering inward, hiding behind walls. It has been China's gravest mistake."

"Yet the wall still stands."

His fingertips skimmed across her wrist as he moved his hands to his pockets. He found her eyes. "Yes," he said, "but for this moment, we stand on top of it."

♫♫♫

In early November Yen ordered the house outfitted for the cold months. Thick woven mats were suspended from rafters to cover the thin wooden walls, and others were joined into carpeting. Then, in place of the asphyxiating braziers used in most Chinese homes, Hope instructed Yen to find two coal-burning stoves with proper stovepipes, one for the living room, and one for Paul's office. When set up on bricks, the stove created a warm zone where she could read, Pearl could have her lessons, Morris could play. The warmth did not extend into their sleeping quarters, but there the thick camel's hair comforters were as good as heating pads at night.

To this point Hope had resisted Chinese dress for herself or the children. In part she was following Paul's lead, as even he held to Western clothing, except when attending traditional functions—from which she was routinely excluded both as a woman and a foreigner. She was also still a *little* mindful of Sarah's East-West advice, but most of all, she had been acting on her own biases dating back to her youth, when other children used to taunt her by costuming themselves in feathered headdresses and war paint, mimicking native dances and whooping, fawning, and dancing backward as they begged her to "be our squaw girl." She had seen more than her fill of the "trinkets"—beaded belts, fringed buckskins, moccasins, painted pipes, and buffalo robes—sported like trophies by the Fort Dodge cavalry. In the same spirit, the San Francisco police and other scavengers who had picked over the rubble of Chinatown after the Quake would pose for pictures sucking opium pipes (scrubbed clean of all coolie germs, one presumed) or leaning hunchbacked on the dragon handle of an ivory walking stick. While it was clearly a show of respect for men like Paul to adopt the fashion of Western culture, she had decided long ago that whites who "dressed native," as the British were so fond of saying, only did so as a means of ridiculing the conquered.

Her resolve broke down one night when she lay in bed fully clothed with both children huddled against her and all their teeth chattering like castanets. Outside, the wind howled. Yellow loess dust scratched against the roof and oil-paper windows. Their hair crackled with static electricity, and sparks flew with each touch to their heavy woolen sweaters. The tweeds, gabardines, and muslins from which Hope made their clothes would be no match for the winter Peking promised.

Yen, of course, knew a tailor who was delighted by the prospect of outfitting a foreign family. He came to the house, calculated the list of garments to be furnished, and named a price that Hope thought embarrassingly low. Yen brought it down by half. Within the week the man arrived back with armfuls of wrapped paper packages out of which tumbled apple green silk pajamas, satin underpinnings, padded socks, felt puttees, brocade vestments lined with squirrel and rabbit fur, and black velvet boots lined with camel's hair.

Paul, who had ordered his own winter wardrobe to be brought from Wuchang, was at home the afternoon the new garments arrived and insisted on a fashion show. Pearl was excused from her lessons. Morris's nap was delayed. Paul enthroned himself in Hope's upholstered armchair while Ah-nie and the other female servants instructed on the proper order

of garments, working from tight to loose, silk to satin to fur-lined brocade and velvet. Hope imagined this must be how a swaddled baby felt—
surprisingly comfortable!

"Next time," Paul said when the children had gone off, "order ermine.
Much warmer than squirrel or rabbit."

"Ermine!"

"Or mink," he said blandly.

"I hardly see how the trim can make that much difference."

"No trim." He turned up the hem of her vest. "See, Chinese put fur
inside. This way the warmth is next to your skin. Only Westerners are
foolish to wear fur outside."

"I'm sorry. I think that would be a terrible waste of ermine or mink."
She tilted her face coquettishly.

He let go of her vest and patted it smooth. "I forget to tell you. I have
arranged a post for William Tan in my department. He and Daisy will
move into the third court next week."

"Why, that's wonderful news, Paul! I confess, I could use some company—"

He stood up and went to the stove with his hands outstretched, a tic
working his left cheek. Hope felt an instinctive flash of alarm at his distraction, but running a quick inventory, she noted that his hands were
steady, his shoulders relaxed. If another dire political turn were taking
place, his mood would be much darker. "What is it?" she asked.

"You remember," he said slowly, "when we meet Madam Shen outside
Yüan's palace few weeks ago and you take our picture?"

"That woman you said was the palace procuress?" She could hardly
forget. Madam Shen was as gaudy as a Chinese opera star, with her ruby
lips and white powder mask, and as saucy as a Toulouse-Lautrec harlot in
her ostrich plumes and frills. East had never before met West with such a
resounding bang. As a lark, Hope had taken Paul's picture with this vision
against one of the dragon friezes that ran along the palace wall. The
madam pouted for the camera, while Paul struck a Napoleonic pose. It
was a frame for the books, and Hope had had such a good time taking it
that only after they'd bid their goodbyes did it occur to her to ask how
Paul was acquainted with Madam Shen. That was when he explained that

she directed an "agency" that served all Yüan's high officials, though he was quick to add that he had never availed himself of her services.

"Well?" Hope folded her hands in her lap. "What about her?"

By the time Paul finished his story, she was laughing so hard she was weeping. "Oh, it's too incredible. Just wait till I write Mary Jane about this. No one back home will believe it!"

"This business is not finished yet," Paul warned. "There is to be a trial and I will be called as key witness."

"A trial!" Hope leaned forward. "How fascinating. Are spectators allowed? I should say, are women allowed?"

Paul strutted toward her with an air of comical menace, arms folded tight across his chest. "And why do you ask this thing, my wife?"

"Because I've few enough chances to watch you in action, and this sounds like one I'd be a fool to miss."

He placed his hands firmly on her shoulders and gave her forehead a smacking kiss. "As usual, dearest, you are right. I only wish I, too, could be fool enough to miss it."

ॐॐॐ

Ta Hsing Hsien Hutung
Peking
December 5, 1914
Dear Mary Jane and Dad,
Paul is embroiled in such a delicious, utterly absurd affair that I cannot resist writing the juicy details. You especially will appreciate this piquant view of women's "emancipated" role in politics here, though I must preface by stating that there *are* a surprising number of genuinely modern-thinking women in China, including several Paul knew as revolutionary students in Japan who now call themselves the Movement Sect. Unfortunately, it is still the women who apply more traditional keys to power who make the biggest waves. In Peking, these latter "ladies" are known as the Vagabond Sect. Our story concerns the Vagabonds' leader, Madam Shen P'ei-chen, who is posed

with Paul, in the first of the enclosed photos, outside Yüan Shih-k'ai's palace.

How does Paul know Madam Shen? Well, this "madam" has made it her business to know every influential man in Peking, beginning with Yüan's top henchmen! Family ties being the primary source of strength and allegiance among the Chinese, she has "adopted" the General Supervisor of the Palace Guard for her godfather, and Minister of the Army, General Tuan Ch'i-jui, for her uncle. She won over the rest of the President's men by providing them with "women volunteers," and ultimately gained the favor of Yüan Shih-k'ai himself. Being both too ambitious and too modern for concubine status, Madam Shen persuaded Yüan—who boldly claims that he is eradicating vice!—to appoint her Woman Minister of a General Palace Agency in charge of "entertaining" officials and their guests. Her office is around the corner from Paul's.

Well, last month, Madam Shen was entertaining her "godfather's" Palace Guards at a brothel called the House of Wakening Sexual Desires (!) when the guests—well into their cups—started playing a wager game of smelling feet, akin to poker, but with a uniquely Chinese emphasis on that most incomprehensibly erotic of private parts, the bound foot. This game continued for *three days*. Word leaked out, and soon the story was splashed all over the anti-Yüan newspaper *Shen Chow Daily*. Madam Shen immediately demanded that the paper's editor, an old friend of Paul's named Wang, issue a retraction. Mr. Wang responded with a profile of Madam Shen in which he detailed her manufactured kinships and described the true mission of her Palace Agency. He then wisely fled the city.

Within hours of his departure Madam Shen arrived at his house with a battalion of Vagabonds and Palace Guards. Though the gates were locked, Madam ordered the guards to break in and smash the contents of the receiving halls. She then sat down to wait for Wang. The house was not wholly unoccupied, however. A friend of Mr. Wang's, one Mr. Kuo, was staying in a rear court. When he came out to reason with the women, they smashed up his quarters, too. Then they swarmed around him, tearing his hair and ripping his clothes. Finally, with a great shout, the ladies tossed him into the courtyard, where he landed square on a pomegranate bush.

Paul was driving home from a banquet when he saw scores of police and hundreds of spectators crowding around Wang's gate. As a friend of Wang's, Paul pushed through to find poor Kuo covered with mud, holding his trousers by one hand and threatening the women with the other. Madam Shen waved Paul forward. "You are a gentleman. You tell this man. We have been slandered!" The leader of the Guards said his men would not leave until Wang returned.

Poor Paul was surrounded by lunatics, but he held sway. "Remember," he said to the soldier, "you are in uniform. If the President learns of this incident, your superior must be punished." So, too, he implied, must this man himself. Then Paul offered his own carriage to take Madam Shen and her ladies home. A few days later Mr. Kuo filed an official complaint listing Paul as witness.

To this point, everything I've told you comes from Paul, but when the case was presented before the magistrate, I was able to watch the shenanigans firsthand from the observation balcony above the courtroom. I suited up in Chinese clothing to attract as little attention as possible. Fortunately, the Chinese press was out in force, including one or two Movement Sect ladies, so I was not the only one with a camera. These poorly lit photos, however, do not do justice to the chaos of the scene. As in a Chinese theater, there was constant chatter, nibbling of nuts, spitting, coughing, yelling, stamping. My fellow observers' silk brocades and sateen top hats did nothing to polish their behavior.

The principals all, in turn, gave predictable accounts. Paul's remarks coming at the end, however, were colored by his own peculiarly vaudevillian humor. He seems to know just how to dig under his adversaries' skin, to their extreme irritation and his own amusement. Asked to describe what he saw that night at Mr. Wang's house, he began with a straightforward account, but when he came to the verbal exchanges, he stopped and said to the magistrate, "These ladies and this gentleman were using words which are embarrassing to the decent ear. Will I be going against the law to repeat them?"

To which the mob in the balcony roared, "No! No!"

So Paul delivered a string of slang words, and the audience hooted so that even I understood the gist. Within moments the examiner was reprimanding Paul for obscenity. "If Your Honor does not wish to listen," Paul replied, "I shall not carry on, for to do so would be to go against—"

Again the balcony erupted, "Let him speak!"

So you see, Paul maneuvered himself into the hero's role, telling the truth while treating the proceedings like the circus they really were. How I grinned when I got him home that night. The more because his lighthearted tactic worked, and the case ended in Mr. Kuo's favor, with a sentence of six months house arrest for Madam Shen and public ridicule and excoriation of Yüan Shih-k'ai. You can see the Woman Minister in that final photograph, tripping down the courthouse steps and braying with outrage. Such are women's rights and justice, Chinese style.

Well, there is so much more to tell, of our beautiful home here and the stealthy way this city seduces one with its glorious architecture and energy, as well as this absurd theater. I feel a part of Paul's life—or at least attached to it—in a way that I haven't since Berkeley. I can even think and speak now of our sweet baby girl without lapsing into despair. But Pearl's afternoon lessons are beckoning, and I am invited to tea with our friend Daisy Tan, and the cook needs me to help him make a pound cake, and the children need mistletoe for their Christmas wreath. . . . How I wish you two could be here with us. Second best, that you are having equally lovely and loving times of your own.

Always your adoring daughter and friend,
Hope

ৡৡৡ

3

Nothing compares with a Peking blizzard. The snow flutters weightless as talcum, crunching underfoot and filling the recessed pools and streams with rounded pillows of whiteness. The precision of dry snow is such that it exaggerates rather than distorts the shapes that lie beneath it, bestows perfect caps on all the magical spirit creatures that line the city's rooftops, and renders even more majestic the swooping silhouettes of the architecture as a whole. The effect on the city's noise is like that of a quilt over a snarling cat. All movement is muffled, all color stayed. Until the Gobi wind picks up.

When all that talcum takes back to the air, and those foolish or impoverished enough to be outside must walk doubled over like a snail, anyone with an ounce of privilege will stay home. On evenings like these Hope blessed her husband for bringing the Tans to live in their compound, for the two couples would take refuge together and, as the winds outside twisted and howled, they would play bridge or mah-jongg (patiently schooling the poor novice Hope) or simply cluster around the stove and enjoy the comfort of Hope's overstuffed chairs.

"You see Yüan soldier parade last week-ah?" Daisy clapped her childlike hands. "Just like German every one!" She hopped up and cocked one forefinger against her upper lip in imitation of the Palace Guard's handlebar mustaches, swung her other arm rigid by her side, and goosestepped across the room.

"You need a better uniform." Hope sprang from her seat, returning seconds later with a gold sash, a broad-brimmed feathered hat, a pair of Paul's round-lensed glasses, and her camera with a new magnesium flash. Daisy donned the props over her long maroon gown, struck a pose worthy of the Kaiser himself, and, with a click of the shutter, the room clouded with smoke, everyone batting their arms and coughing. Hope shooed them aside and hauled open the door. An instant of that swirling snow-wind cleared the air.

Paul poured cups of rice wine for William and himself. "You know why Yüan has his military imitate the Kaiser's troops."

William raised his cup in a mock toast. "Kaiser Wilhelm has the greatest, most powerful fighting force in the world!" He lowered his voice to a stage whisper. "And he has agreed to recognize Yüan as Emperor if China sides with Germany in the war."

"Surely the Kaiser is busy enough at home without playing footsie with Yüan Shih-k'ai!" Hope said. "Anyway, between George Morrison and Ambassador Jordan I thought Yüan was already tied to the Allies." George Morrison was an Australian newspaperman who had insinuated himself into Yüan's inner circle and had recently been appointed "political advisor" to the President. Jordan was Britain's ambassador, a good man by Paul's account, who had helped to negotiate the surrender of the Manchus in 1911 and remained in Yüan's favor ever since. Hope, who had met the two men only fleetingly at a Legation tea, considered them both opportunists, but in a city ruled by opportunists, they seemed the least predatory of the lot.

"I believe the English tell a story about a goose that lays golden eggs," said William. "Well, the foreign powers see China as just such a goose, golden with trade and mining and other riches. They will not share it willingly, nor will any one give it up to another. But now this goose is for sale. Price is Yüan's enthronement. So they bid, thinking the bird can have only one master. Only Yüan does not agree. His scheme is to take all offers and still keep the gold for himself."

"Yes," said Paul. "But Hope is right. Jordan and Morrison are working hard to persuade Yüan to refuse Germany. They claim the Allies will reward him by pressuring Japan to return Shantung to China."

"Boys squabbling over their forts," said Hope. "Forget the goose."

Daisy curled herself into the love seat across from her husband. "I hear Japanese ambassador visit to Mr. Yüan palace yesterday. I hear he bring very big paper, demand Yüan give to Japan many territory, many power. If Yüan will not sign, maybe Japan will start another war with China. But maybe Yüan will sign, then Japan make Yüan as Emperor, and England, France, Germany—all other foreign powers in China must bow down before Japan."

Hope braced herself for the men's reaction. It did not surprise her that

Daisy would have gossip from the palace. Tan Taitai chose her household staff less for their quality of service than for their network of informants, and William endorsed this practice, relied on it politically. Paul claimed that once it had even saved William's life. But now, while William's expression remained guarded, Paul got up and began pacing the room.

"So," said William, "it is just as you and Dr. Sun predicted."

"No. Worse." Paul shook his head. "I predicted the Japanese would try bribery, but Yüan's flirtation with Germany has pushed the price too high. No matter their promises, neither the Allies nor the Germans can afford to defend China while they must also fight in Europe, and Yüan's feudal armies alone are no match for Japan's gunboats. So the Japanese make these demands with impunity. Yüan will have no choice but to yield. And you and I, *p'eng yu*, we will be expected to coat this *kou dan* with syrup and encourage the people to swallow it."

In the worried silence that followed Daisy leaned over and plucked at Hope's sleeve. Her eyes shone as if the whole business were nothing more to her than a game. With a look she beckoned Hope away from the men and into the bedroom. As soon as the door shut, she dropped onto the bed, lifting her gown with a flourish. "See, Hop-ah!"

From beneath her pipe-stem trousers poked two black leather slippers. Hope recognized them as a pair she and Daisy had bought together in Shanghai. But at the time, Hope considered them merely symbolic. Daisy had barely begun the process of unbinding her feet, could not even try them on. Now, though her white stockinged insteps bulged over the straps and the black kid gapped and stretched, her foot almost filled the length of the shoe.

"Every day I soak feet. No bandage." Daisy made massaging and prying motions with her hands. "I know, I can do. I do!"

Hope winced at the thought of the pain this must entail, yet heroic as Daisy's accomplishment would have seemed just minutes ago, it now struck her as trivial—the very announcement mystifying. Hadn't Daisy heard what Paul was saying?

"Congratulations," Hope said, but before she could think how to continue, Daisy was tugging at her hand to sit down, come closer.

"You know how I hear this news in palace?" Daisy asked in a conspiratorial whisper. "My sister Suyun have lover!"

"Oh," Hope said. "I'm sorry to hear that . . . Or should I be glad?"

Daisy covered her mouth and giggled. "Lover is official to Yüan!"

"I see." Hope knew instinctively that she was not going to like what was coming, but there was no way, short of clapping her own hand over Daisy's mouth, to stop the rest of the story.

As she lay next to Paul a few hours later, with the snow crackling against the paper windows and her icy feet sliding under his knees for warmth, she asked for his interpretation.

"I do not understand what you ask," he said, and she recognized in his voice the same impatience she had felt at Daisy's coy revelation.

"I guess I'm asking how I'm supposed to respond," said Hope. "Here is this young girl, presumably in love with a man who is already married and she *won't* be his concubine, and he claims he can't divorce his wife, and now the poor thing is pregnant—"

"And Daisy will take this baby because she has not her own. Daisy and William take Suyun in. They are very generous."

"So you condone this!"

Paul turned on his side, pulling her knees up against him and rubbing the cold from her feet. "Other way is for this girl to swallow gold. You think this will be better?"

"The other way might be for her to keep her own child, for this man to support them even if he won't marry her. And for Daisy and William to help her without stealing her child out from under her!"

"Too much face lost," he said simply.

"Ach! Face. It's the same as Yüan Shih-k'ai trading the country for a coronation! It's selfish and shameful and cruel."

Paul squeezed her feet hard and pushed her legs back down. "It is not the same, Hope."

౷౷౷

The Twenty-one Demands, as Japan's bid for sovereignty over China came to be called, were so outrageous that Paul's worst fears were not, in fact, born out. Yüan did not capitulate immediately, but sent Paul and William covertly scurrying for support from the other foreign consuls and ambassadors to oppose the Japanese. Meanwhile, Yüan's negotiators attempted, with only marginal success, to chip away the worst of the demands, which gave Japan authority over China's munitions, railways, mines, and security. The bargaining took almost as long as Suyun's baby did to be born.

The winds and snows passed, fruit trees burst into luxuriant bloom, April's dust storms erupted and ebbed. Suyun, a small, still girl with clear eyes and a startlingly direct gaze, spent these months of her confinement in the Tans' court sewing, playing with Pearl and Morris, begging stories from Hope about America. By June, Yüan Shih-k'ai had submitted to the Japanese. Ambassador Jordan and the other European and American diplomats finally conceded, as Paul had predicted they would, that their governments were preoccupied with the salvation of Europe, and could not help the Chinese against Japan. Hope felt that Daisy was placing her in a position very nearly as distasteful as Ambassador Jordan's.

Young Suyun reminded Hope of Li-li back home. How could she possibly, then, condone this scheme of Daisy's to take the girl's child for her own! It seemed the Tans had brought Suyun to Peking, and Hope suspected, though Paul refused to confirm it, that William was responsible for introducing her to her ministerial lover. But Paul made it clear that William was one of the few men in Peking who had his wholehearted trust. By interfering in this matter at all, much less taking Suyun's side, Hope would betray this trust, upsetting the peace of their extended household and possibly jeopardizing Paul in some way that she could not imagine.

This is none of your business, she told herself firmly the morning Daisy's maid came running to announce the birth—a son.

"Can I go see, Mama?" Pearl pleaded.

"Babies are fragile creatures, sweet pea. Let the poor thing gather its strength before we subject it to your steamy kisses."

"But I'll be good. I just want to see."

"You saw your—" But Hope could not complete the thought. The last newborn any of them had seen was now buried in Shanghai. "I said no," she said, too sharply.

Pearl's face crumpled.

Hope gathered up the tiger shoes Pearl had helped her select. "I'll tell the baby these are from you, and soon as Suyun says he's strong enough, I'll take you over."

"You mean Daisy." Pearl thrust out her chin. "It's Daisy's baby."

Daisy had made a point in these last weeks of treating Pearl to bits of sugared melon and sesame candy. Now Hope understood why. "Be good." She smoothed her daughter's heavy black hair. "Find your Stevenson poems, and later we'll read the one about the shadow."

"But, Mama, I'm not a baby!" whined Pearl.

"Just so. And this is why you must obey without complaining."

Hope gave her daughter a hurried kiss and set off down the outside path to Daisy's court. But her own words sickened her. Was this truly the burden of maturity—to accept without complaint whatever fate doled out? Back home, under Mary Jane's watchful eye and ear, she would never have dreamed such a thing. She might well have raised her daughter with precisely the opposite exhortation. Yet now . . . *mei fatse*. Nothing to be done. As Yen had explained in one of their occasional philosophical debates, "Some winds bring good luck, some winds bring bad. Sometimes two together. No one can stop the wind."

Sometimes two together, Hope thought. She had so much to be thankful for, so much to mourn. The two were as inextricably bound together as these two sisters and the baby now awaiting her visit.

The elderly maid whom they called Bald Crow ushered Hope into a narrow space partitioned off Daisy's bedroom, where a pale and empty-armed Suyun lay on a small square bed. As Hope approached, her eyes darted left.

"Hop-ah!" Daisy cried, beckoning. She was enthroned on a huge blackwood settee festooned with scarlet pillows, the baby in her lap.

He was still pink and wrinkled from birth, the tiny mouth working into a yawn, a full head of bristling hair, and eyes that seemed filled with questions as they quivered this way and that.

"My mother," said Daisy, "she write give milk name Meiling, bad spirits think this baby worthless girl, but William too modern, say no. Already he say Kuochang, this mean Glory of State. Some day big official, this boy."

Such a small child, Hope thought, and such a heavy burden. She could feel Suyun's eyes boring into her back, the weight of the gift in her arms.

Oblivious, Daisy chucked the baby under his chin and sang a high-pitched tune. "Sit! Please. I have Bald Crow bring some tea."

"No, Daisy." Hope suddenly felt suffocated. "Pearl is waiting. I can't stay, but I did want to pay my respects to you both." She looked at Suyun's downcast face. "To tell you how glad I am that you are healthy and the child is strong." She went to the bed and placed the parcel into the girl's arms. "Maybe these will help keep the evil spirits away."

Suyun stared at the package. Without lifting her eyes either to Hope or Daisy, she slowly undid the silk ribbon, pulled open the flame-colored wrapping to reveal the tiny tiger-faced shoes. Now Hope wished she had had the sense to choose something different, less traditional and predictable. Something Suyun might have a chance of keeping.

Though when Hope glanced back and saw the angry burn in Daisy's cheeks, she understood that this unwed sister would be allowed to keep nothing.

಄಄಄

4

That summer, while Yüan Shih-k'ai cranked up support for his installation as China's first "constitutional monarch," and Suyun silently yielded to her role as wet nurse to her own baby, Paul arranged for Hope and the children to escape to Peitaho, where he had rented a cottage for July and August. Just six hours from Peking by train, this summer beach resort on the Gulf of Chihli used to be a favorite retreat of the Empress Dowager Tz'u-hsi. More recently it had been taken over by foreigners. German bakeries and beer halls had sprung up, French cafés and pastry shops, British tea rooms and playgrounds, American hotels and bars. Above all, there were wonderful beaches. The children had plenty of playmates, the diplomats' and Standard Oil wives exchanged pleasantries with Hope, and every weekend Paul came out, complaining of the baking city heat and luring Hope for leisurely walks along the flattened rock coast.

At the end of July Hope decided to hold a proper birthday party for Pearl. Between the distractions of babies and moving and the insufficiency of playmates, the child had never had more than a family party, and now she was seven and very much excited about this celebration. Together she and Hope hand-painted invitations and lettered the envelopes in gold leaf. They bought balloons and party hats and poppers. Hope rolled up her sleeves, pushed the servants aside, and made a Lady Baltimore cake with frothy whipped icing and raisins, walnuts, and figs, and a wreath of candied cherries and violets—a confection not even Mother Wayland could have surpassed. They festooned the bare plaster walls of the cottage with streamers of red and gold, arranged bouquets of purple iris and tiger lilies from their own little yard, and set up seats for musical chairs and a target donkey for Pin-the-Tail. Hope made Pearl and Morrie special party clothes—for Pearl, a white organza dress with Belgian lace at the throat and knife pleats all around the skirt, and for Morrie, a blouse with a sailor collar and short white pants—and both received Lord Fauntleroy haircuts.

Half an hour before the appointed time, as Pearl and Morris, fully dressed and decked out in party hats, stood hovering at the front door, Hope was seized with terror that no one would come. The chits had all been dutifully returned, all accepting the invitation, but now that the moment was at hand, Hope had all she could do not to pull Pearl away, warn her not to wish for too much, prepare her for disaster. It will be all right—Hope bit her tongue—even if it's only us, we'll have our own party. Papa will come. You'll see.

But Paul was not due until that evening. This party was for the children. And if no children appeared, Pearl would be heartbroken.

"Missy no worry," Yen assured her. "All children like party."

Hope looked up and, in spite of her dark convictions, burst into laughter. Yen had replaced his accustomed felt bowler with one of the glittery cone party hats. He pulled his arm from behind his back and, grinning, handed her the Kodak. She was posing him with the children on the front stoop when the first guests arrived—a set of Standard Oil twins from Minnesota, escorted by their amah. The others appeared as if by pre-arrangement—Americans first, then the Germans, then British, and lastly, dribbling in late, the French.

Though the guests had a tendency to cluster by nationality, all sang a lusty "Happy Birthday" to Pearl and cheered as she blew out the candles. They competed fiercely at the party games—none more so than the little Englishmen—and were just settling down for the present unwrapping, when a familiar shout went up out front. The front door opened and Paul strode into the parlor, clapping and shouting for his daughter.

The children stared in mass confusion. Pearl looked as if she'd been struck. Through the youngsters' eyes Hope saw her husband as she had never seen him before—a tall, swarthy, bullish native. His skin was shiny with the day's heat. The stub of a cigarette glowed between his knuckles. He wore a striped linen jacket, rumpled after the long train journey and mismatched with a mustard shirt. His black hair lay damp with perspiration, and his eyes were dark as a pirate's. He coughed and laughed and shouted again.

Hope came up out of her chair to take his arm. "They're just opening the presents, dearest." She applied pressure to steer him around.

"Is that reason I should not wish my daughter happy birthday?" He was obliviously jolly. Loud. Almost raucous. "Presents, ah?"

The children were whispering among themselves, wide-eyed and snickering. What they had thought, what they'd been told of Pearl's parentage, Hope did not know, but none had seen Paul before. He did not come to the beach on his visits. He did not take the children to the playground, and they never went about as a family. Perhaps the children thought Pearl and Morris were Spanish. Perhaps they thought they were adopted.

Slowly, Paul met his daughter's shocked gaze. Slowly he surveyed the scene, took in each small face in the circle below him, the starched pinafores, seersucker shorts and suspenders, the yellow and brown and orange tresses, the freckles and deep golden tans. He turned a bleak, shamed face to Hope as she searched for some word that would soften or undo the wrong, but her mouth opened and closed on dead air. He left.

Three weeks passed. Pearl and Morris were shunned by all the British children and most of the others. Hope had discovered at the opposite end of town a cluster of homes rented out to Chinese, and she now took the children to that beach, though they were only marginally better received there. They were tolerated. Perhaps, she thought bitterly, that was the best they could expect, and anything else had been an illusion all along. But it was her fault, not Paul's, for raising that illusion in her children's eyes—and for seeing it smashed. She should have known better. Hadn't she learned anything from her own childhood? No, in a word, because she kept stubbornly dreaming, wishing that things could be different, that she could *make* them different for her children.

Paul returned, finally, one evening at dusk as the family was finishing supper. He gave no indication of displeasure, did not mention the ill-fated party, only kissed his son and daughter on the forehead, invited them to pick his pockets for sweets.

Then he turned to Hope. "Come walk."

Leaving the children to Ah-nie—and ignoring Pearl's apprehensive stare—Hope gathered up her shawl. Paul clapped his hat back on his head, and they set off along the shore. The darkening ocean spread at their feet, the mist sharp with wood smoke from the Chinese village, and as they walked, without speaking or touching, the sky turned from violent pink to gray.

They reached an outcropping where someone hundreds, perhaps thousands of years before had carved a bench out of a boulder. Paul waved for her to sit.

"Our daughter is seven now," he said as if changing the subject.

"Paul, I have—"

He cut her off, not harshly but firmly. "Do you not think Pearl should have proper schooling?"

"School? I— I've taught her . . ." Hope floundered. "Yes, I suppose . . . She ought to be in school."

"The only schools in Peking are mission schools or the ones in the Legation."

"And," she said carefully, "the children in the Legation schools would all be European or American. Or Japanese."

"That is true. But this is not the problem. Things are very unstable in the capital now. I will worry to have Pearl away from us."

"What's happened?"

"Yüan is becoming Emperor. But he is losing his support. His generals are splitting into camps for and against. The Japanese are playing games. Sun is trying to curry favor with Japanese sources of money and weapons outside the government, but he is making little progress, and without a unified resistance I am afraid each general will attack the throne for himself."

"In other words, civil war."

He clasped his hands behind his head and stretched his legs. "I do not think this will happen right away. Maybe the foreign powers will come to their senses and persuade Yüan not to do this thing. But he is a fool for pomp and glory."

"Trussing up his soldiers like the Kaiser's army."

Paul sighed. "He has dismissed me."

"Paul!"

"I am to retire." There was just enough light for her to see him smile. "He plans to crown Li Yüan-hung prince and I will be one of several marquises."

"You're joking," Hope said weakly. "Oh, Paul, no. Please tell me you're joking."

"I only wish so. Your great revolutionist husband, marquis to the crown puppet of Japan."

"You've agreed, then."

"I have little choice, Hope. This is Yüan's way of pardoning me for my revolutionary history and my association with the Kuomintang. If I refuse, I am announcing as his enemy."

"But you are his enemy," she murmured.

"Sh. The trees have ears."

"I feel as if we're in a Shakespearean tragedy."

"Or farce." He laughed, reaching now and pulling her fingers to his lips. He nibbled them thoughtfully for a moment or two, then said, "We shall stay in Peking as long as it is safe. This may be some months, perhaps another year or more. With this uncertainty, I think it is not good to send Pearl to school. But in China, most children learn at home. I myself study with home teacher many years before entering school with other boys."

"I remember." Hope recalled Paul's story of old Fong thrashing his hands with a bamboo stick. She shivered. "But what kind of a tutor—"

"Your hands always cold," Paul said, tucking them inside his jacket. She uncurled her fingers over his heart, but could not bring herself to move closer.

"A Chinese tutor, then?"

He gave her a deliberate kiss on the cheek. "Thank you, Hsin-hsin, but no. I have learned of a young woman who comes from South Africa to marry a soldier at the British Legation. When she arrive, he has been called back to fight in the war. Now, she must find work. In South Africa she is a governess."

"But what can she teach?"

"You interview her. Decide if she is qualified."

"Pearl will be disappointed."

"Why?"

"She was looking forward to going to a real school, meeting other children."

"Yes." Paul's voice was low and restrained. "I can see she enjoys other children. But this will have to wait."

༄༅༄

Miss Anna Van Zyl arrived for her interview promptly at two o'clock on a warm breezy afternoon the week following their return to Peking. She smelled like orange blossoms and made soft, energetic exclamations at the courtyard's botanic marvels.

"*Punica granatum! Solanum jasminoides. Pontederia cordata. Firmiana simplex!* What a charming garden." Tall, slender as a twig, she had wispy ginger hair and aquamarine eyes that shimmered when they caught the light at certain angles. Pearl was immediately enthralled.

"I studied botany in school, you know. I think that somewhere in this peculiar country I should find a plant no one has yet named and I shall achieve immortality as the *Jasminum* or *Lilium Van Zyl*. What do you think?" Her laughter had an electric quality. She seemed inclined to hold nothing back, and as soon as she was equipped with a cup of tea and a biscuit, she poured out more than Hope could ever want to know about her thwarted engagement and precarious finances.

Paul's version of Miss Van Zyl's history proved accurate. She was twenty-one, a graduate of a Johannesburg normal school, and had spent four years as governess in Pretoria, where she met her fiancé, a British Army lieutenant. They courted in secret, as she was a Boer and hostilities between the Afrikaners and the British were still at a fever pitch ten years after the Vereeniging Treaty, and when her lieutenant was reassigned to the British Legation in Peking, they both saw his move as the solution to her family's disapproval. The following year he sent for her to join him, but while she was sailing across the Indian Ocean, the Great War broke out. By the time Miss Van Zyl arrived in Tientsin, her fiancé had been sent off to Delhi to train the Indian Corps then being groomed to join colonial forces in France. For the past year the young governess had been bumping around the Legation, taking jobs as stenographer or typist, but the British in Peking were hardly more charitable toward a struggling Boer than those in Pretoria had been. "When Mrs. Morrison mentioned that your family was in need of a governess, I thought this could be the answer to my prayer," she said, tilting the last word into a question.

"Your prayer and ours," Hope said warmly. "I know from my own experience what a lonely place this country can be. We're no substitute for your young man, I'm sure, but you will be welcome here."

"Oh, thank you so. Mrs. Morrison didn't tell me how *lovely* you'd be."

"No, I don't imagine she would." Hope stopped there. Jennie Morrison, wife of Yüan Shih-k'ai's special advisor George Morrison, was one of Peking's White Beauties and a reigning Legation socialite. Hope had met her once at a garden party with Paul, but the two women had exchanged no more than ten words. She assumed Mrs. Morrison had referred Anna only at her husband's behest, as a political favor to Paul. "Anyway," she said brightly. "When can you start?"

They set school hours from nine to three, with Miss Van Zyl joining the family for tiffin, five days a week. The curriculum consisted of arithmetic, spelling, history, geography, and penmanship. Hope, reluctant to loosen the ties too completely, would continue Pearl's instruction in literature on her own.

"I think perhaps we should be friends, Miss Van Zyl," Hope said as they parted.

"I would like that, Madame Leon." She took Hope's hands in a warm, firm grip. "And I shall certainly do all that I can toward that end."

Los Angeles
September 19, 1915
Dearest Hope,

I have been presumptuous. Your father called me a "damn fool," the closest he's come to pure invective in all the time we've been together. I understand, though. This is a foolish thing I've done, and typical of me only to question what I've asked for after I've got it.

Oh, best get it out and over with. You see, I was so filled with admiration after receiving your letter about that *Shen Chow* madness that I retyped the whole story as an article and sent it off to *Harper's* under your name—with the photographs and myself named as agent.

Dear Hope, I now cannot imagine what possessed me. When your father learned what I'd done he pointed out fifty ways the article could be compromising to Paul and to the image of China as a whole. I don't necessarily agree. I think perhaps his indignation was caused as much by my identifying myself under my maiden name as by any injustice I've done Paul. Personally, I believe the story offers a wonderful, human antidote to the wooden tracts one ordinarily reads about China. The editors, it seems, take my side.

Now I must eat crow and send this explanation at all speed. It will reach you by October, I imagine, and I've wangled a delay until November for you to return your signature on the enclosed publication contract. I beg you to put me out of my misery by cabling whether you will ever speak to me again (and, incidentally, whether you consent to this publication). I do believe in my heart, Hope, that this kind of reporting and camera work may be your true calling, though I agree with the man at *Harper's* that you should upgrade to one of the newer, more professional cameras.

I must hurry and mail this "post haste" while your father is busy with patients. I know he'll forgive me once you've made your decision, and there's an end to my role in it. Apart from this one collision, we are as happy as schoolchildren, your dad

and I—even if we are grandparents! Love is a very rich and peculiar business. But then, you've always known that.

With admiration and affection.

Always,

Mary Jane

[enclosed]
William Cadlow
Senior Editor
Harper's
September 1, 1915
Dear Miss Lockyear:
I am much obliged to you for sending us this extraordinary
article by your client Miss Newfield about the Shen Chow affair in Peking. Our editorial board has never seen anything like
it—with the exception of myself. I confess that I was on the
staff of *The Independent* when Miss Newfield submitted several
pieces about an earlier era in Chinese history which my senior
editor rejected—over my hearty objections. You can imagine
my delight on learning that this able reporter is still "on the
China beat" and that I am now in a position to publish her
work under my own masthead.

I will need the enclosed contract returned to me as quickly
as possible—I assume you have power of attorney—and then
we can set a publication date.

My one request relates to future submissions. It is evident
from these photographs that Miss Newfield has an artist's eye
and a real feel for her subject matter, but her work could be
greatly improved by a less amateur camera than she has used
here. The new high-speed pocket Premo and folding reflex
models are quite popular with many of our reporters.

In any case, I look forward to regular contributions from
Miss Newfield, and I hope she will forgive me for not having

enough clout at *The Independent* to see her launch fulfilled years ago.

Most sincerely,
William Cadlow

"What do you think," Hope asked when Paul's eyes had dropped to the final line.

He spat into the porcelain spittoon by his desk and tapped his cigarette thoughtfully. The late sun filtering through the papered windows cast a glow over the cluttered office, but there was a chill in his voice when he spoke. "I think Americans are very ignorant about China."

"Yes, but here you have people like Mr. Cadlow showing such interest. He's right, you know, the dry political reports do nothing for America's understanding of the people or the *feel* of this world. Sun Yat-sen's manifestos aren't exactly heartwarming, either."

"But your stories of our brothel games and hysterical women are." He regarded her through the cigarette smoke with that infuriating expressionless expression he used when he wanted her to show her hand first.

"Honestly, Paul! What I wrote to Mary Jane is real. It's human. It's silly and bold and remarkably modern, in a way that Americans just don't associate with China. *That's* why I was interested enough to sit through all those days when you were on the stand, why I couldn't help write her about it, and why she sent it off as she did. You act as though I've shamed you, but you came out the hero. You can't sweep everything under the rug, you know."

He tossed the cigarette into the spittoon and pulled off his spectacles with one hand, rubbing his eyes with the other. His "retirement" was due to begin as soon as Yüan Shih-k'ai officially declared his intention to become Emperor. In the meantime, he was charged with overseeing the propaganda campaign that would garner both foreign and Chinese support for this monarchy. Four and five nights each week he was out at banquets or meetings in the Legation Quarter sounding out foreign diplomats and, while appearing to support Yüan's bid himself, providing them with ample justification for opposing it. Often the evenings would stretch into mah-jongg or poetry parties with his revolutionary friends—parties at which the loud singsong of recitation or the fervor of gambling disguised the political strategizing. But the late hours and strain of the masquerade were starting to take their toll. Paul looked heavier, older, and more tired than Hope had ever seen him. Her plea for truth and honesty now rang in her ears as it must sound to him. Inanity.

She leaned forward with her hands flat on his desk. "Paul, please. I will not send Cadlow a word that you haven't reviewed and approved. I won't write anything serious or political. I won't write anything that could compromise you or Sun."

"What else is there to write?"

The dullness of his voice startled her. "Why," she answered, "I'll write about the crowds of people coughing and talking and cracking nuts and throwing hot towels back and forth in the moving picture houses of Peking. I'll write about the moss that grows on the Great Wall, the smells of markets and how the Manchu women wrap their hair. I'll tell why the children here wear split pants, and how it feels for a woman like Daisy Tan to unbind her feet, and—" She threw her hands in the air, laughing. "I don't *know*, but out of the fifteen *billion* interesting things that I see every time I set foot out of the house, I am sure I can find at least a few things that will not offend you!"

By now Paul was sitting back in his chair with his arms folded and a wavelike motion taking hold of his mouth.

"Aha!" She pointed. "You're trying not to smile, but you can't help it. Admit it, you are a little pleased by this. You must be, Paul, for my sake. Please be proud of me. Please give it your blessing. Then it will belong to both of us."

The smile escaped him and he sighed, shaking his head and slapping the desk with his palms. "Hsin-hsin, how I can say no to you? My modern American wife."

"Oh, *thank* you, Paul." She hopped up and came around the desk. "Dearest, you know I *do* love you."

Still seated, he tipped his head back against her breast. He closed his eyes. "I know."

ৡৢৢৢৢ
5

Ta Hsing Hsien Hutung
December 16, 1915
Dear Sarah,

I am lazing shamelessly this morning, still under the spell of the ball Paul and I attended last night. It is going to make a wonderful article for *Harper's*, but you must have my first report, as you'll appreciate both the evening's extravagance and coincidence.

The purpose of the occasion was to curry foreign favor for Yüan Shih-k'ai's monarchical scheme (a subject that dominates all here in Peking, superseding the European War and the boycott against the Japanese and certainly any of the baser issues such as drought, famine, locust plagues, flooding, or national debt). Thus we were invited to one of the old Manchu palaces to view the would-be Emperor amid all the pomp and majesty he so craves. The extensive gardens, alas, were cloaked in drifted snow, but the swept paths, illuminated by blazing torches, led us to a banquet hall big as a barn, with reception rooms winging out to either side. Picture gaudy brocaded ceilings, overlays of gilt and fluted jade, vermilion columns, and silk-tasseled lanterns. A Chinese orchestra played in one corner. And several *hundred* guests all in Western dress. I wore a cream brocade and ermine, Daisy Tan a royal blue embroidered satin, Paul and William top hats and tails, and our young friend Anna, about whom I'll tell more in a moment, a particularly resplendent apple green taffeta.

With the exception of the Germans, the entire Legation Quarter seemed to have been invited, including French and Dutch, Italians and Belgians, Russians, and, of course, the ever-present Japanese. Paul introduced me to Britain's Ambassador Jordan and Yüan's public apologist that Harvard Professor

Frank Goodnow. The Australian, George Morrison and his wife, Jennie, spent a while talking with us because of Anna, who came to us as a governess by their referral. They are certainly a handsome pair, but Morrison's unwavering enthusiasm as Yüan's political advisor makes him suspect in my book.

There was also, of course, a large contingent of Yüan's ministers and officers. The most impressive of these was Vice President Li Yüan-hung, the former viceroy of Paul's native Hupei Province. He is a broad, stern man with a bristling mustache who bears an uncanny resemblance to Field Marshal Hindenburg, but he and Paul seem to be genuinely in each other's favor—a rarity in the current political climate.

Yüan made his entrance late, wearing a long velvet coat over ill-fitting khaki trousers that looked slept in. He met everyone with the same opaque expression, as if his smile were nailed to his walrus mustache, and I remembered his admiration of the Germans when I saw how he clicked his heels with each greeting and clutched the hilt of his sword. Then Paul pointed out a grotesquely twisted figure poking his head between the curtains at the end of the room. That was Yüan K'e-ting, the half-paralyzed, half-witted son whom some believe to be the true force behind this monarchy scheme! Reason enough to block the whole business, yet the spectacle marches on.

At length we took our seats at table. Given the nature of Peking diplomacy, there were many more foreign men than women, which was why we had specifically been instructed to bring our eligible young Anna Van Zyl. (Poor thing found herself seated next to a Russian minister who brutally fondled her left hand while babbling in some hybrid language that no one could understand.) There were endless toasts and even more endless courses—all sumptuous. Curried lotus root and glazed eel, bird's nest and shark's fin and dragon's eye soups, prawns the size of lobsters, crayfish drizzled with shaved ginger, pigeon eggs in broth, smothered pork, whole legs of lamb, cutlets, stews, boiled abalone, glazed Peking duck, and, of course, all those fantastic Oriental delicacies whose origins one mustn't question. We tasted and marveled as the dishes came and went for nearly four hours. Finally, after that last requisite bowl of rice, we rose with great groans of relief and started toward the reception halls, where two Western orchestras had set up for the ball.

But first President Yüan struck a pose on the dais. His henchmen cleared a wide swath, and Paul whispered into my ear, "Show time." Sure enough, Yüan's chief lackey started a roll call of names like an old royal herald. For the next hour Yüan the Benevolent doled out titles and medals and ribbons to every man in Peking whose favor could help him. This ceremony, the translator announced in four languages, would fulfill the President's promise to see titles of nobility, which had been stolen by the Manchus, restored to Han Chinese. I wish you could have seen the look on Paul's and William Tan's faces as they came up from their bows (thank heavens this buffoonery stopped short of full kowtows!). After a single telling glance at each other they seemed to pour all their energy into keeping their mouths on straight. Fortunately, as mere "marquises," they were only second-rank nobility. The title of Prince of the Realm was reserved for poor Li Yüan-hung. Considering Yüan's affection for assassination as a disciplining tool, I'd have thought Li might pretend to play along with this charade, but he refused even to bow.

At length the "show" was over, and I was able to admire the gold medallion and tricolored ribbon that decorated Paul's chest. I managed neither to laugh out loud nor throw my arms around him, but when the band struck up again, I did persuade him to dance. Anna Van Zyl, an expert dancer, had spent the previous afternoon instructing our whole family in the waltz and fox-trot and grand march. We were a sight to behold, you can imagine, with Pearl and Morris arm and arm, Paul and me tripping over each other's toes. But Anna is an immensely patient and tolerant young woman. As a result we were now able, if not to glide, at least to make the circuit of the ballroom without conspicuously embarrassing ourselves. Anna, of course, was belle of the ball.

I should tell you about Anna. She is adorable. Fine-boned, fresh-faced, high-spirited. She wears her gingery hair in a great, soft pile and has one of those murmuring South African voices—like white chocolate melted to a gloss. Her nose turns up pertly, and especially in a ball gown, her figure seems all perfectly crafted curves. She has a light in her that seems untouched by her many disappointments, as if she believes each setback will lead, however indirectly, to a reward she cannot quite envision. Barely twenty-one, she still has that faith in the infinity of life. I love her for this, as I envy her. She is as irresistible to me as to the men who poured around her, vying for a dance. So, after Paul abandoned me to go off and confer with William and Vice President Li, I willingly served as accomplice to these hankering men. They would dance me once around the floor to Anna, then cut in, switching her abandoned partner off to me.

But you may remember, pages ago, I mentioned a coincidence that would amuse you. Well, here it is. I'd just been abandoned for the umpteenth time and was hunting for Paul to take me home, when a grave voice asked me to dance. I looked up to find myself arm in arm with—can you guess? Yes, our old friend Dr. Mann! He looked splendid, if a little sparer than I remembered, with that same thoughtful seriousness about him. He'd noticed me earlier, he said, after the banquet, but I was so thronged by admirers he dared not approach. I laughed aloud at that, pointing to Anna, and informed him that in approximately fifteen seconds he should thank me and ask her to dance. He glanced at her appreciatively but said she was too young for him. I explained that he could dance with her without marrying her, to which he replied that he thought her young men might disagree. So I told him it was only a matter of time before Anna's British fiancé returned from the war and, if he wasn't going to cut me loose, then he might at least tell me what had become of him since he left Shanghai.

Sarah, your doctor does have an adventurous soul! He didn't last long at the hospital where he was headed when last you heard of him—more sparks with the head surgeons, I surmise—but spent several months going up the Yangtze to Chungking. Then he traveled overland to the Yellow River and followed that up through Mongolia and all the way back to the coast. He slept in abandoned temples and visited with Chinese, missionary, even some Muslim doctors along the way, keeping notes for a medical journal he's writing—a sort of catalogue of Eastern medical practices, including many, he claims, "of inexplicable effectiveness." Now, for the moment, he has taken over an infirmary in Tientsin. The head doctor died of yellow fever last year, and so Dr. Mann has complete control. He is using some of the Chinese medicines he's studied and has traditional Chinese doctors on staff, which has made him extremely popular with the locals.

We shared several dances before Paul found his way back to me, and I was glad for the chance to introduce him to the doctor. I did not make the remark *you* would have wished about Dr. Mann's being present for the birth of Paul's son when Paul himself was not. I explained instead that Dr. Mann was very kind to me during the madness surrounding Sung Chiao-jen's assassination, at which Paul bowed gravely and expressed his deep gratitude to the doctor for seeing to my safety. Then Paul suggested a banquet in the doctor's honor, but Dr. Mann seemed peculiarly disconcerted by this and said he must return to his clinic. Paul laughed, gave him one of those overly hearty claps on the back, and pumped his hand like the seasoned politician he has become. And we parted.

I've come to the end of the story, Sarah. Perhaps you've been to enough Chinese extravaganzas that this all seems trifling, but I thought you would appreciate the personalities involved. I wish you had been here, sure you would have added unexpected spice and perhaps caused a few more fireworks than the sparkling rockets and twizzlers Yüan had set off in the snow as we dispersed.

I also wish I'd been a better correspondent over this past year. Seeing Dr. Mann brought back such fond thoughts of our times together in Shanghai. I have no equal friends here, and I wouldn't dare to guess when we might return south. Part of me doesn't want to, this city is so beautiful, has such a sense of history and magic. And it is even more lovely to be safely away from Paul's mother than it is sad to be so far from our baby's grave. But I do miss you and Jin. And Jed. Please tell Jed, by the way, that I've bought myself a Graflex camera and a pocket Premo, and when I do return to Shanghai I expect him to continue my instruction in darkroom skills.

So know that you have my fondest wishes, Sarah, and give a kiss to your Gerry for me. But I must get up and dress. The children are calling for me to come out and see their snowmen!

Love,

Hope

Toward the end of January, when the last traces of snow had blown away and the winds temporarily died down, Daisy Tan invited Hope and Anna and Pearl for an outing to Lung Fo market. Suyun was not mentioned, which meant, Hope assumed, that the girl would have a rare afternoon alone with her son. More for this reason than to spend these hours shopping, Hope agreed to the plan. Pearl and Anna were both delighted to escape their lessons, and after a rushed tiffin of soup and cold lamb, they joined Daisy at the gate, with Bald Crow coming along to carry packages. As the five of them squeezed into a single horse-drawn cab, it occurred to Hope that Yen and Paul would never have permitted this excursion without a male escort. But both men had gone off with William to meet with the students orchestrating Peking's massive and ongoing anti-Japanese boycott. Sun Yat-sen wanted the boycott called off, since the Japanese had finally come out in opposition to Yüan's monarchy.

At the gateway to the main market square the women left the *mafoo* to wait with the cab, and set off by foot. But just inside the cedar *p'ai lou*, or archway, they met an itinerant dentist whose signage, lettered in English as testimony to the man's advanced education, read INSERTION FALSE TEETH AND EYES, LATEST METHODISTS.

"Don't laugh," said Hope under her breath, clasping both Pearl and

Anna firmly by the wrist as all three nodded to the bowing dentist. "I *must* have this." Showing her camera, she persuaded the man and one of his on-lookers to pose as if in mid-extraction.

"But I don't understand, Mama," Pearl said when they were safely out of earshot. "Why does he only insert the eyes and teeth into Methodists?"

The question was so naive, so plaintive and utterly bewildered that Hope and Anna dissolved into laughter. Daisy gave them an impatient look and explained to Pearl in sharp Mandarin that the dentist was a low-class, ignorant laborer who did not deserve this attention.

"God bless the child," Anna said. "What innocence!"

They proceeded, jostling their way along narrow canopied passageways that teemed with every imaginable form of humanity, from beggars whose rag clothes were tied on with string, to fortune-tellers shaking rhythmic cans of sticks, to blind storytellers and children beating drums, to flocks of silk-robed gentry walking their caged birds. Daisy, who had distinct opinions about every merchant in the market, led Hope and Anna to her favorite shops while Pearl and Bald Crow trailed behind watching the street acrobats and puppet shows.

By Daisy's third jade shop Hope was lagging as well, and paused to rest with Pearl in front of two animal trainers. The first was a tall one-eyed man holding a stripped-down umbrella. From each naked spoke swung a string tied to a miniature pagoda, ladder, or other trinket, while a white mouse raced up and down the strings from toy to toy. The second trainer beat a gong and barked out the legend of an ancient hermit, which his rather mangy blue-jacketed monkey pantomimed. The louder the audi-ence cheered for the mouse, the louder beat the gong.

After several minutes, Hope realized that everyone was looking to her and Pearl to choose the winning act. "What do we do?" she wondered aloud.

"Best give both same and away before they count." Daisy, who had come out to see what was keeping Hope, ducked back into the shop and returned with two envelopes. She had Bald Crow deliver these to the an-imal trainers while she and the others slipped around the corner. Mo-ments later a roar went up and Hope half expected an irate mob to follow. But only Bald Crow appeared.

"People say the foreign ladies must be Christians," she reported, shame-faced. "They cannot tell good from bad."

Hope hushed Pearl's indignant protests that she knew perfectly well the mouse was the better act. "I see Solomon has no place in this country," she said to Anna.

Daisy beckoned Bald Crow to pass her folding bamboo walking stick. The uneven pavement and brittle cold were hard on her tortured feet. But she insisted on one last stop. More grandly appointed than the other stalls, this one sported glass cases and electric lights and a counter with cane-backed chairs where they could rest and sip tea while the elderly merchant brought out diamond necklaces and sapphire brooches and emerald and opal pendants. Hope bought Pearl a tiger-eye charm, which Daisy said would keep evil spirits away, and Daisy bought two teardrop necklaces, which she promptly presented, the star sapphire to Hope and the turquoise to Anna. Of course, both protested that this was too generous. Both were adamant—and overruled. "These stone like you eyes. So pretty." Daisy clenched her right hand and struck her heart. "*Yui*. Friendship. We remember this day always, yes?"

Hope and Anna exchanged glances. There was no point trying to reciprocate, as that would only compound their shame at not having made the gesture first. Both were now obligated to express their gratitude in some equally clever fashion in the future. Possibly, Hope thought cynically, by presenting Daisy with some particularly celebratory gift on her "son's" first birthday, when Suyun was to return to her parents in Hupei.

It was nearly four. Paul and William would be home soon, and the shadows were growing long. But as they started back toward the main square, a cry went up and the street filled with running boys and men braying harangues and curses. At the end of the alley two government soldiers appeared with raised bayonets.

Pearl clutched Hope's hand on one side, Anna's on the other. "It's all right," Hope said with more confidence than she felt. "We'll wait this out."

Bald Crow cocked her head like a listening parrot, then brightened. "No, Taitai. No problem. Execution. Kidnappers. Soldiers want everyone come this side."

Daisy tapped her walking stick. "No danger at execution. Come. You no need look."

But Hope was worried about Pearl. Her daughter's silence did not mean she'd missed a word of this exchange, and her studious examination of her feet did not hide her curiosity. "Come, sweet love," she said softly. "We'll be fine."

They joined hands and pushed into the throng, but just as Hope spotted the *p'ai lou*, a line of soldiers roughly pushed them aside, wielding their rifle butts as prods. Behind came another line of men pulling five crude carts of the kind normally used for hauling wood. Today each cart held two men, hands and necks locked into the wooden stocks called cangues.

"*Jang lui!*" the soldiers shouted. The crowd packed together so tightly that the women could not take another step. Hope lifted her elbows out to the sides to prevent Pearl from being crushed—and to gain enough air to stop herself from fainting. At the same time she sifted through the dialects for recognizable phrases. These men, it seemed, included certain high officials and members of the Hsinhua Palace Guard who were accused of concealing themselves in the palace and conspiring to kidnap Emperor Yüan. Their supposed motive was to collapse the monarchy and reinstate the Republic. This was deemed a capital crime.

"Shoot them!" shouted one impatient spectator.

"The garrote!" suggested another.

"The Empress would have chopped their heads off!" cried an old woman watching from the balcony of a teahouse.

Nausea, heat, cold, and panic gripped Hope's body in waves, but she steadied herself and leaned to whisper in Anna's ear. Then she stooped to Pearl. "We're going to divide up, love. You hold tight to Anna and Daisy and follow around to the side there. Don't let go of Anna for anything, hear? I'll meet you at the cab."

"But where are you going, Mama?"

Hope pressed her bloodless cheek against her daughter's warm one. "Something I must do. It won't take long, then we'll be on our way."

She kissed Pearl and gave Anna's elbow a squeeze, took a step, and they were gone. The noise, crush, and dark stink of the crowd instantly seemed to multiply, but she threaded her way forward to the raised platform of an open-air noodle shop. Though it was already packed with spectators, Hope was the only white woman, and as she moved toward the front, hands pounded backs, fingers pointed, mouths opened—people made way.

The square appeared from this higher vantage as a field of domed, woven, and fur-flapped caps, all pointed toward the clearing where the prisoners now bowed against a wall not forty feet from Hope. She pulled out her camera. Paul had told her about these men, arrested only yesterday. "Heroes of the Revolution," he called them. No kidnappers, their actual "crime" had been to spirit documents out of the Presidential Palace that proved Yüan had conceded to the Twenty-one Demands in exchange for Japan's secret promise to support him as Emperor. Britain's Ambassador Jordan had used the documents to pressure Japan, at the eleventh hour, to oppose Yüan's bid for the monarchy. While this hadn't stopped Yüan, it had weakened his position—and humiliated him. Now that he had caught these heroes, he would martyr them.

She adjusted focus as she scanned, from the gaping, riveted faces around her to the exploding gold of the dropping sun, the little puffs of dust rising like gunsmoke from between the tightly packed bodies. She aimed over the heads of the soldiers, found the kneeling prisoners. Then the executioner lifted his broad steel crescent. The first young prisoner, lips pinched, eyes staring and hard, had been released from his cangue, spread his hands on his knees. Hope was transfixed by the smoothness of his naked forehead.

The blade chopped down. The man's head dipped forward, blood spurting from the neck, but it was still attached to his shuddering body. The roar of the spectators echoed through the square. Everywhere mouths split open in laughter, in cheers and shaming hoots. The dripping sword lifted and fell again. The face, now twisted in agony, rolled from the kneeling man's shoulders.

Behind the lens, Hope held her breath against her own body's revolt and continued by dogged force to capture the dark boil of blood from the gaping neck, the slow, twitching collapse of the torso. The faces of the other prisoners stretched like masks, their eyes stripped by resignation. By horror. By paralysis.

The leash that had held her, photographing this carnage through some demonic sense of necessity, now broke abruptly and sent her flying down into and through the crush. She didn't wait for a path to open but shoved with the best of them, forcing her way toward the towering *p'ai lou*. But these were northerners, many even taller than Paul. She barely reached to their armpits, and they were so engrossed in the execution that they did not even notice the foreigner. As the bloodthirsty clamor rose again, she felt she was going to faint or vomit, or both.

She fought the sensation by screaming, kicking out like a child in a tantrum. "Pearl!" She swung her fisted arms. "Anna! Daisy!"

Her brain was closing, the will leaving her limbs, but she was dimly aware of men on either side of her backing away, gaps appearing between their bodies, a pale glint of light. She heard someone call her name. Her eyes were shut. She could not push them open.

Suddenly she saw the carriage, Pearl with outstretched arms, Bald Crow and Anna racing to catch her. Daisy's face floated like a tranquil petal above the hordes.

BABABA

Paul laughed. "The poor fool. He can't reveal the crime that's been done so he makes up this story and kills two innocent men!"

"There were ten men." Hope spoke in a low, cautious whisper from bed. Her skull felt as if it were being ground between two millstones.

"For show." Paul sat at the dressing table, watching without seeming to see her. "It is easy torture to force men to watch an execution thinking they will be next to die. And it creates a larger spectacle to have these extra prisoners."

Hope groaned. "How can you speak like this? As if the murder of innocent men were nothing!"

"But the heroes—the men who committed the real crime of leaking those documents—they were freed shortly after the execution. Surely you see this is good news. Yüan's hands are tied."

"His executioner's aren't." Hope started to rise, but the pain and nausea spun her back into the pillow.

"You and Daisy should not go to market without Yen or me."

"I suppose the execution would have been canceled if you or Yen had been there!"

"Ah, Hope. Even in pain you show your anger."

They were interrupted by a knock on the door, and the children trooped in to say their good nights. Hope took them in her arms. Pearl claimed to have seen nothing, but Hope could tell by the dazed widening of her eyes that she was lying. More, what she had seen would stay with her, would mark her in some inexpressible way for the rest of her life. Hope didn't blame herself for leaving the child. She doubted she could have stopped her seeing, nor could she have softened the view. What she did regret was the fact of the execution itself, what it told of this place, these people—Paul. She had forced herself to take those photographs, but she was not sure she could bear to look at them.

"Ch'eng-yü!" Paul waggled his hand for his son and swung him over his shoulder, then commanded Pearl to sing the Moon Lady's ballad, which Joy had taught her in Shanghai. Paul and Morris strutted around the room while Pearl sang in a high, excited voice. The noise was excruciating to Hope, and the instant Pearl had finished, she called for Ah-nie to take the children to bed.

"You *are* angry," Paul said, rubbing her feet through the bedclothes.

"I watched a man die stupidly, viciously, and needlessly today and I have the worst headache of my life, and you can't seem to comprehend either of these simple facts." She yanked her feet away from him.

"Should I leave you?"

They stared at each other as in a standoff.

"No."

He drew her legs back and slowly worked his hand up and down the length of her calf.

"Perhaps you are less innocent than they were."

He smiled at his moving hands. "That is why I could not have been one of them."

She raised herself on her elbows, motioning him to stop. She felt swollen and throbbing and nauseous, but it was not the shock of the day that made her so. For four weeks she had been resisting this malaise—and denying its implications.

"We have two small children, Paul . . . and another coming."

As this news took hold, she could see each thought rippling through his mind: memory of their lost son and daughter; the prospect of another bout of grief, if this child, too, went wrong; concern at Hope's ability to hold up; but then, the old paternal pride at the chance for another son; the inevitable swagger of masculine conceit; and finally, curiosity.

She gave him a wan smile. "I suppose we have Yüan to thank for this. Remember our lazy morning after the ball when we celebrated your marquis-ship?"

His eyes widened, amused, fingers dawdled on her ear, and she slipped an arm around his neck. "So you see," she whispered "No more palace intrigues. No more cloak-and-dagger. You have a wife and family who can't live without you."

Paul drew back, gliding his hand over the quilted contours of her body. "I promise," he said solemnly.

஭஭஭

Los Angeles
February 27, 1916
Dearest Dolly,

I am sorry for the time it has taken me to write, but perhaps you can understand and forgive if I tell you that I can hardly bear to write these words even now. Mary Jane passed away on the eighth of this month. She was taken by scarlet fever, so quick, a fire it seemed to consume her soul. You would not have recognized her at the end, my poor, beloved wife—oh, daughter, believe me when I tell you I loved our Mary Jane.

Perhaps it will give some solace if you know, I was not alone. There was abundance of flowers and hosts of friends to say their farewells. But she did so wish to see you and the children and I do wish you were here with me now.

Dolly dear, you are all I have ever more.

I love you.

Dad

VIII
FLIGHT
TIENTSIN
(1916)

ॐॐॐ

1

Sun Yat-sen finally agreed to command a full-scale revolt against Yüan. However, other rebel leaders had preceded him with weaponry and muscle of their own. In January one of Sun's former allies in Canton, the warlord Ch'en Chiung-ming, had launched his own rebellion, and other generals were proclaiming independence in the southwestern provinces. Beleaguered and beset by defections from both his bureaucracy and military staffs, Yüan canceled his monarchy in March, saying that he had been urged only reluctantly to the throne and was now reclaiming the presidency at the will of the people. Paul and William decided the time had come for Sun to strike. They evolved their plans with the collusion of the American and Japanese Legations and prepared to launch them the first week in April.

Paul did not discuss these plans with Hope. In part, he held back out of concern for her and the children's safety, but more, he dreaded her reaction. Doc's news of Mary Jane's death had caused Hope to withdraw once more into that familiar ghostly sadness. Paul had tried to comfort her, brought enticing teas, English novels and butterscotch from the British Legation, even a new Remington typewriter with the thought that work on her articles might raise her from this shadow. Mary Jane had been his friend also and he had a clearer understanding of this grief than he had for Hope's mourning of the lost babies. But he also accepted the inevitability of death in a way that his wife apparently could not. To despair over a loss that could not be reversed seemed to Paul a waste of life. When Hope descended into this state he was torn between anger over her withdrawal from him and fear that her depression would persist and worsen. Since he could find no words that would lift her mood, he took to saying nothing at all.

But on the night of his departure, he could delay no longer. It was late. Hope sat by the stove with a book lying open in her lap, her eyes listlessly traveling the same page over and over again. The children and most of the servants were asleep, and though the parched winds stirred as usual outside, the house felt abnormally still. That morning Daisy had removed her entire household to Taiyüan, where she planned to show off the baby to relatives. Paul had considered prevailing on Daisy to postpone her trip until his and William's return, but Hope's continuing anger toward Daisy warned him against interfering. If his wife would not understand the ways of Chinese families, if she would jeopardize a valued friendship for the sake of that unwed Suyun, then perhaps it was just as well that the third court stood empty in his absence. After all, Yen would watch over her and the children. And Anna Van Zyl came almost every day. In the state she was in, Hope would hardly miss him.

He stubbed out his cigarette and laid a hand on her shoulder. "I must go to Tientsin tonight." She did not look up. "If all goes well, this will be the end of Yüan."

She shut the book, and he saw that it was an edition of *Uncle Tom's Cabin* given to her by Mary Jane in the first years of their friendship. "How long?" she said in a dull voice.

"Two weeks. Maybe three." The volume slid from her lap and he stooped to catch it, placed it on the small inlaid table beside her. "Not long, Hope."

She looked at him, hard. "I wish that weren't my name."

Shaking his head, he moved to pick up a hobbyhorse from the floor. The red paint was worn off the long stick body, the leather ears fingered to satin from affection. The horsehair mane was tangled and one glass eye had come loose. Prancer, Ch'eng-yü called the toy.

"Love comes so naturally to children," Hope said. "Why is it so difficult for grown-ups?"

"Is it difficult for you?" He tried to screw in the dangling eye.

"Morris can't bear to be parted from that horse. He fell asleep in front
of the fire tonight, else he would have dragged it to bed with him."

"We are not children, Hope. We must heed our minds as well as
hearts." The glass eye fell back into his palm.

Hope got up and took the broken pieces from him. "Children, too,
play at being bandits and spies. Pearl and Morris wage full-scale battles
here in the courtyard. They send coded messages back and forth. They
even dress up as Empress and Emperor. But for all that, I never doubt
their love for each other, or for us."

There was a soft knock, and the door slid open. Yen dropped his eyes.
"Master Tan is waiting, Laoyeh."

"Moment," said Paul, and the door glided shut.

Hope had found some glue in a drawer and was restoring the glass eye
to its socket, her preoccupation a clear rebuke, but Paul did his best to ignore it. He stood at her back with one hand to the early rounding of her
belly, the other to her shoulder. He softly kissed the side of her neck, expecting her to turn. She did not move.

"Just come back to us, Paul," she whispered.

∾∾∾

Two nights later she dreamt of San Francisco—a brilliant sea-blue day,
brimming with life and enterprise. Suddenly the tide surges over the far
hill and down in a glassy wash. Up over the second hill, and again, down
the closest rise. The street is a black glistening line in its wake, and she is
far enough removed that she cannot see the submerged faces, believes that
life will resume, only freshly bathed. Then another wave comes. She sees
a shadow. A black whale flings itself into the air, shimmers in the sun. He
brushes a tower on the highest hill. Cornices fall. Windows shatter. He
descends, then leaps again, large as a monument himself. But this time
when he falls, the tide has fled. He hits that glistening line. His body fills
the ruined street, crushing the drowned and gasping. Only then does she
think of the damage, families destroyed, homes lost forever. Up to the
moment of the black whale's death, all she could see was his magic . . .

Yen stood over Hope's bed, shaking her awake. Paul had sent a messenger from Tsinan. She was to gather up the children, pack only essentials, and travel with Yen by cart, not train, to Tientsin, and from there by British steamer to Shanghai. Paul would meet them or leave further instructions at the Nantao house.

Hope pushed herself to the edge of the mattress, neither blinking nor breathing, but violently alert. "What's happened?"

Yen lifted his hands in a pretense of ignorance.

Over the years Hope had learned to be judicious in challenging her head man's authority. She no longer questioned the running of the household, the minor disputes with other servants, even Paul's willingness to confide in Yen plans he would not reveal to her. But when Yen's jurisdiction overlapped her own and he still tried to withhold information, she could be every bit as hardheaded as he was. "We don't leave this house unless you tell me what danger we're in and why."

"Master's plan has gone wrong," he said simply.

"And what *was* the plan!" But Yen's contorted face gave her pause. If Paul had sworn him to secrecy, then she was severely compromising his loyalty. "I insist you tell me," she said, more softly. "And if he asks, I will tell him you refused to speak. I will tell him I left you no choice. Now hurry, I must know if we are in danger. And I must know why."

So, as best he could, Yen poured out the botched plot. Paul and William had arranged for Vice President Li Yüan-hung to escape from Peking under protection of American and Japanese troops. He was to travel secretly to meet Dr. Sun, already en route from Japan, and establish a new revolutionary government based in the south. Given the support of the foreign powers, Sun and Li believed they could coerce Yüan to step down without firing a shot. But Li had failed to appear at the designated time and place. Now Paul and William feared that Yüan had uncovered the scheme. Hope and the children were not likely in danger, but they must leave right away to be sure.

"Where is my husband now?"

He shook his head. "The messenger will say only that he is safe."

Safe, she thought. Overhead, the ceiling's painted vines and lotus petals writhed in the flare of Yen's lantern.

"Please, Taitai. The cart is outside."

"Yes." She sighed, still unable to move. Her throat felt strange. If it weren't for the children . . . She flinched with a sudden cramp as Yen stooped to light the oil lamp by her bed.

He gestured insistently toward her wardrobe. "Western dress is better," he said. "Take only clothing and valuables for the journey. We leave Ah-nie to attend the rest and meet us in Shanghai."

"Tell her not to wake the children," Hope called after him. "Let me wake my own children . . ."

Better because bandits would think twice about kidnaping a white woman and children in Western clothing, or because Yüan would be more likely to leave them alone? Hope grimaced as she pulled the first layer of her Chinese silk underwear up over her roiling belly. Within its band she secreted her jewelry, including the necklace Paul had given her before the first inaugural ball and his marquis medal, which he had left with her for safekeeping.

Safekeeping. The word seemed to dangle over her as she breathed against another onslaught of nausea. She thought of the withered baby girl they had buried in Shanghai, the blue skin of her stillborn boy in Berkeley. Of Li-li and her baby, whom she'd never even seen. Of Mary Jane and Hope's mother and grandmother before her. Safekeeping was a nonsense word, she thought, and her stomach quieted abruptly at the certain knowledge that followed.

She would not survive the loss of another child.

She entered the nursery to find Ah-nie piling clothes and the children's most cherished stuffed and carved animals into a single wicker suitcase. Pearl and Morris, on either side of the room, were curled deeply into their pillows, rosy-cheeked, tousled, hands fisted as if for a fight. As Hope bent over her daughter she was suddenly overwhelmed by the brutality of what she was doing, what was being done to her. Her anger wrenched her. Tears coated her cheeks, and she began to shake. She wanted to take her children in her arms, to hold them to her, not to wake them, but to join them in their hard, defensive sleep.

"Missy?" Ah-nie dangled a handkerchief.

Hope took it and scrubbed her hot face. "Pearl." She tested her voice. "Wake up, my sweet. We're going to Shanghai."

Pearl's eyelids fluttered. She yawned and stretched. "It's dark out."

"I know. That's what makes it—" She searched. "An adventure. Yen's taking us on an adventure. Come. Put on your warm clothes and your good gray smocked wool over."

Pearl groggily dressed while Hope roused Morris. The little boy reached for his hobbyhorse, and Hope proceeded to change his clothes around the wooden appendage, talking boldly about their moonlight ride, the magic journey ahead of them. She had almost persuaded herself that this ploy was working, and all the evenings spent reading *Kidnapped* and *Captains Courageous* had finally paid off, when Pearl said, "I like Peking."

"Me, too," Morris echoed.

"Shanghai's sticky and smelly and the children in the park are mean."

Morris nodded emphatically, squirming out of Hope's grasp.

"Put your shoes on, Pearl."

"But, Mama—!"

Pearl broke off in stricken silence, head flung back, jaw slack. Her cheek flamed where Hope, for the first time in her life, had slapped her. Hope's hand, too, stung. Her whole body was shaking, and she could feel the layers of sorrow and regret descending like armored gates. She wanted to take her daughter in her arms and rock her, beg her forgiveness. Instead she heard her own icy voice. "These are your father's instructions. Hurry."

Minutes later they left the lamp-whipped quarters they had all come to love, marched like convicts down the covered gallery and past the writhing spirit wall for the final time. It was one o'clock in the morning, the earth black under a dense shield of cloud. The air sparked against their skin. "Rain," said Hope.

Yen nodded. "Maybe better. Keep police inside."

"With good reason," she answered grimly. Spring rains in northeastern China were as treacherous for travelers as a hail of artillery fire. They washed out bridges, flooded streambeds, blinded animals and drivers alike to the changed contours of the road. "Let's hope we make Tientsin before it starts."

The cart that stood waiting, with its wizened driver, derelict donkeys, and tightly arching hood, was indistinguishable from the thousands of such vehicles that plodded through the city each day, but at this hour, when only soldiers and robbers were about, its waiting presence was like a beacon. Yen's eyes flashed up and down the shrouded *hut'ung*, and he came as near to losing his temper with the dawdling children as Hope had ever heard him. Finally they were jammed with their few hastily packed bags into the goatskin-lined wagon. Hope's spine was wedged against the side board, her hat crushed against the arching canopy, and only after considerable experimentation did she manage to tuck her legs, angling and folding them around Pearl's. Morris, lying across their laps, whimpered as he realized that Ah-nie was to be left behind, but the amah shushed and handed in his hobbyhorse. He clung to it silently as the wooden wheels began to creak and Yen, sitting up with the driver, lowered the hood's front flap.

Hope whispered for the children to stay quiet, though the monstrous transformation of her character had effectively struck them dumb. She said nothing to comfort them, nothing to inform them. Instead she kept her eyes fixed on the small string grid that served as a one-way window. As they wound through the shadowed alleyways, avoiding the wide public avenues, her head filled with the images that seemed as inextricably bound to China as its dust, and smells, and walls. The detached head of the innocent man she'd seen murdered in the market. The slumped figures of Paul's fellow revolutionaries shot dead on railroad platforms or poisoned at state dinners. The ruffled streamers of flesh crossing Paul's own back. From every black gateway, around each new corner she expected the sudden gleam of a bayonet or the shivering nose of a pistol. Paul always assured her that Chinese respect for family preserved the lives of wives and children even when men were targeted for treason. And even the most bloodthirsty of today's generals knew to leave foreigners alone. But if this was true, why were she and the children being spirited away under darkness?

All the gates of the city but Ch'ien Men were locked at this hour, and even Ch'ien Men was deserted. Beggars huddled in shadow clusters. Sentries dozed against the city wall. There were no camels or mule trains tonight, only a few stalwart vendors hunched by their ovens, and three or four straggling revelers. The latter wore the regimental green of Yüan's municipal troops, and Hope shrank from their erratic laughter, clutching the children tightly.

"*T'ing!*"

Morris's hobbyhorse drove its wooden head into Hope's jaw as the cart jerked to a halt. The voice that had commanded them to stop was slurred and, judging from the exchange up front, only the *mafoo* understood the man's dialect. But there was no mistaking his intent when, with a blow, he shoved Yen aside and peered under the flap. His grin, fully visible even in the darkness, was reptilian.

Hope squeezed Pearl's hand, transferred the slumbering Morris into her lap, and inched forward. The stink of garlic and liquor very nearly overpowered her as she leaned through the opening, but she caught her breath and swallowed hard. "Why have you stopped us?"

The soldier was as short as he was broad, and the cart gave Hope just enough height that she looked down on him. Yen made a single motion with his eyes to the man's scraggly mustache, the buttons of his epaulets, and his holstered Mauser. Behind him three infantrymen stood at attention. Yen was armed, she knew, but that would hardly help this situation. They were dealing with an officer.

He spat thickly, then snarled at the driver. Yen eased a wad of bills from his pocket, but the soldier knocked them from his hand and made him kneel in the mud to retrieve them. Hope hugged herself. It was a rare misstep for Yen. He should have slipped the money to the man while being cuffed, so the others would not see the bribe. Now it was too public and too late. The officer raised his boot to Yen's head.

Gripping the cart, Hope hauled herself to a standing position, so that she towered over them all. "Yen," she said in peremptory English, as if she neither noticed nor concerned herself with his peril. "Tell this man I am wife of President Yüan's personal advisor George Morrison. My husband is awaiting me in Tientsin, and if we are further detained here, this man will have to answer to both the President and the British Legation."

Yen's jaw dropped at the baldness of this lie, but he duly translated to the *mafoo*, who in turn translated for the officer. Their assailant knit his heavy eyebrows as he assessed Hope's crushed fedora, her navy tweed coat and leather gloves, the muddied spats over her button boots. He teetered as he considered his options. Finally he swatted in front of his face, spat again and threw Hope a look of such undisguised hatred that she could feel it burn into the pit of her stomach. One of the subordinates drove his rifle into Yen's ribs, sending him sprawling against the wooden wheel. The driver scurried to help him up.

"*Chi hsü tsou!*" Hope ordered the driver. To Yen she whispered, "Don't look back."

As they jerked forward, she withdrew behind the flap and enfolded the children, pulling them as flat as possible against the cart floor. Morris was awake, but Pearl had planted her thumb in his mouth to silence him. Behind, the commander was screaming at his men. Even above the rasp of the wheels, Hope could hear the slap of flesh. In that most Chinese of ways, she thought, the commander had diverted his rage from the hated Westerner, turned it against his own.

"Mama?" Pearl whispered. "He's wet." Morris stirred in denial, shrank into the corner.

Hope started to respond, but as she opened her mouth she realized that she could not catch her breath. The burning in her stomach had spread to her throat, and the soldier's stench was still on her. She held herself as they lurched and slammed down one rutted lane after another, but they had traveled little more than a mile when she suddenly pitched forward, grabbing the *mafoo* by the shoulder, and hurled herself into the road. There was a ditch, visible only as a black line against the marginally lighter darkness. As Hope reeled toward it she clutched at the ghostly figure of a sapling, all that stopped her headlong fall. The smells of night-soil and donkey, her own sweat and imminent rain overcame her, and she was as sick as she had ever been in her life.

Yen, ever-dutiful Yen, stood by as the emotions she had been holding inside now erupted with volcanic imprecision. When she could retch no more, he offered a canister of boiled water, and she realized she was parched with thirst. She poured the liquid down her throat and let him help her back into the cart. They had to continue. They were nowhere, and at any moment the storm would begin. She braced herself against the violence of the cart and tried to comfort her terrified children. "It's going to be all right," she whispered. "I'm sorry—" Tears sprang to her eyes, and she bit down to stop them. "I'm sorry I was short with you, Pearl."

"I understand, Mama. You feel bad."

"Want to hold Prancer, Mama?" Morris asked tentatively.

"No, darling." Hope forced her burning cheek away from the little boy's forehead. "You keep your Prancer."

"Is Papa going to meet us in Tientsin?"

"No."

There was silence then as the cart tipped and rattled deeper into the countryside. They dared not light the driver's lantern for fear of attracting unwanted attention, and the thickening night swallowed the least glimmer of milestone or landmark. A soft watery slapping suggested a nearby canal, and every now and then a spate of birdsong or batwings broke above their heads, but the cold had grown clammy, and the trees along the road were beginning to heave with the approaching storm.

Hope fought for these observations as a distraction from her body's continuing rebellion. Her bones were burning, her stomach yanked in knots, and her throat felt as if it were filled with stones, making it impossible to swallow and difficult to breathe. When she closed her eyes, the darkness whirled. She drew her daughter's head against her shoulder, held both children against the vehicle's battering waves. The rain began, a brittle scatter across the canvas top, and she felt the motion of an arm reaching to secure the flap.

"Yen."

"Yes, Taitai." His voice sounded cool on her melting skin.

"I—I can't . . ." These few whispered syllables consumed every reserve of energy Hope could muster, and she sank back, depleted, as the storms within and without rose in competition. The night was splitting in a battle of purple, gold, navy, and orange so brilliant that it glowed through the canvas. The thunder's force rocked the cart, and the rain beat now, solid and relentless, swamping the rural lane. Through the string grid, Hope watched the river ignite with lightning, the dark forms of sampans shadow-boxing trees along the shore. Seconds or hours passed, the same. She was only dimly aware of Yen and the driver out in front, dragging the donkeys through mud.

Dawn was paling a low line of sky, and the torrent had steadied to a downpour when the outline of a two-story inn at last materialized by the roadside. Yen tucked the children under his coat and carried them to the unlit door, then came back with an oil-paper umbrella to cover Hope as she staggered from the cart. She leaned on him, panting, insensible to the rain. Her skin was streaming anyway, her corset spongy with perspiration, but she could rest here, at least, lie quiet, stop moving.

By the wavering light of a single stump candle planted inside the door, she could see her children waiting down a long, low-ceilinged passageway with crumbling, sooty walls and a dirt floor strewn with moldering grass. There were goats and chickens underfoot, and the smells of excrement and rot and seeping damp were unbearable. Hope's stomach clenched and she turned, groping for the door, but instead stumbled into a windowless antechamber where the stink of decay was replaced by a sweet, tarry, green perfume, like medicinal incense. Her stomach relaxed, and it occurred to her to wonder if the sickness had caused her to hallucinate. She fought the impulse to close her eyes and succumb to the fragrant haze. Slowly her vision adjusted. She became aware of figures slumped about the room. She saw the walls were lined with shallow bunks, like so many coffins stacked to the ceiling, and from each one stared the starved, motionless skull of an opium addict.

Reeling, she fell back into the light. Yen's face rose before her, an exaggeration of her own disorientation and terror, but she lunged toward it. She was burning and shivering in the bitter damp, her tongue swollen in her mouth. She shook her head, unable to speak, and while Pearl strained to support her weight, Yen clutched the sleeping Morris and argued with the proprietor, who had a harelip and black teeth. Painstakingly, Hope came to understand that this disheveled man wanted nothing to do with the foreign woman and her children. He could see she was ill, he had no interest in housing a foreigner's corpse. Then Yen reached into his pocket, and in her delirium, Hope was convinced he was reaching for his gun.

A choked, guttural protest fought its way up her throat. She wobbled against Pearl's shoulder and felt inside her waistband. At the same time, she arched her neck, tipped her chin, working her perspiring head in the attempt to free her vocal cords.

But when her fingers at last fastened on the concealed packets, she felt herself sliding again. She couldn't remember which was which, and in any case, she couldn't decide . . . If she showed the necklace, the man would admit them, but would surely attempt to steal it. If she showed the marquis medal, he might be sufficiently cowed to help them, but he might not believe it real.

They were all watching her. The innkeeper clicked his teeth. Morris had wakened without a sound against Yen's rigid shoulder, and Pearl looked up with a spellbound expression, as if praying with her eyes open. Hope worked her hand slowly free of the folded liner. She held the smaller of the two pouches out to Yen, who opened it with great ceremony. The innkeeper's eyes widened as Yen explained the medal's significance.

Before he had finished Hope was overcome by a sudden, shimmering light that seemed to start from the base of her skull. She heard words, a rustle and stamp, felt the folds of Pearl's taffeta bow, a pressure at her arm. Somehow she managed to haul herself up the rope-bound ladder to the second floor. They entered a square room with a plank table, a single wooden chair, an open chamber pot and brick *k'ang*, a sleeping platform under which a fire could be made during the cold months. The fire was unlit. There was no mattress or bedding. The single oil-paper window flamed with the lightning outside, while the thatched ceiling rustled with rats, the floorboards with roaches, and rainwater ran in a dark screen down the wall behind the *k'ang*.

Pearl was stepping gingerly to join Hope on the *k'ang*.

"No!" Hope winced at the pain of speaking, but held up her hand, palm out. "Germs. Take Morris. Stay . . . table." She tried in vain to swallow, turned to Yen. "Doctor. Go."

There was no doubt in her mind what was going to happen. Her mother's fate was to be Morris and Pearl's legacy as it had been her own. And the new child would go with her.

But she would not submit willingly.

Yen gave Morris to Pearl. The children huddled together in the middle of the table. The candle twitched as Yen bent to light the fire, but Hope was already burning, and the coal smoke would make it even harder to breathe. She reached out a hand, pushing him roughly. "Go."

Yen backed away. The door latched behind him. Her children's faces were gray in this light, their arms and legs entwined. Hope remembered the tree she and Paul had seen in Wyoming, the sycamore and oak growing into each other, and she thought that was how her children seemed, growing up in this raw, brutal country. Paul's voice wound a slender thread through her mind now, and though at first she couldn't hear what he was saying, she could feel the effect working up her spine. She saw his face, one eyebrow ruffled, the pale sienna of his skin alight in the lantern flame that leapt in a ruthless cat's dance. He was reading. "We could not understand because we were too far, could not remember because we were traveling in the night of first ages, of those ages that are gone, leaving hardly a sign—no memories."

"No memories," Hope mouthed, and vomited a thin trail of bile.

Some time later the door slammed open and Yen entered, accompanied by a squat, bent-back man cloaked in black with eyes like two tarnished razors. Even through her fever Hope felt the sting as his gaze sliced into her.

"*Yang kuei!*" The Chinese doctor raised his arm as if to ward off a blow. Yen tried to hold him, but the man slapped him away, barking something about Chinese graves. Hope saw rain spitting against the sodden window, seeping down the wall. She thought of that headless body in the square, the dark shimmer of its blood easing into the earth.

🐦🐦🐦

2

Shadows goose-stepped across her mind. Her thoughts themselves were white, empty except for the barren light of a distance too great to travel. If not for the shadows, this far light would settle and bury her like snow. But the shadows stalked the whiteness. They assumed the shapes of palm fronds rattling in a dry wind, of hard-cut puppets acting out tales of infidelity or defilement. A sword. A whale. A dangling figure, sexless and free. The curled and pulsing shape of a heart. Beating. Beating.

Emotion was a stranger in this universe of whiteness, silence the one consistent note, but the shadows danced on, faces now. Or parts of faces. Lips curled back. A heavy-lidded eye. The probing slide of an overgrown nose. Someone was putting a name to these shapes, but who? Where? Shadow and light were the sole inhabitants of this noiseless, rimless desert. Perhaps it was they who labeled themselves. A self-contained universe, needing nothing. Wanting nothing . . .

"Hope?"

She moaned, tried to turn their head.

"Quiet now."

The shadows darkened. And shattered in a blinding rain.

ॐॐॐ

A sound like bells woke her. She could not open her eyes. Her arms were lifeless, her lungs searing. But that sound called her.

"Pearl." The effort ground her throat like a fistful of gravel.

"There she is." Something cool and damp moved over her face. "Can you open your eyes, Hope? Atta girl."

She felt a fluttering and clawing at her breast, and her head filled with the shadow of a bird being ravaged by a cat.

"Slow. Take it slow." The voice climbed over her, shading her as she struggled to work her eyelids. "Pearl and Morris are fine. Yen's here, too. They're all waiting to see you."

She strained, rocking forward and back, still in darkness. Were they all dead, then, and she the last to join them? She found her tongue and moved it over her lips, tasted dead skin, moisture left by the dampened cloth.

"You're going to make it," said the voice again. A man's voice. Familiar but unplaceable. "Wherever you've been, you can put it behind you now."

The cool sensation moved again over her brow, resting briefly on her closed eyelids. When it lifted, she blinked. The light was excruciating, but after a few more trials, she was able to look at the man seated beside her. A thin, angular man with long ears, full lips that continued to move. "I knew you could do it. Come, take a sip of water if you can. It'll help the burning."

He slipped an arm around her shoulders to brace her, held a glass to her mouth. She choked on the water, but he insisted she try again. The effort, though agonizing, helped force her to consciousness. By the time she'd figured out how to let the drops trickle down her throat, her mind was a clutter of questions.

"My children," she mouthed.

"It's all right. They're outside, you hear them playing? When you have some strength, we'll call them in. By some miracle the fever missed them both."

She lay back. From the filthy chamber where she lost consciousness she had come to a soft, clean bed in a whitewashed room filled with books and pictures and sunlight. The wall beside the bed was hung with Chinese phrenological and acupuncture charts. A third was blocked by a tall folding screen with images of cranes. There was an enamel basin and chamber pot, a rough-hewn door, and an open rectangular window through which Hope could now distinguish the children's voices, Yen's low growl behind them.

She raised herself up. "I told them," she whispered, "stay on the table."

Her attendant wrung out the cloth in the basin. "They did, too. That's right where we found them. They're good kids. You've done a fine job with them. Can't be easy."

Their eyes met. His were a mossy brown struck through with glimmers of blue and green. Again, she felt the tug of recognition, but something he had said, she wasn't sure what, started her crying.

"Hey," he murmured, coming closer. "You had a bad streak of luck. That's all." He glanced down. "By all signs, the baby's pulled through, too."

She followed his eyes. He—someone—had removed her clothing and placed her in a soft white muslin shift, which was all that covered the low swell of her belly. The baby. She drew the blue counterpane up to her chest. The baby.

"My husband," she rasped. "Have you—"

"I've telephoned around Tientsin. He's known here, and I'm told he left safely for the south the night before you arrived. But no one knows where he is now. Sun Yat-sen's called an emergency assembly in Canton. That may be where he's gone. Don't try to talk out loud, Hope. I can understand if you mouth the words slowly."

It dawned on her that she had no more idea of her own whereabouts than she had Paul's. "Where?" she mouthed as instructed. "How did we get here?"

"You're in Tientsin," he answered. "Thanks to Yen. You were ten miles upriver. Not many servants would run that distance for a foreign mistress. Fortunately, he's from around here and knew of my clinic. You're very, very lucky."

She nodded, tears starting again. She remembered the lies that night and the sickness that followed, the menace of the river, the storm. Cold and sleet. Pearl's sodden hair. Morrie's reaching arms and the rats, the throb of her own hateful voice as she ordered her children not to touch her.

She shut her eyes. When she opened them she understood at last that it was Stephen Mann staring back at her. She became conscious of the fever still firing her skin, the fall of her unpinned, dirty hair on her shoulders. She attempted to lift her hands, but she had no strength. Her only defense was to look away.

Jude the Obscure, read the spine of the first book her eyes came to. *The Tempest. Dante's Inferno. The Scarlet Letter.* Beneath them stood a low oval table with a shaving pot, brush, and towel, and a small gilt-framed photograph of an elderly man and woman smiling down from a Model T Ford.

Mann was following her gaze. "Let me confess before you accuse me. This is my house. The clinic is down the road, but I wouldn't have dreamt of leaving you in anyone else's care, and my attentiveness—" he glanced at a neatly made-up cot in the corner "—might have been misconstrued."

She dragged one shrunken arm across her lap. Her hand appeared in her still uncertain vision as an assemblage of match sticks. "I'm sorry," she mouthed.

"Sorry! You've been to the river and back again, and you're apologizing to *me*? I've never seen anyone work so hard to hang on to life. You fought like a tiger."

She looked up. The circles under Mann's kind eyes were dark as nickels. His shoulders slumped from fatigue, and, judging by the stubble on his lean cheeks, that shaving pot hadn't been used in days. "How long have we been here?"

"Almost a week."

"What kind of fever?"

"Diphtheria."

A chill ran through her, so strong and sudden that she began to tremble. In her urgency to explain, she choked on the words, "My mother—"

"I told you not to talk. It's the fever. It coats your throat and tonsils. That's why you must keep drinking." He drew a blanket around her shoulders and gave her another sip of water. "Your mother?"

Her lips moved in this new silent language. "Died of diphtheria."

"You were very young?"

She nodded. "A baby."

"You're not going to die, Hope."

He sat with his elbows braced on his knees, one hand cupped in the other. The contradiction between his determined words and this pleading gesture confused her. She tried to reassure herself by picturing Paul in the doctor's place, but the image that resulted was so still, so closed and unreadable that it started her trembling all over again.

જ⟩જ⟩જ⟩

For days Hope remained too weak even to manage a spoon. She had lost so much weight that her wrist-bones stood out in knobs and her chest sank beneath her collarbones. Mann's maidservant Fresh Rain had to carry her to the chamber pot and bathe her, but the fever had broken. Hope's voice was gradually restored. She could smile. Yen brought news that Paul had been in Shanghai and was now on his way to Canton. The infant in her womb sprang to life, as if in defiance of the rest of her body, and the children were regular and enthusiastic visitors.

"Dr. Mann has a puppy!" Morris reported. "He let us play with him. His name is Mister Bacon 'cause he's all stripey. Isn't that a funny name?"

"And there's an old man who lives next door who keeps a canary," said Pearl. "And every afternoon he opens the door and the bird flies to the top of the willow tree here in our yard, and when the man calls, the canary flies right back into her cage. Imagine!"

"Imagine." Hope smiled and shook her head.

"Are you feeling better, Mama?"

"Much better, my sweets."

"Will we have to go home soon?"

"Dr. Mann says I'll need a few more days."

"It's nice here," said Pearl.

"Dr. Mann's nice."

"Yes," Hope said. "I know."

Evenings, when he returned from his rounds at the clinic and the children had gone to bed, Mann would sit by her side in his garnet wing chair, and they would talk of books and medicine, and music and photography, and writing and China—and home. He told her about the forests and mountains of his native Washington, of trees so big around that loggers made houses from their hollowed-out trunks. He described the green of the place, a dense, drenching, limitless color. "You can feel the life beneath your feet."

In her turn, she talked of the plains, the humility of space when the horizon unspools in a perfect circle and the sky feels taut as a drum. She told about the dust storms and twisters, of crouching in a dank, lightless cellar while the earth flies apart overhead, and of other nights so still it seemed you could cut the air into slices. She told him about the family that had raised her, about her father and Mary Jane and Li-li and Thomas. During the breath in which she was debating whether to begin the tale of her marriage, Mann announced he was one of a family of fifteen children, all born on a land-grant farm in Alberta before his parents decided that not even potatoes would grow in Canadian soil. They'd retired to Seattle and started a boarding house, which grew into a successful hotel, the children working as staff. All the others were still there.

"And what made you different?" she asked.

"I was the youngest." He knit his hands across his lap and stretched his legs straight. He had about him an ease, a complete and unguarded presence, that reminded Hope acutely of Frank Pearson. "Fourteen brothers and sisters all assuming authority over me. I guess it made me a bit power hungry."

"You don't seem very power hungry to me." She smiled. "I always wondered what it would be like to have real brothers and sisters."

He pulled the lantern closer between them. "Now you have children instead."

The door was open. The air smelled of lilac and oranges. Mann's house lay outside the city wall, and so he had offered, when she was well enough to be moved, to take her and the children to another doctor's home inside the concessions, but he'd also confessed he enjoyed their company and didn't mind at all sleeping in his study, where he had moved his cot once she was past the fever. So they remained his guests.

"You're power hungry," she prompted. "Is that why you became a doctor?"

"In part." As he pulled up the cowl of his sweater, she noticed that his hands were thick and flat at the joints, ringless under short golden hairs.

"When I was ten," he said, "there was a little boy who lived at our boarding house—about the same age Morrie is now. One day his mother said she'd give me a quarter to look after him. There was a park nearby, so I took him over. He was a real little lad, if you know what I mean. He looked up to me in the way I looked up to my favorite brother. And he was a goer. I taught him to throw a ball, and we climbed some trees. He asked to swing, and he was laughing so that I pushed him higher and higher. He was even with the top bar when suddenly he cried out my name. As I looked up he pitched to the ground, landed shaking and kicking, eyes rolled back. I yelled for help, but there was no one around. 'Course, I had no idea what was wrong with him, never heard of an epileptic fit. I was terrified to touch him, afraid to leave him. His skin was turning blue, and the convulsions got worse. I tried to grab him, hold him still, but it was too late. His head had struck a rock."

He leaned forward, caught the drape of the blue counterpane and rubbed it between those squared-off fingers. "I never got over that feeling of helplessness, watching him die and not even knowing what was wrong."

"Poor child." Hope touched his hand. His fingers curled around hers.

"The thing is, all my medical training, all the problems I've learned to cure only make me more aware of the ones that continue to defy me."

"Defy you!" Hope shook her head and, suddenly uneasy at the sight of their clasped hands, let him go. "You sound like Ahab chasing his Great White Whale. I hardly think incurable disease has a vendetta against you personally."

"Your reaction was personal enough," he said quietly, "when you learned your fever was diphtheria."

"My reaction was based on superstitious fear," she retorted. "Anyway, you cured me."

"Did I?"

The unexpected emotion behind these two words brought her head up with a snap. For the briefest of moments they locked eyes.

She looked away. "I'm afraid we're overstaying our welcome."

"That would not be possible."

She tried to deflect his intensity, but the combination of feelings he had aroused made her flustered, unsure of herself. She fixed her gaze on his shoulders. Wide, athletic shoulders, which he squared with deceptive confidence. "Stephen," she said.

He didn't answer. It was the first time she had used his Christian name.

She lifted her eyes and found his expression changed again. The fierceness had left him. Now she was aware only of the yearning that had underscored it. And the regret.

"That's how I'd like to think of you."

"*Do* you think of me, Hope?"

"I'd be pretty ungrateful not to." She forced a laugh. "You saved my life!"

"Yen and fate deserve more credit than I do. That's not what I'm asking."

Her wrists, as if by some warning instinct, had settled on the low, flinching dome of her belly. She sighed, looking down. "Pregnancy is a curious condition. Like carrying your conscience in your womb."

"I was wondering what you had in there." He threw her a deadpan smile and stood abruptly to leave. "I understand conscience is a heavy burden. You carry it better than I would."

෨෨෨

The following evening she read to the children from a book of poetry by Bret Harte, which Mann (even, and perhaps especially, in her thoughts, now *Stephen* seemed dangerously familiar) had given them. Morris had fallen asleep in the armchair, but Pearl begged for one more poem. Hope sighed, and turned the page. "It's titled 'Fate.'"

The verse was short. It opened with cloudy skies and tempestuous waves warning against a sail, darkness and danger discouraging a hunt. " 'But the ship sailed safely over the sea,' " she concluded, " 'And the hunters came from the chase in glee; and the town that was builded upon a rock was swallowed up in the earthquake shock.' "

Hope lifted her shoulders in a sudden shiver and closed the book.

"What's it mean, Mama?" Pearl wanted to know.

"Nothing." Hope shook her head. "*Mei fatse.* That's what it means. No matter how strong and safe you think you are, the earth can still open beneath your feet. Now run and get Yen. Poor Morrie will have a terrible crick if he sleeps in that position much longer."

But after Yen had carried Morris off, Pearl stole back again. Seeing that Hope was neither reading nor writing nor sleeping but only lying with her eyes fixed on the far wall, she curled herself at the foot of the bed, and waited to be noticed. With Morrie asleep and Dr. Mann at his clinic, this was a rare chance to have her mother to herself. At length Hope sighed and shifted her position, drawing her daughter against her hip. "What is it?"

"Mama," Pearl said, "why don't we go to church?"

"Church!" Hope studied her more closely. The wide dark eyes were graver than usual and deadly earnest. "Do you wish we did?"

"When we were all alone," said Pearl, "and you were so sick and I didn't know what would happen to us, I thought maybe God could help, but I was afraid to ask because I didn't really know how." She laid her cheek thoughtfully against her mother's leg. "And also I thought maybe I couldn't because we don't go to church."

"Oh, Pearl, you don't have to go to church to talk to God. You can talk to Him anywhere. Whenever you feel upset or uncertain. That's better, I think, than saving your feelings for a particular day or place."

"But how?"

"Just be very still and listen carefully to the voice that speaks deep inside you. The voice only you can hear. That always tells the truth. You know the one I mean?"

Pearl nodded doubtfully, but squeezed her eyes shut, clasped her hands tightly, and moved her lips. For a minute she sat perfectly still, then her eyes fluttered open. "I think He heard me."

"See?"

"Want to know what I told him?"

"No," Hope answered firmly. "I do not."

The child straightened her mother's bedclothes. "Aren't you even a little curious?"

Hope restrained a smile. "Pearl, you know you can always tell me what's on your mind and I'll do my best to help. But your prayers are like a very, very private conversation. Something you should treasure, that becomes all the more valuable because it is yours alone."

"Like a secret?"

"Not exactly. Secrets are often mean, sneaky. Something said behind another's back. Oh, this is hard to explain, but it's also important, so listen carefully and try to understand. Everyone has a special place—like a little room inside." She tapped Pearl's chest. "In this room you are completely free of what anyone else in the world may think. And because you are free in this way, you are also safe. No one will judge you there, so you've no reason to lie. This is where you and God talk. Now you may have similar conversations with other people outside this private room. You should always try anyway to tell the truth. But with other people you have to be careful, you have to think how they will interpret your words, how they may react. That's what makes the world outside so much more complicated and dangerous, why it is important to have this inside place where you can be safe."

"Safe even from earthquakes?"

After a pause Hope said gently, "It's a different kind of safety. But yes, I suppose in a way . . . it's where you go to piece things together after the earth's fallen apart."

Pearl wound the corner of the bedsheet around her finger.

"Does this make sense to you?" asked Hope.

"Yes." She let the sheet unwind. "But will I get in trouble if I tell?"

"Pearl. I'm trying to make you see that you don't *have* to tell, that no one in the world has the right to enter this private place of yours without your permission. And yes, sometimes you might get in trouble for opening your heart, for saying what you really believe." She paused. "That's why, when you do open yourself in this way, it should be with someone who loves you absolutely, someone who would never, ever betray your trust."

"Do you love Papa that way?"

Hope winced at the unexpected question. "I . . . Yes, Pearl. Of course."

"What about me?" Pearl asked. "I love you. I trust you. Why can't I tell you?"

Hope leaned down and kissed the warm dark crown of her daughter's head. "I treasure your love. Of course you may tell me what's in your heart, my sweet. But you must understand, it's not necessary. I want you to have your own hopes and dreams."

"What if I just tell you one of those dreams and don't say it was what I prayed for?"

Hope took the small face between her hands. "All right you! I will remember this moment when you're twenty, and you'll tell me it never happened."

"What I dream," said Pearl deliberately, "is that Papa will come get us and never go away again."

Hope inhaled sharply. "Yes," she whispered as Pearl's large eyes continued to watch her. "I dream that, too."

The next morning Mann brought the following cable:

Relieved you and babies safe stop thanks to doctor stop letter to follow stop Paul stop

ৡৡৡ

3

Canton
6 April, 1916
My dearest Hope,

I receive a cable from Dr. Mann telling me only that you have diphtheria but will be well in few weeks, he is taking care of you. This makes me wild with worry, you know. He does not say if our babies are ill or well. I do not know if your recovery continues. Please write to me as soon as you are able, set my heart at ease. I know Yen will always take best care of you, that you are safer with him than with me in many times. You know I would not leave you to his care if it were otherwise. And this Dr. Mann I remember from Peking. A good man, I think, to cable to me at his own expense.

It is difficult to write of my life, our future, not knowing the state of your health. I worry all the time, but I must believe you will return to me. I have arranged passage for you with China Line steamship, all paid, tickets cut when you are well to make this journey. Our new home is ready at 50 Range Road in American Settlement. This house has very much space. Tell Pearl that she will have her own room and Joy is eager to see how big she has grown. Morris and new baby can share one nursery, and there are good quarters for servants, and a large yard with tree for a swing for children. Ah-nie has returned to Shanghai with all house goods from Peking, and our former servants wish return my employ also. Other ways, all is ready for you return.

Of the rest, I dare not write. William and I have made a safe journey, but I fear for the unity of our hard-fought Republic. And so I fear for us all.

You must know my thoughts are with you morning and night. I remember that you are my true wife. I remember all that you once told me about your early years without your own mama, and your fear that this same fate awaits our own children. So when I receive Dr. Mann's cable I went to the Buddhist temple in Nantao and made many prayers before the Goddess Kuan Yin. I know you do not believe in such things, but the temple was a place of comfort for me in my boyhood, and I find it still has that effect during times of greatest hardship and pain.

I long to hear in your own words that you are well and ready to return my side.

I am your Paul

Tientsin
April 15, 1916
Dearest Paul,

I have your letter in my hands and in my heart. I am indeed your true wife, Paul, and you cannot imagine how your assurances have healed me. You are right that the specter of death loomed very large before me that first awful night. You are also right that Yen takes better care of us than we deserve. Were it not for his fortitude and the miracle that he was from Tientsin and so knew of Dr. Mann's clinic, I assure you I would be in no condition to answer you today. But the good doctor has done everything but turn himself out of his own home to make us all comfortable, and we owe him as well as Yen a great deal.

We have stayed these weeks in his own very pleasant compound, and he has a fine library, so I have regained my strength
with the help of Hardy and Dickens.

Dr. Mann also has a puppy, to whom the children have become very attached. I'm afraid they will not leave here without,
at the very least, a promise of a dog of their own upon our return to Shanghai. The house and the yard sound lovely, and sizable enough even for this addition. As for me, the doctor says I
will be well enough to travel by the end of this week, and I've
already sent Yen to arrange for a berth on the SS *Yantai*, so we
shall be chugging into Whangpoo harbor Monday afternoon.
It is said that absence makes the heart grow fonder, but illness
has a similar effect, and the combination of the two have made
me miss you more than I ever thought possible. I will ask this.
Just this. Please be standing on the wharf to meet us. Please be
there.

  With all our love,
  Your true wife,
  Hope

☙☙☙

The day before the family was to sail, Mann hired a motorcar to take
them on a farewell excursion. It had running boards and chrome head-
lights and a spacious tonneau and, within minutes of its arrival, was surrounded by admiring neighbors.

"It's extravagant, Stephen!" Hope protested. "You've already done too
much."

"Quite the opposite, I'd say." He swung the picnic basket into the
trunk, tipped his cap to the children already in the car and mugging
through the rear windshield. "Anyway, you're overruled."

It was a jaunty cap, Hope noted, charcoal tweed to match his suit, and
he had slipped a sprig of peach blossom into his lapel. He looked as
though he had been planning this outing for weeks. She smiled. "It's doctor's orders, then."

"As you wish." He twirled his hand in the air and bowed, then opened the car door with a flourish. She climbed in, and, tooting the horn to disperse their onlookers, they were off.

It was a warm day. The sky was stippled with filmy clouds and the air blew soft through the open windows. They sat facing each other, Mann next to Pearl and Morris beside Hope, Yen and the liveried driver up front. Everyone exclaimed at the smooth, purring motion and the speed, in spite of the uneven roads.

"Not a bad alternative to the Peking cart," Mann said with a grin.

"Do you think Papa could buy us a motorcar?" asked Pearl.

"Yay," said Morris. "I want a big black motorcar just like this one!"

Hope rolled her eyes at Mann. "Now see what you've started?"

But he looked back at her without a hint of regret, and said nothing. She faltered, finally answering the children, "It's because we *don't* have an automobile that today is so special. Mustn't ruin what you do have by wishing for what you haven't."

"Words to live by." Mann lifted an eyebrow. "Is that a Kansas pioneer slogan, or something you picked up here?"

She felt herself redden. "Don't mock me," she warned, turning away. But he had made his point.

They turned the corner past his clinic. The gates were open, and Hope could see through to a courtyard filled with white-tunicked attendants and patients resting under shade trees. The scene was peaceful, almost bucolic, in stark contrast to the antiseptic atmosphere of most Western hospitals. She thought of her first encounter with Dr. Stephen Mann at Ste. Marie's, his recommendation of the Native Hospital, her automatic assumptions about his character. And her hostility.

He was now pointing out the sights to Pearl and Morris—the distant boats in the harbor, the old Tientsin drum tower poking up above the city wall, the usual fantastic assortment of roadside vendors and entertainers—but every now and then his eyes would wander back toward Hope. They would stop and rest until she noticed, and only then slip back toward the window. Over the past month, through breakfasts and dinners and evenings with the children and daily walks (her "physical therapy") around Mann's courtyard, this had become an all too familiar pattern. Though Hope tried to deflect his gaze with laughter or shrugs or blithe conversation—or references to her husband—such efforts had proven as futile as they were halfhearted.

"Look, Mama. It's Ch'ing Ming." Pearl pointed to a series of low hills on which families dressed in springtime colors were picnicking among burial mounds. Ch'ing Ming, or Clear Bright, festival was the annual celebration of the dead.

"Actually," said Mann, with a glance toward the front seat, "I have an ulterior motive for this expedition. With your approval, of course, Hope. I thought we might thank Yen for his good services by paying our respects to his ancestors."

"What a wonderful idea! How could I not approve?" In fact, she had expected to be toured through Tientsin's drab Legation Quarter, which she had already glimpsed from the train, and the prospect of seeing Yen's home village seemed much more appealing. It was just the sort of thing Stephen would think of.

Once again, she felt his eyes on her. She smiled and shook her head.

Yen made the mandatory protest, but when Hope and the children insisted, he assumed the role of navigator with such energy and accuracy that it was only minutes before they turned off the main road and down a dirt lane bordered by lush fields of *kaoliang*. They raised a storm of dust, and Hope was beginning to wonder if their fancy coup would survive this route when Yen pointed to a cluster of broken walls. This was where he was born, he said calmly. He grew up here. Then, during the 1900 uprising, some of the farmers were accused of befriending the foreigners, so the Boxer rebels attacked the whole village. He shrugged. "*Mei fatse.*"

Yen had the driver stop at the base of a neglected slope strewn with toppled grave stele. He sprang from the car clutching his hat to his head, and motioned for the children to follow him. They did so eagerly, gathering fallen branches for brooms, and sweeping the ancestral ground as they had seen Chinese children do.

"It should have been my idea," Hope said to Mann as they waited for the driver to open the trunk. "You shame me."

His voice darkened, even as his smile held steady. "I would never shame you, Hope."

She looked away to Yen's ambling form, now halfway up the hillside. "He rarely mentions his family."

Mann took the picnic basket from the driver, then they left him with the car and began walking slowly after the others. "Yen and I had quite a lot of time to chat before you came out of your fever. He told me his people were killed by the Boxers. Everyone in the village who survived fled. That's how he came to be in Shanghai—where, I gather, he met your husband."

Hope smoothed her perspiring palms on her skirt, conscious of the quickened breeze against her clothing and her shortness of breath at the steep incline. She was still weak. "Yen's devoted to Paul," she said abruptly.

"Yes." He waved to the little band above them, now plucking buttercups to lay on the graves. "He's devoted to you, too, Hope. And the children."

"Maybe I should have married Yen!" She meant this as a light remark, to defuse the tension gathering in her chest, but it drew a quizzical look from Mann. Rather than risk further discussion, she pushed ahead to catch up with the others.

As they moved from one weathered stele to the next, Yen recited his relatives' names. These spun past Hope without her being able to tell the men from the women or how they connected to Yen—except for his mother and father, who had died when he was little older than Pearl. Before their graves, Hope pressed her hands together and bowed three times, thanking them aloud, on behalf of herself and her baby and Morris and Pearl, for giving life to Yen, who in turn had saved their lives. Stephen Mann followed her example, adding that Yen had "given me great happiness by bringing the Leon family to my home."

To the children's delight, Mann had brought along a brilliant, multi-paneled kite shaped like a whiskered dragon. It required both his and Yen's efforts to get skyborne, but when this was accomplished, he handed Pearl the spool of kite string and assigned Morris the task of weatherman. The boy's disappointment at being denied the controls was overwhelmed by his delight at the trick Mann taught him of licking his finger and testing which way the wind was blowing. Yen, meanwhile, schooled Pearl in the intricate maneuvers that would make the kite soar and dance.

Stephen rejoined Hope on the picnic blanket, where she was assembling their provisions—sliced sausage and ham and cucumber sandwiches, *paotzu* in a little hatted wicker basket, sweet rice wrapped in lotus leaves, almond cookies, and a thermos of green tea. He lay on his side watching her hands.

She pointed to the children. "You don't make it easy to leave, you know."

"That's the idea." His voice dipped awkwardly, a breezy delivery gone wrong. He had removed his jacket and rolled up his shirt sleeves before helping Yen with the kite. Suddenly his forearm, with its golden hairs and freckles and long, slender bones, stretched toward her like a lure.

The cup shook as she filled it with tea, set it down on the blanket between them. "They're going to miss you terribly."

"Are they?" He lifted up on his elbow. "And what about you, Hope?"

She circled her thumb on the thermos's smooth surface. From the corner of her eye she watched him reach for his cup. Instead, his hand veered, closing over her own.

"Please, don't," she whispered.

"Are you sure?"

She shook her head. "Yen," she said. "And the children. They'll see us."

"I don't care."

For four weeks they had lived together. This was the first they had touched since Paul's cable arrived. She wrenched her arm away.

For a long time neither of them spoke or looked at the other. Mann lay back twisting a stalk of grass between his fingers. Hope watched the paper dragon climb and dive, fighting the wind above them. The wind would claim that kite, she thought, were it not for the children tugging its string.

He sat up. "Hope, I know what you're thinking, but I can't let you go without, at least—"

She glanced at him with a longing so pure it felt like hatred, then turned quickly back to the sky. Beyond the whipping figure of the kite, the clouds had stiffened. Their brilliance made her eyes water.

He continued very slowly, "I would give you a different life."

But Morris had tired of the kite and was running toward them with his small zigzag steps. Just before he reached them, she turned, her voice breaking. "Write to me, Stephen?"

For the merest fraction of a second they looked at each other fully and without evasion. She recorded the colors of his eyes. The square line of his jaw. His straight, full lips and backswept hair and his scent of brilliantine and pipe smoke. The low, rumbly voice that had stroked itself so stealthily into her consciousness that she only now realized it was part of her.

On the steamer the next night, while Yen and the children slept in their berths, she wrote: *I have chosen this life. One life. One man. One love. In sickness and in health. There are too many witnesses, too many hostages, too many dangers to question this choice. If only I had known . . .*

IX

SEPARATION

SHANGHAI

(1916–1919)

჻჻჻

1

They entered Whangpoo harbor on a clear, treacherously calm afternoon four days later. As Hope waited at the rail, the children chased each other around her skirts, and three Persian businessmen, the only other passengers, huddled at a polite distance. Apart from the junks and cargo vessels by the godown wharfs, theirs was the lone boat coming into dock, and she could see the pier from the middle of the river. It was empty but for the stevedores and two figures at the bottom of the gangway. One was William Tan. The other was Paul.

The men were so deep in conversation that the steamer was docking before they noticed it. At Pearl's shout, Paul looked up sharply. William pointed. Paul waved. The children jumped and yelled. As the gangplank was moved into place, Yen began gathering up their baggage. Hope took a deep breath and moved forward.

Paul scooped Morris into one arm, placed his free hand on Pearl's upturned head. His hair was uncombed, and his glasses rode low on his nose. Behind them, his eyes seemed dark and small and studious. Hope could feel his caution as he searched for indications of her health and mood. Like a divining rod, her hand dropped to her swollen belly.

Pearl squealed. William had conjured a coin from behind her ear, now produced another from under her collar.

"You are well, Hsin-hsin." Paul smiled.

"And you're alive."

He put Morris down and straightened the boy's cap. Both children were transfixed by the magic.

Paul turned back to Hope. "I am standing on the wharf to meet you," he said. "As you wish."

As you wish. Hope felt something thin and tender falter inside her chest. Stephen Mann had kissed her goodbye on the wharf in Tientsin. He had held her publicly, brutally. He had kissed her full on the mouth.

"It's been a long trip," she said. "Do you think we could go home now, Paul?"

༄༅༄

April 27, 1916

I feel like a pillow that's been shaken out, all my stuffing flung to the sky, floated to parts unknown and forsaken, then recovered and stitched back into the original casing, placed on the same old bed, with the same man cupping his face against me. I tell myself that I'm really here, yet it is inconceivable that I could be.

Last night, our first in this new house, this new stage (as I feel it to be) in our married life, Paul was so gentle toward me. He worried about my illness, about the baby. I don't believe that our separation entered into his consideration—certainly he could not see it as an obstacle, as it was to me. But another factor, which I dare not even put into words, drove me in a way I could hardly have expected. I pulled him to me, all but ripped off his clothes in my hurry. I felt as if I had been starved for months—it was that visceral a hunger, with nothing spiritual about it. I devoured him, exhausted him, sated him, and when he lay dazed and adoring by my side, I turned away.

I fear for this child inside me. All the deceit and bitterness pulsing through me is being fed directly to this growing soul, and there is nothing in me now to nourish the sweetness, the light, the innocent trust a baby—every baby—deserves. Always before, my pregnancies graced me with the illusion of maturity and courage, that my days of chaos were over and I could be entrusted to hold and protect. This time the illusions have all come crashing, and I feel I am twelve again. Lost. Powerless. And hopelessly unreliable.

As the steamer turned into the delta coming back, we passed a British gunboat and I remembered that strange mirage I suffered the day Pearl and I first arrived from America. Frank Pearson's ghost. Then I remembered that in Tientsin Stephen Mann said he, too, arrived in China just after the revolution. He spent his first months working as an assistant medic on a navy vessel. Yesterday I understood that it was not Frank's ghost calling me home, but Stephen.

50 Range Rd.
May 5, 1916
Dearest Dad,

I imagine by now you have received the letters I wrote back in March. I hope that the sharpest pains of your grief have faded and you can think of Mary Jane with as much love and sweetness as sorrow. I've found some comfort in the knowledge that this point does eventually come—like a light that beckons, however dimly. Too often I've had to rely on it. But surely you know this. You've more experience than I, and you've always bounced back.

I am sure I've missed Mary Jane almost as much as you these past weeks, missed her wisdom and humor and relentless honesty, but life here has allowed me little peace to mourn her as she deserves. As you can see from the address, we are back in Shanghai. The new house Paul's found for us is large and solid and comfortable. A glassed-in verandah runs the length of the garden side, so I can write there while watching the children play. There is room in the yard for badminton and croquet, in which Morris's enthusiasm more than makes up for his lack of skill or size. Pearl excels in her role of athletic coach, and they are both ecstatic to be reunited with their old amah Joy (I should say *former* rather than old, as she's barely twenty), who views sports as a prime example of Western inanity. Like all those born of the peasant class, Joy and our other amah Ah-nie equate leisure with rest and cannot imagine why anyone—even children—should choose to run and jump like wild animals.

Speaking of animals, the servants' faith in our judgment has also been tested by our most recently acquired pets. You see, gentry class Chinese rarely keep any pet more demanding than a canary or carp—and many consider dogmeat a delicacy! But one cool gray afternoon a few days after our return to Shanghai, Paul appeared in his inimitable way with not one but two canines under his arms. Small, yapping, wiggling madly, the furred creatures immediately captured the children's affection. Pearl wanted to know their names and breeds, neither of which Paul could provide. I am proud to tell you I was the one who identified the stumpy tan bitch as a Welsh corgi and the little male as a fox terrier. The Wayland boys taught me something, after all! Paul was immensely impressed. He has such respect for this sort of categorical knowledge and so far outstrips me in most areas that it takes us both aback when I best him.

I suppose you are wondering what Paul is doing now that the political winds are shifting again. So am I, but as usual I am not privy to the details. At the moment he is off to Canton, where a number of the southern generals are establishing a counter-government to Yüan's in the north. I'm afraid this will lead to massive civil war here soon, which not even Paul's sainted Dr. Sun Yat-sen will be strong enough to win.

There was a time when I entertained fantasies of Paul pulling out of the fray and leading what I might call a "normal" life, and for a time after we first arrived in China I think the state of affairs here so demoralized him that he, too, seriously considered this possibility. But I've come to realize that the quest for democratic government is a kind of sickness with Paul. He genuinely believes not only that it can be accomplished but that, through it, the Chinese people will recover their ancestral greatness. This sickness is fueled by Paul's elite status as a returned student. So many of the foreign-educated are frauds, rich bureaucrats, or sycophants, and they are the ones whom Yüan has hired to pad out his palaces. The genuinely bright, dedicated revolutionary returned students like Paul are few in number and greatly admired, and they can virtually write their tickets as to position and access within the Nationalist movement. That's a lot to ask him to give up, and I no longer even try.

I guess, by pouring all this out to you, I'm trying to talk myself into understanding why Paul has left us here on our own yet again. As I always talked myself into understanding why you had to go off on your ventures leaving me as a child with the Waylands. Well, I survived that well enough and still love you in spite of it, so I should survive these separations from Paul. You are both good, honorable men, and for that I must be grateful. Also, the children are really getting to be wonderful company, and here in Shanghai I am reunited with my old friends Jed Israel and Sarah Chou, whom I've mentioned in past letters. Jed has helped me to set up my own darkroom, and Sarah recently gave birth to a second boy, little Ken, which gives Pearl and me a great excuse to go over for visits. We also see a bit of Paul's older son, Jin, who is at university here. And, of course, this baby of mine is due in no time . . .

One more bit of *good* news. My first article and photographs from China will be published in the June edition of *Harper's*. You must obtain a copy or two, as I've wired my friend Mr. Cadlow to include a dedication to Mary Jane. One of so many things I have to thank her for, and one of the few ways I have to honor her.

But I must go. I am taking Pearl to visit a school this morning. She'll be eight this summer and Morris has just turned four, can you believe it! So many changes, Dad, but know that you have my love always,

Hope

She told no one the truth, least of all those closest to her. And so the children chattered happily on about their time in Tientsin, reprimanded the new dogs to "be good like Mister Bacon," and debated whether Papa could ever have a motorcar as nice as Dr. Mann's. They asked Dahsoo if he could make sweet rice in lotus leaves like they made it in Tientsin. The louder and more gleefully they bantered, the more the baby in Hope's womb seemed to squirm.

She retaliated, at least initially, by immersing herself in the project of getting Pearl enrolled in school.

May 20, 1916

Pearl is now a week's veteran of the Thomas Hanbury School for Eurasian girls. Our only alternative would be the missionary schools where, given Pearl's odd notions, I expect she would become a staunch believer and probably set her sights on becoming a nun. Besides, as Sarah advised us (her Gerald attends the Hanbury boys'), "Pearl really *is* Eurasian. You've no idea the hazing Gerry endured his first year, given his confused background. But Pearl should be in her element." How very reassured I felt at that!

Sarah's candor over her children's paternity and her calm acceptance of Shanghai's racial hierarchy confounds me. Yet I can no longer fault her. She was right about the school. As noxious as I may consider the admissions bias, there is something touching about that hopping sea of girls, all with the same mix of dark and light features. Most of Shanghai's Eurasian children come from miserable homes, their mothers poor Portuguese or Chinese prostitutes who married across race lines out of desperation and now lead hidden lives in Chapei. You can spot these children in an instant by their dirty smocks and ripped leather shoes, their hair in Chinese braids, eyes either downcast or fiercely belligerent. Most barely speak English. And when your typical Shanghailander looks at a Hanbury student, he will make no distinction. But in fact, the Hanbury girls, in their neat print waists and embroidered dresses, are as different from the Chapei Eurasians as the Shanghailanders themselves. Their fathers are merchants or compradors or bankers or lawyers, their mothers Chinese, German, French, or

Italian. They have money, intelligence, confidence. And among these girls, I think, my daughter may find some real friends.

I think back to my own childhood, how often I wished for a friend who was "like" me, who could understand the confusion and hurt I felt, who could help me to fight back. Of course, just when I think the situations are comparable, I realize there can be no comparison . . .

As her body grew heavier and her confinement loomed, and the children and household established their own separate rhythms, Hope felt herself withdrawing. She tried to write her way out, attempted to interview Yen for an article about the sad history of his home village, but he protested that he had been too young, could not now remember, he had never thought it necessary to understand, only to protect himself when the fighting came. Though Hope did not really believe he suspected her, Yen's evasiveness felt like an accusation.

June 2, 1916

The cruelest twist of betrayal is the temptation to confess. I am hounded by the impulse to unburden myself to Paul, even though I can imagine too well what it would do to him . . . and us. The part of him that has embraced our union with all the romance of the West (for which I myself am to blame) would feel injured and betrayed. The part—the larger part, I fear— that still judges marital happiness by the Chinese traditions would condemn me without the least shred of understanding. I wish I could believe otherwise. I do think Paul is capable of a different response, but in the end, I am far too cowardly to test him. He is my husband, and we must hold our family together at all costs. I must find my way back out of this, pretend the detour was never seen. No codes of conduct were broken, after all. The only law violated was the law of the heart.

I see Paul again as I watched him in the court in Peking, taking his oath and bearing witness against a woman whose emotions had borne her out of any rational control. Paul's testimony proved her guilt. She was sentenced, fined, and jailed. To

Paul, to us all, it seemed a grand farce. A comedy. Evidence more of humanity than criminality. But by which standard should he judge me?

⌘⌘⌘

2

Wuchang
June 7, 1916
Dearest Hope,

Do you hear the news? Yüan Shih-k'ai has died, and Vice President Li Yüan-hung has assumed the presidency. After all his many intrigues and with so many enemies, you may think Yüan was poisoned, but I am told he died of apoplexy. Here in Wuhan there is much celebration. Today I have met with representatives of several opposing generals and all say they will unite under President Li to restore the Republic. Dr. Sun, too, has decided to support Li as the constitutional leader.

Li has cabled request my return to Peking. William already is there advising him. I believe I am to be given post as Minister of Information. This is good news, yes? I leave here tomorrow. Perhaps I can arrange bigger house for you and babies to come early July, that still two months before new baby if you are well to travel. What are your wishes, dearest? Please advise me.

Other news, my mother is well. Her second daughter takes good care of her. It is good I make this visit, however, as the journey is much greater from Peking, and I do not know when I shall be able to return home again.

You may write to me in William's care at Ta Hsing Hsien Hutung. I stay with them until my own arrangements secured.

With love and my kisses to you and babies,
Your husband Paul

50 Range Road
Shanghai
June 15, 1916
Dear Paul,

I have your letter from Wuchang. The news of Yüan, of course, I had heard, but surely you cannot have imagined that I would receive your plan for removing to Peking with anything but disbelief. Pearl is at long last enrolled in school. You have us in a grand house here. The baby's arrival is but weeks off (and, to judge from its size and energy, possibly much sooner). Yes, I loved Peking, but I barely survived our escape from it. How can you believe this government will be any more stable than the last?

I am not happy about proposing this, but I really think if you take this post, then we must, for now, be parted. You will doubtless have business in Shanghai, and you will come to us then. If the new government takes root, then of course I will reconsider, but right now, I must put the interests of the children ahead of our happiness. I know this is exactly what I've always said I wanted to avoid. I know and I hate it. But I cannot see any other way.

If you must do this, I will not oppose you. But I will not join you.

I am sorry, Paul. More than you can know.

Hope

Ta Hsing Hsien Hutung
Peking
July 3, 1916
Dearest,

Of course you are right. It is best you and children remain in Shanghai until our baby come. Everything is changing very fast here. President Li is taking things in hand, and National Assembly will reconvene in August, so there is great optimism. I am very busy to keep the legations informed and also the student groups, who are concerned that Li will not be strong against the Japanese.

Daisy Tan sends you her most sincere wishes and hopes you and children are well. Suyun has returned to Hankow, but Daisy proved herself a doting mother. Kuochang will be well tended and well educated under William and Daisy's care. However, your feelings unchanged, perhaps best you no longer must greet Daisy each day.

Also I saw Miss Van Zyl yesterday, and she sends the enclosed marigold seeds for you and Pearl. I apologized that you could not say goodbye to her in person, but she was most understanding. She has taken position as governess for an Australian family in Tientsin to start next month, so all is well.

Yen will take good care of you always. You know I trust him with my life.

Please give babies kiss for me.

Your husband Paul

August 13, 1916

Sarah has taken the children off for a beach expedition to Pootoo. Bless her! It is so stifling, the air like wringing gauze, and the children's boundless energy defies me. I've managed to finish off four articles about Peking for William Cadlow, but in this weather the mere prospect of starting any new work exhausts me. If not for this somersaulting watermelon I must lug about with me day in and out we might have gone up to Kuling this summer. To think that first summer I assumed we would return year after year, and now four years have passed without our once getting back. I loved that place. But more, I loved being with Paul there, and that would certainly not be possible now.

Ludicrous, even fantastic, the turns my thoughts take in this withering weather, in my condition, and especially in my solitude. Stephen's face comes back to me now only in pieces—the flecks of strange, drifting color in his eyes, the rugged cleft in his chin. The way he smiled at me, so slow and seriously gentle, but with the force of a riptide. I can still see the slivers of early gray run through his hair. I touched that hair only once, when he lifted me in his arms from the bed to the wheelchair, but I can still feel its softness against my palms. And his size, all lank and strength, his voice low, rich and intent. I remember hearing that voice through the fever, and it was like a sounding for someone lost underwater—far away, barely audible, but booming with the promise of reprieve.

I've not had a word from him, yet I've no doubt that if he drove up this afternoon with four steamship tickets and a plan, I would take the children and leave Paul. I dream of nothing more, even as I can imagine nothing worse.

Fortunately, I am in no danger. Sarah stopped by for tea yesterday with the news that Eugene had met Stephen at a banquet in Tientsin last week, and he said he was moving to the Philippines. My face gave me away, but for once Sarah did not seize the opportunity to humiliate me. I suppose she was shocked because she'd always made such a show of her own flirtation with Stephen, but she put that quickly aside, as she did her disappointment when I insisted there had been no physical infidelity. She showed genuine sympathy and offered advice far more sensible than I would have expected.

"Be careful, Hope," she told me. "The heart is a powerful instrument, but it can do as much harm as good."

50 Range Road
Shanghai
September 17, 1916
Dear Dad,
I enclose a photograph of our newest little Jasmine in her proud father's arms. She was born on the morning of the tenth and we had quite a party for her arrival, with Pearl and Morris and her half-brother, Jin, and my friend Jed Israel snapping pictures mere hours after she was born. Surprised me, after all the fuss she made when she was inside what a *little* body she turned out to be, but she has spirit to make up for what she lacks in

size. My friend Sarah took one look at the snapping black eyes and mischievous mouth and decided her nickname ought to be Jazz. And Jazz, I fear, she will be, at least to Sarah and the children.

Paul has left this afternoon to return to Peking, but the house is such abuzz with the new baby, and all I seem to want to do is sleep, so there wasn't much to keep him. He's promised to return for Christmas, if not before, so it's not so bad. (You see how reconciled I'm becoming to life as a Chinese politician's wife!)

Anyway, I really am too sleepy to keep my eyes open any longer, so I'll close for now. All of us send our love and kisses,

Your Hope

᭨᭨᭨
3

Jasmine screamed. She clenched her small body and turned magenta. She cried and kicked and panted so hard that Hope thought her heart must give out, and if not, that she or Ah-nie must smother her until it did. The colic stretched from hours into months. Ah-nie fed the child elixirs of ginseng and motherwort through a tube. Hope tried swaddling, rocking, singing, walks. She nursed her, starved her, fed her on and against demand, but nothing consoled the maddened infant. The piercing screams drove Pearl to the homes of her school friends, Morris outside with the dogs. Poor Ah-nie and Joy bore the brunt of the agony. Hope could not stand it. Each wail, each new contortion of the baby's impossible power dealt a fresh accusation. Her fears had been realized. The child had absorbed all her mother's anguish in utero, and was now bearing eloquent testimony.

Paul did return home once that fall, but within minutes of Jasmine's afternoon fit, he removed himself to the Nantao house and stayed there, entertaining colleagues and friends. Hope thought bitterly of those first years in Berkeley, when she forgave him his distance from Mulan and Jin, accepted as excuses geography and exile, flight from his mother and first wife, the demands of revolution. But ever since their escape from Peking, his ongoing preoccupation with politics seemed a monumental betrayal. That he abandoned her to this squalling, writhing demon only added to his culpability.

Her reprieve was her work. Cadlow had responded promptly and effusively to her last Peking articles—one about Ambassador Jordan's theft of Japanese documents from the Hsin Hwa Palace and the subsequent market beheading, another about Yüan Shih-k'ai's ball, and two dealing with the rigidity of Chinese family hierarchy, in which she gratifyingly skewered (without identifying them) Daisy Tan and Paul's mother. After Jasmine's birth she had started a new series, about the state of medicine in China. She wrote about her experience giving birth at the Shanghai Native Hospital, about Western doctors who were open-minded toward Chinese medicine. She wrote an article about the self-mutilation of Shanghai's street children, and the reluctance of doctors to treat them. In other words, against her better judgment, she indulged her continuing thoughts of Mann.

Fortunately, other story ideas came by way of Jed Israel and Jin. Hope's hunch had paid off, and a solid friendship had developed between the two young men. Now that Hope was back and working, the three regularly went out "scouting," as Jed called it, into the industrial zones or countryside, orphanages and riverfront squatters' camps that Hope would never dare enter alone. Jin would sketch while Jed and Hope took photographs or conducted informal interviews with children and peasants and laborers.

Still more, and considerably different, suggestions for articles came from Sarah Chou. New dance and fashion trends were among Sarah's favorites, or brawls that erupted in the red-light district involving prominent Shanghailanders. But in late November she learned that the Mother of Birth Control, Margaret Sanger, was to lecture about the role for contraception in modern China. Sarah suggested that, after three months of shattered sleep and infant colic, Hope might have a special interest in Mrs. Sanger's arguments. Jin said he'd come along, too, and that most of his college friends were going. Perhaps Mrs. Sanger would grant Hope an interview.

So she left Jasmine pummeling the sainted, beleaguered Ah-nie and took her camera, notepad, and perpetually leaking breasts, and met Sarah and Jin at the International Institute—the one forum in Shanghai willing to grant Mrs. Sanger's request to speak before a mixed audience. As they took their seats in the full house, Hope noted a small complement of bombastic white men and tittering ladies, but the bulk of the audience, as Jin had predicted, were Chinese students—both male and female, and most in Western dress.

"She hardly looks a renegade!" Sarah whispered when Mrs. Sanger stepped to the podium. Hope was equally surprised. According to the biographical handout, Margaret Sanger was only two years older than Hope, yet she had borne three children, been divorced, worked as a nurse, and published and traveled all over the world. Earlier that year she'd been forced to flee America after publishing "obscene" materials containing contraceptive instructions. But the woman who stood before them could pass for a minister's wife. She had kind, searching eyes, fair curls, and an almost timid set to her mouth.

Mrs. Sanger smiled and opened with an overview of women as slaves of Chinese society. She described the pattern of Chinese men spending whole days and evenings in the company of male friends, while reserving their wives solely for sex and childbearing. "Since sex is honored rather than despised, they contend, the wife should not feel any more humiliated or unhappy than a prized animal achieving the purpose for which she is bred. But let us suppose that this instinctive animal has larger thoughts, emotions, desires that transcend her husband's walls. What then?" She peered out over her glasses.

Hope looked uncomfortably at Jin, who had folded his arms across his chest. Sarah twirled a strand of hair around one finger.

"If woman truly desires an individual life," Mrs. Sanger went on, "she must be honest and frank about her instinctive nature. Maternity has historically forced this issue. While her husband may divorce himself from his children as he pursues his independent friendships and ambitions, no loving mother can so separate herself. Nor can she divorce sexual love from the eternal prospect of pregnancy."

An embarrassed hiccup ran through the white audience, while the Chinese students were rapt. Hope pressed her pencil into her pad, trying to ignore the icy sensation that had rooted itself in her stomach.

"However much she may love the child born of a free and passionate union, she is captive to it in ways that are too often detrimental to her own and to her family's well-being. What if the new baby is born hard or sick, so demanding that she has no reserves left for her other children? What if she herself becomes ill, or her husband is taken ill or dies and she is left without support? What if she has no family or friends? What if the child is *illegitimate*?"

Again she stopped and peered out over the audience. Hope's pad had dropped into her lap. She flinched as the speaker's gaze ran over her, and suddenly she wanted nothing more than to leave before another word was uttered. But if she got up now every eye in the room would follow her.

"Chastity," said Mrs. Sanger. "In China as in the West, this has been the good woman's only safeguard against the confinement and shame of unwanted pregnancy. But what, then, of her own instinctive passions? What of her partner's sexual demands? Chastity is as unnatural a condition for women as for men, and yet it is imposed exclusively on the female sex."

The whole audience erupted now, with outraged boos and applause and mutterings. Sarah's elbow dug into Hope's ribs. In the waver of afternoon light the crimson bunting above the stage appeared to pulsate. Hope squeezed her eyes shut.

Mrs. Sanger plunged on, describing her vision of a sexually emancipated woman moving at will through a world of opportunity, experience, discovery, and love. Hope heard Jin crack his knuckles, Sarah sigh.

In China, said the speaker, contraception was key to reducing poverty, famine, illiteracy, because it alone would enable women to take their rightful place *beside* men in the march toward modernization. "Indeed," she concluded, "without this one, most basic of human freedoms, there can be no lasting economic, political, or spiritual freedom for society as a whole, and women in China will remain the prisoners of tradition and of fate."

A second of stunned silence passed, then the audience sent up shouts of damnation and cheers. Jin was waving his arm with a question. Sarah leaned toward Hope, calling out above the uproar, "There's a girl after my heart!"

Hope stared at her coldly. Students were distributing free copies of Mrs. Sanger's paper, *Woman Rebel*. She left before they'd reached her.

When she got home, a letter from America was waiting, with a return address she didn't recognize. Upstairs, Jasmine and Ah-nie had collapsed, asleep. Joy and Morris were out walking the dogs. Pearl was at school. The house reverberated with a rare and delectable quiet, but Hope could not relax. She still felt that icy knot in her stomach. It was absurd, of course. Margaret Sanger was a total stranger, had been speaking in generalities. Why, then, did she feel so exposed?

Impatient, she slit open the envelope. All thought of the lecture vanished as she scanned the first few lines.

> Sunset Lime Co.
> Dealers in Lime, Lath, and Cement
> Colton Cement—Atlas White Cement
> 317 E. Third Street
> Los Angeles

> November seventeen, 1916
> Mrs. Paul Leon
> 50 Range Road, Shanghai China
> Dear Madam:
> It is my sad duty to advise you of the death of your father, Theodore T. Newfield, 1311 South Hill St. He passed away very suddenly and unexpectedly Wednesday morning, November 3, 1916, at nine o'clock AM . . . .

The words on the page flickered and blurred. Her arms holding the paper went numb. Phrases such as "your father and I were bosom friends," "they finally sent for a pulmotor, which they used without result," and "bank account of $500 and various stocks of negligible value" barely scratched her brain. She knew what it meant—that her fate was sealed, the last way back not just closed but locked—yet it could not be true. It wasn't possible.

She had never said goodbye.

జ్ఞాజ్ఞాజ్ఞా

4

March 1, 1917

War is everywhere now. The rivers and creeks are swollen with the dead, the alleys with the homeless and maimed. Across China as across Europe thousands lie pruned of their limbs and heads or shot through the eyes and hearts. Girls and mothers are raped and gored by rampaging soldiers. Tattered bodies fall spread-eagled, the sepia shreddings of wives' photographs, letters from lovers, identification cards strewn like petals across lifeless faces. I have gone out into the countryside to see them, but they have also come to me. In the harbor, floating fields of pink, white, and red paper funeral flowers bob among gray-skinned corpses of soldiers and peasants washed downstream. Meanwhile, in Peking, Paul attends victory banquets for the fast-footed bureaucrats and nobles who pledge their undying support—until the next conquering battalion swarms across the horizon, and allegiances switch again.

There are times when I think I would have made a better man than woman. Like Paul, like my father—or Stephen—I would take my refuge in the world, in the uniform of war and motion and impersonal ideals. I would work outside myself instead of forever burrowing inward. I would be permitted, by virtue of my sex, the luxury of courting death.

However, I am not my father or my husband or any of my brave, truant, voyaging friends. I may go out under escort, with Jin or Jed or Yen, and I may take my notes and pictures, talk to the combatants, but the leash does not stretch far. As Mrs. Sanger stated so succinctly last fall, as Jasmine's intermittent colics still remind me, I am tied to my children. And willingly so. But, oh, the restlessness. Dad's passing cut the last cord, and now I am spinning in my moorings, with nowhere to go and yet still straining, for what I dare not say.

As the bodies pile up around us, Paul and I live on in increasingly separate worlds, preoccupied with losses that never intersect, with ambitions that stink of secrecy. Even our bodies have become strangers to each other, insensible to the months apart. This is not the life I swore to live or the love I vowed to keep. Yet I am as much to blame—or more—than Paul or any whiff of fate.

As Sarah said to me today, in that most banal of settings, while swinging our boys at the park, "Two things to be said for tragedy. For one it's never dull. Then, too, there's nothing compares to it for showing the mistakes you've made and who you really are."

⁊⁊⁊

The months trudged by. Throughout China the Japanese continued to savor the treaties and extortionist loans that Yüan Shih-k'ai had granted through the Twenty-one Demands, which the succeeding Republican government lacked the power to refute. Then, at the end of June 1917, competing northern armies of renegade warlords overran Peking, terminating that government. Paul, William, and ousted President Li Yüan-hung once again fled south to Canton, where Sun Yat-sen and the rest of the former Kuomintang stalwarts were already reestablishing a separate southern capital. For the next two years, except for the frequent periods when Sun was driven out by some rebel faction, Paul's primary residence would be the Presidential Palace in Canton.

Whenever the southern government did collapse, Paul would return to Shanghai—sometimes for days and other times for months—to teach and to conspire with William Tan for Sun's next resurgence. During these visits, he would feed Hope stories of his military encounters, describe the scholars and merchant patriots who were his banquet companions in Canton. From the pleasure in his voice, she knew that he was in his element there, with his hero Sun and a round-the-clock whirl of politics. He never once suggested that she or the children visit him, but he did now actively encourage her writing as a means of aiding Sun's renewed push for foreign support. And though she no longer harbored the illusion that these collections of words could bring any true insight into her husband's world, she kept writing them because Cadlow praised and paid for them.

But while Paul continued to immerse himself in Dr. Sun's struggle for national leadership, Jed Israel and Jin were becoming enmeshed in Shanghai's local labor and student movements. They said Hope should not write about China's politics unless she looked beyond the warlords and battlefields into the changing society. To this end, Jed took her into the Japanese silk mills where she photographed children as young as four plunging their hands into boiling water to extract and unravel the softened cocoons. In the dining halls at St. John's University she listened to Jin's pomaded, Western-clad friends argue the relative merits of socialism and democracy. In his secret (from his father) studio in the Chinese City, she photographed Jin and other friends making anatomical drawings of street urchins and elderly beggars. Outside Shanghai's dingiest bars and cabarets Jed introduced her to some of the White Russian "royalty" who were flocking to China as a safe haven from the Bolshevik revolution. All the tensions that lay hidden and seething in the rest of the country, Hope's friends suggested, were exposed by Shanghai's collision of cultures.

None was more exposed, Hope thought, than the increasing tension between the races. But she needed no help in seeing this problem; it was her family's particular affliction.

In the fall of 1918 quiet, bookish little Morris joined his sister for the daily rickshaw rides to and from Thomas Hanbury, and though the children rarely spoke of it, Hope knew they were subjected to the same sniggers and petty exclusions, the cruel undercurrent of ostracism that she herself felt whenever she was in public with them. Outside the concessions they were trailed by stone-throwing parades of Chinese children screaming, "*Yang kuei tzu! Hun hsüeh erh! Ta pitzu!*" Foreign ghost. Mixed blood. Big nose. Within the territories, they were only slightly less obscenely snubbed by whites. As Eurasians, the children were expected to keep to their own schools, their own neighborhoods, their own kind, and most especially, they were not to mix with the exalted Anglo-Saxon Shanghailanders. When Morris got older, Hope could look forward to him taking up arms as a member of the Eurasian company of Shanghai's

Volunteer Corps, but he would never be admitted to Shanghai's social clubs or permitted to join the city's ruling elite. As for marriage, the papers routinely reported the suicides of young Eurasian girls who made the mistake of falling in love with white men, and of the "accidental" shootings, drownings, and disappearances of Eurasian men who became engaged to Shanghailander daughters. Tragedy, indeed, in Sarah's words, to make you see who you really are.

Hope tried to counter the bigotry by maintaining a fastidiously ordered, clean, Americanized home in which her children were the prized jewels. She made cakes for their birthdays, fashioned dresses and suits after the latest Stateside magazines, took them to the circus and cinema and for ice cream at the Chocolate Shop on Nanking Road. She sent them out with Yen to buy kites and puppets and chewing gum. She read to them religiously from the classics, took reams of photographs of them in the garden, and annually marched them down to Denniston's for Jed to make a formal family portrait that at least included Yen and the amahs, if not Paul.

At the same time, Hope worked strenuously to conceal her growing estrangement from Paul and to encourage the children's admiration and respect for their father. He was a high government official, she reminded them, a close associate of the great Dr. Sun; a scholar in five languages; a nobleman and a revolutionary. He was an idealist. A poet. A dedicated patriot. Their father was a good, gentle man, and he loved them.

Reciting over and over the qualities that had caused her to fall in love with and marry Paul, Hope struggled to connect these memories to the stout, indomitable figure her husband was becoming. But he did not make it easy. On one of his periodic returns to Shanghai, she noticed the thick, sickly sweet smell of opium on his clothing. Sometimes he invited his friends to the house for mah-jongg or poetry sessions, and they would file straight past her into his study as if she didn't exist. Then for hours the house would throb with their voices, laughing, arguing, chanting their verses. Passing the open door she often saw piles of money on the table, though Paul never divulged his gambling wins or losses. Later, when he came to her, he was flushed and clumsy, with the sour-sharp smell of *mao-t'ai* liquor on his breath. That he was often more affectionate, more ardent on these occasions did little to endear him to her. Inevitably, she wondered if he did not indulge in other "customary recreations" when he was away.

From the beginning (if she were honest with herself) and certainly from the moment she learned of Nai-li's second "daughter-in-law," Hope had twinges of unease about Paul's fidelity. He had never made a secret of his familiarity with the brothels in both Canton and Peking. There had been that business with Madam Shen and the House of Wakening Sexual Desires, but even more recently he had told her stories, which she grimly wrote down for Cadlow, of the family sagas and downturns of fortune that had led certain "flower girls" to their fate. And, of course, there were his infrequent, but usually prolonged visits to his mother's house in Wuchang. Afterward, he would attribute the length of these visits to his negotiations with local officials, or the pressure of old friends, or the state of his mother's health, and if he mentioned Ling-yi at all it was only to commend her for attending to and (implicitly) anchoring Nai-li in Hankow where she would not irritate Hope. In the past, Hope had forestalled suspicion by harboring a certain pity for this woman so doomed to a life of chastity and servitude. Ling-yi was, after all, performing the duties that traditionally would fall on Paul's true wife, and even if Hope, as a foreigner, was excused from such traditions, Paul was not. But now, Hope was torn between an upsurge of jealous suspicion and the faint wish that Paul might go ahead and take Ling-yi or some other. For, though nearly three years had passed, during which she had neither sent nor received a single word from him, she was still plagued by thoughts of Stephen Mann.

જ⁀જ⁀જ⁀

5

March 13, 1919. She shut the door and leaned back against it, listening. In spite of the yapping dogs in the yard, Jasmine's shrill cries, and Ahnie's weary pleadings upstairs, the house seemed ominously empty.

It was in fact emptier than usual, since Joy had left them two days ago—to marry a clerk from Sincere's department store. She said Pearl and Morris were old enough now, they no longer needed two amahs, and Ahnie should be the one to stay, as she had no desire to marry. Pearl had gone into a sulk, complaining that this young man couldn't possibly love Joy as much as *she* did, and only Paul's presence defused her theatrics. Though it was pure serendipity that he happened to be on hand for the moment.

Paul had been back nearly a month, but, as one of the delegates sent by Sun to the Shanghai Peace Talks, he was hardly home. These talks, inspired by the Western Powers' Versailles Conference, were meant to bring together representatives from the northern and southern governments to end China's three-year-old civil war. But negotiations had repeatedly collapsed, and yesterday the northern delegation was abruptly recalled to Peking. Paul had spent most of last night closeted with William Tan in crisis meetings. Then, early this morning he left for Nantao to consult with Jin on his plans for the future, now that the boy had completed his degree in political science.

But less than two hours later Paul had returned, thrusting aside Hope's darkroom curtain and ruining the batch of prints she had just exposed. "You knew what he is doing!" he accused her. "Pictures of naked women. Cartoon drawings like the scribbles of a child. You encourage him in this!"

She untied her apron and took an uncertain breath, came out into the hall to meet him. "I think he has talent, Paul."

"Talent," he spat back. "I should not let you know my son!" He took a step backward and his heavy leather heel struck the wall, reverberating down the corridor.

Hope dug her teeth into her lower lip, trying to rouse herself to the assault. She wondered distractedly where Yen was, whether Dahsoo and Lumei could hear from the kitchen. But she felt queerly unmoved herself by Paul's anger, as if, like one of Jasmine's tantrums, it were more an embarrassing nuisance than a personal attack.

"Perhaps we should go into your study." And without waiting for his reply, she led the way into the dusky chamber that even through part-time use had become a clutter of papers and books and smelled of stale tobacco.

The midwinter light gave Paul's flesh a gray tinge, and without his accustomed jovial veneer, his features seemed to sag. "Do you know what he is doing these last months," he demanded, "when he *says* he is completing his studies?"

Hope shook her head. "He told me St. John's had granted him an extra semester to finish his degree, so he could take some additional courses."

Paul reached into his jacket pocket and flung a crumpled pamphlet onto her lap. Smoothing it out, she saw that it was a comic strip. Caricatures of foreign men and women running arm in arm, with Chinese in regimental uniforms thrusting bayonets at their backsides. Another of the Forbidden City going up in smoke, surrounded by jeering crowds. And another of Dr. Sun Yat-sen holding hands with a man wearing the *jintan* mustache favored by Japanese. Jin's name was inscribed in block ideograms at the conclusion of each strip.

Hope folded the pamphlet in half and ran her thumbnail down the crease, then resolutely placed it on the octagonal table that stood between the chaise where she was seated and Paul's ladder-backed chair. She could have told Paul it was his own fault, for pushing Jin into political science. She could have reminded him that he was the hothead who, at Jin's age, had stood on a table in front of hundreds and called for the overthrow of the Manchus. She could have suggested that the cartoons were just retribution for the *North China Daily*'s buck-toothed caricatures of Chinamen. Instead she said mildly, "I had no idea."

"He tells me you approve."

"I approve of his studying art. Yes, why shouldn't I?"

"Western art!"

She looked at him curiously. "Why are you so angry? Do you even know?"

His chin sank into his starched collar. His eyelids squeezed behind the round lenses. "This," he said, jabbing a bitten forefinger at the paper. "This is not art. It is disgrace."

Something about her husband's fury piqued Hope, and yet, in spite of his accusations, she felt personally detached. She might have been a doctor diagnosing an illness that she could neither catch nor cure. The disgrace that Paul felt, she suddenly realized, had little to do with Jin's radical sentiments—which were, after all, but an exaggeration of Paul's own. Nor was it specifically aimed at the corruption of his son by the Western Learning, which he also had encouraged. His anger was, in fact, directed at nothing that Jin *had* done but, rather, all that he had *not*.

Her gaze fell on the intricately carved ink sticks and slates that sat always ready on Paul's desk. The bamboo pot full of brushes with their bristles pulled from ponies and goats and mink. The pressed rice paper and china pot of vermilion paste into which he sank his onyx seal. Beside the desk were piled fresh copies of Paul's verses of the "Imperial Age of Hong Hsien," a lyric account of Yüan Shih-k'ai's "reign" that had been published to great acclaim among Paul's fellow literati. On the wall hung Paul's marquis medal from that same era, framed with dismissive simplicity in blackwood but displayed prominently enough.

Smoothing her palms absently over the lawn of her skirt, Hope felt the stiffened contour of her pocket and jerked as if she'd burned herself. Paul tipped his head at the sudden movement, but the light from the high windows caught his lenses so that she couldn't see his eyes. Struggling to regain her equilibrium, Hope stood up, folded her arms tightly against her waist.

"You're angry," she said, retraining her thoughts on the issue at hand, "because Jin's not exactly like you. He didn't suffer through all those years of recitation. He never got to the Forbidden City, no one ever shut him up in one of those examination cubicles or rode him through the streets as a triumphal scholar. And no one ever will. But he *is* like you, Paul. He was born twenty years later. That's all."

His jowls quivered as he clenched his teeth. She knew she was right. She knew also that she could never begin to understand what at this moment was clicking through her husband's brain. Names, faces, rules, assumptions, codes of tradition so deeply embedded in his blood that they defied articulation. The source of his rage was neither his head nor his heart but some deeper chamber where the controls had been set centuries ago and, for all his revolutionary intentions, still remained unmoved. No matter what intimacies, what secrets, what travails they might share, this compartment would always lie beyond Hope's reach. For this reason, and this alone, Paul blamed Hope for her stepson's "betrayal."

They stared at each other. Paul's fingers fumbled absently at the pocket of his weskit. His broad shoulders curled inward. He made no move to stand, and yet she felt he was poised to leave. And she was grateful.

"It's not my fault," she said tightly, getting up. "I've given Jin nothing but friendship." But her defense sounded like accusation. So did his reply.

"I do not know what you do when I am gone," Paul said. "And yet I trust you."

She froze for a split second, then yanked open the study door. The crown of Yen's derby was just appearing at the top of the stairs, and his tread had the firm, hurried thud of news. She raced to her room before he could see her, and fell on the bed with her face in her hands.

Barely an hour later, she descended to find Paul whirling about the parlor, collecting his extra spectacles, today's *Shen Pao*, the notepad on which he'd been scratching out suggestions for Sun Yat-sen's memoirs. As he located each item he tossed it into his black satchel, on top of his hastily packed clothes. Haste also showed in his uncombed hair bristling over his collar, his loosened tie, and the ruffled twitching of his left eyebrow as he made a mental inventory of the belongings he was still missing. From snatches of his instructions to Yen, who was to escort him to the station and then proceed with the news to William Tan and Li Yüan-hung, Hope deciphered that Sun's bodyguard and naval minister had been murdered. It was time to close ranks again.

Paul did not kiss her as she stood waiting, dry-eyed, to bid him good-bye, but he instructed her to kiss the older children for him, gave the roaming Jasmine a perfunctory hug. He straightened his hat, checked his gold pocket watch, and told her not to worry. His gaze was alert, impatient, impenetrable. He made no further mention of Jin, or of trust, or the bottomless hole widening between them.

Now Hope lay her head back against the door, listening lest he return. But the gate had shut, his rickshaw gone. Slowly her hands, which had somehow come to rest in a cross at her throat, began to creep downward, following the curves of her breasts, the straight decline of her rib cage, the indentation of her waist to the abrupt widening of her hips and thighs beneath the gathers of her skirt. She had not emptied her pocket. Had he come to her, run his hands over her body even as she did now, he would have discovered the letter that had arrived that morning. But he had trusted her.

> Hong Kong
> March 10, 1919
> Dear Hope,
> I have been a wretched friend. Halfway around Asia and not a word. If you can find it in your heart to forgive me, I think you will also understand. Have been in contact with your friend Anna Van Zyl, who reports that your baby arrived safely and that you and all your children are well. I am so happy for you and your husband.
> But this is not exclusively a note of congratulations. After too many aimless months, I have decided to return to a hospital I visited some years ago in Chungking. Hope, my return will bring me through Shanghai. If there is a chance of seeing you, I would like nothing more.
> I arrive on the seventeenth and will be staying at the Metropole. If you telephone me there, we can arrange to meet. However, if you do not ring, I will understand.
> Yours,
> Stephen

6

They arranged, in a terse, falsely cordial telephone call, to meet at a coffee shop in Chapei. It was not an assignation, Hope instructed herself firmly as she rung off, just a place and a time. But she told Yen she was going to meet Sarah, told Sarah she was going out by herself to photograph the Lunghua Pagoda. She arranged for Pearl and Morris to go home after school with Pearl's friend Iona McDonald, while Jasmine stayed with Ah-nie. She put on a new hyacinth blue linen suit with knife-pleated skirt and matching slouch fedora and chewed Sen-Sen with unconscious fervor as she set off by tramcar to Thibet Road. She felt light and nervous and oddly transparent, as if anyone who saw her must read her thoughts, though she herself could not.

The instant she saw him, at a table in the window of that shabby café, she caught her breath in the same way she had at her first anonymous sighting on the river—only now there was no mistaking him. His narrow patrician nose and cleft chin, the earnest profile and back-swept hair—his face was more drawn than when she'd last seen him, his hair a little thinner and grayer, but as he leaned forward, lighting his pipe, she saw that he had the same full lips, the same expression of solemn, heartrending intensity.

At last he raised his eyes. She shook her head as he started to rise, pushed inside to join him, and he took her gloved hands, smiling.

"You're the same."

"Hardly!" Her voice boomed in her ears.

"I was afraid you wouldn't come."

"No," she answered in the Chinese way.

His smile faded. "I thought three years would be enough."

"It's been a long three years."

"Hope . . ."

Unwillingly, she reclaimed her hands and applied herself to the deliberate removal and pocketing of her gloves. They sat down and ordered coffee, which arrived so weak they could see the cracks at the bottom of the cups, but they would not drink it anyway.

"You know," he started again, frowning at the table, "or I think you know why I never wrote. I've tried everything to forget you. It's stupid, my carrying on this way. But I finally gave in because nothing's worked. No sense beating around it, I've never met a woman with your courage. Your strength." He gave her a hard look. "I can't stop thinking you're the reason I *came* to China, Hope. To find you . . . and bring you home."

She swallowed. Every muscle in his body seemed to be straining toward her.

"Of course," he raced on, "you're concerned about your children. But

you know how I feel about those kids. I'd do anything for them. For you."
He stopped, biting his lips, and cradled his pipe between his palms.

"Stephen . . ." But after a moment's hesitation, she could not bring herself to speak.

There seemed nothing further to say, and the impassive stares of the
Japanese shopkeeper and his wife made their silence all the more uncomfortable. Finally they rose and moved into the street. They discussed no
destination, but let the flow of traffic carry them past the barred black
doors of the surrounding ironworks, mills, and machine shops. They kept
close enough that the backs of their hands grazed each other as they
walked, each union lingering just a fraction of a second longer, until their
fingers caught and locked. At his touch, Hope became acutely aware of
her vivid blue clothing, Mann's hatless height. She looked up at him. "We
stand out here."

"You would stand out anywhere," he answered, without breaking stride.

She was struck at once by the stilted flattery and the maudlin tone of
this response. She didn't doubt his sincerity. It wasn't that. But something
in his voice made her feel suddenly and miserably distant.

The sky closed, dark and damp, and the pace of the throng immediately quickened against the coming rain. He took her elbow and guided
her between two godowns along a short alley that ended at a locust tree
and a muddy patch overlooking Soochow Creek. A low brick wall
shielded the drop to the bank. Behind them rose the windowless flanks of
warehouses and factories. Except for the boatloads of river people below
and the miniature figures across the creek, they were alone.

Stephen turned to her, his eyes gravely searching the edges of her face
as if uncertain how to enter. He slipped his fingers under the brim of her
hat and lifted it with a tentative movement, reached and set it carefully on
the little wall. The jaunty shape of the thing, the soft texture, the sharp
blue made an alien spot against the rumpled dusk, and Hope found herself gliding backward, distancing her body from the silent object as from
a signature she disowned.

She had not registered the locust tree's nearness until its trunk found
her back. Then, suddenly, she smelled its white flowers clustered above her
head, felt its living warmth cradling her shoulders. He had to stoop to
avoid the thorny branches as he came closer, whether following or press-

ing her against the tree she could not distinguish. His face was close and dark, his breath warm on her forehead. His fingertips played across her cheeks. She touched his skin where the collar of his shirt parted, felt the join of muscle to bone, the fibers of hair working up from his chest. These few discoveries mesmerized her. She felt she could pour herself into them and never emerge again, but before she knew what was happening he had found her with his mouth and all her hesitant wonder collapsed under the weight of his crude power, his haste, the ravenous pull of his kiss and the clumsy workings of his hands over her breasts and throat, his hips moving urgently against her waist. Now she flailed at these sensations, reaching with every nerve to hold and sharpen them until they marked her as plainly as the deep-grooved tree digging into her spine.

When his lips moved to the side of her neck, she tried to say something, but the words garbled with her own desire. His hands closed on her shoulders. His soundless speech breathed into her ear, and the mingled scents of warm skin and cherry pipe tobacco and locust flowers pressed away the latrine stench of the creek. She brought one of his hands around to her lips, ran her tongue across the scalloped hardness of his knuckles. He continued to move against her and she shut her eyes as his fingers wormed inside her jacket, under the belt of her skirt. She found herself mirroring his movements, feeling down into the back of his trousers and up beneath his shirt, had just drawn a breath at the unfamiliar touch of this lean, furred back when the sensation of his hands traveling against her own skin shocked her into nervous laughter.

"It's the war you have to thank."

He drew back, dazed. "What?"

"The corset drive. Three years ago you'd have been fighting your way through a cage of steel—now it's all gone for the war."

"So much the better." But his mouth was lost again somewhere below her ear, and she could hardly hear him. They held each other awkwardly, and now that her mind was functioning, however dimly, she realized their difference in height was an encumbrance that would vanish only if they could lie down. The mud here was sucking at their heels, and there was not a blade of grass.

"I have a room," he said.

She started, simultaneously surprised that he had been paying such close attention to her thoughts and dismayed that their intimate fum-blings had obscured rather than illuminated this closeness. "Where?" she said.

"Here—just around the way."

Above, the sky had deepened to a bruised purple, and across the creek, though it was not yet four o'clock, the lights of the Settlement were blink-ing on. Here in this neglected corner, Hope could just barely see Stephen's cheek twitching, the lines of uncertainty straining at his eyes, but she could feel the ferocity with which he was looking at her, an expression so serious he seemed almost wounded. His hand tightened around her fin-gers. They began to walk. Suddenly, inadvertently, she glanced away and, though she at once looked back, he had followed her eyes. He left her, turned in the direction she had looked, and grabbed her hat from the low guard wall as if it were a burdensome child.

"If only—" she started to say, but her words were blunted by the wind that now jumped and snapped with the nearing storm. Impatiently, heed-lessly crumpling the fedora's brim, he reclaimed her hand.

The mist was thick and heavy now, but before she could think to ask for her hat, he had turned into a narrow doorway and was fumbling for his key. The building was unmarked except for a string of colored Christ-mas lights blinking intermittently above the entrance. The once red door was cracked and peeling, the threshold high and scuffed to bare wood. They stepped over it into a dark, steep stairwell reminiscent, Hope thought with a twinge, of the approach to Paul's San Francisco newspa-per office.

"You all right?" Stephen regarded her with concern, the warmth of his hand radiating up the inside of her arm. She had never envisioned him in such a place, could not have conceived of being here with him, but she nodded. He was free. He could go anywhere. It was for her sake they had come here. Where no one would know them. No one would care.

As they reached the third landing a woman appeared, her head wrapped in a loose gray shawl, her face averted. But her hands were bare and scarred and white, and a few blond hairs escaped the shawl. The sight of those telltale wisps started a tremor in Hope's throat that did not stop after the woman had gone. She noticed now the greasy smudges, the rank smells of mildew and decaying wood, the moisture that seeped down the walls in dark patches. From within those walls she heard moaning and the scatterplay of vermin. The stairs were so steep, hardly more than a ladder . . .

A roll of thunder broke outside, and she fell against his arm.

"It's all right." It was no longer a question. He turned her onto the next landing.

But as he inserted the key, Hope suffered a vision of Yen firing lamps around the house, tidying the mantel, straightening the clock. She heard Lu-mei's gentle chiding for Morris to emerge from his hiding place under the stairs, Ah-nie's rough voice singing a lullabye to Jasmine, Pearl calling for Dahsoo to fix her tea. She watched Paul, unexpectedly hurrying home, glance from his rickshaw to a foreign couple furtively embracing across the creek.

And now she saw, not in her mind's eye, but a mere step away, the place where Stephen had brought her. A wrought iron bed with a sagging mattress, a stained water jug and basin, a bamboo table and two chairs, on the wall a mirror with a crack running through its blackened surface. It was not his fault. She could see the effort he had made to camouflage the room's true nature. He had covered the table with a pale blue cloth and a bowl of oranges, shaded the bare bulb with a wicker hat. There were silk cushions on the rickety chairs. The bed was draped in an Indian print, and a crock beside it bloomed with purple asters. In another life, another time, the transformation he had wrought would have struck her as enchanting. It would have won her.

"I can't," she said.

"Hope, please." He loomed in the doorway. "I won't touch you. I won't do anything you don't want."

"I know that." She met him with her fingertips as he moved toward her. She touched his lips and cheeks, not in invitation, but with the memorizing intensity of the blind. To her astonishment he began to cry.

"If only—"

"No, Stephen," she begged. "Please, don't." Below them a door opened. Voices called out in Shanghai dialect, and there was the rasping, heavy sound of bundles being dragged.

He cradled her head in his hands, but made no further attempt to draw her into the room, and when the sounds below had ceased he said,

"I didn't bring you here to seduce you. Please, Hope, you must believe that."

She glanced through the doorway at the muted light and flowers. She swallowed. "I have to go."

He nodded slowly, pinching his lips into a tight, pale line, and ducked back inside to shut off the light and relock the door. When he returned, his face was ruthlessly composed. He set the blue fedora back on her head and lightly stroked her throat. "Do you have any notion how beautiful you are?"

Outside, her heel skidded on a patch of grease. He caught her, but let go as soon as he'd righted her, and the next thing she felt was the warm, flaring softness of his lips on her cheek. The rickshaw lurched into motion. And it rained.

BOOK THREE

Two or three grass huts,

Rattan walls and a thousand willows,

Meandering paths connect to deeper paths.

Beyond the bridge, another bridge.

A woman and a wise man gather herbs together,

Their son will grow to be a woodcutter.

The mountain calendar knows no new or old.

When meeting an outsider, they ask what dynasty holds power.

X

SICKNESS AND HEALTH

SHANGHAI

(1919–1925)

᭜᭜᭜

1

On a cool, bright morning in April, three weeks after her meeting with Stephen, Hope was out on the verandah singing "Ride a Cocked Horse" with Jasmine on her knee when she heard Paul's heavy step behind her. She finished the song without looking up.

"Wi' wings on her fingers and bells on her toes, she make music wherever she go!" Jasmine sang along, her black bob jumping as she twisted to command her mother to bounce her harder. Then, over Hope's shoulder, she saw her father and froze. Hope tried to put her down.

"No, no, no, no!" Jasmine screamed and hugged Hope to stop her turning.

"Jazz," said Hope sharply. "Don't pull so. It's time for your nap."

"No!" Jasmine repeated, clamping her hands to Hope's cheeks. But Ah-nie came now, her strong arms opening and closing, sleek head wagging in consternation. The toddler's outraged bawls echoed through the house as Ah-nie carried her inside.

Throughout this display Paul stood swaying slightly, valise in hand, hat askew. With her ears still ringing, Hope got up to face him.

She started to apologize, but he cut her off. "Warlords overrun everything," he said as if picking up in the middle of an argument. "William and Daisy back to Hupei. Sun here with me."

His skin was flushed, his voice breathless. He was squinting and seemed not even to have noticed Jasmine's fit. Hope touched his forehead.

"Paul, you're burning!"

As if in reply, he threw back his head and shoulders. His jaw locked as he simultaneously gasped for air and tried to swallow. Hope put her arms around him to help him onto the lounge and realized his jacket was soaked through the back. "Easy now. Here, can you drink a little water? It's your throat, then? And your neck? The light hurts your eyes, doesn't it . . ." She spoke in a low, diagnostic murmur. No sudden movement. No loud noise. But she could feel his fever rising by the second. He kept talking about betrayal, broken promises, traitors, rebellion. Out of the corner of her eye she spotted Yen entering the yard, and summoned him.

"Laoyeh is very ill," she whispered. "Tell Dahsoo I need a bowl of ice and boiled water and cloths, and you go for—"

Paul grabbed her hand. His eyelids fluttered, and out of his delirium he managed, "Yu Sutan. No foreign doctor."

Hope struggled to think. If only Stephen hadn't left. And then the absurdity of this thought erased it.

"Help me," she said to Yen, sliding an arm behind her husband's sopping back. "Help me get him into the dark."

෨෨෨

For four weeks she packed his alternately unconscious and delusional head in ice. She laid chilled compresses over his eyes, wrapped his body in wet sheets, placed shavings of ice and frozen broth on his thickened tongue. She blackened the windows, for even a sliver of light could be excruciating to a patient with meningitis. She instructed Ah-nie to keep the children quiet, and only Yen and the doctors were allowed in the sickroom. Hope had finally called for the American woman Dr. Harris, who had delivered Jasmine. She was a bony, ether-scented individual who spoke enough Shanghainese to converse respectfully with Yu Sutan, though she and Hope were certain the bearded old man was a quack. Once, when Pearl was stricken with worms, Paul had insisted she take the black waxy pill that Yu prescribed, and Hope was up all night with the screaming child, whose eyes had turned bright green. The only reason she gave the Chinese doctor any leeway at all was that the pill had killed off the worms. But Dr. Harris assured Hope that she was already giving Paul the most effective treatment.

And so she kept her vigil. He muttered about Chang Chih-tung and the crescent blade, shouted unintelligible pleas to his dead father and warnings that the police were about to raid the SK *Nagasaki*. He spoke a patchwork of Mandarin, Russian, Japanese, English, Shanghainese, and his home dialect, of which Hope could decipher only a fraction, but it was enough to rekindle her wonder at her husband's intellect at the same time that it reminded her what a relatively minor role she and the children played in his life. When the shaking so wracked him that he lifted and wailed, she would hold him and counter his mental meanderings with whispered memories of the secret glen where he had proposed to her, the twined trees they'd discovered by that Evanston stream, their first nights together, under the stars in that roofless miner's hut. "We'll have times like those again," she promised. "When you're better, we'll go back to Kuling. We'll swim in the Three Graces Pool. We'll sit and talk and watch the stars."

Paul gave no sign of hearing. His labored breathing seemed to take all his effort, and when his eyes opened, they rolled like a blind man's across her face. Hope slept in a chair beside his bed, in unwilling catnaps only. She hardly ate, ordered Dahsoo to brew pots of strong black tea, and dragged herself from the room but once each day, when Ah-nie tentatively knocked to announce the children's bedtime. Then she would stumble out to kiss them good night and instruct them in the bewildered prayers that she insisted they say for their father.

"He needs your help," she told them. "He will get well, but he needs you to believe. To know that you love him. He needs your prayers."

In the dismal fuddle of her sleep-deprived mind she did not think how bizarre this request must seem. Fortunately, Pearl took matters in hand and by the second night had both her siblings kneeling, hands clasped, heads bowed like dutiful cherubs. Sighing, Hope staggered back to the sickroom.

If she had to call out all the saints in heaven, every Taoist deity and the Bodhisattva himself, she would, but in the hours of Paul's deepest sleep, she forced herself to imagine the worst. The income from her articles and photos averaged no more than twenty to thirty dollars a month, and though she had some three hundred saved out of her father's "estate," that would not begin to cover passage for a family of four—and after they got to the States, what then? She had no citizenship, no family, no friends. But if they remained here, Paul's mother would give them nothing and might well claim Morris for her own. Sarah could take them in briefly, but only at her husband's mercy—and since he had recently taken a White Russian girl as yet another concubine . . . Jed Israel and Jin would certainly offer comfort and sympathy, but Jin was living at Nainai's pleasure in the Nantao house, while Jed camped in a cubicle above Denniston's and never had more than a few coppers to spare.

No, her situation offered only one recourse. And the irony, after these three persistent years of yearning, was that it filled her with dread. Whatever she and Stephen might have had together if they had met when both were free, if they had tested themselves with a proper courtship, if they had come to each other under normal circumstances, they could never have that now. Even if she could locate him, even if he had the wherewithal to help her, how could they possibly find joy in each other—or solace, or relief?

Falling forward, Hope pressed her husband's hand to her cheek.

"Forgive me," she breathed. "Oh, Paul, please forgive me."

ॐॐॐ

The sun was high and bright in her face when the blister of gunshot woke her. Voices rang out. The whole house seemed to throb. With effort Hope lifted her wooden head and got her body upright. She was in Paul's study. The children were calling to each other in the hallway, Ah-nie shushing them in vain. Hope pressed her knuckles against her forehead, trying to get her bearings. The fever had broken. She recalled a faint smile jerking across Paul's face. His eyes had opened, his lips parted, then he groaned and went back to sleep. She had swabbed his face, toweled the sweat off his hair, removed the cold plasters from his chest and back, thrown the damp sheets into a pile and draped him with clean ones and an eiderdown. Finally she'd called Yen to stand watch, and dragged herself to Paul's study, where she instantly fell asleep, fully clothed, on the chaise.

Another gunshot shook the walls. It registered as a disconnected thud, like a newspaper thrown against the door, something unasked for and beside the point that nevertheless demanded attention. Too exhausted to be afraid, she dragged herself to the window. Below, young men and women were streaming down Range Road waving banners and slogans, the Kuomintang flag, chanting at the top of their lungs. With effort Hope translated a few basic phrases. They were calling for a strike, decrying injustice, and condemning the foreign imperialists. At first the gunshots seemed to be coming from a zealous protester firing into the air, but as Hope watched, a phalanx of helmeted Settlement police blocked the procession's path. The chief officer waved an arm and shouted something inaudible above the noise of the mob. The hundreds at the back pressed against those who'd stopped, compressing the bodies into a solid mass between the street's bordering walls. Suddenly the narrow channel erupted with gunfire, smoke, and screams, the raw animal thundering of panic as the protesters turned and fought for escape. Bodies were tossed against the compound walls, hands clawed at each locked gate, the human tide rose in sequential waves as the strong climbed over the top and the weak were sucked under.

A few seconds, and it was over. The tide forced itself out and did not return. The police moved forward kicking at bodies. White-jacketed medics came from behind, tending to those who moved. Those who did not included a woman in a bloodstained white gown with arms flung above her head and, behind her, three small children.

"Mama," said a small, cautious voice behind her. "Is it going to be all right?"

Hope blinked, coming haltingly out of her paralysis. Morris stood in the doorway.

She took the room in two wobbly steps and gathered him into her arms. Burying her face in his hair, she managed to choke down her sobs, then took his hand, and they found his sisters, Pearl huddled in the hallway with Ah-nie, and Jasmine obliviously dismembering a stuffed bear in the nursery. "It *will* be all right," Hope said firmly. She frowned, again disoriented, and glanced at her watch. "Why aren't you at school, Pearl?"

"Today's Sunday. Besides, the Volunteers came by telling everyone to stay in."

There was a stir at the end of the hall, and Jin came bounding up the stairs. His face had a fresh-slapped look of excitement, and he was so breathless he could hardly speak.

"Pa—" he said, stopping and bending from the waist to get his wind. "How—is—he?" Jin had visited several times since Paul's fever struck, and though the two had not actually spoken since their argument back in March, in Hope's mind a truce had already been declared.

"I was just going to see," she said. "His temperature broke last night."

Jin nodded. His shirt was torn and wrinkled, his hair falling into his eyes, and his leather oxfords looked as though they'd been run over by a truck. "He does not know, then."

Hope eyed the children and Ah-nie, who were listening with unusual attentiveness, but was saved from sending them away by Yen's appearance in the bedroom doorway.

"Taitai," he said. "Laoyeh is awake."

Hope touched Jin's shoulder. "Come. We'll talk later."

Dispatching Yen to reassure the children, Hope replaced him at bedside while Jin parted the black drapes. Even this sliver of light made Paul grimace; however the very energy of his protest was encouraging.

"*T'ai liang le,*" he muttered, putting up a fist.

Hope caught his arm and guided it down. "Can you see, then, Paul?"

He started at the sound of her voice, then quieted. "It's all right," she said. "Jin's here. Can you see him?"

But Paul was looking only at Hope. His eyes had filled with tears.

ᏰᏰᏰ

Jin said nothing to his father that day about the student protests, or the shootings, or the Versailles treaty that had spawned them, and when Hope learned the news, she asked that he refrain until Paul was significantly stronger. While she had been sitting in the dark, it seemed, the Western Powers had dashed China's future against the rocks.

For months, Woodrow Wilson had been raising the expectations of China's West-leaning students and intellectuals with all sorts of puffed-up talk about self-determination for nations and bringing an end to the colonial era. In 1917 both the northern and southern Chinese governments had declared against Germany—marking the first time that China had entered a modern war on the winning side. The two-hundred-thousand-man Chinese Labor Corps had subsequently dug trenches, exhumed and buried bodies, cooked, hauled, mined, and fought alongside the British and French for the duration of the Great War in Europe. Certainly, the young moderns thought, their country deserved some compensation. But at the Paris Peace Conference, Wilson joined the European Allies in siding with Japan against China's national interests. They made no effort to reverse the extortions Yüan Shih-k'ai had ceded to Japan under the Twenty-one Demands, nor would they restore to China the former German Concessions in Shantung. These were to remain under Japanese control, and so Japanese troops would also remain on Chinese soil. The final twist that had sent the marchers into the streets was the disclosure that the band of warlords who currently controlled the northern government in Peking had taken millions of dollars worth of Japanese loans for their own enrichment—which the Chinese people would be obligated to repay.

On May 4, three thousand students had marched in Peking, burning the home of one northern official, beating another, and colliding with police. In the weeks that followed, the demonstrations spread to more than two hundred cities. The students were joined by workers. The boycott against Japanese goods was renewed. Protesters marched and rallied and were gunned down in foreign concessions throughout the country, but in Shanghai the killings Hope had witnessed were soon overshadowed by the general strike that was to paralyze the city for the next two months.

Jin was one of the organizers. He rallied students to parade around the concessions; brought food to striking workers' homes; printed and distributed anti-imperialist pamphlets; arranged public bonfires of Japanese and Western books, toys, machinery, and clothing; orchestrated the midnight hangings of Japanese ministers in effigy along the Bund; excoriated the Western Powers in cartoons, which he somehow managed to paint, without being arrested, on the whitewashed walls along Avenue Joffre. Hope and Paul knew nothing of these activities at the time, of course. Paul was still convalescing, and Jin, when he asked if he might move in with them for safety, merely said that the Chinese police were conducting sweeps for all students living in Nantao, and several of his friends had been tortured. But while he stopped short of divulging the full extent of his activities, he made little attempt to contain his excitement over the changes he saw coming.

"Power of opinion and allegiance are everything," he said over supper one night. "Always before, only elders have this power. Young can do nothing, know nothing. Now all this will change. The young are China's future. We must decide for ourselves. Self-determination. Independence. No more kowtowing to the West, and if this means war with Japan, then we fight!"

Hope made a patting motion with her hand. "Keep your voice down, Jin. Your father hasn't the strength to lift his head, but if he hears you talking like this there'll be no containing him."

"Why not?" asked Pearl. The Hanbury Schools were closed because of the strike, so Pearl and Morris were allowed to stay up and take supper with Hope and Jin while Ah-nie wrestled Jasmine to bed. Eleven-year-old Pearl made a point of asking questions to prove her maturity.

"Because," Hope answered her, "our Jin is a perfect replica of his father."

Jin's face reddened and he coughed into his napkin.

"No, really." She handed him a glass of water. "If I closed my eyes I could hardly believe it wasn't Paul making the speech you just gave. And now that you've taken up those wire-rimmed glasses, you even look like him."

The two children studied their half-brother with renewed interest.

"I'm curious, though," Hope continued. "Won't this revolutionary fervor interfere with your painting?"

Jin held one of his chopsticks like a brush and "painted" across his plate. "Political movements require artists as well as writers or soldiers or politicians. Art and music and poetry can move the people's soul, make them hungry for freedom as for food. This my father never understand!"

Hearing Ah-nie's slow, ponderous tread on the stairs, Hope motioned Morris to finish his supper. "How can you say that?" she answered Jin. "Your father is both a revolutionary and a poet."

"Classical poetry!" he snorted. "And Sun Yat-sen's failed Republic. These are dead man's games."

"Jin!" Years ago, when her stepson had first confessed his admiration for Western art, she had encouraged him, but there was a belligerence in his attitude now that went beyond aesthetic preference.

"You have read his poetry?" he demanded.

"Well, no. I'm afraid the classical language is beyond me."

"Yes. And all but this many Chinese, as well." He pinched his thumb and forefinger. "This so-called art is device to keep people out. Say, we literati so educated, so special, only we possess true learning. All you others, nothing! What use is art if no one can see? What use words no one can read?"

"But surely you respect the years of study that went into this poetry."

"Games for rich men who do nothing else. You know, for centuries only scholars can be officials. Of course this is why my father has taken his palace examinations, why he is so esteemed. But it is no better than the British with their exclusive all-powerful clubs! Or Catholic missionaries delivering sermons in Latin, then wonder why Chinese peasants do not take Christ as their savior. What has classical language to do with governing?"

"Nothing. It was precisely this system that your father worked so hard to overturn."

Jin slapped the table. "But he is one of them!"

"Am I?"

Paul stood white-faced, leaning in the doorway. Hope rushed to him and drew his arm around her neck, summoned Morris to support his other side. He had lost so much weight that his black silk gown might have been draped over broomsticks, but he squeezed her hand with a warmth that surprised her.

"You belong in bed," she scolded, sitting him down.

"I come from bed. I return to bed. Anyway, I have nothing to do but write poetry no one will read."

Jin grimaced, but said nothing.

"Can you eat?" Hope inanely cleared and replaced dishes, calling for Dahsoo to bring Paul some supper.

"You know why you think these things?" Paul tapped his thumb on the edge of the table. "You do not study. You do not know history. Yes I compose poetry. But what I do in America is not poetry. What I do in Peking and Canton is not poetry. It is revolution."

"Yes, revolution," said Jin with a subtle but unmistakable toss of his head. "Your idea of revolution is to write a literati's ode to Yüan Shih-k'ai. And you teach—not principles of revolution, but the language of elitism."

Paul's hand clenched. "How do you know what I teach? Never once do you set foot in my classes!"

"I hear what you say, Father. I see those who admire you."

Dahsoo shuffled in with Paul's supper, and Hope motioned with her eyes for Pearl to take her brother upstairs, but the children sat riveted by Jin's defiance.

"A man can be many things," said Paul. "And a man whose life shades two centuries must be many things."

"In mathematics," replied Jin, his voice quavering, "when a negative number is combined with its positive, the result is zero."

Paul stared as if he did not recognize his son. No one made a sound.

Finally Jin stood. His eyes met Hope's. Then he turned and strode out through the kitchen. The next day he returned for his clothes and left word with Yen that Jed Israel would know where to find him.

᭞᭞᭞

By July the strike was ended. China had refused to sign the Versailles treaty, several Peking ministers had been dismissed for colluding with the Japanese, and, for the time being, the protesters were mollified. While Jin kept his distance, Paul seemed determined not to let this breach affect him. His health was improving steadily, and with the consent of both his doctors, he arranged for the family to vacation in the nearby mountain resort of Mokanshan.

Hope found this resort less beautiful than Kuling (more bamboo forests than breathtaking vistas), but the reprieve from Shanghai's soggy heat and rotting garbage, as well as from the ongoing political and personal tensions, made such comparisons seem piddling. Paul had rented them a small Taoist temple, and although the paper windows were cracked and the ancient beams gaped with woodpecker and termite holes, there was a pleasant brook and a prolific vegetable garden on the grounds, and a nearby hot spring for Paul's aching bones. The family rested and read, hiked and swam, played badminton in the temple courtyard and cards by lantern light. Evenings, after the children were in bed, Hope and Paul sat and talked and watched the stars. More than Paul's health was restored.

Upon their return to Shanghai, Paul began teaching again. They did not discuss or hear from Jin, but the political climate was calm, and Hope told herself that the boy was bound to come to his senses. In the meantime, she had her hands full with the children and her articles ... and, with somewhat less enthusiasm, gardening.

When the family went to Mokanshan, the two dogs had stayed behind with Dahsoo and Lu-mei, but the servants had no love for these animals and left them loose in the backyard. The Leons had arrived home to find the flower beds in shambles, pots broken, piles of dirt everywhere. So it was that on a gray afternoon in early September, with a typhoon threatening, Hope and Jasmine were planting chrysanthemums. Or rather, Hope was planting while Jasmine played in the dirt.

"Mama! *Pao tsang!*"

Hope looked over to find the child up to her knees in the hole she was digging, both cheeks and her forehead black, the wind whipping her pinafore. "Jasmine," she said. "I think you've had enough."

"But look!" Jasmine stamped triumphantly. "Treasure."

"You should have been born a dog," said Hope, reaching to pull the child out of her mess. Jasmine's face hardened and she slithered from her mother's grasp. "What I meant," Hope adjusted, coaxing, "was that you've done as much digging as Betty and Dinky."

Hearing their names, the dogs began leaping in their enclosure across the yard. But the pout was on. "No!" Jasmine screamed, bringing Ah-nie from the house. "No! *Wo pu shih! Wo pu shih kou!*" I am not a dog.

"Of course not. Now give me that trowel and come out of there before you hurt yourself." What Hope really feared was that the child would hurl it at her or Ah-nie. Last year one of her tantrums had nearly put Joy's eye out, which doubtless helped precipitate the amah's departure.

"No!"

Ah-nie tried to cajole her, but Jasmine stamped her foot again and began reciting coolie insults. This so impressed—and mortified—Hope that it was several seconds before she noticed the noise coming from Jasmine's feet. Hard to hear, between the yapping dogs and rising wind, but it sounded metallic.

"Jazz!" she said sharply. "Where is the treasure?"

Jasmine brightened, pointing down, and Ah-nie swooped her into her arms. "Look!" Jasmine cried. "I tol' you."

The first drops fell as Hope knelt to examine the package that Jasmine had been drumming with her feet. It was large and round, wrapped in cotton batting that was still clean beneath the surface dirt.

Very slowly, Hope rocked back on her heels. In a controlled voice she said, "Good girl, Jasmine. Now go inside with Ah-nie and get cleaned up."

"I want to see the treasure!"

Hope managed a smile. She knew if she downplayed this, Jasmine would forget it, but if the child did not forget, there could be no silencing her. "It's just a pipe," she said. "You did a good job, darling, but there is no treasure. Now go on, it's starting to rain."

Only after Ah-nie had carried the disappointed child inside did Hope pull back the layers of batting. As she'd suspected, Jasmine's "treasure" was round, iron, and lethal. And as the storm began to soak the earth, three more just like it emerged.

It took four calls, the lines crackling wildly, before she tracked him down. She did not bother to identify herself, but said simply, "I found them."

The voice at the other end sounded amused. "Do not worry. No one will search the property of an American woman."

Through the window Hope watched the typhoon now unleashing its full force. The roaring filled her head. Trees were bending, shutters clapping. The rain was blowing sideways.

She said, "I want them out of here, Jin. Every one of them. Now."

4

That winter was wet and gray and cold to the bone. It was the end of Jin, as far as Hope was concerned. After she'd stood in the hammering rain and watched him, wordless and unrepentant, pack his cache of bombs into a cart and haul it out of her yard (there were five in all, which he'd buried during the family's Mokanshan holiday), she told herself she didn't care if she never saw him again, but she would not give him the satisfaction of revealing his trespass to Paul. Since nursing him back to health she had felt a tenderness for her husband that was new and deeply reassuring. For the first time in years, she sensed that she had the capacity to protect him, to make decisions on his behalf, to shield him from hurts that he himself could not or would not avoid. The illusion—for she recognized that it was largely an illusion—was the greater because Paul had spent so much of this time at home and because of his frailty after his long illness, but it was fed, too, by the sweet regard in which he now held her. She would look up from her reading and discover him watching her through half-closed eyes, or wake to the weight of his palm over her heart. "I remember," he would say, and describe the day they first met back in Berkeley—how she had taken him by surprise. During their stay in Mokanshan he had asked her to read to him the way she used to in California, and so, together, they discovered the works of Theodore Dreiser and Upton Sinclair—Literary Revolutionaries, Paul called them. He appealed to her now for advice on matters ranging from his foreign wardrobe to Dr. Sun's marriage. (Hope said she believed that, between the thirty-year age difference and his refusal to divorce his first wife before marrying the Methodist Ch'ing-ling, Sun could not have designed a more unacceptable union, as far as the Western Powers were concerned, but it was good they had married for love.) Paul seemed to cherish her presence in a way that he never had before. He simply liked to have her near him. Hope basked in this new affection and would do nothing to jeopardize it—even if that meant keeping Jin's violation a secret.

Then, one morning in early March, Jin came to visit. His face was so thin that his eyes and mouth seemed grotesque. He wore a shabby blue cotton worker's jacket. His hair hung long and uncombed, and there was a smudge of ink on his lips. When she addressed him, trying to mask her distress at his appearance, he looked at her with the polite formality of one who has just been introduced. He said he had a telegram to deliver to his father.

While he was upstairs with Paul, Hope decided the cable must have come from Nai-li. Jin had moved back to the Nantao house last fall after the police sweeps subsided, and Paul had heard from his mother that, even though she was displeased at her grandson's failure either to make a marriage or choose a profession, she would continue to pay his regular stipend for caretaking her Shanghai courts and readying them for her annual visits. Usually she stayed in Shanghai from February through April, but this year she was late. The telegram, Hope decided, must contain the date of her pending arrival.

After an hour she heard the front door open and shut. Then Paul came to her. "We must pack," he said in a toneless voice. "My mother is dying."

ᏸᏸᏸ

For years Hope had listened to Paul talk of the three-city region known as Wuhan with a respect that bordered on reverence. Here in Hankow, Hanyang, and his native Wuchang were laid the seeds of the Chinese Revolution. From this intersection of the Yun and Yangtze Rivers came the proudest and most venerable literati, the most responsible leaders, the most courageous warriors. This was where Paul had run as a boy, where his mother had stood up to the Taiping Big-Foots, where he had taken his first Imperial exams, where his ancestors were buried. Here was where Paul's first loyalties lay. And here, too, was where his mother kept the woman she considered his true wife.

On the river steamer Hope tried to talk to Paul about Ling-yi, but she felt ashamed giving voice to this ever-present, yet unmentionable concern. Their tacit agreement of the past seven years, not to discuss or acknowledge Ling-yi in any way, made the whole subject embarrassing. Hope felt as though she were announcing that she would have her menstrual period at Nainai's house, or that Jasmine was bound to have a tantrum, or that she knew Paul would humiliate himself again by knocking his head against the floor. "Of course she will be there," was all he would say. He might have been talking about a family pet.

So Hope swallowed her misgivings and tried to look forward to the famous Wuhan, but what greeted her as the steamer pulled into port was not what she had expected. The air was ashen not only with the blanketing mist but with a pervasive and irritating veil of industrial smoke. The chimneyed factories, Western-colonnaded office buildings, crouching godowns and shops all seemed fashioned from the same dead gray as the water. Behind them, the three walled Chinese cities loomed on their promontories like fortresses.

There were no carriages at the docks, so they climbed into rickshaws and rode for half an hour through Wuchang's seeping alleyways. The *hut'ung* where they finally stopped was indistinguishable from the others, nor was there anything remarkable about the gate, but the stature of Paul's family announced itself the moment they stepped inside.

The Liang wealth was signaled by the towering jadeite spirit wall just within the gate, their illustrious history by the curtained sedan chair on display in the first court. This chair had red lacquer shafts, purple and gold props, and an embroidered canopy of blue and imperial yellow—the grandest Hope had ever seen.

"My father used this sedan during his appointment as Viceroy of Canton," Paul told the children.

Jasmine immediately tried to climb inside, but Jin restrained her. "There is plenty to explore here, little one," he said in a subdued voice. "Be patient."

The bearers caught up their trunks and an elderly maid beckoned them down a long painted gallery. Pearl and Morris clung to Hope. Yen carried Jasmine. Paul and Jin strode ahead, talking in low tones. The scenery of the mostly vacant courts appeared and disappeared like lantern slides through the rounded and diamond-shaped gateways—rockeries and waterfalls, stone terraces with feathered bamboo, zigzag walkways and painted pavilions, all cast in twilight. Paul pointed through a lamplit doorway, and Hope recognized the ancestral library he had described in some of their earliest conversations, lined floor to ceiling with yellowed scrolls, "some old as Jesus." A wonderful and terrible burden, she thought with a glance to the two solemn men in front of her, to spend your childhood with such history constantly tapping your shoulder. Yet this place represented everything that Paul and Jin both claimed to reject for China's future.

Winter Plum and Mulan were waiting for them in the main court. The old maidservant looked as confidently proprietary and not an iota warmer than Hope remembered her. Mulan, however, had changed dramatically in the eight years since Hope last saw her. She had acquired a beaten look, and, though only in her mid-twenties, she seemed unaccountably older. Her hands fidgeted constantly, tearing at her cuticles, and her posture was slumped, her black hair pulled severely away from her face. Her makeup

was equally severe, her brows plucked thin as wire, and she wore no jewelry. But it was her eyes that bore the brunt of the change. Where before
they had been electric with pride and disdain, they now had no luster at
all, but flicked restlessly here and there, as if imprisoned behind that powdered skin. She greeted her father with a downcast gaze, and though she
did not address anyone else directly, Hope had the distinct impression
that this greeting was meant to encompass them all. So was her announcement that Nainai wished to receive them right away.

Mulan led them through several anterooms before they reached
Nainai's chamber. The scent of incense and medicine became stronger
with each step, and by the time they reached the central hall, the smell and
smoke were overwhelming, but not even the children dared complain.
Nainai watched them from an enormous canopied bed in the center of
the room. She wore a black embroidered jacket with a collar that stood
nearly to her jaw and thick gold hoops in her earlobes. Her sparse gray
hair was stretched back tight into its accustomed knot, and Hope wondered idly, as Paul knelt down, why the old woman could not at least on
her deathbed be permitted to release her hair.

But Nainai was not one to yield to discomfort. At length she signaled
for Paul to rise. Next she summoned Jin, and finally Morris, who, to his
credit, strode forward without a twinge of protest. The old woman raised
her eyes then to Jasmine, whose hand Hope was squeezing in a forceful
warning not to open her mouth, and the stalwart Pearl, and finally, belat-
edly, to Hope.

Nai-li squinted down, her gaze softened none by her suffering or by
the nearness of death. Hope felt a hard, dry current like a shock of electricity pass between them. Neither of them flinched, and Hope almost
believed that she had bested the old lady, when Nai-li unconcernedly
turned away and, with a flutter of two long-nailed fingers, dismissed
everyone but Paul and a woman Hope now noticed for the first time, in
the shadows on the far side of the bed.

Her throat contracted as Paul's other wife moved into place beside him.
Long ago, Paul had assured her that Ling-yi had buck teeth and an axe-
shaped birthmark, and she realized that through all these years she had
subconsciously clung to this disparaging description as a kind of shield.
But now, though it was difficult to see in this dusky light, across some

twenty feet, she had an impression of roundness that was at odds with Paul's remark. Ling-yi was soft, feminine. Her mouth was small, her eyes and brows angled demurely toward her nose. She did not part her lips to show her teeth, and any facial marks were invisible beneath her ivory powder. As Hope trailed out behind her family, she had the sinking feeling that she had been trapped at her own game. If Paul had, in fact, refused his standing invitation to this woman, then he had shown far more fortitude than she had in drawing back from Stephen Mann. And if he had not refused . . . She looked back, hoping for some sign, some indication in his face or posture that would quiet her confusion, but Paul stood straight, hands flat on his thighs. His eyes were on his mother.

Mulan led them to a nearby court with a rockery, where rooms had been readied. Supper was laid out for the children, and Hope settled them at table, then beckoned Jin and Mulan into the receiving hall and shut the door.

"What is her illness?" she asked.

"*Ai cheng.*" Mulan lifted her hands.

"Breast cancer," Jin translated.

"It is bad," said Mulan. "I help to bathe her. The flesh here and here, all black."

Hope winced. "I don't suppose she has seen a Western doctor."

"No. Priests, Chinese doctors. Nainai will not accept Western medicine."

"Priests?"

"Buddhist and Taoist."

"Ah." Hope chewed her lower lip. Jin and Mulan shifted uneasily. It appeared none of them dared speak of the matter that was foremost in Hope's mind, yet she could not bring herself to dismiss them and wait for Paul alone.

"There's no knowing then," she said, "how long she will remain sick."

"Oh, yes," Mulan said. "Nainai has told us she will die before the next moon."

"She has, has she?"

Jin smiled. "She is Nainai."

"I see," said Hope doubtfully, and realized they were still standing in the middle of the room. She asked them to sit, offered to call for tea, but Jin excused himself to go to his own court, and Mulan said she should return to wait on Nainai. Hope saw them out onto the gallery. "Thank you both for talking to me."

"It is our duty," said Mulan. Her eyes met Hope's as if she wished to say more, but abruptly glanced away.

"Surely not to me!" Hope said.

"You are our father's wife," Jin said quietly.

Hope hesitated. He was staring at the sky, hands clasped behind his back.

"Thank you," she said again.

ⒷⒷⒷ

The children were in bed by the time Paul reappeared. He sat with Hope in their bedroom before a low table set with steaming noodles and pork and heated wine. "You were gone a long time," she said.

He took a swallow of wine.

"So that was Ling-yi." She waited, then added, "She's quite attractive."

Paul laid his hands, palms down, on the table in front of him. "My mother agrees that once she has died, Ling-yi's duty to the family will be fulfilled."

She stared at him.

"It is awkward, because Ling-yi will be neither widowed nor divorced, and her own parents have died. As a traditional woman, Ling-yi cannot remarry, and my mother has grown fond enough of her that she foresees humiliation if she remains under the family roof. Also, my mother does not forgive me for continuing to refuse Ling-yi." Paul took another drink. His cheeks flushed with the alcohol, and he removed his dark wool jacket. "Tomorrow I must change to Chinese dress. Morris and Jin also. My mother understands if you and our daughters do not."

Hope held her own cup of wine to her nose and breathed in the sharp, sweet fumes. The specter of death seemed to have brought Nainai an unprecedented capacity for empathy. She said quietly, "Go on."

"Ling-yi will need income. Our family's principal wealth lies in this and our Shanghai house. Our farms were sold on my father's death to pay off his debts."

"I thought there were also some businesses."

"Yes, and my mother has proposed to give to Ling-yi our jewelry shop in Ichang. There is an apartment attached, where she can live. I have given my approval."

She nodded, unable to fully grasp what he was explaining. "The other—it's a tea shop, isn't it?"

Paul shrugged. "Traditional Chinese funerals are very expensive. Because Jin and I are more modern, my mother fears this may be the last such funeral in our family. Also she does not trust us to know the correct arrangements, so she has planned it herself, sparing no expense. She has sold the tea shop to pay for it."

"How perfectly ghoulish!" Hope shuddered. But Nainai's behavior was not really what bothered her. She was as appalled by Paul's casual recounting as she was relieved by his apparently genuine disinterest in Ling-yi. His emotions were as tightly controlled as his mother's!

"Chinese are more accepting of death than you Westerners," he continued. "Those who believe as my mother does, look forward to the afterlife."

Hope remembered sitting with Paul through those long weeks of meningitis, her terror that he would not survive. She thought of all the risks he ran, his conviction that he was not "important enough" to die. But she merely said, "Mulan told me it was breast cancer."

Paul looked up, blinking. Then he placed a slice of barbecued pork on Hope's noodles and motioned for her to eat. "So Mulan spoke to you."

"Mm." Hope frowned. "She's changed a great deal since she married, hasn't she? Friendlier to me, maybe, but she doesn't seem very happy."

"Mulan has no happiness. She is filled either with rage or sorrow. She has always been so."

Hope wondered how he could possibly know, since he had been absent her entire childhood, but this was not a defense she, of all people, could make on Mulan's behalf. He would say no more about either Mulan's problems or the matter of inheritance, and they retired to a vast lacquered bed heaped with red and gold pillows and overhung with tasseled lanterns. There was a heavy scent of anise in the air, and a soft rain pattered against the roof. As she lay back beside him Hope asked if this was the same chamber where his first wife had received him on their wedding night—a scene that had played so often in her mind that she has half eager, half dreading to see the actual setting.

He ran his fingers through her undressed hair, fanning it over her shoulder. "That court was closed after her death. This court I had prepared for you when I first returned from America. It has stood ready all these years."

The rain quickened, tapping now at the oiled paper panes. Paul's other arm was trapped beneath her waist, his hand curling at her hip with a familiar insistence.

"Why did you never tell me?" she whispered.

"Mei fatse." There was just enough light for her to see his smile.

"No," she said, yielding at last to the truth of this hated phrase. "I don't suppose there was."

෪෪෪

In spite of her prediction, Paul's mother took twelve weeks to die. For Hope they were the longest, most frustrating, and arguably the most interesting weeks of her life. Strong as she had always known Paul's mother to be, she had never imagined powers of endurance and stubbornness such as Nai-li showed in her final days. There were daily visitations by three separate sets of black-gowned physicians who doctored her with herbal plasters and infusions, pills that looked like asphalt marbles, and elixirs that smelled of ether, ammonia, or rotten eggs. They inserted needles in her face, neck, and feet to ease her pain, applied hot cups, which left dark red wheals across her back and chest. They adjusted the incense, the position of her bed. They soaked her in cold water, then in heat for varying durations. Many of these ministrations required an audience, and only Jasmine, by reason of her age and uncontrollable outbursts of disgust and boredom, was allowed to be excused.

Not even Paul could explain why, without any other cessation of hostility, his mother insisted on Hope's presence in the sickroom. Had she been commanded to stand watch alone or solely in Ling-yi's company, Hope might have ventured a guess, but she and Ling-yi were not singled out and, in fact, had nothing more to do with each other than to stand and watch along with the rest as the old woman's skin blackened and withered, grotesque tumors appeared at her neck, and the disease gnawed away at her brain. After the first week, Morris and Pearl, who could not understand why their sister's abominable behavior always seemed to be rewarded, made long impassioned pleas for their own release.

"It's the price we pay for Nainai's leaving us alone all these years," answered Hope.

"Leaving you alone, you mean," sulked Pearl. "We've had to see her plenty."

It was true. The children had been subjected to audiences every time Nainai came to Shanghai. She always favored Morris, but criticized his ignorance of the Confucian classics. She routinely insulted the girls. One of the things that had endeared Jin to Hope over the years was that he softened these visits by playing games or doing tricks for the children when Nainai wasn't looking.

"Well, you won't much longer," said Hope. "For your father's sake, we must do this."

"Will we be rich after she dies, Mama?" Morris twisted his neck against the unfamiliar mandarin collar. He was wearing one of Paul's own boyhood gowns of a deep black-brown shantung, and he looked elegant, much older than his eight years, and alarmingly well suited to this fashion, though he claimed to hate it.

"I don't know about that," Hope answered. "But Papa has promised me one thing. He says we'll be able to build a house in Kuling."

"Where we went that first summer?" asked Pearl.

"You remember? You called it Cloud Mountain."

"We went swimming."

"Yes, and Papa, too. I've always thought if there is one place in China that I could call home, it is Kuling."

From that day on, the prospect of a mountain home became their secret charm, making almost bearable the sight, smell, and sound of Nainai's physical disintegration. It was less effective, however, against the treatment Hope now received from Jin and Mulan. Although she felt no specific hostility, it was clear that Paul's two older children had been instructed to have nothing to do with her. After that first night, they did not speak to her except in the most cursory fashion. During their audiences in Nainai's chamber, they stood beside Ling-yi, and although Jin remained friendly with the children, he would invite them to play in his own court or the old Children's Court, rather than coming to Hope's. When she mentioned this to Paul, he dismissed her concerns, reminding her that Nainai had raised the older two, and they were merely distressed at her passing. Paul's own distress was eclipsed by the cables Sun Yat-sen was routing to him, about a new war erupting in Hunan, Japanese troop movements along the Eastern Railroad, and the arrival of Bolshevik agitators in Shanghai to launch a Chinese Communist Party. Evenings when his mother did not ask for him, he frequently went out to visit old friends, and fellow revolutionaries. Sometimes he persuaded Jin to accompany him. By the tenth week, Hope was ready to give up her dream house in Kuling, if only they could leave this purgatory.

Then the cancer spread. The old woman's legs, arms, and bowels were affected. No amount of incense could erase the stench of decay in her room, and no amount of face paint could cover the agony tearing at her mouth and eyes. She twitched. She rolled her head. She emitted a low, throbbing moan from the base of her throat. She could not swallow. Each breath was a labor. Still she insisted on controlling her death watch, the elegant clothing, the binding of her feet, the daily inspection of those she considered her own.

It was now that Hope felt most like an intruder, now when she longed to escape as much for Paul's mother's sake as for her own. And she understood at last that this was precisely why she'd been summoned. She had not stolen Paul away, and she had even given a son to this family, some daughters, however worthless. But she herself had never—could never—be more than a trespasser. And by dying under the forced gaze of her violator, Nai-li was getting even.

ॐॐॐ

June 19, 1920
Dear Sarah,
    What hell we have come through, I cannot describe, but finally it is over. I will have one unbelievable article for Cadlow! I even managed photographs of the funeral, to Paul's chagrin. I had to promise him I'd leave out all personal references to the family, though I've decided the most interesting thing about

this whole affair is my own relationship to Paul's mother, which I can finally permit myself to find interesting, now that she is gone. How she hated me! And yet I realize that none of it was personal. I think if she had been capable of recognizing me as a fellow woman instead of as a foreigner, we might even have established some mutual respect for each other—perhaps we did at the last, in a bizarre way. But as a foreigner, I was as much an enemy as the British with their gunboats and opium trade, or the missionaries with their stolen land, or the French with their opportunistic lies, or America, God help us, with her infinitely retractable promises of aid and assistance. Paul's mother supported him going off to study abroad, she aided and fed his revolutionary friends—even saved a few of their lives—and she never, despite repeated threats, did disinherit him after he married me, but she was of the old school to the end, and she made sure every one of us knew it.

What I will write about is the funeral, and as you told me you've never been on the inside of one of these shows, I'll rehearse the content of the article for you, beginning with the rites on the day she died—a day which she herself announced in the strongest, clearest voice I had heard since our arrival. It was three o'clock in the morning, and we had all been called from our beds. She ordered her coffin, built ten years ago and relacquered every year since, to be brought into the Court of Dignity. Then she informed us that the hour of her death was auspicious, and those who occupied the family home would continue to eat well (a bribe, I thought, to persuade Paul and Jin to hold the fort). Paul and Jin and Morris threw themselves into full-length kowtows, but she never said another word. When she was quite unconscious, a few minutes before dawn, we gathered out in the courtyard while Paul climbed up to the roof and raised his arm in a plea for the departing soul to stay a little longer. That was a strange moment for me, vastly more moving than anything I've ever experienced in a church, and also more cleansing. I heard genuine grief in Paul's voice and felt such a welling of forgiveness and—you will not believe it, but gratitude that I was present for that particular instant at that particular place in the universe. The dawn was just breaking, all blue and purple and pink, with Paul in his long black robe against it, arms outstretched and head flung back. I could practically feel the spirit brush my skin as she took her leave. I suppose that was the one instant when I felt truly present and a part of all that Paul was experiencing here. The irony that Nai-li was responsible for this is not lost on me.

There were candles to be lit and the body to be washed. This, at least, the children were spared from. I was not. Paul gave me the option, said that his mother had failed to give directions on this one point—my participation. But had I not gone, Paul would have stood beside Ling-yi washing his mother's cold form.

Water was brought from the temple, but it neither perfumed nor concealed the ravages of illness, which she had endured without a whimper. We were quick to dress her in layers of silk gauze and embroidery, an emerald and gold headdress, jade earrings, and the shoes she had embroidered herself specifically for the occasion. (The experience of cleansing and binding the dead woman's feet should give me material for three articles. Would that I had snapped a picture of that, no one alive could deny the barbaric inhumanity of this practice. Alas, the introduction of a camera during this ritual would have seemed equally barbaric.)

We tucked her into her silk-lined coffin with everything necessary to provide her comfort during the journey to the Western Sky. Changes of clothes, books, a pipe and tobacco, money, of course, and spiritual passports. Then the coffin was sealed and at its head were placed a stone tablet in which her name had been carved, a bowl of sesame oil, incense, and a vase full of blue "virtue flowers." I dressed the girls and myself in loose white dresses, and Paul and Jin and Morris put on the coarse sackcloth mourning gowns, the same sort of head fillets and straw sandals that we have all seen so often in Shanghai's native funerals.

Some servants were dispatched with funeral invitations. Others moved about the house replacing red candles and lanterns with white. The kitchen staff went into high gear, turning out the banquet that Nai-li had ordered, and poor Jasmine sat in a corner and sucked her thumb—it has taken so much out of her to be so very NOT the center of attention that I suspect we may see a permanent alteration in her disposition! Paul and Jin and Mulan went over the guest list and tutored the rest of us in the expected protocol. The next day a Taoist priest with one of those square turned-up hats and flowing black robes stood beating a gong at the entrance court as local merchants, officials and their wives, neighbors, former tenants and servants, even a few men who had been students with Paul came to pay their respects. Paul and Jin knelt beside the coffin as each guest bowed three times, Ling-yi and Mulan bowing in unison while the cacophony of stringed instruments and priestly chanting went on and on and on in the courtyard. It was drizzling, and the air was so warm and heavy that it muffled some of the noise, but the ceaseless throb of it got into your bones. The guests moved on to the banquet hall, where they were clearly astounded to find me and the children waiting to thank them. But as these exchanges follow a certain regulation code, we all muddled through without losing too much face.

Jasmine finally had a role, which she accepted with great excitement and much officious supervision from her big brother and sister. She took possession of the Heavenly Gifts, which the guests brought to accompany the soul on its journey. To Jasmine, of course, all these papier-mâché articles were toys. There were dolls to serve as spiritual servants, horses to carry the soul, pots and cooking utensils and chopsticks, sets of chess and mah-jongg, books, money, baskets of peaches (for longevity!), elaborate necklaces, a pet canary, and finally, the pièce de résistance from the mayor of Wuchang, a cardboard Model T Ford with uniformed chauffeur! As I watched Jasmine, in her own heaven, creating a private playhouse for these goods, I mentioned to Mulan that Nai-li couldn't have assembled a more impressive array if she'd ordered them herself. Mulan gave me a peculiar look and informed me that, of course, Nainai had told all the guests what to bring—at least she had made oblique suggestions, which amounted to the same thing.

The following day was beastly. Humidity and a relentless white sun searing through the mist. The funeral catafalque was the size of a stagecoach, draped with thick white satin. It required ten bearers, who made up only a fraction of the procession. Others carried Nai-li's sedan chair and an easel with her portrait. Another contingent walked with brooms sweeping the path to heaven, and still more carried the Heavenly Gifts. Morris and Jin and Paul carried the spirit tablet ahead of the catafalque. The rest of us walked behind. There were more chanting priests, half Taoist, half Buddhist, more musicians blowing and twanging, the local watchman adding to the din with his wooden clappers. At one point, to my utter astonishment, this hodgepodge orchestra broke into a uniquely Chinese rendition of "Yankee Doodle Dandy," apparently in honor of Paul's status as a returned student! Every so often, silver paper cash was thrown to bribe any lurking devils. I am sure the throngs of gawkers along the route were thinking I was the real devil and poor Nai-li must therefore not stand a chance. However, judging by the calls and jeers, my presence attracted far more spectators than would otherwise have watched Nai-li's crossing, and her spirit must have appreciated that.

It was about two miles to the gravesite. We formed a circle as the coffin was lowered, each of us throwing in earth. Then the priests made a bonfire of the Heavenly Gifts. Fortunately, that was the conclusion of the ceremony, for there was no consoling Jasmine. Paul and Jin had to bodily restrain her from plunging in after "her" horse and canary, and I'm afraid at this point the family did lose substantial face. We put her into a rickshaw and I brought her, sobbing, back to the house. Poor little thing, I knew exactly how she felt and I couldn't be cross with her, but Paul was livid when he returned. He has so little patience for Jasmine. She's a trying child, but still . . .

Well, you have enough family tribulations of your own without my burdening you. The news that I'm sure you've been waiting for came when Nai-li's banker called (as she had instructed him to do) that evening. It was the equivalent to the reading of a will, though as I'm sure you know, only the most modern Chinese have actual wills. Ordinarily, all property belongs to the family and everyone shares equally, both profits and indebtedness. But given the peculiar nature of this family, Nai-li made special arrangements. I have already written you of her plans for Ling-yi (who is beginning to seem to me the true heroine of this family; certainly, though I am glad she will be off to her own separate life, I do not begrudge her reward). The only remaining mystery was the amount of liquid property. As it turned out, there is a round total of approximately one hundred thousand Mexican dollars, one third of which are to go to Jin and two thirds to Paul along with the houses, which are as good as useless financially, since Paul would never dream of selling them. So there we are, not as well off as your Eugene, perhaps, but far more solvent than we have been. Paul is making arrangements now for us to stop in Kuling on the way back to Shanghai, so that we can look for some land and begin the delicious process of planning our new home.

The only lingering mystery is Mulan. She and Jin have been so remote through this whole process, and for a while I assumed they had reverted to their old hostility toward me, but now I think there may be something more at play. Mulan was visibly distressed when the banker had finished his news, and I think she really believed Nai-li might break the time-honored custom and include her—a female—in the inheritance. She said not one word to anyone, and it's now twenty-four hours later and I haven't seen her all day. Jin claims to know nothing. Paul went to her court more than an hour ago, so perhaps I will learn something when he returns. You, my girl, will have to wait for this story, though, for I can hardly keep my eyes open.

Trust you are getting some cool breezes while we steam in

this forsaken pressure cooker. Thank God for mosquito netting is all I can say, and good night.

Love, Hope

Paul was already up and gone when Hope awoke the next morning. Jasmine had stolen into her bed in the night and was still asleep, with her bangs fanned up and her lips parted in a rare peaceful smile. Hope spread the sheet loosely over her, and climbed out from under the net. She had just finished bathing and dressing when she noticed a shadow falling across the translucent window. Mulan was pacing the outer gallery.

The girl's face, for once, was free of its white mask, and she looked at Hope with uncharacteristic directness. "May I speak with you, please?"

Hope sighed. "For three months I've been wishing you'd say that. Of course."

They went out to sit in the rockery. Mulan was worrying her hands. "I have been a poor daughter to you and my father," she said.

I'll grant you have not been particularly welcoming, Hope remarked to herself, but to Mulan she said, "You have been a very filial granddaughter."

"This is not how my father thinks." Mulan spoke haltingly in excellent but unpracticed English. The care with which she formed her words heightened their undertone of urgency. "I have made a worthless life for myself. When I meet you, I believe that my father accept this doctrine of free love. I want to show him, I, too, am modern woman."

"You *are* a modern woman. You went to college. Aurora University! How many women in China could make such a claim?"

"I want to punish him as well as to follow him." Mulan lowered her eyes. "I tell myself I love this wealthy man. He takes me in his automobile. He has a Gramophone. He dines with me in restaurants. I think he is handsome, and when he says he will marry me, I do not refuse him."

"I see." Hope recalled Paul's comment when he first told her of Mulan's marriage, that the family would lose much face if he forbade it. She straightened her back, motioning Pearl, who was skipping toward them, to go back and check on her sister. "And so you got your way, and now it's awful, and you don't know how to get out of it."

Mulan looked up.

"I understand better than you can imagine. Not that I know if I can help. But how bad—why are you unhappy with him?"

Mulan answered by pushing up her long gauze sleeves.

Hope stifled a cry. The scars rivaled Paul's in violence, but were more erratic, as if a blade had been simultaneously dragged and twisted, plowing through almost to muscle.

When she had regained her breath, Hope covered the girl's arm with her own hands. Mulan did not pull away. She did not react at all. "You've shown your father this?"

Mulan shook her head. "It is shameful."

"But if he is to understand—" Hope couldn't help asking, "Are there more?"

Mulan gestured toward her ankles, the collar of her gown.

"But *why?*"

Mulan's eyes shivered. "I wear the foreign dress. These are exposed. Dalin is Muhammedan."

"Surely, even for a Muhammedan, that does not justify . . . this!"

"Everything is different for the wife. Must stay inside. Must not read. Must have relations with him whenever . . . Because I bring him only one daughter, no son, he beats me."

"What of this *have* you told your father?"

"Only I must leave Dalin."

"But Paul is a reasonable man. If you explain—"

"He say whatever I suffer, I bring on myself. I join my husband's family, my duty is to that family."

"Does he indeed?" Hope stiffened. "Let me talk to him."

"He has gone with Yen to the cable office." Mulan hesitated. "I must leave today. I am to travel with Ling-yi."

"Why did you wait so long to come to me!"

"I think Nainai will help me. Leave money to buy my freedom."

"What would that cost?"

"I think many thousands."

Hope shook her head. "I've nothing like that much. You've told Jin and Ling-yi, then?"

"Not Ling-yi. She could never understand . . . Jin knows. He will divide his money with me, but only if Father approves."

"Why would Jin, of all people, make such a condition?"

Mulan frowned. "This is a family matter. And Jin is first son."

Hope threw up her hands. "Well, you can't go back, Mulan!"

But the girl was picking at the fabric of her gown, avoiding Hope's gaze. "One of my husband's guards will come at noon."

This brought Hope's agitation to an abrupt stop. Mulan had sabotaged her own request!

"I'm at a loss," she said after a wary interval. "Of course, I'll try to talk to Paul, but you must agree to show him these scars. Whatever your mistakes, they're no worse than any of us have made in our turn. No one deserves such treatment."

But Paul and Yen still had not returned when Dalin's guard arrived, early, with strict instructions to see the young women onto the two o'clock ferry. He was a broad, mustachioed Yunnaese wearing soldier's uniform with a holstered Mauser. He ordered the bags loaded into one cart, then positioned himself impassively beside the second, in which Mulan and Ling-yi were to ride. Hope tried to stall by bringing the children out to say their goodbyes, but they were indifferent to Ling-yi, whose dialect they could not understand and whose position in the household had never been revealed to them; they were wary of Mulan, whom Pearl early on had nicknamed the Ghost Wife; and they were eager to return to their play. Jin's farewell was hardly less perfunctory. He apparently had little patience for Mulan's woes and showed benign contempt for Ling-yi's old-school docility. Finally they could delay no longer.

Ling-yi was already in the cart when Hope drew Mulan back and overtly pressed a small paper packet into her hands. It contained the star sapphire that Daisy Tan had bought for her in Peking . . . and the aquamarine and pearl necklace that Paul had given her when she first arrived in China. "Maybe Ling-yi can sell these for you," she whispered. "I'm sorry there's nothing more I can do."

Mulan's protests were interrupted by the clatter of arriving rickshaws. Paul descended red-faced and perspiring heavily under his straw boater. He seemed not to know why the women were gathered at the gate. Both Ling-yi and Mulan had told him the schedule, but he was preoccupied with news that Sun had yet again dissolved the Canton government. Hope tried to get his attention, said he should call Mulan back inside, but the guard clicked his heels and respectfully informed Paul that the party must leave at once. Mulan drew her hands—and the packet—up inside her long sleeves, and climbed into the cart.

"You heard him," Paul said when Hope again protested. "The ferry will not wait."

Then his eyes went to Ling-yi. He studied her with a finality that chilled Hope, for it told her that he would never give this woman—this wife—another thought. He waved with equal finality to his daughter, and she bowed her head and was gone.

Hope followed Paul to his study.

"You should not have forced Mulan to go."

"I did not force her!"

"You did not intervene. It is the same thing."

"I did try once to intervene." Paul pulled off his glasses and rubbed his eyes. "Eight years ago I did everything in my power to persuade her not to marry this man."

"Did you?" The words turned up with an ugly curl, and Paul looked at her sharply. He pushed back the door to the adjoining room, where Pearl and Morris were studying, and told them to take their sister to the old Children's Court and wade in the sand pool there.

When they were gone he said, "Why this sudden interest in Mulan's marriage?"

Hope considered her words, the various approaches. Mulan had laid a minefield through territory that was, even on its face, treacherous.

"Her sleeve happened to pull back this morning," she lied. "I saw those ghastly scars and asked how she got them. She didn't want to tell me, but I insisted, and then it all came out. You must help her get a divorce, Paul!"

She expected him to ask what scars she was talking about. Instead he tapped the pad of one thumb against his lips and stared at the latticed window. A mosquito buzzed Hope's ear, and she slapped, crushing it against her cheek, then, sickened, whisked it with the back of her hand. What was it about this country, these people—Paul!—that made honest compassion seem shameful?

"You will stop at nothing," she said, changing tack. "You'd fight to the death to achieve Sun's ideal of a free and unified China. Why won't you do the same for your daughter?"

Paul lowered his hands to the arms of his chair and articulated slowly, as if to a dim-witted child or foreign speaker. "Mulan was given every advantage. She was pampered, educated. I gave instruction, she and Jin were to follow my example, have all liberty of modern men and women. On this my mother followed my instruction exactly. *This* is what my daughter chooses with her liberty."

He was looking past her now, his face contracting with such emotion that Hope knew she should leave the matter here. But she kept seeing that butchered flesh, kept imagining the horror of intimacy with a man who could do such a thing. "You speak as though she volunteered for crucifixion just to spite you."

"And you mistake her for a victim."

"She was a child. Children make mistakes. They should not be made to carry those mistakes like millstones around their necks for the rest of their lives."

"When mistakes change the course of fate they cannot be undone."

A chill ran down Hope's spine, though she did not at first know why. Then she realized she was no longer thinking of Mulan. She had in her mind's eye her own children. Herself. "We've made our bed," she said under her breath. "Now we must lie in it."

"What is that?"

"*Mei fatse*," she said bitterly. "American translation."

Beads of perspiration broke across Paul's forehead. "You think I am cruel and uncaring."

"I'm sure I'll get over it."

"What would you have me do?"

"Help her." She watched him light a cigarette. His hands were trembling. "At least offer to help her."

"How do you think Mulan's husband knew that her duty here was fulfilled? After three months, knew to send his guard today?"

Hope got up and moved to the open doorway, fixing her gaze on the rockery. Given the morning's confusion, she had not thought to question such logistics. The obvious answer was that Paul had notified him, but she held her tongue.

"I tried to describe for you once the powers of this man," Paul said. "There is no greater source of wealth than the traffic of arms and ammunition in a country at war. There are no more sinister friends than those of the man who runs such traffic. In your country such men are called gangsters. When I first learned of Mulan's fascination for this man, I told her what life he would give to her. Do you know, she laughed like a monkey, mocking me."

"But she had no choice—"

"Ah. She tells you a great deal, this daughter of mine. But I learned of her flirtation with Dalin when I first return from America. I confront her then. Two more years pass before her daughter was born. So you are wrong. She had choice. Now not I but her husband and child hold her to it. And she would dare to leave them both."

The damp heat pressed against her face. She had not considered the fate of Mulan's child. "But if she and her daughter came to visit us in Shanghai, we could arrange to get them out of the country—"

Paul threw his cigarette into the bronze spittoon beside the chair. "Did he allow the child to come to her *nainai's* funeral? This man is not stupid."

"She's your grandchild." Hope stared at him. "You've never even seen her, have you?"

"For eight years you do not speak of Mulan. Her child does not exist. Now you are filled with pity and concern, and you do not take time to think. No, I do not see the child. She belongs to his family, Hope, not mine. There is no crossing a man such as Dalin."

"But men like that surely respond to money?"

He tore at his thumbnail. "Would you give up your house in Kuling?"

Hope hesitated, thinking of the necklaces. "If that bought their freedom . . ."

"It would not even begin."

"How do you know, if you've never spoken to him—"

Paul opened a small cedar box on his desk and pulled out a folded square paper. "Your Chinese should be good enough to read this. He is practically illiterate."

Hope bit her lip at this condescension, but took the note and returned to her chair. Though the brushwork was crude, the characters uneven, the basic message was clear: "In return for your daughter, I will accept your house in Wuchang—with your most admirable library. In return for my daughter, I will accept your house in Shanghai plus an order from your friend Sun Yat-sen for one million dollars in artillery and ammunition."

She frowned, her brain scrambling still for resolution. "Would Sun put up the money? He needs the weapons."

"Hope." He rose with a sigh and came around the desk. "You try my patience. Remember when Yüan Shih-kai accepted a loan from the Japanese with condition that it buy Japanese guns? And do you remember that the guns they sent were old and rusted? They exploded in the Chinese soldier faces. For three years Dalin has supplied the warlords in Peking. They have promised to make him governor of Szechwan. This is no deal he is proposing. It is an offer to ruin me and bring down the revolution around me." Paul reclaimed the note from her stiffened fingers. "You must believe, there is no way other than war with Dalin. And if such war is declared, he will stop at nothing. Not Mulan or her daughter. Not me. Not our children. Not even you, Hope."

He uttered these words softly, clearly regretting them. They might have been razor blades applied the same way. Hope turned on him. "No," she said brutally. "Not even me. Because I belong to you."

But he would not be baited. "She was wrong to speak to you."

"She was helpless," she said. There was a long silence and then, without realizing it was happening, she began to cry.

ॐॐॐ

5

July 4, 1920
My dear Hope,
Happy Independence Day! The American clubs are giving quite a show here in old S-town, with red, white, and blue streamers, sparklers, watermelon picnics, and the Grand Old Flag dangling limp from every Marine warship and Standard

Oil tanker in the port. Tonight we're to be treated to a show of fireworks off the Bund—those of us who wish to drag out into the evening bog to stand wilting as we watch. I don't think there's been a breeze through these streets in a month, and the bodies of cholera victims are piling up at an alarming rate in Nantao. I do envy you going to Kuling!

Now, as to this business about your stepdaughter. I really am surprised your Paul puts up with you, you goose! He must either have the patience of a saint or this must honest-to-Pete be true love that you've managed to steal. Will you not come to your senses and understand, once and for all, that you're in China? This girl has gotten herself into a desperate trap, it's true, but Paul's right, she has done it to herself. Think of all the poor women who are sold off like slaves, or your maid back in Berkeley you've told me about, being sent by her own father to the Frisco brothels! You mustn't blame Paul for his reluctance, nor must you box your own ears for being unable to help. Something about this story does not ring true to me. Maybe it's my cynical nature, or maybe I've been around certain tracks more often than you, but your Mulan may have done more than wear a short dress to earn those scars. Mind, I'm not excusing her husband, he sounds a proper cousin to this "Dogmeat General" up north—the one they say favors braised beagle and has fifty concubines from different countries, each with her "conquered" flag on her washbowl! Be that as it may, you must realize, my dear innocent, that some of these wives are up to quite as much mischief as their husbands. Oh, I can see you holding your nose and tossing your head, but it's true. I advise you to think long and hard before you wade in any deeper.

As for *my* happy family, Eugene is off with his new Number Three to the cool of Tsingtao, where he is doubtless cranking up some scheme to borrow money from the Japanese to loan to Old Man Sun. If he's taught me one thing, this man of mine, it's that everything—honor, business, duty, and affection—revolves around an axis. And that axis is survival. Call us Godless

if you must, but on this my Chinese "lord" and I understand
each other perfectly . . . and I'll bet your Mulan would agree.

Anyway, I imagine you have your hands full with your own
children and Paul and your work and now, your dream house in
the hills. By the way, I do think your rendering of old Nainai's
funeral should sit very well with Mr. Cadlow, and Jed says he's
a truckload of funeral shots to contribute if your own don't
turn out.

So see you in September, dear heart, and build fast! Gene
says, if you (and Paul!?) invite us, the boys and I may come up
for a stay with you next summer.

Boodles of love,
Sarah

August 23, 1920
Kuling
Dearest Sarah,
We have returned at last to Paradise. The same house Paul
secured for us before, the same clear, shimmering cool air, the
same scents of pine and moss and altitude that are like the
purest elixir after the sludge and stink and death and drama we
have endured below. I feel healed and energized, almost as if
this place had cast a spell on me. I think we all feel it. The children run like Banchees, stripped down to the bare necessities.
Pearl gloats at the authority I give her over Morris and Jasmine,
but she takes it seriously as a Scout leader and has made energetic hikers of them both. Yen, too, poor soul, as he's the one
who generally trudges along to make sure no harm befalls them.
But, in a way, it's just as well, since he loves them more than Ah-
nie does, and he tells them all sorts of mythic stories about the
old shrines and temples they discover. Even way up here, it
seems the very earth is alive with history. Part of me wants to
go with them, but another part is so enjoying this time with
Paul, all our excited preparations for our home, that I rarely
leave his side.

We have found the loveliest site for the house, directly above a running brook, surrounded by hillsides of pink and white azaleas, rhododendron, and mountain laurel. There is a gently rising slope for a path and a wide pad that will serve perfectly for the foundation. Back a bit and up, the pines begin, and in the evening there starts the most beautiful soughing, like some sweet, sad string instrument, though it's only the wind. We are in the upper valley, happily apart from the pious scorn of the lower valley residents. That said, many of the American Y people seem to be genuinely friendly and supportive, inviting our children down to play and Paul and me to tea, and offering many sound construction suggestions. One Randolph James, who built his own lodge in the Adirondacks before being assigned to China, has agreed to draw up some architectural plans, which we can noodle with over the winter and begin building next spring, as soon as the snows melt off. He and Paul seem to get on famously—you should see the two of them standing with the local carpenters and bricklayers arguing ad nauseum over measurements and window placement and materials. My only absolute demand is a wide framed porch and bedroom windows facing east. The sunrises here are truly so majestic that to do otherwise would be a crime. Beyond that, we have hit on a stylistic compromise of East and West, which we are calling "mountain style." Fieldstone and timber beams, gently peaked roof, glass-paned windows but with Chinese proportions, and everything low-slung in the shape of an ell except for a small upstairs sitting room/guest room, which will perch rather like a tower overlooking the whole valley.

All right, I've allowed myself to get carried away with this rapture, at least in part, because I'm ashamed. The cool light of reason and your sage advice have prevailed. Why is it that we accept wisdom so much more readily from friends than lovers? Your reprimand was hardly different from Paul's and yet I was willing to listen instead of bullheadedly ducking and dodging as I did with him. The answer to your question of infidelity is, I don't know. When I asked Paul, in as musing a tone as I could muster, what he thought on that score, he insinuated that there had been rumors, and though he stopped short of saying he believed them, I'm quite certain he does. So perhaps Mulan is lucky to be alive at all, as Dalin would be well within his rights to lock her up and starve her to death—or worse—for such a crime. And perhaps she was trying to use me by painting herself as the victim, the way some play on the heartstrings of missionaries. How easily truth and deceit are exchanged in this land of mirrors! While we can't help those who refuse to help themselves, there's such a fine line between refusal and helplessness that I often can't find it even within myself. I think you will understand why I feel I have been embroiled in a cautionary tale, and I must step back out of it if I know what's good for me, whatever the truth of Mulan's plight may be. Still, there's no pretending I feel any better about it than I would if I were watching her slide over the edge of a precipice. Survival may be the axis around which we revolve, but it's a painfully bleak world if that is all that we have in common.

So, my dear, I must close and go rouse young Princess Jasmine. We are going for a last swim with Paul at Paradise Pool before he leaves us for Canton. I suppose you have heard Sun's sometime ally Ch'en Chiung-ming has taken the city back again, and so the Ping-Pong game continues, and my husband with it. We will stay on here until the first, and be home the week before school starts—in time to move back to Frenchtown in October! I am writing madly to stockpile some articles, as I know I won't get a word down once that onslaught begins.

Thanks, as always, for bearing with me—and for the significant contribution you've made to the peace that currently reigns in my marriage. I do try to remind myself daily that *that* and the children are my primary concerns, but I am unforgivably distractible.

See you in September,
Love, Hope

6

She would think of the early twenties as accordion years, a time of continuous squeeze and expansion, with Sun in power in Canton, Sun out of power and back to Shanghai; a push toward modernization, a pull toward tradition; civil war against the north, truce with the various warlord cliques; drought and famine, rain and flooding; the Kuomintang dissolves, then reorganizes; the foreign imperialists are the enemy, the foreign powers allies. Paul's moods and movements on any given day mirrored these various switchbacks so exactly that Hope gave up trying to gauge his mental outlook, as she had long ago given up trying to predict when he would come home. But every few weeks—or months—he *did* come home, and they would sequester themselves in their second-floor suite in the new house on Rue de Grouchy (their last neighborhood, Hongkew, had become so overrun with impoverished White Russians and other war refugees that Paul decided it was no longer suitable for Hope and the children), or in the book-lined study of the house in Kuling, and Paul would update her. He told of Sun's grand military plan for a Northern Expedition to sweep the country under Nationalist control, and of the Bolshevik emissaries who were bending Sun's ear with promises of arms and expertise—if he would embrace a socialist agenda. Sometimes Paul was didactic, often irate, and occasionally dejected. Increasingly he seemed plain worn out.

Paul had lived, breathed, and dreamt the revolution every day for more than thirty years. To Hope's mind, he had little to show for it. The country had become a patchwork of ever shifting and proliferating warlord fiefdoms, and while Dr. Sun was lionized by those like Paul who still credited him with overthrowing the Manchus, his real power in the current state was nonexistent. By remaining tenaciously in his service, Paul often worked months without pay and, though he was careful to see the Kuling house finished, the remainder of the funds Nai-li had left him soon vanished into Sun's bankrupt coffers, to be doled out to the hundred men who formed Sun's personal bodyguard—the only troops over whom Sun had any real control. This financial transfer, of course, was accomplished without Hope's knowledge, nor was she ever notified ahead of time when Paul disappeared into the interior to negotiate the support of warlords who, likely as not, would be killed or ousted before the pact was sealed. Upon his return he would tell stories of pirates he'd passed on the river, or bandits he'd watched robbing graves, or the smoking funeral pyres he had seen in areas of cholera or smallpox epidemics.

After sitting through one particularly long and grisly account of a warlord battle in which four schoolboys were killed in crossfire, she asked, "When are you going to realize that *you* also are vulnerable?"

He smiled, and gave the familiar refrain. "I am not important. Nothing will happen to me."

"You *are* important to me and the children. That's precisely what I wish you would get through your thick head."

"If my head is so thick," he said blithely, "it will protect me."

Nothing changed and yet, for all the strains, these years introduced a new peace between them. Though Paul spent weeks at a stretch in Wuchang, where he was forever hammering out deals with local warlords on Sun's behalf, she no longer recoiled from his embraces when he returned from these home visits. Nai-li was dead, and Ling-yi, as Hope had predicted, was erased from Paul's thoughts as if she had never existed. While his capacity for oblivion gave her some pause, she trained herself to view it as affirmation of their own love.

Gone were her early fantasies of working by his side, of translating his writings or being a political helpmate, yet Hope realized now that she *was* his partner in more meaningful ways. When he was tired and discouraged she gathered him into bed. Through her articles for Cadlow, she would flatter him with anonymous portraits of China's returned students "striving for modernization," and at those still rare events when it was politically helpful to display a foreign wife, she would appear publicly by his side. Sometimes she even went forth as his emissary, as on one memorable occasion when she and the children were driven in a Stutz roadster, with armed bodyguards on the running boards, to a banquet out by Siccawei with the head wife of Shanghai's director general—who conversed in her thudding Hakka dialect for three solid hours without noticing that Hope understood not one word. Finally, there was her role as intermediary with Jin, who had sworn to her that he would never again let his politics endanger her or the children—but who nevertheless was becoming an ardent socialist. This meant that he and Paul continued to clash, and it fell to Hope to deliver the conciliatory messages and reports of Sun's softening toward the Bolsheviks that would bring the two back together.

At the same time, even if she had to secure an advance from *Harper's* or borrow from Sarah, Hope made sure that Pearl and Morris and Jasmine, in her turn, were enrolled in school every fall, with new shoes and books and the latest fashions—white duck trousers and flannel jackets for Morris, pleated knee-length skirts and blouses for the girls—which Hope made from Parisian and American patterns. Summers they would spend in Kuling, usually with Sarah and Gerald and Ken (though Paul encouraged Hope to call on Daisy Tan, who was now living in Shanghai, he no longer opposed her preference for Sarah), and Paul joined them sometimes for as long as three weeks at a stretch. The children grew brown and sturdy during these idyllic months, and Hope put endless finishing touches on their home, convinced this was where she belonged.

Yes, she and Paul did have business together—business that was curiously enhanced by their largely separate lives. Their shared purpose was to keep the family together, to persevere—in Sarah's words, to survive.

To this end, there were certain matters that Hope now banished from her thoughts. Stephen Mann was foremost. She told herself to consider him dead. To Sarah's inquiries she would shrug or laugh. And on the rare occasions when the old longings threatened to rise again (usually during Paul's prolonged absences), she would take herself out and photograph the meanest, most devastating images—maimed one-eyed babies, streetwalkers in rags, opium eaters crouched by the road selling scraps of paper and used tin cans, corpses encrusted with rats, or human heads dangling in cages in the Chinese City—anything to remind herself how trivial were her own regrets.

The other name she rigorously shut from her thoughts was Mulan's. The autumn after Nainai's death they had received a terse note from Dalin stating that Mulan had disappeared in the night. She had not taken her daughter or any of her belongings, and had poisoned Dalin's four pet keeshonds to prevent their barking when she left. Paul wrote back that he had not seen or heard from his daughter, but would notify Dalin if he did. For days afterward, Hope was aware of a black Pierce-Arrow parked around the corner and a figure wearing a blue scholar's gown and Homburg who hovered up the block. She kept the children home from school. Then Jed told her that a member of the Green Gang, Shanghai's most notorious criminal syndicate, had demanded duplicates of her film, which, at Paul's insistence, she authorized Jed to hand over. Paul assured her there was no basis for her gravest fear, that Dalin would try to get to Mulan by kidnapping the other children. "Such tactics are a last resort. If he really suspected that I had helped her he would confront me directly."

"That's very reassuring," Hope retorted, but soon the Pierce-Arrow and its occupants disappeared. There was nothing further from Dalin, and Paul said they should put Mulan out of their thoughts.

Then, one evening in early May 1922, Hope received a note summoning her to an inn in the Chinese City. It was written in English and signed "Your Daughter." Paul was in Canton, Jin in Hankow, and Yen had gone to the cinema for the evening. Hope was terrified the note might be some kind of trap and wanted someone to go with her. Sarah was unlikely to be either sympathetic or discreet, so instead, Hope telephoned Denniston's. Fifteen minutes later Jed Israel was in front of her house with two rickshaws.

Having never mentioned Mulan before, she quickly filled him in. Ever prepared, he had his Speed Graphic slung over his shoulder, but she instructed him that the subject might be less than cooperative. He dashed a hand through his thick red curls and answered noncommittally that he was used to that. The sinew in his voice startled her, and for a moment she was distracted by the recognition that the stammering adolescent she had met in Evanston had long since matured into a professional "China hand."

She gave a false address near French Park, but there was no sign they were being followed, and so, keeping as much as possible to back streets, they proceeded to their true destination. It was nearly ten o'clock when they reached the inn, a squat shadowy building, closely shuttered and barred, flanked by piece factories. Hope shuddered, recalling her last Chinese inn.

Jed laid a hand on her shoulder. "Don't worry," he said. "I know this place. The owner's a g-good man."

She looked at him.

"I know his son. He's trying to organize the local sweatshop w-w-workers."

Jed knocked at the door, identifying himself by his Chinese name, and after a pause, a short tubercular-looking man opened up. But his smile faltered when he saw Hope, and faded completely when she asked to see Mulan. He led them to the opposite side of a court that must once have been a stately home, though the original halls had been divided and subdivided, the spaces between hemmed in, so that some twenty cubicles now surrounded the flat paved yard. The full moon was bright in a cloudless sky, but to Hope the pale dazzle only made the place seem more desolate.

The room into which the innkeeper showed them was grimmer still. Even before the door opened they were assaulted by the stench of a full chamber pot and the strains of a tango pitching and dying at low volume from a box Victrola. One bare electric lightbulb flickered above the mattress where Mulan's body lay.

Hope's first thought was that her stepdaughter was dead. The girl did not move, and her eyes were glassy. But then she saw Hope and tried to smile. Her head lolled back and forth. Hope crouched beside her and took her hand. The face was bare and she wore a man's trousers and shirt many sizes too big for her. Suddenly she grimaced, and made an unearthly noise. Milky fluid trickled from the corner of her mouth, and a sweet metallic smell cut through the room's general stench.

Hope had a hand on her forehead, was searching for a pulse and shouting for Jed to get help, when Mulan tried to raise herself. "No!"

Hope hesitated, then put an arm around the rigid shoulders and shook her head for Jed to stay.

"It is carbolic."

Hope looked up with a start and discovered a bulky blond man, dressed in the same manner as Mulan, sitting in the darkened corner on the other side of the bed.

"I tell her ve better alone, but she vant you come." The stranger's voice was like a trampled animal's.

"Why?" demanded Hope. "Why has she done this?"

"Dalin."

The girl's head rocked to the right, and a bizarre brightness came into her eyes. She breathed, "Ivan, look. Pictures."

Hope glanced around and, to her disgust, saw that Jed had placed his camera on a stool and was training his lens on the couple. Ivan knelt beside the bed and took Mulan's hands. Mulan pursed her lips in a grotesque stage kiss.

"Don't move," said Jed in a low voice, his stammer overcome, as it always was, by the intensity he applied to his work. Hope wanted to fly at him and tear the stupid little machine from his grasp. She wanted to take Mulan and shake her. But she couldn't move.

"Two years ve live in secret," said the Russian. "Dalin, he track us."

Jed slid his improvised tripod closer as the man bent to kiss Mulan's forehead. The camera snapped. The tango wheezed and rallied. Mulan's body convulsed.

"Your friend, Jed." Hope blocked the lens. "He must know someone around here with opium. Morphine. Anything to ease her pain."

They locked eyes for a moment like enemies, then he nodded and left the room. Hope took a rag that Mulan had clenched in her fist and wiped the sweat from her forehead. It was cold. "*Why* have you done this," she murmured. "Why?"

Mulan was trying to swallow. Her lover held a dirty glass to her lips. "Little bird," he murmured.

Hope said to him desperately, "Couldn't you get her away!"

His large, deep-set eyes welled up. "I try. I beg her, com vit me back to Russia. She vill not."

"Tell Father," Mulan panted. "You see. Picture. Show him."

Hope backed away. "Is that why you sent for me? To punish your father?"

A wild look of panic crossed Mulan's face. Her knees seized up to her chest and she clung to Ivan's arm as if she meant to climb it. The stink of the chamber pot, which the horror of the situation had overwhelmed, now rose to Hope's notice once more. She crossed the room and yanked the needle off that grinding record, found the pot behind its screen. The contents slopped from beneath the lid, but she got it outside and herself to the pump in the center of the courtyard. She scrubbed her hands, her wrists, soaking her sleeves to the elbows, and struggled to compose herself.

She was still standing there when Jed returned. "Better than opium." He opened his palm to reveal a small black capsule.

"What is it?"

"Cyanide. Carbolic can take hours, and it's agonizing. This, immediate."

Hope's hand shook violently as she took the thing, so deadly it seemed alive.

Ivan had settled onto the mattress beside Mulan with one arm cradling her shoulders, the other stroking her cheek. Hope held out the pill. "You can end this now."

But as Ivan lifted the capsule to her mouth, Mulan noticed Jed back behind his lens. "Picture," she begged. "For my husband."

Hope turned away, repelled. The next instant she heard a faint gasp and the snap of Jed Israel's shutter.

It was her wish, Ivan told them, that he bury her at sea.

Hope and Jed walked the darkened streets in silence back to Nanking Road. An American man and woman, they entered the lobby of the Cathay Hotel and turned toward the bar. It was well after midnight, but no one tried to stop them. No one gave them a glance. Jed ordered two scotch whiskeys. Hope, who rarely drank anything more potent than a thimbleful of wine, swallowed hers in a gulp. The alcohol made her head throb. Her thoughts were consumed with Paul.

Suddenly Jed's hand covered hers. The sharp glitter of the bar lights and mirrors reflected in his eyes. Around them couples leaned, cuddled, nuzzled necks, clasping each other and swaying to the blues of the black pianist in the corner. The Annamese bartender smiled.

A new revulsion came over her as she saw how she must appear to Jed. How she would, at this moment, appear to Paul. "No," she said. "Don't."

Jed gazed at her steadily, then slid his hand away and ordered another drink. As she stood to go, he lifted his glass and said, "F-f-from the w-wedding to the deathbed. I feel like a member of the f-f-family."

"That's cruel."

"Is it?" He tilted his head and looked at her with one eye closed, as if taking her picture. "Why'd she h-hate Paul so much?"

"Because he married me."

"Married you? Or l-l-loved you?"

Hope murmured, "Loved."

Jed turned back to his drink, head down and shrugging. "Then you shouldn't care."

She touched his shoulder gently, and kissed him on the cheek.

ॐॐॐ

The following Sunday Hope was waiting at the pier when Paul returned from Canton.

He gave her a grim smile. "You could not wait for me at home?"

"The children have their friends over. The dogs were barking, and Dahsoo is in a pique because he burned this morning's biscuits—I wanted to see you alone."

He glanced at the bustle of coolies and tourists streaming to either side of them. "We are hardly alone."

"We could go to the Confucian Temple. I just . . . The children know nothing about all this, and I don't want to risk their hearing us."

He nodded.

The Confucian Temple consisted of a pagoda and several low, open halls of the Sages where elderly men and women lit incense or knelt in contemplation. Behind was a small, empty garden where Hope and Paul found a bench beside a lotus pool, and sat for some time without speaking. Hope thought Paul's eyes seemed unbearably heavy, his face drawn. Yet there was the same tenderness in his expression that had made her fall in love with him, that had checked her whenever she thought this love was gone. Or that it was not enough.

She had cabled him only that Mulan had died, that he must return to Shanghai. She had told herself this was for his sake, so she could tell him in person and comfort him. "I received a letter," he said first. "Same day as your cable.

"She explained her intentions, that she would summon you as her witness." He lifted his eyes. "I am so sorry, Hope."

She let his words sink in, the depths of Mulan's cruelty—and desperation.

"Was it very bad?" he asked.

"For her, it was agony."

"And this man, this Ivan. He was there?"

"For the good it did. He seemed a rather stupid brute. He grieved. Clearly he adored her in his way, but I think she considered him little more than a device."

"Device?"

"Or excuse. I think Mulan's tragedy is that she was unable to love."

Paul squinted at the reflections on the surface of the pond.

"She wrote you about Ivan, then?" Hope asked.

He coughed and lit a cigarette. "Bolshevik. One of Dalin's customers. He spoke no Chinese, only Russian and English. Dalin speaks neither, but Mulan spoke English. So she was their translator."

"Do you think Dalin knows?"

Paul reached inside his jacket and handed her a telegram. The message read, *"Kung hsi."* Congratulations.

Hope shuddered. "What a monster."

"Yes." He stared at the paper for a moment, then took it and folded it back into his pocket.

"Paul?"

"Mm."

"Was I wrong to go to her?"

He blew a stream of smoke and ground the cigarette under his heel. "There is no wrong or right in such matters. She would have her way. I regret only the sorrow she has brought to your eyes, Hsin-hsin. For that, I can never forgive her."

૭ઙૐ

7

Are you out of your bloody mind!" Sarah slammed her cup down in its saucer, splashing tea all over the new teakwood table. "You're forty-two years old. You've a child old enough to marry. You hardly ever see your husband, and half the time you're scraping bottom just to keep everyone fed and clothed. You *can't* be serious, Hope!"

"I didn't invite you all the way to Kuling so you could scream at me like some underfed fishwife." Hope shoved her sewing aside and bit into a piece of salted plum, which Ah-nie swore would settle her stomach.

"Surely you don't *want* this baby," pressed Sarah.

"How could I not?"

"Easily. Isn't Jazz enough of a handful?"

Hope looked down past the verandah railing to the stream, where the younger children were fishing with bamboo poles and bits of duck fat for lures. Eleven-year-old Morris and Sarah's little Ken were perched on a rock, carefully angling their rods out to the deepest pool, while six-year-old Jasmine pranced along the edge, her dress soaked nearly to the waist. There was a time when Hope would have called her in and upbraided her, sent her to her room. Now she merely sighed.

"She is that. But it's nothing to do with this baby. If I *can* pull it off at my grand old age, I'm sure not going to refuse!"

Sarah folded her arms. "The odds aren't good, you know."

"Thank you for pointing that out. I'd remind you, Sarah, that in my case, the odds have never been good, yet I've beaten a few of them."

"Indeed." Sarah squinted at her. "You *really* still feel . . . ?"

Pearl and Gerald came out of the house, slamming the screen behind them. Pearl wore a loose blue shift and had a towel rolled under her arm. "We're going to pick up Dottie Cheung and meet some chums at the Paradise for a swim." Pearl leaned down to give her mother a kiss. "Be back by six. Need us to pick up anything in the valley?"

"No thanks." Hope hesitated. "A swim sounds good, though. Would you die of embarrassment if we brought the younger ones over?"

Pearl laughed, shaking her curls back from her face. "Spying on us, eh? Well, sure, Mama. It's a free country."

"Is it, now?" said Sarah. "First I've heard."

Gerald piped up. "It's what that American bloke Donald Osborne says all the time. Pearl's soft on him."

Pearl punched him in the arm. "Am not!"

"You're too young to be soft on anyone," said Hope firmly. "Now off with you. If we see you, we see you."

"And you don't think you've got your hands full?" said Sarah as the two chased each other down the trail.

Hope ignored her. "I really could use a swim."

"You never did tell me about you and Paul."

"You never did ask," Hope retorted.

"Well, there *was* a time I thought things had pretty well dried up, least on your part."

"Times change." Hope stood and stretched her arms above her head, twisting from the waist. "Remember corsets? That awful feeling you couldn't *breathe.*"

"You're changing the subject."

Hope turned and shouted to Morris to bring the others in.

Behind her, Sarah said, "Do you never even wonder about Stephen Mann?"

The nausea overcame Hope so suddenly that she vomited over the porch railing. Unperturbed, Sarah handed her a damp napkin to wipe her mouth. "You poor sop. You do, don't you?"

"What a question! No. I don't."

Sarah pointed to the boys hauling Jasmine out of the stream. "Looks like she hardly needs more swimming." Then, "Would you like some help? At forgetting him, that is?"

Hope threw her a suspicious glance.

"A few weeks back, when I took the boys over to Ste. Marie's for their physicals, I heard one of the nurses mention Dr. Mann's name. I asked how he was, and she showed me an announcement they'd just received about his appointment as chief of surgery at Chungking Inland Hospital."

Hope leaned back against the railing. "Good for him."

"The notice included a short biography." Sarah paused. "It said he was married, Hope. To Anna Van Zyl."

Sarah's face brimmed with concern. In that moment, Hope despised her.

"I only tell you," she hurried on, "because you are carrying your husband's child, and you said you want to forget him."

"And since when did you become so wise and noble?"

"Touchy!" Sarah waved to the fishermen tramping up the path, then reached into her shirtdress pocket. "Here."

Hope looked at the professional card Sarah had given her. *T. C. Wong, M.D., Ladies' therapies and remedies.*

"In case you change your mind about this baby," said Sarah.

"You snake." Hope started to rip the card, but Sarah stopped her.

"He's first-rate." They locked eyes.

"I don't want to know."

"You needn't," Sarah said. "But for once in your life, Hope, don't close off your options."

Hope shoved the card into her sewing box to hide it from the children. When she turned, Jasmine stood dripping on the verandah steps, her face a delirious shimmer of pride, in her hand a wriggling trout.

ॐॐॐ

By the following Christmas Hope was six months pregnant, nearly free of morning sickness, and (against her better judgment) expecting Paul home for dinner with William Tan and family. She had decorated the house with boughs of holly and monkey pine, had found a splendid miniature gray fir tree on Flower Street, which the children had trimmed with tiny silver bells and blown glass baubles collected over the years. Dahsoo had a suckling pig roasting, a wood fire was blazing, and the big house on Rue de Grouchy felt as homey as any on the Kansas plains. By four o'clock, the table was laid, the children were dressed in new velveteen and serge outfits, and Daisy had arrived with young Kuochang, now a handsome boy of eight and the mirror image of his mother—or aunt, as he was taught to call Suyun. Paul and William had been scheduled to arrive two nights earlier, but both wives were experienced enough to proceed on their own—the men would turn up or not.

Unfortunately, Hope had been unable to rekindle her original warm feelings for Daisy. Quite apart from her treatment of Suyun, Daisy had, since her return to Shanghai, embraced her role as a "modern woman" with a zeal that Hope found offensive. She had become enamored of foreign-style nightclubs, racetracks, and casinos. She had pursued friendships with the wives of the city's most powerful men, including the concubines of the legendary Tu Yueh-sheng, the rags-to-riches mobster who reputedly controlled the city's opium and arms trade. "The wives are simple girls," she told Hope, "but what jewels they wear! What influence they have at their fingertips!" As the daughter of a favored fourth wife to a well-to-do silver merchant in Hupei, Daisy had a cultivated appreciation both for wealth and "influence" and for the ability of certain women to access both, via the bedroom. Since William's political status was as precarious as Paul's, Hope was not altogether surprised when rumors floated back through Pearl's school chums (particularly the boys, who, at sixteen, already frequented the city's most decadent entertainments) that Daisy had been seen on the arm of men who were decidedly not her husband. There was, however, no intimation that William disapproved. Paul went so far as to speculate that Daisy was serving as William's, and by extension Sun Yat-sen's, spy. If Sun needed reports on how many sables Chingmei wore over her beaded gown or the number of diamonds sparkling on Jade Bell's fingers, Hope decided the revolution must have fallen into a terminal stage. Certainly, when Daisy spoke to Hope about her adventures, this was the level of intelligence. Hope resisted her visits unless, as tonight, Paul himself had made the invitation.

And so the two women sat as twilight descended. Pearl and Jasmine were pounding out a ragtime tune on the piano. Morris had his nose in a book, and Kuochang sat with his hands between his knees, silent as a deaf-mute. Hope asked, "Where are you in school now, Kuochang?"

"I have him enrolled at the Ecole," Daisy answered for him. "He is very happy there. Look, Ho-pah, did I show you what my William gives to me?" She pulled up the sleeve of her raw silk jacket and twisted her wrist to the light. The gold watch was encrusted with emeralds, a seed pearl embedded in the stem.

"Ah," said Hope. "It's after five. I suppose we should go ahead without them."

Daisy's face crumpled. "You no like?"

"It's lovely." Hope sighed. "William must adore you, Daisy. Morris, would you put that book down and take poor Kuochang up to your room. He must be desperately bored sitting here with us."

"Kuochang no mind," Daisy protested, but before Hope had a chance to press her case, the telltale flutter of voices sounded out by the front gate, and she heard Paul and William calling loudly for their suppers and their wives.

Half an hour later the two families were assembled around the large circular table in the reception hall that doubled as a formal dining room. The children sat at one side, the adults the other, with Pearl and Morris poised in between and struggling to keep up with two very different conversations.

"I hear the Chinese boys at Ecole get paddled every day," said Jasmine, "and you're made to carry the French boys' towels and shine their shoes."

"Jazz!" hissed Pearl.

Kuochang shrugged and spooned his soup. "Sometimes."

"But you get back at them, too," said Morris. "Don't you?"

Hope was about to break up this discussion when she was distracted by the men's laughter at her own side of the table. "Hope," said William with an injured look, "do you know your husband has replaced me with a Russian as his new best friend?"

"A Russian!" Hope saw that he was joking. Nevertheless, she recoiled at the image he'd prompted, of Ivan standing over Mulan's dead body.

Paul, seated beside her, poured some claret into her glass and urged her to drink. "William provokes you. It is Sun who is this Borodin's best friend—to hear the Bolsheviks tell it."

"What *are* you talking about?" said Hope.

William pulled himself up in his seat and placed one hand across his breast, drew a finger mustache and intoned, "Mikhail Borodin, come to save Chinese Revolution in name of Comrade Lenin."

"I hear something about this man." Daisy licked her spoon like a cat. "His wife is American, I think. But very plain and fat."

"In Daisy's mind, the only thing of interest about any man is his wife," laughed William. "I wonder what that says about me."

"But what's he to do with you, Paul?" There was an excessive brilliance to this banter that alarmed Hope.

"Nothing more, if I can help it."

"Humble!" cried William. "I have never met a more humble man. I will venture that you do not know you are married to a national hero, Hope."

"I believe I am."

"Ah! But I hear in your voice some uncertainty. You do not know of his secret missions."

"Which ones?"

The word "secret" had registered at the other end of the table, and now all ears were directed to William. He raised his glass and drank to the health of Paul's children. "Your father can make a dragon smile. He can make a snake shake hands. He can change the course of rivers and turn the tides of the sea."

The children rolled their eyes and went back to arguing about which was the best bonbonnière in the Settlement.

William continued, once more addressing Hope. "Your Paul's silver tongue has held off more than one warlord from Sun's door. He has traveled to Peking under cover of darkness. He has brought troops to the rescue when our Dr. Sun was in his darkest hours. And for this, young Borodin comes along and puts our hero on trial!"

Hope's spoon struck her bowl. "On trial!"

"Let William tell the story." Paul patted her hand. But for Hope, who knew little of the rapidly mounting influence of Russian advisors in Sun's ranks, and even less of the young *sovetnik* Borodin, it would take the entire dinner, plus hours more over tea and brandy, before she had a clear understanding of just what her husband had endured these past weeks.

Mikhail Borodin was a veteran of Russia's recent Bolshevik revolution, a friend of Stalin's, and a professional revolutionist who had come to China by way of England and America (where he had indeed taken a wife and produced two American-born children). He had arrived in Canton not three months earlier to woo Sun with promises of Russian funding, arms, and all the military expertise required to secure Sun's power base in the south. Sun called Borodin his "Lafayette," and looked to him to help the Kuomintang develop its own army while, at the same time, building a secure and self-supporting government. Borodin had promptly proven his usefulness by directing Sun's victory against a new rebellion by the Cantonese warlord Ch'en Chiung-ming.

Paul, who was on the Kuomintang's Executive Committee, had his first run-in with Borodin during the negotiations for this campaign. The key to Sun's success, said Borodin, lay in mobilizing the masses into a volunteer army of millions. But in order to attract these peasants and workers, Sun's government must promise labor reform. Land must be redistributed to those who actually worked it. Wages must be raised. Workdays must be shortened, taxes controlled.

Recalling the strains between Jin and Paul on these very issues, Hope could imagine her husband's response to Mikhail Borodin. "Big mouth," Sun Yat-sen used to call Paul in jest. He still had not learned his lesson.

Paul explained to Borodin that these reforms would constitute treason against Sun's strongest supporters: the scholars, gentry, and merchant classes responsible for China's liberation from the Manchus. They had given their blood and millions of dollars for Dr. Sun's vision of a new China, and they did not expect as repayment to be stripped of everything they owned. Moreover, they would marshal their considerable resources to *ensure* that this did not happen. Paul informed Borodin that the Executive Committee refused to sign his decree.

Borodin went ahead and organized a patchwork of troops from the Chinese Communist and socialist organizations and local volunteers. Some six hundred recruits were sent to the front. The warlord backed down, and Borodin claimed Sun's confidence. He needed the "old man," as he called Sun, to achieve his aims in China. But he did not need opposition like that mounted by Liang Po-yu.

Two days before they were to return to Shanghai for Christmas, Paul and William, who was also a member of the Executive Committee, were called to meet with Borodin at the old cement factory on the outskirts of Canton, which Sun used as his headquarters during periods when the Presidential Palace fell to warlord control. Guards in Kuomintang uniforms stood by the rear door and bowed respectfully as the two entered. More guards stood inside. The two men were ushered into a large square chamber, empty except for a bank of straight-backed chairs and a single table at which Borodin was seated. Borodin was a decade younger than Paul and William, but several inches taller, powerfully built, with a large square forehead, glowering dark eyes, and a thick mustache that seemed to give him a perpetual sneer. He nodded to Paul and William and asked them to be seated while they awaited the other "witnesses."

The atmosphere was highlighted, William said, by a continuous rain of dust particles and the incessant flapping of a pigeon trapped beneath the exposed roof beams.

At length three more members of the committee entered, all clearly as mystified as William and Paul. "Comrades," Borodin addressed them in English, which, because Borodin spoke no Chinese, was rapidly becoming the "official" language of the Kuomintang. "Russia's Supreme Soviet was not fully established until Vladimir Lenin killed a few of its oldest members—those whose true hearts still lay with the bourgeois regime. It has been decided that the Chinese Kuomintang should do the same."

With this encouraging introduction, he went on to reinvent several of Paul's secret missions to northern and local warlords as treason against Sun Yat-sen. "You were the intermediary who arranged for warlord Fan's troops to pressure Dr. Sun into accepting an alliance. And you—" he glared across the row of committee members, "were his accomplices."

By this point in the telling, William was fully fired with claret and brandy, and he jumped up and strode about the room. The children straddled stools and perched on chair arms. Paul had tried to shoo at least his own children away after dinner, but now the scent of blood was in the air and Pearl insisted they deserved to know *something* of what their father did for a living. Hope silently remarked that of all the reasons Paul did what he did, a living was hardly one of them, but to the children she held her peace. If their father was a hero, as William insisted, then they did deserve to know of that.

"You have twisted the meaning of these missions," Paul had said as he stood and marched up to Borodin. "You know nothing of my loyalty to Sun or anything about these men. But if you want to know who was in charge—who is responsible—then do not go further. I am responsible, Comrade Borodin."

Borodin sat dumbfounded, the more because Paul had delivered this rebuke entirely in Russian. It was the first time the Bolshevik had ever heard his native language spoken by a Chinese.

Seconds passed while Borodin considered his options. At length the Russian gave a grim smile and stood, reaching into the pocket of his frayed green jacket. He pulled out one of his Russian cigarettes, handed it to Paul, and, shaking his head, said, "You, my friend, are a man."

Even Borodin's handpicked soldiers lowered their rifles at that. The Russian let out a roar of laughter, as if the entire proceedings were some Machiavellian joke. Then he bade them farewell, saying that he was traveling north for the next few weeks, but would see them when the National Congress convened at the end of January.

"Dr. Sun was moved to tears when he learned what had happened," said William. "He issued a proclamation of our loyalty and dedication to the party. And that was the end of the whole sordid business. But if it had not been for your husband, I think we might well have ended like that pigeon."

"What happened to the pigeon?" Jasmine asked in a husky voice.

"As we were leaving one of the soldiers shot it to end its misery."

"William!" Daisy covered her face.

"Unfortunately, that is not quite the end of the story," said Paul. "Borodin was berthed next to us on the steamer, so we have had the pleasure of his company for the past three days."

"Your new best friend, eh?" Hope lifted her eyebrow. She could not decide which was the stronger emotion: rage at William's jocular attitude or horror at the peril they had barely managed to escape.

Paul drew a fistful of gold from his pocket. "I don't think our comrade would quite agree."

William let out a guffaw. *"Pai gow,"* he said. "He had never played it before, and he refused to stop. This is a bad combination when faced with an expert like Paul."

Hope made no comment about William's story until after the Tans had left, and she and Paul were alone in their room. He lay on the bed, catching up with the Shanghai papers. She sat at her dressing table brushing her hair. She spoke to the mirror. "You would never have told me, would you? If William hadn't started in?"

"William exaggerates," he said.

"He did not make it up."

"Borodin is a mosquito parading as a tiger." He laid his papers aside and came behind her, still speaking to her reflection. He had removed his spectacles, so that she was aware of the deep gray circles beneath his eyes. Much of the weight the meningitis had taken off him was now returned, but he still had a tendency to look gaunt and exhausted.

"You were about to be put before the firing squad, Paul."

"That was never his intention."

Hope dug the bristles into her scalp and pulled in long, measured strokes. The white streaks running from her temple and nape highlighted the absurdity of her pregnant condition. He touched her hair as if he couldn't see them.

"I understand you can't quit," she said, twisting to face him, "but why must you continually *raise* the stakes!"

"Would you have me be a clerk?" Paul lifted an eyebrow. "Or perhaps I could serve as the young Madame Sun's assistant?"

"Oh, stop!" Hope jerked back toward the mirror in vexation. "Is there no middle ground for you?"

Paul smiled, stubbornly sliding his hands over her shoulders and down the front of her silk dressing gown. He cupped a breast in each palm. "This will be a very happy baby, I think."

When she did not respond, he caught her eyes in the mirror in such a way that, between his gaze and the solid warmth of his body, she felt pinned inside him. "You, Hsin-hsin," he said softly. "You are my middle ground."

ॐॐॐ

8

Theodore Newfield Leon was born laughing. "Never have I seen such a baby," said the Danish woman doctor who delivered him. "Not a cry, not a wail, but a grand, gurgling giggle. A little Buddha, you have here!"

Indeed, to Hope's somewhat surprised relief, Teddy was none the worse for his mother's advanced age, had all the requisite digits and appendages, and showed such a hale constitution that when Jasmine broke out with chicken pox three days after his arrival, Teddy alone of the children was immune.

Paul, who made it a point to be on hand for the birth, took a special pride in this son. He insisted on a Completion of the Month party for the child, at which the Tans and Eugene Chou and Sarah (Paul was courting Eugene as a financier for the Kuomintang) all bore witness as the baby was presented with the career tray of scholar's brush, toy sword, abacus, official seal, herbs, compass, and slide rule. When the little arms shot out simultaneously for brush and sword, the men, who had placed drinking wagers on the selection, shouted their approval for this young scholar of the revolution.

But the pride that Paul lavished on this newest child did not make up for the time and attention he withheld from the others as they grew older and become preoccupied with their mostly foreign friends and activities. Nor did it halt the stealthy erosion of respect for their father that Hope had detected (in spite of William's heroic tales) over the past few years. More than once she had caught Pearl and Jasmine mimicking the singsong of his late-night drinking parties, or lampooning his poems as if they were children's limericks. Pearl flirted openly with the German boy who lived next door, often wondering loudly what Papa would think if his daughter were to marry "the enemy." Morris responded to his father's presence by retreating to his room and his books—not the histories of the Taiping and Boxer Rebellions that Paul urged on him, or even the Conrad and Hawthorne that Hope gave him, but newly imported works by writers such as F. Scott Fitzgerald, D. H. Lawrence, Apollinaire, and Aldous Huxley. Hope suspected that the children's resentments were exacerbated by their continuing affection for Jin, who had secured a position (of which Paul approved) as artistic designer for a publishing company on Honan Road, but spent his free time organizing a new workers' political party (of which Paul disapproved). She tried to talk to them—including Jin—to encourage their respect and to demand at least courtesy toward their father and his friends. They would answer her with patient, long-suffering faces, nod politely, and fold their hands, but she knew that, while she might force their conduct, their hearts were closing.

That summer an incident occurred in Kuling that brought this conflict into painful focus. They had been woken before dawn by a shattering cry, followed by shouting and slapping, the thump of flesh against wood. Lamps were lit, and the whole family assembled on the porch, where Yen held a slight, darkly clad figure, lifting him practically off his feet.

"Thief!" Yen declared, yanking the boy's elbows to show how his threadbare pockets bulged. Yen had caught him halfway out the window.

The children smirked. Ah-nie shook her head and padded back to check on the sleeping Teddy. But Paul was beside himself. He began screaming for Dahsoo to go straight away and fetch village police chief

Liu. At the same time, he turned on the children, waving his arms and barking at them to stand back, then at the boy to—quickly!—turn out his pockets. But the sight of their silverware, a brass clock, Pearl's tiger-eye pendant, and a silver matchbox that had belonged to Nai-li proved more than he could bear. While Yen jerked the thief back from the trove, Paul clapped his hands and paced, roaring at the boy. With wide, desperate eyes he looked to Hope, to the children, then back to the thief, who stood rigid, staring at the floor. There was a moment's stillness. Then, as if jabbed by a pin, Paul began flailing his own cheeks, bringing tears to his eyes. He shouted at Yen, "Slap his face! Slap his face!"

Jasmine burst out laughing and tripped over the threshold, sprawling across the parlor floor. This only made Paul more furious, and he began hopping from foot to foot. Hope was mortified. She had never seen such a display, and hoped she never would again. She instructed Pearl to get Jasmine to her room—Morris was already long gone. Then she shook out a cigarette from the pot by the sofa and handed it to Paul. He took it without looking at her, then the match that followed. The cigarette wobbled as he lit it. At last the bouncing lantern announced Dahsoo's return with Chief Liu.

Paul stood silent while Yen delivered his account of catching the thief. Then, with an exactitude that surprised Hope, given his agitation, Paul provided a full inventory of the retrieved goods. Chief Liu, a self-important character with gap teeth and unruly eyebrows, accepted a cigarette as the boy turned out his pockets again and Yen shook his sleeves and trousers. A costume ring of Jasmine's was added to the recovered pile. Then the chief demanded the boy's name. He recognized it from the list of sedan chair bearers, which was routinely submitted to him by the Gap transportation office because, as he said with a scowl at the thief, "These coolies no good."

Yen was noted as a witness and the thief led away with his wrists in chains. Without a word, Paul slipped upstairs to his study, leaving Hope alone to the sunrise.

It was a glorious one, with slivers of magenta and molten gold shooting across the valley, but Hope felt as if it were mocking her. Only the baby would be spared, she thought. For the others, this morning's slapstick image of their father would remain as damning as her own memory of Paul prostrating himself for his mother. No revolutionary act of heroism, no exquisitely reasoned essay or acclaimed poetic composition could erase the memory of such ineffectuality. Nor would they take into account whatever bizarre childhood torments must have accounted for this lapse. What mattered, what made Paul's outburst so indelible was that this was the truest, most intimate glimpse of him that his children had ever known.

ᔥᔥᔥ

Presidential Palace
Canton
October 12, 1924
Dearest Hope,
A new warlord, Feng Yu-hsiang, has taken Peking. He is Christian, a pragmatist, an admirer of Sun. This is good news. He wants peace talks between key factions by January. But this gives less than three months for us to build a unification plan that will satisfy all—Borodin, the Kuomintang's merchant supporters, and the warlords who will be seated at this table.

I leave today for Hupei to arrange with leaders there to support this peace plan, then on to meet Dr. Sun in Tientsin. I hope maybe I can return to Shanghai for Christmas, but now I cannot predict. I am sending what I can, six hundred dollars for you until my return. I so miss our little Teddy. And all our babies.

Take good care of our home.
Your husband, Paul

Tientsin
December 20, 1924
Dearest Hope,
Sun has arrived from Japan, and we have met. He is gravely ill, but in good spirits in spite of fact that peace talks have been thwarted. You remember Madame Shen's old "uncle" Tuan Ch'i-jui? Well, he brought his troops into Peking while Feng

Yu-hsiang was here in Tientsin, and seized government for himself. This ends all hope of cooperation among the northern warlords; however, Dr. Sun wishes now to go forward with a plan William and I have brokered to establish new Nationalist capital in Wuhan. There on his sickbed, Dr. Sun affixed his seal to the document of intent. I am hopeful this may lead to some good.

Now that the agreement has been sealed, however, William and I must go to Wuhan for some weeks to negotiate terms of this agreement. I am sorry to miss our Christmas together, but I have enclosed some little cash for you to buy presents for the babies.

I will be home as soon as possible.

Your husband, Paul

Peking

March 13, 1925

Dearest Hope,

I feel as I have lost my elder brother. I was summoned from Wuhan just few days ago. I arrived to find that Dr. Sun had lost faith in Western medicine, and had taken some Chinese herbs. His eyes were bulging and he could not speak. Soon he was gone, and all the future—my own and China's—forever changed.

I have been traveling a great deal these past weeks. Many times it has seemed that we had peace at our fingertips. Now all dreams are dashed. We have no leader with strength or vision to replace Dr. Sun. Borodin toys with his puppets. The northern warlords again circle like vultures. Young marshal Chiang Kai-shek, the commandant of the new soldiers' academy in Canton, talks of going ahead with the great military march northward from Canton which was Sun's dream for unifying the country under the Kuomintang, but there is little support for this now.

Sun's funeral will take place next month, here in the Western

Hills. Many hundreds of thousands will march in his procession. I must join them. Then I return to Shanghai.

Beyond this, I do not know. I face a mountain with no way around. I wish you were here, my wife. I wish you with me.

Your husband,

Paul

XI
FIFTH SEASON
KULING AND WUHAN
(1926–1927)

᭰᭰᭰

1

A shimmering June day at the Three Graces Pool. Hope and the children had come up to Kuling a couple of weeks earlier, Sarah and her two just days ago, but the summer crowd was still light, and they had the small, spring-fed lake almost to themselves. The older children were out on the raft. Jasmine and a White Russian boy she'd met that morning were wading along the shore. Hope lay back on the blanket she and Sarah were sharing while little Teddy napped on his quilt beside them.

"Your figure's come back nicely." Out of the corner of her eye Hope could see Sarah's long, slender legs gravitating toward a wedge of sunlight. "Considering your age," Sarah added.

Hope threw her a teasing moue. "I detest people who dole out compliments to their inferiors. It's a perfectly transparent ploy, you know."

"Inferiors!"

"I'm afraid, dear heart, when it comes to figures, you have me knocked. You needn't play games to make me admit it."

"Well, I . . ." But having the satisfaction she'd baited, Sarah fell judiciously silent.

She sat as if she were one of the Three Graces herself, thought Hope, the way her arms clasped loosely around her knees, her bobbed hair catch-

ing the light. It was true that Sarah had become steadily *more* beautiful over
the years. She often said her looks were her ticket to satisfaction and escape. For that very reason the subject disquieted Hope, and she resented
Sarah's not infrequent allusion that beauty was a tool they had in common.

The sun slid behind a cloud, and Hope looked up, startled, as darkness swept across Lu Shan. She wondered if the same shadow would pass
over Paul—wherever he was. The thought made her shiver.

Sarah pointed to her boys and Morris racing each other to land. Pearl
and her friend Shirley Tsai cheered them on. "They really are happy here,"
Hope said.

"So are you," said Sarah.

"Be happier if Paul were here with us."

"Nothing new in that."

"Maybe." She considered. "I hope not."

"Eugene seems to think they've actually got a chance of making good
on this Northern Expedition. And Gerry tells me Jed Israel says the same."

"I don't know, but at least it's brought Jin and Paul back onto the same
team. Paul says this young commander Chiang Kai-shek means to prove
himself as Sun Yat-sen's successor—and so is determined to make the Expedition a success. Jin's pleased because Chiang seems to have embraced
the students and workers in the process. Even Borodin has backed down
and is claiming to be a friend . . . The question is whether any of them
can be trusted."

"*Any* of them?" Sarah gave her a hard look.

Teddy stirred in his sleep. Hope tidied his coverlet, but Sarah's challenge unnerved her, and after she'd made certain that the baby was not
waking up, she reached into the pocket of her wrapper for Paul's most recent letter. She had been rereading it this morning before they set off for
the pool. Now she scanned it again, searching for the reassurance that he
had so clearly meant to convey.

> Hong Kong
> May 7, 1926
> Dearest Hope,
> I am in Hong Kong for a few days to negotiate toward end to
> the general strike here, which labor unions backed by Communists

have conducted for more than one year. We have agreement from Borodin and his faction to support a truce, but we must take care. British have fired on strikers here as they did in Shanghai, and each death raises the passion for revenge—which can only bring more slaughter and defeat. This was lesson of Taipings and Boxers, but the radical students and unschooled workers have not learned it. I spend no fondness for Borodin, but at least he now understands that power lies still with foreigners and generals, and it will take a firm union of merchant and landowner money combined with manpower of the masses to wrest China from their grip.

Young general Chiang Kai-shek understands this, too. He has studied in Japan, taken military training in Soviet Russia, and has many rich and powerful friends, so he sees all sides. He has had many tensions with the Communists and Soviet advisors in Canton, but as new commander-in-chief of the National Revolutionary Army, he has upper hand now, and so has ordered us to begin Northern Expedition next month. Our goal is Yangtze Valley. We will march in two sections with Russian aviators overhead and saboteurs assisting. I am to push northwest with first section toward Wuhan. Second section led by Gen. Chiang to travel northeast toward Nanking.

Forces are strong, morale high, many hundreds of cadets from Chiang's new military academy, plus many thousands of volunteer propagandists. Maybe Jin told you, I have requested him for my unit. If all goes well, perhaps we both meet you and babies in Kuling during August.

Please do not worry for me, Hope. There is goodwill in the countryside. People are tired of fighting and hunger. If Borodin and Chiang stand together, the country will follow.

Enclosed money will pay for steamer to Kiukiang and keep you in Kuling this summer. I am sorry not to send more, but pay is scarce. I am promised another sum when we reach Wuhan, will send to you then. For safety, best go to mountains when children's school end and stay until you hear from me. All will be well there, no fighting.

Your husband,

Paul

Sarah peered over her shoulder. "Do you know where he is?"

"Marching north from Canton. Somewhere in Hunan. I try not to think about it."

"It's hard to picture Paul and Jin as soldiers."

"Soldiers! Is that what you thought?" Hope gave a peremptory laugh. "You'd have to count words as weapons, which I guess they do, but not the way you mean. My husband is a propagandist, my dear. He may be schooled in military tactics, but he's never so much as touched a bayonet. The plan, as I understand it, is for his unit to travel *ahead* of the troops, not with them. He meets with the local officials, village leaders, and warlords, persuades them to join the United Front of the Kuomintang. Meanwhile his volunteers—like Jin—tout revolution to the villagers, so that when the soldiers march into town everyone's throwing flowers."

"Or spears. What, exactly, does Paul say to prevent them putting his head on a block?"

Hope grimaced. " 'Only the United National Front can exterminate the foreign oppressors who enslave and murder workers and children.' A cheery appeal, don't you think? But according to the reports Yen brings up from Kiukiang, it's working like a charm."

"I've lost track. Do we count as foreign oppressors, or collaborators, or both?"

"I try not to think about that either," said Hope. "Whatever the answer may be today, it's bound to be different tomorrow."

"You sound positively jaded."

"I'm tired. Poor William Cadlow. I haven't written a thing since Teddy was born, and he keeps sending pep notes to start me up again, but the truth is, I can't bear to look too closely anymore. It's getting grim, Sarah. Pithy little stories about students doing the Charleston and dressing like Theda Bara trivialize China. Yet whenever Paul tries to explain the current political situation I feel myself going numb."

"Seems to me, you could use a diversion."

Teddy rolled over, chortling, scrambled to his feet and made straight for the picnic hamper. Hope sighed, "You'd think I had enough."

Sarah, who was seated closest to the food, handed the toddler a tea biscuit. "When Jasmine and I went down valley this morning," she continued as if Hope hadn't spoken, "there was quite a commotion outside the

Fairy Glen Hotel. A man had arrived on a litter. His wife was shouting for medical help and the man was telling her to pipe down. Seems he'd decided to walk up the mountain instead of riding, and he'd slipped and broken his leg—"

"Sarah," Hope interrupted. "You're bright red."

"Oh, this good-for-nothing Irish skin. You could at least indulge me my little run-around. All right, guess who they were."

"No." Hope passed back the India rubber ball that Teddy had just tossed in her lap. "Not now, love."

"Ball," the child insisted, this time rolling it over her shoulder. "Mama p'ay."

Sarah said, "It's Stephen Mann."

Hope dropped the ball. It bounced into the lake with Teddy lurching after it. Hope grabbed him in time, but he let out such a pitiful wail that Sarah reached for her bathing cap. "I'll go." Seconds later she surfaced in the water with the red ball between her teeth. Teddy clapped and laughed uproariously.

"Was he very hurt?" Hope asked as Sarah dried herself off.

"He was sheet white. But he said hello, and apologized for not getting up. Same old gallantry." Sarah pursed her lips at Teddy, now busily admonishing the runaway ball in his own unintelligible language. When Hope failed to comment, she went on, "He introduced me to Anna. I—I didn't tell that you were here, Hope, only while he was having his leg looked after she said they meant to find a place for the summer. Then I remembered Pearl's friend Shirley saying her family could only stay the week and wanted to let their house, so I mentioned it. Anna was awfully grateful—"

"A diversion," Hope said bitterly. "You really are something, Sarah."

"What! I'm only the messenger. Don't go blaming me."

"You're evil."

"Evil, am I? And what are you? What's your Dr. Mann? We're all of us evil in our own ways. All scrambling for the good. Might as well face up to it, Hope. Think a bit, you should thank me."

ॐॐॐ

June 28, 1926

I could kill her. Strangle her with my bare hands. To a woman like Sarah love is nothing but a game or a tool. I don't think she knows the heart's even involved, but oh, how she delights in watching others writhe.

I have not seen them yet, but Shirley came this evening to say goodbye. She told us the Manns were to take their house, and I had everything I could do to keep Pearl from bounding down the valley that instant to say hello. Of course, Yen was on hand, and he flashed me a look that I could only take as a warning. Teddy was bouncing at my knee, Jazz "tightrope walking" along the porch railing, and Morris chose that moment to venture in with one of his father's cigarettes dangling from his mouth. It seems to me that all that, plus a glance in the mirror, ought to be plenty warning enough, but Yen sometimes seems the wisest of any of us. His memory is long, and his insight into human nature far deeper than we realize. There have been times, when I was taking his picture, that I felt he truly pitied me. Other times when he admired me. Never have I doubted his sympathy, and yet, for all that, his loyalty is to Paul. As he reminds me, mine is, too.

2

The Tsai house stood less than a mile from the Leons', in a meadow nestled down by the stream. From the main trail, the welcoming procession could see over the surrounding wall and into the yard. A manservant stood talking to someone inside the house, and a maid was sweeping the brick walk that connected the outer buildings. The yard was shaded by a tall silver birch, under which lay a chaise longue draped with a red plaid blanket.

As the party started down to the gate, Anna stepped from the house.

Though still at some distance, Hope was shocked by her plump, ungainly posture, the pinched expression of her face. She wore a beige chemise that fell formless to the knees. Her once ginger hair, now in an Eton crop, had gone much grayer than Hope's own, and her eyes squinted shortsightedly behind wire-rimmed glasses as she strained to make out who was coming.

"It's us, Miss Van Zyl!" Pearl waved wildly. "Pearl and Morris Leon. And Mama and her friend. Do you remember?"

Anna clapped a hand to her mouth and darted to the gate, calling behind her, "Stephen, do you hear? It's Hope *Leon* and the children. They're *here!*" By the time they reached the bottom of the hill, the gate was flung open and Anna was hurling herself into Hope's arms. "I can't believe it! After all these years? And here, of all places. Hope, it's *so* good to see you. And Pearl! No, it can't be. Morris! Little Morris. The size of you! Oh dear, you all look so wonderful." Before Hope could open her mouth, tears were spilling from Anna's still incandescent blue eyes. The glasses came off. She busied herself with a handkerchief, and hugs were exchanged all around.

"I always meant to write," said Anna. "Even before Stephen and I married, but we were always so busy—always on the move . . ."

"Never mind. It's good to see you again." Hope stopped, momentarily losing her train of thought. Sarah caught her eye. "Oh. Yes, this is Sarah Chou. You met, of course, but perhaps you didn't make the connection. Remember, I used to tell you about her in Peking?"

"The one with the beautiful auburn hair! Of course, you are." Anna looked as though she might cry all over again as Sarah munificently embraced her.

"Anna!" Mann's voice boomed from behind the birch. "Bring them, will you?"

"Beware." Anna touched Hope's elbow. "Doctors make the world's worst patients."

"Do they?" Hope's smile felt pasted on.

The red plaid of the chaise lengthened with their approach, its occupant suddenly visible. Then Anna's hand dropped away and the children fell behind her, and Hope was facing him again, saying hello, what a surprise and how was he feeling, how *had* the accident happened . . .

"I was trying to be a stoic, as usual." The familiarity of his voice caught her like a wave. His hair had receded, squaring back his forehead, and was now silvery brown. He had grown a boxcar mustache, was thinner, bonier, but the same restless colors moved through his eyes. Even with his leg in a cast and his torso cranked up onto his elbows, he seemed to tower over her.

"I thought doctors were invulnerable," she said.

"Have to be made of stone to be invulnerable." He studied her. "You look wonderful, Hope."

She turned abruptly and motioned to Pearl and Morris. "Remember the children?"

"Pearl." Mann shook his head. "You're a grown lady. And Morris. I guess a lifetime's passed."

"We've brought some things to welcome you." Pearl lifted the basket she was carrying. "And to make you well. You'll find it quite impossible to be unhealthy in Kuling."

"Delighted to hear that. Thank you."

"You are so lovely," said Anna, the old inflection turning her words to a question. She beckoned to her maidservant. "Let's have some of that ham right away, shall we? And here, An-ying, put these glorious lupines into water and bring some tea for our guests."

"So, Doctor." Sarah moved next to Hope, lacing an arm around her waist. "Do you hate me too much for keeping them a surprise?"

"Not *too* much." He grinned, and Hope pulled away. Her heart was pounding so that she was sure they must be able to hear it. She refused to look at Sarah.

"Yen's at the house with the others," said Morris, bringing two wicker chairs from the terrace. "He says hello."

"Hello to Yen," said Mann. "What others?"

"Jasmine and Teddy." Sarah fell into one of the chairs. "Hope's younger children. And my boys, Gerald and Ken."

Hope sat down. Stephen's undisguised pleasure irritated her almost as much as Sarah's glee. For her part, Anna seemed oblivious. "So many children," she sighed. "What a lucky life you lead."

"Aye, lucky!" Sarah laughed. "Now that is the word, if ever I heard one."

The servants returned with two laden tea trays, and the children seated themselves on the grass. Anna thumped her husband's pillows and raised him to a sitting position. Helping him with his teacup, lathering a biscuit with honey, she was resigned in her movements, her calm, her discipline. All the while, she talked of the ordeal of their trip. The previous week torrential rains had hit the Yangtze Valley, flooding the plains as they had two years earlier, when Hope and the children had themselves witnessed what Anna was now describing. The rain brought the river over its banks and stretched it to an inland ocean. Fields, farms, roads, and trees were all submerged, and the turgid waters would thicken here with the thatch of a roof, there the carcass of a pig or child. Steamer passengers watched whole families clinging to treetops, men paddling wooden troughs, women sitting stone-faced and mute on the island of a village parapet. Around them, water for as far as the eye could see.

"Those poor, poor people," said Anna. "Not a sign of help but what they could do for each other."

"God forbid the steamers should stop and take the poor souls aboard," said Sarah. "I know. The river was already rising when we came up. The Brits traveling with us were placing wagers on death toll predictions."

"Ugh!" Pearl wrinkled her nose. "Can't we change the subject? Here, Mama." She reached into the basket and brought up Hope's Graflex. "Let's do the picture now."

Hope sighed. She hadn't wanted to bring the camera, but the children insisted. "I hardly think Dr. Mann—"

"No," he said. "Absolutely, we should have something to remember this day."

"I still have that picture you took of us at the races." Sarah pinched Hope's arm. "Remember, Doctor?"

"How could I forget?"

Hope pretended to busy herself with the camera. In the aftermath of Chapei, she'd destroyed her own copy of that photograph, and the negative.

She stared into the viewfinder. "Something's wrong."

"Oh, Mama!" Morris spoke with disgust. At fourteen, he was a wizard at things mechanical, and only too pleased to point out when others were not. He lifted the lens hatch. Hope had no choice but to proceed.

The children posed in rakish attitudes. Anna perched behind Mann's reclining figure and smoothed her rumpled bosom. Sarah leaned against the silver birch, tugging her cloche down vampishly over one eye. But it was Stephen who thwarted her. Each time she brought the group into focus, his gaze would press through the lens so insistently that she had to look away.

Finally, she gave up. She pointed the camera, felt for the release. And shut her eyes.

∽∽∽

Pearl was right about Kuling's healing powers. Within a week Stephen Mann was up on crutches and circling his garden. Two and he was venturing as far as the Taoist shrine up the trail. By month's end he and his canvas crusher and cane were regular visitors at the Leons', often joining the family for a swim, boat ride, or round of croquet, and all remarked on the good spirits that seemed to accompany his restored athleticism. Anna took advantage of her husband's independent wanderings to go off on her own to hunt for mountain wildflowers. And Hope would maneuver around Mann's attentions by snaring the children into a game of bridge just before he arrived to make a fourth, or starting a planting project with Yen in which Mann was spontaneously included, or luring Jasmine and Teddy to a butterfly hunt or fishing expedition with Mann as wildlife expert. He bantered easily with the children, though she noticed from the first introduction that his dealings with the two younger ones were suspiciously imbalanced. "She's a feisty gal," he'd say when Jasmine jumped with both feet into muddy puddles, but little Teddy's ability at age two to pair words and pictures in Jasmine's first-grade reader drew no comment. Sometimes Hope caught him watching the boy with such a sour, resentful expression that she was tempted to shake him, *Yes, that is our baby—mine and Paul's.*

She never acted on this temptation. She never touched his hand, even in passing, and their conversation was forcibly slight. They did not speak of their time in Tientsin, much less the meeting in Chapei. But the combination of Mann's restored vigor with all that remained unsaid made Hope increasingly tense. She knew that whatever had not transpired between her and Mann had been of her own choosing. It was she who had stopped short of the open door. She who had ridden away. Yet as the weeks passed, everything twisted until she found herself blaming him for leaving, condemning him for not answering her unspoken thoughts.

Then, one languid, overcast day in early August, they sat beside each other on a low stone wall dangling their toes at Paradise Pool. The older children were swimming. Teddy toddled up the beach under Ah-nie's watch. Clusters of summer people strolled about the bathhouses or basked on the rock-strewn shore, but all were well out of earshot.

"We're even now," he said suddenly. "You needn't erect a fortress, you know."

She kept her eyes low and steady on the water. "What do I need, then?"

"That depends."

She leaned forward and smoothed her skirt across her knees. "You and Anna have never said how it happened."

"It?" Though she refused to look at his face, she could hear the sneer in his voice.

"How you fell in love."

She sensed, without knowing, that she had raised her voice. Now she overadjusted, felt him tilting closer to hear as she continued, "Was Yüan's banquet really the first time you met?"

There was an awkward moment filled with laughter from the beach and the skitter of footsteps behind them. Teddy was coming to play, but Mann took the ball from the child's outstretched hand and tossed it back to Ah-nie. Teddy turned on cue and was off and away, commanding her to throw it "like that man."

"You learned that from your dog," Hope said. "What happened to him, anyway?"

"Left him with the Dutchman who replaced me in Tientsin. His wife needed company, and the pup kept bringing up difficult memories for me." He held his eyes on her as he filled his pipe. The aroma of that cherry tobacco brought up difficult memories for Hope, too, but she said nothing.

"Yes," he continued, "that was the first time we met. Though you may recall, my attentions that evening were otherwise engaged."

She gave him an anguished look. "Don't do this."

He paused, smoking. Then he cleared his throat and went on as if she hadn't spoken. "I ran into Anna in Tientsin after—well, a few months after

I last saw you. Mrs. Morrison had her out—to cheer her up, she said. We went for tea, and in the middle Anna broke down. Seemed she'd only recently learned her fiancé was killed at the Somme." He studied the pipe cradled in his hand. "You know what they say about misery and company."

Hope lifted her face. The top of Lu Shan was buried in clouds.

"Hey, Mama! Watch!" Jasmine did a back flip off the boat dock.

"It's none of my business," said Hope, "but Anna used to talk about having a big family . . ."

He let out a short, derisive laugh. "Yes, someone sent me that article you wrote about Margaret Sanger's triumphal visit! Unfortunately, she never made it to Chungking, so I can't very well blame it on her, can I?"

"I'm sorry—" The bitterness of his tone jolted her. She should have known better.

"Why? It's hardly your fault." Mann snapped his pipe against the wall, emptying it into the water.

"But Anna seems," Hope faltered, "—she seems happy?"

"Ah." He nodded. "Well, yes, and if you believe that, you must believe the change in her is the kindly mark of time. Maybe so. Maybe she was destined from the start to become a fat, humorless matron by thirty, but for some reason I didn't see that seven years ago."

"That's unkind."

"No, vicious. After all, she's my nurse, my escort, my guardian angel. But there's one thing she's not, Hope."

A sudden leveling of his voice forced her to look him full in the face. His eyes were burning and the whole length of his body stretched taut as he reached for her. "Hope," he repeated urgently.

But in that breath she was up and racing for the beach. Her skirt pushed against her legs, her cries sprang out ahead of her. She took Teddy by surprise, caught him into her arms too suddenly, spun him too rapidly, but he laughed as she knew he would, his straight black hair flying into her mouth, his wide eyes snapping, little fingers grabbing her ears and neck. The boy squealed as he pulled her hat free, sent it sailing over the waves. Then mother and son ran pell-mell, splashing heedless as the water crawled up her skirt and Teddy, sensing nothing but fun, scooped up the boater and plopped it on his head, biting the sodden streamers.

"I love you," she cried. "You know, you know, you know I love you!"

வெவெவெ

A few nights later Hope woke from a dream of the Great Earthquake. The floor had opened and she had fallen into the arms of a man she could not see. He held her, rocked her, stroked her bare skin, but when she tried to look at him, she could not move. When she tried to speak, she could not open her eyes. And when she tried to think, she was convinced that she had died.

For several minutes she sat in the dark, desperate for consciousness. She could hear the rain on the roof, now stopping, and a dull whisking sound marked some small creature scurrying beneath the floorboards. Otherwise, the household was asleep. As you should be, she told herself, pressing her head back into the pillow. But the dream had left her restless, and her eyes, which had refused to open, now would not stay closed. She was thinking of Paul in some village hut, billeted with propagandists and guards. She was thinking of Stephen at Paradise Pool, still reaching . . .

She lit the lamp beside her bed. It was three-thirty. She had long intended to photograph the sunrise from Lion's Leap, and this morning, after the rain, it would be a beauty. Hurriedly she put up her hair and dressed, threw on an old wool jacket and Paul's broad-brimmed hat. She snuffed the lamp and tiptoed out in her stockinged feet, walking boots under one arm and the Graflex slung from the other. A few weeks ago Stephen had been talking about the role of mountains in Taoist philosophy as the birthplace of "the ten thousand things," the place where *yin* and *yang* are forever trading places. Perhaps she could fashion an article out of this for Cadlow.

The path to Lion's Leap followed the ridge above the Manns', and though it was too dark to see her watch—she hadn't brought a lantern— Hope calculated that it was about four when she reached their turnoff. She saw no lights. The only sounds were the soughing treetops and the hiss of the running stream. Yet she stopped as if she had detected something out of the ordinary. She scanned the moonlit walls, the black square windows. The courtyard was empty. There was no sign of a prowler, she thought, and she had no business standing here, watching in the dark.

Still, the quiet held her. She could hear each drop of moisture fall, each rustling leaf. Each breath.

She shuddered and moved on. But she had gone only a few feet when a loud crack sounded from inside the house. Then a more measured creaking, as of furniture being moved, unwilling doors being opened. A bat swept over her head, so close that she could feel its wings. She choked back a cry and crouched down low, covering her face as Stephen's voice rose through the darkness. "For me," he was saying, "that's why."

But then the creaking began again—"Goddammit, woman!"

Hope fled. The camera beat against her hip. Her hands were coated with sweat. Her hair had come loose and her boots untied, but she kept on without stopping, stumbling over tree roots and slipping in mud. It was two miles to the Leap, straight uphill. Never once did she look back.

When she reached her destination, she could not think why she had come. The sunrise was nothing but colored air. And the valley was underwater.

Hope stepped back from the three-thousand-foot drop, kneeling against a spasm of vertigo. She was about to turn and leave when she noticed, off to her right, a finger of land rising out of a cloud. On its back grew two stunted peach trees, late fruit still clinging to the limbs.

Peaches, Hope recalled, were considered the food of Immortals, a symbol of longevity, and so, even though they were foreign to the mountain terrain, Taoist priests planted these trees in hopes of pleasing the gods. Doubtless there had once been a whole orchard on this spit of land, but the winters here were hard. These two rugged spirits alone had survived, standing side by side, close enough together that their roots must touch, though not their branches.

She lifted the camera to her eye, adjusted for the changing light. But the closer she looked, the less interested she became in the trees themselves, and the more in the space between them. Fluid, open-ended, slightly uneven and so eternally unpredictable, that empty shape had a beauty all its own, which she was only beginning to see.

∽∽∽

Hengyang, Hunan
August 10, 1926
Dearest,

I am told dispatch will be sent to Kiukiang this evening and with little cumshaw, this letter may reach you one week's time. It is first opportunity I have to write. I trust you can understand.

We have many victories with little bloodshed during our march from Kwangtung. Countryside people know little of revolution. Many do not know even the Manchus have fallen. All that is far away. But they know the warlords still seize their homes. They know dams and aqueducts are broken, fields flood in rain, dry up in drought, governors do nothing to fix. Or to stop usurers double their fees after each plague of locusts. All our friend Mr. Borodin and his *sovetniki* exploit very well.

The students of my unit remind me of myself, my days in Hupei and Japan. They keep me awake late at night to discuss theories of Marx and Abraham Lincoln, ask if I defend the slaves and American Indians when in California! They amuse themselves to write manifestos and debate if social justice means all men should have only one wife or all women have many husbands. They call everyone "comrade," distribute handbooks to villagers who cannot read, and sing Internationale in Russian that no one can understand. I am glad Mr. Borodin does not travel with us. I have heard him sing in Canton. His voice very much like a frog.

My role as elder statesman is not to sing or distribute pamphlets. I meet with local governor in each town. I drink tea and thank this warlord for receiving me. All have heard of the discipline and training of General Chiang's cadets and of the Soviet weapons they carry. Warlord knows better than I how many of our revolutionary troops follow close behind us. But I cup my ear when one of our airplanes flies over. I comment that our National Revolutionary Army has doubled with new volunteers since leaving Canton. Then I invite this warlord to join our most honorable campaign, that our troops may consider him ally rather than enemy. Sometimes we visit two or three times before we reach agreement. But never more than four times.

I describe these things that you will not worry. Our progress is slow but steady. Until last week, Jin was assigned to this same unit. Now he goes ahead to Changsha. There is talk of a push to Wuhan in next weeks, and we are promised full pay with this victory.

Hope, I have no money to send now, but please do not worry. I will be paid soon. I will send to you. Still possible I can bring to you. For now, I am sure Yen takes good care of you and our babies. You are safe in our house. I keep your picture against my breast as I march. I sleep with it near me. There are many young girls in these propaganda units. They are strong and proud of their independence. Today as I watch one of them pasting up her wall poster, I remember you and Mary Jane with your banners for suffrage. My heart weeps at such memories. I do not forget you are my wife.

I am your husband, Paul

3

August 26, 1926

They're gone. The fighting that Paul wrote about reached Hankow this week, and Anna announced rather shrilly that she and Mann must return to civilization. As the river back to Chungking is closed, they are traveling with Sarah and the boys to Shanghai. Anna is making noises about returning from there to South Africa, and Mann seems indifferent, so I expect they'll have left by the time we get back to the city. Sarah tried to persuade me to go with them, and for practical reasons that might have made sense—if we had the funds. But Paul's letter has taken its toll on me, and the prospect of four or five days on the river in the Manns' constant company seemed about as inviting as a week in chains.

I'm relieved, frankly. It was never more than infatuation. I understand that now. I look at the transformation in Anna, and I cannot help but think that it takes two. I always imagined Mann was destined for greatness—a free thinker, a champion of the poor and downtrodden, a compassionate human being. Yet now I'm inclined to believe he is not so different from those men who hang about the Shanghai clubs—men imprisoned by that fatal combination of dashing good looks and an inborn craving for control. Oh, he means to do well. I expect that's why he spent all those years adventuring—trying to submerge his true nature under the banners of Good Works and Meaning. Only to end up in Chungking—the end of the world—with a barren wife. He warned me clearly enough in Tientsin, but I refused to listen. I heard only that he was in love with me.

How could any two men be more opposite than Paul and Mann? One so indefatigably genuine and the other so full of unconscious guile. I think it quite possible that Paul never should have married, while Mann, I see now, would wither up and die without a wife. Yet I would not exchange my husband. Not for all the comfort and security or companionship he's denied me. The difference between Paul and Stephen Mann is that Paul, for all his distractions and divided loyalties, genuinely loves me with all his heart, while Mann can love only the reflection I provide him of himself.

ॐॐॐ

But Hope's relief at the Manns' departure faded as the weeks trudged on and there was no further word from Paul. While August passed into September and the days grew shorter and colder, the twin valleys rang with the hammering of boards over windows, the clink of silver and china being packed, husbands arguing fares with sedan chair carriers and wives with household servants over their season's-end tip, or cumshaw. At last the chairs would line up by each gate, belongings piled high, restive children scolded, and the bearers would grunt their signal to hoist the poles. By the middle of the month, the valley was empty. All the local servants—including their own cook—returned to winter homes and jobs down the mountain in Kiukiang. The rafts at Paradise and Three Graces were beached, the dressing rooms padlocked, rowboats tarped. The hotels of the lower valley were shuttered, the main resort's churches, shops, and clubs all closed. There remained only a minuscule year-round colony, the two-man police force, and, on the far side of the valley, the Kuling American School. This boarding school, with its incongruously solid and austere Tudor campus, was attended primarily by children of foreigners assigned to the interior. Its grim presence and the occasional appearance of a uniformed student in the deserted village were stark reminders, as if the family needed any, of the Leon children's limbo.

Hope did what she could about this. Over the years, along with Pearl's nickel romances and Morris's Sherlock Holmes adventures, copies of *Ivanhoe, Bleak House, Sister Carrie, Paradise Lost,* and *Howard's End* had come to Kuling. Hope now used these as assigned reading and required critical essays of the three older children. She also contrived math and physics problems, drilled them in vocabulary and geography from Paul's tattered atlas. And while Ah-nie amused Teddy, Hope assigned herself a new series of articles for Cadlow. She wrote about building a mountain home in China, life in a Chinese resort, catching a thief in Kuling—in short, mined as much of their personal life as possible. If she was *lucky*, it would be three months before she saw a penny from these articles, but the work gave her the illusion of action and renewed a long neglected pact with herself, never to depend on Paul financially.

Concerned that soldiers might either fight their way into the valley or flee here from battles below, Hope gave strict instructions that everyone was to remain within sight of the house. They made group excursions to pick apples and pears in the orchard up the trail, and Yen and Morris went down to the stream to fish for the trout that was becoming their daily diet. But there were no hikes or "explores," and cabin fever soon descended. The children played backgammon, chess, or cards, scavenged Hope's sewing scraps to make coats, hats, and mufflers, or helped Ah-nie and Yen. But mostly, they bickered. Pearl lorded over Morris. Morris taunted

Teddy. Jasmine picked on everyone, wrestling each adversary to the ground, and often bringing on tears. An imagined slight, a crumb of biscuit, the line of a song, even memories became fodder for dispute.

"I wish I had a yellow blazer like your friend Millie Lim," Jasmine would say to Pearl.

"It's Doris Hoagland who has that blazer."

"No, it isn't."

"I should know, she's my friend."

"No, she's not. You hate her."

"Do not."

"Yes, you do. You told me, she has a face like a turnip. Anyway, I *saw* Millie wearing that blazer."

"You little liar, you don't even know what Millie looks like."

And so it would go, hour after hour, until at last, one of Morris's drawers turned up a whistle, which Hope used at regular intervals in a Pavlovian and only minimally successful attempt to reign them in.

Her only consolation was the mountain itself. By October the overnight snaps of frost had turned the valley into a patchwork of magenta and gold. At the higher elevations there was snow, and in between, the pine-covered slopes smoked with mist. Every morning now a crisp filigree of ice edged the stream, and the smell of burning wood from the stove was so singular and piercing that you could practically hear it against the surrounding silence. Under other circumstances Hope imagined that this same solitude and beauty might have moved her to tears. As it was, she could not afford to cry.

"Fifth season," Yen said one sunrise when she joined him on the verandah.

"What is fifth season?"

He waved his arm toward the view. "Old times, we have summer, winter, spring, and autumn, but also one more. Five seasons, five elements, five colors, five tones. Harmony. Fifth season comes between summer and autumn. Very short. Very bright."

Hope clasped her fingers around her teacup. "Yen?"

He squinted, watching the light.

"What do you think we should do?"

There was a pause. Then he answered quietly, "Laoyeh will send for us."

"I know how much rice is left, but only you know exactly how much money we have."

His eyes crossed slightly as they did when he was deep in thought. He did not speak.

"I need you to tell me, Yen."

She knew that for Yen to admit what she suspected would involve a catastrophic loss of face. That's why she had let the matter go this long. But, while he had stretched their funds as best he could, she also knew that he had originally budgeted only to the end of August. Frugality could take them just so far. The one shop still operating in Kuling was a combination butcher and dry goods store where they could obtain fresh pork or venison, flour, honey, cornmeal, and a few winter vegetables, but the prices were exorbitant, the black-toothed butcher Wu and his wife full of explanations why the same haw candies they had sold for a single copper a month ago now cost a thousand cash. And why the credit they had routinely extended all summer was withdrawn with the change in season.

Yen ruefully pulled from his pocket the little Moroccan-bound ledger in which he kept the household accounts—in a completely indecipherable scrawl.

But she shook her head. "I'm not accusing you, Yen. You mustn't think that. I know you've accomplished miracles, and I wouldn't blame you if we were penniless right now. But I need to know how much trouble we are in, so we can decide together what to do next." She tilted her head back to look him in the eye. "How much do we have left?"

He spoke so softly she could hardly hear him.

She felt for a chair and sat down. "That won't buy us even a week's worth of rice!"

Yen pulled on his ear, his eyes calling her attention to the swaying curtains inside. The children were up.

"All right," she said at last, with more courage than she felt. "Don't worry. I have a plan. Come with me down to the village after breakfast?"

Yen didn't answer. He had gone with her to the village after breakfast every day for a month.

The hike around the ridge to the lower valley took fifteen minutes in summer, half an hour when the rocks, as now, were skinned with ice. They encountered no one on the trail, and only a mangy dog and a curious goat in the deserted village. When they reached the low bungalow that passed for a police station, Hope stepped over the threshold without knocking, and Yen stooped under the eaves behind her. The police chief and his deputy, as usual, were playing chess, drinking tea, and smoking the American cigarettes that were part of their retainer for "guarding" the foreigners' properties. They did not look up.

"Any word?" she asked, as she did every day.

The chief's reply was, as usual, a slow and exaggerated gap-toothed grin. He wore a grease-stained brown uniform with a leather-banded cap and dangled his cigarette from the corner of his mouth as he must have seen some American actor do in a moving picture. His deputy was a wide-faced peasant boy who seemed to develop an acute interest in his fingernails whenever Hope appeared. Both of them stank richly of garlic. Unfortunately, any word from Paul must come through this station, and Hope didn't trust these men to bring it to her. When the Leons first came to Kuling, the chief had been solicitous, doffing his hat when he met them on the trail, demanding only minimal squeeze in exchange for signing their building permits and adding their property to his protectorate. Paul would chat with him about local warlords or military campaigns, and the chief seemed to respect him. At least he nodded vigorously and scratched his head rather than glowering as he did around the foreigners. But the bearer who had broken into their house two years earlier must have reported Paul's tantrum during his interrogation, for the chief's solicitude vanished thereafter.

"No word," he said now in his thick mountain dialect, bothering neither to remove the cigarette nor to address her in the English that he spoke perfectly well.

Ordinarily she would have left it at that. She wanted no more to do with this man than was absolutely necessary, but necessity had caught up with her.

"Chief Liu," she said, squaring her back. "Are you aware that my husband is a close associate of General Chiang Kai-shek?"

The man's large wadded lids slowly rose, then descended in a reptilian blink.

"He is engaged even now in the great Northern Expedition, which has liberated all of Hunan and will soon sweep the warlords out of Kiangsi. I expect his unit to arrive here in Kuling any day."

Behind her, Yen cleared his throat and swung the rough wood door shut. The room turned abruptly dank and claustrophobic, and Hope felt more than a little ridiculous standing there in her old plaid cardigan and drop-waisted linen, the brown fedora from another era yanked down over her eyes. A waking snore issued from the deputy's slack mouth, and the chief leaned back, casually flicking his cigarette stub into a chipped spittoon.

"I tell you these things," Hope forced herself to continue, "because I know you, Chief Liu, are a man of honor."

The corners of his mouth toyed with a smile, but rejected it. "You wish me to assist you in some matter I think," he said, adding as an afterthought, "missy."

"Certainly in this valley you are a man of importance," she said, "and persuasion."

He nodded, stroking the short black tuft that passed for his mustache.

"I have seen with my own eyes how Mr. Wu and Wu Taitai look up to you."

He grunted.

"If you were to say to Mr. Wu that my husband is a man of importance, I know that he would listen to you." She glanced at Yen for moral support, but he looked as close to tears as she had ever seen him, and he refused to meet her eyes. "All I am asking is that the Wus allow us to purchase goods by chit, the same as we do all summer."

The chief scratched his nose, as if genuinely considering this request. "Summer is not autumn," he said eventually. "I do not tell Wu Yao-lu how to run his shop, he does not tell me how to police this valley. You talk to Wu Taitai, tell her these things. Maybe she can help you."

"I *have* talked to her—" But she could feel her temper starting to boil. "Thank you, Chief Liu," she concluded. "I appreciate your advice."

Bless Yen, there were no recriminations, no sour looks or gentle adages on the way home. Whatever shame she had brought on the house of Liang, in his mind it was he who had failed to keep the family solvent. She knew it was as useless to console him as it was to berate herself, yet she did briefly touch his arm as they started up the front steps. "I hate to think where this family would be without you, Yen."

The large flat lips pinched together and he looked at her steadily. "Laoyeh will come," he said. "I know this."

She smiled. "I know this, too."

But any dim glow of encouragement was dashed by the scene that met them inside. Jasmine, Morris, and the baby were gathered around the wooden card table with scissors and a stack of old magazines. From these they had cut out pictures of food, which they were busily "devouring" with knife and fork.

"Mm hmm." Jasmine speared a square of brown paper. "Beef Wellington!"

Morris sucked on an empty fork. "Devil's food cake and custard." He moaned, "Tinned peaches, too."

"Oh, yes, tinned peaches!"

"Cake!" clamored Teddy, bouncing on his short, stockinged legs. "Want some!"

Ah-nie, who stood ready to catch Teddy if he fell, had her own eye on a picture of turkey roast from the Thanksgiving issue of *Harper's* that had carried Hope's last article.

"Dear God," Hope said under her breath, "what is to become of us?"

But in the next instant she was bustling about the room, stoking the fire, straightening her papers, directing Yen to put on water for tea and Ah-nie to put Teddy down for a nap. If the children could make a game of this, she was damned if she'd fall apart.

"Where's Pearl?" she asked suddenly.

Morris shrugged, licking a picture of baked Virginia ham.

"She went out," said Jasmine, "just a few minutes after you and Yen. Thought she was going to catch up with you."

"What do you mean, out?" demanded Hope. "Haven't I told every one of you, you are never to leave this house alone!"

"Don't yell at us."

"Didn't she tell you where she was going, Morris?"

"I hope she was going to the store," he said sullenly. "What I'd give for a box of chocolates."

Jasmine fell sideways off her chair and writhed melodramatically across the floor, nearly tripping Yen as he came in from the kitchen with Hope's tea.

"Never mind that," she said to him. "Pearl's gone off somewhere—"

But at that moment the door opened. Pearl's marcelled bob hung limp from the drizzle that had begun just as Hope and Yen got home. Her pink sweater and skirt were also soaked, but her round moon face was beaming.

"I'm back," she said.

"So we see." Hope wavered. "Better get those muddy shoes off."

Pearl darted a glance around her audience. "I've been up to the school," she announced. "They're ever so nice there. Helpful."

"Helpful," repeated her mother.

"Yes." Pearl hesitated, then turned out her sweater pocket onto the table. Silver, copper, and paper cash in small denominations covered the demolished magazines.

"I heard you and Yen talking," Pearl started to explain, but Hope waved her to silence.

Her voice failed her. She knew just what Pearl had done. What now had to be undone. Whatever the cost.

ᏬᏬᏬ

She went alone that afternoon, as soon as the rain had stopped. She wore a businesslike green gabardine suit and matching feathered toque. Her Graflex, the only offering she could think of, was tucked under her arm.

The school seemed even larger and more ominous up close than from a distance. The front door was massive. The main hallway had that dour institutional smell that has nothing whatsoever to do with schooling, yet always seems to accompany it, and the headmistress, one Miss Edith Eaton, looked every bit as upright and puritanical as her name suggested. She wore her brown hair in a wispless bun, her tortoiseshell glasses on the exact center of her nose, and her starched round collar perfectly flat across perfectly angular shoulders. She knew precisely who Hope was, and she knew all about Pearl's visit.

"The children were only too happy to take up a collection." She leaned across her desk with a confessional smile. "Most of them are from missionary families. Charity comes naturally, you see."

"Well, I'm afraid there's been a dreadful mistake."

Miss Eaton lifted her chin. "Really."

"I've come to return the money."

"I see." The headmistress picked up a pencil and turned it between her fingers. "I think that would be rather awkward. Like sending back the Sunday collection plate. Not a tidy process. And rather a slap in the face, after the children have shown such generosity."

"Ah." Hope moistened her lips. "Well, you understand that it is quite impossible for us to accept this as charity."

Miss Eaton continued to manipulate the pencil. "We have one or two Eurasian boys here. One's father is with Standard Oil. The other's is a French consul in Hankow. It's their *mothers* who are Chinese."

Hope clenched her hands in her lap. "I wonder," she said, full of false brightness, "if I might repay your students' generosity by taking their photographs. I have my own equipment, as you see. And I'm fairly experienced."

"I imagine you are."

"Under the circumstances," Hope went on, closing her ears, "I'm not as well supplied as I'd like. But I have enough stock of film to take several group pictures, say one of each class."

"Mrs. Leon," said the headmistress severely, "we ordinarily take class photographs at the end of each school year."

"Well—"

"However, the teacher who generally takes these photographs is on sabbatical in France. He has left behind a fully equipped darkroom with a proper studio camera and a supply of film and mountings that should more than meet your needs. Each student will require a portrait, so of course your offer to do the work in exchange for this morning's collection is quite unthinkable. We generally pay Mr. Claire one hundred dollars above his salary for this service. I am willing to offer you the same. There's just one thing."

"Y-yes?"

"I would appreciate you keeping your daughter away from our campus." She gave Hope a sharp look. "She caused quite a stir among the boys this morning. I am quite willing to give you and your family a helping hand, but I try to run a decent, orderly school here."

Hope felt the color drain from her face. Her hands were like ice, and if she'd had even an inch of leeway she would have hammered them into Miss Eaton's skull. But she could see no other way out.

"Of course." Hope stood up. "I understand completely, Miss Eaton. Decency, at all cost."

ॐॐॐ

October 23, 1926

If only Mary Jane could see what her innocent gift of a Kodak hath wrought! My days for the past two weeks have been a seemingly endless succession of chip-toothed grins and crossed eyes. Tow-headed boys with cowlicks and brown-haired girls with freckles. Their careless faces populate my dreams, driving out my own children almost completely. I have photographed them singly, in their cricket teams, Scouting uniforms, and chorus formation. I have been the brunt of their jokes, their protruding tongues, and blatant speculation. My Chinese husband is known around the Kuling School to be alternately a fallen Manchu prince, a Communist, a bandit, a viceroy with fifteen wives, and a publisher of Mandarin Bibles! Pearl, who so severely threatened Miss Eaton's moral order, has been described to me by those (mostly younger boys) who encountered her as "chipper," "pert," "a good egg," and "wholesome." I think, on balance, Miss Eaton is right that I should confine her movements, but the moral order that needs protecting is not the school's but Pearl's! I forget too easily, because she does look and behave so innocent, that she is eighteen years old. If we ever get back to Shanghai, this will be her last year of school, and then our worries will really begin.

But that seems brutally far away. According to the coolies, there is fighting all around the base of the mountain. Even if I had the fare for the steamer, we could never get out now. I cannot allow myself to believe that we shall be stuck here all the way through winter, yet the possibility is real. When this job for the dreaded Miss Eaton is done, the specter of poverty will rise again. By then the children may well have cannibalized each other. We have run completely out of reading material. The girls spend their days unraveling old sweaters to knit into new ones. Yen is teaching Morris all his old childhood songs and stories, and Ah-nie entertains Teddy endlessly with that poor little India rubber ball.

But there are small triumphs to be gained from this. Jed Israel, for one, will be so proud when he sees what his reluctant pupil has made of his random darkroom lessons. It was pure bravado—and desperation—that drove me to offer my "photographic services" to Miss Eaton. What I would have done if the school had no darkroom I can't imagine, for the small quantities of developer and fixer I brought from Shanghai had mostly evaporated after Morris and Ken fooled with them— and left the caps off. Also, the shed where I played at developing this summer is like an ice house now. And though I suppose I might have muddled through, I am becoming quite an accomplished printmaker with the help of the proper tools.

Doubtless Miss Eaton would not approve if she knew about it, but I have used the facilities to produce some exceptional portraits of Chief Liu and his deputies and also the Wus, which I've used to barter my way back "into the chits." In exchange for the portraits that are now prominently displayed on the shop and police station walls, we have added portions of noodle, buns, pork, and vegetables to our daily rice. I only wish I'd thought of this trick in September, before the first pangs of starvation set in!

The other boon of this crisis has been my writing. I have a sizable stack of nearly completed articles for Cadlow, including a profile of Yen, an interview with Chief Liu, and an account, compiled with the help of Morris and several Kuling students, of the enthusiasm for Boy Scouting that has gripped China in recent years (it's my opinion that Scouting is a precise blend of missionary zealotry and military trappings—both of which are much in evidence in today's China and therefore appeal to young boys trying to make sense of these seemingly contradictory forces).

Anyway, the photographic work, the articles, the children all help me to keep my mind off the larger issues. I must believe that Paul is wending his way toward us, that he will reach us before we are destitute again, that we are no more vulnerable to this war than Miss Eaton and her students believe themselves to be. I must believe all sorts of things about who I am, who my children are, what place we hold in this lunatic world—and so I do believe.

But every now and then I think of this summer, of Stephen and Sarah and my foolish preoccupations, and I suddenly feel so many centuries old that the bottom drops right out from under me. It's a feeling I am quite certain Miss Eaton would find positively indecent.

བབབ

On November 16, Hope was working on her final batch of prints in the Kuling School darkroom when the walls began to reverberate with the students' cries. She timed out the exposures, finished moving them through the sequence of baths, and carefully pinned them to the drying rack before washing her hands and removing her apron. She put on her jacket, ran a hand over her hair, and emerged from the darkroom with as much dignity as she was ever able to muster when perfumed by chemicals and half blind from light deprivation.

"What is it?" she asked a small pigtailed girl galloping toward the stairs.

"Soldiers!"

"What kind of soldiers?"

But the girl was gone, and Hope didn't wait for further details. Half an hour later she was home with the children, Yen standing guard on the porch. She had seen not a soul along the way, nor were there any signs of encampments, gun placements, or reconnaissance. She had no idea what kind of soldiers had been sighted, whose army they belonged to, or what their reasons for coming up the mountain might be. But she did not intend to be separated from her children while the facts presented themselves.

They crowded around the windows, Morris in the upstairs study, Jasmine in the kitchen. Pearl and Hope took the north and south watches, while Ah-nie and Teddy hid in the nursery, Ah-nie as near to being under the bed as she could possibly manage. There were periodic alarms, once when Morris spotted a movement that turned into a leaping doe and several times when Jasmine's fertile mind transformed rocks and bushes into gun-toting warriors. But Hope had come home at two o'clock. By four the sun had slipped below the ridge, and they were all getting jumpy.

Suddenly Yen called to Hope. Two men were coming up the trail. One was Chief Liu, with his chest puffed out and his most officious scowl on. Behind him strode a man in the brown uniform of the National Revolutionary Army.

Hope lowered herself into one of the porch chairs and labored to even out her breathing. At the bottom of the steps Chief Liu saluted and banged his heels together. His companion bowed his head briefly, and approached.

"Mrs. Liang?" His accent was American—Yankee, and now that she saw him more closely she realized he could not be more than three-quarters Chinese. He had the same length of face as Morris, though his eyes were slightly less round, his forehead marginally squarer. Sturdy, youthful, and vigorous in appearance, he had an openness of expression that one almost never saw in full Chinese. His bearing was respectably official without being the least bit grave.

"Yes," she answered.

"I am Lieutenant Jung. I have a package from your husband." Turning to shield the motion from Liu's eyes, he reached inside his jacket and pulled out a thick envelope. She slipped it into her skirt pocket.

"You've seen him, then?"

"We were in the same unit entering Wuhan. He is there now."

"I expected him to come himself."

"I am to convey his regret. Also to tell you, he tried twice before to send word. I was by his side when he telegraphed Shanghai. He was very distressed to learn that you had not returned there. When I was assigned to one of the details sent to capture Kiukiang, he requested for me to come here. I have known your husband for many years. He was friends with my father, and I'm honored that he trusted me." The lieutenant's attention strayed momentarily to the children clustered at the window.

He smiled. "You have a son."

"Two."

He saluted the children, and at a nod from Hope they came tumbling out.

"This is Lieutenant Jung," she said. "He's a friend of Papa's."

"Where is Papa?" Pearl demanded. "Is he all right?"

Teddy showed the soldier his new back teeth.

"Have you been in the fighting?" Morris wanted to know.

"Is that a real pistol?" asked Jasmine.

Hope silenced the brood. "It's late. If you can stand the assault, you're welcome to stay here tonight."

"Thank you, no. I am billeted with a small detail in the village, but tomorrow morning I will accompany you and your children down to Kiukiang and see you safely onto the steamer."

"At least some supper?"

Lieutenant Jung replied with an almost imperceptible tilt of his head toward the police chief, who by now had slid halfway up the stairs and was leaning to catch every word. The soldier gave Hope a slow wink and, turning, signaled Chief Liu that he would be with him in a moment. The chief jerked backward, nearly losing his balance, and landed with another salute at the bottom of the steps.

"I don't know how to thank you," said Hope.

The man slid his left thumb under his leather bandolier. His eyes had crept back to Morris, whose jaw hung slack with admiration. Suddenly the lieutenant stuck out his hand. Astonished, Morris gave a quick look as if asking permission, but before it could either be granted or refused, he was gripping the soldier enthusiastically and pumping the poor man's arm.

"Lieutenant?" said Hope.

The soldier looked up.

"Who is your father?"

He let Morris go. "His name was Morris Jung. He died in Peking last year."

They stood facing each other like two distant relatives at their first introduction. There was that vague sense of relevance, of some nonspecific mutuality or connection, yet at the same time utter bewilderment. In the end, there was only one link between them. One reason for the soldier's curiosity. Why Morris was his father's namesake. And why Hope should allow her family to follow him into a war zone.

"Did my husband tell you to say that?" said Hope.

The young man looked offended. "But it is the truth."

"Why couldn't he come himself?"

He winced. Hope looked past him and signaled Yen to move the children inside. They went reluctantly, and the soldier forced a smile, assuring them he would see them tomorrow. Hope moved to the far end of the porch and glared at the police chief to keep him out of earshot.

"What's happened?" she insisted, lowering her voice to a near-whisper.

At last the emissary let down his mask. He kept his voice in a quiet monotone, his body in regimental posture. "He has been placed under house arrest. Borodin has denounced him as a counterrevolutionary and threatened to seize your husband's property. He insisted I should not tell you, but . . ."

Hope looked away. Darkness had fallen across the valley. Every now and then a low white light shivered behind the mountains. After the usual interval, distant thunder would follow.

Wuchang

October 29, 1926

Dearest Hope and babies.

On Double Ten Day, our National Revolutionary Army has "liberated" my home city. As we crossed the river, the Bund of Hankow was lined with workers and merchants waving banners, the shining sun of the Republic, shouting "Long live the revolution!" There was little fighting, as most of the local generals had joined with us, and the people here were unanimous in support. That has changed some now. Every day brings change.

This is why I must stay here for the time and cannot come to you. I am sorry. I have cabled to Shanghai and received word from Sarah that you stayed on in Kuling. I think you must not receive the moneys I sent to you from Changsha in August and September. Yen will take care of you. I know this. But I worry now. I trust Lieutenant Jung to deliver this letter, these moneys to you without fail. If our troops are successful in Kiukiang, I know this will reach you. When the lieutenant explains our family connection, you will know to trust him, and he will see you return safe to our home in Shanghai.

It is dangerous to write of particulars. I cannot say when I may join you. Neither have I news of Jin. When I arrived in Changsha, he already departed. But know that I am well. My old servants here in Wuchang take good care. I do not know what will happen to my property here. The mood of this city now is uncertain, but when I hear that you and our babies are safe and well, I be content. Sometimes during the Expedition, I look up into the mountains and think of the song of Wang Wei.

> *I walk until water checks my path,*
> *Then turn to the rising clouds.*

I send you my love, my sorrow. My heart. Hsin-hsin.

I am your husband, Paul

༄༄༄

4

Only after Hope and the children had threaded their way through the mobbed streets of Kiukiang and were spat on by striking rickshaw pullers; after they'd been taunted by a crowd hoisting an effigy of a Catholic priest with a rope around his neck; after she noticed the machine guns rimming the foreign concession and read the wall posters announcing the public beheading of factory workers by the British-backed warlord in Shanghai; after they'd reached a Yangtze River bristling with gunboats and heard the rumors that the Kuomintang had split into two factions, with General Chiang Kai-shek taking Nanking as his capital for the right wing and Mikhail Borodin setting up a left-wing government in Wuhan—only then did Hope fully grasp the extent to which Paul's beloved revolution was spinning out of control. Exactly why he had been arrested and the true danger of his situation remained for the moment unclear, though Hope assumed Borodin had targeted Paul as a member of the right wing. The lieutenant could tell her only that he had received Paul's letter and the enclosed hundred dollars from William Tan, who had made a late-night visit to Paul before leaving for America, where he was to be Chiang's ambassador. William had made light of the arrest, saying Paul was just protecting his home. The city of Wuchang was a hotbed of agitation, Lieutenant Jung explained. Workers were storming the foreign concessions, and Borodin had begun confiscating all properties belonging to absentee landowners. Paul's, the young soldier said, was "a voice of reason at a time when common sense was branded as treason." With this phrase ringing in her head, Hope shepherded the children onto the British steamer *Tuk Wo* and spent the next three nights writing fervent confessional letters to Paul, which she burned before the ink was dry.

They arrived back in Shanghai on Thanksgiving afternoon and hired a cab to take them home. It seemed to Hope that the whole city was holding its breath. They passed Holy Trinity Cathedral as the service was breaking, and the congregation pouring out onto the streets was both enormous and unnaturally quiet. The lights were blinking on Nanking Road, the windows of Sincere and Wing On chock-a-block with displays of imported toys and liquors, fruit and puddings, and the holiday crowds were out in force, but the faces were more troubled than gay. In and around the strolling foreigners huddled permanent encampments of refugees.

"I feel as though we've been gone years," said Pearl. "Has the city changed, or is it me?"

Hope wiped the fog from the window for Teddy to look out. "I'm afraid it's both."

"Will Papa be home to meet us?" asked Jasmine.

"I don't think so." After much deliberation, Hope had concluded that both the family and Paul would be best served if she kept the lieutenant's news to herself. She had not even told Yen.

But when the cab drew up in front of the house, a hollow cry rose in her throat. The lights were on, smoke curled from the chimney, and shadows moved across the parlor curtains. In that moment the sensation of relief drowned out all the fear and anger and heartache—even the exhaustion of the last days. She was ahead of the children, racing up the walk, leaving Yen to manage the fare and luggage. The key was in her hand. The door sprang open. The voices inside stopped abruptly.

She turned into the sitting room and made a rapid survey of its occupants: four young men, two women. Chinese. One of the women was seated at Hope's desk, with Hope's pen poised over a tablet. The men were variously standing and sitting, paper-bound books in their hands. The other woman was just coming from the kitchen with a laden tea tray.

They all stared at Hope, at the children behind her. Hope's relief evaporated. Three months they'd been delayed. Paul had told her he paid the year's rent in advance, but who knew what the arrangement really was? She'd never even seen the landlord. No occupants, no rent. Of course. Their home had been given away.

She could feel her face thickening with tears, her shoulders start to quiver. She spun abruptly, but her way was blocked. Someone had stolen up behind her, and now hands were gripping her shoulders. She pulled back. The children started giggling as she lifted her face, met the familiar stretched black eyes.

Jin.

∅∅∅

December 10, 1926

I am in an agony of waiting. Since Jin left for Wuhan over a week ago, I've heard nothing, and I alternate between berating myself for inflating the situation and damning myself for trusting him.

Justifications run like ticker tape. A son would never betray his father. Jin's position as a student organizer and former Expedition propagandist gives him access to information. He knows the maze of Wuhan, both physically and politically, could escape if it came to that. And what is the alternative, after all? If I went myself, I'd have to leave the children, and what could I realistically accomplish? Paul has kept our lives so scrupulously separate that I don't even know where he places in the current chain of command. I thought of sending Yen, and it's possible he could contact Paul through the servant underground, but he has neither the status nor the savvy to negotiate his release. William, of course, would have been the one—of all the times for him to be out of the country! But William could not (or would not) do more when he *was* in Wuhan than to act as Paul's messenger. Eugene Chou is in Peking, and Jed . . . well, I did go to see Jed, but whatever he witnessed here this fall has changed him in a way that scares me. He started in on some of the street executions he'd witnessed—friends of his, he said. Summary beheadings. One girl out by Siccawei was disemboweled and strangled with her own intestines. I became faint, but he wouldn't stop talking. His eyes took on the most terrifying glow. We were in the back of the shop, where he has his studio, and before I left he insisted I look at his "collection." I thought he was talking about cameras, but he showed me a box full of stilettos and hatchets and automatic guns, all stolen, he said, from the local warlord's police.

So I told Jin. He said he knew "channels." Through these "revolutionary study groups" he's been conducting, he's acquired status as an "organizer." I recoil from the verbal tyranny of revolution, as well as from its cloak-and-dagger aspects. I want so desperately to believe that this is really what it seems—a game played by overaged boys that will disintegrate into a pillow fight as soon as the referee finds his whistle. But who is the referee now that Sun is gone? Chiang? Borodin? The British, with their gentlemen's clubs and battle stations ever ready? Or the French, who everyone says are playing footsie—alongside Chiang—with Tu Yueh-sheng's Green Gang mobsters? Or the Japanese, whose intentions no one ever seems to know until it is too late. Paul could be the victim of any one of these, there's so little rhyme or reason. Nothing's really changed from the days when palace counselors poisoned each other's rice to gain Imperial advantage.

If we should ever get Paul back . . .

No, I can't any more. I can't make those promises. Can't form those threats. I've sent Cadlow my articles and pictures. I am forcing myself to write more. Two a month plus photographs will bring one hundred dollars. No *mei fatse*. No. I will not be fate's pawn any longer.

*　　*　　*

But the weeks wore on. Still nothing from Jin. No word or money yet from Cadlow. On the surface, Hope maintained an appearance of routine by writing, sewing, working in the darkroom, managing the household on a severely curtailed budget. She had tea with Sarah, whom she had not told of Paul's arrest, and learned that the Manns had set sail for South Africa less than a month after leaving Kuling. Hope had all but forgotten Stephen Mann in her fear for Paul.

The only time she succeeded in shrugging off this fear was when she replaced it with worries over the children. With some considerable persuasion and penalty payments for overdue tuition, Hope had gotten Pearl and Morris and Jasmine all reinstated in school, but they had barely started back when classes broke for the Christmas holidays. With no money for their amusement and grave concerns about their safety, given the city's combative atmosphere, Hope tried to keep them at their books, making up the work they'd missed in the fall. Of course, they all complained, Jasmine by strapping on her roller skates and furiously tearing up and down the block, Morris by shutting himself in his room, and Pearl by assaulting Hope with long, teary protests about all the "holiday fun" she was missing with her chums.

On Christmas eve a check arrived from William Cadlow in the amount of five hundred dollars—payment for the articles Hope had written in Kuling. However, her relief at receiving the money was tempered by the accompanying note, which suggested Hope comment more in the future on the political climate in China. The recent successes of this Northern Expedition had fired the American public's interest, as well as concern over the investments of American companies in China. Who were these two power brokers Chiang Kai-shek and "Michael" Borodin? How was it that they were partners one minute and mortal enemies the next? Could she possibly interview one of them?

Hope traveled through the next days in a haze. On Christmas, the children were so thrilled by the unexpected profusion of gifts—silk scarves and stockings, colored beads and strap shoes and a wooden push-toy for Teddy, which she'd collected in a single blurred hour before Sincere's department store closed for the holiday—and by the equally unexpected feast of roast duck and crab apples, that they did not notice their mother's uncharacteristic silence. They did not ask if anything were bothering her.

They did not question her disinterest in their jokes or think twice when she retreated to her desk. It struck Hope, watching them, that they were all four like spinning tops. Teddy pushing his wooden goose across the room, Morris utterly absorbed in his crossword puzzle . . . Jasmine accompanying the Gramophone on a ukulele that one of her Hawaiian school friends had loaned her, and Pearl practicing the Charleston . . .

You could disappear, Hope told herself, and they would notice your absence no more than they notice their father's. Ah-nie would stay with them. And Yen. It would only be for a week or two.

On January 3, the morning the children returned to school, the phone rang. Jed wanted her to come to the store to see "a new camera that's just in." When she arrived he gave her a warning look and turned the shop over to his assistant. He motioned Hope toward the back.

"A messenger came last night with a note from Jin." He handed her a wad of blue paper. "It was stuffed into a shell casing."

She bit her lip as she smoothed the crushed note. Jin wrote that he could not arrange Paul's escape without assistance, and time was running out. Perhaps her friends at the American consulate could intervene, or if William Tan had returned yet . . . ?

Hope asked Jed for a match and an ashtray, and burned the message. "Can you get me an introduction to Borodin?"

He put a pot of water on the hotplate. It was cold in the studio, and gloomy. Jed's bony figure and shorn, flaming hair seemed to jump among the imitation Chippendale and Ming furnishings he used for props. He busied himself with measuring tea leaves, and only after he'd prepared her cup did he answer. His voice was clear and charged, with no trace of his stammer.

"Why?"

"I've been asked to interview him." She drew Cadlow's letter from her purse.

"I thought you steered clear of politics."

"I prefer to. But it seems American readers want to know what's transformed those pathetically inept Chinese Nationalists into a respectable fighting force." She seated herself in one of the Chippendale chairs. "Besides, Jin and Paul tell me that Borodin was quite the darling of the young moderns' salons in Canton. He speaks English and he likes to talk."

"You don't sound like yourself, Hope."

"No?" Her eyes fixed on a calendar—a giveaway from some paint company—that Jed had pinned to the wall. A black-green mountain beneath vaporous clouds weighed over the grid of days. "Whom do I sound like?"

"Whom." Jed shook his head. "Always gram-matically correct. That's you, all right. But the rest . . . Where is Paul, anyway?"

Her shoulders rose mechanically, dropped. Jed's haggard look, his unshaven chin, twitching green eyes, and refusal to sit down did not inspire her confidence. She thought of his arsenal behind that gilded screen. Was it possible that she had changed, by any measure, as much as Jed had in the decades she'd known him?

"You know what they call w-women like you?" he said.

"I didn't know there were enough women like me to be called anything."

"Sun w-widows." Jed set his cup among the lenses and light filters and empty film boxes that littered his table. "Sun's the symbol of the revolution—"

"I know what it means," snapped Hope. "Can you help me?"

"There's M-madame Sun, the original widow herself, working by Borodin's side. Paul must know her. Why not ask her to introduce you?"

"I'd rather Borodin receive me as an American journalist than as Paul's wife."

"How very un-Chinese." Jed yawned, showing badly neglected teeth. "You're not p-planning to go alone?"

"I think I'm better off that way."

"I hear things are pretty tense in Wuhan. Lots of anti-foreign protests."

"So the papers say. But I'll only be there a day or two. I don't want any company, Jed."

"Oh, don't worry. It was a w-w-w-warning, not an offer." He slid his thumbs into the pockets of his faded blue jacket and stood chewing on his cheek. Finally he shook his head and reached for a scrap of paper. "This fellow is one of Borodin's assistants. You'll find him at the headquarters in Hankow. If you bring that letter, he'll put you through. If I were you, though, I'd dress Chinese and avoid the British steamers."

Hope stared at him. It was the longest she had ever heard him speak without stammering. Though she wasn't sure why, this realization saddened her. She took the paper and wrapped her arms around him, thanking him with her face pressed into his shoulder, which smelled of photographic chemicals and cigarette smoke, saltpeter, and faintly but unmistakably of chocolate. He returned the hug stiffly and wished her good luck.

Hope walked from Denniston's to the Confucian Temple, where she sat for an hour reviewing her choices. All were distasteful or terrifying, or both. She could try wiring William Tan. Or appeal to Madame Sun. Or beg for Eugene Chou's intervention. Or, she could go to Borodin. Trust. That was where every choice broke down. Trust, the essential, the impossible—the lesson, she saw now, that had been defying Paul all these years. Those who had power were never to be trusted, yet when you needed that power you had no choice.

She sank forward with her elbows on her knees, rubbing her thumbs into her temples and trying to remember the stories Paul used to tell of palace intrigues and ministerial deceits, the twisted chains of favor that scholars and eunuchs routinely used to gain influence at court—and how often these turned deadly when the favors unexpectedly reversed. The Chinese way was never to do anything directly. They were forever side-stepping spirit walls, averting their eyes, walking in zigzags, relying on go-betweens, all for fear of offending or being offended—or trapped—by evil or shame. Yet there was Paul, trapped. Wuchang was his home. He had friends, powerful friends who could surely have helped him escape by now. Why was he still there?

She knew, though for weeks she'd refused to admit it. He had stood up to Borodin once, when his life was at stake. This time their face-off was over property. Paul was gambling his freedom for his home. "If my head is so thick, it will protect me," he'd joked. Even now, Hope thought, he will not *believe* he's in real danger.

Finally she decided she had only one choice. She went home and worked until early afternoon, going through her notes from her earliest conversations with Paul about his student days in Tokyo and from ten years later, when he was plotting Li Yüan-hung's abortive "escape" from Peking. When she had found the names she needed, she changed into her most tailored, businesslike black suit, tucked the necessary identification documents into her purse, and made her way to the Japanese consulate.

For two hours she asked one stone-faced undersecretary after another for information about Mr. Nakai Mitsuru, whom her notes described as an "old friend of Paul's from Tokyo days, now counselor of the Japanese

Legation in Hankow." Though no one admitted to recognizing the name, at length she found herself before the consul general himself, who bowed stiffly and informed her that Mr. Mitsuru was indeed still in Hankow, and how could he assist her? This short ramrod of a man had the power to help her, and so she forced herself to trust him. In return, he checked her credentials with grim deliberation, double-checked the documents proving Paul's association with Sun Yat-sen and his years in Japan, and grilled her with obvious suspicion about the circumstances of her marriage, but she never wavered. Finally he yielded. If she could get her husband to the consulate in Hankow, he would instruct Mr. Mitsuru to provide asylum.

The next morning, having left a worried but now fully informed Yen in charge of the household, Hope boarded a Belgian river steamer on which she was the sole female. It took but a few hours to realize that the ratios were starkly reversed on vessels traveling into Shanghai. There had been massive demonstrations against the Hankow concessions, she was told, and the British Marines had refused to fight back. Now the concessions—European, American, and Japanese alike—were evacuating women and children by the hundreds. For the first time, the Chinese first mate gloated, the imperialists were giving back some of the land they had stolen.

It was dusk six days later when the steamer docked in Wuchang. Though bitter cold and heavily misted, the narrow streets winding back from the port seethed with voices and bobbing yellow lanterns. Hope pulled the thick quilted coat—a relic from her days in Peking—tightly about her neck, tugged her fur-lined cap over her ears, and wound her arm around the carpetbag that contained a single change of clothing, her camera, her wedding ring, and the notes she hoped would sustain her through the interview to come. Paul was somewhere at the other end of this blackened maze. She had debated trying to go to him first, but the rickshaw pullers' resentful eyes and the absence of any alternative transportation dispelled all thought of this. The river captain, a fat, bearded Welshman who habitually fingered his pocket change, had told her the pullers were among the most belligerent of the anti-foreign forces in the Three Cities, "demanding a steamship fare for a trot across town—and whistling up their pals against anyone stupid enough not to pay it. Insanity's the norm in Wuhan these days."

Besides, she told herself, Paul's house was under guard, and any unauthorized visit might endanger him further—possibly jeopardize her own safety, as well. She needed to locate Jin. So she took the next ferry to Hankow and crossed the Bund as Jed had directed her, to the gloomy three-storied villa Borodin had taken for his headquarters.

The gloom lifted abruptly as she entered the foyer. It was like stepping into the eye of a storm. Rooms opened off to either side of a once-grand mahogany staircase, each crowded with tables and books and stacks of paper and about a dozen workers busily pasting up leaflets, laying out copy, folding, punching, marking up pages. They were mostly young men and women wearing the barren colors and rumpled cotton of the proletariat. A few stood talking in rushed, earnest bursts, which were punctuated by the steady thwack of printing presses and the tapping of typewriters from adjoining chambers. Standing unnoticed in the vacant hallway, Hope thought of Paul's old newsrooms in Chinatown, her own uncertain activism in Berkeley. She felt as if she were being dragged simultaneously backward and forward in time.

She shut her eyes and steadied her breathing. Then she turned into the larger of the two rooms, advancing just far enough to make eye contact with one of the faster-talking young men, a dark-skinned fellow with Chinese facial features but nappy, brilliantined black hair, who had an air of authority. "I'm looking for—"

Hope stopped, suddenly confused, blood rushing to her face even as her mind seemed to empty. She tossed out the only name she could think of. "Mr. Su." Jed's friend.

She could feel her heart pounding against her ribs as the man scrutinized her. He stood very straight. "I am Su," he said in clipped English.

She mentioned Jed's name, which elicited a laugh and a nod, then she explained that she'd been sent by the American magazine *Harper's* to interview Mr. Borodin. She showed the letter to identify herself. Hope Newfield.

Without comment, Su strode into the hallway and disappeared upstairs. Hope followed as far as the foyer. All the way upriver she had been in a state of revolt against the subterfuge and danger that had been thrust on her. The proof of this revolt was her inability now to believe that any of this was real. Not the smell of ink and sweat, or the humming, uneven floorboards, the candy wrapper falling from one young girl's fingers as she reached to fold her next pamphlet. Not the unwashed green drapes and curls of ivory enamel flaking off the windowsill, the unshaded lightbulbs buzzing overhead—none of these or a hundred other details made the situation any more believable. This world that Paul and Jin and Jed inhabited, this realm of revolution, was so apart from her own experience, however long she had observed it from the sidelines, that she had to stifle the feeling that she had been thrown into one of Morris's boy adventure stories. But worse than the sense of unreality was the confusion it engendered. Her mind refused to sustain the thread of her plan. She had intended to ask for Jin when she came in, not Su. Jin was with these people in some capacity; this was the address given in his note, and she had come through the door with his name on her tongue. Now, caught at her own game, she would have to play it through. But there must not be another such lapse.

She heard a blur of voices upstairs, the opening and shutting of a door, then the thud of boots descending the uncarpeted steps. She drew back, but there was a familiarity about the uneven rhythm, and as soon as its owner, a jug-eared man wearing the uniform of the Northern Expeditionary Army, came into view, she called out softly.

Jin blanched at the sight of her, his eyes flickering with alarm. He gripped her wrist, pushing her around behind the staircase into a narrow alcove stacked with boxes and broken typewriters. They spoke in urgent but almost inaudible whispers. When she told him her pretext for coming to Wuhan, he sucked in his breath. "Did you tell Su . . ."

She shook her head, showing her naked hand. "I am only a journalist, here to interview Borodin. But I've arranged for Paul's protection at the Japanese consulate. Can you get him there?"

He looked at her in disbelief, and for one terrible second, she thought he would refuse. Then, grimly, he nodded. "Interview Borodin, right away if possible, and keep him as long as you can—he is to give the Chekka his blacklist tonight." He hesitated to make sure she understood. The Chekka were Borodin's secret police—specifically, the secret police used against counterrevolutionaries. "Afterward, go to the Japanese. I will bring Father."

For the first time in all the years she had known him, Jin hugged her. It was a hard, trembling hug fraught with terror. An instant later, he was gone.

She waited for several seconds, leaning against the alcove wall. Then, biting the color back into her lips, she returned to the hallway just as Su was on his way down. He said she could have fifteen minutes, and led her upstairs to a plainly furnished sitting room presided over by a large dark-haired man in an overstuffed armchair.

She would have recognized Borodin even without Su's introduction. There was the woolly black mustache William had described, the world-weary eyes with their heavy lids. His black hair was cut short and parted to one side, eyebrows thick and straight. His face was lean and as sharply creased as his trousers, but beneath his loose embroidered Russian tunic, he had the build of a bear.

"So Miss Newfield," he said in perfect English, and waved her to the opposite seat. "You come to us from *Harper's*?"

"I come," she said, conjuring a mental image of the last American soil she'd seen, "from San Francisco."

And so the farce began. A manservant dressed in white served her a sticky sweet digestif. Borodin poured tea from a silver samovar. He delivered a rambling discourse about Shakespeare's genius, Chekhov's craft, and his own passion for Tchaikovsky. She asked his opinion of Chinese ingenuity. He explained that the key to China's revolution lay in the liberation of precisely that ingenious spirit, so long downtrodden and divided by the competing demands of family, warlords, and the Imperial system.

"Unification and dedication to the national good—this will release the true greatness of these people." He laced his broad fingers across one knee. "Unification of the world as a whole will have the same effect on us all."

"I believe you refer to unification under socialism, Mr. Borodin," said Hope.

He sucked in his cheeks. "If you wish."

"I suppose, then, you feel that the return of the foreign concessions to Chinese control is also to the good."

"To the extent that the concessions were imperialist excesses. But I believe my Chinese friends display their own excesses. I am not against foreign investments in China, so long as the terms are fair and justified. Slavery, Miss Newfield, is never fair or justified. But neither is the emancipation of those slaves overnight and without any preparation for their freedom. This, unfortunately, was the effect of the Chinese overthrow of the Manchus. My good friend Dr. Sun Yat-sen was a truly great man, a visionary. As you know, his young wife is with us here in Wuhan. However, Dr. Sun was sadly betrayed by his reactionary friends, whose true interest in revolution was to claim the Manchus' power for themselves."

Hope brought the glass of liqueur to her lips, and drained it.

"What of Chiang Kai-shek?" she pressed, once she'd regained her nerve. "People credit him with almost as many of the Northern Expedition's victories as they do you."

"Comrade Chiang is an excellent general. A pity you did not come to Kuling last month. You could have interviewed us together. We are not such enemies as people suggest."

Hope dropped her eyes to her notebook. "Kuling?"

"The mountain resort so favored by foreigners, above Kiukiang. Have you never been there?"

She hunched her shoulders ambiguously, writing.

"A very relaxing place for a meeting of the minds. Especially in winter when there are no foreign tourists."

She halted her mental calculations of dates and near-misses, and met his glittering gaze. "Forgive me Mr. Borodin. But aren't you also, in a way, a tourist?"

He laughed. "I am indeed. A revolutionary tourist, just as you, yourself, are a journalistic tourist. I like that. I hope you use it in your article. Yes, I am only passing through to offer advice and observation. Exactly." He laughed again. "Exactly!"

There was a knock on the door. Su strode across the room and whispered in Borodin's ear. The door cracked open to reveal a man wearing jackboots and the black uniform of the secret police. The Chekka.

"I almost forgot!" Hope cried, rummaging in her bag. She hoisted the Graflex. "My editor will never forgive me if I don't include a photograph."

Borodin smiled.

"Please. I know you're busy. Just a couple of minutes more."

He gave a careless shrug and told Su to hold off. But his aide did not leave. The door didn't close. The wide pockmarked face above the jack-boots was now watching her intently.

Still, Hope took her time. The lack of light would necessitate some ad-justments, she told them. A square of white cloth across the lap. A re-arrangement of lamps. She apologized for not bringing a flash. The exposure had to be slow, and she didn't have a tripod, but (remembering Jed's improvisations at Mulan's deathbed) that table would do nicely. Now if Mr. Borodin would just turn his body, oh, and did he have a comb? That blouse with its embroidered flowers—however evocative—might not command as much respect as his uniform jacket. Yes, much better. Al-most ready. And she'd neglected to ask, how had he liked the United States? He attended Valparaiso, wasn't it? She'd never been to Indiana. He met his wife there? Fanny. A pity she couldn't be here tonight, but cer-tainly she should be included in the article.

By the time she was finished, Su had attempted to interrupt three more times and Hope had stretched her fifteen minutes to nearly two hours. Borodin asked if she would like to wait and, after he'd taken care of some business, she might join him for supper with Madame Sun. Hope man-aged to keep her voice steady enough to thank him, but politely refused. "I have some business to attend to up in the concessions."

"We can give you an escort."

"No. Please, I find I can get a better feel for things on my own. I'm used to it."

"I admire your spirit, Miss Newfield," said Borodin. "You are an im-pressive woman. But these are uncertain times for a foreign woman alone in Hankow. At least take this card. If you are stopped, it will assure you safe conduct."

She smiled, ducked her head benignly at Mr. Su, and with forced com-posure, accepted the square of paper signed in Borodin's round, even hand.

శ్రీశ్రీశ్రీ

Outside, the destroyers and gunboats still lined the blackened river, their strung lights like festive ornaments haloed in the mist, their cannons silently sitting guard as clusters of diplomatic and civilian stragglers picked their way down out of the concessions and up the waiting gangways. Hope ducked into a shallow archway where she was hidden but had a clear view back to the villa.

No guards stood watch. No faces appeared at the brightly lit windows. She would surely have noticed if anyone followed her, yet still she trembled and waited. Wheels ground into the pavement. Hooves sounded their dull staccato. Wagons deposited cargoes of household treasures, then moved off in numbing procession. All the while, as in another world, street vendors hawked the noodles and gruels that would stay a poor man's hunger, and oil lamps smoked in the mouths of shops and on the decks of sampans huddled among the warships. What felt like an hour was, by Hope's watch, only five minutes.

Suddenly the villa's front door flew open, and five uniformed policemen filed down the steps as a gleaming black touring car slid from the shadows. Though she was too far away to read their faces, she could tell by his limp that the man in the lead was the Chekka chief who had been waiting for instructions while she prolonged her interview with Borodin. He barked an order at the driver, fired a salute at Mr. Su, who stood above him in the entryway, then the car doors slammed, and the tires spun on the damp pavement. The police were heading in the direction of the ferry to Wuchang. It was nearly ten o'clock when Hope resumed normal breathing.

She was stopped a few minutes later by a soldier in the uniform of the Revolutionary Army, but Borodin's card worked as advertised. Instead of detaining her, the sentry gave her directions to the Japanese consulate and warned her to use the side entrance, as the front was ringed with pickets from Japanese-owned iron mills. There were several hundred camped overnight. She thanked him and told him he reminded her of her eldest son, which he did. He smiled and said he was honored, saluted, and strode off.

Hope was fighting tears all the rest of the way to the consulate. She told herself it was irrational. Whatever might happen to Paul, she would be back with the children within a few days. But the darkness, the mist, the unconsolably ancient echoes of this place made her feel that she had passed into a realm from which there was no return. She fumbled in her bag for her ring, slipped it onto her left hand. Then she wiped her eyes and proceeded.

Hope did not exhibit Borodin's card to the Japanese sentries. Instead she pushed her scarf back so they could see her face, and asked to speak with Mr. Mitsuru. She was shown through a warren of passageways into a large underfurnished salon deep inside the building. In a few minutes, a middle-aged man in a Western suit, with alert, semicircular eyes, entered the room and bowed.

"Mrs. Liang," he said in meticulous English, "you have arrived safely."

She forced herself through the courtesy of bowing. "Is he . . . ?"

"Not yet. My instructions were to await his arrival. This is correct?"

"Yes. Yes, he will be here." She curled one hand uncertainly inside the other.

"Please, be seated." Mr. Mitsuru waited for her and then sat down himself. "I have known your husband for many years. We were students together—"

"I know." Hope's voice shook. Her hand had found the mahogany side table and her thumb was rubbing circles. She knew that her husband could make finer distinctions than she between allies and enemies. This was more difficult than she had expected.

"He has been under house arrest for some months. I am wondering if it might be necessary to send an armed escort."

Hope tried unsuccessfully to read her host's face. His eyes seemed kindly, but his expression never changed. If he'd known Paul was under arrest, why hadn't he sent an armed escort months ago? "No, thank you, Mr. Mitsuru," she said at last. "We wouldn't want this to become an international incident. I have arranged for my husband's rescue in a more discreet—and I believe, safer manner."

Mitsuru sat as if his chair had no cushioning. "I mean only that you may trust me, Mrs. Liang."

She remembered the warmth and tension of Jin's arms about her shoulders. "Trust," she said, "is not easy for a woman in my position."

"I understand."

"But I wouldn't be here if I didn't trust, Mr. Mitsuru."

"Then we must wait." He went to a mirrored bar in the corner and brought back a brandy, which she refused, and a bowl of peanuts, which she attacked with unexpected appetite. Seeing this, he announced that he had not yet dined and invited her join him for a simple meal, which he ordered through the white-jacketed servant stationed outside the door.

"Provisions are sparse," he explained. "The radicals have applied pressure on merchants to discourage their supplying us."

Hope didn't answer. Mitsuru's impenetrable control made her feel like an exposed nerve, but she would not let him know that.

The consulate dining room was even less furnished than the salon. The long table and chairs, bilious green carpet and electric candelabras were still in position, but there were empty spaces where the sideboards and more decorative pieces must have stood. The cries of the protesters, which had been bare whispers in the other room, here were clearly audible.

"You're preparing to evacuate," she said.

A servant brought bowls of miso soup and Mitsuru gestured for her to start. "It is only prudent. But the greater wrath of the masses has been directed toward the British. You understand, they are the true aliens here, the invaders. The Europeans are colonizers and imperialists, and therefore a far greater enemy to China than her brethren in Japan."

Hope grimaced at the soup's pungent saltiness. He sounded, for all his earnest intensity, like a wind-up toy. "When did you last see my husband, Mr. Mitsuru?"

"It was in October, shortly after he arrived in Hankow. He was in good health—trim, fatigued from the Expedition, but in excellent spirits. I remember him saying that he believed Dr. Sun would have been very pleased."

"About the success of the Expedition."

"Yes. The unity."

Hope sighed. "I'm afraid that optimism has always been Paul's Achilles' heel."

"Paul?"

She shunned his questioning glance. "Po-yu's American name. He—he rarely uses it outside of the family."

Mitsuru nodded.

"And how did you first get to know my husband?"

"We were students together at Seijo Gakko." He lifted his napkin to his lips. "I am ashamed to say that our friendship began when we alone of all our class failed at target practice."

"I'd say that's to your credit."

"Ah yes. I remember Po-yu once telling me that his American bride was a pacifist. I find it amusing that the same nation that produced the cowboy and Indian wars now champions the cause of peace."

He remained unflappably gracious even as their conversation now acquired a distrustful edge. He apologized again for the poor quality of the food and she lodged the mandatory protests that, no, the dishes of pork and cuttlefish were excellent—a culinary feat all the more astounding considering the hour and circumstances. But Hope's appetite had left her, and she refused the warm rice wine he offered. Though they did not speak again of Paul, her husband remained at the center of her thoughts, and she was relieved when one of Mitsuru's assistants interrupted.

"I must excuse myself," he said, "but you please remain here as our guest tonight. I have sent—discreetly—for information. As soon as we learn anything you will be notified."

At that he gave her over to a maid who showed her to a dimly lit guest chamber on the second floor. It was after midnight. Heavy woven shades covered the room's two vertical windows. She shut off the lamp before pushing them aside. The room faced the front of the consulate and, beyond the circular entry court, she could see the encampment of protesters, including several women and children huddled beneath dark blankets, with pamphlets and posters scattered at their feet. It was a forlorn and desperate scene, yet frightening as well. These impoverished creatures were responsible for driving the all-mighty British from one of their prize strongholds. They were ignorant, starving, cold, and angry—in short, they had nothing to lose. The organizational skills that Borodin had taught them were like a match to the fuse of a bomb.

Hope scanned the edges of the demonstration fruitlessly for some shadow or movement that might be Jin or Paul, then let the shade swing back. She had so decisively rebuffed Mitsuru's suggestion of sending an armed guard. Why? She wasn't sure except that she knew, instinctively, Jin alone had the better chance of rescuing his father—and, especially in the current climate, they could not risk bloodshed by Japanese troops on Paul's behalf. She lay back staring at the outline of the motionless ceiling fan, recalling the shock in Jin's eyes when she had instructed him to bring Paul here. He despised the Japanese as the revolutionary rhetoric had trained him, and in that look she had seen every fiber in him straining against this solution. Was it possible that he would rescue Paul and take him elsewhere? No. The Western Powers had already demonstrated that they would not fire back even to protect their own, and there was nowhere else Paul could be assured of protection. If there had been, surely Jin would have gotten him out before . . . Surely.

She thought of the military drill Jin was wearing, the ease with which he passed through Borodin's villa—the fact that he knew the Chekka had met, that Paul's name was on the blacklist. But that hug. She had to believe . . . she *did* believe.

She pressed her knuckles hard against her closed eyes until the darkness exploded. The silence was deafening. Not the tick of a clock. No clapping watchmen or clattering honeycarts. Not even the groan of a settling floorboard. It was as if the entire city were in a state of suspension.

She started once more to think of the children, but then she began to cry. She stopped herself and forced her thoughts forward. She had no choice but to rely on Mitsuru. If dawn came and still—

"Hsin-hsin."

Paul stood in the doorway. Unharmed.

ॐॐॐ

At dawn the next morning, disguised as an evacuating Japanese couple and escorted by two consulate Marines, they made their way through snow flurries to a Japanese merchant vessel docked within view of Borodin's villa. When the port official asked for papers, the Marines supplied documentation for Tokutomi Ichiro, a Yokohama haberdasher, and his wife, Nomi. The official mentioned an embarkation fee, which the Marines translated for the "Ichiros," who unfortunately spoke no Chinese, and "Tokutomi," whose face was masked against the snow and cold, made an impatient motion and deposited three times the named fee in the official's moth-eaten glove. The official bowed, turned on his heel. Fifteen minutes later the *Kuriyama* was underway, chipping ice with her bow and shooting plumes of white steam into the steel wool sky.

They spent the next week in the narrow cubicle designated as their compartment. They spoke haltingly of their children, the long months that had passed between them, the letters they had written that were never received. They touched. They wept. And then he told of the gunshots, the cries of his gate man being pistol-whipped, finally the terror that had driven him to break through the thin plaster wall behind the Kitchen God's altar, to find his son digging toward him from the other side. Then the race to asylum with the Chekka's shouts ringing in their ears, and Jin's haste as he slipped back into the night, promising to meet Paul in Shanghai.

Of her own role, Hope said only that Jin had summoned her, to smooth things with Mitsuru. Jin saved your life, she told him.

XII
BETRAYAL
SHANGHAI
(1927–1932)

☙☙☙

1

The Shanghai to which the Japanese steamer returned them was a changed city. Even before they reached port, they had seen the gunboats and riverboats stuffed to the bulwarks with pale-faced refugees, mostly men now following the earlier evacuation of women and children from the interior. Through the *Kuriyama*'s crew Paul learned that the surrender of Hankow to the National Revolutionary Army, followed by the fall of Kiukiang on January 7, had sparked panic among the taipans. Standard Oil, Jardine Matheson, Butterfield, Royal Dutch Shell, U.S. Steel, Asiatic Petroleum, American Tobacco—all the major "imperialist" enterprises had recalled their employees from the interior to the one city in China where there were sufficient foreign troops to protect them.

As soon as they stepped onto the pier, Hope could see that those troops had multiplied many times over, just in the days she'd been gone. The streets were now thronged, not only with refugees and beggars and Concession patrols, but Punjabi police shipped from Bombay, British Bluejackets, French Annamites, Japanese and American Marines. A three-foot-deep barbed-wire barricade now ringed the foreign compounds, fortified by sandbags, tommy guns, and armored cars. When Hope's and Paul's rickshaws were stopped at the checkpoint, the British officer turned up his lip and demanded identification. Paul had nothing but the Chinese clothes he was wearing when he fled his home in Wuchang. Hope pawed through her carpetbag. When she had left Shanghai, no documentation was required. At last she hauled out Cadlow's letter. It gave the address on Rue de Grouchy and implied that— present Chinese garb notwithstanding—she was an American. She said merely that Paul was "with her." The officer grudgingly let them pass but warned them, from now on, to "carry credentials."

She could see, looking over to the other rickshaw, how furious Paul was at this ultimate insult, but within minutes they had reached the house and her own anger gave way to relief at seeing the children. With a cry, she scooped Teddy out of Ah-nie's arms and surprised the others at a game of rounders with some neighbors in the backyard. The children gave their father a restrained, uncertain glance, Hope a more genuine hug, and asked, wasn't it exciting with all the soldiers, and did they think there might really be a fight? The Eurasian Volunteer Corps conducted daily drills in front of the house, and Morris reported that Gerald Chou said he could enlist in three months, soon as he turned fifteen.

Suddenly Jasmine burst into tears. Two days earlier she'd left the gate open, and the dogs had run off. No one had seen them since.

಄಄಄

February 25, 1927

All right. I surrender. I have had my fill of this madness. Getting Paul back alive was excitement enough to last me two lifetimes, but there is to be no end to the uncertainty, it seems. Last weekend Shanghai went on strike again—nearly half a million workers walked off the job. No trams. No dockworkers. No factory whistles. Chapei was a ghost town, the concessions under siege. Almost the only sounds were the cries of the student protesters, the soapbox organizers haranguing the "masses" as everyone insists on calling them. Of course, the schools were closed, though I wouldn't have let the children out in any event. Paul spent most of these days closeted with Eugene Chou, who seems to have become a close ally in the aftermath of Wuchang. I am afraid that Paul's loathing for Borodin may be driving him into league with equally detestable, though opposite, men. I've never trusted

Eugene as far as I could see him. All his money, I suppose, and the shabby way he treats Sarah—the latest is he's *arranged a marriage* for Ken, and according to Sarah he's promised to turn her out on the street without a cent if she opposes him. She says she's less afraid of poverty than that Eugene will set some local thug against her—and has sent Gerry to seek his fortune in the States rather than risk his attempting to protect his brother. Apparently Eugene is financial "advisor" both to Shanghai's most notorious mobster, Tu Yueh-sheng, and to our local warlord, Sun Chuan-fang. Paul's affiliation with Eugene sickens—and frightens—me almost as much as Sarah's marriage does, but Paul is as dismissive as Sarah is sanguine. She laughs; Paul nods and closes his eyes. The children play, and the workers strike.

We all go along in our separate universes, scheming, worrying, fantasizing, and accusing, and the only times our interests ever truly intersect are when the blades are drawn and the guns begin, as they did again last night. There was no violence in the concessions, of course, and if Paul had his way we'd never learn what happened, but Jin came this afternoon. His clothes were torn, he was bleeding from the neck and covered with mud. Paul was in his study, but Jin begged me not to tell him he'd come. I cleaned him up and gave him fresh clothing—the wound was superficial. I instructed the servants to keep the children away and made Jin tell me everything he'd witnessed. Of course, it was retaliation for the strikes, only this time the British got the warlords to do their dirty work. Instead of foreign troops firing at students, the execution squads—and the methods—were Chinese. Two of Jin's close friends were beheaded as they were trying to get back onto St. John's campus. A dead Chinese baby was hurled over the gates of the Episcopal mission, and an old man—a mere street peddler—was shot for crying out "Cakes for sale!" because in Shanghainese this sounds like "Overcome the soldiers." Anyone handing out leaflets was paraded through the Chinese City, then lined up by Sun Chuan-fang's troops and shot. In retribution the Communists have been killing off any worker who dares to oppose unionization. Jin was so scared he was shaking. It was worse than Wuhan, he said, and I thought, of course, he would think that. In Wuhan, his father's life was at stake and only secondarily his own. I wish they could both see that, in spite of so many divisions and striations, we really are in this together.

But Jin refused to stay for fear Paul would come down and they would get in a shouting match. I took Teddy into my lap for a story. Jasmine sat down to listen. Morris was in the corner working on a model automobile. Then Pearl came in with her hands full of knitting, and every so often I'd glance up and see those long needles . . . I felt as if we were inside a cocoon, while outside the silkworms had all gone mad, and soon we alone would survive.

﷼﷼﷼

Late in March, Shanghai's labor unions called for another general strike, and workers throughout the city began arming themselves. At noon on the twenty-first, Jin stopped by—jubilant—to announce that the strike had begun and throughout the Chinese neighborhoods union pickets were routing the gray-uniformed troops and police allied with Shanghai's warlord, Sun Chuan-fang. Though the workers were armed only with clubs, axes, and small arms, Jin's report proved accurate, and exactly twenty-nine hours later, all Shanghai outside the foreign settlements was under Nationalist control. Even before the fighting ceased, the streets were festooned with blue and white Kuomintang, red Communist flags, and banners welcoming the troops of the Northern Expedition, which arrived just in time to celebrate.

To Paul's dismay, Chiang Kai-shek played no part in this victory. The uprising had been organized and executed by the students and Communists, and so was perceived primarily as a Communist rather than a Nationalist triumph. There was widespread talk that Chiang was finished, that the Communists were poised for a takeover of the Kuomintang. Thus, instead of calming fears within the concessions, the arrival of the Northern Expedition, for which Paul had worked so hard, was heightening the foreigners' alarm.

In the weeks that followed, Paul ruminated endlessly over these developments. Often as he lay awake into the night, he would turn to Hope, reciting some article he had read in the *North China Daily* and asking if his interpretation of editorial mistrust for Chiang Kai-shek was correct. Since Wuchang he solicited her opinion more than ever in the past, and though he did not say so outright, she knew he was trying to plan his own next political alliance. Since the uprising, Chiang Kai-shek had appointed Sarah's husband, Eugene Chou, to his inner cabinet and abruptly recalled William Tan from his ambassadorship in America to serve as commissioner of foreign affairs. It was only a matter of time before Chiang reached out for Paul, but whether Paul would—or should—agree to serve was far less clear. Hope said he had read the papers correctly and reminded him, tersely, that Chiang had been strolling about Kuling with Borodin while Paul was under house arrest.

"He may not have sanctioned your execution," she said, "but he certainly didn't lift a finger to stop it."

"He did not know. I am not important."

"You were important enough for Borodin to order you killed! Why? Because he felt a personal vendetta, or because he believed you'd already allied yourself with Chiang? Either way, Chiang should have thought you important enough to rescue, shouldn't he?"

But the shrillness in her voice seemed to weary Paul. He would confide his ambivalence, but rarely his choices, and in retracting from her he would invariably fall back on that hated phrase, "You do not understand."

Then, one evening as she was getting ready for bed, he said, "We must celebrate."

"Celebrate?"

Paul's reflection in the dressing table mirror showed him sitting at the foot of the bed, elbows planted on his pajamaed knees, the stem of his neck sunk between his shoulders. His hair stuck up in graying tufts, and his voice had a strange, metallic timbre. He seemed to be talking to the wall. "A simple dinner. Chinese style. To celebrate William and Daisy's homecoming and the new appointment. I will ask Eugene Chou. You will like to have Sarah—" his eyes flicked in her direction "—so you are not too much in Daisy's company. And Jin will come." He drew a cigarette from the lacquer box beside the bed and prepared to light it.

"Jin!" Hope half turned toward him. "Is that wise, with Eugene?"

Paul replanted his elbows on his knees, smoking. "William will want to know everything that has happened. He enjoys the details of battle. Jin was in the streets during the uprising. He can tell about it. Don't worry, Hope. I will instruct him."

"But Eugene is notorious for his hatred of the left. And you know how outspoken Jin can be, especially when his back is to the wall. Why risk it?"

The corner of the room around her husband was sliding behind a haze. "Jin will come."

"You sound as if you've already asked him."

"I have told him."

"But *why?*"

Paul held the cigarette inelegantly between the pads of forefinger and thumb. At length he stood and looked at her. "This is between Jin and me, Hope. Do not trouble yourself."

"Trouble myself! Paul, you don't—"

"No!" The ash from his cigarette dropped to the floor. He flicked it irritably with his bare toes, then ground the stub into an ashtray on her table. "You do not question me. Jin will come. You arrange the meal, whatever you like. You talk to Sarah. Talk to Daisy about America. You do not question me and Jin." He pulled his robe from the back of the chair, then, a measure more softly as he shrugged it on and stepped into his slippers, "I will be in my study. You go to sleep."

Though he wasn't wearing his glasses, she could see the circular impressions of his spectacles in the puffy skin around his eyes. His jaw thrust forward as he swallowed. He made no move to open the door.

"Paul." She leaned, touched the fall of his sleeve, and met his eyes. "Just tell me whose cause you are serving here. Jin is your son. He saved your life."

His eyes skated past her, and she felt a compression in her chest as she thought again of their talk during those long days on the steamer back from Wuhan, the half-truths she had told about the circumstances of his rescue and her own part in its execution. She had given Jin the credit, reconstructed the story so that he had returned to Wuhan of his own accord, that the idea of contacting the Japanese had come from Jin, and she had come only as a last resort, to plead for Paul's life with the Japanese and, foreigner to foreigner, with Borodin in the event Jin's rescue plan failed. She did not mention that she had, in fact, met with Borodin, and later, when she typed up the article for Cadlow, she sent it under a pseudonym that could not be linked to either her or Paul. Meanwhile, she instructed Jin and Jed Israel to say nothing of her true role in Wuhan. Her reasons for drawing this veil were more intuitive than specific. She told herself it was right that a son should save his father's life, and Jin had taken the greater physical risk. Maybe now the rift between the two men could be closed for good, and Jin could once more assume an active role in all their lives. But underneath the justifications she made to herself lay another, more ominous awareness. As she'd written up her interview with Borodin, later as she developed the pictures she had taken and recalled the horror and exhilaration of those two nerve-racking hours, she found she could not disagree with all—or even many—of the points the Russian had made. He spoke her language. He seemed a reasonable man. He made *sense* to her. Yet he had ordered the execution of her husband. How could she possibly explain that to Paul? How could he trust her if she did? The truth was, she no longer trusted herself.

"Yes," Paul interrupted her thoughts. "I owe Jin my life. That is why, Hope. *That* is why."

Two nights later the party raised glasses and drank to the Northern Expedition's success. Although Jin was clearly uneasy in his role as partisan observer, he did not shrink from the retelling of the skirmishes, the eagerness of certain police battalions to retreat, the joy with which students and workers reclaimed the streets. "When the Nationalist flag rose above the post office," he said with a sidelong look to Hope, "I thought of the years Father spent in exile, his long association with Dr. Sun, all that we endured last summer, and I felt such pride. Tears came to my eyes—"

"Yes." William, who sat beside Daisy in the place of honor, waved his spoon impatiently. "Good filial son. But what about the fighting?"

"The warlord's troops were happy to throw away their weapons, and the rebels were happy to let them run. In Nantao, the Chinese City, there was no real fighting."

"No fighting." Pearl had insisted that, at eighteen, she was too old to be excluded from the party. "But lots of flags!"

"I never saw so many flags," Sarah concurred. "My tailor said his wife stood outside his shop selling every one as fast as he could turn it out."

"Very patriotic." Eugene turned and spat thickly into the brass spittoon Yen had knowingly placed behind him. His presence had lost none of its power over the years, but the elegance that once impressed Hope had long since been replaced by a coarseness of both features and manner. His bullet-shaped head and neck had grown fat, and his eyes had taken on the same yellow tinge as his skin. He reminded Hope of an enormous pit bull.

Jin went on, "By afternoon the only gunfire I hear was coming from Chapei. There the White Russian mercenaries were surrounded. I saw flames rising taller than the Commercial Press. And so many people pushing to get through the barricades into the Settlement."

Paul cleared his throat, and Jin stopped talking.

"Yesterday," said Daisy in her usual oblivious fashion, "before I even unpack my things, William insists we go to see Chapei. Nothing is left there! I think this bad, sure, many factories burned, but also good. Now Chapei rebuild, all new and clean."

Hope met Jin's disgusted gaze. The others continued eating.

"You might consider," said Hope, "that thousands of people lost their lives, between the fires and shelling. And fifteen hundred homes were destroyed."

"Hope—" Paul's voice was sharp, but William stopped him with a casual wave of his hand.

"Hope is right. Daisy's words were thoughtless. Her tongue is made stupid by her admiration of America where everything seems so new and clean."

"Did you see Berkeley," asked Pearl. "Did you see where we used to live?"

Daisy's small fine head swiveled complacently toward Pearl, as if she had forgotten that this young woman was the same child she used to favor with treats and trinkets. "I am sorry, we visit New York and Washington only. I very like the tall, tall buildings. Everyone so elegant. My Kuo, he say, 'I come to university here, maybe marry American bride, same as Uncle Liang.'"

Hope turned away. The thought of this vain, grasping, heartless woman flitting over American soil made her sick with envy and resentment. But Paul and William erupted in a bluster of laughter. "No need go to America," corrected Eugene, jerking his goatee at Sarah.

"How is New York?" said Sarah, with a steadying glance at Hope. "I lived there once."

Hope signaled Yen to bring the next course, and Jin continued with details about the White Russians who had been trapped inside an armored train, the thousands of red-ribboned execution swords the workers had confiscated, the sight of northern soldiers stripping off their gray uniforms as they ran, pleading to be let into the concessions.

Suddenly Eugene, who had been shaking his big head sullenly throughout this last recitation, looked up with interest and interrupted. "I hear talk of you," he said, narrowing his yellow eyes at Jin. "I think you are too modest, my nephew."

Paul's hand, half lifted to his lips, descended.

"I hear that your father owes you his life," continued Eugene. "You are a true filial son!"

"What is this?" William's voice lifted, raucous and laughing, as it had when he regaled them with the story of Paul's first confrontation with Borodin.

Jin rubbed his lips together, glancing at Hope. Paul busied himself apportioning the sea bass Yen had brought in, leaving it to Eugene to describe the rescue in Wuhan. His version matched the account Hope had fed to Paul, so she assumed it had come from him, but the thought of his exchanging this confidence with Eugene made her acutely uncomfortable. Sarah's arched brow as she listened to the account only intensified this discomfort. If Hope had not felt free enough to tell Sarah, her most trusted friend, then how could Paul have told—*why* would he have chosen to tell Eugene?

"*Gan bei!*" the men thundered, raising their glasses in Jin's honor.

"Now, Liang," said William, "it's your turn. Three times you must drink to your son's health, for if his health had failed, you would not be here to drink at all!"

Eugene gave a hearty laugh and pounded the table. Paul made a show of sighing and shaking his head, but dutifully lifted and emptied his glass three times. When he finished he went around the table to Jin. Father and son embraced. Paul scuffed a hand through Jin's hair as if he were a child, and Hope was struck by the unnaturalness of this gesture. Of all his children, only Teddy received such treatment. Never Jin. The laughter continued with artificial volume. The women clapped their hands. The men fell on the successive courses of food, but both Jin and Paul were fidgety. Paul smoked throughout the meal. Jin tapped his chopsticks against his glass, turned to Pearl and showed her how to make the napkin swans which used to delight her as a child. Daisy and Sarah talked of shopping in New York. The men's conversation returned inexorably to politics. The recent movements of Communists under this young man Mao Tse-tung in Hunan. The territories yet to be taken by the Expeditionary Army. William's impression of a warming among the foreign powers toward Chiang Kai-shek. Hope's attention drifted. Their fixation was so incessant, like the roll of waves against the shore, each new development bringing minute shifts of light and sand but never any definitive answer or conclusion—never anything to hold on to.

She was drawn back to the conversation by a subtle but unmistakable shift in Eugene's tone. "But you," he was saying to Jin. "You have a head for politics, I think. How is it that you learned Mr. Borodin had condemned your father?" He opened his eyes wide and looked around at the other guests. "Could it be you are a *spy?*"

Daisy covered her mouth with her hand and tittered appreciatively, while Pearl, who had been listening to Daisy's and Sarah's descriptions of Fifth Avenue, looked up with a bemused expression. Sarah determinedly sipped her wine, as if to react to her husband would only encourage him.

"It could be that any of us are spies," Jin answered evenly. "Or all of us."

Hope was aware of Paul beside her lighting yet another cigarette. The smoke already encased him.

"All of us?" Eugene pursed his fleshy lips and cast a glance around the table. "I hope we are on the same side, then."

"And what side is that?" Jin countered.

Eugene stroked his beard. "The side that is fighting for a free and united China, of course."

"And what side is that?" pressed Jin.

Paul's cigarette dropped in his plate. He fumbled for his glass and lifted it toward Eugene. "To the Kuomintang!"

It was a dreadful misstep. Everyone but Jin lifted a glass.

"You do not drink to the party of your father," Eugene observed.

"I do not drink to the party that employs thugs to murder patriots. I do not drink to the party that is ruled by traitors."

"Traitors!"

"My son knows nothing of politics." Paul was rising to his feet, leaning behind Hope as if to grab Jin by the collar, but Jin was already standing.

"Traitors such as Mr. Chou's own good friend Gangster Tu."

There was a shrill, suffocating moment of silence. Then Paul's hand flashed through the air, his knuckles slamming into his son's jaw so hard that the reverberation shook the tableware. Jin's head spun back over his right shoulder, then snapped forward again with a shudder. Paul barked at him in their home dialect, a voice wrung from his throat. But Jin's eyes, though glittering with tears, held fast on Eugene's smile. Then he stepped away from the table, pivoted, and left.

To Hope's horror, Paul began to laugh. He tugged on his ear. *"T'a tsui le!"* he said. He's drunk!

"T'a chen te tsui le!" Eugene and William echoed Paul's hoots. He's drunk, all right.

Hope sat rooted to her chair, unable to answer Pearl's bewildered stare, to hear Daisy's banter, to receive Sarah's telepathic sympathy. She was aware only of the hysterical darkness that underscored her husband's laughter. He had brought his son into the tiger's cage to win the tiger's protection. Instead, Jin had jabbed the beast in the eye—and fled with the cage door open.

2

Paul refused to speak of Jin in the days that followed. He ignored Hope's questioning glances, turned away from her touch. He instructed Yen to stockpile provisions for a month. He forbade the family to leave the Concession—and Hope, in particular, to go anywhere near Jed Israel. He spent his days and evenings in meetings, most nights hunched over his desk. Hope begged him to tell her what he knew, what had him so pre-occupied—and frightened. But he would only stare back at her from behind those round lenses like a fish inside a tank, and she knew that some irreparable line between them had broken.

One night in mid-April Hope woke with a vague sense of alarm. The bed beside her was empty. She got up and checked Paul's study, the kitchen, the drawing room. It was overcast, the shadows deeper, more sinister than usual, yet she felt certain that he had not left the house. From room to room she padded, on bare feet so as not to alert the servants. Yen heard anyway, and met her at the stairs. She reassured him that, no, she hadn't heard anything. She'd been hungry was all. He gave her an incredulous look; in the fifteen years of his employment he had never known her to night-walk. But he returned to bed, and she continued her search through the nursery, Jasmine's and Pearl's rooms. Morris's door was ajar.

Paul sat at the end of the bed. It was too dark to read his expression, but his posture was slumped, elbows resting on his knees and chin in his hands. He was not watching Morris the way she sometimes watched her children sleep. His was not an attitude of love . . . it was more like that of a lapsed Christian who, in a moment of weakness, finds himself in church.

He gave no sign that he noticed her, though she could see well enough that his eyes were open. The iridescent hands of Morris's alarm clock read almost four A.M. A few brave nightingales were chirping, and from the direction of Nanking Road came the low continuous reverberations of movement and music. A cold damp breeze stirred the heavy drapes, and she thought she heard a dog bark.

She hesitated, then came forward, lightly touching Paul's shoulder. The touch did not startle him and, to her surprise, he did not reject it.

"He's nearly grown," she whispered. In fact, Morris would turn fifteen in just a few days. He had already gotten someone to give him a helmet like the ones the Eurasian Volunteer Corps wore, though Hope had forbidden him to join.

Paul sat up and placed his hand over Hope's. "He must not stay here."

"What?"

"When he finishes school, I will arrange it. He will go to Berkeley or Yale. America."

"Yale! Paul, what has possessed you?"

But his eyes were fastened on the sleeping boy. He merely squeezed her hand.

At fifty-one, Paul was a powerful man, but the events of the past years had left their mark in subtle ways that surprised her at moments such as this, when something he said or did made her experience him like a stranger. Suddenly she would notice the crepey softness of his neck, the concentric wrinkles that had formed beneath his earlobes, the deepening crow's-feet, the brittleness of his collarbone under his thin silk robe. He smoked and chewed on his nails constantly, so the tips of his fingers had become callused and yellow, the pads spatulated—she could feel the scrape of his ragged nails even now against her wrist, smelled the nicotine in his skin. His hair had receded back behind his crown, and the loss of four teeth had brought a downward cast to his once firm mouth. But none of these changes explained this uncharacteristic concern for his son's future.

"Of course, I want this—" She was silenced by a bugle blast, immediately echoed by a watery siren. Paul stood up so violently that Hope was thrown off balance. "What is it?"

But he had gone to close the window, and when he turned back he threw a quick glance at Morris, who had not stirred, and motioned her out of the room. By the hall light she saw a muscle throbbing in his cheek. He pushed her ahead of him.

They entered their bedroom, and with a single movement, he peeled off her nightgown and jerked her toward him. Not a word. Not a sound. He lowered himself to the edge of the bed and buried his face between her breasts. Hard and tight, his knuckles drove into the flesh beneath her shoulder blades. A hot, wet stream slid down her belly, and the breath she'd been holding unfurled as she felt him howling into her skin.

ᏦᏦᏦ

Within minutes of that siren, the guns began. Small arms, at first, spraying the pickets stationed near the Tramways Company and Commercial Press. Then squads of soldiers moved against the railway and docks, positioned machine guns outside guild houses and union offices.

By dawn a hard rain was falling, the stammering of machine gunfire seemed to issue from every direction, and the gutters were running red.

Gangster Tu's White Armbands killed Jed Israel as he attempted to defend a picket station across the river in Pootung. His body was found in a drainage ditch two days later, his long red hair turned green with sewage, his head all but severed from his neck by an automatic weapon that fired more precisely than any camera he'd ever owned.

Jin's body was dumped on Hope and Paul's doorstep that same evening, though it was weeks before they pieced together the details of his murder. He had survived the first night of the massacre to march under that relentless morning's rain with some hundred thousand men, women, and children through the ruins of Chapei. They were appealing to Chiang Kai-shek and the Kuomintang and the forces of peaceful justice to stop the slaughter. They were unarmed. Chiang's soldiers stood in two military lines on either side of Paoshan Road and watched as the demonstrators marched into the gauntlet, women and children first. Then the troops raised their bayonets, Mausers, and tommy guns. The back of Jin's skull split like a pomegranate, spilling its gleaming fruit.

ৡৡৡ

3

One could hardly say that was the beginning of the end. The beginning of the end had been the beginning, but that was so long ago that when Hope thought back to the first warning cannonade in Berkeley, she could not remember the smell of exploded flesh and bone for the stronger memory of roses. The smell of death now was fresh and the faces of the executed still pulsed in her eyes. The even greater difference, though, was Paul.

After the White Terror had ended, if it could be said that it ever ended, he became another man. Not just older or harder or more withdrawn. He became the man that he had been struggling for twenty years to change.

He had Yen give away his American suits and ordered a tailor in the Chinese City to make four new black and brown shantung robes, two velvet waistcoats, and three sets of white silk underwear, one wide-sleeved mandarin jacket, and three round black silk scholar's caps. He adopted an ivory cigarette holder and a tight, tripping style of walking, the habit of rolling two silver exercise balls as he stood for endless hours pondering his lecture notes or compositions. Scholarly pursuits seemed to absorb virtually all his time, energy, and affection. He no longer dined with the family, avoided Western foods, and resumed his old habit of playing mahjongg or singing poetry criticism with his friends late into the night. He would withdraw to the Nantao house for days at a stretch, and seemed hardly to notice his children, except to criticize the shortness of their dresses, demand why they were not studying, or admonish them to show some respect. No more was said of his proposal to send Morris to college in America, but one day he called the family into the drawing room, and there was Old Yu, the doctor who Paul now maintained had "cured" him of meningitis. Yu was to be the children's Chinese tutor, Paul announced. He would come for one hour every evening to teach them their native language. Yu Hu-hsu, the children mockingly called him, for his long trickling beard. His voice was like the squeak of chalk on blackboard and he had the disgusting habit of picking his nose with the three-inch scholar's nail on his little finger. Soon he had the children parroting classical verses from the Tang and Ming Dynasties, though when Hope tested them they retained not a word.

She supposed, in some twisted way that defied her understanding, this cultural reversion was Paul's means of grieving, his compensation for the fact that the political climate deprived him of a proper funeral and mourning for his son. He would accept no other comfort, refused to talk of Jin's death. He left Hope to her business as the mother of his children, and once or twice a week she would awake to see him disrobing at the end of the bed, or to the weight of his hand on her breast, and he would take her without a kiss, without tenderness. He would take her with the same inattentive greed with which he now drank his wine. On other nights he either slept in his study or stayed out at his meetings and banquets until morning. She did not oppose him. She did not complain even when she noticed the sticky green scent of opium on his clothes, or when, one morning after a particularly drunken night, he fell asleep in the rickshaw and "lost" ten thousand dollars he'd won at the gambling table.

The truth was, Hope envied his ability to retreat, however destructively, however incomprehensibly. She thought, if only she'd known her mother or Seneca grandmother, they might have taught her some native rituals of her own to answer the horror, the sorrow, the *impossibility* of what had happened. But the one thing she had accomplished by coming to China was to erase that piece of her heritage finally and completely. She was no longer American at all. She was a white Chinese. What was it Jin had said? When a negative is combined with its positive, the result is zero.

ॐॐॐ

In July, Mikhail Borodin fled Hankow and returned to the Soviet Union. Paul immediately went to Wuchang to reclaim his home. "It is well," he reported on his return. "Workers lived in some courts, but the library survives, and my father's sedan chair." For the first time in weeks, he looked at her as if he expected some reply, but Hope could find no words to answer him.

She knew now, the family had to leave, else the weight of this madness would crush them. But when she suggested to Paul that the time had come for her to take the children home, he would not hear of it. Steamship fares had escalated sharply with the demand of the inland refugees fleeing back to the States. A new government post for him had not yet been found, and with all the strikes and disruption of classes, his university pay had been halved. Besides, it was impossible for Chinese citizens to get visas.

She had only one way out, but that ironically would force her back into the very business she now wanted desperately to escape. After the Borodin article, Cadlow offered to raise her rate to one hundred dollars or more per article—on condition she write about the "guts of China's civil war." Word of the White Terror, as the April 12 slaughter was now called, had excited a great deal of interest across the Pacific. To the Americans, the blood that had streamed from her stepson's head was far enough away and "exotic" enough to be titillating.

So for weeks she forced herself to listen with widened ears whenever William or Eugene came to visit. She searched the *North China Daily, Shen*

Bao, the *Kuowen ch'ou-p'ao*, the *China Weekly Review* for the discrepancies that revealed hidden truth. She kept notes on the gossip her children brought back via school chums. But the men did most of their talking behind closed doors. The editorials swam together. And the children were hardly reliable sources. She knew that the kind of reporting Cadlow wanted would require her to take her notepad and camera to the streets, to the parts of town Jin and Jed used to show her, to hotel lobbies and bars such as the Cathay, to the docks and mills and godowns and the ruins of Chapei, where she would find what was left of the blocks where once she had attempted to escape with Stephen Mann—where Jin had been shot in cold blood. She could not bring herself to set foot outside the Concession.

Sympathetic Sarah was a frequent visitor, bringing "intelligence from the field," as she called it. Eugene's nights with her now were not frequent enough to yield much more than Hope overheard between him and Paul, but Sarah's own adventures were more colorful. She had been present for sailors' brawls in Blood Alley, could describe all the newest, gaudiest nightclubs down to the last pink-tinted chandelier and which of Tu's mistresses sang or danced where. She had tales—through the woman who dyed her hair—about Shanghai's most fantastic perversions and illicit liaisons, in varying sexual, animal, and drug-induced combinations. Hope tried to sponge up Sarah's prurient delight and pour it through her pen, but the resulting articles turned her stomach. While she spoke at length of Shanghai's nightlife, Sarah never mentioned young Ken's forced engagement to one of Chiang Kai-shek's cousins.

Gradually, reluctantly, Hope gave up trying to satisfy Cadlow and earn the cash to go home. Instead, she began to write for herself. She wrote about idealistic young men catching the thrill of revolution, about a tragic young wife who poisoned herself rather than submit to her husband's brutality. She wrote of a lonely, alienated doctor who deluded himself into thinking he was in love with a married woman, and of a beautiful Irishwoman who had become a Chinese gangster's concubine. She told the story of a father forced to abandon his son to execution by the White Terror.

September 14, 1927
Harper's
Dear Miss Newfield:

Imagine my surprise on opening your latest collection. After your searing portrait of Borodin last spring, I thought we had agreed you should pursue this more aggressive political reporting. I wish you had mentioned your desire to write fiction, as we could then have taken it step by step.

I'm afraid these stories, while poignant and full of colorful detail, are both too fantastic and too overwrought for our readers to "buy" them. Please understand, we do publish short fiction pieces, but far fewer than articles and essays, and they generally must follow a certain arching form, with a beginning, a middle, and a surprise at the end. They must be as focused and controlled as your photographs (which were also missed in this collection), the emotion contained rather than bursting, the details judiciously selected rather than thrown out scattershot.

I have the sense, Miss Newfield, that you are somehow unburdening yourself in these pieces rather than crafting them into literature. If you care to refine them into proper stories I will be only too glad to review them. However, I'm afraid, as they stand, they are unpublishable, and under the circumstances, I am unable to forward the advance of five hundred dollars you have requested.

I hope this has been helpful rather than hurtful, and that you do not discontinue your journalistic efforts while you experiment in other directions.

Sincerely,
William Cadlow

She replied to Cadlow's letter by mashing it into a ball and throwing it across the room. Damn him. She could no more write a straight, clinical report on this massacre or Chiang's farcical government than she could have suppressed the hysteria that gripped her when she heard in July that Chiang had awarded Gangster Tu the Order of the Brilliant Jade and appointed him Chief of Opium Suppression. Cadlow was right. She was an amateur. She was overwrought. And he was right, too, that she had done the stories for other reasons. They had released some of the chaos bottled up inside her. At least she could now speak Jin's name aloud, could remember Jed's pure, painful stammer without weeping. She could forgive Paul his mystifying transformation, even if she would never be able to accept it. And she could go on as mother to her children without her heart leaping into her throat every time they left the house. Though this came the hardest.

That first morning, within hours after the machine guns subsided, Morris had slipped away. Hope immediately sent Yen in pursuit, but Morris had met a couple of neighborhood boys and they ducked under some shrubbery and disappeared. When Morris finally returned, nearly two hours later, Hope slapped him across the face and boxed his ears, weeping. It was the first time she had struck any of her children since that awful night leaving Peking. Much later Morris confessed that he had seen a Chinese boy no older than himself pinned under the barbed-wire barricades—his mouth sliced back from ear to ear and bullet holes punched in his chest. Though he became a Boy Scout that summer, Morris never again spoke of joining the Eurasian Volunteer Corps, and whenever the subject of his future came up, he said he would very much like to attend university in America.

But Pearl's future was more imminent. In spite of the Terror—or more likely because of it—neither her incomplete record nor her dubious grades had prevented her from graduating that June, a month shy of her nineteenth birthday. Yet Pearl remained a child. Seemingly immune to the horrors and hardships around her, she was given to bursts of tittering laughter, expressions such as "skidoo" and "toodles" and "Oh, you kid!" She marcelled her hair, turned down her stockings, and rouged her knees and cheeks. And though she kept a diligent scrapbook from the *North China Daily*, she ignored all news of politics, instead clipping articles about U.S. Marine Corps parades, the annual race club meetings, drownings of coolies in Soochow Creek, and colorful car accidents and fires along Bubbling Well Road. While she spoke of Jin with sadness and a kind of awe, talked of praying for his soul, there was no depth to her grief. It was as if she did not quite believe that he was—*could be*—dead.

In much the same way her father retreated to his Chinese traditions, Pearl had responded to the Terrors by immersing herself in Shanghai's social whirl. Parties and boys, she joked, were her new religion. She had wormed her way into a circle of silly but well-to-do girls whose fathers were American or French Catholics and whose suitors were the boys of the Concession Volunteer Corps. The Volunteers, she said, were "just swell" when you got to chatting with them. When Hope tried to explain precisely why those boys would act so particularly "swell" to a pretty little Eurasian girl, Pearl cried, "Mama, these are boys from the *best* families, and they're only being friendly. Besides, why would they trouble me with all that when they can have an *experienced* White Russian princess for a song!" Finally, Hope had no alternative but to tell Pearl bluntly that neither her sweet, but rather unassuming looks nor her father's "position" made her more than a marginal marriage prospect. Besides, if they were ever to get out of China, they would need more money than Hope's writing could bring, even if she did get it back on track. And Pearl had neither the inclination nor the grades to go to college. So that summer, while fighting kept the river—and Kuling—closed to civilians, Hope taught her daughter how to hunt for a job.

They circled ads in the *North China Daily*, telephoned for appointments, bought American patterns and sewed trim linen suits and collared "work dresses." They rehearsed her presentation for interviews (discovering in the process that eleven-year-old Jasmine had an uncanny eye for the nuance of smile or turn of phrase that would make Pearl seem more sophisticated), and within two weeks Pearl had landed a secretarial position with Asia Realty, typing and answering the telephone for a rotund cigar-smoking Cockney named Jim Yeardley. Pearl was so naive that she thought her new boss was just being friendly when he offered her whiskey at the end of the day, but those bedroom eyes lost their luster when Pearl, while tidying the back storeroom, stumbled on some old account books stuffed with Yeardley's pilfered cash. Mr. Pedersen, the company's mild goggle-eyed owner, became Pearl's eternal champion, but the poor girl was terrified for weeks by the booted Yeardley's threat of revenge. She insisted either Hope or Yen walk her to work and pick her up every day, and though there was no further trace of the dreaded Cockney, by the following spring Hope suspected her daughter might make a better bride than working girl after all.

There was no shortage of beaux. Eurasians, Frenchmen, Americans, and Italians. The problem had to do with their intentions. Hope insisted that Pearl introduce any boy who meant to take her out, and she restricted her to double or group dates. Pearl scoffed at her mother's cautiousness, but she did not disobey. Yeardley had taught her a lesson, and there were too many sailors and soldiers swaggering about for even Pearl to be cavalier. She narrowed her escorts finally to one. Trevor Noble was a sweet if consumptive boy whose father worked at the American Mail Line and whose sister Googoo was an old school chum of Pearl's.

Paul did not approve. "She should be married," he growled. "How can she spend so much time with him, still they do not marry?"

"They're getting to know each other."

"She can know him after marriage!"

"She's only twenty," Hope reminded him. "I was twenty-five when you married me."

"That is different," he said. "You were American girl."

"According to her passport, so is Pearl."

He reached for his cap from the stand by the door. They were having this conversation, like most lately, in passing.

"She should be married," he repeated, and left.

෨෨෨

August 3, 1928
c/o Noble
Lot 112, Mokanshan
Dear Mama,

Well, we got here safely, and it's lovely. The swimming pool is just beside the garden, and the tennis court is on the left side of the house. My room is on the ground floor.

The first night something woke me up and I listened and listened till I couldn't hear a thing, then as clear as anything, I hear something at my shutter, just as tho someone lifted it to try and get in. Oh my! I was scared. I tried to scream, but not a sound came out. I could only listen and listen. I told myself it was Mr. Noble or a servant, but it kept on for what seemed hours, besides there being a rat in my trunk and another by my bureau

gnawing away. Well, after I plucked up courage to sit, I flashed
Trevor's big torch onto the shutters and I coughed and said,
"Get out." Then the dog that sleeps outside my verandah shutters barked like blazes. I told Trevor and he came down the second night without telling anyone (in case it was someone
playing a joke), and caught the morning coolie trying to see
what he could steal. Just like that bearer Yen caught in Kuling!
Only Mr. Noble handled it in stride and merely kicked the old
boy out for being so cheeky. Not like Papa.

I'm not wearing my nice dresses as I'd look too foolish. Mrs.
Noble changes off and on with only two dresses. We have to
make our own beds as there are no amahs, and I wouldn't let her
make my bed for me. Also I shall have to wash my own things.

I wonder what Papa says about things?

Love you!

Pearl

Pass. 125 Rue de Grouchy
Shanghai
August 9, 1928
Dearest Pearl,

Card and letter both received. I certainly hope your adventures are over now, as it sounds quite an alarming welcome!

I am glad to report that it is raining here. A cool, gentle rain.
I've hardly been out of the house since you left, trying to work
on my articles, though I'm afraid I'm in a bad rut, as my father
used to say, and I don't know how to get out of it.

We do miss you a lot, but never mind that. Enjoy yourself all
you can. Watch out that Trevor doesn't get overfatigued, though.
TB is nothing to kid about, as you must realize. Have you been
able to take walks yet with Trevor? Go slow if you do, and try
not to quarrel. Rest and eat well, those are your marching orders.

As for how Mrs. Noble dresses, that's her business and no
gauge for you. You are young and sweet and attractive, and
you've no reason not to flaunt it. Trevor will get tired always seeing you in the same old dress. Besides, I went to considerable

trouble to get that red voile and the organdy ready in time for you to take with you. I'll be put out if they come back unworn.

Papa hasn't said anything except, "Blossom has only two weeks?" So he doesn't mind. By the time you return he'll be up in Kuling, where he's stopping to check on the house before he goes to Nanking. He's been appointed to the Supervisory Yüan, which means that he's supposed to keep all Chiang's bureaucrats in line and the government free of corruption. At least he'll have a salary again. But it also means that he'll be spending most of his time in Nanking. I don't know, maybe for all our sakes, it's best. Anyway, don't you worry. Just take good care of yourself.

Lovingly,
Mama

☙☙☙

4

May 15, 1929
En route to Nanking
Dear Sarah,

I have tried several times these past weeks to reach you, but you have not returned my calls. I suppose this must mean Eugene is favoring you again, or are you busy making arrangements for Ken's wedding? At any rate, I have a favor to ask. I am taking Jasmine and Teddy up to Nanking to join Paul for the ceremonies at Dr. Sun's new mausoleum, and we've left Morris (has to finish his exams) and Pearl (couldn't get leave from her job) home with Yen. Would you mind awfully looking in on them? I know that Pearl's a grown woman and Morris is practically a man, but in Shanghai, how can a mother *not* worry? Especially since Trevor Noble died at Christmas, Pearl's been in a keen state of nerves, giddy gay one moment and sobbing the next, and the only thing that seems to calm her is going to church, but then her friends will take her out nightclubbing "to cheer her up," and . . . well, you understand. Indulge me, Sarah, and make sure they don't get into trouble.

As for yours truly . . . You are doubtless wondering why, given the current state of things, we are winding our way to Nanking. Well, as always, I hope to get some photographs and make a story out of it. Generalissimo Chiang is reportedly taking between three and six million dollars from the national coffers to pay for Sun's new mausoleum, and I'm sure there will be plenty of colorful pomp and what-not when our hero's body is dragged down from Peking. The children are wound up because Paul's promised they can ride ponies along the top of the old city wall the way Pearl remembers doing with Yen in Peking. They're very pleased at last to have an adventure that excludes their older brother and sister, and Jasmine will doubtless lord this over them for the rest of their lives.

Yes, but what about *you*, Hope? I can just hear you, Sarah. I can, but I honestly don't know how to answer. Paul is full of beans over Chiang's rebuilding campaign, says the new government is turning Nanking into a fully up-to-date city, and— now that the Western nations have recognized the Nationalist government—a very cosmopolitan center, as well. Chinese and English are spoken interchangeably and, much more than in Shanghai, there is respect among the races. So he says. Perhaps this will form the subject for another article, but we will see if it persuades me to uproot the children yet again so that we can move there, as Paul claims he wishes.

I say *claims* because I can't believe he really cares a whit. No use pretending, you know how things have been with us since Jin died. It's as though he's on one side of the looking glass, and I'm on the other, and even if we put our hands up and press our palms together, all we can feel is the cold flat line between us. You laugh, I know, and say more the fool I for thinking it was ever otherwise, and maybe you're right. All I know is, it's this way now, and I don't know whether to feel more sad or angry. Paul is as good a man as ever. Dear, kind, gentle, patient in his way, and generous to a fault. But his distance now is hard and obdurate, and his addiction to this country's political intrigues and upheavals seems even still to grow unabated. No matter how glaringly corrupt, savage, deceitful, or tyrannical its leaders might be, he would rather see his son murdered and decried than be excluded from its government.

I should not go on. The pen can be a treacherous weapon, and I do not want to compromise you. It is just that, even within four walls—palm-to-palm, as it were—Paul and I are so far apart that we might as well be in different cities. I no longer see the point in pretending otherwise, unless it is for the children's good, but their lives are firmly planted in Shanghai. And there is some protection there, is there not?

It is late. We have a comfortable wagon-lit, and the children are in their bunks fast asleep. Outside, it is so dark we could be traveling through the high Sierras and I would be none the wiser. Can you believe that was twenty-three years ago? I can still see that fiercely determined expression on your face after Kathe tumbled into those coolies in Oakland! And feel the tension of your back when we were bunked together in the train. I wonder if, ten years from now, I'll have equally powerful memories of sitting here, rocking through Kiangsu with my sleeping children, my pen slipping and jerking as I write these words?

But I must close. I'll post this from the station when we arrive and call you as soon as we return—the fifth or sixth of June.

My best to Ken, and love to you always,
Hope

June 1, 1929
I am in hiding tonight. It has been a brutal day, and, I fear, irreparably damaging.

I should have expected as much when I first laid eyes on the mausoleum that we came to celebrate. Chiang Kai-shek has built in Dr. Sun's "honor" a horror of marble ugliness and excess—eighty thousand square meters of hard, blistering stone. But as inappropriate and brutal as this tomb may be for a man of Sun's naive modesty, the ceremonies that Chiang ordered for the reinterment were, quite simply, a travesty. Thousands stood for hours in the suffocating heat, waving flags and singing Nationalist anthems, listening to interminable speeches by anyone and everyone in Chiang's circle who stood to profit by association with the Father of the Republic. Jasmine's badgering and Teddy's questions were almost as incessant as the ceremonial noise, but far more sympathetic, as far as I'm concerned. Dr. Sun may have always desired to be buried in the Purple Mountain, but I'm sure he would rather have had an unmarked grave than be dragged out and used as he was today. I begin to wonder if there isn't something innate in Chinese society that grinds all truly noble ambition to dust.

At length Paul climbed up on the dais and made his own speech in Sun's memory. He was perfectly genuine, heartfelt in his words and expression, yet whatever came out of his mouth was overpowered by the sight of the Generalissimo behind him nodding, squeezing those glittering eyes down into a benevolent viper's smile. Sarah tells me Chiang's personal gain has risen into the tens of millions since he's come to power, yet Paul is paid as irregularly as ever, and the government debt climbs almost as fast as the Generalissimo's wealth. I remember Paul's tirades against the Manchus for stealing China's riches, against Yüan Shih-k'ai for pocketing money borrowed at the people's expense, against the warlords for building palaces and buying concubines with the farmers' taxes. Can my husband honestly believe that anything has changed?

So we quarreled. We'd come back to this hotel, where Paul lives in a suite that is as plain and utilitarian as the outer lobbies are gaudy with red carpets and gilt. The children were in their room. I had collapsed in the sitting room, and Paul was pacing around in obvious agitation. He said he wanted me to accompany him to the reception and banquet tonight. He'd arranged for a woman to come and stay with the children. Now,

I was soaked with sweat and limp with exhaustion. My head ached so that I felt it was being split with a cleaver, and I would rather have spit on most of the people attending these festivities than speak to them. Besides, this was the first notice he'd given me. I refused.

"You are my wife," he said. "You must come."

"Is that an order?"

"If you like."

"I don't like. I am not your servant. And I want nothing to do with this city or the people who rule here."

Then he said, "This is my business. It is what I do. Who I am."

"It's been your business since before we were married, and you've consistently done everything in your power to exclude me from it. Now I see why. And I want no part of it."

His face darkened the way it does, as if his rage is trapped and cooking inside him. I braced myself for him to slap his cheeks at the same time that I prayed he would not. At some core point I would rather he throw a chair out the window, rather he plunge his fist through the wall, rather, even, that he strike me if I am what has enraged him than that he turn all fury, all frustration and humiliation first and only against himself. At least if he struck me, we could have it out. It would *be* out, this awful, invisible tension between us. We could brawl and claw and scream—and perhaps in the process we might remember what it is to feel each other.

He did not slap himself or me. He simply shrank away. His face seemed to wither before my eyes. He let out a single tremulous sigh, and two tears broke and slid down his cheeks. His fists were clenched, his arms cocked, but it was the pose of a paralyzed child rather than a threatening man.

So many words came into my throat that I choked on them and no sound at all would come out. He sickened me. I pitied him. I hated him. But more than anything, his palpable fear of me terrified me.

"Let us go, Paul," I said at last, with as much effort as if I had been lifting a concrete block by breath alone. "I haven't been back to my country in seventeen years. I want Morris to attend university in America and for all the children to know their other home."

Paul drew himself up, slowly and with almost enough dignity to command me. "My children are Chinese," he said. "And you, my wife, a Chinese citizen."

"China is not my home, Paul. It never will be."

But suddenly I felt unmoored. My legs rocked beneath me. His tears had dried and his face pulled into a strange, downturned grimace that seemed at once cloying and shamed. He laid a hand against my cheek, just for an instant, but he didn't look at me and I felt no connection, no emotion in his touch. I realized this is the way he now touches our children and what I was feeling was what they feel for him. I couldn't respond, and after a moment he passed into the bedroom. I went in to the children and a few minutes later we heard the succession of doors opening and closing, signaling his departure.

June 4, 1929
En route
Dearest, peachiest, squarest Hope,

You must (tho I know you won't) forgive me for not saying goodbye. I've met the dreamiest boy. Jimmy Marlowe. He's from San Diego, California, and he has the loveliest blue-green eyes and arms like twists of train tracks. You can see I'm quite gone on him, and in spite of the age gap (I daren't tell you how wide!), he says the same of me. We met at the Casanova just a few weeks ago, tho he's been in Shanghai almost two years. Lucky, lucky timing. He's a sailor, you know, and most conveniently he's due for home leave. Yes'm, we sail tonight. I've written Gerry all about it and asked him to meet us on the other side—did I tell you Gerry has a girl, and they're living in Dallas, Texas, of all places?

'Course, I can't say a word to anyone else. Oh, I know Eugene will be in a stew. The really hard part is, I can't take Ken. If I did, the Chou clan would send out all their posses—they've got cousins in every Chinatown in America—and I'm sure I'd be dead in a month and Ken right back where he started. Oh dear, Hope. I know what you're thinking. I know you could never do anything like this. But please try to understand. For twenty years I've been kept like some creature in a bottle. I've survived, and I've managed to have some fun, and my boys are good boys, both of them. But I haven't been free, and I really haven't been living, and this is a chance that won't come again. I hate this country. It's squalid, it's twisted, and it's cruel. Trapped in Shanghai I suppose I see the worst of it, but there's nothing for that.

I think of America. I think of the space, the color, the taste of the air. It's freedom I remember, Hope.

So please look in on my dear Ken. As I write this he's studying for his exams with Morris. They are both nearly grown men, you know. They hardly need us at all anymore, and as I haven't any other little ones I mustn't delude myself that I'm indispensable. I'm not. Not to anyone but me.

I do hope you understand a little. I'll write when I land and have an address. Perhaps someday you'll come back as well, and we'll reminisce about our Shanghai Days and think them all perfectly ducky. I'd like that.

Good luck, Hope. And love.

Sarah

ぶぶぶ

She could feel herself hardening. Her skin, her spine, even her hair, now streaked with heavy branches of silver—seemed to have become stiff and tough. She hated this change. It made her think of the coffin at Nainai's house. That coffin had been there for more than fifteen years, waiting for Nainai to die, and every autumn it was relacquered to strengthen it for death. But her own hardening promised no strength. It promised a grave and permanent loss.

There was no one now in whom she could confide such feelings. Sarah had vanished without a trace. Not even Ken, whose wedding the Leons attended just weeks after his mother's flight, had heard any word of her whereabouts. In any case, Sarah had gone too far this time for Hope ever to confide in her again. Leaving Eugene she could understand better than she could Sarah's submission to him all these years. But leaving her son, running off with a man she barely knew—a *sailor* half her age!

Hope tried to bury her emotions in writing and the photographs she had resumed taking in a haphazard way—more of an excuse to get out of the house and be alone than to capture "the essence of Shanghai," as Cadlow kept exhorting her to do. But it was all slipping. Though Cadlow was sympathetic, he now rejected one or two out of every three articles—virtually everything Hope submitted under her real name. Only the pseudonymous pieces held up, in his view. "If you are afraid, for some reason," he urged, "we will let Hope Newfield slip away and welcome our new contributor Isabelle Wayland—as long as the work is consistent." But identity was only part of the problem.

"Come to church, Mama," Pearl would beg. "It's so grand and mystical. You can't help but feel a part of something larger than your own problems."

Pearl had started going to St. Joseph's Cathedral after Trevor Noble died. His family was in the congregation, and his funeral had been there. Several of Pearl's friends went to mass on Sundays, and over time she had taken to going along. "It's a comfort," she had explained after Trevor, then later, "It's smashing pageantry. The Catholics give even the Chinese festivals a run for their money." Sometimes she dragged Jasmine and Teddy along, enticing them with the prospect of joining her friends for socials afterward. There was a young priest whose mission seemed to be to attract the "lost" Eurasian youth of Shanghai into the Catholic fold, and he had hit on the highly successful strategy of treating these youths to ice cream and soda pop after mass. The circle widened, and soon poor Trevor Noble was all but forgotten as Pearl and Jasmine squabbled over which of the young men they'd met at church was the most handsome, the better dancer, dresser, or prankster. Hope reasoned that there was no harm in their going, better the Catholics than Shanghai's gangsters. But she herself had spent too many years listening to Paul's harangues against the missionaries and especially the Catholics, who had cut privileged land and taxation deals with the Manchus, carving out their own fiefdoms and brutalizing nonconverts in the name of the church (that running joke about all the blue-eyed Chinese unique to the inland mission villages). Hope despised hypocrisy, and it seemed that the Christian religions specialized in the art of preaching one thing and doing another. So, although she kept the children well supplied with Sunday dresses and suits and some small change for the collection plate, she refused Pearl's pleas to join them.

The house was now routinely deserted on Sundays. Morris, having graduated in the spring of 1930 (and having even less enthusiasm for church than his mother), had taken a job as cub reporter for the *Evening Mercury*, and was assigned to the Concession police beat every weekend. The servants had always had every Sunday off, and though Yen used to idle around the house, he now was gone for good. For years Paul's friends had given Yen tips for serving them his special roast pork and for keeping them well lubricated at their mah-jongg and poetry parties. For years Yen's only indulgence had been the picture show he treated himself to each week or the occasional toy he bought from his own pocket for the children. Everything else had been carefully saved until, one day in late 1929, he announced that he had bought a small inn in Hongkew. Ah-nie would help him run it. The children no longer needed tending, they said, and Laoyeh did not require Yen's service in Nanking. There was a tearful goodbye, and several weeks later Yen invited the family to come see their establishment. As soon as she entered, Hope let out a cry. Then the tears streamed down her face. Dear, dear Yen and Ah-nie. There, above the desk in the narrow, dimly lit lobby, hung a huge grainy enlargement of a photograph Jed Israel had taken of Hope the year after Morris was born.

Ordinarily, she fended off the dismal mood she had come to call her Sunday blues by hiding in the darkroom she'd set up in Yen's old quarters under the stairs. Or she'd work on an article, or sew, or write in her journal. In good weather, she might work in the garden. Certainly, she was never without tasks to occupy her hands and mind, if not her heart. But there came a Sunday in mid-November of 1931 when the emptiness of the house threatened to engulf her. It was a bleak day, nothing inviting about it except that it offered an alternative to her own solitude. And Shanghai's guarantee that by stepping outside she would be reminded of her own comparative good fortune.

She set off toward Hongkew with a vague notion of stopping to visit Yen. A new miniature Leica was tucked into the pocket of her old tweed coat. The traffic was brisk, whole families jammed into wheelbarrows on the way to market, the usual flow of street merchants waving their hand-made toys and confections, touring cars and rickshaws streaming to and from the Bund. In the middle of Route Père Robert the red-turbaned Sikh on his pedestal still performed his curious traffic dance. Colonial puppets, Jed used to call the Sikhs.

She turned up the velvet collar of her coat, tugged her jersey cloche down low, and took the policeman's picture. A few minutes later she pho-tographed a group of uniformed Boy Scouts in front of a toy shop burn-ing wooden cars and airplanes while their leader harangued the sullen merchant for disobeying China's latest boycott against Japanese goods.

At the entrance to French Park she stopped again, for a very different display: the Sunday promenade. Formal Europeans in full plumage, tight-lipped and strolling compulsively; clusters of young Chinese dressed like flappers; lovers who clung to the shadows. Odd, thought Hope, how it was the lovers who wanted so to be discreet who stood out most of all. Like that middle-aged man going off on the side path with his young girl-friend—he in his sharp-brimmed hat and pin stripes, she with her shin-gled hair and red silk. She so very animated, he almost paternal in his bearing. But not quite.

Hope edged behind a nearby yew, debating whether to photograph the pair. The man was removing his gold-rimmed spectacles, slipping them carefully into his breast pocket as he whispered into the girl's ear. She laughed and tipped her head up, turning so that his lips could not help but brush her cheek. He caught her elbow and their bodies tensed, mov-ing against each other, but at the precise moment Hope lifted her camera, the man straightened abruptly, looked right and left, showing his full face. Hope was sheltered. He did not see her, and after a moment the couple drifted away. But she could not move.

The man was William Tan.

She took a deep breath. She should hardly be surprised. She'd sensed as much about William from the very first, yet she had so thoroughly mas-tered the art of suspending assumption that she was as shocked as if it were not William but Paul having an affair. She *would* be shocked, she realized with a start, even now, if it were Paul.

She turned, pocketing the Leica, her eyes still pulling toward the two figures disappearing behind the shrubbery. She had the impression that her mind, her reflexes were resisting her will, and though some part of her brain knew already what the next instant would bring, she could not access this information. Only when William and the girl had completely vanished and she started back toward the street did she realize that she had been seen, after all. But not by William.

"Still taking pictures, eh?"

"Stephen!" She clapped her hand to her mouth.

Mann smiled. "It's all right. Good photographers are supposed to snoop."

She lowered her hand with a feeble wave. "I didn't get anything."

There was a long pause as they studied each other. He was as changed from her memory as she must seem to him. Always spare, he was now bony, his skin deeply lined, and the once full lips now thin and pinched. The hands he extended were crisscrossed with coarse gray hairs and protruding veins. Only his eyes still bore the restless drive that had once so deeply stirred her.

"How long have you been back!"

"A year. More. I lose track. Say, it's bitter out here. Shall we get some coffee?"

She chewed her lips, thinking. "All right. There's a pastry shop a few blocks from here. French. They have coffee."

"You don't drink coffee, do you?"

She smiled. "No. But it's only habit."

"All of life is habit," he said. "Or the breaking of it."

He took her arm. They walked in the direction she had indicated and came at length to a pink box of a shop with glittering cases full of napoleons and puff pastries, eclairs and petits fours. A row of pink-shaded wall lamps gave the place a cozy glow, and it was filled with young Chinese and Shanghailander couples trying to look "Continental." Pearl had told her about this café, but Hope had never been here herself.

"I don't know." She balked. "I think I'm too old."

"Nonsense." Mann held the door.

They found a table toward the back where they would be less conspicuous. A young girl with dark bangs and moony eyes took Mann's order for two café au laits. He emptied his pipe into the ashtray in the center of the table, kept tapping it against the glass rim.

"Sarah's run away, did you know?" said Hope. "With a sailor—"

His tongue flicked across his lower lip. He started to nod, then glanced away. "Anna left me, too. Four years ago."

"Oh—" This time his name twisted on her tongue. "Stephen, I'm sorry."

He would not meet her eyes.

The girl brought their coffees. Hope sipped suspiciously. "Why, it's good!" her relief at this minor discovery startled her.

He smiled. "It's all right."

They began to talk. She brought him up to date on her children, described Yen's new enterprise, Paul's assignment to the Control Yüan in Nanking, their exile from Kuling since Mao Tse-tung's Communists had occupied Kiangsi. He told briefly of Anna's desertion in Pretoria for a botanist who had been her teacher at normal school. Of his life in Tientsin since then, back at the same clinic where he had worked before, and the general tenor of life in the north under Peking's last warlord, whose preferred method of execution was the garrote.

"It bewilders me," he said, "how the Chinese can continue to call us barbarians when they have beasts among them like this man."

"You know . . . about Jed Israel?"

He nodded slowly.

"At least you missed that." She trained her eyes on the pressed tin ceiling, fighting tears. "They killed Paul's son, too. Jin."

He moved his hand closer, but did not try to touch her, and they sat for several minutes without speaking. The bell over the door jangled almost continuously. Young couples laughed and chatted, watching each other with interest and Hope and Mann not at all.

"Where are you working now?" she asked finally.

He gave her a long look and removed his hat. Underneath, the top of his head was bald. He grinned. "We get old, we come full circle. Shanghai Native."

"No!"

"Still the most humane hospital in Shanghai."

She covered her face. The tears that she had contained before now rolled freely down her cheeks. She was laughing. Crying. They *were* so old. They barely knew each other, yet they went back forever. She didn't know what they were doing here. She didn't really care. It was as though she'd reached the end of the earth and discovered a friend there waiting.

She wiped her eyes with the pink linen napkin that had come with the coffee. She sneezed. She touched his sleeve. He made no move to return the touch, only watched her with amused tenderness.

"I'm going home in February. Back to Seattle." For a moment his lips remained parted, as if he meant to continue. Instead he finished his coffee.

She had no reason to be surprised. No business being sorry. But she was. "Why now," she blurted, "after all these years?"

His eyes rested on her with an ease that she did not recognize. "I'm finally old enough to admit I've failed," he said. "And to realize there's no shame in that."

After a long pause, she asked, "Was it a coincidence, our meeting today?"

He smiled sheepishly and shook his head. "I've been meaning to see you for the longest time. Come to your house, gotten as close as the gate. Today I turned the corner just as you were leaving. Forgive me, I followed you."

"Why?"

Mann gave her a long studied look, then filled and lit his pipe. He smoked for a while, still watching her as if considering his options. At last he said deliberately, "I keep feeling that we're unfinished, Hope."

She forced a laugh. "People are never finished—except in death."

"You know that's not what I mean."

She avoided his eyes. "I know, but I'm trying to tell you, that notion of completion is an illusion. Nothing ever turns out as we imagine it will. It's impossible, what you mean."

"I can believe in failure," he said. "But I don't agree with you."

"I think—" But her gaze fell on the gnarled, careworn hand that lay clutching that dull pink napkin. The bones stood out like starved ribs, the knuckles pressed white as tiny bleached skulls underneath the blue-veined skin. Her hand.

"Walk me home?" she asked.

"If you like."

"Yes." She rose. "I'd like it fine. And we'll say goodbye properly. You'll sail to America. And maybe one day I'll have a postcard from Seattle?"

Mann pulled the pipe from his mouth and sat watching the smoke continue to curl from its bowl. Then, in a single movement, he dumped the burning embers into his cup and replaced the empty pipe stem between his big ivory teeth.

Fifteen minutes later he left her at the corner of her street with a dry, embarrassed kiss that landed just east of her lips. He told her to give his best to her children. Regards to her husband. Take care of herself. He did promise to write, and he'd look for her articles when he got back to the States. When he smiled the lines radiated from the corners of his eyes. He tipped his hat, and walked away.

ஒஒஒ

5

Teddy and Jasmine wore her down. Pearl had gone off to a tea at the rectory, to be followed by supper with Googoo Noble and friends. Morris was going out to the pictures to celebrate the government sponsorship Paul at last had secured for him to attend university in California the following fall. But he was taking his friend Flossie, which meant the younger two were not welcome, and besides, he was seeing some Greta Garbo movie. Teddy and Jazz wanted to see the new Gary Cooper western, *The Virginian.*

"Wasn't it Virginia where you grew up, Mama?" Teddy coaxed.

"Not Virginia. Kansas."

But Jasmine was already putting her coat on. "There's a five o'clock show at the Lyceum. We can make it if we hurry."

Within the hour Hope was transported back to a world in which men rode horses and called women "ma'am." She remembered the long, flouncy skirts she'd worn as a child, those sausage sleeves and droopy bonnets that made her feel like a reluctant sunflower. She saw in the faces of those cinema cowboys both the tormentors and protectors of her youth, and cringed when the fateful moment came (volubly anticipated by the more experienced cinemagoers in the audience) for Gary Cooper to put an insulting Walter Huston in his place: "If you want to call me that . . . smile." There was nothing quite like the innocence and simplicity of this exported vision of America. No wonder the Chinese could not get enough of it.

It was nearly nine when they got home, and with school the next day she hurried the children to bed. Within the hour Morris, too, returned, mimicking Garbo. "Gif me a visky—ginger ale on the side—and don't be stingy—" he batted his long, thick black eyelashes "—baby."

Hope threw her slipper at him. "Valentino, you may be, but Garbo you are not. You didn't see Pearl outside, did you?"

He shrugged and affected a coquettish moue. "I haf seen no vun who von't gif me a viskey." Then he draped one hand across his brow and slunk down the hall to his room.

She watched him enviously. Was it even remotely possible that her children were as lighthearted as they seemed? No. In a word. Yet their capacity for pretense seemed inexhaustible. That was one thing they'd gotten out of Shanghai.

She lay back against the sofa pillows, adjusted her glasses, and opened *The Right to Be Happy*, by Mrs. Bertrand Russell. She'd heard Mr. Bertrand Russell give a lecture in Shanghai several years ago, and was impressed with his sympathy for the Chinese and his criticisms of British colonialism. She wondered if Mrs. Russell could possibly be as outspoken as her husband. Certainly, if the chapter entitled "Sex and Parenthood" was any indication, the answer was an emphatic yes. *There is no instinct that has been so maligned, suppressed, abused, and distorted,* Mrs. Russell wrote, *as the instinct of sex. Yet sex-love is the most intense instinctive pleasure known to men and women, and starvation or thwarting of this instinct causes more acute unhappiness than poverty, disease, or ignorance.*

Hope gently closed the book. She snapped out the light and lay star-

ing at the ceiling. How *was* it that, even when sex was stripped of its pro-
creative function, it could still have such a preoccupying pull? She sighed,
recalling Paul's urgent attentions during his visit last week. No matter how
little passed between them in other aspects of their lives, he still came to
her. And then Stephen returning the other day, after all this time . . .

A car door slammed, and the street out front echoed with youthful
good nights. There, Hope thought, there's Pearl, and I can go to sleep. But
the jangle of keys and door-clicks that followed came from the neighbor's
house. She checked the clock. Nearly midnight. Surely they wouldn't have
gone over to Hongkew to dance. She'd warned Pearl, with all the pickets
agitating against the Japanese, it was too dangerous. But Pearl had retorted, she was twenty-three years old and knew perfectly well what was
what, and besides, they were all in a group coming from church. Pearl was
twenty-three going on twelve, and the boys in her crowd hardly inspired
confidence. Pearl was always reminding her that Trevor, at least, had been
a good one. But Trevor was dead.

Another hour passed. Hope got ready for bed, lay down and closed her
eyes, but every ten or fifteen minutes she'd get up to look out the window.
It was wintry damp out, the streetlights blurring the leafless plane trees,
reflecting on the wet pavement. At one-thirty she called the rectory. No
answer. Then she woke Googoo Noble, who said Pearl had never turned
up for supper. Hope telephoned the police. No, they had picked up no
one of her daughter's description. No Eurasians all night, they said pointedly.

She told herself: Once, when you were Pearl's age, you met a man who
swept you off your feet. He took you sailing. You lost track of time. It
was three o'clock in the morning when he brought you home, four before
he let you go.

"Maybe she's met her Frank Pearson," Hope said aloud.

Ten minutes later footsteps sounded on the pavement outside. The gate
creaked, there was a fumbling at the lock. Before Pearl could get in, Hope
was downstairs, clutching her wrapper and stammering with anger and relief. Whatever words she had thought to utter went out of her head when
the door opened.

Pearl's face was like a chalk painting caught in rain. The kohl with
which she had rimmed her eyes now ran in black tracks down either side

of her nose. Her mouth was a disfigured blur of cherry red lipstick, her hair twisted in wild black knots. Her skin beneath its smash of paint was ashen, and her eyes were empty and dull. She looked at her mother with no recognition, no emotion. The lumpen mouth moved but no sound emerged. Only then did Hope notice the ripped stockings, the torn green voile, the open coat.

She took her dazed child by the shoulders and shook her. "Who did this?" she shouted. "Who did this to you?"

"I don't know." Pearl's nose was running. "Father Desmond was handing me some punch, and then—" The darkness spilled down her face. "I can't remember."

Hope lost her mind that night, but not in rage or despair. She lost it in control. She started the water from the tap and helped her daughter to stand in the tub while she gently washed the blood from her legs, cleaning deep inside, replacing the smell of human brine and iron with the soft, sweet scent of lavender. She rinsed her with the hand shower, sent the residue down the drain, then scrubbed the porcelain around her feet until all trace was gone. Only then would she fill the bath and permit Pearl to lie down. She massaged her shoulders and neck, rubbed her arms and legs, hands and feet and spine as the hot water rose about her, soaking out the stupor and pain. She shampooed the girl's hair with rose water, salved the bruises and minor abrasions, then powdered the doctored skin with talcum. She fed her aspirin and apricot juice for the headache that started when the drug began to fade, and put her to bed on immaculate linens, sat watching and tenderly holding her hand as the sleeping eyes flitted back and forth beneath their translucent lids. She burned the clothes.

All night she kept her vigil, haunted by the filth, the laughter that filled her imagination. The trust violated and crushed. She is alive, Hope kept telling herself. She will live beyond this. I will take her away. She at least has a chance to recover. But Hope could not complete any comparison between her daughter and Jin and Jed or even the women and children who had been mowed down during the Terrors. The martyrs had been warned of the risks, and they were striking, protesting, marching *for a cause*. They had suffered and died with honor. Pearl had realized nothing, had suffered for nothing except the amusement and contempt of monsters. A priest!

But her sickness and outrage were stayed by her own guilt. This was the fate that she had run from Fort Dodge to escape, only to bring it on her daughter.

At breakfast she told the others that Pearl was ill. A fever, Hope said, perhaps the grippe. She would stay in bed until they were sure. In the meantime, she was to be left alone. Teddy and Jasmine argued over who would have the last piece of bacon. Morris complained that his article on the murdered racecourse *mafoo* had been bumped for a piece on the anti-Japanese pickets. Exhausted and frantic, Hope shooed them away, took a tray up to Pearl, who was just waking.

She remembered nothing from the moment she was laughing at Father Desmond's joke about a Chinese beggar knocking on St. Peter's gate. She had finished her punch, was setting the empty glass on a small round table next to the piano, and before he could get to the tag line, everything just stopped. Next thing she knew, she was at the end of their block. Some men were steadying her on her feet and telling her to go on home. She tripped several times and lost her direction. When she looked back, the men were gone. No, she didn't know who they were. She didn't know if she knew them. She wouldn't know if she ever saw them again.

Then she laughed. "I'm all right, Mama. You're being a silly. Someone spiked the punch, and I got drunk, that's all. Let me up, I'll go to work."

Hope pulled back. If Pearl did not remember, what purpose would it serve to force her? "You were bruised," was all she said, in the end. "I want to make sure you're all right."

The next day Pearl went back to work. For the next four weeks Hope waited. By the time Paul returned for Christmas, her fears were confirmed.

Pearl refused to leave her room. "You tell him, Mama," she pleaded. "I can't."

Hope said Pearl was blameless, and he was her father. He loved her. But even to her own ears these words had a tinny ring. Finally, she told Pearl not to worry, she would take care of it.

彭彭彭

Paul leaned his elbows on his desk, smoking hard as Hope told what had happened. He did not interrupt or react in any way until she had finished. Then, when there was nothing left to tell, he stubbed his cigarette out, folded his hands back into the sleeves of his mandarin gown, and said, "She must be married."

"Married! But who? They—"

"I will arrange," he said in a grim tone.

"Arrange what?" Hope was enraged as much by his impassivity, his lack of outrage as by his presumption that marriage could set anything right.

"Arrange marriage," he said, and on the third repetition, his meaning finally sank through. An arranged marriage. A stranger. Chinese.

"No!" She stood abruptly, dizzied.

"There is no other way, Hope." There was neither hardness nor sadness in his voice. He might have been delivering one of his lectures. "Soon no one will have her."

She felt something snap within her chest. It was a hard, dry, brittle sensation like the breaking of a wishbone. She stared at the rounded flesh of Paul's face, at the incipient wattles beneath his chin, the still delicate ears and sagging shoulders, the distant strain behind his glasses. She remembered the way he had discarded Mulan, his recurring contempt for Sarah, the pitiless expression he had turned on Ling-yi. For this man she had felt passion and remorse, despair and sorrow. She had loved him, honored him. God knows, she had obeyed him. She had given up her homeland, her passport, left friends and family, watched four of his children, two of her own, die without his speaking one word of grief at their passing. More than once she had risked her own life for him. And for all his trespasses, his incomprehensible lapses and absences, she had forgiven him in the name of his father, his mother, his childhood, his country. No more.

There was no forgiveness left.

"You can't," she said. "I may have lost my citizenship when I married you, but Pearl did not. She is an American citizen. You cannot—you will not touch her!"

"And you will not save her," he replied quietly.

He went to Pearl then. Hope watched him place the ragged tips of his fingers to her forehead, saw her daughter's lips tremble as he held her. He never spoke a word of blame, or of consolation. By nightfall, he was gone.

ॐॐॐ

Never had she despised herself as she did that Christmas. First she ordered Pearl to bed, told the other children and the servants that she had a contagious stomach illness and was not to be disturbed. Then she told a miserably disappointed Teddy that, after less than twenty hours, his father had been ordered back to Nanking. Next time, she tried to console him, you can recite the new poem Yu Hu-hsu taught you, next time you can take Papa to visit Yen. But there was no comfort in her voice, no truth to her promises, and the boy's slight frame stiffened under her arm, his little jaw trembling less with disappointment than resentment. It was not Paul but his mother he pushed away.

Then Hope announced there would to be no Christmas presents. "We must save every bit," she said, raising her hands at the shrillness of her own voice. "Pearl is sick!" She looked at them pleadingly. "Pearl is sick, you see! And if we save enough, perhaps we can all go back to America with Morris next summer." They didn't say a word.

But they would not know. They must not know. Teddy was too young, and Morris, Hope knew, would feel compelled to avenge his sister— probably by trying to expose Father Desmond. But that would only intensify Pearl's shame, and who would believe a Eurasian's word against a Catholic priest—especially when there were no witnesses? As for Jasmine—well, Jasmine was like Sarah. She was as street-smart at fifteen as Pearl had been innocent at twenty. Hope knew that nothing would prevent her younger daughter from rushing headlong into whatever disasters or adventures awaited her, but she had an innate toughness, too, that made her emotionally invulnerable. Hope's children had been subjected their entire lives to Shanghai's warning leers, the crude whispers and crass innuendos—*Eurasian trash*—and they were past masters at denial and dismissal, evasion, distraction, reinvention. She had groomed these skills in them. Brush it aside, she would say. You're beautiful. You're brilliant. You're better than all of them put together, and any day now we'll get out of here. We'll go back to America where you'll be free. She still said these things.

No, there was no gain in revenge or confrontation, even if either one had been possible. This place, these people were nothing but transients, a whole city of failures and frauds who would descend on innocence like a pack of vultures and rip its very heart out. How could she tell them the real reason she had turned her back on Christmas? This most holy of Christian rituals—she could just see Father Desmond lifting his accursed hand in benediction. Perhaps a better woman would have mounted a charade—the customary tree, the garlands, the smell of roasting meat, and laughter, and the glitter of little surprises filled with promise and love. She recalled the delight of that first Christmas in Shanghai, that stupid bent monkey pine under the laughing Buddha, and the three of them dancing together as Pearl crowed, "Ooh la la!"

On Christmas day William and Daisy Tan held a gala party. Hope sent the three younger children, dressed in holiday finery, with Pearl's and her own regrets. Pearl spent the day curled around her pillow. Hope ransacked her closets.

She turned her purses inside out. She hunted through files of letters, articles, searched old journals, and emptied drawers. Pearl was not the first girl to be defiled by these bastards.

Think, she told herself. You know you kept it. And now you know why. She could still see the day, the slant of light through the leaves, the twitching silvered death of the trout in Jasmine's hand. She recalled Sarah's vehemence, her own defiant repulsion. How many babies had she seen die. To cut off her own lifeblood? Never!

The black lacquer sewing box she'd brought back from Kuling sat on an open shelf above her desk. Underneath the bottom tray the creamy vellum lay, preserved.

> *T. C. Wong, M.D.,*
> *Ladies' therapies and remedies.*

ವಿಶ್ವ

6

Dr. Wong's office was located in Hongkew, around the corner from the Japanese consulate. It was an immaculate place, startlingly white with gold leaf scrolls painted along the molding of the waiting room and around the rims of the round white tables and matching chairs. The lights were encased in frosted glass, the windows in drifts of snowy damask. On a hunch, Hope had introduced herself as a friend of Mrs. Eugene Chou—which Mrs. Chou she didn't specify—and the nurse had consented to an appointment after normal office hours. So there were no other patients, only one Chinese nurse and the doctor himself. The nurse was fat, her eyes and mouth squeezed between rolls of pink flesh, but she had a warm and sympathetic smile and nodded confidently as Hope explained their mission. Dr. Wong inspired no less confidence. He was a grandfatherly figure, short and slight, but erect, with thick white hair brushed straight back and alert, incisive eyes. His questions were solely medical in nature. Blood type. Any allergies? Prone to infection? History of seizures or fainting? And discreet. No mention of the father.

Hope stayed, holding Pearl's hand throughout the procedure. She made sure every instrument had been sterilized, every surface of the operating room was antiseptically clean. She noted with approval the gallon jug of Jeyes' Liquid, the vat of boiling water, the laundered towels and spotless masks with which both doctor and nurse covered their mouths and noses. She saw that the hypodermic was wiped with alcohol and made sure that Pearl's grip had relaxed, her breathing steadied before they began. She smiled. Oh, she smiled into those young, glazed eyes, and she talked about Berkeley, the beautiful white cottage where Pearl was born, the way the mists would pull over the hills in the evening like the world's softest, thickest blankets.

An hour later they were in a taxi heading home. Pearl was moaning a little, a faint perspiration breaking across her forehead, in Hope's pocket a vial of sedatives. She had her arm around the girl's shoulder so that the bobbed black hair fanned across her sleeve. Pearl's eyes were closed, and every few seconds she would wince with a spasm of pain. Dr. Wong had said everything "went textbook," that she would bleed for about a week, discomfort only one day or two. "Then good as new." Dr. Wong, it seemed, had many American patients and had picked up some of their phrases.

It was nearly seven o'clock, and cold. The moon was blocked by thick quilted clouds, so the reflections of electric light on the hoods and chrome of surrounding automobiles and on windows of the small Hongkew shop fronts had an even more artificial quality than usual. Many of the nearby cotton and paper mills had just changed shift, and the streets were thronged with wagons and tramcars packed with workers. Traffic crawled.

Suddenly several dozen Japanese pickets streamed around the corner, waving banners and lighted torches, screaming anti-Chinese rhetoric. The taxi stalled as people dashed in front of it. Pearl groaned, and Hope wiped her forehead.

The pickets were heading toward a Chinese towel factory a hundred yards or so ahead. Chinese workers tried to block their path, pushing and shoving, yelling curses. The mob was multiplying. The driver lay on his horn, but it did no good, and the noise seemed to aggravate Pearl's pain. Hope begged the man to move forward, but he turned in his seat at that, loathing in his face. She tried to tell him that she hadn't meant he should drive over the Chinese workers, but, of course, that's precisely what she had meant. Drive over anyone necessary to get her daughter safely out of here.

Now eyes and lips and flat swatches of cheek and forehead pressed against the glass. Hope laid her hand across Pearl's eyes, shielded her with her own body. The driver had locked the doors, but people were drumming on the hood and windows. A terrifying jungle sort of drumming, primitive and insatiable. The faces had pulled back by inches, but the car was ringed with outstretched arms. It began rocking violently from side to side. A brick skittered across the hood. Hope heard screams through the cries of the Japanese pickets, and ahead orange flames started licking from the lower windows of the San Yu factory. Still sheltered by her sedation and pain, Pearl curled deeper into Hope's arms. Her words slurred as she asked what was happening. The driver was yelling at them to get down as he tried to back up, now frightened enough for his own life that he didn't care whom he ran over, but the street was jammed behind, as well, not only with the rioters but abandoned trucks and rickshaws. Beyond them now appeared an armored car, black with the rising-sun insignia of the Japanese Army. The driver threw open his door and was instantly swallowed into the seething darkness.

Now a flurry of hands began to dance through the open door. The windshield seemed to be liquefying. The cab rang with a metallic splash as shots burst overhead. Machine gunfire. Hope lifted the lock, grabbed Pearl by the shoulders, and fell out of the car. A cry went up as three boys pushed past them, climbing onto the vehicle's hood and pouring something from a canister. They ignored the two women. Hope was dragging Pearl, who could hold her weight but moved in a daze and kept asking if this was a nightmare. They had covered barely twenty feet when someone threw a match, and the cab exploded in two-story flames. The heat sucked at their clothes. Hope could feel her stockings melting. Another concussion shook the ground and pitched them forward, toward the creek.

"Mama," Pearl moaned. "Mama, please stop."

But it was too dangerous. They were caught in a screaming sea, not attacked directly but shunted and thrown, swept along by the violent motions of the riot. Around them, rickshaw pullers were being trampled and beaten. Beggars were kicked, shop windows stoned. The Chinese workers who tried to leave the burning building were driven back inside. Uniformed Japanese stood on street corners watching, doing nothing to stop the madness.

They had reached the Garden Bridge before the first klaxons and fire sirens sounded. Suddenly Pearl jerked violently and twisted over the bridge's railing, vomiting into the blackness.

"Mama," she whispered in an agonized voice. "I've wet myself."

XIII
FATE

SHANGHAI
(1932)

᭞᭞᭞

1

The earth will open and swallow us. The wars will ignite and surround us. There is always danger outside the walls, beckoning at the gates. We will perish or persevere. Fate will decide.

These words became Hope's private canticle through the endless days and nights that followed, as she stood watch over her unconscious daughter. As she struggled to follow her husband's example, to *accept*.

But Paul embraced fate as instinctively as he did the presence of spirits, the inevitability of warlords, the power of gangsters, the rise of Chiang Kai-shek and his thugs. He was trained in the arts of compromising with evil, learned early to value the humiliation of knocking his head on the stone floor or feeling the knife in his back. At the same time, he understood the inherent treachery of pride, would refute each triumph and understate each gain with the same cunning by which his own mother gave him a girl's name on the day of his birth, berated him during infancy that the spirits would consider him worthless and not bother stealing him away. He knew to keep his true heart secret, that it should not betray him—or his family.

Hope had clung too long to her faith in safety, that place she once promised Pearl, where there was no right or wrong and truth was all that mattered. She had told her the danger lay outside, in what others would think or do, that the truest safety lies with those we love and trust absolutely. But the gravest danger to Pearl had come through those she trusted the most, and Hope now saw that no truth was more duplicitous than the truth of her own heart.

All she wanted was to protect Pearl, to strip away the horror she'd suffered and restore her to the life for which she was intended. To save her. But something had gone wrong. Pearl had become infected. She would not stop bleeding. The panic of fighting erupting around them, toxic drugs she'd been given, the madness starting all over again, and no escape . . . She'd collapsed on the Garden Bridge and gone into shock before Hope could get her to the hospital. The hemorrhage was severe, and within hours Pearl had developed septicemia, required massive transfusions. But for Stephen Mann, she'd have died before dawn. As it was, she lay in a coma.

Outside, Japan's assault on Hongkew had expanded, become official, and Shanghai once again had turned into a war zone. Armored trucks rumbled past the hospital. Bombardments rippled the walls. The night sky was a haze of ocher, the day black with smoke from the fires that raged across Chapei.

Hope stayed at her daughter's bedside, torturing herself with blame and regret and the new memories being etched in her heart—the deadly white of Pearl's unconscious face, the lifeless weight of her hand, the anguish in Stephen's eyes when he said there was nothing more he could do. And the gentle cadence of Paul's voice as he sought to draw her away. *Mei fatse.*

As her vigil stretched into weeks, Hope would hear the two men talking at the entrance to the ward, exchanging details about the bombardments, troop movements, prospects for truce between the Chinese Nineteenth Route Army, which was defending Chapei, and the commander of the Japanese forces, Admiral Shiozawa. Apparently Mann had postponed his departure for America, though whether because of the fighting or because of Pearl or some other reason, Hope didn't think to ask. She gathered that Paul, when he wasn't at the hospital, was seeing to the children at home or making diplomatic missions to the Japanese consulate. He was supposedly in Shanghai to negotiate a truce.

Hope was grateful for both men, she welcomed the murmur of their voices, and sipped from the bowls of tea and soup they urged on her at intervals, but her guilt pushed into the distance everything but Pearl. She had vowed after burying her last baby that she would kill herself before she watched another of her children die. There had been so many bodies since then, so many senseless deaths, yet she would still have given her own life for Pearl's gladly, if it were possible. It was possible, though in a different way than she imagined.

క్రిక్రిక్రి

Pearl was still unconscious on March 8 when the fighting stopped. For almost three months the Nineteenth Route Army, which consisted of some thirty thousand scrappy, mostly unpaid boy soldiers under the command of a defiant Cantonese general, had held Chapei in the name of China. According to Stephen, they had persisted with rifles and machine guns against continuous Japanese airborne and artillery bombardments. But they had received no support from Chiang Kai-shek, who had all but ordered Paul to surrender Shanghai if it would appease the Japanese, and finally the young, battered heroes (as Stephen viewed them) had been forced to withdraw. Now, while the Japanese bluejacket Marines advanced to take possession of North Station, Paul had gone aboard the warship *Azumo*, where Japan's Admiral Shiozawa was entertaining the foreign press.

Though Hope was paying scant attention, Stephen went on to explain that Paul's diplomacy was largely responsible for containing the fighting to Chapei and Hongkew and limiting weapons to bayonets, machine guns, and thirty-pound bombs. If the Japanese officers had had their way, Stephen said, those Cantonese boys would have been pulverized by heavy artillery of the five-hundred-pound variety. But in exchange for yielding to Paul's containment policy, the Admiral had demanded Paul's presence at this press briefing following the cease-fire. He wanted to make sure the Western correspondents understood that Japan had exercised humane restraint.

"Paul has an absolute genius for self-effacement," Mann was saying. "The irony is that he accomplishes far more with it than most of his countrymen accomplish with guns."

Hope leaned back against the hospital wall, staring at Stephen and for the first time fully comprehending that the two men she had so long cast as opponents had become allies. But in the next instant this thought was wiped from her mind by the struggled groan of her daughter.

Pearl's eyes were open, her lips moved. As Hope leaned over her, clutching her hands, she smiled and asked for water.

ॐॐॐ

2

That night Hope came home, and she and Paul sat together, alone for the first time since their showdown before Christmas. She had no more tears left. Pearl was going to survive, might even be able to have children. Paul had seen her briefly after she woke, kissed her forehead, squeezed her hand. That simply, the siege had ended. Now he was going to tell Hope what must be done. And, this time, she would consent.

"You know," he began, "I always want the family together."

She bent her head. The radio was on in Jasmine's room, and the ceiling above them creaked with her dancing. Jazz and Morris had brought Teddy to the hospital this evening. They had laughed and told stories and nibbled chocolates, and Pearl had smiled at them.

"I know you are never happy in Shanghai." Paul squinted suddenly and reached to switch off the lamp beside the sofa. The hallway lights were still on, and outside, the moon was full, but the parlor was now dark enough that his cigarette glowed where he had abandoned it in the ashtray. "I have wished you come to Nanking."

A moment passed. Two. "All right," she said. "But Pearl? Do you still think . . ." She didn't recognize her own voice, couldn't finish the thought.

"No." Paul picked up the cigarette, turned it between his fingers, and put it back down. "No more. I am saying, you were right. From now on, Nanking is too dangerous. Japanese, Communists. Maybe few months, maybe one, two years, who can know? What has happened to Pearl . . . China is being eaten now, inside and out."

She could feel his eyes on her, through the darkness. "And so are we," she said.

"Hsin-hsin," he said softly. "You are my wife."

She tried to recall the slim young man who had appeared before her on that stifling spring day twenty-six years earlier, to fit him into the broad, bulky shape that loomed across from her now. But Paul was hidden beneath his winter layers of cotton and silk, behind his thick lenses, his swallowed grief. She had never understood. He was right about that. Until now.

"I am your wife," she answered.

"Then you will do as I ask?"

"Yes."

"Dr. Mann."

She looked up sharply.

"He has friend from Chungking with American Tobacco, can arrange passage, visas. I pay for your ticket and Pearl and babies. Morris already is arranged through government scholarship. Best you go as soon as Pearl is well. Dr. Mann says he can take care of you."

Suddenly she understood why he had extinguished the lights. The shadow of the room was like water, enveloping and sedative. Invasive. "You are sending us away."

"Many years you ask to go home."

"And many years you've refused. So I made my home in Kuling—"

"No one can go to Kuling now, Hope. Maybe not for many more years. Maybe never."

She wanted to cry, but couldn't. Already Kuling seemed a dream. She said, "I thought we could not afford it."

His shoulders lifted and dropped. "The Nantao house."

Paul had rented out his mother's house soon after Jin's death, but in his inimitable fashion, he'd let it to one of his poet friends, for next to nothing. "What do you mean?"

"I sold it to Eugene Chou. He wants all his family inside same walls."

She swallowed hard. "You mean Ken and his wife."

"Everyone. Except Sarah and Gerald, of course."

As he brought the cigarette to his mouth, the glowing tip trembled.

"But you wouldn't sell your mother's house just to send us to America."

"No." His voice altered. "I owe Eugene . . . and William."

"Owe?" For a second she was lost. "You mean . . . gambling."

He smoked, not answering. She went to the window. There was a time when such matters as Paul's gambling seemed crisp and inarguable as the color of whitewash. Now the distinguishing lines had melted. The white wall along the back of the yard turned black with the angle of shadow, blue with the fall of moonlight. Was it, then, black, or blue—or white? We are mortals, all of us, she thought, with moments of weakness, moments of strength, the capacity to love and hate, interchangeably at times, to delight and fatally disappoint. We entice and betray, wound and scar and die. And there is nothing to be done.

When she turned, he had put out the cigarette and sat with his hands splayed across his gowned thighs, facing the seat she had vacated.

She said, "America is not my country anymore."

He sighed. "You remind me, Pearl is still American citizen. And Dr. Mann says that laws have changed. Now, if you return, sign declaration, you are citizen also."

"If I renounce you."

He hesitated. "I think so."

She reached for one of the low blackwood side tables she had bought during that early redecorating frenzy on Pushi Road. As her thumb circled the inlaid leaves of ivory and mother-of-pearl, she was suddenly, forcefully aware of the minute changes of surface, the slip from polished grain to wavering shell to slivered bone. She tried to muster anger at Mann for cajoling Paul into this scheme, but he was only offering what she herself had schemed and begged Paul to grant her.

"I won't renounce you."

"No?" He sat very still—straighter than before—yet there was something ultimately relaxed about him, the way he cupped one hand inside the other, the murmur of his breath. He would not judge her.

"No," she said. "Any more than you would."

"But for me there is no need."

She found herself inspecting these words as if he had spoken a foreign language or perhaps did not accurately express himself because he was speaking English. It occurred to her that someone else—Mann, for instance—would have layered this statement with ulterior meanings and innuendo. They would have veiled an invitation or accusation or plea. But Paul, though a classical master of metaphor and allusion, meant precisely what he said. He had no need to renounce his wife. He had his home, his friends, his work, his faith, his nationality intact. She had provided him with children and the comfort of her body. Now, for the sake of their children, she was leaving and he was staying, and yet they were the same.

ॐॐॐ

3

They left on Morris's twentieth birthday, twenty years and four months after Hope and Pearl had first arrived in China. It was spring, bright and blustery, the trees along the Bund cruelly green. The children were happy, Hope decided, not so much to be leaving as to be going to America. Even with all they had lived through, they were still young enough to view life in terms of its possibilities. Pearl, too, though wan and wobbly, was looking forward to long days in the sun and seeing again the country of her birth, which she remembered now only through occasional dreams. But as they made their way down the dock, in their gabardine suits and jersey frocks, laughing excitedly with the friends who had come to see them off, her children seemed to Hope to already occupy a separate universe from their father.

Paul hung back, reticent, smoking, preoccupied even now with the emergency discussions he had left in Loyang and the squeeze of Nationalist power, between the Japanese on one side and the Communists on the other . . . He let Stephen Mann take charge of the baggage, turned over the tickets to Hope. Paul alone wore Chinese dress—a long black gown and navy vest, dark stockings and cloth shoes. His head was bare, his spectacles slipped, as always, to the tip of his nose.

A horn blasted, and a man's voice came through a megaphone. Passengers began to board. Jasmine was unabashedly kissing all her beaux goodbye, while the other children shook hands. Stephen cried out a greeting to

Yen, now hurrying down the gangplank, with Ah-nie in tow. There were cries of delight among the children as Yen made them all presents of camphorwood beads, which he said would keep them safe. Hope clasped his hands and embraced Ah-nie, and they all began to weep.

Suddenly, there was no more time left. The children and Stephen went ahead. Paul lifted his hand to Hope's cheek. She went up on her toes and kissed him, publicly, shamelessly, winding her arms around his neck as her tears soaked both their faces.

He gave her a final, gentle push, and she was into the boat with the others. From somewhere in the middle of the river, three more blasts of a siren sounded, and the tender cast off.

The sun's brightness made her squint. The boat's rocking made it difficult to keep a steady eye, but all the way to the bend in the harbor she held him in her sight—a tall, broad, darkly clad figure, one arm raised and waving slowly, as the water widened between them.

EPILOGUE

To the north I see a span of mountains
To the south I see water flow in peace.
In one year my beard has turned white,
In the heart of night, rain falls on a lonely boat.
When the tide rises, the sails descend,.
The cold river rings with stone chimes.
The golden sun drops its slanting rays,
Multiplying the pavilions beneath my gaze.

REPLY

CHUNGKING

(FEBRUARY 1942)

☙☙☙

1

Control Yüan
Chungking, Szechwan
April 2, 1939
My dearest Hope,
I have received letter, writing by Morris, on one week ago. Said that you had send a letter to me, but I have not received it. It is long time since I can write to you. I hope you can understand.

Before last year May, I leaved Nanking with a small box to Kuling. But our house of Kuling occupied by Chinese Army, all people drived down the mountain. Old Chief Liu was nearly kill by them, because he told them, do not ruined my things. Now I do not know, can be remained how much.

Last year May to August, I have been Wuchang in my family house. Our books, clothes, and all things, all hold by army, ruined and burned (my father's and mother's things, too). The Japanese airplan have bombared every day. Around my home all destroyed or burned. By my house still well, no broken then.

At last year September I leaved Hankow to Chungking on the river way, by steamer, spend one month. I have one bag summer cloth, only that blanket you give to me in Shanghai,

then in winter I need cloth, because old clothing was left in
Kuling, could not carried away.

I received a letter from Hankow, said that my house was
burned by government order before they leaved there. Then in
Nanking, in Kuling, in Wuchang, my property will be lost all.
Few days ago, here in Chungking, the Japanese airplan has
bombared and burned around my living house, all is ruined
when I was in the mountain hole.

Dearest Hope, here all is gone for me, everything change. I
do not know how to do in future. I think, if I come to you, now
will be better. Only so much time passed. Do you keep place
for me in your heart, your home? I cannot be certain unless you
answer.

I await your answer

Your husband, Paul

Now, at last, Paul will have his answer.

I am on my way to Chungking. William Cadlow, on the threshold of
retirement, has given me one last chance. "You're lucky I haven't died or
moved to Timbuktu," he wrote when I contacted him last month. "Ten
years. You drop off the face of the map, and now you want me to send
you to Chungking, just like *that?* I have every right to refuse, you know.
Would, too, if I didn't somehow feel I owe you this—price of history and
friendship, however long-distance. Anyway, since Pearl Harbor, I've been
scrambling for someone to send to Chungking. Our readers are hungry
for the insights that will show our Chinese allies as living, bleeding, passionate human beings—separate and distinct from the Japanese. If anyone can demystify them, you can, Hope."

I laughed out loud when I read that last line, thought, the old Hope
would have bundled this off to Sarah with some cryptic, self-deprecating
note. But the last I heard from Sarah was four years ago, she was about to
marry a fertilizer baron in Boca Raton, and she'd "as soon never think of
China again." She'd be more appalled to learn I was going back than
amused by Cadlow's comment. I am glad Sarah tracked me down after we
arrived in Los Angeles and that we are still, haphazardly, in touch, but I
no longer envy her talent for reinventing herself. What for her is a survival

skill has backfired on me. For ten years, through the Depression, I've earned a decent living teaching English composition and literature, taking class photographs of schoolchildren. I've watched my own children grow up, Morris moving to Washington to become a documentary filmmaker. Jasmine taking bit parts as "exotic Eurasian" singsong girls in Hollywood movies. Pearl has a baby girl and an American husband who forbids her to reveal that she's half Chinese, and now Teddy, still a Chinese citizen, has been drafted into the U.S. Army, becoming American by default— and possibly in exchange for his life. Through all of this I've tried to keep my head down and my spirits up, to push China and Paul out of my thoughts and concentrate on this life apart, but Cadlow's right. My job is—always was—to demystify my Chinese ally. My husband. My lover. My past.

And so the planes that carry us through this interminable journey drone on. We have made eight stops on four continents in one week. We have flown in DC-3s, seaplanes, and stripped-down military transport, over oceans and deserts, blackouts and battle zones. We have traveled with diplomats and soldiers, aid workers and journalists, spent nights in cargo hangars, pensiones, hostels, and USO lounges. More than once I have forgotten where I am upon waking.

What will happen when we finally reach Chungking, I cannot predict. Paul knows only that Morris is coming to produce a documentary on China's war for the International Red Cross. Communications have improved dramatically since America joined the war, and so letters that, before, would have taken months—or years—have been flying back and forth. In this way, Paul has arranged for Morris to meet with various officials and to stay at Chungking's Press Hostel. He has predicted that his son will be proud of the courage with which the Chinese are defending their country. The tone of his two messages since Pearl Harbor is so fondly optimistic that it is hard to believe they were written by the same man who scrawled this letter in my hands.

I, myself, have written Paul only that I received his letter, three years delayed, and am considering his request . . .

But now, as we lift off from Calcutta, we are so near. The cabin is hot and crowded with military and government personnel. Across the aisle sits a youngish Canadian, some sort of industrial advisor, who reminds me of

Stephen Mann in the self-conscious way he holds himself, as if he can't decide whether to act powerful or embarrassed. He has the same cleft chin and angular face, the same thinning sandy hair Stephen used to have. Even Morris remarks on the resemblance when the man pulls out his pipe. I mention the difference about the eyes; our fellow traveler has a clear, piercing green gaze. Morris shrugs and says he never noticed the color of Dr. Mann's eyes. Then he wonders whatever happened to Mann. I watch the industrial advisor stuff the bowl of his pipe and light it with long draughts, his cheeks caving and his eyes intent.

During our three long weeks aboard the *President Coolidge*, Stephen Mann was solicitous of Pearl. He was attentive to me, cautiously jovial with the others. He dined with us, played shuffleboard, raced the children across the pool, and strolled the decks with pipe in hand. He and I danced and took the cold night air. We avoided reminiscence. Three days out of Honolulu, in a gray, coating gloom, he asked me to marry him.

Now, as Morris drifts back to his work, I imagine trying to explain this trip to Stephen. No, I know how I would explain it. What I imagine is his reaction. The flash of those yellow motes in his eyes. The tensed jaw and clutch of his chest as he took in air and let it out, even the slope of his bony shoulders marking his disappointment. His reaction would be no different, I'm sure, than it was on the pier in San Pedro when I thanked him for all he had done for me, and especially for Pearl, and told him to go back to Seattle, to his family, to go home. He said, "There is no going back, Hope. Don't you understand that yet?"

I would tell him, *I am going back because my marriage is not finished.*

ॐॐॐ

2

As we descend to Chungking the clouds open and close, giving us intermittent glimpses of brackish river and chalky gray cliffs. I make out the charred hull of a cathedral, the pinched streets of a medieval town that passes at eye level as we drop into the gorge. Mist and rain stream from the wings, and our wheels hit water, driving spume up the windows before grabbing the yellow sand spit runway. As we climb down from the plane the rain stiffens into slanting spikes, and we must run for the end of the spit, where a small open boat is waiting. Morris throws an arm around my shoulders and draws a square of oilcloth above our heads, but within seconds the rain has seeped through my three coats, jacket, dress, and underpinnings (what we wear is not included in our two-pound luggage limit). Meanwhile, high on its cliff, Chungking leans above us like the prow of some great shadow ship, unmoved by our discomfort.

An hour later the rain has dwindled. We have dropped our bags at the former school that serves as Chungking's foreign Press Hostel and are making our way by fading light up the slickened, ice-edged hill to the city. It's two or three miles, all uphill, but the passing motorbuses lurch like death traps, bursting with five times as many passengers as they were built to carry and belching poisonous wood-oil fumes. A rickshaw costs four hundred Chinese dollars. It is war, and so we walk.

Morris trudges silently beside me, climbing, climbing seemingly endless cuts of slimy stone steps, but he studies the passing faces and ruined walls with an air of preoccupation, his thoughts still back with the brace of foreigners clustered in the hostel lobby. Apparently it had not occurred to my son that his mother would be the oldest and one of the only women among the Chungking press corps. He must have asked me six times on the way up to our rooms if I felt quite well, if I didn't want to rest, wouldn't I want to move to Papa's after we'd surprised him. Poor thing. He has no idea, suddenly, what I'm doing here, and he's embarrassed and concerned. Underneath his handsome bravado—and in direct contradiction to the life he's lived, he still believes in order and convention and appearances. I told him *yes, no,* and *no,* and if we expected to find our way, we'd better start before it got dark. Perhaps I should have shown him Paul's letter. Probably I should have solicited comments and advice from all my children months ago. But while I had the nerve to travel more than halfway around the world, I did not have the nerve to confide in my family. Not before I'd seen Paul one last time.

Morris has the address—an alley off the Street of Seven Stars—but we must stop four black-suited policemen for directions before we reach the right lane. It's near the Wang Lung Men steps, the city's ancient access up the cliff from the riverbank, though there is nothing scenic or antique about the stucco facades and mud shells that line this *hut'ung* now. The walls, in this damp twilight, are the color of fetid water. The building where my husband lives is shaped like a shoe box with small square windows, blackened chimney pots, soot crawling in vines down the rough facade. The blackout cloths give it a vacant look in spite of the men—some in uniform and others in traditional gowns—who scurry in and out of the entryway.

"You all right, Mama?" Morris asks yet again. "If he's not here, I think we should leave a note telling him you're with me."

I squeeze his hand. "He might turn us away, then."

"Is *that* what you're afraid of?"

"No!" I scoff. But suddenly I feel a fool. All this distance, all this time, and I'm still toying with half-truths.

I push forward, ask a young man with the vivid red cheeks of a consumptive which door belongs to Liang Po-yu. He points up three flights. I thank him and wish him well. He gives me a curious look, and I realize the stairwell is throbbing with voices. The door he's indicated stands open.

Morris goes ahead now. The stairs are narrow and steep, barely lit. There is no heat, and the smells of must and cheap cooking oil permeate the building, but the voices above are jocular. Their familiarity simultaneously chills and consoles me, and I am pressing with every nerve against the instinct to flee.

Paul is not visible as we approach the doorway, but his friends are. Looking past Morris's shoulder I can see three men of varying sizes and ages, all wearing crude blue cotton robes. An iron floor lamp with a pink tasseled shade casts light up into their laughing faces and down on their mud-spattered shoes. They stand before a wall map studded with red- and yellow- and blue-headed pins, speculating about the most strategic targets for the coming American air strikes. The floor is bare, the ceiling low. The foot of a narrow metal bed is visible, with a butterscotch blanket carefully folded, its once satin edging threadbare.

I am having difficulty breathing. Morris touches my shoulder lightly, steps through, and disappears to the left of the doorway. I hear Paul cry out. It is a ragged noise, but bright with emotion. The men at the map turn and watch. They smile with all their teeth as I follow into the room to see my husband and son embracing.

Morris towers over his father. For a moment I am confused, then stunned. The stained gray muslin padding of his gown. The sparse tufts of silvery hair. His hands, flung around Morris's shoulders, are curled in reflexive fists, the skin leathered and spotted brown. As he pulls back, I see the wear on his face, creasing his forehead, tugging his mouth. His lips have shrunk around toothless gums. The flesh puddles beneath his eyes. He has, in fact, lost almost all his hair, and his once thick, dark eyebrows have turned wispy and white, as if eaten by moths.

The room has fallen silent around us. Paul studies me with the same wary disbelief as I examine him. There is a sadness so full and deep in his eyes that it tears at my heart. Neither of us moves. Then Morris says something. Paul's friends begin to stir, and suddenly I'm conscious that everyone in the room knows exactly who I am. They are bowing and greeting me politely. Someone offers a bowl of tea.

Paul moves past Morris, stands before me. He smells of cinnamon and nicotine and the dampness buried in the layers of his clothing.

"I'm writing again," I mumble, pull from my purse the small chrome Leica I bought especially for this journey. "And pictures. Cadlow sent me."

The heavy skin around his grayed eyes softens. "You will write about China again."

"Yes."

"Look, missus," one of the younger men in the group breaks in, speaking English. I follow his outstretched arm to a cluttered desk on which I recognize Paul's old ink stone, his onyx seal with its carved lion head. "All friends of Liang Po-yu can see his American wife."

I lift my eyes. On the wall behind the desk hangs a photograph—a smiling grandmotherly portrait that Jasmine had one of her studio friends take of me five years ago. She gave copies to her brothers and sister as Christmas presents. She sent one to her father. He took it with him when he fled Nanking, carried it home to Kuling, and Wuchang, kept it even through his month on the river and year after year of war.

My picture, hanging frameless on this spare cracked wall, flanked by misted mountain landscapes and a charcoal stele rubbing, is as jarring to me as my living presence must be to these men—to Paul. Yet it holds the place of honor.

ༀༀༀ

3

It's late and bitter cold out here in the hostel courtyard. The stars are like knife-cuts, the clouds, purple shadows moving west. I know I should go to bed, try to sleep, but I also know I can't.

Nearly a week has passed since we arrived. The weather has cleared some. I've filled three notebooks and shot twenty rolls of film. Paul has shown Morris and me his offices in the Control Yüan, though there is little enough to see besides row upon row of desks and wall paint that peels in yellow scabs and dozens of boy and girl clerk-assistants whose parents are "in government" and whose sole function appears to be clock-watching. Later, as we stood overlooking the south bank, Paul pointed out the grounded European steamers that have been turned into fashionable restaurants for the Generalissimo's intimates. Yesterday we walked past the half-ruined hospital where, he said, Dr. Mann is still memorialized. We visited the crater where Paul's last house used to stand, then he hired a car to take us up to the cave where he hides during the spring and summer air bombardments. The caves are miles out of the city, dug deep into the faces of gray-green cliffs, crisscrossed with bamboo gates, and reachable only by hundreds of steps.

"In winter, this place seems grim and cold, but in summer when the city is so hot, we are surprisingly comfortable here." Paul apologized when he realized he had lapsed into Mandarin.

Today, for the first time, he and I spent a few hours by ourselves. Morris had meetings all afternoon with his Red Cross sponsors, so after Paul finished at his office we walked over to a teahouse at the top of the Wang Lung Men steps. The inside room was crowded and deafeningly noisy, but we pushed through to the terrace outside, which we had to ourselves. Of course, it was overcast and very cold, but Paul, inside his customary padding, seemed hardly to notice. I tucked the collars of my gloves up under my coat sleeves and welcomed the arrival of tea.

Our table had a view of the Yangtze gorge and, beyond, the velvety green foothills and mountains. Paul pointed out the yellow hat-shaped villas scattered across the hilltops. "Many foreign widows still live in these houses. They do not understand."

I winced at the familiar phrase. "Don't understand what?"

"This war. History. We fight. We lose everything, but we go on. They do not belong here now."

"Did they ever?"

He sipped his tea and squinted into the distance. "Sometime, there can be place for everyone. Not now."

The readjustment of his face as he turned back to me was subtle and ambiguous. His eyes did not meet mine, and he did not speak. Below us, on the riverbanks, children were gathering for a procession. I could not see them over the edge of the cliff, but I could hear their voices, sharp and busy and painfully young amid all their cymbals and drums.

"And what about you, Paul?" I said. "In that letter—the one that took so long to reach me—you said everything here was gone for you, too. You asked to come back to America."

He pulled his spectacles from a slit in his gown and tucked the stems behind his ears. They accentuated the owlishness of his face, compared to mine, which made me look like a schoolmarm. Through our respective glasses, we studied each other.

"*Mei fatse*," he said. "When you do not answer, I think, is fate. I lose everything. I go on."

"But now? Now fate has brought me here."

"Now much I have lost comes back to me. My work, my friends. My country." He smiled. "My son and wife."

There rose a clanging of instruments and the muffled stamp of cloth shoes as the children started climbing toward us, up the ancient stone steps. Suddenly Paul reached across the weathered table. Through the jersey of my gloves I felt the flatness of his bare fingertips as he took my hand. I glanced down and saw that his nails, like his skin, had thickened and browned with age, but he no longer gnawed them. As he gained the throat of my glove and gently encircled my wrist, a familiar, though almost forgotten sensation flowed up the inside of my arm. He turned my palm up and pushed back my sleeve, and for several seconds sat staring at the pale blue lines that once had been his weakness.

At length, he restored the glove and sleeve to their original position and drew his hand back across the table. He took off his glasses and rubbed his eyes the way he used to. "It is good you went to America."

Our tea had gone cold. He signaled to a girl standing in the teahouse door to come refill our bowls. At the top of the stairs the parade dragon appeared, many yards of yellow satin pinching and stretching like a concertina, with red lantern eyes and a feathered headdress, at once ferocious and heartrendingly innocent. Child dancers and musicians completed the parade, followed by vendors selling toys—painted balls, wooden monkeys and bears.

Paul raised his arm and called to a girl with a long bamboo stick strung with drum-shaped lanterns. "Hsin-hsin," he said. "For you, this one."

He held up a small lamp made of wood and water-green oil-paper. Inside was suspended a porcelain boat filled with rapeseed oil. The gray day was just sufficiently dark that, when the girl lit the oil, the lamp sprang to life, for between the light and the translucent green screen hung two moving rings of shadow figures. As Paul gently manipulated the strings, two parallel parades rotated: on top, a flotilla of warships and an army marching under the flag of the ancient Han Dynasty; below, a marriage cart trailing ribbons, the interlaced branches of two outstretched trees, a cormorant and his fisherman's boat, and a steaming train with one silhouetted figure peering from each compartment.

The ring of peace and the ring of war revolved at different speeds. Periodically, they reversed course and passed in opposing directions. They were lit by the same light, spun within reach of each other, but though their shadows occasionally touched, they remained separate and distinct. This stole nothing from the lantern's beauty. In fact, it was its magic.

CHRONOLOGY

Date	Event
1840–42	• Opium War. Great Britain forces China to accept foreign trade, particularly trade in opium.
1853–64	• Taiping Rebellion against Manchu rule, crushed by Manchu forces with help from British Army regulars and European and American mercenaries.
1866	• Sun Yat-sen (founder of Kuomintang, or Nationalist Party, 1912) born in Kwangtung Province.
1882	• Exclusion Act of 1882 prohibits entry of Chinese laborers into U.S.
1885	• Armed white miners attack hundreds of Chinese laborers in Rock Springs, Wyoming, killing 28 Chinese, wounding 15.
1894–95	• Sino-Japanese War. China loses Taiwan to Japan, recognizes Korea's independence.
1895	• Sun Yat-sen's first plan for rebellion against the Manchus is uncovered. Sun flees China.
1900	• The Boxer Rebellion. Secret society of the Boxers leads a Chinese revolt against the Western Powers, and is suppressed. Allied reprisals include mass executions, crushing indemnities, new concessions, legalized foreign garrisons between Tientsin and Peking.
	• Sun Yat-sen secretly returns from Europe to China, plots with revolutionary students under T'ang Ts'ai-ch'ang to seize Hankow from Manchu control. The plot is exposed. Sun Yat-sen escapes to Japan. T'ang Ts'ai-ch'ang is executed by Chang Chih-tung.
1903	• Chinese student activists at New Year's celebration in Tokyo publicly call for overthrow of the Manchus.
1904	• Russo-Japanese War begins.
	• Chinese Freemasons in San Francisco give Sun Yat-sen editorial control over their newspaper, *Ta T'ung Jih Pao.*
	• Sun Yat-sen forms revolutionary Alliance Society in

Tokyo (name changed in 1912 to Kuomintang).
- Traditional Chinese examination system is abolished.
1906   • Great Earthquake and Fire in San Francisco.
1908   • Dowager Empress and the Emperor die.
1909   • Sun Yat-sen tours U.S. to raise funds for revolution.
1911   • Oct. 10, Chinese Revolution breaks out in Wuchang. Manchu troops mutiny.
        • Dec. 25, Sun Yat-sen arrives in Shanghai.
1912   • Jan. 1, provisional assembly of Nanking elects Sun Yat-sen President of Republic of China.
        • Feb. 12, boy-emperor P'u-i formally abdicates.
        • Sun Yat-sen resigns in favor of Yüan Shih-k'ai, as President of Republic of China. Sun becomes Director of Railways.
1913   • March 20, Kuomintang leader Sung Chiao-jen assassinated in Shanghai.
        • Summer, Second (Republican) Revolution fails.
1914   • European Great War (WWI) begins.
        • Japan seizes Tsingtao, German colony in China.
1915   • Jan. 18, Japan presents the Twenty-one Demands to China.
        • Dec. 12, Yüan Shih-k'ai attempts to reestablish monarchy, with himself as Emperor.
1916   • Sun Yat-sen incites the southern provinces to form a revolutionary government at Canton.
        • March 22, Yüan Shih-k'ai cancels his monarchy.
        • June 6, Yüan Shih-k'ai dies. Vice President Li Yüan-hung becomes President.
        • Warlord Era begins.
1917   • August, Northern government in Peking and Generalissimo Sun Yat-sen, heading a separate provisional regime in Canton, declare war on Germany. 175, 000 laborers sent overseas to help Allies.
1918   • Nov. 11, World War I ends.
1919   • April, Versailles treaty awards Germany's China concessions to Japan.

- May Fourth Movement. Students riot, protesting Versailles treaty.

1921   • Chinese Communist Party is founded in Shanghai.

1923   • Oct., Mikhail Borodin arrives in Canton.

1924   • Kuomintang is recognized with Russian assistance. Kuomintang and Chinese Communist Party form their first united front.

- Chiang Kai-shek is appointed commandant of Whampao Military Academy.
- Sun Yat-sen plans Northern Expedition for reunification of China.

1925   • March, Sun Yat-sen dies.

1926   • Northern Expedition led by Chiang Kai-shek is launched against northern warlords.

- Kuomintang, led by left wing and Mikhail Borodin, chooses Hankow as its capital.
- Dec. 5–8, Chiang Kai-shek and Mikhail Borodin attempt truce through meetings in Kuling.

1927   • British Settlements in Hankow and Kiukiang are overrun by Chinese demonstrators and are to be renditioned to China.

- Nanking Incident. Foreign residents are killed and molested by Chinese troops in Nanking.
- April 12–13, Chiang Kai-shek launches White Terror massacre of left wing in Shanghai and southern provinces, killing thousands.
- July, Mikhail Borodin flees China for Soviet Union.

1928   • June, Peking falls to the Nationalists.

- October, Chiang Kai-shek establishes Nationalist capital in Nanking.

1931   • Sept., Japan invades Manchuria.

1932   • Jan., Japan attacks Shanghai.

1937–40   • Japanese armies overrun western and central China.

- Nationalists retreat west, establish wartime capital in Chungking.

1939   • March, Japanese begin aerial bombing of Chungking.

- World War II begins in Europe.
1941
- Dec. 7, Japanese attack Pearl Harbor.
- U.S. enters the war, siding with Allies—and China.
1945
- Aug. 6, 9, U.S. drops atomic bombs on Hiroshima and Nagasaki.
- Aug. 14, Japan surrenders.
- Chiang reopens war against Communists.
1946–49
- Second Civil War, called by the Communists the War of Liberation.

ACKNOWLEDGMENTS

My thanks, first of all, to my father, Maurice Liu, whose memories of people and places and unerring recall of history helped to fill in so many blanks. Also to my uncle and aunts, Herb and Aileen Luis and Loti Hipple, and my mother, Jane Liu, for backing up Dad's memories with their own stories and research, and to my cousin Caroline Robertson Brown for the many tales, photographs, and documents she relayed from her mother's "archives." I owe a tremendous debt to the late Blossom Luis Robertson, who sadly died before completing her own China novel, but who opened the way for this book.

From the first, my editor, Jamie Raab, and my agent, Richard Pine, have provided the tough and gentle criticism for which I am ever grateful. I also want to thank Maureen Egen, Liv Blumer, and Nancy Wiese for your unflagging enthusiasm and hard work; Arthur Pine and Lori Andiman for your good humor and diligence; John Aherne for relaying and converting revision after revision; Eric Edson, Cai Emmons, Hugh Gross, Arnold Margolin for steering me through the first perilous chapters; and Linda Ashour for her astute advice in the final hours.

My translators, Adam Schorr, Shu Min Li, and Joy Shaw, not only provided expert advice regarding Chinese culture, history, and language, but by enabling me to read Liu Ch'eng-yü's memoirs and poetry, they introduced me to a man of incomparable humor, intellect, courage, and humanity—who also happened to be my grandfather.

Thanks to Neil Thompson and Suzanne Dewberry for their cheerful assistance in turning up family immigration and citizenship documents; to Denice Wheeler for acquainting me with Evanston's history as "marriage capital" of the Old West; to Esther Katz for her last-minute briefing on Margaret Sanger; and to Thomas Chinn for demystifying San Francisco's early Chinatown, its politics and people.

Finally, for granting me the time, patience, insight, and love that have made it possible to write and to keep on writing, I thank my "men," Graham, Daniel, and especially Marty, with all my heart.